Handsome Women

ALSO BY JUDITH HENRY WALL

Love and Duty

Judith Henry Wall

Handsome Women

Viking

VIKING
Published by the Penguin Group
Viking Penguin, a division of Penguin Books USA Inc.,
40 West 23rd Street, New York, New York 10010, U.S.A.
Penguin Books Ltd, 27 Wrights Lane, London W8 5TZ, England
Penguin Books Australia Ltd, Ringwood, Victoria, Australia
Penguin Books Canada Ltd, 2801 John Street,
Markham, Ontario, Canada L3R 1B4
Penguin Books (N.Z.) Ltd, 182–190 Wairau Road,
Auckland 10, New Zealand

Penguin Books Ltd, Registered Offices:
Harmondsworth, Middlesex, England

First published in 1990 by Viking Penguin,
a division of Penguin Books USA Inc.

1   3   5   7   9   10   8   6   4   2

Grateful acknowledgment is made for permission to reprint an excerpt from
"Over There" by George M. Cohan. Copyright © 1917 (renewed 1945) Leo
Feist, Inc. Rights assigned to EMI Catalogue Partnership. All rights controlled and administered by EMI Feist Catalog, Inc. International copyright
secured. Made in USA. All rights reserved. Used by permission.

LIBRARY OF CONGRESS CATALOGING IN PUBLICATION DATA
Wall, Judith Henry.
Handsome women/Judith Henry Wall.
p.   cm.
ISBN 0-670-82652-9
I. Title.
PS3573.A42556H36 1990
813'.54 — dc20   89–40316

Printed in the United States of America
Set in Sabon

Sisters are forever.
This book is for Peggy.
I love you!

Special thanks to
Colonel William H. Hamilton,
U.S. Army retired,
for technical assistance

And my continuing gratitude to
Pamela Dorman of Viking Penguin
and Phillippa Brophy
of Sterling Lord Literistic

Handsome Women

PROLOGUE

June 2, 1963

The chapel had a splendid organ. Wagner's processional reverberated majestically through the vaulted space of the Air Force Academy Chapel—coronation music for Maggie's day to reign triumphant.

Louise watched as the wedding party took their places in the front of the chapel, then seated herself. There was a wave of rustling throughout the sanctuary as the guests followed her lead.

The khaki collar of the chaplain's uniform shirt showed at the neck of his white surplice. The man had grown up in New England. He sounded like a Kennedy.

"Dearly beloved, we are gathered together here in the sight of God, and in the presence of these witnesses, to unite this man and this woman in holy matrimony."

A queen's beaded tiara graced Maggie's red-gold hair. Such gorgeous hair. Even when she was a toddler, people had commented on it.

This was the day Maggie had waited for, planned for, dreamed of. Maggie and Danny had been in love from the first day they had seen each other. Seven years ago. They had been little more than children.

I fell in love that year, too. In 1957 she had been thirty-eight, Louise thought, but sometimes it seemed as though she had only imagined that love.

Maggie had always known she would marry Danny—in a military wedding just like her parents had had. Louise remembered how her daughters had spent hours poring over their parents' wedding album. Their favorite picture was the one of their just-married parents racing under the crossed sabers as they came out of the old stone chapel at West Point. An honor guard of cadets stood at attention, their sabers forming an arch for the newlyweds, sunlight glittering on the blades. Louise's triumphant smile was frozen in time. Her own coronation day.

"Who giveth this woman to be married to this man?"

Franklin stepped forward and placed his daughter's hand in Danny's, passing her from father to husband. Franklin smiled his blessing. A good match, his face said when he came to take his place beside Louise.

Louise recalled other pictures in her white wedding album. The father of the bride and the father of the groom handsome in their own uniforms. The mothers proper in hats and gloves. Her sister, Marynell, beautiful as maid of honor. Franklin's cousin, David—then a first lieutenant—was best man. David had died a captain—at Tobruk with the British.

And now, a generation later, Franklin's father was sitting on Louise's other side, retired now but uniformed once again for his granddaughter's wedding. But his proud military bearing had left him, and Louise had to remind him this morning who was getting married. Her mother-in-law, Maxine, was still erect, still proud.

"I, Daniel, take thee, Margaret, to be my wedded wife, to have and to hold, from this day forward . . . " His voice was clear and true. When Maggie's turn came, her voice was full of emotion.

Louise's mind wandered back to the photograph with the crossed sabers. She had stared at the magical photograph for years afterwards, first with fond memories, then with puzzlement. How had the young woman in the picture been so certain she would find happiness?

She could recreate the entire wedding album in her head in the correct order. But, like her daughters, she was drawn most by the picture with the crossed sabers. She could recall every minute detail—the way her veil billowed around her. The way her hand rested on Franklin's uniformed arm. The lift of his chin. The cut of his hair—the exact haircut he wore today. He still looked the same. She did not.

"Bless, O Lord, the giving of these rings, that they who wear them may abide in thy peace and continue in thy favor through Jesus Christ our Lord. Amen."

Louise had been a pretty bride, but now she was becoming what people referred to as "handsome." She disliked that word when used to describe women, but Franklin was a general now, and generals' wives were handsome women. Their bearing was erect, even regal. Their hair was careful and makeup subdued. Their manner was impeccable and smile gracious. And even if they had once been homely or pretty or even lovely, they became handsome.

"For as much as Daniel and Margaret have consented together in holy wedlock, have witnessed the same before God and this company, and therefore have pledged their faith each to the other . . . "

Why were her thoughts crowding in like this, year tumbling over year, two weddings superimposing themselves one upon the other? Her thoughts should be focused on her daughter, on her darling Maggie.

Danny loved Maggie intensely, but Louise had never known a successful military officer who loved his wife the way Danny loved her daughter. Something would have to change. What would it be, Louise wondered, his love or his career? But she shouldn't be such a cynic. Maggie and Danny had been born to love each other. At times, it seemed as though they would explode with all the exuberant, young passion they shared. Sometimes the looks they exchanged were so naked, so in love, Louise felt her own insides open with longing.

"Look graciously upon them, that they may love, honor and cherish each other and so live together in faithfulness and patience, in wisdom and true godliness, that their home may be a haven of blessing and place of peace . . . "

Yes, military men needed a peaceful place to come home to, to serve as a beacon in times of war. And a noble wife with welcoming arms.

The congregation was joining in the Lord's Prayer. Franklin's voice rang out beside her, his head bowed.

The chapel at West Point had been a nicer place to get married,

Louise decided. This building, like the rest of the Air Force Academy, was starkly futuristic. And so much space loomed overhead, dwarfing the kneeling bride and groom at the altar. Louise wanted them and the ceremony to seem more important. It was Maggie's day— everything she had lived and dreamed for culminated in this one day. Perhaps that was the flaw. Queen for a day. Never again in her life would she be so honored.

At least all the imposing space was full of sunlight. That was nice. Like a benediction.

The chaplain was giving his final blessing. " . . . and fill you with all spiritual benediction and love that you may so live together in this life that in the world to come you may have life everlasting. Amen."

The recessional boomed forth. "Love Divine, All Loves Excelling."

Maggie stopped at their pew. Radiant, beloved daughter, the best of them both. She was hugging her father, and now her mother, with words of thanks, words of love.

Louise looked at Danny, and he nodded. He loved Maggie, would always love her.

But for a young Air Force pilot with a war to fight, how long was always?

Book One

★ ★ ★

1937–1940

CHAPTER

ONE

"Oh, Louise, it was made for you!" *December 28, 1937*

Marynell exclaimed as she circled her sister, examining the dress from all angles.

Louise wondered if her sister really approved of the dress or was simply trying to hurry her along. Marynell stopped circling and came to stand beside Louise, slipping an arm around her waist. "What do you think, Sis?" Marynell asked. "Is it the one that will make your cadet's heart go pitty-pat?"

As Louise regarded Marynell's and her own reflected images in the three-way mirror, she felt that odd mixture of pride and intimidation she so often experienced with her older sister. The curl in her own brown hair relied on nightly pincurls, while Marynell's was naturally wavy. Marynell wasn't afraid of makeup or anything else. She smiled and walked and laughed like a movie star—beautiful, flirtatious, self-assured.

Marynell had made her own choice immediately. A dress in the department store window reminded her of one Myrna Loy had worn in *The Great Ziegfeld*. She tried the dress on only to make certain it fit. It was white satin with a deep V in back and a peplum flaring from a gold belt.

Other shoppers in the better dress department stopped to stare at the beautiful young woman in the glamorous dress. Salesladies hurried over. The dress, they declared, looked better on Marynell than on the mannequin in the window. Louise had known that no such fuss would be made over her when her turn came to try on a dress. Marynell was the beautiful sister. Louise was the smart one.

But now, as Louise studied her own image, she wondered if she might not pass for pretty in this dress. If her hair hadn't lost its curl from pulling too many dresses over her head, if she had some color in her cheeks and perhaps pearls at her throat, Louise thought she would look quite nice, especially if she could remember to smile. Marynell said she always looked too serious, and boys expected girls to smile. "And tilt your head to one side," she insisted. "That makes you look more feminine, less serious."

She slipped away from her sister's arm and turned around, enjoying the swish of taffeta as she moved. With its dropped waist and high neck, the dress was more demure than Marynell's bare-backed white satin. The lavender lace over lavender taffeta was fitted and showed that she had a figure, and there were rhinestones and white sequins encrusted in the lace. Louise had never owned anything with rhinestones or sequins, and she'd never had a dress that swished.

"You wear lavender well, honey," the saleslady commented. "It brings out the green in your eyes."

Louise looked in the mirror at her hazel eyes. They did look greener.

"What do you think, Mother?" Louise asked.

Elizabeth Rodgers sat on an upholstered bench near the mirror, her coat in her lap. She was still wearing her beige kid gloves.

Elizabeth shook her head slightly as she brought her attention into focus. She studied the lavender dress, her own hazel eyes magnified behind rimless spectacles.

"It's very pretty, dear, but so grown-up." She turned to the saleslady. "Are you sure it isn't too mature for a young girl? Louise just turned eighteen."

"Mother, we're going to a West Point hop, not Sunday school," Marynell protested. "I think the dress is perfect for Louise. We'll both look smashing."

Marynell would be smashing, Louise thought, but for herself she'd settle for looking appropriate. She liked this dress the best, but she hesitated. Did it look too fancy for the daughter of an Army doctor?

A princess could wear such a dress. But then, she had always imagined a West Point ballroom full of dashing young men in full-dress uniforms with their dates looking like princesses—like a scene out of *The Student Prince.*

At their daddy's suggestion, the sisters and their mother had ridden the bus from Fort Belvoir into Washington to take advantage of the after-Christmas sales. Their daddy said he wanted his girls to be wearing the prettiest dresses at the hop. "Have your mother buy a dress, too," he told his daughters. "I can't remember the last time she had a new dress."

"What about it, dear?" the saleslady asked.

"I'd like to think about it while we look for something for our mother."

Elizabeth looked up, her face alarmed. "Oh, no. I don't need a dress."

"Daddy expressly said you were to have a dress, too," Louise said firmly. "He said for us not to come home unless we all three had something beautiful to show off for him."

"Your father can't afford for all three of us to buy a dress," Elizabeth protested. She took off her left glove and began twisting it.

Louise nodded at the saleslady, who scurried off to the racks.

Marynell caught her sister's eye and shrugged helplessly. Mother was such a problem, her look said. Marynell sat on the bench beside Elizabeth. "Wouldn't it be fun to have something special for the New Year's reception, Mother?" she asked. "Something with a little color for a change?"

Elizabeth shook her head no. "I'm comfortable in what I have."

"But just think how nice you'd look in a beautiful new dress," Marynell insisted.

Louise sympathized with her mother. New clothes were frightening. The night before Louise had something new to wear to school, she couldn't sleep. She worried that she'd look out of place, that she would be noticed, that she wouldn't be noticed. A new hairstyle was the same—maybe worse. Even when other girls said they loved it, Louise wondered if they really did.

Marynell could never understand the worry of something new. She had never agonized over clothes, over whether to wear a ribbon in her hair.

The saleslady bustled over with an armful of dresses. Elizabeth shook her head. "It's time we start home," she protested. "Your father will be needing his dinner."

"Mother, it's only two-thirty. We've got plenty of time."

The saleslady quickly held up one of her collection for Elizabeth's inspection. A yellow sale tag hung from its sleeve. Elizabeth looked at the dress for a long minute, a soft sigh escaping her lips. It was a silk paisley print of pale blue and yellow, its skirt softly pleated, with a deep ruffle of ecru lace rimming the neck and wrists.

The woman had read her well. The dress was pretty, but muted, a perfect dress for a lady like Elizabeth Rodgers. "Your husband would be pleased, dearie."

Elizabeth blushed.

She blushed again at her daughters' exclamations when she came out of the dressing room. The dress draped softly about her thin, almost bosomless figure. The lace at the neck and wrists was appealingly feminine. The soft colors were flattering to Elizabeth's complexion. Louise wished her mother wouldn't part her hair in the middle and pull it back in an old-lady knot at the nape of her neck. If it weren't for her hairstyle and the thick glasses, Elizabeth would look lovely. It amazed Louise to realize anew that her mother was beautiful, even more beautiful than Marynell. After all, the sisters had always been slightly embarrassed by their reclusive, colorless mother who never achieved the social patina of the other officers' wives. But Elizabeth's cheekbones were high and patrician, her nose narrow and delicate. Her skin was still flawless but for the network of fine wrinkles that now radiated from the corners of her eyes. But her hair had been graying for years, as had her wardrobe.

"It's too expensive—even on sale," Elizabeth said at once. But the image of herself in the mirror was pleasing. It showed in her expression. Tears welled in her eyes. "Do you really think your father wants me to buy a dress?"

· · ·

Eddie Rodgers was already home, his Saturday afternoon hospital rounds accomplished, his newspaper in hand.

He reassured his wife. Of course it was all right that she had bought a dress. No, he didn't want her to return it. He insisted his three "girls" model their dresses for him.

"But your dinner," Elizabeth protested.

"Dinner can wait," he told her in the gentle but firm voice he often used with his wife.

After the impromptu fashion show, Eddie marched wife and daughters to the west side of the house to catch the waning rays of January sunlight and took their picture with his box camera.

The sisters stood arm-in-arm, shivering without their coats, and offered proud smiles. Louise wished her hair looked better.

Then Louise photographed her parents together—Elizabeth shyly smiling, Eddie handsome in his uniform, his hair still jet black, his arm around his wife's slender waist as they stood beside the two-story quarters that had been their home for the past two years. Before that, they had lived at Fort Bragg, North Carolina, and before that, Jefferson Barracks near St. Louis. Before that, other posts. For military families, a sense of home was more dependent on familiar furnishings carted around from post to post than an assigned set of quarters. No matter where the Rodgerses lived, they sat around the same dining room table; over the sideboard inherited from Great-aunt Beth hung the same scene of horses, riders and dogs milling about in front of a British manor house, waiting for the hunt to begin.

Louise's dormitory room at Mary Baldwin College had never felt like home. The furnishings were impersonal. And her roommate was not her sister.

Next Friday, she and Marynell would depart for a weekend at West Point, a very daring, very grown-up thing to do. She was not a little girl anymore. In a few years, she'd probably marry and make a home of her own.

Louise and Marynell helped their mother with dinner, their new dresses safely put away. Elizabeth warmed up leftover turkey and dressing. Marynell tossed a salad while Louise set the table. After dinner, the sisters put on their coats and mufflers and walked to the post theater to see the latest Charlie Chaplin movie. When they got home, their parents were still in the living room, Eddie hovering near the radio for the nightly news program, a stack of medical journals at his elbow, a lost game of solitaire still scattered across the round table. Elizabeth was sitting in the wing chair, the cat curled on her lap and a shawl draped over her shoulders as she squinted at the pages of her book. If Elizabeth was sitting down, she was reading. Every year, she retreated more and more into her novels. Louise noticed the difference in her mother just since September when she and Marynell had departed for college. Louise wore wrinkled blouses and the house was less tidy in spite of the cleaning woman who came on Monday and Thursday mornings. A stack of library books on the console table by the front door was overdue.

With both daughters gone, Louise could well imagine her mother reading away the morning in her bathrobe until time to dress and fix lunch for her husband, then returning to her books for the afternoon until time to prepare dinner, breaking her routine only to do grocery shopping at the commissary and get a new supply of books from the post library.

Louise wondered how her mother would ever get through hostessing the Christmas reception for the hospital staff when her daughters no longer came home for the holidays.

Marynell brought two glasses of milk from the kitchen, and the sisters sat for a while listening to the news. Reports on the civil war in Spain. More government regulation for the coal industry. Roosevelt was advocating naval expansion for the nation's self-defense. The former king of England and his bride of six months, the former Wallis Simpson, were enjoying the nightlife in Paris and drawing crowds wherever they went.

At the end of the news, Eddie—without asking—poured Elizabeth a glass of sherry from the decanter on the credenza. As an afterthought, he poured a glass for each of his daughters and placed them by the empty milk glasses. For himself, he poured a finger of scotch.

Louise concentrated on not making a face as she forced herself to sip at the sherry. She couldn't believe her mother really liked the stuff.

"I don't want a marriage like that," Marynell said later as she sprawled across Louise's bed. Louise picked up her hairbrush from the dressing table and began giving her hair its nightly one hundred strokes.

"They don't argue," Louise defended, sitting on a corner of the bed and leaning forward to brush from the roots up.

"I'd die of boredom. God, how can they stand it?"

"What would you do differently?" Louise asked.

"Entertain. Go dancing. Play bridge. Anything but sitting there night after night for a lifetime."

"Yes," Louise said, resuming an upright position, "but isn't it lovely to always have them there when we drink our glass of milk?"

And it had been, she realized, suddenly appreciating what had been taken for granted all the years of her growing up—the constancy of evenings with her parents either in the living room or propped up in their bed, looking up from their reading to respond to a good-night peck and ask if homework was done, if shoes were polished for tomorrow. Of course, there had been the years when Daddy still had to go back to the hospital for emergencies. But since he had been promoted to major, he was really more of an administrator than a practitioner, leaving the after-hours medicine to his subordinates.

"I couldn't believe the sherry," Marynell said.

"I think it was his way of saying we've grown up," Louise said, as she mentally counted seventy-eight and -nine.

"Mother didn't even notice," Marynell said. "Sometimes I think those books are her real life, and we're just filler."

"Let's read the letters," Louise said, deliberately changing the subject.

"Good idea," Marynell said, bouncing off the bed and racing down the hall to her own bedroom.

Louise had taken her own two letters out of the leather jewelry box on her dresser. She knew their contents by heart. "At the suggestion of your parents' friend, Mrs. Willard Fentriss, I am writing to invite you for the Winter Hop at the Academy on January 5. Yours sincerely, Cadet Sergeant Gerald Lincoln Worth III."

The second note said, "I am delighted that you have accepted my invitation and will be my date for the Winter Hop. I will be dining with you at the Fentriss home before the hop, and I look forward to meeting you at this time. Yours sincerely, Cadet Sergeant Gerald Lincoln Worth III."

Her first letters from a boy, Louise thought, staring dreamily at the carefully penned notes with the gold embossed crest of the academy at the top of the page. But a cadet wasn't a boy. Gerald Lincoln Worth III was a man, a third-year cadet at the United States Military Academy.

The sisters sat on the bed, lost in their separate daydreams. Louise realized that part of her was already in love with a cadet she had never met. And the rest of her hoped she would get sick and not ever have to meet him.

"Wouldn't it be romantic if we both fell in love?" Marynell said with a prolonged sigh. She drifted off the bed to the mirror and fluffed her wonderful hair.

Taking a deep breath, Louise leaned back in the train seat and willed herself to relax. She must stop mentally packing and repacking her suitcase. Whatever she had forgotten she would have to do without. She and her sister were going to a West Point hop—the stuff of countless daydreams, except in her daydreams she hadn't been nervous and afraid.

Marynell was traveling in her standby navy-blue gabardine dress. Louise was wearing a plaid wool dress to which she had added a white satin collar in hopes of giving it a dressier look. Like Marynell, Louise was wearing a cloche hat. Their leather gloves were tucked away in their purses.

The floor of the train trembled under Louise's feet. They waved one last time to their father. He blew them a kiss, a very unmilitary gesture for a man in uniform, but then he never looked quite as military as other officers. His posture was too relaxed, his tummy too soft, and he had never mastered the art of spit-polishing his shoes.

Marynell nudged Louise and pointed out the window at a couple locked in a farewell embrace. "Like in the movies," she sighed.

Louise nodded. "Clark Gable and Carole Lombard."

The whistle sounded its warning. The man began to draw away from the young woman, who was weeping, clinging. They kissed again. Louise wondered if the woman wore a wedding band under her glove. But somehow they didn't seem married. Married people didn't act that way in public.

The train began its first tentative movement. The girls waved again at their father, then Marynell grabbed Louise's hand. The sisters looked at each other and giggled. They were on their way to *West Point!*

The young man had boarded, the woman was walking beside the slowly moving train, waving. Marynell sighed at the romance of the little scenario. "I can't decide which will more fun—to be loved or to be in love."

"That couple didn't look like either one of them was having any fun," Louise pointed out.

"But they were living *romance*. I want romance," Marynell said with a dramatic wave of her hand. "I'd like to be that woman, enough in love with a man to weep at farewell. Even if she's never going to see him again, she has a beautiful memory. In fact, tragic romance is even more beautiful than happily ever after, don't you think?"

"You mean like Romeo and Juliet? I'll pass on that. I'd rather be a little less romantic and stay alive."

But a nonfatal romance would be nice, and Louise longed for it more than she longed for good grades or new clothes. She longed for it more than fame or riches.

She wondered if her date for the weekend went by Gerald or Jerry. Mrs. Fentriss had called him Gerald in the letters she had written arranging the weekend, and he had signed his letters that way. But somehow Gerald sounded like a name teachers would use, not one's friends.

Major Fentriss was medical corps like their father. He had been a classmate of Eddie Rodgers' at the Washington University medical college in St. Louis, and immediately after their internship year, the two men had served in the war together in France—and then again years later at Fort Bragg. Major Fentriss was now guardian of the health care for the cadets and military cadre at West Point. Mrs. Fentriss had promised on her Christmas card last year that she would invite Louise and Marynell up for a weekend and arrange cadet escorts. But that had been over a year ago. They knew she had either forgotten or was waiting for Louise to turn eighteen.

The train was picking up speed. Already the outskirts of the city were rolling past. Marynell fished a small tablet and a pencil out of her purse and handed it to her sister.

"Conversation topics," she said firmly.

Louise nodded.

Marynell had attended dances at Staunton Military Academy, Mary Baldwin College's brother school, and had had a steady beau during her freshman year. They had even kissed, Marynell had confided to her sister. But the boy had been a senior and graduated. Marynell went out with a variety of boys in the following year and a half. Since arriving at Mary Baldwin for her freshman year, Louise had double-dated with her sister three times, but none of the boys—all SMA cadets—had called her back. Marynell said it was because she never said anything. Louise was determined to talk at West Point, and Marynell had promised to help her prepare.

"Ask him about his family," Marynell instructed.

Louise dutifully wrote "family" in her notebook. At Marynell's instruction, she added subtopics of siblings, father's career, mother's hobbies, pets.

"If he's an Army brat, ask about all the places they've lived," her sister continued.

Louise added "places he's lived" to her list.

"Has he always wanted a military career? What branch does he want to serve in? Does he likes West Point? What's his toughest class? His favorite class? His major? Does he play on an athletic team? Who are his best friends? Does he ever get homesick? Does he think there will be a war?"

Louise wrote fast to keep up with her sister's suggestions. "How can you think of all that?" she asked.

"Oh, it's easy after you get the hang of it. Boys like to talk about themselves and give their opinions. Just keep asking them questions, and they'll think you're wonderful." Louise stared at her notebook. She'd never be able to carry this off.

She didn't want to envy her sister. Always before, Louise had accepted their differences with good grace. When they were younger, it hadn't mattered that she hung back, that she was quiet, that she was less beautiful than the self-assured Marynell. After all, Louise made better grades, kept her room neater and could make a chocolate cake better than either her mother or her sister. But now Louise acknowledged that she'd gotten the short end of the stick. Boys would rather flirt with a pretty girl than a smart one. And the way to a man's heart was not through his stomach. Whoever said that was dumb.

It seemed like a terrible thing to be jealous of one's own sister.

CHAPTER

TWO

The small station was built on the edge of the Hudson River. Most of the passengers getting off the train were young women. Many were wearing fur coats, obviously not the daughters of Army families. Looming above them were massive granite battlements. "Creepers," Marynell said. "Looks like something from the Middle Ages."

A plump, middle-aged woman was making her way across the platform. "Marynell. Louise," she said. "My goodness. I hardly recognized you two. What happened to the pigtails?"

Louise wasn't sure she would have recognized Millie Fentriss either if she'd seen her on the street. Seven years ago, when they'd lived next door to the Fentrisses at Fort Bragg, Mrs. Fentriss had been a slim brunette. The woman beaming at them now had crossed over into plump, graying matronhood.

"Well, I see that Louise still has her mother's eyes, and Marynell still has her father's smile," she said between hugs. "Your parents are such dear people. I don't know what I would have done without them when our Robbie was sick and I had my surgery. He's in medical school now in St. Louis and sends his best to you girls. Your parents are saints, you know. I always wanted to do something nice for them, and it dawned on me how old you girls were by now, and that you just might be interested in coming to a hop. Am I right? Just the words 'West Point' are enough to make any self-respecting Army daughter's heart skip a beat. Last June, you wouldn't believe the weddings that went on around here. Of course, every Army girl dreams of tying the knot at the West Point Chapel."

As she led them to her car, Millie babbled on, often asking questions but leaving no time for them to be answered. Maybe that was why Millie and her mother had become friends. Millie did the talking, and all that was required of Elizabeth was to nod from time to time.

Once past the fortress walls, the reservation itself was a comfortable Army post with ancient trees, stately buildings, carefully kept grounds, handsome rows of identical two-story brick officers' quarters. Millie took them on a tour, chatting away about academy lore and traditions. "You girls know about Kissing Rock, don't you? The cadets are forbidden from making any public displays of affection, but no one's ever gotten demerits for kissing a girl under the rock."

The Fentrisses' furniture was the same as Louise remembered from Fort Bragg, except for new slipcovers on the sofa and easy chairs. While his wife had grown rounder, Major Fentriss seemed to have shrunk. Louise had been certain he was tall at Fort Bragg, and he certainly had possessed more hair. Like her father, Major Fentriss never looked quite at home in his uniform. Military physicians often seemed to lack the crispness of other officers. And they never wore boots. Louise thought officers looked especially handsome when they wore high, polished boots and jodhpurs.

Millie gave them tea and cookies, then showed them to the guest room. "The young men are expected at seven," she told them and giggled like a girl. "This is so much fun. I've never played matchmaker before. As I wrote your mother, both these young men come highly recommended by the cadet hostess. They're both from Army families."

Both girls were ready in plenty of time. Louise went down to ask Millie if they could help with dinner, only to be shooed away. "Heavens, no. You might get something on your wonderful dress."

Louise went back upstairs and sat on the bed with Marynell, careful not to wrinkle her dress, waiting for the doorbell to ring.

Marynell insisted on adding a second coat of mascara to Louise's lashes and color to her cheeks. "You've simply got to wear more rouge," she chastised.

Promptly at seven, the doorbell rang. Louise's heart pounded so hard it hurt. Marynell gave her sister a reassuring hug. "It'll be all right, honey. Underneath the uniforms, they're just college boys. And I'll bet they're as nervous as we are."

Marcus Remington, Marynell's date, was a young Ichabod Crane complete with Adam's apple above the high collar of his uniform jacket. He was nervous and cleared his throat a lot. Gerald Worth was coolly blue-eyed and slender, not nervous at all. During dinner, his knee touched Louise's leg. The first time it happened, Louise jerked her leg away and assumed it had been an accident. Then it happened again. Louise angled her body in her chair to avoid further contact.

"You haven't dated much, I take it," Gerald said softly, leaning toward her ear, his shoulder brushing hers.

Louise shook her head no and concentrated on her salad.

Major Fentriss helped his wife serve. Marynell hopped up, insisting she would help instead. "Nonsense," the diminutive major said. "Millie has me well trained. You young people enjoy each other."

With both Fentrisses out of the room, Gerald said, "Officers should not do kitchen duty."

"He's also a husband," Louise said, surprised at her own boldness, but it seemed ungrateful for Gerald to criticize their host. And her father helped out in the kitchen, too. When she and Marynell were growing up, more evenings than not, Eddie would send his daughters off to their homework after dinner while he helped Elizabeth clean up. But Louise could feel Marynell's warning gaze and immediately regretted her words. *A girl did not contradict her date.* Louise knew that without having written it down in her little notebook.

Millie chatted incessantly during the meal, sparing Louise the need to use any of her conversation topics. She was relieved to be able to save them for later.

She picked at her veal, fighting off a depressing sense of disappointment. The night was not going to be wonderful. Gerald was surely wishing he'd been paired off with the vivacious older sister. His knee did not stray again.

After dinner, Millie supervised the bundling up, even buttoning the top button on Louise's coat as though she were a child.

"She does the same thing to me," Major Fentriss said with a chuckle. "Millie's got to have someone to mother."

Louise avoided looking at Gerald.

On the walk across the reservation, Gerald's firm hand on her elbow made Louise feel awkward and off balance. She realized the gesture was intended to be courtly—a gentleman making sure his lady did not trip in the darkness—but she held her upper arm away from her body to put distance between his fingers and the side of her breast. Soon a cramp grabbed at her muscles, forcing her to relax a bit. In spite of the chill, she could feel perspiration gathering under her arms and between her breasts. She was supposed to be having fun. She and Marynell had squealed and hugged when the invitations arrived.

Marynell was chattering away brightly to Marcus in front of them, asking him questions from the list.

Louise cleared her throat. "Mrs. Fentriss tells me you're from Cleveland."

"Cincinnati," Gerald corrected. "Actually, I was born in Cincinnati and have relatives living there, but you know how it is when you're Army. We've lived all over."

"What branch is your father?"

"Quartermaster."

"Is that what you want? Quartermaster."

"Heavens, no. I want to be a pilot. The Army Air Corps is the branch of the future. My second choice would be field artillery. I made excellent grades in ballistics."

Louise wasn't sure what ballistics was. She wondered if it would seem dumb if she asked.

"My best class is French," she said, wondering if it was all right to say something about herself at this point.

Louise knew her voice was as stiff as her body. When Gerald offered no response to her comment, she struggled to remember the next question on her list.

"Have you always wanted a military career?"

"Yes."

They fell silent, listening to Marynell's chatter. "Oh, Ingrid Bergman is my favorite, too," she cooed. "Have you seen *Intermezzo*?"

How did Marynell do it? She didn't even have to stop and think.

"Do you think there will be a war?" Louise asked.

"Yes."

She wanted to cry.

By moonlight, the Gothic architecture of the granite buildings seemed softer. West Point. For years, the very words had conjured up romantic fantasies.

At Cullum Hall, cadets and their dates had already formed a line up the marble staircase to the second-floor ballroom, waiting for their turn in the receiving line, where they were first greeted by a short, plump woman who reminded Louise of Millie Fentriss. "And you girls must be the Rodgers sisters," she announced. "I'm Mrs. Renfrow, the cadet hostess. I understand your father is medical corps and that you both attend Mary Baldwin. We don't get many Virginia girls up here at the Point. They mostly go to Annapolis, I guess. But then Army girls have no business dating Navy boys, do they?"

"My goodness," Marynell said, when they were out of earshot. "Does she memorize the names of each boy's date in advance?"

"She has a New York detective agency check out each girl," Gerald said. "Only refined young women are allowed here, lest some cadet become smitten with a chorus girl or someone equally inappropriate."

When Marynell laughed, Louise realized Gerald had been joking—at least about the detective agency.

Gerald presented Louise with her presigned dance card. He had the first and last dances, as tradition required. And Louise noted that he also had taken dance number seven. She looked with apprehension at the other names. But at least she wouldn't have to think of twelve dances' worth of conversation to share with Gerald.

Louise was too nervous to enjoy the brilliant setting around her, but she took it all in to consider later. The ballroom was impressive with white and gold walls, rich red upholstery on the chairs. Around the huge room were life-size portraits of important-looking men in uniform. The cadet orchestra was good enough to be professional. All the cadets were identically clad in dress uniforms, their dates in fluffy, pastel formals. Louise kept looking down at her own dress. It really was pretty.

Somehow she managed to make her way to intermission, asking each of her partners where they were from, if their father was Army, what branch they were interested in. The young men offered polite questions of their own. Where she was from, if her father was Army, if she had ever been to a West Point hop before. She wished her hands didn't sweat.

At intermission she and Gerald stood silently sipping ice water, which seemed to be the only refreshment. She looked around the room for Marynell. Gerald understood. He took her glass from her hand and guided her across the room to the security of her sister.

Marynell and Marcus were sitting with another couple. Having seated Louise next to her sister, Gerald soon fell into a conversation with the other cadets about the fighting between Japan and China and Roosevelt's calling for a boycott of Japanese goods.

Marynell tugged at her sister's sleeve. "Talk," Marynell whispered out of the side of her mouth.

"I can't," Louise said.

Marynell regarded her sister perched on the edge of her chair like a bird about to take flight. Poor Louise. She was pretty enough but so backward when it came to boys, and no boy was going to court a backward girl. Marynell worried more about her sister's future than her own.

After intermission, Marynell's first partner was Marcus's battalion commander, Cadet Captain Franklin Cravens. Cadet Cravens was much better looking than poor gangling Marcus. And self-assured. Marynell liked a man who knew what he was about.

She smiled and asked several questions. Thank God she wasn't like her sister. Franklin told her she danced well. Then he said she was very pretty. It was too easy. Her questions revealed that Franklin's father was Army and stationed at Camp Dix, New Jersey. The post commandant. That meant his father must be a general! Marynell's heart soared. A cadet captain with a general for a father! When the music ended, Franklin thanked her and started to escort her back to Marcus. "Oh, couldn't we go out on the balcony until the next dance begins?" Marynell said, fanning her face with her hand. "It's so stuffy in here."

Franklin studied her face before offering his arm and escorting her out onto the balcony, where several other couples had stepped outside to smoke. The moonlight reflected on the river, but it was too chilly to be romantic. The other girls had evening wraps about their shoulders. Marynell tried not to shiver.

She leaned over the wall and made a great show of admiring the view. She knew Franklin was admiring her profile, her smooth white throat made pale in the moonlight.

"Oh, isn't it just perfectly beautiful!" she exclaimed, tilting her face in his direction.

Franklin nodded, his look noncommittal.

Marynell felt a moment of unaccustomed indecision. How *did* one talk to a general's son?

"Is this your last year?" she asked.

Again he nodded. "You're going to freeze," he said, taking her arm and guiding her toward the door. "And I imagine your next partner is searching for you."

"Is your girlfriend here for the weekend?" Marynell asked as they strolled back inside.

Franklin shook his head no.

When the familiar strains of "Stardust" began, Franklin abruptly took her in his arms. Marynell struggled to keep a smug smile from her lips. "What about number eight on my little card?" Marynell asked coyly.

"Whoever he is, I outrank him," Franklin said.

The lights dimmed and colored spotlights played over the dancing couples. Franklin took advantage of the darkness to pull her hard against him. Wordlessly, they danced, his erection growing against her belly. She wondered if she should be indignant, but she did nothing.

"You're the most beautiful girl here," he whispered in her ear.

Marynell relaxed and lifted both arms around his neck, making it easy for him to sneak a feel of her right breast. She closed her eyes, imagining a succession of Saturday night hops as the date of Franklin Cravens. And since he was a first classman, a wedding at the end of the semester. She was a lucky girl. But then she'd always known things would work out for her. It was as though it was written in a big book someplace that Marynell was special, that good things would happen to her.

Marynell pulled away long enough to tell him, "This is my first time here. I just met my date this evening."

Franklin's thumb rubbed up and down the outside of her breast.

She wondered if he'd try to go all the way before they were engaged. She wouldn't let him. She'd heard too many horror stories about girls who didn't save it and ended up jilted—or pregnant. But she'd let him feel her a lot. She could hardly wait to get him hot and begging.

When the music ended, he thanked her formally and escorted her back to Marcus. Marcus called him "sir."

For the rest of the evening, Marynell kept looking around for a glimpse of Franklin. She only saw him once more, dancing with a blonde. She wanted to give him her address and make sure he remembered her name and that she went to Mary Baldwin College, but surely he had taken note. She rubbed her upper arm over the side of her breast where he had touched her. *Surely.*

At midnight, the orchestra played "Army Blue." Once again the lights were dimmed. Marynell allowed Marcus to hold her close while she pretended he was Franklin Cravens.

The sisters walked two by two with their dates back to the Fentrisses' quarters. Louise tried only one question. "Do you have any brothers and sisters?"

"One sister," Gerald answered.

Louise waited nervously for him to take her elbow, but instead he slipped his arm around her waist. She stiffened, and he withdrew it.

Louise was thankful for Marynell's happy chatter. It saved them from silence.

She expected chastisement from her sister, but Marynell seemed distracted as they got ready for bed.

The beds were twin with a small lamp table in between. "Well, good night," Marynell said as she turned out the light. In the darkness, she asked, "You okay, Sis?"

"I suppose."

"I'll come lie with you for a minute, okay?" Marynell said.

Louise felt better with her sister's warmth at her side. "I don't think I'll ever get married," she said in the darkness.

"Sure you will, but not to him. You need someone who's shy, too."

"If he's as shy as I am, we'll never have children," Louise said matter-of-factly.

Marynell giggled.

Louise supposed it was funny, but she couldn't bring herself to laugh.

After a minute of silence, Marynell asked, "Do you think about it very much?"

"What?"

"Making love with a man. Sex."

"I think about being loved," Louise said, "about having a man be nice to me and court me and bring me flowers. Kissing, too."

"But never being naked and having a man touch you?"

"A little, I guess. It'll have to be in the dark. I think I'd die if a man ever saw me naked."

"Me, too," Marynell agreed, "except that sometimes I wonder if it would be exciting. I wonder if Mother and Daddy ever look at each other."

"*Marynell!* You shouldn't think about our parents in that way."

Silence again.

"Of course, Daddy's seen lots of people naked," Marynell said. "Even if your husband doesn't look at you, a doctor sure gets a bird's-eye view when he delivers your babies."

Louise's stomach contracted at the thought. She'd long ago decided that would be the worst part of childbirth.

The silence surrounded them again.

"Well, I guess I'll get some sleep," Marynell said and swung her feet to the floor. "Are you going to cry?" she asked Louise.

"No."

"I'd hoped we'd both be in love by now."

"Are you?"

"Not with Marcus. He's too ugly ever to be a general. And he clears his throat every six to eight words. I counted. I'd like to be a general's wife someday." Marynell paused then added, "I danced with a real dreamy boy. I hope he asks me back next time."

"I hope so, too," Louise said.

Marynell bent over and kissed Louise's cheek before returning to her own bed.

Louise wondered if a general couldn't be ugly and decided that he could as long as he was physically impressive. Marcus was neither. Gerald was handsome and well built, but she didn't think she wanted to marry Gerald—not that he'd have her.

She was a failure as a date. She wished she was alone so she could cry.

Gerald and Marcus came at ten-thirty in the morning to take the sisters to services in the famous chapel where so many Army marriages had begun. The stately sanctuary was lined with regimental flags, and the tremendous organ could have served a cathedral. Louise got goose bumps when the cadet choir sang "A Mighty Fortress Is Our God."

Marynell was restless during the service, twisting in her seat to look behind her. Louise knew she was looking for the cadet from the dance.

After the four young people lunched with the Fentrisses, they attended a horse show in the great riding hall. Louise relaxed a bit. Horses were easy to talk about. She asked Gerald if he liked to ride, and he told her about the old roan mare his family had taken from post to post until she died three years ago. "I loved that old nag," Gerald said affectionately. "She was like a member of the family. We all cried when she died."

She started to tell him about the mare she and Marynell had ridden for years, but she asked him about his family instead. She was being a better date, Louise told herself. Gerald even smiled at her a couple of times.

After an ice cream cone at the Boodles, the cadets walked the girls back to the Fentrisses' in time to get their bags and make their train.

Millie gushed a bit too much. "Now when will we see all you young people again?"

Marcus looked eager. "How about week after next?" he asked, looking at Gerald for confirmation.

Gerald shrugged. "Sure." Louise wished he seemed more enthusiastic. She really had been a better date this afternoon.

For their second trip to West Point, they left before dawn directly from the Staunton station and didn't arrive until late afternoon. No wonder girls from Mary Baldwin didn't go to West Point hops. Louise felt a little foolish going all this way for a boy who didn't seem to like her very much. She had tried to study on the train but found it difficult to concentrate. Maybe Gerald liked her more than she thought. Billie, her roommate, said he probably respected her because she didn't let him get fresh.

Louise couldn't decide if she would like Gerald if he liked her.

They had a light supper with the Fentrisses and hurried off to get ready for the evening. They were wearing the same dresses to this hop but decided they would trade if they got invited back a third time.

Once again, Louise and Marynell were ready in plenty of time. But no sooner had they seated themselves carefully on the bed to wait when the doorbell sounded. "It's too early to be them," Marynell said, but they both rushed to the mirror for one last look, just in case. Marynell patted her own hair, then turned to fuss a bit over Louise's. Louise wasn't sure about all those finger waves. Somehow they suited Marynell better than they did her.

Voices drifted up from downstairs. After a time, Millie tapped on the door and let herself in.

"My, how lovely you girls look. Come along now. There's someone downstairs you need to talk to, Louise. There's been a change of plans."

Louise and Marynell exchanged puzzled looks.

Mrs. Renfrow, the cadet hostess, was waiting in the living room with Marcus and a cadet Louise had never seen before. Marcus stepped forward and stood by Marynell. The other cadet stared for a minute at Marynell, then turned his attention to Louise, offering her a nod and a half smile. Louise's stomach was churning with dread. Millie Fentriss was smiling too sweetly, Mrs. Renfrow too graciously. Even Marynell hung back, then tugged on Marcus's arm, pulling him into the hallway.

"Louise, dear," Mrs. Renfrow said in a voice dripping with kindness, "Cadet Sergeant Worth was taken ill this afternoon and sends his deepest regrets. Cadet Captain Franklin Cravens has stepped forward and asked to be your escort tonight in Gerald's stead."

Mrs. Renfrow averted her eyes as she spoke. She felt sorry for Louise.

Louise felt her cheeks go hot with humiliation. She knew Gerald wasn't really sick.

She turned to Cadet Cravens. Without really looking at him she said, "That's very gracious of you, but I would prefer not to go." She had to escape before she cried. Please, just go, she thought. Please.

"May I suggest that Cadet Remington escort Miss Marynell and Mrs. Renfrow to Cullum Hall," Franklin Cravens was saying in a take-charge voice. "Perhaps Miss Louise and I can join them later."

Everyone hastened to follow his instructions. Louise looked at him. He was handsome, impressive. Military from head to toe.

Louise was aware of Millie bustling about, seeing Marynell, Marcus and Mrs. Renfrow on their way. She announced from the entry hall that she'd make coffee.

Louise turned to go upstairs.

"Please stay," Franklin said. "I'd like to explain."

"You don't need to. I didn't think he liked me. Now I know."

Franklin took her arm and led her to the sofa. Why was she letting him? She didn't want to be led around by the arm any more. Franklin pulled up the ottoman and sat in front of her.

"Cadet Worth is a gentleman and would have fulfilled his responsibility to you if I hadn't asked him to say he was sick," Franklin explained. "He went with me this afternoon to talk it over with Mrs. Renfrow."

"And she agreed?" Louise said, her head beginning to hurt. She wanted to take off her dress and lie in a dark room with a wet cloth on her head. She never wanted to date again. If she were Catholic, she'd become a nun. Maybe she would anyway. Catholics weren't so different from Episcopalians.

"It took a little persuading. Gerald wasn't sickly enough to suit her, but she is easily impressed by rank and I'm not only the senior battalion commander, I have the highest ranking father of any cadet. Sometimes that is advantageous."

"I don't understand," Louise said. When could she escape and go upstairs to darkness?

"Gerald is supply sergeant on my staff. After drill this morning, I heard him complaining about his date for tonight. I'd seen you with him two weeks ago, looking a bit overwhelmed. Everything Gerald said about you made me think I would like to escort you to the hop myself, and I saw no reason to put you through an evening with a reluctant date."

Louise rubbed her temples. Would he let her go if she cried? she wondered. "What did he say about me that was so intriguing? That I was tongue-tied?"

"He said that you were pretty but too shy for comfort, that you were an officer's daughter and wouldn't play footsie with him under the table or let him put his arm around you. That you'd probably never dated before."

"Do you think that's good?" Her head was throbbing. The rubbing didn't help.

"Yes."

"Why?"

"Because I'll graduate in June, and I've had my fill of young women who are neither shy nor reluctant. Will you please accompany me to the dance?"

"No. Everyone will know Gerald stood me up. In addition to my other faults, I'm not very tough."

"Only an hour ago, Major Fentriss was kind enough to put Gerald in the infirmary to be observed for a possible appendicitis. Now, I suggest we have a cup of coffee with Mrs. Fentriss and be on our way."

Louise sat dumbly, not knowing what she should say or do.

"You won't run off, will you, if I go get you some aspirin for that headache? I really do want to take you to the hop."

His expression was serious and sincere. She actually believed him. She nodded.

She heard him talking to Millie in the kitchen. When he returned, he was carrying a glass of water and two aspirin. Millie was following him with the tray for coffee. Franklin put the aspirin in Louise's hand and stood over her while she took them.

Louise's coffee had sherry in it. She sipped it quietly, trying not to make a face and listening to Franklin ask Millie about how she liked being assigned to West Point, if the picture on the upright piano was of her son. She seemed flattered by his attention.

Louise realized she would go to the dance with this strong-willed young man. A high-ranking cadet and the son of a high-ranking officer. How strange that she would end up with a date like that.

When she had finished her coffee, Franklin sent her upstairs to freshen up. She stared in the mirror and could see why. She was pale. Her hair was mussed. She put on lipstick, added some of Marynell's rouge and brushed out the finger waves a bit.

Going back down the stairs, she felt like a windup doll.

The evening was easy. Franklin took charge and did the question asking. When they danced, he led so competently, Louise could almost relax. Almost.

She needed desperately to talk to Marynell and get some sisterly reassurance, but Marynell always seemed to be in another part of the ballroom.

At the end of the evening, Franklin shook her hand at the Fentrisses' front door and invited her to chapel in the morning. And he said he planned to write to her. He didn't ask if she would write back.

"He said he was going to write to me," Louise told Marynell as they got ready for bed.

"Then why aren't you more excited?" Marynell challenged.

"Because it all seems so strange. I don't understand why he's interested in me, of all people."

"Did he dance close?" Marynell asked.

"Oh, no. He was a perfect gentleman."

There was no sisterly cuddling after the lights were out. Louise felt neither exhilarated nor depressed. She tried to feel in love but was too tired to feel much of anything. And anyway, she wouldn't want to be in love yet just in case he didn't write to her. But if he did, that would mean she'd had a successful date. Marynell said a successful date was one when you heard from the boy again.

Franklin had said he liked her dress. And he complimented her on the way she answered the polite questions of the assistant commandant's wife when they went through the receiving line.

He also asked if she'd ever worn her hair long. She knew it had been a bad idea to cut it, but Marynell had insisted.

So Marynell didn't know everything.

CHAPTER

THREE

*F*ranklin wrote twice the following week. That in itself amazed Louise, and she was shocked by the status his letters gave her among the girls in Hill Top Hall. Letters from West Point! A fourth-year cadet no less. And everyone thought she was a mouse.

They had been right. Louise knew that letters from West Point did not change who she was—a shy young woman who was more comfortable studying her lessons than going to a dance, who would never be able to flirt, who in spite of her intensely romantic daydreams worried at times if she was one of those women who should never marry and should love nieces, nephews and small animals instead. She longed for a grand passion but feared she did not have it in herself to give.

What did Franklin Cravens want of her? No matter how hard she tried, Louise could not conjure up images of him kissing her throat, of being in bed with him. He was so correct, so in control.

The following week, two more letters arrived.

In addition to Franklin's letters, Louise also received a letter from her father, who wrote each daughter on alternating weeks with the expectation that the letters would be shared. His letters included hospital gossip, comments on the weather and current events, and news of their mother—usually that she was fine and sent her love. Elizabeth often added a handwritten note at the bottom of Eddie's typewritten page. She missed them. The cat was sick. Study hard. The name of a book they might enjoy reading. And there were always newspaper clippings—the latest linking the high incidence of tuberculosis among young women to poor dietary habits and another profiling Eleanor Roosevelt. Elizabeth greatly admired the president's wife, which puzzled Louise a bit. Her mother and Mrs. Roosevelt couldn't have been more different. Louise could dash off a "Dear Mother and Daddy" letter in ten or fifteen minutes, but her answers to Franklin's letters took hours. The campus security guard reported after-hours dorm lights to the housemother, and in order to avoid demerits, Louise sat in the dimly lit hallway studying, one ear tuned for the tiptoeing housemother making her rounds. Lonely, cold, Louise found it hard to concentrate during these late-night sessions, but she persevered. She had always been a good student, and doing well in her college classes was very important to her. Marynell was majoring in elementary education, which seemed far more practical than the difficult and time-consuming study of French, but elementary ed was for girls who didn't study much.

Of course, most girls got a certificate to teach in their major field in case they should be widowed young and left without resources. Or in case they never married, but no one discussed that possibility. Never marrying was considered a worse fate than being widowed young.

Marynell suffered from all the attention her sister was getting. Marynell deserved a man like Franklin more than her less glamorous sister, but Louise wished Marynell could take some joy in her good fortune. When Marynell announced she had no further interest in Marcus Remington, Louise wondered if poor Marcus's crime was that he wasn't as grand as Franklin Cravens. The sisters sat together less often at dinner, and while Louise had become good friends with her second-semester roommate, Billie Cottingem of Charlotte, North Carolina, she missed her sister's companionship.

"You need a picture of your young man in his uniform for your desk, sugar," Billie announced. "If you had that, you'd be the envy of every girl at Mary Baldwin."

Billie had six older sisters, five of whom were married. She knew a lot about everything, and in lieu of her sister, Louise sought her roommate's help in making her letters to Franklin have just the right friendly tone. She didn't want him to think she presumed anything. Franklin signed his letters "Sincerely," and Louise felt as though she needed to come up with something else. "Love" would never do. "Yours truly" sounded like a business letter. Billie suggested "Your friend." Louise wasn't happy with it but could think of nothing better.

Franklin wrote in a precise script about his life at the academy, his philosophy, his career goals. He was impatient with being a cadet and looking forward to graduation and a military career in the field artillery, a branch he considered more dignified than infantry, more realistic than the outdated cavalry, more versatile than armored and one that offered greater opportunity for advancement than the non-combat branches.

He asked Louise specific questions about her studies, her family, her religious beliefs. Louise felt as though she was doing a school assignment each time she prepared a letter for him.

Franklin invited her to the St. Patrick's Day hop and arranged for a fourth-year student from his staff to serve as Marynell's escort. He had spoken to Mrs. Fentriss, and once again she invited the sisters to stay at her house.

Louise kept examining and reexamining her emotions. She was writing to a man. He had invited her to a dance in the last semester of his senior year. This meant something. How did she feel about him?

She wanted to be in love.

At night Louise resolutely hugged her pillow and tried to force romantic thoughts of Franklin into her mind.

She touched her breasts and tried to imagine Franklin's hands. His mouth. Billie said that boys did that—sucked on a girl's breasts like a baby. Louise had giggled about it at the time but couldn't stop thinking about it. A boy's mouth on her breasts. "You're so lucky to have nice titties," Billie said, bemoaning her own boyish chest.

No matter how she tried, Louise could not imagine an adoring Franklin sucking her breasts.

She would die if anyone knew how much she touched them, but she avoided touching anyplace else. Except sometimes in the bathtub. When she was little, her mother would slap her hands for "fiddling" with herself, but somehow it didn't seem as naughty to allow soapy fingers to stray inside her mysterious, already exposed opening as it did to pull panties aside at night.

"You know 'bout erections, don't you, sugar?" Billie asked one day while she was going her sit-ups.

"Like a building?" Louise asked from her desk.

Billie giggled between grunts. Her toes were tucked under her bed, her hands behind her head as she performed elbow to knee on first one side then the other. Billie often said if she could move the roll of fat on her belly to her chest, she'd be happy.

"No, I don't mean buildings. I mean penises—or is it peni?— getting erect. That's what you call it when they get hard. An erection."

"Are you talking about a boy's *thing*?"

"You don't know 'bout any of this, do you?" Billie asked, straining as she changed to leg lifts.

"I know about them putting it in," Louise said defensively. "I know about vaginas and sexual intercourse."

"Well, 'their thing' has to get hard before they can put it in. They're usually limp as old celery."

Louise sat on the floor beside her roommate. "Okay, if you're so smart, how do they make it hard? Soak it in ice water?"

"No, sugar, they get *aroused*," Billie drawled in her woman-of-the-world voice. "When they get 'round a girl they like and start thinkin' about sex, maybe kissin' and touchin', the ugly old thing gets all big and hard so they can put it in if they get the chance."

"You're making this up," Louise accused.

"Didn't you every have a dog and see his thing come out?"

"We had cats. But I've seen a horse. It was slimy and horrible. I thought his insides were coming out."

"Well, normally a man's penis just dangles there between his legs. But when he wants sex, it sticks straight out from his body like a big, red battering ram."

"How do you know?"

"My sisters told me."

"It sticks out straight," Louise repeated in disbelief, unable to imagine such a thing. "No, I don't believe you. That'd be just too queer for words."

Billie got up and rolled a piece of notebook paper in a tube, then started strutting around the room pelvis first with the paper tube substituting for an erection.

"I know you're making all this up," Louise said, doubling over with laughter.

"Oh, no, I'm not. If it didn't get hard, it'd be like tryin' to stick a stalk of limp celery up a hole."

They were both hysterical now. Louise was laughing so hard her neck hurt. "You're going to make me wet my pants," she squealed, clutching at her belly.

The girls from across the hall came across to see what the ruckus was about. Soon Billie was explaining about limp celery to a half dozen squealing girls. "My mother told me about sex," said Cindy Willis from Richmond, "but she never said one word about erections."

At lunch the next day, Billie held up a stick of celery and a whole table of girls laughed until tears rolled down their faces.

But even as Louise laughed she felt in awe of men, their sexuality, their maleness, which seemed so alien to Mary Baldwin College's comfortable community of young females and aging spinster teachers. There was so much she didn't understand, and in spite of the laughter, Louise felt afraid.

For even if she signed her letters to Franklin Cravens as "your friend," she knew they weren't friends at all. They were participants in a ritual that could lead to his penetration of her body and her life.

The Friday before the next hop, Louise and Marynell rode the bus home to celebrate their mother's fortieth birthday. Eddie took them out to dinner at the officers' club. Elizabeth protested the extravagance of the angora sweater he had presented to her, but she kept touching it throughout the evening, pleased. All Marynell and Louise could afford was bath powder and a box of everyday hankies. Even with their father buying their train tickets, the extra expense of their West Point weekends meant nothing was left over from their allowances for other things. After all, one couldn't wear darned stockings or worn-out gloves at West Point, and a hostess gift was in order for Millie. As it was, they were dropping pennies in the collection plate at chapel and hadn't seen a movie in weeks.

They left the Fort Belvoir station before dawn in order to arrive in time for a regimental volleyball game. Louise tried to study, but her mind wandered as the train carried her closer to Franklin and the next stage in what seemed like a courtship. Her stomach churned with nervousness, but her thoughts bobbed around in a sea of anticipation.

Franklin seemed taller and older than Louise remembered. He took her shoulders in his hands and kissed first one cheek and then the other.

"I'd wondered if you'd still seem as pretty," he said solemnly. "You do."

He was impeccable. His uniform, his posture, his haircut, his manners. Louise felt like a child in his presence, but it wasn't an uncomfortable feeling.

Marynell offered Franklin a polite handshake, then turned her attention to her date. Bert Russell, Franklin's second in command, was powerfully built but only slightly taller than Marynell.

"From Dallas, Texas," Marynell said. "My goodness! You must tell me all about Texas. Does everyone down there really have oil wells in their backyard?"

Louise could tell by the tone of Marynell's voice that she was trying to forgive Bert's shortness.

"I've enjoyed your letters," Franklin said as they strolled across the reservation.

"Oh, and I yours."

Louise felt good. More than good. Hopeful. The hop was going to be wonderful. Franklin complimented her new hairstyle that waved softly instead of sporting the more fashionable finger waves. She felt better in her last year's Easter dress than she thought she would. At Marynell's insistence, she was wearing more mascara and rouge and had to admit she looked better for it.

"Do you write to any other man?" Franklin asked.

Louise was surprised by his question. "No."

"You seem very different from your sister. I imagine she has lots of beaus."

Nodding, Louise felt a pang of jealousy. She struggled for some response, then gave up and listened to Marynell going down the list of questions. Bert's father was an infantry major. Bert had always wanted to come to West Point.

Marynell and Louise sat in the stands while Bert and Franklin played an intense volleyball match. The sight of Franklin in his athletic suit fascinated her, but she almost felt as though she should look away. The muscles in his legs looked hard as steel under their covering of heavy, dark hair. The front of his shorts covered a rounded bulge, his shoulders were powerful under his jersey. He played with intensity, sweat dripping from his body, yelling encouragement to his teammates.

After the game, they went to the Boodles for sodas. Marynell and Louise had to pay. Cadets were not allowed to carry any money, and even so much as a dime in their pocket could bring about demerits.

The four of them sat with two other cadets from Franklin's battalion and their dates. Louise admired the easy camaraderie of the men. The other two girls, students from Mount Holyoke, exchanged girls'-school stories with Louise and Marynell. At first, Franklin was careful to draw Louise into the conversation, but gradually, he and the other cadets seemed to forget the presence of their dates. The talk turned to global politics. Germany had annexed Austria. Japan persisted in its aggression against China. Hitler and Mussolini had made an agreement for a "common foreign policy."

Only last month, Hitler had broadcast his decree throughout Germany that he personally had taken over command of the country's armed forces.

"It's von Ribbentrop's doing," a cadet from Georgia insisted in his unmilitary drawl. He sounded like the male professors at Mary Baldwin. "That travelin'-salesman-turned-diplomat has convinced Hitler that the aristocracy's hold over the military has to be broken."

"It's like the Treaty of Versailles never existed," Bert said. "The German army is estimated at six hundred thousand."

"Not even Britain or France will stand up to Hitler," Franklin said. "I think he's out to gobble up Europe, and who's going to stop him? Britain and France are unprepared for war."

"Why should he stop with Europe?" a broad-faced blond cadet from Minnesota asked. "Congress is going to have to fund a military buildup pretty soon, or we all better start brushing up on our German."

"You're right about that," Franklin agreed vehemently. "This country has about as much military preparedness as a flock of sitting ducks."

"It's just a matter of time," the Georgian drawled. "Two years. Three."

"You know," the Georgian continued. "My ol' man didn't want me to come to the Point. He said that there'd never be another major war, that a peacetime army wasn't much better than a Boy Scout troop. He wanted me to study medicine or law. I'm glad now I didn't listen to him."

The cadets seemed so sure, so gleefully sure the world was building to another war. And they wanted it. Louise had grown up on Army posts, but this was the first time she realized that the business of professional soldiers really was war. The peacetime army of her lifetime was an aberration. These young men, in electing to come to West Point, had gambled that there would eventually be an opportunity for them to make their marks on the battlefield. Now it seemed they might win their gamble.

"Do you really think there will be a war?" she asked Franklin on the way to the Fentrisses for dinner.

Marynell and Bert listened for his reply.

"I think there will always be another war. It's just a question of when—in this case, a question of how long Hitler will be allowed to go unchecked. He spelled it all out in a book he wrote in the twenties. It's there in black and white that he means to get back the territory that Germany lost in the World War—and more. 'Living space,' he calls it."

"Is that why you wanted to come to West Point—to fight in a war?" Louise asked.

"I believe in serving my country. It will need me more in a war than otherwise. And the military is a highly disciplined way of life. I believe in that, war or no war. Now enough war talk."

Louise was relieved. Maybe it was frivolous, but tonight she wanted to be young and gay and not think of ugly things. Nothing was going to ruin the evening for her. She didn't even mind that Franklin would realize that she and Marynell had traded dresses. This hop was going to be different. She was still nervous, but she trusted in Franklin's ability to smooth the way for her.

Throughout the afternoon and evening, Franklin had carefully avoided looking at Marynell, and she at him. But it would have seemed strange if he hadn't signed her dance program, and now he was escorting her onto the dance floor.

He regretted not having the presence of mind that first evening at Major Fentriss's quarters to acknowledge having met Marynell before. But he had been so shocked to see the girl who'd let him touch her breasts on the dance floor come walking into the living room that he had said nothing. He'd wondered if she would ever bring up the episode or if they would go through life pretending he hadn't had a hard-on against her belly.

Franklin watched Louise and Bert dance away from them before turning to take Marynell in his arms. He held her carefully, not at all like last time. Such a beautiful girl. Her hair was an incredibly thick, rich brown, her lips full and enticing, her eyes vividly green. Her beauty was much bolder than her sister's. He knew all he had to do was pull her close and his body would react.

"I'd like an explanation," she said, looking up at him, her brows arched, her chin jutting.

"Of what?" he asked, stalling.

"Of everything. Why you danced with me like that at the last hop, then ignored me for the rest of the evening? Why you chose to humiliate me by asking out my sister?"

He had hurt her. The knowledge surprised him. "I had no idea I'd see you again," he explained. "I didn't know that you were the sister of the young woman I'd offered to escort to the hop. I didn't even know she had a sister. I just knew she seemed like a nice girl and didn't deserve to spend a miserable evening with a cadet who wasn't interested in nice girls. I'm sincerely sorry if I upset you, Marynell."

Franklin felt himself wavering, wondering if he'd misread the beautiful young woman. He had assumed she was just another easy girl, a camp follower. But her eyes were glistening with hurt feelings, her chin quivering. Easy girls had feelings, too, he supposed, but a man couldn't risk falling for a woman like that. He'd never know when she'd rub up against someone else, like Brenda Copeland had done. Brenda had been sweet when they were in high school, but at college she had acquired a taste for making conquests. And after Brenda, he himself had been a willing conquest of one of the regulars from Sarah Lawrence—a luscious girl named Angela. He'd been shocked when he realized Angela expected an engagement ring.

"Why did you dance with me like that if you had no intention of ever seeing me again?" Marynell demanded. "That was a pretty crummy thing to do."

"You were beautiful and exciting," Franklin tried to explain. "Last year or the year before, I might have given you a real rush. But I'll be graduating soon, and I don't want to marry the sort of girl I've been dating. I don't have time for any more exciting girls."

"Louise doesn't excite you?" she demanded.

It was Marynell's mouth that set her apart, Franklin decided. Her lips on another face would have been too full, but on her they were sensuous, ripe. He found himself waiting for glimpses of her teeth and the tip of her tongue.

"No. But your sister pleases me in a different way." Franklin hesitated. How upset was Marynell? "Look, Marynell, I don't want there to be bad blood between us. If this relationship between me and your sister is uncomfortable for you, maybe I should reconsider courting her."

"You haven't danced with her like you danced with me that night?" Marynell asked.

Franklin shook his head. Louise wasn't that sort of girl.

"She'd probably let you if you tried," Marynell said.

"Perhaps," he acknowledged. "She might be too timid to say no."

"Whereas I invited it," Marynell said flatly. "It's just a game, you know. I wanted you to like me. But I . . ." She looked away, composing herself.

Franklin decided she was a virgin. She wasn't the sort of girl who went all the way—just part of the way. And enjoyed it.

"And to think I'd worried about Louise being an old maid," Marynell said ruefully as the music ended. "You don't have to worry about me, Cadet Cravens. I wouldn't dream of standing in my sister's way. And now, I think we should agree not to speak of this again."

Franklin took her hand and planted a soft kiss on her fingertips. "Thank you," he said. "You really are beautiful."

"You thought about making love to me, didn't you?" Marynell asked.

Franklin understood. She needed that much satisfaction. "Yes. But I never will," Franklin said. "You understand that, don't you, Marynell?"

She nodded. "I suppose I should thank you for the lesson on how to get a man. I can act just as chaste as Louise."

"With Louise, it isn't an act."

Marynell's chin went up. "Are you sure, Franklin Cravens? After all, she is *my* sister."

The evening was everything Louise wanted it to be. This afternoon, Franklin's athletic, sweating body had been vaguely disturbing, but tonight his masculinity was irresistible. Meticulously attired in his full-dress uniform, his West Point posture commanding, his manner courtly, his smile just for her, Franklin seemed like a prince of royal blood. Even the commandant of the academy and his handsome wife courted Franklin's attention. General Connor pumped Franklin's hand and asked about his parents. Mrs. Connor called him "dear boy." When they paid their respects to Mrs. Renfrow, the cadet hostess all but curtsied to Franklin before kissing Louise on the cheek.

Franklin had broken with tradition and allowed only three other names on Louise's dance card—Bert and the two other battalion commanders. With Franklin leading her around the floor, Louise felt almost perfect. All she had to do was relax in his arms and let the music flow through her veins. In Franklin's arms, she was the princess royal dancing at the ball in glass slippers and with a fairy-tale heart. Perhaps it would all end at the stroke of midnight, but for this evening of magic, Franklin was both prince and fairy godmother. He had made this happen for her, made her princess for a night, and she would be forever grateful for a special memory to tuck away—no matter what.

At intermission, General Connor's aide invited them to sit with the general and his wife. When Louise took the seat beside Mrs. Connor, the older woman grabbed Louise's hand. "You children are so young and beautiful it makes me ache," she said, her smile tinged with poignancy. "Enjoy it, my dear, and remember every moment well."

Louise wondered if she would look back on this night as the most wonderful of her entire life. She didn't know if she loved Franklin, but she loved this night, being at his side, feeling special. When the orchestra played the last dance—"Army Blue" followed by "Auld Lang Syne"—she got tears in her eyes that it was over.

CHAPTER

FOUR

On the walk across the moonlit reservation, Marynell and Bert fell behind. Soon it was just Franklin's and her footsteps echoing on the sidewalks. She was going to have to face the end of the evening alone, and Louise felt her earlier elation slipping away. What should she say to him on the Fentrisses' front porch? Franklin deserved more than a mere thank you, but how could she ever put into words the wonder of tonight?

Would he try to kiss her? Louise wanted to slip into her bed tonight and think back on a beautiful kiss at the end of her fairy-tale evening.

"Have you ever kissed a man before?" Franklin asked as they approached the front walk of the Fentrisses' quarters. The porch light was on.

"No."

"Good." And he pulled her into the shadows between two cedars. With her face between his hands, he lightly kissed her lips, her nose, her eyes.

Louise stood with her arms limply at her side, feeling more awkward than frightened.

His lips found her throat. "Like a swan," he said between kisses. "Pure and white."

Louise relaxed a bit. She knew that later, as she remembered this moment, it would seem more wonderful.

Then he was at her mouth again; this time his tongue parted her lips. Such a strange, unnatural feeling, to have someone's tongue in her mouth. Her instincts told her to pull away, but she didn't.

Very soon, however, he stopped, stepped back from her and took her hands from her sides. Into each palm he placed a kiss.

"I don't want you to go out with any other man," he said. "Ours is an exclusive relationship, and I place my trust in you. I know you are a woman of character."

Louise nodded. Exclusive. This princely man had chosen her for his own. She could come back and dance with him again, and next time the kissing would be better. She would put her arms around him. It all seemed like a miracle.

At the door, under the light, he kissed her cheek and said, "I will write."

"Thank you for tonight," Louise said. "It was the most beautiful night of my life, and I'll never forget it."

Franklin's lips brushed hers one last time. "Dear Louise," he whispered.

Millie had milk and cookies waiting. Louise wondered if she looked different for being kissed. She sat on the edge of her chair waiting for Marynell.

The two women waited twenty long minutes. Bert would be given demerits for returning late to his barracks.

Marynell rushed in breathless, her hair mussed. Her mouth looked bruised, and her face and neck blushed a splotchy red. Millie pretended not to notice.

Dutifully, the sisters drank their milk, and each ate a peanut butter cookie.

As soon as the door to their bedroom was closed, Marynell challenged, "Did he kiss you?"

Louise nodded.

"With his tongue?"

Louise nodded again.

"Welcome to the club," Marynell said, kicking off her shoes and sprawling across bed. "Well, did you like it?"

"Yes, I think so. I liked having him want to kiss me, but it felt strange."

"Did he rub up against you?"

"No. Did Bert do that to you?"

"Yes. His thing was hard as a rock. I could feel it right through his britches."

Louise reached for the hooks in back of her dress. For the first time in her life, she felt superior to her sister. Franklin admired her purity and wasn't the sort of man who rubbed up against a girl he admired.

From her bed in the darkened room, Marynell said, "Bert asked me back next month, but you'll have to come alone."

"Why?"

"I don't like him."

"But you let him kiss you."

"That's how I know that I don't like him. He didn't make me feel anything."

"Like what?"

"Like I might want to do more than kiss."

"Marynell!"

"I wouldn't *do* it," Marynell said peevishly. "I'd just like to feel like I want to. And besides, Bert doesn't look like general material to me. You don't know how lucky you are. Franklin Cravens is a dream come true. I guess you know I'm so jealous, I can't stand it. I'm sorry, Sis, but I really am."

Yes, Louise knew, and it made her uncomfortable. "If Bert did seem like general material, would you like him better?" she asked.

"I might. But it seems to me it's all mixed up together. I don't like him to kiss me because he's not handsome or important or commanding. I want to be proud of the man I marry. After all, whatever happens to me depends on him."

"Do they always put their tongue in your mouth?" Louise asked.

"Uh-huh. And they like it if you do it back."

"I couldn't do that!" Louise turned to face her sister's profile in the darkness. Marynell was on her back, her arms out of the covers across her chest. Louise couldn't tell if her eyes were open.

"Sure you could," Marynell snapped. "Don't be such a little prude.

I don't care how bashful you are, you aren't that different from any other girl."

"I think Franklin would be shocked if I did. He seems pleased that I've never had a boyfriend before. He really is a perfect gentleman."

"Well, next time, rub up against him a bit and see how *gentlemanly* he is. They're all the same. Every time you're with a boy, they want to go a little farther, and after you neck a long time, it gets to be a real problem to keep them from touching you."

"Then why neck so much?"

"Because it's exciting to have a boy get crazy over you and beg you to let him do things. They want to touch you and kiss your breasts. You wait and see."

Marynell went to sleep first. Louise was chilly and pulled up the extra blanket from the foot of the bed. The branches of the winter-bare tree outside the window swayed slowly back and forth, and the moonlight projected their eerie shadows on the opposite wall.

Louise stared at the hypnotically swaying shadows, her mind spinning. She thought of Franklin, in his imposing uniform, wanting to touch her body. Her pulse quickened. He had kissed her throat, just like Clark Gable had done to Vivien Leigh in *Gone With the Wind*. How could a girl not fall in love with a man like Cadet Captain Franklin Cravens? She still couldn't believe he had chosen her.

But what if he changed his mind? The thought struck fear in her heart. No other man as wonderful as Franklin Cravens would ever want her. Not in her entire life.

Marynell wasn't asleep. She had pretended she was to end the conversation.

Why had she talked like that to Louise, saying things to shock her? Urging her to be more aggressive with Franklin when she knew how he felt about aggressive women?

She was jealous of her sister, and the harsh, ugly feeling eating at her insides disgusted her.

In their family, Daddy had looked after Mother, and Marynell looked after Louise. Louise wasn't as vague as their mother, but she wasn't tough enough to get by without someone bullying her into wearing the right clothes and keeping her from sitting at home studying all the time. Marynell sometimes got tired of playing big sister, but being needed wasn't so bad and made it easy to love her sister—until Franklin Cravens came along.

Marynell still couldn't believe it. Louise was such a dud as a date that the good-looking Gerald Worth had dumped her. And where did he dump her? Right into the lap of the prize catch of the entire academy!

It wasn't fair. It just wasn't fair. The refrain had been drumming itself through her head for over a month now.

After Marynell had met Franklin, she'd been certain that she had found the man of her dreams. The disappointment of being rejected was made a hundred times worse by the fact that he had chosen her vestal-virgin sister over her.

Franklin was wasted on Louise. Louise would be just as happy with some bland professor. She was just going to end up reading books all the time like their mother. She had no flair, no ambition.

Marynell had seen him first. Damn, it really wasn't fair! How was she supposed to know he was looking for chaste? She could be chaste, too. Damn him. Damn Louise.

Well, if Franklin Cravens wanted to marry a Madonna, so be it. She herself wanted a marriage with passion. She liked the way it felt when she necked with a boy. She wanted more. Lots more. She wanted eternal love *and* eternal lust.

Except that Franklin Cravens was surely the Class of '38's most likely to succeed. Marynell knew that if given a chance she would have sacrificed passion to be married to a man like that.

Marynell had lied to Louise about Bert. She liked him just fine and had used his obvious admiration for her to salve her damaged ego, but Bert confessed he already had a serious girlfriend back in Texas. "Almost engaged to be engaged," he had explained. All he wanted from Marynell was heavy petting, and in return she could be his date to West Point parties.

Well, she'd love to heavy-pet with Bert, but she wasn't coming back up here just for that. She was going to change. She was going to start being demure and sweet. She wanted to marry a West Pointer because ninety percent of all generals were graduates of the academy. She wanted to marry a young, dashing, passionate officer who would someday make her a general's lady.

But this one last night, she had eased the hurt of Franklin by letting Bert lift her dress and stroke the bare skin above her stockings. She had let him ease a finger inside her panties, inside her wet vagina, and slide his finger up and down inside of her. And now, as she lay in the darkness remembering, she felt herself getting wet again.

She wished his finger were still there. She wished Louise were in another room so she could put her own finger in there. Of course, the girls at school would say that was nasty, that nice girls didn't do such things. Which was nastier, Marynell wondered, touching herself or letting a boy touch you? At least no one need ever know if she did it to herself.

What if Bert told his friends? What if the cadets told each other which girls let them touch?

She cupped her hand between her legs and pushed hard to relieve the yearning, but she left her underwear in place. She had to start training her body not to want so much.

True to her word, Marynell did not go back to West Point in April. Louise had hinted for Franklin to arrange another date for Marynell, but he hadn't. Louise felt a bit relieved. She wouldn't have to feel bad if Marynell suffered another disappointment.

At the April hop, Louise was only a little nervous as Franklin introduced her to an endless succession of classmates and their dates. Many of the couples had been going together for a long time and would be marrying after graduation during June Week activities.

"Mary Baldwin? Where's that?" asked one of the other dates, a pert blonde from Vassar who looked like an adult version of Shirley Temple.

"It's in Virginia."

"No kidding. Franklin must like you southern belles. His last girlfriend was from North Carolina."

"Oh. What happened to her?"

"She came north to school and turned into too much of a party girl to suit Franklin. He likes girls like you—reserved, ladylike. Keep up the act. It seems to be working. By the way, are you an Army brat?"

Louise nodded.

"Good. I'd hate for someone who didn't appreciate what they were getting to land Franklin Cravens. Scott says he's sure to be a distinguished graduate. And it sure can't hurt to have a high-ranking father when it comes to getting plush assignments after graduation."

Sunday, Franklin and Louise had lunch at the Thayer Hotel with Colonel and Mrs. Garrett Fittshugh, Franklin's uncle and aunt. The aunt, a tall, aristocratic-looking woman, was the older sister of Franklin's mother. Her steel-gray hair fit her head like a cap. Marynell would have wanted to pluck her formidable brows. His uncle was a full colonel in the ordnance corps and commandant of nearby Picatinny Arsenal. He reminded Louise of her father—slightly plump, slightly rumpled, smiling eyes. She wondered if ordnance was like the medical corps—not quite mainstream Army.

The men talked of Hitler, Japan and munitions deployment in the event of a war. The aunt quizzed Louise about her family, about her visits to West Point, about her school. Louise wondered if the colonel's wife had been sent by Franklin's mother to look over Franklin's new girlfriend. "Has your mother enjoyed being an Army wife?" Mrs. Fittshugh asked.

Louise considered explaining her mother's retiring nature but decided against it. "Yes," she said. "We've been very fortunate in being assigned to lovely old posts with nice quarters. I've had a wonderful life."

Later, as Franklin took her on a walk about the lake, he praised her "performance."

"They're nice people, and I enjoyed meeting them, but I hadn't realized I was on stage," she said. But that wasn't true. Louise was conscious of playing the kind of girl who would be an asset to a man's military career. Did that mean she wanted to marry Franklin?

But of course she wanted to marry Franklin. She was forever acting out scenarios of him proposing, of their wedding, of their wedding night. She thought about him all the time, hugged her pillow and pretended it was him.

"What I mean," Franklin explained, "is that I'm sure my aunt will tell my parents what a lovely girl I've been keeping company with. It will make things easier."

At Kissing Rock, he kissed her tenderly. The April sunshine was like a warm blessing on her shoulders.

Louise's arms went easily around Franklin. It felt deliciously grown-up to be in his arms, to return his embrace, his kiss. His tongue didn't feel so alien now, just intimate and exciting. It made her flush with pleasure.

Louise took her midterm tests the week before her next visit. Studying had never been so difficult. She went to bed each night exhausted, but, once there, thoughts of Franklin made it hard to sleep.

The next visit, after the dance when Franklin kissed her in the shadows, her lips were already parted, waiting for his tongue. He stroked her neck, her back. "I'm glad you're slender," he said, "and that your skin is so clear and white."

Louise was sorry when he pulled away and glanced at his watch. She wanted to pull him back, to kiss him again. She wondered if he had been aroused, if he had an erection, but it seemed no great problem for him to walk her the rest of the way to the Fentrisses' front door, kiss her forehead and leave her.

Sunday morning, Millie fixed pancakes, then shooed Franklin and Louise outside with their second cups of coffee. The morning felt of spring, and a riot of bird sounds filled the air. A row of daffodils in full bloom lined the back walk, and a dwarf pear tree was white with sweet-smelling blossoms. And there among all that fresh beauty, sitting on lawn chairs behind the Fentrisses' quarters, Franklin slipped a miniature replica of a West Point ring on her finger.

"You're all I've ever wanted in a wife," he told her.

Louise stared at the ring, thinking of the commotion it would cause back at school. A West Point miniature! She was proud and scared.

She wished they could have known each other longer and prolonged these sweet times of courtship. But Franklin would be graduating soon. If there was to be a June Week wedding, they didn't have much time. And maybe they knew each other well enough. He was a certain type of man, and she was a certain type of girl. After a year of courtship, would they have known more?

But after a year, she would have been older. Right now, she was just playing at being adult.

The small diamond in the ring's crest was dazzling in the sunlight. Almost blinding. She looked at Franklin. He was smiling expectantly. Was an answer required? But there had been no question.

"Don't you think you should ask me?" she said softly.

Franklin was taken aback. "I assumed we were of one mind."

Louise smiled. "I suppose. But a girl likes a proposal."

Franklin's brow wrinkled, and Louise wondered if he was angry. But he decided to make a game of it and offered a great show of straightening his gray tunic jacket, smoothing his hair and kneeling in the grass in front of her. "Miss Louise Victoria Rodgers, would you do me the great honor of becoming my wife?"

She wanted him to say that he loved her, but then he must love her if he wanted to marry her. And she must love him if she was going to say yes.

And what else was there to say but yes?

"I respect you more than I've ever respected any other girl, Louise," Franklin said, suddenly earnest. "You are so lovely, and I'll always cherish you."

She was foolishly pleased that he thought she was lovely. And he would cherish her. The words of love would come later. She would say them, too. *I love you, Franklin.* She already whispered it to him dozens of times in her fantasies even though she wasn't sure what love between a man and a woman really meant. Was it sex, or was it reading comfortably side by side in bed before turning out the lights? She always imagined she would feel more uplifted at the moment of commitment, that music would play in her head and her heart would leap for joy.

But the air smelled of spring and promise. And he was so very handsome.

She said yes and kissed him, then helped him brush the wet grass from the knees of his uniform and told him she was honored.

And she was. A West Point marriage. A succession of well-tended

Army quarters. Children. The preferential treatment that came from a husband's rank. And passion. She wanted passion. It was what she longed for most of all.

They'd be going first to Fort Sill, Oklahoma, he told her, where he would take the field artillery course for regular Army officers.

"God, it's a good time to be going in. A man can really make his mark. I'm so lucky."

When they kissed, Louise met his tongue with her own and felt her insides leap in approval of her daring. She wished they weren't sitting down. She would like to feel his body pressed against her. She wanted to know that he wanted her in every way.

Franklin waited until the departing train had rounded the curve of the river before heading back up the hill, a self-satisfied smile tugging at his mouth. The weekend had gone well. The ring even fit. He wasn't quite sure why he was one of those blessed people for whom things usually worked out well, but he was, and he accepted the fact with proper humility and good grace.

Oh, there would be minor setbacks, like the unpleasant business with Brenda Copeland when she convinced him to go to bed with her the night he proposed. They'd done heavy petting before, but he'd assumed she was a virgin and never tried to do more. But she wasn't, and in bed, nothing was too vulgar, too dirty for her. He still got aroused, thinking about it.

"I can't marry you now," he told her afterwards. She had raged and thrown things, then she wept and knelt at his feet, begging. It was the most unpleasant scene he'd ever been a part of, but the experience had made him more determined that the woman he married had to be above that sort of thing. The physical side of their marriage would be conducted with dignity and respect. After all, she would be the mother of his children.

He hadn't planned to stop at the chapel, but suddenly he was there, entering the impressive, hushed sanctuary, kneeling at a pew near the front. This was where he would marry Louise. She would be veiled in white, unsoiled.

Kneeling, with his hands folded, Franklin looked up at the symbols of his faith and promised he would be a good husband and, in doing so, felt more a man. He was grateful he was mature enough to select a wife with his head and heart and not his loins.

And oddly enough, Louise's chastity filled him with its own kind of desire. A virgin bride. A virtuous wife. Their marriage would be a holy thing, their lovemaking a sacrament. He understood now the value of keeping oneself in check in order to achieve a higher love. He would never defile Louise. And when he marched off to war like a crusader of old, he would go with an easy heart.

CHAPTER

FIVE

*L*ouise felt more engaged after telling Marynell. The sisters hugged and wept and hugged some more, then Marynell raced up and down the halls of the dorm, knocking on doors, telling everyone her little sister was engaged. Marynell and Louise's roommate Billie organized an instant pajama party in Louise's honor. Girls from all over the dorm came to stare reverently at the miniature, to find a corner of floor or bed to sit on, eat peanut butter and saltines, and hear the details of Franklin's proposal. A makeshift throne in the center of the room was fashioned for Louise out of a desk chair, pillows and blankets. Billie made a cardboard crown for her roommate's head. Louise had completed only her freshman year, but in the estimation of Mary Baldwin's girls, her college career had been a glorious success.

When Louise told them Franklin knelt to propose, they offered a collective sigh.

"What did he say?" demanded lanky Betty Lou Holland. "Come on, Louise, share with us less fortunate females."

"Well, he asked me to be his wife and said he would cherish me," Louise was blushing furiously.

This was greeted with another sigh and a moment of silence.

"And what did you say?" asked Cindy, her across-the-hall neighbor, her hair in toilet-paper-wrapped pincurls.

"I said I would be honored to be his wife. We'll be married during June Week in the West Point Chapel."

"Will there be crossed sabers like in the movies?" asked June Kay Vaughn from the corner. June Kay was also engaged, to a junior partner in her father's law firm.

"I suppose," Louise said. And already she could see a picture of herself in a wedding dress, rushing under the crossed sabers, her uniformed groom at her side. What could be more romantic? The affirmation in the eyes of her dormmates made her heart beat faster. How lucky she was to be engaged to Franklin. It was the most exciting thing that had ever happened to her.

Even Mrs. Leigh, the dour housemother with overdyed black hair, came upstairs in her bathrobe carrying a tin of butter cookies to congratulate Louise and touch her ring. "We haven't had a girl engaged to a West Point cadet in years. Be sure to send me a picture of your wedding."

When Mrs. Leigh left, Marynell stood to make a speech. Her short dark hair was a thick, lustrous mass about her face. Her wonderful green eyes were bright with unshed tears. Even without her precious makeup, she was the prettiest girl in the room. Louise felt a pang of guilt that she was on the throne and not her sister. Marynell should have had her day first. "As a baby," Marynell began, holding up her hands for quiet, "Louise walked late and talked late, but she sure got engaged early. Of course, she wore my incredible white satin dress to the hop, and I'm sure that's what tipped him over the edge."

Marynell picked her way through the room to stand beside Louise and take her hand. "My sis and I have always been close. I kept her nose wiped and her collar on the outside of her cardigan sweater. She was always there to laugh and cry with me, and I wonder if Franklin Cravens knows what a sweet girl he's got. I'm happy and sad all mixed up together. It's always been my sis and me, and now it won't be that way anymore. Of course, we always knew it'd happen someday, but I'm going to miss her."

Marynell was crying now. She turned to Louise. "I love you, honey, and I'm happy for you. Really I am. Jealous, too, but happy."

Louise jumped up and hugged her sister. Her crown fell on the floor. The overflowing room was quiet but for the sniffling from two dozen misty-eyed girls.

Louise called home the following evening. "He's riding the train to Belvoir next Saturday to meet you and Mother. Are you proud of me, Daddy?"

"You bet, honey, if that's what you really want. Your mother's going to be disappointed that you're not finishing college, but Franklin sounds like a worthy young man and I look forward to meeting him. I hope he doesn't expect any sort of a formal announcement party. Your mother . . . "

"Oh, no, Daddy. We just want a quiet family evening so you and Mother can get to know him. Franklin wants us all to go down to Camp Dix weekend after next to meet his family. They'll probably have some sort of party."

Louise insisted that a reluctant Marynell come home with her for the weekend. "Please. You can study on the bus. It's a family time, and Mother will be so nervous, she'll need us both to help. I'll bet the silverware hasn't been polished this year."

Elizabeth wasn't nervous at all.

"You're not even nineteen yet," she admonished, sitting on Louise's bed while her daughter dressed for dinner. Elizabeth was wearing her gray wool in spite of the fact that it was April and warm, but she'd put on some makeup in honor of Franklin's visit and had on her pearl necklace and earrings. Louise had felt proud when she introduced her pretty mother to Franklin.

"You were only nineteen when you got married," Louise said, putting her mirror and brush in their accustomed place on the maple dresser that had been a part of her bedroom in a succession of Army quarters for as long as she could remember.

"Get a job," Elizabeth said. "Go to New York—or Europe. Find a way to get to Paris even if you have to wait tables when you get there. I would have liked to do that—to wait tables in Paris, to have gone someplace and done something."

Louise was shocked. "Aren't you glad you got married and had a family?"

"A girl has lots of years to get married and have a family. What's your hurry? You've had only one year of college. I thought you liked college."

"Oh, I do. But Franklin's graduating and feels it's time for him to get married. You know how hard Army life is for bachelor officers."

"He could manage for a year or two. I should think he would want his wife to have more education."

"I don't think it's important to him, and what if he wouldn't wait? What if he married someone else?"

"Would that break your heart?" Elizabeth asked, pushing her glasses higher on her nose and focusing her gaze on her daughter.

"Well—not exactly. But, Mother, I'm not special. I've always just been the good little girl with the neat notebooks and the clean bedroom. I've never had anything special happen to me. I guess I'm afraid to let this chance go by. And besides, what possible reason could I give for saying no to a man like Franklin? A girl would be out of her mind."

Louise sat on the bed and took her mother's hand. "Please be happy for me. Please."

"But just think of the possibilities of being young and in Paris."

"Mother, be sensible. How would I get to Paris?"

Elizabeth cocked her head to one side and grinned. "I could sell my mother's brooch."

"What brooch?"

"It's a joke. In stories, that's how they get the money. You know—a sacrifice. Sell their brooch or their hair. My dear Louise, I'll give you my blessing if you promise me it's what you really want. No. On second thought, don't do that. No one ever knows what they really want at eighteen—or nineteen—and even if they could figure it out, it would probably be impossible to accomplish."

"Aren't you happy, Mother?"

"Life isn't a happy state, dear. The best one can reasonably hope for is to be content."

Louise and Elizabeth went downstairs to join the two men and Marynell for a late supper. The table, set with a white linen cloth and wineglasses, seemed too formal for the simple meal of cold cuts and potato salad, as did the uniforms on the two men. Louise noted that her father's tie was neatly tied, his shoes freshly polished.

Over coffee, Franklin asked Eddie about his experiences in France, and the three women listened indulgently to Eddie's oft-repeated "war stories."

Fresh out of medical school, Eddie had worked in a field hospital set up in a convent. "Sometimes I felt like all I did was cut off arms and legs. We were constantly being overrun with casualties and were so understaffed, we didn't have time to save limbs, just lives. Terrible time. Terrible. I'll never forget the screams and the smells. You can diagnose gangrene from down the hall before you ever lay eyes on the patient. The ground got so frozen, it was impossible to dig holes. We had to haul off the amputated limbs and burn them. I hope Roosevelt can keep us out of another war. I often thought if politicians could just spend a day in a military hospital in a war zone, they wouldn't be so all-fired eager to start another war. I can't tell you how pitiful it was, the way we had to send some of those boys home. Just pitiful. If it was up to the medical corps, there wouldn't be another war, I can promise you that."

Eddie took out his handkerchief and blew his nose. He meant what he said. Franklin listened quietly, but Louise sensed that the words of a middle-aged Army doctor had little effect on an eager young West Pointer. Louise wondered if each generation of men had to find out about war anew.

"I don't think there's going to be much of a choice, sir. It looks like this war is being thrust on us," Franklin said politely.

"Yes, I suppose so," Eddie admitted. "But sometimes I wonder if weapons manufacturers don't really rule the world."

Louise hastily changed the subject by asking her father about his golf game, knowing this was the time of the year when he was full of plans for improving it. By fall, he would swear he was giving up golf for good.

Eddie gave his daughter a little look to let her know he knew he was being manipulated, then asked Franklin if he liked to play golf.

After dinner, the two men went into the living room for their "talk." Louise felt ridiculously nervous. Of course, her father was going to say yes. It was a mere formality. But she needed very much for the two men to like each other.

"Don't misunderstand me," Eddie told Franklin. "I think you're a fine young man with a wonderful future ahead of you, but somehow Louise seems a mismatch for you. Do you think she's tough enough to be the kind of wife you need? Army wives don't have permanent homes. They don't have the support of mothers and sisters and aunties. They have to live and breathe Army. In wartime, they have to raise children alone. Of course, it's harder on some women than others. I often wonder what would happen to Elizabeth if I dropped dead. After all these years as an Army wife, she has no place to go back to. I was sort of hoping Louise would find a banker or lawyer down here in Virginia. Elizabeth and I have talked about retiring around here someday. A small town probably."

The young man was intimidating. Eddie found himself talking too much and wishing he'd polished his brass along with his shoes. He wished Elizabeth had thought to straighten the books on the shelves and empty the ashes from the fireplace. He sat up straighter and sucked in his stomach.

"But Louise has been raised on military posts," Franklin said, his voice patient, "and I think she understands the commitment she is making. I realize that she is a sweet, vulnerable young woman, but I don't admire strong-willed women. I promise to care for her to the best of my ability and help her to grow into her role. And if the day ever comes that she is the wife of a high-ranking officer, she will be ready. She's very special, sir. Surely you see that."

Eddie nodded, then realized he was going to cry. Damn. He took out his handkerchief to wipe his eyes and blow his nose. "Excuse me, son. I just wish she could stay my little girl a while longer. Pretty soon, Marynell will marry too—probably another Army officer—and then I'll only see my girls once a year if that often. Sometimes I wish I hadn't stayed in the Army after the war and had established a civilian practice instead. My girls might have married hometown boys and raised some grandchildren I'd get to see once in a while."

Eddie blew his nose again. It had a very unmilitary sound. "I don't know how much Louise has talked about her mother, but she never could have managed if I'd been anything other than medical corps. We docs get to play by an easier set of rules."

"Are you saying that Louise is like her mother?" Franklin asked.

"No, not at all. Elizabeth should have run a little bookstore in a seaside town or worked in a library. She never did well with teas and bridge, but Louise will do a good job. She's conscientious to a fault with everything she does. I just hope that's what is best for her. Be kind to her, son," he said, folding his handkerchief and replacing it in his pocket.

"Yes, sir. Always. You have my word."

"Well then, there's a bottle of champagne cooling in the icebox. Shall we call in the ladies for a toast?"

Eddie took comfort in the fact that a man like Franklin Cravens did not give his word lightly. He was a soon-to-be officer and already a gentleman. A West Pointer. And he had to admit he would be quite proud to have him as a son-in-law. He'd already done some boasting at the hospital.

Eddie worried, however, that he had not been quite truthful. There was a lot of her passive, accepting mother in his younger daughter.

Elizabeth had tried to be a good officer's wife. In the beginning she had attended the club meetings, served on committees, returned social obligations. She had worried over bridge, attempted golf, saved recipes, agonized over dinner parties, worked at remembering names. But gradually, she slipped away from it and into her books. The role of the wife wasn't so vital in the medical corps. Promotions tended to be more automatic with Army physicians, who didn't place much credence in efficiency reports and put patients before protocol.

But the wife of an officer like Franklin Cravens would play an important role in his career. She couldn't bring him advancements, but she could hold him back. High-ranking officers did not have incompetent wives.

A bookstore by a seaside. Now where in the world had that come from? What a foolish notion. Elizabeth couldn't run a household much less a business. She had forgotten to buy toothpaste for two weeks now. She forgot social engagements. She forgot to bring groceries in from the car. Sometimes Eddie wanted desperately to be furious with her, to shake her slender shoulders and force her to remember things. Sometimes he wondered what his life would have been like if he had married that feisty little Missy Moyer with the carrot-colored hair. Sometimes he felt like he was married to a wisp of smoke.

Yet there was something oddly fulfilling in having a wife who could not survive without him. Elizabeth couldn't balance a checkbook. She didn't like to drive off the post alone. When Elizabeth's mother died, Eddie took care of the arrangements. When her father needed to be put in an old folks' home, Eddie had arranged that, too. The girls had always asked him for permission—if they could pop popcorn, go to the movies, have someone to spend the night. Sometimes Elizabeth woke up crying for no apparent reason and needed him to comfort her.

And at other times, her arms would slip around his neck in the night, and her soft, breathless voice would whisper in his ear for him to love her. Her body was still thin and flat, like a girl too young for lovemaking. When he slid himself inside of her, it was always exciting, like he was entering a virgin.

Marynell scoffed when Louise told her what Elizabeth had said about going to Paris and getting a job. Franklin had already been installed in the guest room. Their parents were propped up in bed reading themselves to sleep. The two sisters kept their voices low so as not to disturb the quiet household.

"Mother reads too many books. Don't pay any attention to her," Marynell said, holding out her hand admiring the polish she had just applied to her fingernails.

"But I know what she means," Louise said softly from where she sat cross-legged on the floor of Marynell's room, looking at pictures of bridal dresses in a magazine. "Once you are married, your life is set."

"Maybe you can go to Paris with Franklin someday."

"Yes, but it wouldn't be the same."

"My God, Louise, do you want to wait tables in Paris?"

"Of course not. But I understand what Mother means. If you don't do things like that before you get married, you never will."

"If you do things like that before you get married, you will ruin your reputation, and men like Franklin Cravens won't want you. They marry inexperienced schoolgirls. There are some more magazines in the top of the closet. Don't get a wedding dress with a high neckline. I think I should have some say about it, since I'll have to wear it, too."

The second week in May, the Rodgers family drove their aging Oldsmobile to Camp Dix, New Jersey, to meet Franklin's parents. The military policemen at the main gate saluted smartly and directed them to the home of the commanding officer.

Every curb was whitewashed. Speed-limit signs were posted on every block. The trees were all pruned at the same height, every shrub precisely trimmed. Spring flowers grew in carefully tended beds outlined with white picket fences. Franklin's father ran a tight ship, it seemed.

Eddie parked in front of the general's residence. "It'd make three of our quarters," Marynell said.

"She must have lots of help," Elizabeth said half to herself. "I wonder how many bathrooms there are."

"Have you ever seen such a beautiful yard?" Eddie said. "Maybe I could retire and grow roses for the commander of Camp Dix."

Louise had nothing to say. It's a good thing her family was with her; otherwise, she'd never have the nerve to go into that house.

The front door opened, and Franklin came out accompanied by an attractive, gray-haired matron in a mauve dress. "She looks just like a general's wife," Louise whispered.

"Yes," Elizabeth and Marynell agreed in unison.

Maxine Cravens was smoothly gracious, shaking hands all around and giving Louise a kiss on the cheek and a hug. "My dear, you are as lovely as my Franklin promised. Welcome." She turned to the rest of the family. "Welcome to you all. I am so pleased to have you here."

General Cravens arrived promptly at one o'clock with his aide, a ruddy-faced captain, who joined them for lunch.

The general was taller and huskier than Franklin, but father and son shared the same ramrod straight posture, square shoulders, determined jaw and military bearing. From his mother, Franklin had received his elegant slimness, his brown eyes, his heavy brow.

Louise calculated that both the general and his wife must be in their fifties, and Franklin was their only child. She wondered why.

After lunch, Franklin drove the four Rodgerses around the sprawling camp, which served as an infantry training center. Founded in 1917, the base still lacked the stately trees of older Army posts but was otherwise much the same, with well-tended grounds, a flagpole and cannon in front of headquarters, hospital, church, post exchange, officers' club, noncommissioned officers' club, theater—all in khaki-colored stucco. The field-grade officers' quarters were segregated from those of junior grade, with the noncommissioned officers in yet another neighborhood—each with a small, street-side sign announcing the name and rank of the officer whose family lived within.

Endless rows of barracks occupied other areas of the base, and Franklin drove past shooting ranges and outdoor teaching amphitheaters, then out onto the vast reservation where infantry troops were trained for combat.

Louise sat between Franklin and her father in the front seat, with her mother and sister in the back. Eddie asked knowledgeable questions, and Franklin gave detailed answers. Her father knew more about the military than she had realized.

After the post tour, Maxine took Louise into her garden for a "chat." Louise wondered what would happen if she didn't pass muster with Franklin's mother. Would Franklin still want her as his wife?

The roof of the summerhouse was dripping sweet-smelling wisteria blossoms. Maxine sat in a thronelike chair with a high fanned back of filigreed metal. Louise wondered if Maxine had always been regal or if it came to her as her husband moved up the ladder of rank.

Everyone expected Franklin to be a general someday like his father, but Louise couldn't imagine herself with power, prestige, servants, a house like this one. All she'd ever considered having was a life like the one she'd always known, with a comfortable husband who loved her the way her father loved her mother, with children and cats and tomato plants in the backyard. She wasn't cut out to be a queen any more than her mother had been.

Franklin should be marrying Marynell. Marynell could pull it off.

As Maxine directed their conversation, Louise realized her future mother-in-law had conducted an investigation of her son's intended. Maxine had spoken not only with her sister, Mrs. Fittshugh, but with Mrs. Renfrow, the cadet hostess at West Point, who had referred her to Millie Fentriss.

"I heard the same words used to describe you, dear. Shy. Reserved. Ladylike. I can see why Franklin was drawn to a girl like you. The young woman he was engaged to before experienced a rather distressing metamorphosis during her years at Barnard. It was a difficult experience for my son. Quite frankly, I had worried he'd gone too far in the other direction, but you seem a bright girl who will grow in the job."

Maxine paused while the orderly served iced coffee garnished with mint leaves. "That's fine, Wilson. It looks very nice. And you did a splendid job on the hall floor. I've never seen it look better."

After the soldier was out of earshot, Maxine continued. "An officer's wife can help or hinder his career. Right now, you have no presence, but if you work at it, that will come in time. Keep your eyes open and be careful of every word that comes out of your mouth. Never criticize another officer or his wife. Be gracious even it kills you. And guard your own and Franklin's reputation as though your life depended on it. I want you always to call me if there's any problem at all that I can help you with. I've seen all the pitfalls, Louise, and fallen in a few of them. I've always wanted a daughter, and I'd be honored if you would turn to me for advice."

Louise nodded. "Thank you. That's very comforting."

"My son has a promising future ahead of him," Maxine continued. "One of the things that could interfere with his future is a bad marriage. Wives make marriages, Louise. 'For better or worse' was written for wives."

Then Maxine smiled and reached for Louise's hand. "Dear child, I'm frightening you, aren't I? I don't mean to paint such a serious picture. My life has been so rich and full as Harold's wife. We have come up through the ranks as a team. Can you imagine the pride that I feel when I look at this man I've loved and served all these years? Sometimes when he's standing at attention reviewing his troops or greeting dignitaries during a reception, I feel like I could burst with pride. *My* husband, a general with stars on his shoulders. I can think of no other life that would have brought me more fulfillment. And someday, my dear, you will have the respect and the gracious life that goes with being the wife of a high-ranking offer. But you must earn it. You must be diligent and wise. And make Franklin feel like a general in his own home, even when he's a lowly lieutenant. If a man's wife doesn't honor him, he loses his ability to inspire it in others."

Maxine released Louise's hand, then reached across the table to touch her cheek. "How young you are. Do you love my son?"

"Yes," she said softly. "I'm a little in awe of him, but I love him and want to be a good wife."

"And so you will," Maxine said, standing. She embraced Louise warmly and shooed her off to rest before dinner.

Maxine watched the slim girl walk across the yard to the house, then reseated herself. With her head resting against the high back of her chair, her eyes closed, she waited for Wilson to bring her afternoon sherry.

Her son had chosen the wrong sister. Maxine wondered why, for she had seen the look in Marynell Rodgers's eyes. The girl would gladly have traded places with her younger sister. Marynell was more beautiful and tougher than the quiet Louise, and seemingly more clever. But she hadn't been clever enough to attract Franklin, apparently, and that was a pity. Franklin probably thought he was marrying a woman as fine as his mother when, in fact, it was in Marynell that Maxine saw a kindred spirit. Servants didn't fluster Marynell. She was self-assured, poised, and when she looked around the Camp Dix commandant's quarters, it was with more than a casual interest. Maxine could almost see inside Marynell's head as the girl tried the house on for size. Maxine could have worked with that girl. But Louise. What did one do with a Louise but hope for the best? A girl like that didn't understand about marriage at all. Marriage didn't flow a natural course like a river. It was more like a ship that had to be kept on course. And it was wives who piloted marriages through the shallows.

Maxine had been married once before. No one, not even her sister or her husband, knew her secret. Only the young man she'd run off with, her parents and her mama's colored maid had known, and now all of them were dead. Maxine had breathed a little easier when she heard Ryan McBlain had died, then she cried a bit, as much for her departed youth as for a lost love. Ryan promised he would never tell, and he hadn't. "I knew you were too good for me," he had confessed when they said good-bye.

It was in 1906, the week after her sister Grace's marriage to Warren Fittshugh, that Maxine met Ryan at the county fair at Bowling Green, Kentucky, where her daddy was a doctor and her mother was from an old family. Ryan was a local boy, hired by the carnival folks to run the ring toss. He presented her with a Kewpie doll prize even though she missed every throw, and he made her promise to come back the next night. His grin was cocky, his eyes admiring. The third night, he whispered for her to meet him in the shadows behind the Ferris wheel. The rest of her summer she spent in a dizzy haze, her body moist and eager as she waited for the night, for her stolen time with Ryan, which was often spent in the summer house of her own backyard. Maxine knew that his daddy used to have a dry goods store but was now a no-account drunk and his mother took in laundry, but Ryan drove her crazy with his kisses. He put his hand between her legs and made fire come there.

Ryan had planned to go to sea, but he wondered how he could possibly live without Maxine. More than anything in the world he wanted to make love to her, to marry her, to make her pregnant with his baby, to come home every night to her arms. He knew she was too fine for the likes of him, but she swore she could live without her family's money, that they loved each other enough to find a way.

The running away seemed like a wonderful game, secreting a valise away in the carriage house, then riding the night train to Evansville, where a cousin of Ryan's had promised to get him work on the river.

Maxine and Ryan were married at city hall and in a shabby room at a seedy boardinghouse finally tasted fully of carnal delights. Maxine loved Ryan's body, but she hated the boardinghouse. Honeymoons were supposed to be spent in beautiful places with satin sheets and a beautiful view. She'd never slept on dingy sheets or shared a bathroom with strangers before. She'd never been among people who belched in public and wore sweat-stained clothing. She wondered what would happen next. They couldn't stay here. She couldn't go home. The game was no longer fun.

Maxine's daddy found them three days later, and within the week arranged for a quick annulment using some of his wife's old money to grease the necessary wheels, and he provided a generous settlement for Ryan, who cried and swore he'd love Maxine until the day he died but took the money her daddy offered. Even as she rode the train back to Bowling Green, refusing to talk to her daddy, acting like her heart was permanently broken, Maxine felt the euphoria of relief. Whatever made her think she could live her life married to an ordinary boy whose daddy got arrested on Saturday nights? She wondered if Ryan, too, was relieved. Surely he had begun to wonder what he was supposed to do with a wife who expected a fresh pair of white gloves every time she went out.

Her mama sent Ruby to Maxine's room that first night back. Ruby gave her a putrid, thick potion that smelled of rotting plants and urine. Maxine tasted it and gagged, but Ruby stood by her bed until she finished every drop. "Now, chile, if you still miss your monthly, you come to me right away," Ruby instructed. And then, arms folded under her ample bosom, seated in the same chair where she'd rocked Maxine as a child, she explained how to fake virginity. "Your mama says you don't go 'fessing to no man 'bout what happened. Or to no one else. Not ever. Your mama don't want any of this spoken of ever again."

Maxine's period arrived on schedule. She wondered if it would have anyway without Ruby's potion, and she wondered what Ruby would have done if she'd turned up pregnant. She thought of whispered stories about girls bleeding to death, about families with unexplained babies to hide away. What a goose she had been to risk her safe, beautiful existence on a whim. Life, she now realized, could not be lived on impulse. Everything—even lust—must be carefully thought out.

Maxine met Harold Cravens the following summer at a cotillion in Memphis, where she was visiting her Aunt Lukie. Harold had just finished his third year at the Point and was dramatically impressive in dress whites. His older brother was Army. Their daddy was a general, a hero of the Indian wars. Maxine looked Harold over carefully and liked what she saw. He was handsome and smart and ambitious.

She loved Harold's uniform, his courtly manners, the way he crossed out the remaining names on her dance program and kept her for himself. Maxine allowed Harold to court her, and at the end of the month, he followed her home to Bowling Green to ask her delighted father for his daughter's hand in marriage. They would be married the following year, after Harold's graduation.

Maxine didn't feel as passionately in love with Harold as she had with Ryan, but she felt wiser. She liked Harold Cravens well enough, and he would be a husband to make her proud.

With time and marriage, she came to feel for her young officer a comfortable kind of love that even poured over into passion on occasion. Harold brought her security and respect, and she supplied him with a backbone when his grew soft.

The two finest days in Maxine's life were the day her son was born and the day Harold received his first star. But nothing ever matched the excitement of sneaking out at night to meet Ryan McBlain. Never had kissing been so sweet, the fondling so enticing, the yearning so intense. For many years, she dreamed of seeing Ryan one last time, but she never dreamed of more than that. And now, months, even years could go by without Maxine thinking of the blue-eyed boy with the cocky grin. It had been such a long time ago. Ryan had earned medals in the war, then read for the bar and eventually won a term in the Kentucky state legislature. Maxine had been proud when she heard but felt no regret. Even if Ryan had become rich and bought the whole of Logan County, she would not have been regretful. She belonged at Harold's side. In the Army, a wife was taken seriously and respected, not just indulged the way her daddy had always indulged her silly mother and her mother's gossipy friends.

During the long years when Maxine was praying continually for a baby, she wondered if her childlessness was God's punishment for the loving and leaving of Ryan and for not being the chaste bride Harold thought he had married. But she had gotten away with her crimes, apparently.

After a buffet dinner, the three Rodgers women rushed to dress for the reception. As usual, Marynell worked on her mother's and sister's hair with her curling iron and tinted their faces with her rouge and mascara. "I swear, you two are so timid about these things."

"I look painted," Elizabeth said.

"No, you don't. You look beautiful," Marynell said.

The reception was held in the Cravenses' quarters with the serving done by enlisted men in dress uniforms. Louise, in her lavender dress, smiled until her face hurt.

She was amazed at her mother. Elizabeth left her glasses upstairs, smiled graciously if somewhat myopically and remembered names just like a seasoned Army wife.

"How lovely she is," Marynell whispered. Elizabeth was wearing the paisley silk purchased after Christmas. "I wonder if Daddy's told her how beautiful she looks."

"Daddy tells her that all the time."

"I guess he does," Marynell acknowledged. "But their marriage seems so boring, nothing but books and the radio. Why did Mother get so drab, and why did Daddy let her?"

"They seem happy enough to me," Louise countered, but she knew what Marynell meant. If courtship had to be proper and marriage was supposed to be content, why were there deep longings that erupted in the night? There was too much about what happened between men and women that she didn't understand, and she was beginning to realize that answers didn't automatically come with a white veil and wedding vows.

CHAPTER

SIX

*L*ouise had always been thrilled by military parades, but no parade had ever impressed her like the marching cadets at West Point.

The sunlight glistened on the nation's finest; every white-clad leg, every gray-clad arm moved in unison. Even the "swish, swish" of bayonet scabbards brushing against trouser legs sounded as one.

When the corps was in position, it stretched the entire length of the parade ground. The long gray line.

"There he is," Louise said, tugging at Marynell's sleeve. Then she leaned across to her parents to make sure they recognized Franklin standing at the head of a battalion. On the other side of Eddie and Elizabeth, General and Mrs. Cravens were handsome and proud, her posture as erect as his. Behind them were Franklin's aunt and uncle—the Fittshughs—and his cousin David, who had graduated from the academy three years ago.

At the thundering words "pass in review," Louise reached for Marynell's hand, and her sister offered an answering squeeze.

Louise realized she was marrying more than a man; she was marrying a tradition and a way of life. Pride swelled so strongly in her breast, it was painful. It was not the sort of passion she had dreamed of, but it was real. She silently pledged herself to the fine man she was marrying, a man who was entering a lifetime of service to his country.

And during her wedding ceremony in the West Point chapel, Louise thought again how special it was to be marrying not only a man but a way of life.

She had worried that she would whisper when she took her vows, but her voice rang out clearly in the chapel. "I, Louise, take thee Franklin . . . " Then she looked into Franklin's dark eyes and listened as he promised to love and honor her, to take care of her for the rest of her life.

Marynell stepped forward to lift her sister's veil, and Louise was in Franklin's arms, his mouth soft and sweet on hers. And he said it then for the first time—"I love you, Louise," whispered in her ear. She loved him, too. Always would. For a lifetime.

As Marynell watched, she felt her cold heart melting and actually found herself weeping, and that made her like herself better. Marynell wanted her sister to be happy, and she would find a Franklin of her own.

The carefully rehearsed honor guard drew their sabers as the just-married couple left the altar and formed an arch for them to march under. Then the men exited by a side door, hurried around the chapel and reformed their gleaming archway at the front door for the couple to make their triumphant exit.

Marynell took note of everything. Someday she'd be the bride in that wonderful dress, only she wanted a longer veil. Louise's looked skimpy. But still, Louise was radiant. Franklin could not help but love her, but he'd never take as good care of her as her older sister had.

After the small wedding reception at the Thayer Hotel, Louise and Franklin said good-bye to their families and friends and drove away in the brand-new 1938 Pontiac sedan Franklin's parents had given them as a wedding present to begin their new life together. Franklin would attend the regular officers' course at Fort Sill, Oklahoma, where the Army trained its new artillery men.

Gone were Franklin's cadet grays. Dressed in civilian clothing for the journey, he looked strange to Louise, more ordinary. The trunk and backseat had been packed with their summer wardrobes and household essentials selected from their wedding gifts. The rest of their things would be shipped later when Franklin had a permanent assignment.

I'm married, Louise kept telling herself. *Married*. From daughter to wife. She had a strange feeling that she'd missed something in between, like when she fell asleep on a long motor trip and woke up in a different state.

The first three nights of their journey were to be spent at an isolated cabin on Greenwood Lake in New Jersey's Bearfort Mountains. Now owned by friends of Franklin's parents, the cabin had once belonged to Franklin's grandparents.

Louise only half-listened to Franklin's stories of fishing, hunting, mountain climbing, of how he had learned to drive on these roads in his granddad's truck and learned to shoot in those woods with his granddad's rifle. Her mind had moved on ahead. Soon they would arrive, unpack, eat dinner, bathe and spend their first night together. She was too exhausted to feel nervous, although nervousness had prevented her from sleeping well for weeks. If she could just take a nap, even a short one, she would feel better. As it was, she felt lethargic, slightly ill.

Marynell and the girls at school all thought a honeymoon in a lakeside cabin sounded terribly romantic. Moonlight on the water, soft rustling breezes, time to be alone.

When her mother asked her if she had any questions about her wedding night, Louise had said no.

"Sometimes it seems strange at first, but you'll get used to it," Elizabeth said, not looking at her. "Have you talked to other girls or read books? Do you understand everything?"

Louise nodded, willing her mother to stop. She would ask Marynell.

"Do? I don't think you do anything except just let him do what he wants to," Marynell had said. "Have you ever felt excited by him kissing you?"

"Kind of," Louise admitted from her accustomed perch at the foot of Marynell's bed, hairbrush in hand.

"Well, just let him kiss you a whole lot and get you in the mood."

"I wonder how much it hurts."

"I've heard it's not bad at all if you just relax."

"*Relax!*" Louise's voice was too high.

Marynell scrambled from under the covers and put her arms around her sister. "Yes, honey. Relax. It's going to happen whether you're a nervous wreck or calm, so it seems to me a girl should just close her eyes and relax. Then after she gets used to the way it feels, maybe she can figure out how to enjoy it."

"What if it doesn't work? What if he doesn't get aroused enough to have one of those erections?"

"I'm not sure," Marynell had admitted. "I guess you try again another time."

Last night, Louise had shared a bed at the Fentrisses' with her sister. Tonight she would sleep with Franklin. Everything seemed to be going too fast.

She wondered if Franklin was nervous about tonight, if he had ever had sex before. She thought of his former girlfriend from North Carolina who had gone to Barnard. Did girls who gave up their virginity before marriage really want to, or were they just afraid to tell a boy no?

The cabin, an impressive two-story log affair, had been cleaned and stocked with provisions by a local couple who served as caretakers.

Franklin carried in the bags while Louise explored the kitchen. As Franklin's mother had promised, there was a meal prepared by the caretaker's wife waiting in the icebox. A baked ham. Scalloped potatoes ready to put in the oven. Fresh green beans already cooked with a ham hock and ready to warm. A bottle of champagne stood in the icebox. For later. A chocolate cake was in a saver in the middle of the kitchen table.

"May I help?" Franklin asked. Still in his sport coat, he had a newspaper folded under his arm. Louise wondered if he had brought the paper with him, or if the caretaker had left it. She thought of all the evenings of her life when her father read his paper and listened to the evening news while her mother finished up dinner.

"No. I just need to warm a few things," Louise said. "It won't be long."

She took off the jacket of her going-away suit and found a bibbed apron to tie over the peach-colored gabardine skirt and matching silk blouse, then stood in the middle of the kitchen feeling bewildered. It all seemed so ordinary—just like any other night in her life. Then she saw the new candles in heavy glass holders. She was sure Maxine had included candles in her instructions to the caretaker's wife. Louise smiled at their message. It was up to her to make it special.

She lit the oven for the potatoes and put the beans on a low burner. As an afterthought, she sliced some ham and put it in the oven with the potatoes. Cold ham seemed too much like a picnic. She could hear Edward R. Murrow's voice coming from the radio in the living room. Hitler had accused Prague of deliberate brutality against the German minority in Czechoslovakia.

Louise arranged some homemade pickles in a dish and found a can of applesauce to serve with the ham. Then she spread the table with a freshly laundered cloth, placed the candles in its center, then stepped out back to pick some greenery. The dishes were everyday and the utensils utilitarian, but she set the table carefully, then went upstairs to unpack her suitcase and freshen her makeup. She avoided looking at the bed, avoided thinking about the bed. Dinner first. And spending the evening together. Like married people.

Her hand trembled as she served the food and lit the candles. "We can eat now," she told Franklin. He folded his newspaper and straightened his tie. Louise took off the apron and replaced her suit jacket.

"Do you have bread?" he asked.

Louise went back to the kitchen for bread. When she returned, Franklin offered thanks for the food and asked a blessing on their new "endeavor."

She could manage only a few bites of her dinner. She listened while Franklin talked about jumping out of planes. He wanted to take special training to become a paratrooper.

"Why?" she asked.

"There's talk of units being formed—airborne artillery. Special fighting teams are the coming thing. It would be a good opportunity."

"But isn't it dangerous—jumping out of airplanes?"

"Not if one follows procedure."

She cleared the table and served the chocolate cake, helping herself to a small test bite. It was good, but she could make better. That would be fun, making a cake for Franklin and having him compliment her.

"I like coffee with dessert," he said as she put a slice of cake in front of him.

"I'm sorry. I didn't think to ask." She hurried out to the kitchen to make coffee, all too aware of Franklin waiting at the table with his cake.

At the end of the meal, Franklin helped her carry the dishes to the kitchen. "They'll wait until morning," he said when she started to run water in the dishpan.

She followed Franklin into the living room and watched him reseat himself by the radio. She sat on the other side of the small table in a rocking chair. Music was playing on the radio—Tommy Dorsey's rendition of "Stars Fell on Alabama." Louise wondered if she should have brought something to read.

Franklin was looking at her. She closed her eyes and rocked.

"Are you all right?" he asked.

"Yes. But nervous." She kept her eyes closed.

"Go put on some walking shoes. I think we should take a stroll down to the lake."

The moonlight on the water was like a painting, the air crisp and clear. Louise inhaled gratefully. Franklin took her hand, and they walked down the gravel path to the boat dock. He told her about fishing there as a boy, rowing across the lake to see the cave on the other side. "We can do that tomorrow," he said. "And hike up to the top of the hill. The view is splendid. Tomorrow night, we'll drive into the village for dinner at an inn I like. But tonight, I didn't want to share you with anyone."

He was making it better. Louise wondered if he knew how grateful she was.

They didn't talk on the way back to the house. The gravel crunched under their feet, and the night sounds were all around them—owls, cicadas, rustling sounds in the underbrush. If she were alone she would have been afraid, but with Franklin she felt safe. Her hand fit nicely into his larger one.

On the front porch of the cabin, they turned for a final look at the lake, and his arms slid around her. He held her for a minute, tenderly, like she was something fragile. Louise could feel his heart pounding in his chest.

"Why don't you get ready for bed first," he said, holding open the screen door for her.

Louise climbed the steps, concentrating on putting one foot on the next step and then the next. She felt strange, as if she'd just awakened from a long sleep.

She bathed and put on her satin gown and peignoir, a horrible extravagance that Marynell insisted every bride should have. Louise wondered if she should give the set to Marynell after tonight. Her sister had already taken custody of the wedding dress, but wedding night lingerie might be too intimate to share, even for sisters.

Her scrubbed face looked pale, but it seemed silly to put on makeup before bed. She stared in the mirror for a long time, trying to make a decision. Finally, she added a little rouge and just a bit of lipstick. Maybe he would think it was her natural color.

She slipped her feet into satin bedroom pumps with a bit of ostrich fluff on the toes—another of Marynell's ideas—and made her way to the top of the stairs.

She stood there for several seconds. The radio was still playing. "In the Still of the Night." She was so weary. Her shoulders ached. Her arms. Her legs.

Louise knew she absolutely must not cry now. Maidenly tears after the marital act might be all right, but not before.

She concentrated on walking downstairs in the backless slippers.

"How lovely you look," Franklin said, rising to meet her at the bottom step, to embrace her again, to kiss her forehead. "I won't be long."

Louise sat on the sofa and stared at the deer head over the fireplace. It would be all right. Women had been having wedding nights since time began, and no one ever seemed to suffer permanent damage from the experience. She just hoped he didn't want to look at her, at least not the first time. That would seem more of a violation than the act itself.

When Franklin returned, he was wearing a robe and pajama bottoms. He headed for the kitchen. Shortly, Louise heard a loud *pop!* and he returned with the champagne and glasses.

He poured the champagne and lifted his glass. His toast sounded as if he'd practiced it. "Every man dreams of a sweet, pure bride. Every officer needs a lady for a wife. I'm grateful to have found a bride as lovely as you, dearest Louise, and you are a born lady. I will be gentle with you tonight and for a lifetime, and we will have a good life together."

In spite of her resolve, tears rolled down her cheeks. Franklin knelt in front of her and offered the comfort of his arms. Her tears seemed to please him.

Louise wiped her cheeks with a corner of her peignoir and dutifully drank her champagne. Considering what lay ahead, they carried on a surprisingly normal conversation. Franklin told her the history of the cabin, asked about her family vacations. "Indiana mostly," she said. "I used to love to feed the chickens and gather the eggs. And listen to the grown-ups talk. That was the most fun."

She accepted a second glass of champagne and felt light-headed enough to sing along with the radio as Mildred Bailey sang the "Whiffenpoof Song." Franklin joined her for the chorus. But finally, there seemed to be nothing to do but go hand in hand up the stairs to the bedroom.

With averted eyes, she got a towel from the bathroom to protect the bed. One of the many things she had worried about during her sleepless nights was staining bed linens—or even the mattress. When Franklin turned out the light, Louise offered a silent prayer of thanks that the first time would be in the dark.

He held her for a long time, kissing her, stroking her back and thighs, telling her how special this night was for him. He loves me, Louise thought. He really loves me. And that made her love him all the more. She wanted to please him, to make the night perfect for him. That's all she asked, that everything be all right for him.

She welcomed his kisses, and when he reached inside her gown and felt her breasts, she was proud she wasn't flat-chested like her mother. She wondered if he would put his mouth on her nipples.

"Do you want me to touch you?" she asked.

"No," he said. "It's not necessary."

But he touched her, lifting her gown, putting a finger inside her, moving it back and forth, back and forth. She didn't like it and had to fight the urge to push his hand away.

Then at last, he was hovering over her, one hand supporting his weight, the other hand moving his penis up and down between her legs several times until it found the opening.

He pushed gently at first, then harder. It hurt, but not a lot as resistance gave way, and he was inside of her.

It didn't last long. Suddenly he was groaning and collapsed on top of her, a suffocating, dead weight. "Are you all right?" she asked, wondering if he had had a heart attack.

"So lovely," he gasped. "So very lovely."

His heart pounded heavily in his chest for the longest time as she lay very still in his arms.

Finally, he kissed her tenderly and sat on the side of the bed to pull on his pajama bottoms.

He turned on the lamp and stared at the blood-stained towel. Then he wadded it up and clutched it to his bare chest. Louise looked away, embarrassed.

With his arm across her middle, Franklin slept. Her husband.

She wondered if he would want to have sex often. She was glad he had liked it. As for herself, all she felt was relief that it was over. Next time, maybe it would be different.

CHAPTER

SEVEN

"**A**re you really a major's daughter?"

Marynell was standing on a stepladder, arranging boot boxes from the new shipment. She glanced over her shoulder.

The questioner was a private. And he was beautiful.

Marynell carefully backed herself down the ladder very aware of his eyes on her fanny.

"You're new, aren't you?" he asked.

Marynell nodded. "May I help you?"

"I need corporal's stripes."

"Congratulations," she said.

The soldier was reasonably tall, with thick, wavy black hair and incredibly long lashes that rimmed smiling black eyes. He had a strong nose, good cheekbones and a full, sensual mouth that was at this minute formed into a cocky grin. He was something to behold, but an enlisted man. What a pity.

"Well, are you?"

"What?"

"A major's daughter."

"Yes."

"And your old man would have a stroke if you ever went out with an enlisted man.

"Something like that."

"And even having a Coke in the canteen with an enlisted man would cause a scandal that reached all the way to the White House."

"Absolutely."

"And you're not even tempted by this charming specimen of stalwart American manhood you see standing before you?"

She should be furious at his disrespect but had to laugh. "If Clark Gable was a corporal," she explained, "I'd have to say no. It's carved in stone someplace."

She wished she could tell him he was better looking than Clark Gable, that she wished he were a lieutenant, but what would be the point?

She sold him his stripes and climbed back up the ladder.

Marynell considered her summer job at the post exchange somewhat beneath her status as an officer's daughter. But the job was available and convenient, and she needed to earn money for clothes in which to conduct her fall assault on West Point—more and better clothes than her father could afford, especially after the expense of her sister's wedding and trousseau. She had visited with Millie Fentriss while she was at West Point for Louise's wedding, and she had gone to call on the cadet hostess. Marynell was officially on the drag list for fall, and Millie promised to put out feelers. But Marynell would be in competition with girls from Vassar and Swarthmore who had well-to-do fathers and chic clothes. And she was determined to have a West Point miniature on her finger by the end of the year, preferably by the end of the semester. No girl wanted to graduate from college without a fiancé.

In the letters she wrote to her Mary Baldwin friends, she didn't mention her job, only bridge and swimming at the officers' club, picnics with other officers' kids home for the summer from their respective colleges. Most of her friends at school didn't realize how little money Army officers made, that Army kids were as poor as professors' and ministers' children. Of course, some Army families were subsidized with family money, and Marynell hoped the man she married had some inherited wealth. She would like to have nice furniture and clothes.

Sometimes Marynell almost convinced herself it would be all right to work a few years. She'd felt quite proud when she received her first week's paycheck from the post exchange. When she graduated, she would be qualified to teach elementary school and would actually be able to support herself. But supporting oneself was something women did only if they didn't have husbands, or if their husbands were invalids or failures.

Marynell doubted if she'd ever be able to top her sister's marriage to Franklin Cravens. For a time, she had entertained the notion of marrying a "civilian" to avoid comparison, but the very word "civilian" was boring. Men in civilian suits looked ordinary to her. Sometimes the girls at Mary Baldwin got crushes on the more youthful professors, but not Marynell. Professors wore baggy pants with shiny seats and cardigans with moth holes. And people who lived and died in the same little town seemed limited, no matter how educated they were or how successful their shoe stores or law practices might be.

What appealed to Marynell the most about an Army marriage was the fact that an officer's wife had to achieve right along with her husband. Wives of high-ranking officers were, as a rule, socially adept and politically savvy.

Like Maxine Cravens. Marynell had been very impressed with her sister's new mother-in-law. No other woman Marynell had ever known had as much power or prestige. Surely not the wives of ministers or businessmen. Or the professors' dowdy wives at Mary Baldwin.

Marynell wanted a cadet who was smart and handsome, who was a born leader and brave, who was ambitious and wise. He would love her passionately and appreciate her contribution to their marriage. Together they would be unbeatable. She'd know him when she saw him. He was there in the United States Military Academy Class of '39.

And in the meantime, she was not going to damage her reputation by flirting with a soldier. But over the next week, she couldn't help being aware of Howie Newman when he made his late afternoon visits to the post exchange. And he knew she was aware. She could tell by the way he sauntered about, buying candy or razor blades, deliberately not looking over the military accessories counter in the far corner of the store. Then he would amble over, pretend he had just noticed her and say, "Well, if it isn't the major's daughter."

She always made him buy something. "I don't need any more brass polish or boot strings," he protested.

"You can't just stand there and *talk* to me," Marynell said. "People will notice."

But she'd let him stay a few minutes, learning a bit more about him each time. He was from Utica and had flunked out of NYU because he didn't study. He had joined the Army to escape the wrath of his father, a Jewish grocer who had sacrificed to send his only son to college.

"Why didn't you study?" she asked.

"New York seduced me. It's the most wonderful, beautiful, exciting city imaginable. When my enlistment's up, you can run away with me, and we'll live in Greenwich Village, and I'll write a great book while you charm the literary types with your soft southern ways and corn-pone cooking."

"I'm not southern and I don't cook corn pone. Go away," Marynell said. "I have to work."

"I want to kiss you," he whispered, his teasing tone suddenly gone. "I can't stop thinking about it."

"*Go away*," Marynell repeated. She was angry. He had no right to talk to her like that.

His mouth flitted in and out of her presleep musings. She hugged her pillow to her breasts and pressed her lips against her palm, imagining his kiss. His lips. His tongue.

Her route to and from work took her down an alley behind a row of quarters that included the post commandant's. One sunny morning the last week of June, Howie was polishing the general's car. Marynell stopped in her tracks. He grinned.

"I'm the general's new striker," he explained with a shrug.

Marynell didn't know how he had managed it, but she was certain Howie Newman had engineered his new position in the general's household to be near her.

She hurried by. That evening, the money in her drawer didn't match receipts by almost two dollars. The manager lectured her. Marynell wondered if she would have gotten more than a lecture if her father hadn't commanded the post hospital.

For three days, she took another way to and from work. Then she forgot, and her footsteps automatically sought the old familiar route. As she approached the back of the general's house, she slowed, her heart pounding.

He was there, sweeping out the garage.

"Meet me out back of your quarters tonight at nine. It'll be dark by then."

"No," Marynell said, furious. She looked around to see if anyone was nearby.

"I just want a kiss. Only one. You want it, too."

"You're an idiot. I don't want to kiss an enlisted man, and don't you ever talk to me again."

"I'll be out back by the lilac bush at nine. Just one kiss."

Marynell started running, her feet making a crunching noise in the gravel.

He was crazy. She had absolutely no desire to kiss him. She'd be a fool to kiss him. Her reputation was the most precious thing a girl possessed, and a girl who kissed enlisted men was not the sort who married a West Point cadet.

She had a headache all day that neither aspirin nor coffee helped. At dinner, her father reached over and felt her forehead. "You're a little flushed, honey. You feel all right?"

"Not really. I think I'll go to bed early."

She took a bath and was in bed by seven. At eight, her father came in to check on her. "Would you like some aspirin?" he asked.

"I've already taken a couple, and I feel better. I think I'll just read a while and go to sleep early."

"Well, good night, honey," he said, kissing her forehead.

At nine, she decided to get a glass of iced tea. The radio was on in the living room. Barefooted, she walked toward the kitchen. The back door was open, the screen door hooked.

Marynell unhooked it. The concrete was cool on her bare feet.

He wasn't there. She felt stupid and angry. She looked around one more time, then turned to go back to the house.

She heard footsteps on the gravel, her name being whispered.

"They had guests for dinner," he said. "Cleaning up took longer."

He did not express surprise that she was there. Marynell felt cheap. She was stiff as he pulled her into the shadows and folded her in his arms.

His lips teased, nibbling, rubbing against hers. The tip of his tongue outlined her mouth until it was wet with his saliva. She kept waiting for the real kiss, wanting it more and more.

Her arms slid around his neck as her lips parted. His tongue went deep, very deep. A small sound arose in her throat. It was so naughty. She shouldn't.

They kissed endlessly, devouring each other's mouths. No boy had ever kissed her like this before. She had never kissed anyone back like this before. She couldn't get enough of his tongue, his wetness, his lips.

Finally, with great effort, Marynell pulled away. "I have to go in." But he crushed her back against his chest and reached inside her thin robe to pull her gown from her breasts. Marynell's knees would have given way if he hadn't been supporting her.

"Please. I have to go in. They'll lock me out when they go to bed."

She looked down to see her right breast made silvery white in the moonlight, pushed high and full by his cupping hand. She watched his head bend over her nipple and felt his mouth covering, the tug of his sucking. Nothing had ever felt so wonderful.

Fear made her pull away. "Tomorrow night," he whispered.

"No," she said and hurried back to the house.

Marynell had promised herself she would not touch herself anymore. She knew other girls didn't do that, but tonight, her gown pulled up around her waist, her body arched toward her rubbing fingers until release came. It was intense, yet not deep enough, didn't reach the part of her that wanted it the most. When she woke in the night, she did it again. She didn't understand what was happening to her. She couldn't meet him again. Howie was no inexperienced boy begging for a tiny touch. He was a man wanting sex.

"You have a fever," her father announced, feeling her forehead at breakfast. "Why don't you call in sick?"

Marynell was tempted, but what would she do? Stay in bed all day? She promised to come home if she started feeling bad.

"I absolutely can't have sex with you," she told Howie that night by the lilac bush before he had even kissed her. "I have to be a virgin when I get married."

"I know," he said. "Marry me."

"No, I can't marry a Jewish boy, even if you went back to school and went through ROTC."

"Why not?"

"Because I want to marry a man who will be important. I don't think ROTC officers ever make general. I don't think Jews ever do either." Marynell realized she was being tastelessly blunt, but she needed for him to know how she felt.

"You're a calculating little bitch."

"That's not fair. I have a right to plan my future just like you do. What happens to me depends on the man I marry."

"So what do you want from me?"

"Kissing."

"The MPs could arrest me for sneaking around officers' quarters at night."

"Then go back to your barracks," Marynell challenged, feeling a rush of power.

She worried that her parents would discover her empty bed and started leaving mounded pillows under the covers. She had no idea what she would say if called upon to explain herself, but the pull of Howie outside was too much for her. Some nights he wouldn't come, his service at the general's quarters having lasted longer than he expected. The tension of waiting in the shadows, the disappointment of giving up made her sick to her stomach.

But most nights he was there. Throughout July, they'd hurry across the alley to the row of garages and crawl into the backseat of the Rodgerses' Oldsmobile sedan.

They would undress, and she would let him do everything but go all the way. He masturbated her to climax. He moaned when she made him come with her hand, and finally, after several nights of begging on his part, she put her mouth on him. It made him crazy. She didn't really like to do that, but she did adore making him crazy, and then he didn't beg her so much for the other. Her virginity didn't seem in as much peril as before. She thought about her virginity all the time. She absolutely had to keep it.

And she worried that someone would see them sneaking into the garage or hear their moans from the backseat.

She wondered if Howie really could write. The wife of a literary giant. She tried it on for size, but the only thing she knew was Army, and Zelda Fitzgerald surely hadn't fared too well.

"Do Jews ever get to be generals?" she asked her daddy at dinner. "Or even colonels?" Yes, if she could have Howie, she'd settle for colonel.

"I suppose," Eddie answered. "Why?"

"Just wondering. Do you know of any?"

"Well, a couple of Jewish docs are majors and lieutenant colonels. But I don't know the religious persuasion of most officers."

"What about ROTC grads?" Marynell asked. "Do any of them get to be high ranking?"

But why was she asking? Howie had no interest in a military career. He hated his hair short, hated uniforms and regimentation. He was counting the days until his enlistment was up and was already sending out applications to colleges who gave students a second chance. Howie told her he loved her, over and over with great conviction, and sometimes she worried that she had fallen in love with him. It was so hard to think, so hard to see the other side of this sensuous fog through which she was navigating her days and nights. At work, she kept forgetting what she was supposed to do next. At home, she kept forgetting to eat and sleep. Maybe she should be adventurous and go where the road and Howie took her. But did she have the courage for that? And what if it wasn't love? She suspected that whatever "it" was, it couldn't continue with this intensity. It made her forget who she was.

It came to an end with a military policeman's flashlight illuminating their naked bodies.

Marynell had suggested they go to the post golf course. No one ever went there at night, and it would be safer than the garage. They spread a blanket deep in the shadows of a clump of trees by the fifteenth hole. The freedom of unrestricted movement had been glorious.

The flashlight beam went from their naked bodies to the stripes on Howie's discarded uniform. Marynell felt the hysteria rising in her chest. She had to get away. The MP must not find out who she was. Her father would be put on report. Everyone would know.

"Well, well, well," the man said, returning the flashlight beam to Marynell's body. "You've got yourself a real nice piece here, corporal. Give you something to remember those long, cold nights in the brig. Get your clothes on, you two. We're going to take a little ride."

"Please," Howie begged. "Her father's an officer. Can't you just let her go on home?"

"My, my," the MP drawled. "What would your daddy say, honey? Fucking an enlisted man."

"We don't do that," Marynell said indignantly, covering herself with her blouse. "We just do . . . other things."

The MP laughed and turned off the flashlight. "Sure you do. I'll tell you what, sweetheart, we don't want to get you or your officer daddy in trouble, do we? Why don't you and me just do a little bit of the real thing, and maybe I'll just forget that I ever saw you here tonight."

Marynell grabbed Howie's arm.

"You son of a bitch," Howie's voice said into the fresh darkness. "You can't do that! I won't let you."

"Fine. Then I'll just take the two of you in right now."

"Marynell?"

"Shut up, you idiot. I don't want him to know my name."

The MP laughed. "Smart little thing, isn't she. Beat it, kid."

"Not without her," Howie said, his voice quavering.

"You ever seen anyone beat up with a billy club, soldier? I can fix that pretty face of yours so no girl will ever want to kiss it again." And to prove his point, the man hit Howie hard across the shoulders with a brutal-sounding whack. Howie sucked in his breath, then scrambled to his feet.

The MP knelt beside Marynell, a huge, hulking form in the darkness.

"Howie, do something," Marynell demanded, reaching out to him. If he loved her, he wouldn't let this happen. But he was backing away, sobbing.

Marynell gathered herself together like a cat and made a spring for the woods. The MP caught her ankle and dragged her back. "Oh, no you don't, honey chile. I'm goin' to get me some sweet pussy tonight."

She tried to push him away but felt overwhelmed at his size and strength. Already he was hovering over her, his hand pawing between her legs. She beat at his chest with her fists, wanting desperately to scream, but what if someone came?

And as if reading her mind, the MP warned, "I'll kill you, little Miss Officer's Daughter, if you so much as whimper. Some colonel's wife will find your dead, naked body when she hits her ball out of bounds." He put a large hand around her throat and squeezed hard.

"I won't," she promised. "Please, don't hurt me."

She gasped as he thrust himself in a vagina made slippery and wet by Howie's ministrations, but that was the only sound she made.

She was aware of Howie grabbing his clothes, his footsteps running through the trees. She hated him.

CHAPTER

EIGHT

"Can't your father use his influence to get us some sort of lodging on the post?" Louise made the mistake of asking as they looked at a dank basement apartment that had water marks on the walls and a stained, sagging mattress on the bed. The previous apartment they looked at had been in an attic with a ceiling so low Franklin had been unable to stand up straight. Because of a growing housing shortage at Fort Sill, the junior-grade student officers had to find accommodations in the nearby town of Lawton.

"Why should we be treated differently from other couples in our situation?" Franklin demanded. "I don't believe in using my father's rank to get housing or anything else. Whatever success I have in this man's army, I will have on my own."

God, he sounded pompous. Louise wanted to point out that he'd used his father's name to get the time for their wedding in the West Point chapel changed from nine o'clock in the morning to a more reasonable two o'clock in the afternoon. But that was childish of her, and these were different circumstances.

They continued to look throughout the day at attic and basement rooms, converted garages and live-in arrangements with families, then returned to an apartment house they had visited earlier. What had seemed unsuitable earlier now seemed like the best the town had to offer.

The rent had gone up two dollars since morning, but Franklin didn't argue. Louise worked hard at not crying. Their first home had torn linoleum floors and a rickety bed, but they were fortunate to have found housing even remotely livable in Lawton, Oklahoma. At least this mattress had new ticking.

It was only until Franklin completed the battery officers' school, she reminded herself as they unpacked the car and carried their possessions up three flights of stairs to the two-room, sparsely furnished apartment. When he got a permanent assignment, they'd get a set of quarters.

The town and post had more than the usual number of students at Fort Sill's field artillery school and other training facilities. The Army was moving lethargically into a preparedness phase. And the Navy, too. Congress had just voted for a billion-dollar shipbuilding program. It boggled the mind. A *billion* dollars. Strange how everyday life went on while the world was moving closer to war. She had worried more about planning her wedding than about Adolf Hitler, yet sometimes when she saw the strange little man in the newsreels as he gave his speeches and observed the fanaticism in the faces of the masses, she felt the danger. She wanted to believe that Roosevelt would keep America out of a war, but it was difficult when she was married to a man preparing for one.

The first morning, Franklin took the car to the post, leaving Louise to finish cleaning and settling in. She wanted to surprise him with how homey she had made things in his absence. By evening, the apartment was cleaner but still looked just as shabby.

As summer progressed, the apartment's two rooms became unbearably hot by ten o'clock in the morning. The heat coupled with a two-burner hot plate in lieu of a stove curtailed her plans to "cook up a storm" for her new husband. The tiny gas refrigerator was old. Milk soured quickly. She shopped almost daily, buying only what she could carry.

Her greatest domestic challenge, however, came not from cooking but from laundry. The laundry room in the basement of the apartment building seemed to be in constant use, and Louise had to start early in the morning to keep up with Franklin's unending need for fresh uniforms. Her life seemed to be focused around endless trips up and down the steps to the laundry.

Oddly enough though, some of the best moments of her day came at the clothesline, visiting with other young wives—another lieutenant's wife and five enlisted men's wives, two of whom were pregnant. Over laundry, rank was forgotten. They shared tips on stain removal and hot-plate cookery. The pregnant women answered Louise's curious questions with good humor.

Louise dreaded ironing her husband's heavily starched uniforms and wondered how long it would be before they could afford to have them done. The fabric needed to be almost wet before the wrinkles would come out, yet she had to push the iron back and forth countless times to dry the garment to the required board-stiff, starched perfection. Franklin had to have a fresh uniform every day, and every time he broke the starchy seal of a fresh shirt or pair of trousers, Louise felt like she been slapped. All to do over again. And Franklin reached for a fresh towel every time he showered. Louise wanted to ask him to conserve but feared her request would sound petty. After all, what was another towel?

Her reward for getting caught up with the washing, ironing, shopping, cooking and cleaning would be to escape from her apartment for an hour or two to the shade of a nearby park. Sometimes the other lieutenant's wife, Jessie, would bring a magazine and come with her. They'd read a bit, then stretch out on a blanket and fall into a heat-induced stupor.

Jessie's husband was an ROTC graduate of Georgia Tech. She wondered if the time he was now serving would spare him from being called up if there was a war. They both had majored in journalism and wanted to go back to Turner County and start a weekly newspaper. Louise thought that sounded like a good life—a husband and wife working together.

Their neighborhood was near the colored section, and Louise would see colored women shuffling by the park on their way home from work with tired feet and sagging shoulders. She felt a kinship with them. They'd probably been washing clothes, too.

Franklin came home at night exhausted, sweaty, grimy and smelling of horses but nevertheless excited and challenged by the adventures of his day.

After dinner, Franklin would sit in front of the fan shining shoes and brass or studying his copy of Burger and Handy, the battery officer's bible. When Franklin wasn't studying, he was talking. He seemed almost boyish at times, more human than the West Point cadet she had first met. The Army was living up to his expectations.

"I commanded a firing battery today. It was fantastic—to lay the battery, feel the power of those French 75s going off. I'll tell you, Louise, it's exciting—a little like being God. You just can't imagine what it's like—it's almost spiritual to have control of that much power."

"Spiritual?" Louise turned from the sink and stared at him.

"Yes, in a way. Inspiring. Meeting the challenge."

"You're having spiritual experiences while I do the laundry and step on bugs," Louise said. It wasn't an accusation so much as an observation. How had things gotten divvied up like that?

Franklin stared at her for a minute. "I guess this has been pretty tough for you. If I'd known your life here was going to be so grim, I'd have left you with your parents until I got a permanent assignment."

"No, that wouldn't be right," she said slowly, wiping off the wooden counter top. And she meant it. Her place was with her husband.

But she thought of Marynell and her parents in the comfortable quarters made cool by shade trees, of daily swims in the officers' club pool, of evening walks and occasional horseback rides with her sister. She thought of Marynell going back to college in the fall without her and felt tears of self-pity well up in her eyes.

Franklin came to hold her, to rub the small of her back. She felt better just having him acknowledge that she was having a tougher time than he was.

Franklin needed a fresh shirt for tomorrow. Louise set up the ironing board, only half listening as he continued his evening monologue.

Ironing the heavily starched shirt took forty-five minutes. She'd timed it. Her blouse was soaked with sweat. Franklin reached over and touched the crease in one of the sleeves. "Could you try and get them a little sharper?"

"No," Louise snapped. She turned her back so he couldn't see how angry she was.

"My God, Louise, I thought you were a better soldier than that."

"I'm not a soldier," she said, her back still turned.

"But you're a soldier's wife. They've got to be tough, too." His tone was that of a patient father talking to an errant child. She hated him for it.

Defiantly, she folded up the ironing board and put it behind the bedroom door.

He got two bottles of beer from the icebox, opened them, poured one in a glass and handed it to her. The beer wasn't very cold, but Louise sat down on the sagging sofa and drank it gratefully.

Franklin turned the fan so it was blowing on the sofa, then came to sit beside her. His arm went around her shoulders. She willed herself not to stiffen.

"I love you," he said.

Louise softened a bit. "I love you, too. And I'll try to be tougher, but I'd like you to find a laundry for the uniforms. And I want you to stop using a clean towel every time you take a shower."

He didn't respond.

"Did your mother ever iron your father's uniforms?"

"I don't know about when my dad was a lieutenant. But as long as I can remember, a woman came in." His tone was wary.

Louise realized she was not playing by his rules, that she could win this skirmish, but she would pay a price for it. She'd learned that lesson at her father's knee. Little girls who coaxed and said please had far better results than those who were demanding. She took a long swallow of her beer.

"Please, Franklin. I could try extra hard to save on groceries. It would mean so much to me not to have to iron those uniforms."

He looked relieved and gave her shoulder a squeeze. "Well, if it would make things easier on you, I suppose we could see how much it would cost."

"Thank you, dear. I'd really appreciate it."

"Is your period over?" he asked, leaning over to plant a kiss on her moist neck.

"Not yet," she lied, wondering how much he knew about periods. "Tomorrow night," she added to placate her guilt. She was a bride of one month and already avoiding sex, already lying to her husband. Why did everyone think getting married was so romantic? Or was it just her marriage that wasn't?

The next night, when they made love, it was suffocatingly hot in the tiny bedroom. Louise's batiste nightgown stuck to her body, but Franklin gave no indication he wanted her to take it off. She was less tense than before, though, and he talked to her more. He valued her. He loved her. They would have a baby someday. And he touched her breasts longer, just kneading, not fingering her nipples like she enjoyed doing to herself, but it was nice.

In the park with Jessie, she asked, "Is marriage what you thought it would be?"

"Yes and no," Jessie offered, pushing a lock of damp hair back from her forehead. "I feel sorry for myself because our first home is such a dump. But my Ricky and I, we have our dreams, and I know it will get better. And after three years of neckin' behind bushes, I'm glad to finally . . . " Embarrassed, she covered her pretty mouth for a minute. "Well, you know what I mean. Being *married*. That part is just fine."

The uniforms came back from the laundry with all the buttons broken. When Louise tried to force a needle through fabric made board-stiff with starch and sew on new ones, the needle broke. Her reprieve had been short-lived, but she promised herself that when they got quarters on a post, she'd find a woman to do the ironing.

Franklin started carefully spreading his towel over the shower curtain rod to dry. Louise didn't know whether to feel pleased or guilty.

"You're not going!" Marynell's roommate stared at her in disbelief.

"No, I don't think I will," Marynell said, staring at her empty suitcase open across her bed. She sat down beside it.

"But why, honey?" Beth Anne asked.

Why? Marynell struggled with an an answer. She had sent her

acceptance to the cadet hostess, but her feet felt too heavy even to walk across a room, much less dance.

"I just don't feel like it," was the best she could do.

"What happened to you this summer, Marynell? You haven't been the same girl since you got back. Everyone's noticed. You know what the other girls are saying?"

"No. What?"

"That some boy broke your heart."

Marynell closed the lid of her suitcase.

"Well?" Beth Anne demanded.

"Well what?" Marynell stalled.

Always a day student in the past, Beth Anne's parents were allowing her to live on campus her senior year. Poor girl, Marynell thought dully. What a dud of a roommate she'd gotten.

"Is that what happened?" Beth Anne demanded. "Did you fall in love, and some boy threw you over? Or was it a man? A *lieutenant*?"

Marynell considered. It was tempting to say yes and be done with explanations and speculations. But she still had her pride, it seemed, and didn't want anyone thinking a boy had thrown her over. Marynell signed.

"No. I broke up with him," she explained. "He was from NYU. I loved him."

"So why did you break up?" Beth Anne prodded, dropping to her knees in front of Marynell, her pale blue eyes wide.

"He was Jewish."

Beth Anne sank back on her haunches and nodded wisely. "And your parents were opposed. Oh, you poor dear. You poor, poor dear. Was he just gorgeous?"

"Yes. I wanted to marry him, but we couldn't agree on what faith to raise our children. And my parents would have died. They're such dedicated Episcopalians."

"No wonder you've been so down in the dumps. I'm so sorry, honey. Have you heard from him?"

"No. We agreed not to write." Marynell sighed. "There was no point."

"Did you kiss—or anything?" Beth Anne asked, wide-eyed.

Marynell nodded. "Kissing Jonathan was like kissing a god."

"Jonathan." Beth Anne said the name like a prayer.

Marynell knew that soon every girl in school would know the story. She would come to be regarded as a tragic figure, a romantic heroine. She supposed it was funny, or at least ironic, but maybe everyone would leave her alone supposedly to do her grieving in peace.

Marynell rubbed her temples. "I'm out of aspirin. Do you suppose you could go borrow me a couple?"

Beth Anne fairly exploded out of the room, thrilled to have the opportunity to repeat the story of Jonathan.

Marynell decided she would work on her algebra instead of going to West Point. She shoved the suitcase under the bed, then sat on her bed, exhausted from the effort but relieved to have made the decision not to go. Beth Anne could call Millie Fentriss for her, pretend Marynell had influenza or whatever.

So bizarre. Actually to choose a weekend of studying instead of a West Point hop. But the girl who dreamed of West Point weekends seemed long ago and far away.

Her interest in math had come as a surprise to both her and the professor who taught "Mathematics for the Elementary Teacher." She'd liked her algebra and geometry classes in high school, but most girls didn't study math in college. They studied home economics or humanities.

But Marynell had asked to change from the simplistic teacher's math to an algebra class. Math soothed her. It never played tricks. She escaped into algebra for hours on end these days and decided to take solid geometry and advanced algebra next semester. She wished she'd majored in math, even though the only girls who did that were the ones who might as well have "future spinster" tattooed across their foreheads.

Marynell seldom thought about the cause of her malaise. Howie Newman and the shadowy MP were buried deep in her subconscious. That was how she survived.

On the way home that night last summer, staggering and sobbing, frightened that the MP would follow her and attack her again, she had to stop every few steps to accommodate the cramping pain that doubled her over.

Home. She had to get herself home. Cleaned up. She wanted comforting, but there was no one to turn to. She would rather die than have anyone know what had happened to her. It was disgusting, degrading beyond belief. Her body was covered with his smell, his stench. He had gone on and on with her, for hours it seemed. But she didn't scream. She didn't cry out, for fear that he would carry out his threats or that someone would hear. The screams stayed inside her head.

After he left her there alone in the darkness, she had wiped herself with the blanket and stuffed it in the underbrush, but his coming and her blood still oozed down the inside of her legs as she made her way home—the long way, through shadowed alleys.

She hurt down there something fierce. He had pounded at her again and again, saying vile things, making her say them back to him. If only she'd had a knife in her hand, she would have plunged it in his back. She hated men, herself, sex, being female. If she could find the MP, she'd cut off his penis. She made chopping motions with one hand and clutched at her belly with the other. Glorious retribution. Thoughts of glorious retribution got her home. She crept by the open door of her parents' darkened room. "That you, Marynell?" her father's sleepy voice asked. She managed a normal-sounding, "Yes, I'm home."

She showered with the hottest water she could stand, lathering herself repeatedly, scalding her skin for as long as she could bear it. When she finally pushed the curtain aside, her skin was lobster red and the room was thick with steam. She sat on the toilet and cried so hard she made herself sick. After she had vomited, she rested her head against the cold porcelain of the toilet bowl and wondered what was going to become of her.

While she healed, she avoided looking at her bruised body even when she bathed, which she did frequently, the water always very hot.

God was punishing her for sneaking off with Howie. She had been a wicked girl and was paying the price.

Howie actually sent her a letter. He had requested a transfer. He was dreadfully sorry for everything. He'd never forgive himself.

So much for undying love. Marynell hoped he got run over by a train.

She kept going to the bathroom to see if her period had started. And she kept looking in the mirror to see if something showed in her face. She had come very close to letting Howie put his penis in her, but the MP had *raped* her. The word bounced around in her head. Rape. Like a tennis ball going from one racquet to the other. Rape. Rape. Rape.

She was strong, she told herself. If it had happened to Louise, it would have different, but Marynell was the strong sister.

But just the thought of seeing an MP made her breath come in short, ragged gasps. She'd refused to go to work and stayed in her room most of the time, sleeping more than she was awake. She had trouble eating. Her parents worried, her father obviously not believing her pleas of sick headaches. She had never had a problem with headaches before. "Now, show me exactly where it hurts," he asked repeatedly.

When Eddie tried to make her speculate about the cause of her "headaches," Marynell wouldn't cooperate. She didn't want to talk.

"No. Nothing's happened. I just don't feel good and need to rest."

"It's not normal for a young woman to hide from her friends, Marynell. They come over and call. Everyone's worried. Would you like to talk to another doctor?"

"No! I don't want to talk to anyone. Just let me be. I want some time alone before I go back to school."

"Are you upset about your sister's leaving?"

"Yes. I miss her. But I'll be all right if you'll just leave me alone."

"You aren't having boy troubles, are you?"

"Daddy. *Please.*"

"You know your mother and I love you. No matter what's happened, we'll always love you."

"I'm not pregnant," Marynell said flatly, "if that's what you're worried about."

That very night, after eighteen agonizing days, her period began. She stared at the blood on the toilet paper and wondered if there was a God after all.

Eddie didn't try to get her to talk anymore. He just patted her a lot and made her milkshakes and popcorn that she couldn't eat.

Elizabeth tiptoed and talked in a whisper for the rest of the summer. Marynell wasn't sure what that was supposed to accomplish but understood it was her mother's way of expressing concern.

Marynell stopped opening Louise's letters, not wanting to read about the newlyweds. She was grateful Louise was gone. If her sister were here, Marynell was afraid she might tell her what had happened. Louise was the only human being she could possibly tell, but she wouldn't do that to her sister. She would protect Louise like she always had.

She imagined the look of horror and disgust on her sister's face. Louise treating her differently. Poor pitiful, defiled Marynell.

No, she would bear her shame alone.

Yet, in an incomprehensible way, she blamed her sister for everything. Marynell had gotten involved with a soldier because her sister had abandoned her, because her sister married out of turn, because she would be the woman Marynell wanted to be.

So why couldn't she go to West Point and find another Franklin Cravens?

Because everything had somehow gotten ruined out there by the fifteenth green of the Fort Belvoir golf course. Because she was afraid she would scream if a boy touched her.

She did start screaming—night after night—screaming the screams she couldn't when it actually happened. And the smell of that man's sweaty body, of his semen and her blood, hovered about her.

That was when she knew she must train herself not to think about it any more.

Marynell could feel her father's fear. He thought she was going crazy, that she was going to starve herself to death.

She couldn't really think of any reason to get better except to spare her family. But maybe that was enough.

Finally, late one night toward the end of August, she woke up in a sweat.

She knew she'd been about to start screaming. She got up, grabbing the foot of the bed to accommodate a flash of dizziness. Then she went into the bathroom and stared at the stark face in the mirror.

She was more afraid of dying than living.

She made her way down to the kitchen and forced down a glass of milk. It was cool and tasted white and clean.

Her mother had always said it was best not to think about bad things. Marynell realized how weary she was of thinking about the MP. After weeks of reliving the horror with every breath, it would be a relief not to.

It was easier than she thought. She simply dug a hole in her mind and buried it. Sometimes bad thoughts erupted, but she shoved them back down again. Still, the sadness hung over her like an acid fog that ate away at her beauty and her spirit. She neither cried nor laughed. She just was. But she ate and went for walks with her parents. When the second week of September arrived, she packed her trunk. Elizabeth didn't want her to go, but Eddie insisted that school would be good for her.

At school, everyone asked her if she had been sick. She had had stomach problems, she said. It was better now.

"That explains why you're skinny. But how come you never laugh anymore?" Beth Anne had demanded the first week.

"Don't be silly. I'm just tired."

And she was. Still. Too tired to pack her bag and go to a silly dance.

Beth Anne came bursting back into the room, her face flushed. Marynell wondered to which girl she'd told the Jonathan story first. She'd forgotten the aspirin.

At Thanksgiving, her father suggested she see a psychiatrist.

"Oh, Daddy, I'm fine. I'm making the best grades I've ever made."

Their Thanksgiving table seemed incomplete without Louise. Someday it would be just her parents.

"I always want you to come see me on holidays," she told them. "You will always be welcome in my home."

Her home. Did that mean a husband and children around a table with a turkey to be carved? Marynell realized that deep inside, she still wanted that.

She missed her sister. She wished they were girls again, sleeping in each other's beds when thunderstorms came.

Marynell started to cry. Immediately her parents were on their knees beside her chair. "I wish Louise were here," Marynell sobbed. "Why does everything have to change?"

"Some things don't change," Elizabeth said. "I still overcook the turkey."

"And we'll always love each other," Eddie added.

Marynell could sense the relief in his voice. She was acting like a human being again. But coming back from the other place meant a return to pain and vulnerability, and it meant she would once again have to deal with being a woman.

Her parents sat down, and Eddie offered the blessing. " . . . And finally we ask a special blessing on our president and his efforts to keep our nation at peace, and on our beloved Louise, whom we especially miss on this family day."

Then they recited the Lord's Prayer as they did for Thanksgiving and Christmas dinner.

Forgive us our trespasses as we forgive those who trespass against us.

No, she couldn't do that. To that faceless MP, she had been nothing but a receptacle for his lust. If he remembered that night at all, it would be with mirth. He would swagger a bit remembering he had done that to an officer's daughter. Yet he had altered her for life, and she would hate him forever. And Howie, who hadn't loved her after all. She would never feel the same about men again. Her ability to love a man would be tarnished by his very maleness, by the fact that their marriage would be tainted by deceit. For no man wanted a woman who had been defiled.

And lead us not into temptation but deliver us from evil, for Thine is the kingdom and the power and the glory forever. Amen.

The turkey was dry. Marynell would have had it no other way. She ladled on lots of gravy and scooped out a large helping of mashed potatoes. She was getting so skinny her breasts had started to disappear.

CHAPTER

NINE

*L*ouise stood in the middle of the living room, hands on her hips, feeling extraordinarily pleased with herself. The crisscrossed curtains didn't look homemade at all. With the new curtains and the slipcover she'd made for the secondhand sofa they'd purchased, the living room didn't look quite so "quartermaster," with its Duncan Phyfe furniture that was handsome but identical to all other furniture issued for use in officers' quarters.

Louise remembered the months spent in two shabby rooms in town and was grateful for her clean, spacious new apartment, for the regulation Duncan Phyfe. She hoped they stayed at Fort Sill for a long time. Franklin had finished in the top ten of his class in the officers' course and been assigned to one of the units supporting the school, but she knew "permanent assignment" in the Army probably meant only a year or two.

Louise bent over to pick a piece of lint from the navy border of the beautiful new hooked rug, then walked across it to look at the room from a different angle. She had to smile. Everything looked so nice, almost like a picture in *Good Housekeeping*.

The disquieting sound of hollow footsteps on the apartment's bare wooden floors had prompted putting area rugs at the top of their priority list, and Franklin had gone rug shopping with her in Lawton. On a Saturday morning, the town offered a strange assortment of uniformed military personnel, dusty cowboys, pigtailed Indians and rural families in horse-drawn wagons.

Shopping with her husband at her side made Louise feel smugly married, and her serious face was only a mask. She was having a wonderful time as they looked over the rugs in the town's three furniture stores. They discussed their options over a cafeteria lunch. The braided rugs were cheaper, but Louise had pointed out they really didn't go with Duncan Phyfe furniture. "We won't have quartermaster forever," Franklin countered.

"That's true. And braided rugs look very nice with informal furniture." Louise knew the word "informal" would tip the scales in favor of the rugs she wanted.

"No. I suppose not," Franklin said. "But if we buy the hooked rugs, we can't afford to buy curtains or a bedspread."

"I'll make them," she promised.

Louise suggested five rugs, knowing to ask for more than she really wanted. Franklin agreed to three. She was quickly learning the art of manipulation but disliked the dishonesty of it. Why couldn't they simply discuss things and come to a mutual decision? But the words "I think" coming from her mouth seemed to make her husband instantly intractable.

She searched all over Lawton for fabric she could afford and borrowed a portable Singer from one of the other wives to make curtains, a bedspread and dust ruffle, all for less than the fifteen dollars Franklin had allotted. And now, she could hardly wait for him to come home and see the final effects of her handiwork, which she'd finished in time for their first dinner guests tomorrow evening. Already, she and Franklin had been entertained several times in the homes of other officers, and Louise wanted to show Franklin that she could manage as well as the other wives.

Of course, she was limited by her budget in what she could serve, but entertaining among junior-grade officers was a study in various ways to stretch a chicken.

She and Franklin had discussed the household budget at great length during their honeymoon drive to Oklahoma. A second lieutenant only made one hundred dollars a month plus a small quarters allowance, and Franklin thought they should save at least ten dollars a month.

Even though his parents and her parents both had joint checking accounts, Franklin decided to give Louise a weekly allowance until he felt she was ready for the responsibility of writing checks. Every Saturday morning, he presented her with the week's household money in cash. She and Marynell used to get their allowance on Saturday morning from their father and it felt the same.

Louise had to petition Franklin for every dollar she received above her allowance. She wondered what he planned to do when he went overseas to fight in his wonderful war. Send her a weekly allowance from a foxhole in Europe? He'd have to put her name on the checking account then. She could buy a pair of stockings without having to justify them.

She had eloquent one-sided arguments with herself. To Franklin she said nothing, for even though she wanted to be treated like an adult, she worried about the responsibility. She'd never kept a checkbook before. What if she made mistakes? Telling Franklin she was overdrawn would be worse than asking him for money to buy stockings.

Now that they lived on the post, it was Franklin who suggested Louise hire a colored woman to help with laundry and heavy cleaning. Help was cheap, and Franklin wanted her to use more of her time participating in the various women's activities. Wives of career-minded officers needed to be involved.

Soon a tired, graying woman named Dora came in two mornings a week to wash and iron the cursed uniforms. Louise's burden became Dora's. Somehow it didn't seem fair.

Louise would have preferred to be a library volunteer instead of working at the thrift shop, to which she was assigned by the volunteer coordinator of officers' wives' club. She wasn't very clever at bridge and preferred coffee klatches with her neighbors to the more formal coffees and teas sponsored by the wives' club. Her downstairs neighbor, Cecilia Beckman, had very quickly become her best friend. Cecilia was pregnant and jolly and had a delightful Texas drawl.

"Ya'll just look here in Louise's cupboard," she instructed the wives gathered around Louise's kitchen table. "All the cup handles are turned *exactly* the same direction."

Cecilia kept telling Louise not to work so hard, but she loved keeping house. Maybe if she hadn't been so miserable in that awful town apartment, she might not have felt so grateful about her Fort Sill quarters, but she was. She liked the beautiful old post itself with its red tile roofs, well-kept parkways and colorful history. It had been built to control warring Indian tribes in the 1870s. General Philip Sheridan himself had come close to being massacred on the front porch of the commandant's house. There had been a program about it at a wives' club meeting.

Every afternoon at five o'clock, the cannon on the New Post parade ground would be fired, the flag smartly lowered by a color guard, and a bugler sounded "Retreat." Most of the officers were home by five-fifteen.

When Franklin came in tonight, the first thing he would see was the new curtains.

At four-thirty Louise put on a clean cotton dress and fresh makeup. She set the table and put the tuna-and-rice casserole she'd made this morning in the oven. Then she fluffed pillows, snapped a yellowed leaf off the philodendron and rearranged the magazines, until she heard Franklin's footsteps on the stairs. She stood by the mantel, feeling a silly grin on her face.

He stopped inside the door, surveying. His uniform was sweat-stained, but his shirt was still neatly tucked. He was a remarkably good-looking man, this husband of hers, with his dark hair and determined jaw. She still couldn't believe that such a man had married her.

"Wow! They really look terrific, honey," he said with genuine enthusiasm. She stepped into his hug, still wearing her grin. He smelled of horses and leather and sweat.

"It's great you got them up before tomorrow night," he said, nuzzling her neck. "And it's only two weeks until Mother and Dad come for their visit. Are they going to be impressed! You've done an A-1 job."

Her in-laws. Louise felt a stab of apprehension. "Do you really like the curtains?" she asked, leaning back in the circle of his arms.

"I like them and you," he said, kissing her forehead. "You're a prize among women, dearest Louise, and I am a very fortunate man."

"Can I have another hug? I'm feeling pretty fortunate myself."

While Franklin showered, she made a salad and heated the green beans. As always, Franklin was generous with his compliments about the meal. And he often praised her homemaking prowess, which apparently gave him the right to call her to task when he didn't like something. He had been upset when she forgot to RSVP for a cocktail party. He got irritated if she forgot to buy shaving soap or shoe polish. Occasionally she forgot the salt in his oatmeal. Sometimes she felt like a schoolgirl getting a grade, but she was proud when she pleased him.

Louise wanted very much to prove herself at their dinner party tomorrow night. She fantasized about Franklin complimenting her after the guests had gone, maybe even toasting her with a bit of leftover wine.

"What are you fixing tomorrow night?" he asked, helping himself to a second serving of casserole.

"Chicken divan—it's the casserole with broccoli. I've already stewed the chickens. And we'll have a gelatin salad, relish tray and warm French bread with garlic butter. I bought a jug of that inexpensive Chablis you like. And for dessert, spice cake."

"Sounds good, but why don't you try something a little more imaginative than cake?"

"I think I'd better stick with something I know how to make. I'd rather experiment on nights we don't have guests."

"I suppose, but could you try something a little fancier before my parents come? We'll have to entertain for them, you know. They have friends here."

"Entertain *their* friends? Oh, Franklin, it's bad enough to have people near our own rank. Not your parents' friends. What about the budget?"

"We can manage," he said.

Franklin read the paper while Louise cleaned up the kitchen, then they went for a walk. Autumn evenings in Oklahoma were lovely, and she'd miss this ritual of the junior-grade officers' neighborhood when the weather turned cool. People took walks, pushing baby buggies or strolling with a dog. Sometimes groups ended up sitting in a yard on kitchen chairs carried out, drinking iced tea. Louise already felt very much a part of the post's community of young couples. Life was good here—Army at its best.

This evening they made the loop around the officers' club and back. Johnny and Cecilia Beckman joined them. Louise and Cecilia chatted about an upcoming tea but fell silent when the men's talk turned to the situation in Europe. Last spring, Germany had annexed Austria. And only last month, Czechoslovakia had ceded the Sudetenland to the Nazis. Both men scoffed at Chamberlain's claim that the Munich Agreement meant "peace in our time."

"Don't sound like such skeptics," Cecilia chided. "I know you guys will be disappointed if you don't get to fight the Huns and be field grade by the time you're thirty, but I'd rather be married to a career junior grade than a dead hero."

"What about a live husband with a field-grade rank?" Johnny tossed back over his shoulder.

Cecilia patted her pregnant belly. "Only if I have a guarantee you'll survive to help me raise this kid," she said.

The Beckmans invited them in for a beer. The men got into a discussion about an upcoming training exercise, and the women retreated to the bedroom so Cecilia could show off the latest additions to her layette.

"Just shut me up if I bore you about pregnancy," Cecilia told Louise. "But I swear, it's all I ever think about. I sit around making lists of names or crocheting baby clothes. I can't believe I'm the same girl who had intellectual discussions back at the university, because I'm a nestin' hen now."

Louise understood. Someday soon, she'd like to have a baby herself. Up until now, Franklin had used a condom on the "dangerous days." They had agreed to wait a year before trying to have a baby, but Louise was ready for him to put the condoms aside. Just thinking about it now made something inside of her contract. *Her husband making her pregnant.* An arousing thought. Strange how she had sexual thoughts throughout the day yet felt a small knot of dread in her belly when Franklin turned out the lamp on the bedside table.

He made love to her almost every night, except when she was

having her period. Louise had grown accustomed to his ritual of kissing, kneading her breasts, pulling up her nightgown and manipulating her until she was moist, rolling on top of her. Some nights she enjoyed it, especially when he kissed her for a long time, other nights she wished they could just read themselves to sleep like her parents used to do.

She always found his touching her more arousing than sex itself. His fingers made her insides stir, her vagina open. It made her want something that somehow never came.

Franklin always seemed satisfied enough. He groaned, his body shuddered, and then she'd feel his wetness between her thighs. He always told her he loved her and held her for a time before dropping off to sleep. Sometimes he thanked her, which seemed peculiar. Did that mean she had had a choice? She wanted to have sex with her husband, but she didn't want to feel like she had to.

His sleeping body next to her was a comfort and somehow seemed more what the marital bed was all about than the sex that preceded sleep. Sometimes she touched his arm or back in the night and delighted in the intimate, secret pleasure this brought. He was warm and male. Her husband.

And sometimes she felt him touch her in the night, tentative fingertips so as to not wake her or perhaps to reassure himself that she was still there. But of course, she was still there. She would always be there for him. She cared about him—very much, and she believed that he did indeed love her. She understood that Franklin's rules concealed a vulnerability of sorts; he could function only within carefully defined boundaries. Passion, it seemed, was something beyond those boundaries, in the dim outer reaches where he couldn't take her.

After they said good night to the Beckmans, Louise took her shower, then sat with Franklin at the dining room table while he balanced the checkbook. She looked through her *Good Housekeeping Cookbook*. What *would* she cook for her in-laws?

In bed, she kissed him before he could reach into the drawer of the bedside table for a condom.

It made a difference, kissing him first. She felt herself becoming aroused. They kissed deeply before he slid his unprotected penis into her body. Louise felt positively triumphant.

Louise wondered if the reason for the senior Cravenses' trip to Oklahoma was a status check on their son's marriage. Thank goodness for all the care she had taken with the apartment. Maxine took in everything from the curtains to the cleanliness and seemed pleased.

Louise fretted that their sparsely furnished guest room seemed an inappropriate place for a major general and his wife. Cecilia had lent her a small table and a mirror, which helped some, and so did the small pot of ivy she'd bought.

The post commandant at Fort Sill was a West Point classmate of General Cravens's, so Franklin decided they should be invited to dinner during his parent's visit, as should two other officers—both full colonels—who had served with his father in the war.

"I think it's above and beyond the call," Louise challenged. "If given a chance, I'm sure General and Mrs. Sullivan would be delighted to entertain your parents in their home. My God, Franklin, generals don't come to a lieutenant's quarters. Don't do this to me."

"Never pass up an opportunity to shine," Franklin said.

"Even if the opportunity involves using your father's rank?"

"I am who I am, Louise. I will never ask for favors because of my father, but neither will I turn my back on the recognition that comes from it. You can have extra money to buy a standing rib roast or whatever's necessary to make the evening a success. And get a uniform for Dora so she can serve."

"If I must do this, I will entertain them like the second lieutenant's wife that I am."

Franklin was angry. "This is important," he said, his jaw clenched.

"I am aware of that," Louise said coolly. She hoped she sounded more confident than she felt.

"I'd be petrified if I were you," Cecilia said when she brought over her sterling chafing dish for Louise to fill with the reliable chicken divan. "I want you to know you have the condolences of all us girls."

Louise made lists. Cleaned with a vengeance. Lost sleep. Wondered if she was right in insisting on doing the evening her way.

But the evening could not have gone more smoothly. It became a trip down memory lane for the senior officers and their wives. Quartermaster furniture. Homemade everything. Chicken casserole. Jug wine. A baby crying in the apartment next door. The older couples had all been there. Sentences all seemed to have a way of beginning with "remember when."

The colonels and generals pronounced Louise's chocolate cake one of the best they'd ever tasted. General Sullivan asked for seconds. Louise wrapped up the remainder of the cake to send home with him.

The two generals' wives, who admitted they hadn't washed dishes in years, pulled rank and shooed Louise and the colonels' wives out of the kitchen, insisting they were going to man the cleanup patrol.

The evening was pronounced a tremendous success all around. Franklin was told repeatedly what a fortunate man he was to have a wife like Louise.

After the junior and senior Cravenses had said good night to the guests, General Sullivan with his chocolate cake in hand, Maxine turned to Louise and hugged her. "Charming, my dear. Absolutely charming."

Louise felt drunk with her sweet success. In bed beside her husband, she wanted his praise, too. She wanted him to tell her what a terrific wife she was.

She slid her arms around him. "Make love to me," she whispered.

His body tensed. "My God, Louise. My parents are in the next room."

"We can be quiet. I want you to." It was true. Tonight she felt open, wet, excited.

"I can't," he said.

Franklin stared into the darkness. They could be quiet, he supposed. He could feel the beginnings of desire stirring in his penis.

But it would seem indecent to make love with his mother on the other side of the wall.

He remembered when he was ten or eleven and they lived at Fort Benning, his room had been next to his parents' and he'd hear them in the night. The creaking of their bed. The animal-like grunts and moans. He'd creep down the hall and put his ear to the door.

He wanted to hate his father for doing that to his mother. But she had moaned, too. Louder than his father. He'd look at her sometimes and think of her moaning in the night and feel a sense of disgust, of betrayal. His mother.

Louise didn't moan. Usually, she accepted his lovemaking with sweet passivity—with soft sighs, gentle caresses, warm kisses. But not always. Some nights her eagerness made her more exciting but made him have less control. And when she was eager, he wondered what was in her head.

Harold shaded his eyes with his hand and watched his ball soar down the thirteenth fairway and fall just short of the dogleg sandtrap. Not a bad shot for a man of fifty-five, he thought smugly. He'd outdriven Franklin by a good ten yards. Not a bad shot at all.

Of course, his son preferred tennis. Adored tennis. Franklin was one of those fierce competitors on the court who played every game as though it were for the Wimbledon championship. Harold never had been a match for him, and in spite of nightly push-ups, he huffed and puffed too much now to play tennis with a younger man. The only reason he'd ever taken up the game in the first place was time. And exercise. Tennis was more concentrated in both respects. But golf was more civilized, more friendly, more relaxing, and it could be a man's game or a couples' game. Maxine was an excellent golfer, and sometimes they'd go out together before a late dinner and hit around three or four holes just because it was a good way to share the peace of the evening. And Army courses were well-maintained, beautiful places, like this one, with its magnificent oaks and elms. The course at Dix was newer but already beautiful. But back at Dix, Harold only had time for nine holes every now and then. For him, vacations meant golf. He'd played with old comrades in arms yesterday, but today his son was being forced to indulge him.

Harold replaced his driver, and the caddies picked up the two bags and headed down the fairway. Harold and Franklin fell in behind them.

"So, Mother thinks Louise should be able to write checks," Franklin said, taking up the thread of the conversation begun on the twelfth green.

No wonder his son had hit a bad shot, Harold thought. Franklin was peeved.

"If Louise wants to write checks, why can't she discuss it with me directly instead of telling Mother? I can't believe she had this conversation with my *mother*!"

"Hold on a minute, son. Your mother asked Louise if her name was on the checking account. You could hardly expect the girl to lie."

"And Mother asked you to talk to me about it. Why couldn't she talk to me herself?"

"She asked me what I thought about the situation, and I *volunteered* to talk to you about it. Get off your high horse, Franklin. There's no conspiracy here. I'm your father. I'm older and more experienced at marriage and life, and I felt the need to point out that your wife is young but she is not a child. You need to give her a little room to grow. The girl is actually afraid of you."

"Nonsense! Whatever gave you such an idea?" Franklin increased the length of his stride.

Harold scurried to match his stride to his son's. "The way she hopped up from the table when you asked her if there was more bread. The way she apologized twice for the sugar bowl being empty. The way she's always looking at your face for a reading."

Franklin hooked his next shot.

"I know what you're thinking," Harold said after he'd hit a fine four iron to the apron. "You're thinking your parents should keep their noses out of your marriage. And you're probably right, but indulge me one more observation. A good commanding officer delegates responsibility. Ultimately, he is responsible, but he can't be personally involved in every decision made by his subordinates. Let Louise have some authority, Franklin. One of these days she'll resent you if you don't. Your mother has authority over all things domestic and social. Just like the men on my staff, Maxine has the right to make her own decisions over matters within her jurisdiction, and she has the right to make mistakes."

"It always kind of bothered me," Franklin said almost to himself.

"What?"

"Mother having so much authority. After all, you're the husband."

Harold stopped in his tracks and grabbed his son's arm. "That's right, boy. A *husband*. Not a warden. And a father to his son, not to his wife."

Franklin hit the green with his next shot, then three-putted. A double bogey. He'd be glad when his parents left. A week was too long.

Louise afraid of him! What a stupid idea. She respected him, and Franklin was proud of the fine marriage they had achieved. He supposed that eventually she would have more control over their household, but right now, Franklin rather enjoyed being in charge. And he would never want a wife as strong-willed as his mother.

Sometimes, he was embarrassed for his father when his mother told him what to do. A general who commanded thousands of men!

Louise watched her mother-in-law emerge from the pool. Maxine's body was firm in a skirted bathing suit, her legs muscular.

"You really swim, don't you?" Louise asked.

"Oh, that was nothing," Maxine said, slipping a terry-cloth robe around her shoulders. "Too many people are in the pool for a real swim. At home, I usually go early in the morning and do laps before the pool opens—one of those little privileges of rank. Harold does his nightly push-ups and plays tennis. I swim and play golf. It's not so important at your age when you have to push mops around and carry grocery sacks and laundry baskets up and down steps, but when you're a pampered general's wife, you'll have to do something to ward off sagging underarms and a spreading fanny."

"Do you ever miss cooking and housekeeping?" Louise asked, thinking how much of her current self-worth depended on her prowess in the kitchen and the cleanliness of her home.

"Not the cleaning," Maxine said with an amused laugh. She

paused while a waiter served the Tom Collinses that Louise had ordered. The two women were sitting under a poolside canopy. Other tables were occupied by foursomes playing bridge and golfers enjoying a beer after a round on the adjacent golf course. Franklin and his father were going to meet them here after their game.

"I still get in the kitchen every now and then to cook up something special for Harold," Maxine continued. "Would you believe one of his favorite things is my meat loaf, something I cooked for him back in our JG days. But most of the time, I'm perfectly content to leave the cooking and everything else domestic to others. It's another privilege of rank I enjoy. You will too someday, my dear."

"I hope Franklin has a successful military career," Louise said carefully, "but I don't want either one of us to count on his being a general. I'd rather be surprised than disappointed with life."

"Yes. I can see that," Maxine said, "but disappointment becomes less of a likelihood if you set goals."

"Lots of men make a contribution without being generals," Louise insisted, thinking of her father. "They aren't failures."

"Of course not. Many men who received their commission through ROTC or a direct commission like your father have fine military careers. But the Army looks to West Point for its generals. Men like Franklin set their goals high and have a reasonable expectation of success if they have good efficiency reports and are fortunate enough to receive career-building assignments. Franklin has an advantage there, being his father's son. We've made friends along the way."

"I don't think Franklin will ever ask for favors because of his father's rank," Louise said, remembering how he'd chastised her for suggesting such a thing.

"Ah, but he'll get them without asking," Maxine said. "I liked what I saw at your little dinner party last night, Louise. Your instincts are good. I think you understand that you can't be like your mother, and that relieves my mind. Quiet and retiring won't do. Charm and competence are essential. You have both, just don't be afraid to flaunt them a bit. Speak up more. You don't have to let Franklin do *all* the talking."

"It seems so calculating," Louise said.

"It is. It's a big game for high stakes, with surprisingly simple rules. Always conduct yourself as though your husband's future depended on your actions. In some instances, it will. And you must learn to be gracious even when your feet hurt and your heart is breaking."

Maxine took a long sip of her Tom Collins, then regarded Louise carefully.

"You aren't pregnant yet, are you?"

"No."

"You know he'll go to war when the time comes."

"Yes."

"Don't let him go childless, please." She grabbed Louise's hand and kissed it. "Please. I got everything I wanted out of life for so many years—except a child. Then a child became all I wanted. When Franklin was born, it was like a miracle. I could face his father's death more easily than I could face his."

A mother's fear was written on Maxine's face. Louise felt embarrassed and confused.

"If you are so afraid for him to go, why did you encourage him to pursue a military career?" she asked.

Maxine's chin lifted. "I can't imagine my son doing anything else. He would have seemed less a man."

CHAPTER

TEN

When Franklin came to bed, Louise's mind was going over her schedule for tomorrow. He fussed with the alarm clock for a minute, then turned out the lamp.

She needed to boil the potatoes and eggs first thing so they'd be cool when she made potato salad. Then she'd bake—cinnamon rolls, chocolate cake, a custard pie. She needed to iron the blue tablecloth and napkins.

Tea. Had she remembered to buy tea bags? Her mother didn't drink coffee.

Her father said they'd arrive sometime tomorrow evening. Louise had been in a frenzy ever since he called. They were driving all the way from Fort Belvoir for a visit, before she and Franklin left in August. Mother, Daddy, Marynell would all be here tomorrow! God, how she'd missed them. She'd been married for over a year, but her heart was still with her family.

When Franklin started touching her, it was hard to shift gears. She feigned passion to hurry him along, wrapping her legs around his thighs and moving with him.

"No," he protested. "I want it to last."

She relaxed and let her thoughts drift away. Tomorrow.

When she sensed he was close, she stroked his back and moved with him. "Yes," he said over and over in cadence to the movement of their hips. Who was he saying it to, she wondered, himself or her? And what did he think about during sex? He always seemed so far away from her when they made love.

"Darling, Louise," he gasped. "Thank you. So sweet."

He rolled off of her and into a sitting position on the side of the bed to pull his pajama bottoms on.

Then, stretched out beside her, he said, "Good night, dear."

"Good night, Franklin." Then she couldn't resist saying, "They'll be here tomorrow. I can't believe it."

"Yes. I'm happy for you, dear." His voice was sleepy. Soon his breathing was deep and even.

A week. They were staying with her a whole bittersweet week, for it would be more than two years before she saw them again. After all those timeless years, her relationship with her family would now be lived out in carefully controlled segments—the length of a phone call, a letter, an Army leave.

But there would be only letters for the next two years. She and Franklin would be living in the Philippines—a two-year assignment unless there was a war. Japan had been gobbling up Asia almost unchallenged for years. Everyone feared that the Philippine Islands would be next. And Hitler in Europe seemed just as greedy. Louise knew that war would change everything, but she wasn't sure how.

They didn't know she was pregnant. It would be fun to tell them, to see their faces and share her happiness with her family. She wondered if Franklin would mind terribly if she and Marynell stayed up late talking at least a couple of nights. That's when they always did their best talking—late at night. He was funny about bedtime, though, peevish if she didn't come with him, even when she was having her period. He claimed that he fell asleep more easily if she was there. She marveled at times how quickly they had settled into marriage and how cast-in-stone the rituals had become.

How long could pregnant women have sex? She'd be too embarrassed to ask the doctor, but the nurse who ran the obstetrics clinic at the post hospital seemed approachable. Next visit, Louise would ask her.

She was glad her family would see her apartment before it was dismantled and she and Franklin moved on. And she had a wonderful week planned for them. They'd tour historic Fort Sill, visit the buffalo herd out on the wildlife refuge and drive up Mount Scott on the WPA-built road to enjoy the truly splendid view and perhaps have a picnic lunch there among the boulders if it wasn't too windy. She'd take her mother and Marynell to the wives' club luncheon and style show at the officers' club. She had invited the Fort Sill medical corps folks who had served with her parents during previous assignments for cocktails on Thursday. A regimental parade was scheduled for Saturday morning, a polo game for Sunday afternoon. Louise planned a picnic dinner in Rucker Park on Sunday evening with the Beckmans from downstairs. She hoped they'd bring their wonderful baby. A little girl—Nancy. Louise couldn't get enough of her.

Then her family would head home. Each minute of their visit that went by would mean they were closer to leaving.

She hoped she wasn't nauseated tomorrow when she got up. There was still so much to do. The nurse advised eating crackers in the morning before drinking anything. That helped—until she fried Franklin's bacon. She doubted if she'd ever be able to eat bacon again.

Franklin was definitely asleep now. Quietly, she padded down the dark hallway to the pantry. A box of tea bags was there by the Ovaltine she had bought for her and her sister's bedtime glass of milk.

"Your letters sounded like you'd just copied the ones you wrote to Mother and Daddy."

Marynell shrugged. "I've never been much of a letter writer, and I resented having to write to you. I wanted you there with me. We were supposed to have two more years of college together."

"That would have been nice, but it didn't work out that way." Louise's voice sounded too matter-of-fact to suit Marynell.

"Didn't you miss not going back to college?"

"Yes, but the hardest part was being away from you and Mother and Daddy."

Marynell finished rolling out the biscuit dough, cut it into circles and put them on a baking sheet. "What now?" she asked as she wiped the flour from her hands.

Louise was peeling carrots at the kitchen sink. "Why don't we have a cup of coffee? The meat loaf's already in the oven. I'll get these carrots on to cook, and we can sit awhile."

Marynell got two heavy mugs from the cupboard and turned on the burner under the half-full enamel coffee pot. Then she sat down, watching her sister's efficient movements. Louise was definitely at home in a kitchen, not like their mother at all. Strange. She always assumed her sister would be a carbon copy of Mother.

Louise looked more mature. She was actually quite lovely in spite of that awful chignon and a crying need for more mascara. They used to play house; now Louise was doing it for real.

"Are you happy?" Marynell asked abruptly.

Louise poured the coffee and slipped into the chair across from her sister. "I suppose so. I've loved living here at Fort Sill. The Philippines will be a wonderful opportunity. Imagine—living someplace like that. I'll be a world traveler."

The coffee was hot and good. Franklin had gone back to the office. Mother was lying down. Daddy was playing a round of golf with a former colleague from his days at Jefferson Barracks, claiming his daughters needed some time by themselves. It was nice to be here having coffee and conversation in the kitchen with Louise. It made them seem like the grown-up sisters they were, but Marynell still preferred the late-night girl talk they used to share. "How do you and Franklin get along?" she asked. "Do you like sex?"

"God, Marynell. I can't believe you'd ask a question like that."

"I'm your sister. Remember? We're supposed to be able to talk about anything."

Louise considered for a minute as she took a sip of coffee. "Well, Franklin and I get along very well. Sometimes I resent how in charge of everything he is, but he is always kind and appreciative. And as time goes by, I hope he'll get less bossy. Or maybe I'll learn to speak up more."

"And sex?"

"It's just sex, something you do." Louise took a sudden interest in the back of her hands.

"But do you like it?"

"Sometimes it's nice. Other times, it's to accommodate Franklin."

"But do you feel like you have to do it whenever he wants?"

Louise carried the mugs to the stove for refills. "That's awfully private," she said with her back to her sister.

Marynell relented. Maybe some things were too private to share, even for sisters. But if Louise had opened up to her, maybe then Marynell could have told her about the MP. She had thought about that on the drive out. A year had gone by, a long time to keep something inside. But if Louise wouldn't discuss sex with her husband, how could Marynell talk about rape? And how could Marynell ever explain the circumstances, that she'd been naked with a soldier when another man attacked her? By keeping the secret within her, she didn't have to look at it, didn't have to see it written on the face of her sister. She could imagine the disgust and disappointment on Louise's face, her sister who had always been unrelentingly good. And then there would be pity. Marynell couldn't bear for Louise to pity her.

Their daddy was fond of saying that mistakes weren't sins. The sin was not to learn from them. If she had stayed within the boundaries of acceptable behavior, the rape never would have happened. She would never leave those boundaries again.

The loneliness and isolation Marynell had felt over the last year would never go away. Once she had had the ability to sail through life, but now she wasn't the same person. Even sisterly love was not as perfect as she had once thought. And no man would ever seem princely to Marynell again.

"Now, what about you?" Louise asked, too brightly. "Is there a special someone?"

Marynell shook her head no. "I seem to have lost my taste for dating."

"But why? You always enjoyed it so much before and were so popular. What changed?"

"Oh, I just got bored, I guess, and suddenly felt too old for all that flirting stuff. Believe it or not, I had more fun with calculus than boys. I won the math award at graduation."

"You did? Why, that's wonderful! Are you going to teach math?"

"Just to sixth graders—along with readin' and writin'. I got a job through the college. The letter came right before we left. At a little town in Georgia. Amber. Pretty name."

"And where will you live?"

"In a boardinghouse, I imagine."

"I thought you'd get a job in the D.C. area. There are lots of young, single officers stationed there."

Marynell didn't try to explain that was why she took the job in Georgia, that she had decided to put military life behind her. "Do you think every girl should get married?" she asked.

Louise looked surprised. "The alternative isn't very attractive. Remember Daddy's cousin Clare? She lived with her parents, and everyone felt sorry for her. 'Poor Clare,' they'd say. When I was little, I used to think 'poor' was part of her name."

"Yeah, but remember when you read that book about Madame Curie and said you wanted to do something wonderful like she'd done?"

"But I also read fairy tales and wanted to be the Princess Beautiful. And let's face it—I'm no Madame Curie. But why are we having this conversation? Of course, you'll get married—if not to an officer then to some other man."

"So, if you had it to do over, you'd still get married?"

Louise took a sip of coffee. Then she smiled. "I have a secret. Franklin was going to announce it last night, but you all arrived so late and were exhausted. Tonight we're going to make the official announcement. We even have a bottle of champagne."

"You're going to have a baby," Marynell said.

Louise's smile widened. She nodded.

"A baby," Marynell repeated. Her younger sister had married first so she got to have the first baby. Her body would swell with new life. She would give birth and suckle an infant at her breast. She would be a mother.

The tears were instant. Blindly, Marynell reached for her sister's hand. "Oh, Sis, that's terrific."

Then she was kneeling beside Louise, hugging, laughing, crying. A baby.

Marynell pulled her chair closer and clung to Louise's hand. "What did Franklin say when you told him?"

Louise laughed. "He threw his hat in the air and gave a war whoop. We danced around the room like two crazy people until he decided I was fragile. Then he called his parents. His mother couldn't talk for crying."

"Have you felt it move?"

"No. It's too early. I just found out for sure last week."

Marynell held her breath, feeling changes in her own body, the emptiness defining itself. A baby would fill it up. She wanted a baby, too. The need was like hunger and thirst. It was as real as anything she had ever felt before.

Louise began bleeding the third night of her family's visit. Her doctor recommended complete bed rest. Eddie concurred. Neither physician made any predictions.

By morning, the bleeding had lessened, but it persisted into the next day and night. Marynell wondered if she should pray or hold her breath. Elizabeth tiptoed up and down the hall. Eddie insisted Franklin should go to work. "There's no need for all of us to sit here waiting. We'll call you if there's any change."

"I'm going to stay with you until you're all better," Marynell announced to her sister. "You'll need someone to look after you, and I'm more practiced at that than anyone else."

She set up the card table in the master bedroom along with the dining room chairs and the radio. "We came to visit Louise, and visit we will," she declared.

With her mother's help, Marynell served their meals on the card table. She and her parents sat there during the next three days, keeping Louise company, playing cards, drinking coffee and lemonade. In the evening, with Franklin, they listened to the news and evening programs—Jack Benny, Ed Wynn, the new quiz show "Information Please."

"It's really not necessary for you to stay," Franklin told Marynell when he realized she did indeed plan to play nursemaid to Louise. "I can hire a girl to come in."

"Nonsense," Marynell said, pouring pancake batter onto the griddle. "I wouldn't hear of it."

"Actually, I'd prefer it," Franklin said, his words measured.

"She is my sister, you know."

"But she is *my* wife. And this is my home."

"Are you forbidding me to stay?" Marynell felt herself wilting under his scowl but refused to back down. "Are you going to tell Louise and my parents that you won't let me stay and take care of her?"

He stormed down the hall without answering.

As she flipped the pancakes, she wondered if he ever thought of when they met at West Point, when he got an erection dancing with her.

Franklin didn't like the way Marynell had taken over his household, and he didn't like her. Well, that made them even. He was a twenty-three-year-old stuffed shirt and a tyrant to boot. No, she didn't like him at all.

But Marynell wished she could at least explain to Franklin that she didn't flirt anymore. She couldn't if she'd wanted to.

"I thought you had already left for work," Louise said as Franklin came in the bedroom. His uniform was crisp and fresh, his brass and boots gleaming.

Louise was propped up in bed, sipping the glass of orange juice Marynell had brought her.

Franklin closed the door behind him, sat on the edge of the bed and took her hand. "I want Marynell to leave with your parents," he informed her. "We can hire a girl to come in until you're on your feet again."

"But why should I have a stranger taking care of me when I can have my sister? Daddy has offered to pay for her train ticket back to Belvoir."

"We need our privacy," Franklin said firmly.

Louise put the juice glass on the bedside table. "It's only temporary," she reassured him. "I'd be more comfortable with Marynell."

"And I'd be more comfortable if she left."

"I don't understand. Why does it matter to you one way or the other? I'm the one who's bedridden."

"A man likes to be alone with his wife in the evening. I don't like having people around."

"The people are my family. Are you telling me Marynell can't stay?"

"I'm *asking* you to make other arrangements."

"Then if I have a choice, I choose to have my sister take care of me."

Franklin said no more. Louise kept wondering if she should apologize—or back down. She knew Franklin was wrong, but being right and being comfortable around her husband were two different things.

At the end of the week, Elizabeth and Eddie went to Louise's bedside to say good-bye.

"I'm optimistic, honey," Eddie told Louise, clinging to her hand. "But remember that whatever happens, it's for the best. Nature knows what's best in these matters."

Louise nodded bravely. Elizabeth started to cry. "My poor little girl," she said, sitting on the side of the bed, hugging her daughter.

After the good-byes were said and Marynell had walked her parents out to the car, after Franklin had gone to work, Marynell got the extra pillows from the guest room and curled up in bed beside her sister. Louise was still sniffling. "I can't stand the thought of not seeing them for such a long time," she said.

Louise's poor body ached from inactivity, and Marynell lay propped on her side to give a one-handed back rub. She stayed for the morning, the radio playing as the sisters talked and dozed. That was where Franklin found them at twelve-fifteen.

"Oh, my God. Franklin!" Louise said, a hand against her throat. "Marynell, we forgot about Franklin's lunch."

Marynell could sense that Louise was longing to jump out of bed, go racing down the hall and try to appease her unhappy husband with a hastily prepared meal.

Marynell hurried instead, infected with Louise's anxiety. Franklin could have fixed himself a sandwich, but Marynell was supposed to have taken over Louise's job while her sister was bedridden, and lunchtime sandwiches were part of that job.

The breakfast dishes still littered the table and counter. Scowling, Franklin sat at the table, glancing pointedly at the clock on the wall. Marynell wanted to throw the sandwich at him, but she meekly set it on the table in front of him with an apology, then bustled around, fixing him iced tea and a bowl of sliced peaches.

She tidied up the kitchen while he ate, hovering in case he needed anything, wearing her sister's wifely skin. But why? Their parents weren't like this. Her mother did scurry around at dinnertime and thought it very important to have her husband's drawer full of carefully folded, fresh underwear, but Eddie's control was maintained more with love and reason than intimidation and fear. But control he did, in his own way.

After Franklin went back to work, Marynell breathed a sign of relief and tackled the laundry. Once she'd hung a load of sheets to dry, she dusted and vacuumed, then made chicken à la king for dinner and baked peanut butter cookies. The lord and master would be able to find no fault this evening. She had even remembered to make a list for Cecilia Beckman, who'd offered to do Louise's grocery shopping at the commissary.

Marynell served Louise's dinner on a tray and her own and Franklin's on the card table by the bed. "Very good," he commented when he tasted the chicken. "Do you have any bread?"

Louise stopped bleeding after ten days. The doctor wanted her to stay in bed for two more weeks as a precaution, but he assured Louise that she was still pregnant and had a good chance of staying that way. Franklin was visibly relieved. Louise could probably accompany him to the Philippines. He even started being nicer to Marynell.

Marynell was disappointed. She wanted Franklin to go away. She and her sister could have this baby together.

Finally, after five weeks, Franklin bluntly told his sister-in-law that he appreciated all she had done for them, but Louise could manage now. He had hired a girl to come in to help with the packing, and Marynell could go home. Reluctantly, Marynell took her leave. Louise drove her to the station.

The sisters stood sobbing on the station platform. "Two years," Marynell kept saying.

The conductor called "All aboard." People scurried about them.

"I love you," Louise said.

"I love you, too," Marynell said as they hugged one last time.

"You take care of yourself, hear. I love the baby already."

But she hated the Army, Marynell decided that night as she listened to the monotonous clickety-click of the rails and tried to sleep in the narrow berth. Soon she would have a niece or nephew she couldn't even hold until it was big enough to walk. The Army made it so sisters couldn't share pregnancy and babies. It put uniforms on men like Franklin and made them arrogant. What ever made her think she wanted to marry an officer? Since she couldn't have a baby by herself, she'd find a nice, safe banker or doctor to marry, someone who would install her in a comfortable home, give her babies, allow her to set the terms of their marriage. She was glad she hadn't married Franklin Cravens. He was a real ass. But this husband-to-be wasn't just going to materialize. She would have to find him. She would have to date.

Marynell felt her body shrivel at the thought of a man touching her. Once she had adored it.

Louise stood on the platform for a long time, watching the train disappear. Her tears stopped. The pain of her sister's leaving numbed as she wearily wondered what she would cook for dinner. Franklin would need coddling. Yet Louise felt rooted to the wooden planks.

She'd feel better when the baby started moving inside her, when it became more real. For now, the only reality in her life was Franklin. She would set the table with the good dishes and have wine in goblets. She didn't have enough time to do anything with chicken, but pork chops would be nice. With spiced apples.

Pork. Her stomach lurched.

The train rounded a distant curve and was gone with one final mournful whistle. "Good-bye, Marynell," she whispered. The tears threatened again.

Part of Louise wished she was on the vanishing train with her sister. Part of her was eager to face this evening's challenge of making Franklin happy. But mostly, she felt numb.

The platform was empty. With great effort, Louise turned to go. She felt heavy. Her arms and legs weighed too much.

The stationmaster was smiling at her through his window. Louise nodded, unable to produce a smile.

The blood came all at once, pouring down her legs and onto the boards beneath her feet. Bright red, angry blood. Louise looked to see if the stationmaster had noticed. His eyes were wide, staring. Louise was glad the platform had emptied and that there was only one witness to her shame.

A second gush of blood erupted from her body. So much blood. Should she be afraid?

The blood would ruin the upholstery on the car. Maybe she should ask the man to call an ambulance. Which would be more expensive—an ambulance or replacing stained car upholstery?

But as her knees gave way, she realized the decision would not be hers. She was aware of a third rush of blood, of the stationmaster kneeling beside her. There would be no baby. And she wanted a baby more than she had ever wanted anything.

CHAPTER

ELEVEN

*T*he nightgown was made of fine white lawn with lace ruffles at the neck and wrists, soft gathers falling over her breasts from a lacy yoke. Her hair hung loosely over her shoulders, a shining curtain of reddish brown. Louise studied her image in the mirror as she tied the blue satin bow at the throat. She looked more like a sixteen-year-old virgin than a twenty-year-old wife.

The gown had been a gift from Franklin for her birthday. She had hinted for a new handbag or a chafing dish. The nightgown had surprised her. She could not imagine her officer husband going into a store and buying a nightgown, even one as demure as this. Had he been wearing a uniform? Louise knew the unwritten rules prohibiting a man in uniform from pushing a baby carriage or carrying an umbrella. What else was a man in uniform not supposed to do?

A virginal-looking wife seemed to be what Franklin wanted. While Louise was not altogether comfortable with that image, the reflection in the mirror was not displeasing. She had gotten her color back after her miscarriage. Her silky hair, the rise of her breasts, her young features were all sweetly feminine, and she anticipated the pleased look on Franklin's face when he came out of the bathroom.

They had lived a strangely asexual existence in the weeks before and after her miscarriage—almost three months altogether, their departure for the Philippines postponed, their Fort Sill household still intact. Cecilia had made remarks about how difficult it had been for her husband, Johnny, during the sexless weeks at pregnancy's end and the weeks following her delivery. Abstinence had made Johnny irritable, Cecilia had complained somewhat proudly. But Franklin had accepted the doctor's dictates without question or complaint. He and Louise had lived comfortably like two siblings, seldom kissing—but holding hands during evening walks, friendly pats before sleep, reassuring contact in the night.

But tonight, their sex life would resume, and Louise hoped she would be pregnant very soon. And she found herself looking forward to the sex itself, to being intimate with her husband.

She smiled at her reflected self, then on a whim hurried down the hall to bring the candles from the dining room sideboard. The shower was still running in the bathroom as she placed the candles on the dresser, lit them, switched off the lamp and pulled the covers back.

She picked up her hairbrush and brushed her hair until she heard the shower stop. Her heart beat faster. The candles were a risk. What if he thought they were silly? Louise turned and leaned against the dresser, her hands clasped in front of her like a choir girl.

He was wearing olive-drab undershorts. His chest was bare, muscular, his damp hair wavy and thick. So handsome he was, this husband of hers.

Franklin stood in the bedroom doorway, saying nothing for long, breathless seconds. Then he was across the room, his arms around her. "God, Louise, you are so lovely. So pure and perfect. Do you have any idea how important you are to me? Having you as my wife makes life and the Army and everything else make sense."

It did? She tucked his words away to consider another time.

"When I think that I almost lost you, I get so afraid," he said, holding her head against his shoulder, stroking her hair, his voice catching.

She felt smugly proud that he had suffered so much for her. She had almost bled to death, but the fact seemed strangely remote. She had been unconscious, and Franklin endured it alone. "A close call," the doctor had told her later.

Franklin's mouth was warm on her throat. She wished he would unfasten the ribbon at her neck and kiss her shoulders. She wished he would tear the gown from her body and make love to her on the rug.

Instead, he lifted her in his arms and gently lowered her to the bed. She knew how she looked to him with her hair a dark halo against the white pillow. Her eyes were bright, her lips parted, the outline of her slender body revealed in the drape of the thin fabric. Franklin should be pleased.

A baby, Louise thought as he entered her. *Please, God, let him put a baby inside of me.* She felt her body open to receive him.

She whispered to him how much she loved him. How glad she was to be his wife.

Marynell herded the last of her brood out the door and sank into her desk chair. Teaching school was much more frustrating than she had anticipated, and she was always exhausted at day's end after trying to impose her will on a room full of noisy eleven- and twelve-year-olds. What an awful age! They were awkward and ugly and smelled. Yet, they were oddly sweet at times. The girls wanted to touch her hair, and the boys got crushes. Marynell felt herself becoming a good teacher. The moments when she saw the light dawn on their faces were glorious.

She put her board work up for the next day, straightened her desk, picked up a set of papers to grade and called it a day. She took one last look at her classroom before closing the door. The bulletin board display looked nice, and she liked the new arrangement for the desks. It left more room for the library corner.

She cut across the playground, then headed up Lumpkin Street. Eventually she'd like to have a car, but for now, she didn't mind walking. Her thighs were firmer for it, and someone always offered her a ride when it rained.

Skirting the square with its decaying courthouse, she stopped at Clarkson's Drug Store for tooth powder and shampoo. Mr. Clarkson already knew her by name and called out a greeting. He probably knew the names of almost every white person in the town and a lot of the coloreds. That was nice. Of course, sometimes impersonal treatment would have been better—like when she needed sanitary napkins—but Marynell found a certain comfort, after growing up transient, in having people recognize her, in feeling part of a community.

At Miss Mae Benson's boardinghouse, she loved her second-floor room with its dormer window, white wicker furniture and floral wallpaper. She'd never had wallpaper before. Every morning, it was a surprise to wake up to flowers on her walls. She'd bought plants, her own coffee pot, a radio and a rug.

Amber had been good for her. She was even dating—for almost two months now. Rusty Conklin was the basketball coach at the high school. He was nice, and although Marynell had dreaded the first kiss, when it came it was undemanding. His passion, it seemed, was basketball. He had played for the University of North Carolina Tarheels and now, in addition to his coaching duties, played for a semi-pro industrial-league team that traveled throughout the region. Marynell went to lots of games, and discovered she rather liked basketball.

Tonight they were double-dating with the assistant principal at the high school and the home economics teacher. They were going to see Katharine Hepburn and Cary Grant in *Bringing Up Baby,* at Amber's one theater, the red and gold Emporium. Other times, she and Rusty had doubled with the associate minister at the Methodist church and his fiancée, who was the daughter of a local doctor. Both couples were very nice. Dull. But nice.

Marynell knew that eventually Rusty would ask her to marry him. He wanted sons to grow up and play basketball. He even liked girls' basketball. If she married him, they would live a nice safe life in Amber or some town like Amber, surrounded by safe people, living in the same comfortable house on a tree-lined street for decades. She wondered how much respect the wife of a basketball coach could expect. Maybe Rusty could coach at a college someday. She wished he had more potential, but he let her set the tone, let her bully him into wearing a suit when they went out to dinner and stopped tipping his chair back when she sent him the same warning look she used on her students at school.

She finished grading the papers after dinner. Rusty was his usual ten minutes late. Her heart didn't skip a beat at the sight of him, but her smile felt genuine.

Even if she didn't marry him, she would always feel grateful to Rusty. In great part, she owed these healing months to him.

"You're lookin' great, doll," he said with a wink. "I still can't believe I'm keeping company with someone who looks like a movie star."

She kissed his cheek. "You're sweet."

Marynell traveled to her parents' new home at Fort McClellan, Alabama, for Christmas. Eddie had been assigned to command the base hospital there. Her parents met her at the Anniston station, which was alive with activity of military personnel arriving and departing. The post was the site of the Army's chemical warfare training and testing as well as a training ground for inductees and National Guard units. The Army was awakening from its twenty-year sleep. Germany had invaded Poland in September, and three weeks before, the Russians had invaded Finland. Roosevelt had declared the U.S. a neutral nation, but even so, only last month Congress had authorized "cash and carry" arms sales to "belligerent powers." Marynell wondered if the draft would be reinstated. Eventually Rusty would probably have to go. He even seemed excited about it. Civilians talked about war, too. Somehow, this surprised her.

Her father seemed as robust as ever, but she could see the concern in his eyes for Elizabeth, who had developed a slight tremor in her right hand and seemed as fragile as a crystal goblet. But she was smiling, and her eyes glistened as she told Marynell that Louise was expecting again. Almost three months along. She had waited to tell them this time—just in case.

Franklin's orders to the Philippines had been delayed until February. Marynell wondered if Franklin's father had somehow arranged for the delay so his son would not have to leave his convalescing wife. Louise had almost died. Even now, Marynell couldn't think of it.

"I hope I get a chance to enjoy my grandchildren," Elizabeth said.

"Maybe when your daddy retires, we can be like regular grandparents and have grandchildren come visit in the summer. I loved it so when you girls were little, and I could braid your hair and read you stories. Remember how we had tea parties with those tiny Wedgwood dishes?"

Marynell smiled. She remembered well how Miss Elizabeth, Miss Louise and Miss Marynell would come together for tea and conversation. They all wore hats with veils and white gloves. Their mother had been as good at pretending as her daughters.

As they drove onto the post, Marynell found herself once again part of the orderly military world where curbs were painted white and men wore uniforms. It was five o'clock and the cannon sounded as they drove by the hilltop headquarters building. As military tradition demanded, her father stopped the car and stood at attention, saluting. Hand on her heart, Marynell stood between her parents while the color guard brought down the flag and the bugler sounded "Retreat."

She had never been to Fort McClellan before, but she felt like she'd come home.

One of her father's physician lieutenants dutifully invited the major's daughter to a dance at the officers' club. Marynell hadn't danced in almost two years, and at the first sound of the music, her toe started tapping. But the lieutenant awkwardly two-stepped back and forth to every number. She didn't mind a bit when he was called to the hospital for an emergency. "Don't worry about me," she assured him. "If you don't get back, I'm sure I can get a ride."

She sat with the Simpsons, a major and his wife she remembered from Fort Bragg. She had baby-sat for their children.

Marynell danced with Major Simpson, then with a couple of bachelor officers, a captain who was short and a first lieutenant who was an unimaginative two-stepper like her date. Finally, however, she was dancing with a man who was good. A second lieutenant, slim and tall. She wondered if he was with someone else.

When the number ended, he asked her for the next dance. They talked very little as they twirled and dipped their way through the entire set. Marynell hoped her date wouldn't return, at least until the music ended. The combo was good and played all her favorites—Cole Porter, Irving Berlin, Hoagy Carmichael.

At the end of the set, the lieutenant accompanied her to the table, smoothly introduced himself to the Simpsons and accepted Mrs. Simpson's invitation to join them.

His collar brass was artillery—like Franklin's. He wasn't wearing a wedding band—only a West Point ring. So Lieutenant Jeffrey Washburn had learned to dance at West Point. No wonder he was good. And like other West Pointers, he was polished and mannerly. He was also darkly attractive. He looked a bit like her brother-in-law, but not so much that she didn't want to dance with him.

She asked him if he knew Franklin.

He nodded. Franklin was two years behind him, but he had known who he was. A heavy hitter.

"What does that mean?" Marynell asked.

"His father was regular Army—a general, as I recall—and Cravens was gung ho. On his way to being a Distinguished Military Student."

"I thought everyone was gung ho at West Point."

"There are degrees even at the academy," he explained.

"And you?"

"I was average, not a DMS."

When the music began again, they returned to the dance floor. He was taller than Franklin. Slender. Marynell liked the way he walked. West Pointers had such bearing. Marynell thought of Rusty's slouching walk, the way he was always practicing his hook shot at imaginary baskets.

When Jeffrey Washburn called the next day, Marynell was not surprised. Perhaps she had been too hasty in giving up her goal to be an officer's wife. Perhaps she didn't belong in the civilian world, after all. Rusty was sweet but boring. Towns like Amber were safe but dull. Living in one place forever and ever had its advantages, but so did traveling and meeting new people. She was an Army daughter who had grown up knowing she would be an Army wife. She felt herself veering back on course, but not without wondering what was inside the polished West Point exterior of Jeffrey Washburn. Was he kindly like her father or a dictator like her brother-in-law?

He outranked Franklin by two years.

"Why, Lieutenant Washburn, how nice of you to call."

Marynell pulled Matt Washburn's fingers from his mouth, but he immediately replaced them. "I worry that he'll spoil his teeth if he keeps sucking on his fingers all the time," she told Jeffrey.

The three of them were taking a Saturday drive out onto the reservation, their destination a small lake Jeffrey knew. The unseasonably warm January weather had prompted Marynell to suggest a picnic, and she had worked all morning frying chicken and making potato salad. She had included a bottle of wine for Jeffrey and her and apple juice for Matt. She had also bought two toy cars and hidden them in the basket.

Marynell leaned her cheek against Matt's smooth hair. Poor little motherless boy. The feel of his sturdy little body on her lap was satisfying. She pulled up the leg of his overalls and fondled a plump calf. She took an almost carnal pleasure in touching him, and there was no off-limits with a two-year-old. She could take off his shoes and play with his toes. She could pat his round little rump, and when she changed his diaper, she could even explore his silly little penis and his wrinkled scrotum that looked like a walnut.

The presence of a two-year-old child in Second Lieutenant Jeffrey Washburn's life had come as a shock to Marynell. She wasn't interested in stepmotherhood or at least had never envisioned herself in that role. A widower was something from a romantic novel—with brooding, dark secrets in his soul.

Jeffrey was all of those things. He said nothing about his wife except that she had been a wonderful woman and had died when she fell from a horse. His dark eyes held secrets Marynell wondered if she would ever penetrate. Like Matt. The boy had his father's great dark eyes. And although the memory of his mother must have faded away completely in the year since her death, the boy seemed oddly aware of his tragic circumstances. He was quiet and withdrawn. In novels, the widowed heroes were either childless or had grown children who plotted against their stepmother. They didn't have two-year-olds. Marynell hoped she was up to the task.

"No, Matt," Marynell said again. "You shouldn't put your fingers in your mouth. It's bad for your teeth." She still had little sense of a two-year-old mind and wondered how much the boy understood. When he started whimpering, she stroked his hair with her free hand, having discovered only yesterday how that soothed him.

It was strange to see Jeffrey out of uniform. He was wearing a leather jacket, corduroy pants and a cap. She decided Jeffrey was better looking than Franklin, in a sensitive sort of way. He reminded her of Tyrone Power.

And he was courting her.

But Marynell understood his reasons for courtship were more practical than romantic. Officers needed wives for the sake of their careers, and Jeffrey had an additional motive. His son.

Marynell knew that Jeffrey admired her beauty and had surely observed how good she was with Matt. She understood about Army life and didn't seem to mind the lack of romance in their relationship. She knew she must seem the perfect choice.

Marynell also understood that Jeffrey still grieved for his wife and resented having to get on with his life. Emotionally, he wasn't ready and he knew it. But there was the boy—a two-year-old who sucked his fingers constantly, who showed no signs of talking and spent his days with a hired girl.

A beloved dead wife. Could she really face that? But maybe the emotional distance it put between her and the man beside her would be a blessing. Both of them had been hurt by life and wanted comfort more than passion. If Jeffrey would marry her, she would be a mother to his son and have his other children. In return, he would give her refuge and security. And, in some ways, she could still have the life she had always envisioned for herself.

The breeze blowing across the small lake was chilly, so they buttoned Matt's coat and put on his mittens before following a path through the trees.

A startled cottontail rabbit sat in the middle of the path and stared at them. Matt's mouth fell open as he stared back, his lips forming a soft "Oh," his eyes full of wonder. It was a sweet, silly moment— two innocent little creatures amazing each other. Grown-up laughter mobilized the rabbit, and he dashed away.

"Bunny," Marynell said in her schoolmarm voice. "Bunny."

Matt pointed into the underbrush. "Bunny," he said, his eyes solemn.

Marynell felt pleased with herself. She'd have the boy talking in no time.

They found a sunny spot protected from the wind and spread out their blanket. Matt was taken with the novelty of it all and hunkered down on sturdy little legs to help smooth the blanket. Jeffrey showed him how to throw rocks in the lake while Marynell set out their lunch.

The fried chicken wasn't as crisp as she would have liked, but the potato salad was good. She wondered if Jeffrey's wife had been a good cook and if she would ever have the courage to ask.

After they ate, the three of them dozed in the sunshine. Marynell had her arm shading her eyes when she heard Jeffrey ask, "Have you been with a man before?"

"You mean am I a virgin?" she asked flatly without taking her arm from her eyes.

"Yes."

The sunshine felt like a blessing. It was so peaceful here. Why had he spoiled everything with a question like that?

"Is it important to you?" she asked. Matt was curled against her like a warm puppy dog.

"I'm not sure. I suppose you think I have no right to ask since I've been married before."

"I don't know if you have a right," she snapped. "I wish you hadn't." She was aware of his eyes on her face, but she didn't uncover her eyes.

He touched her hand. "Did someone hurt you?" he asked.

Marynell sighed and rolled away from him, careful not to disturb Matt. She felt the tears welling.

"It's all right, Marynell," he said, stroking her hair. "I'm sorry you weren't left with nice memories."

Jeffrey moved his body close to hers, cupping it around her protectively. She was sandwiched between the man and his sleeping son. She felt Jeffrey's lips in her hair. "Don't cry, Marynell. Please don't cry."

His words made her cry harder.

They were silent on the way home. Matt was content to sit on her lap, his head against her bosom. She didn't try to extract his fingers from his mouth.

She wasn't in love with Jeffrey, but she needed him. She wanted to be a mother more than a wife, but the two went together. If Jeffrey didn't marry her, she'd have to find someone else, and the very idea made her weary. She couldn't go back to safe little Amber and simple Rusty, after abandoning them so abruptly. Her landlady had seemed surprised and hurt by her decision but promised to ship her possessions to Fort McClellan. "I thought you were happy here, my dear," Miss Mae said. "And what about poor Rusty?" The Amber superintendent of schools was angry. "Don't expect any references from this town," he warned her. Rusty was more hurt than angry. "I thought we were in love," he said. Marynell had hung up the phone and cried. She didn't like hurting people.

After the picnic, Jeffrey didn't call for three days. Marynell could almost feel him weighing his options. He wasn't in love either, but maybe that was better.

If she got married right away, Louise might be able to come to the wedding. Surely Franklin couldn't say no to his wife coming to her sister's wedding.

She'd never called a man before, never needed to. "I was going to call you today," Jeffrey said, his tone guarded, defensive. "I'm sorry about the picnic. Maybe I shouldn't have . . . "

"No. I guess I understand. If I were a man, I'd have asked, too." Marynell realized her words were true. If she were a man, she would want a fresh, untainted girl to marry.

"I miss having a wife," he said. "I don't seem to be capable of love just now, but surely in time . . . I do admire you greatly. I would be kind, Marynell. I'd never hurt you."

"I'll take kindness over love," Marynell said.

"This should not be conducted over the phone," he said.

Marynell agreed. They went to the officers' club for dinner. The meal was good, the combo and wine excellent. Marynell looked around her at this carefully monitored world of uniformed men and their decorous ladies, of courteous service and immaculate table-cloths. A world based on order and respect. Many of these same men would leave soon for a world of disarray and death, but they would be secure in the knowledge that all this would be waiting for them should they return.

"This seems so unfair to you," Jeffrey said. "You deserve a wonderful engagement, an elaborate wedding, an adoring groom. I don't think I understand why you are willing to settle for less."

Marynell wished she could tell him why, but even if she completely understood it herself, she would never tell him or anyone else.

"Was she beautiful?" Marynell asked.

"Yes. My wife was beautiful, but Elise is dead. I still have Matt, though. I love him more than anything."

"More than her—than Elise?"

"She's a memory. Matt is real."

"But memories can stand in the way of real life."

"Yes. I suppose I'll always remember the way I felt about her, how we grew up together and seemed connected to each other. We were so sure of everything. I wasn't even afraid when I saw her fall from that horse. I knew she'd get up, get back on and finish the course. Now, I'm afraid."

"Me, too," Marynell said.

"Someone hurt you very much."

"Yes."

"I'm sorry. You don't ever have to speak of it again if you don't want to."

Tears filled her eyes and made glowing halos around the candle flame. "I think I'm very lucky to have found you," she said.

He put his hand over hers. "Will you marry me, lovely Marynell, and be a mother to my son?"

She nodded. It was all right. She would be an officer's wife—competent, admired, poised. And maybe someday there might be more, but she didn't want to count on that. The secret to a successful life was not to count on things too much.

She brought his hand to her lips. The skin was rough and covered with fine black hairs. It smelled of soap. Maybe they could heal each other.

And then there it was in her middle, after all this time, the raw bite of sexual desire.

The candlelight glistened in Marynell's eyes as she looked across the table at him. Beautiful eyes with thick lashes. She was more beautiful than Elise, Jeffrey acknowledged with a tinge of guilt.

Elise's parents had had a cabin on the same Wisconsin lake as his grandparents. There had been summers with Elise for as long as he could remember. She had been his first and only love. They'd learned to water ski behind her father's motor boat. They'd taught themselves to drive in the battered pickup his grandpa kept at the lake, taught each other to kiss in the same truck in the shadows of Pine Ridge. She'd gone to Marymount College to be near West Point. When Jeffrey almost quit the academy, she had assured him she'd love him if he raised cabbages or collected garbage. Their two years of marriage had been like a continuation of all those childhood summers. Even when Matt was born, their baby was like part of a lovely continuum that, begun in childhood, would stretch on into a contented old age of fishing with grandchildren by that same Oneida County lake. Elise had wanted to raise horses as well as children. Jeffrey wasn't sure what he wanted to do, but sometimes he had the distinct feeling that he wasn't cut out for the military. With war looming, however, and his West Point education obligating him for at least eight years of service, everything was on hold anyway. He didn't really think much about what lay ahead. Teaching, perhaps. He was in a training unit here at Fort McClellan, working with National Guardsmen and new recruits. He could see himself as a tweedy professor with a pipe more easily than as a uniformed officer with a swagger stick. His family installed in a house with a porch swing. Elise to come home to. Sunny summers with barefoot children.

Then in a space of an instant, everything changed. Elise had fallen from horses before, but this time she died, instantly, without a final kiss or word of farewell, leaving him a tragic widower, the father of a motherless baby. Summertime ended. He felt angry, cheated and afraid. If Elise could die in a stupid accident, anything could happen.

But as the initial suffocating shock turned into sadness, he considered his options. He had indeed loved Elise, but he had always wanted a bit more. She was his companion more than his lover. Sex was affectionate, not passionate. He missed her as one would miss a favorite sister, the buddy of his childhood.

And now as he looked at the beautiful woman across the table from him, at her graceful hands, the provocative fullness of her lips, the rise of her wonderful breasts, he wondered what it would be like to make love to her.

He wanted to bury his face in Marynell's breasts.

When she took his hand to kiss, then rubbed it against her smooth cheek, desire came thundering into his groin.

He prayed he was doing the right thing. He'd never had to decide about marrying Elise. They'd always known they would be husband and wife. This time was different.

What did Marynell want? Security and kindness, apparently. Whatever her past experience had been, it had taught her to be afraid.

He wished he felt more certain he was doing the right thing.

With his thumb, he rubbed a tear from Marynell's cheek. Beauty wasn't important. Not really. Beauty didn't mean she was fun-loving or reasonable or loyal or even sensual, but beauty was more seductive than he had realized. At this moment, it made him not care as much about other things.

CHAPTER

TWELVE

*F*ranklin pushed a footstool in front of Louise's chair, and gratefully she placed her feet on it. The two-day motor trip from Oklahoma had left them swollen and her back aching, the first real discomforts she had felt with this new pregnancy. She was glad they would be taking the train to San Diego, leaving the Buick for her father to sell.

It seemed a shame to sell their nice car, but Franklin thought it made more sense to sell it than store it for two years. They would be living on the tiny island of Corregidor in Manila Bay. A trolley line made cars unnecessary.

Louise felt Marynell's curious eyes as Franklin pulled her shoes from puffy feet. It did seem strange—a solicitous Franklin. Not only had her miscarriage frightened him, he seemed to regard her new pregnancy as some sacrifice she was making on his behalf. Louise didn't tell him that she was doing it as much for herself as for him. Maybe more.

The miscarriage had made her fearful. What if she couldn't carry a baby to term? What if she couldn't get pregnant again? What if she never had a baby of her own?

She knew now that success was not automatic. She worried over every discomfort, every twitch. But she was in her second trimester. With each day that went by, she became more relaxed. This pregnancy would succeed.

Marynell had outdone herself on dinner. Such a grand meal with sauces and garnishes and wine. She wondered if Lieutenant Washburn appreciated how much trouble Marynell had gone to or noticed that the creases had been ironed out of the tablecloth and the silver was freshly polished.

The boy, Matt, seated on a stack of books, had been surprisingly good during dinner. He was now sitting on Jeffrey's lap, a plump little replica of his solemn, handsome father.

Jeffrey, Marynell and Matt. What an attractive family they would make. But as Louise had watched them throughout the evening, she had felt uneasy. Marynell was trying so hard. It was strange, after years of watching boys hover about her sister to see that the man Marynell had chosen to marry was respectful and admiring of her but clearly not adoring.

Jeffrey Washburn adored his son. Louise wondered how he had felt about the boy's mother.

Eddie served brandy to the men and sherry to Louise. She would have preferred brandy but accepted her glass with a smile. She closed her eyes for a bit and listened to the men talking—about the road to war, of course—and in the kitchen, the sounds of her mother and sister cleaning up. She should help. Tomorrow she'd pitch in. Tonight she was overcome with pregnant languor.

"Our relations with Japan being what they are, I'm surprised the military is still allowing dependents to go to the Philippines," Eddie said. "We don't even have a trade treaty with the Japanese anymore. Are you sure Louise should be going over there?"

Louise sensed her husband's irritation as he explained that the government wouldn't allow military dependents if it weren't safe. Jeffrey agreed with Franklin.

Jeffrey and Franklin were similar in appearance. Jeffrey was a bit taller, but they both had thick dark hair, brown eyes, strong jaws, beautiful teeth. They could have been brothers. But Jeffrey lacked Franklin's bold self-assurance. Louise couldn't decide if he was shy or just quiet.

Shortly, she felt a tug at her skirt and opened her eyes. Matt was standing there, his fingers in his mouth. Louise helped him onto her lap, and he leaned his head against her shoulder. Her soon-to-be nephew. She put cuddling arms around the boy and felt his head grow heavy against her shoulder.

She and Matt dozed until Marynell made a pallet of folded blankets on the floor for the sleeping child. Already she seemed like his mother. The adults adjourned to the dining room table for a game of pinochle. Louise wondered when she and Marynell would have a chance to talk. Tomorrow evening, her in-laws would arrive from Camp Dix to attend Marynell's wedding and see Louise and Franklin off for the Philippines.

The next morning, the sisters decided on a quick walk before breakfast. Franklin was in the shower. "Tell him I won't be long," Louise told her mother. "I'll fix his oatmeal when I get back."

"I can make him oatmeal," Elizabeth said. "You girls need some time together."

Louise started to warn about lumps. Franklin hated lumps in his cooked cereal, but she was afraid she would hurt her mother's feelings.

It was cold. The sisters buttoned the top buttons on their coats and linked arms before thrusting hands into pockets and starting around the officers' circle. The quarters here were identical to the ones at Sill—stucco with red tile roofs. "Why Jeffrey Washburn instead of the basketball coach you wrote about?" Louise blurted out, her breath vaporizing as she spoke.

"Rusty was sweet," Marynell admitted, "but Jeffrey can give me the sort of life I've always wanted."

"Are the military trappings more important than having a man who really loves you? I can't understand why after years of having boys fall in love with you, you decide to marry a man who hasn't recovered from the death of his first wife enough for you to judge what feelings he's even capable of."

Louise felt Marynell stiffen. Probably she shouldn't have blurted all that out at once, but damn it, there was so little time for just the two of them and the wedding was only two days away.

"And I suppose that you and Franklin have the love of the century," Marynell said sarcastically.

It was Louise's turn to stiffen. "My husband and I love each other sincerely," she said, wanting to pull her arm away.

They walked along in silence for a time. Louise began to shiver. It was too cold for a walk, and the words weren't coming out right.

"Yes, I suppose you do," Marynell sighed, ignoring the intervening silence. "But you're not *in* love. You should be married to someone sweet like Daddy, so leave me alone, Sis. I'm doing what I have to do."

"God, I hate this," Louise said. "We can't even talk. We used to talk about everything."

"It's hard to talk about everything when we never see each other."

"I know," Louise sighed. "Sometimes I wish we lived in the same little town right next door to each other and had coffee every morning like the aunts did back in Indiana."

"I know. Maybe we'll live on the same post someday since Jeffrey and Franklin are both field artillery. Fort Sill maybe. It's such a pretty place."

"Yeah. That'd be terrific," Louise said, trying for enthusiasm. Even if that happened, it would be temporary.

She could feel Marynell starting to shiver, too. They needed to turn back. The cold was seeping into her bones.

At the bottom of the back steps, Louise stopped. "Give me a hug," she said.

Louise closed her eyes as they embraced. "You know how much I love you?"

"Yeah," Marynell sniffed. "Would you love me no matter what?"

"Absolutely. No matter what. Always and forever."

At lunch, Eddie offered to take Franklin on a tour of the post, and the sisters found they had the unexpected gift of a few more hours. It was warmer, and they decided to walk to the officers' club to check on the arrangements for the small wedding reception.

Marynell thought the reception area seemed plain. She wanted the palms from the dining room brought in and the framed mirrors from the lobby. The manager balked at first, but Marynell hadn't forgotten how to charm.

When they finished talking to the manager, they went into the deserted bar for Bloody Marys. Their conversation rambled—the tremor in their mother's hand, speculation about the sex of Louise's baby, Marynell's apprehension about becoming stepmother to a two-year-old.

Marynell ordered a second round. "Oh, I really shouldn't," Louise protested. "The first one made me light-headed, and we have to fix dinner."

"Let them eat leftovers," Marynell said with an imperial wave of her hand.

"Jeffrey will be there," Louise reminded her.

"Yeah. We can do something with that chicken you stewed, but let's not waste our time talking about cooking. I'm sorry about this morning. I want to try again. To talk. We used to talk about everything. I want to know about you—about being married. How are things with you and Franklin? In bed, I mean."

"It's nice some times. Other times, I'd just as soon read. What about you and Jeffrey? Do you do much? You know, kiss and touch?"

"Some." Marynell looked away. "Not much."

"Are you apprehensive about your wedding night?" Louise asked.

"Yes and no. How was yours?"

"Okay, I guess. God, that seems like a long time ago. It feels like I've always been married."

"Did you like it the first time?"

"I was so nervous . . . "

"Do you have secrets you've never told me?"

Louise stared at her sister. "No, not secrets exactly. It's just difficult to talk about some things. Maybe when we're both married, it will be different."

Marynell shrugged and looked away. The silence was heavy.

"I want another drink," Marynell said, looking around for the waiter.

"I feel like I'm letting you down," Louise said, reaching for Marynell's hand. "I don't know what to tell you. The first night is just something you have to get through. It doesn't hurt a lot, and Jeffrey's been married before, so I'm sure he realizes it's normal for a girl to be apprehensive on her wedding night. Franklin was gentle." Her voice trailed off. She couldn't think of anything else to say. She was the married woman, but she fell ill-equipped to give advice.

"It's all right," Marynell said. "You don't have to say anything else. Where is that waiter?"

"Maybe we'd better go on home and cook dinner," Louise said.

"I don't feel like cooking dinner."

"What do you feel like?" Louise asked.

"Oh, I don't know. Climbing a mountain. Having an adventure. Going back to Amber and teaching school. But then I think of beautiful Jeffrey and his sad eyes, and I want to hold him and take care of him. Maybe that's what's wrong with me. I'm falling in love."

Louise had made over the bridesmaid's dress Marynell had worn to her wedding to allow room for her expanded girth. She looked more stout than pregnant.

The church was new and rather plain, the wine-colored carpet runner unworn. The baskets of mums on the altar would be taken to the officers' club to do double duty at the reception.

Except for Franklin's parents, their two elderly aunts from Indiana and the Fentrisses from West Point, the church was filled with people Louise didn't know—officers and their wives from the hospital and from Jeffrey's regiment. Jeffrey's mother, crippled with arthritis, had not made the trip from Racine.

General and Mrs. Cravens were striking, sitting there in the front pew by Franklin, the general in his dress blues with stars on his shoulders and rows of ribbons on his chest, Maxine in a peach-colored suit and a mink stole.

Marynell looked like a princess. Louise felt proud and a little jealous as she watched from the front of the church as her sister walked down the aisle on their father's arm. The wedding dress looked better on Marynell than it had on her. Louise wondered if Franklin noticed.

Elizabeth was wearing the same mauve mother-of-the-bride dress she'd worn a year and a half ago. As vague as ever, she had started out the door for the wedding carrying her brown, everyday handbag. Daddy said that the tremor in her hand had nothing to do with her forgetfulness, but he didn't give it a name. "If I go overseas, you girls will have to look after your mother," he told them—twice. The second time he had to blow his nose.

Louise had been touched by her father's concern. He'd always taken such good care of their mother, but she wondered why Elizabeth was the sort of woman who needed looking after. If her father had been a different sort of husband, would she have been a different sort of wife?

On the way to the chapel, Elizabeth started telling about a wedding in one of the Brontë books. Rochester and Jane—not a nice wedding. She was sure Marynell's would be nice. *Good Lord*, Louise thought, *Mother probably read that book twenty years ago*. She couldn't remember what she had done yesterday, but Elizabeth seemed to remember the characters in every book she'd ever read.

Louise looked at Marynell's veiled profile and wondered if Jeffrey Washburn was as touched by her beauty as she herself was at this moment. Her beloved sister. She swallowed to control the swelling in her throat. *Be happy, Marynell. Be happier than I am.*

Not that she was unhappy, Louise reminded herself, stealing a reassuring touch of her pregnant tummy.

Eddie stood beside Marynell until he was called up to fulfill his fatherly duty and place his older daughter's hand in that of her bridegroom. He slipped into the pew beside his wife, his heart pounding. *They're both gone now*, he thought.

His darling daughters now owed their first allegiance to men Eddie would never know well. Franklin, who was too insecure to let Louise blossom. Jeffrey, who was too disillusioned to fall in love. And someday Louise and Marynell would be sitting in church pews watching their own children get married, the endless cycle beginning once again.

Was there to be nothing between this day and old age except long, vacant years with poor Elizabeth? Eddie wondered. He'd be lucky if he saw his grandchildren even for an annual visit. Medicine was a job, military life a comfortable habit, Elizabeth a responsibility. If he were younger, he would enter a surgery residency, but he was too old to shift gears. He didn't want a war, but although he would never admit it to anyone, he almost welcomed the thought of wartime. Wartime had given him the most horrible and the most exciting years of his life.

He reached for his wife's hand. Dear Elizabeth. In some ways, he welcomed the prospect of a time away from her before old age set in.

Marynell was promising to love and honor her husband until death parted them. A shiver went through Eddie's body.

It wasn't West Point, but Jeffrey had arranged for crossed sabers as a surprise for Marynell. The man was trying, Eddie had to give him that.

In the dark bedroom, Louise listened to the activity throughout the house. Doors opening and closing. The toilet flushing. Snatches of conversation. Her in-laws were going to take everyone to the Sunday-night buffet at the club. Louise supposed she would have to get up soon and put on something suitable.

Louise hadn't cried at her sister's wedding, but she wept at the moment of farewell. Marynell looked like a magazine model in her cloche hat and fashionable suit. She smiled and kissed everyone all around until she came to her sister.

"I guess this is really it," Marynell said, her lip quivering.

"For more than two years," Louise said, her composure leaving her. "I don't think I can bear it."

"I know," Marynell said as they hugged. "I know. It doesn't seem right, does it?"

Louise was aware of Jeffrey waiting by the car. Someone had tied streamers and tin cans on the back. "Just Married" was painted across the back window in white letters. "I love you, Marynell. You're the best sister a girl could ever have. You be happy, hear. And write me."

"Send a picture of the baby right away, okay?"

And then they were in the car, driving away, Marynell frantically waving out the window. Belatedly, Louise threw her handful of rice. "I love you, Marynell," she had called after the car.

She assumed the tap at her door was Franklin or her mother, but it was Maxine who opened the door and asked if she could come in.

Louise started to pull herself to a sitting position. "No, stay where you are," Maxine instructed. "Can I get you anything?"

"No. I'll come downstairs in a bit. I need to spend time with the Fentrisses and the aunties."

"You must be exhausted. You were on your feet much too long at the reception." And with that, Maxine pulled the quilt back from Louise's stockinged feet and began to rub.

Louise was astounded. Generals' wives didn't rub feet.

"Relax, dear. They're swollen. It helps if you watch your salt intake, you know."

Louise closed her eyes. It did feel good. But her mother-in-law! Mrs. General Cravens.

"Are you feeling all right?" Maxine asked, her fingers deft.

"Yes, I just needed to be by myself a bit. Marynell and I have always been very close, and now I don't know when I'll see her again. Hasn't it been hard for you seeing your sister only every so often? And when your parents were alive, seeing them only every other year or so?"

"Yes, it has been hard at times," Maxine acknowledged.

"Sometimes I wish I had been born in a civilian family," Louise admitted, "and that I could live out my years surrounded by my family. I don't want to have my baby thousands of miles away from them."

"I can understand that, but there's a compensation I don't think you yet understand."

"What's that?" Maxine was using her thumbs to massage the bottom of Louise's feet. Marynell did that sometimes.

"Military marriages are the strongest there are," Maxine said with great conviction. "Military husbands and wives need each other more because they aren't surrounded by their families. Cruel as it may seem now, Louise, married women who live in the same towns as their mothers and sisters don't have as much time and loyalty for their husbands. In a very real way, it's you and Franklin alone in the world, and that bonds you to each other in a very special way. Yes, I've missed my sister, but Harold is the center of my life just as Franklin is of yours."

"But a husband can't be a sister," Louise protested.

"No, but he can be a brother at times," Maxine said, "if you'll let him."

"I suppose," Louise said, her eyes slipping closed. If it were Marynell rubbing, she would feel free to drift off to sleep.

"If you like," Maxine said, her voice strangely shy, "I'll come stay with you when it's time for the baby to be born."

Louise's eyes shot open. "You'd do that!"

"It's not official yet, but it looks as though Harold will be assigned to Fort Shafter in Hawaii—on the Army staff. I'm sure I can arrange passage to the Philippines on a military transport. One of those privileges of rank, you know."

Louise scrambled to her knees and for the first time in their rather formal relationship hugged her mother-in-law's neck. "I'd like that very much. Very much. Thank you."

Maxine held her daughter-in-law for a moment. She understood well why Franklin had married this soft, quiet girl. There was no artifice about Louise. She wasn't tough or savvy enough, but she was sincere and really quite dear.

Marynell and Jeffrey planned to honeymoon in a beach cottage on Mobile Bay. Marynell had hoped for New Orleans, but Jeffrey only had a five-day leave, and the cottage was an off-season bargain. For their first night, they drove as far as Fairland, a pretty little town outside Montgomery. The inn was a restored antebellum mansion. It reminded Marynell of *Gone With the Wind*.

Their room was lovely with floral wallpaper and softly faded, floral-patterned rugs. The bed had a canopy.

Awkwardly they dressed for dinner, taking turns in the bathroom.

Marynell drank a lot of wine. So did Jeffrey. He kept telling her she was beautiful. It was what she needed to hear, over and over. In bed, he told her again. He needed it too, apparently. Two beautiful, naked people on their wedding night. Their physical beauty reassured them, soothed them, excited them. His words made her more drunk than the wine—not words of love but of desire for her body. He adored her breasts. She wanted desperately to ask if Elise had nice breasts. When the moment of consummation came, she welcomed him with genuine rapture.

But when he began to pump up and down, harder, faster—

unwanted memories came rushing back. Until then she had been all right.

"I'm sorry, honey," he was saying. "It's been so long. I can't wait." And suddenly he was a dead weight on top of her.

Marynell wanted to push his weight off her, to race to the bathroom and wash herself. The male smell of sweat and semen nauseated her.

But she allowed him to hold her, to stroke her back. Would it always be like that, she wondered. Her body wanting, her mind refusing.

His caresses calmed her. He kneaded aching muscles from her neck to her waist. God, she was tired. The last week had been hectic, the tension of today exhausting. "Go to sleep," Jeffrey told her in the same soothing voice he used for Matt.

Not much of a wedding night, she thought as she drifted off to sleep. But then she hadn't allowed herself to expect much. She wondered how often he'd want to have sex with her. Was she going to be accommodating like her sister?

She awoke later and went to the bathroom. When she returned to bed, Jeffrey was waiting for her. They kissed for a while, then he pulled her over on top of him. "This way, honey. You do it to me. I don't want to lose you this time."

It seemed awkward at first, but then she found a position and rhythm. He fondled her breasts while she rocked back and forth. This time, the movement was all hers. She was in charge.

The beat of excitement began to throb in her veins. Maybe this way would be different. Maybe. She thrust her breasts forward to show she liked his hands there. He responded by kneading her nipples between his fingertips—almost too hard, but not quite. Perfect really. God, yes. Perfect.

Yes, if she could keep moving just like this, she was going to make herself have an orgasm using his body. But it was so tiring. She wasn't going to have the stamina to force it, to make it happen. When she faltered, Jeffrey took her hips in his hands and pushed her back and forth. She put her hands flat on his chest and arched her back upwards. Yes. There it was just out there, waiting.

"Come with me now, Marynell," he gasped. "Now!" His hands were strong on her hips, moving her back and forth, helping her. "Now, baby. Now!"

When it started, Marynell was filled with disbelief. The feeling was *inside* her body. No boy's hand or her own had ever done this much for her. This feeling exploded in her belly and radiated down in her thighs. It was the sweetest, most incredible thing she had ever felt.

With Jeffrey still inside of her, she collapsed against his chest. She wanted to tell him it was the first time she'd ever felt it like that. A real orgasm that went all the way to her soul. But she couldn't tell him, of course. They would never speak of what they had and had not felt before. Instead, when she got her breath, she knelt over him and kissed up and down his torso. At that moment, she would have done anything in the world for Jeffrey.

Maxine checked her watch. It was still an hour before their estimated time of arrival in Savannah, where Harold planned to stop for lunch. She reached for the thermos to pour a cup of coffee to share.

She found motor trips tiring, but Harold regarded them as an adventure. Normally Harold was driven every place in the backseat of a staff car, and he considered it a treat to drive himself and wear civilian clothes. He was dressed in a red pullover sweater and navy slacks. Very unmilitary, but he was an impressive-looking man even out of uniform. Still, Maxine preferred him with stars on his shoulders. She always felt a bit cheated when he wore civilian clothes into a restaurant, and no one turned to stare at the general and his lady.

Franklin was handsome like his father. She'd always been so proud of them both. For her, the best years had been with a son on one side and a husband on the other.

But there were still good years left. Of course, there would be a war, and she had no idea how that would affect their lives. She hated the limbo that war had brought more than twenty years before when Harold went off to France. At least if he had to go this time, she wouldn't worry about him getting killed in the trenches. Generals were seldom exposed to danger. It was Franklin she'd worry about this time around.

Maybe Harold wouldn't have to go at all, she mused, taking a sip of the coffee, then handing the cup to Harold. But their three years at Dix would soon be up. Hawaii would be a staging area for the predicted war in the Pacific, and Harold wanted to go there and play a major role. He'd spent the last war in Europe, and the jungles of the South Pacific represented a different challenge.

"Did you get a chance to visit much with Louise?" Harold asked as he handed the cup back to her. "How do you think she and Franklin are getting along?"

"All right. I wish Franklin was more like you, but he's not. She's still intimidated by him, but then she's very young. And basically, they're both sensible young people—both foolishly pleased about the baby."

"Louise is a lovely girl," Harold observed, "I doubt if she'll ever be as brilliant an Army wife as her mother-in-law, but she'll never step out of line. I can't imagine Louise drinking too much or flirting or raising her voice in public."

Maxine nodded her agreement.

"I wonder," Harold said, offering a mischievous sidelong glance, "have you ever wanted to do that—drink too much and flirt and raise your voice?"

"Of course, I have, silly boy. I get tired of being perfect, but it's always paid off. And now, perfect behavior has gotten to be so much of a habit, I don't even think about it. Maybe when you retire, I'll stop putting on my makeup at eight o'clock in the morning and smiling graciously, but in the meantime, I enjoy being who I am. I enjoy it very much."

"What would you think about Hawaii?"

"For what?"

"Retiring."

"Well, why don't we see how we like it? What about an old farmhouse in Virginia, like we'd always talked about?"

"I suppose that would be fine, although I'm not sure what a retired Army officer is supposed to do on a farm, or anyplace else."

"You'll probably be invited to sit on a couple of corporate boards, and you'll write your book just like you've always planned," Maxine said with forced conviction. She didn't like to think about retirement.

"Congratulations, my darling," Louise said, raising her glass to her husband and his new silver bars. News of his promotion had been waiting for him when they arrived this afternoon at Camp Ord. A first lieutenant. She hoped Jeffrey had been promoted, too. The Army was growing fast, and there weren't enough officers to go around.

Franklin smiled and lifted his glass to hers. "To our good life," he said. "God, Louise, you look wonderful."

Louise felt wonderful—rested, full of hope for the future. The train trip west had been delightful. She and Franklin had enjoyed sitting by the window of their compartment, watching the country go by. They had taken their meals in the elegant dining car, slept in cozy berths. She had felt like a little girl on a big adventure. She thought of Maxine's words. Let him be a brother at times. But she couldn't decide if Franklin was being the big brother or the daddy when he explained to her about prairies and timberlines. Why did he always assume that she didn't know anything, and why didn't she tell him otherwise? It had been a wonderful trip, however, and tomorrow they would embark on an even bigger adventure—a two-week ocean voyage to a far-off land. How lucky she was. A wonderful life. A baby on the way. A fine husband who loved her.

"I want you to wear the nightgown tonight," Franklin said over his wineglass, his eyes bright.

Louise was surprised at his words. Their physical relationship was never discussed. She sipped at her wine and felt her pulse quicken. The wine and the desire in his eyes made her brave.

"Yes, I'd like that," she said, "but I want you to take it off me. Let's make it a special night."

Franklin looked away, and Louise was immediately sorry for her words. She'd broken the spell. What an awful thing for a woman almost five months pregnant to say. Of course, he wouldn't want to take off her nightgown. If he didn't want to look at her before, why would he want to look at her now with her thickening middle? She pushed her glass away as though to indicate it had been the wine talking. She hadn't really meant it. But the gesture was useless, the mood already spoiled.

If only she could understand his aversion to nudity. She thought men were supposed to want to look at naked women. Why was her husband different? But then, it really didn't matter since Franklin was the only husband she'd ever have, and his needs were her reality. She wasn't even sure she wanted him to look at her. She just wanted him to want to.

At dawn, Franklin came to her twin bed at the austere base guest house and held her. A child was fussing in the next room. "I love you, Louise, with the purest kind of love," he whispered into the half-light.

"I'm not some sort of madonna," Louise whispered back. "I'm a healthy young woman who wants to feel things. Please, Franklin, haven't you ever thought about putting your mouth on my breasts? Would you do that?"

"But you're pregnant," he protested.

Still under the covers, she wriggled out of her nightgown. Franklin did not take off his undershirt, but soon she was aware of him tugging at his pajama bottoms.

She felt deliciously wanton and wanted kisses, many kisses. "God, Louise, what's gotten into you," he protested, but he returned her insistent kisses. She was wet without the help of his fingers when he slid into her.

"No, it hurts my tummy that way," she said, and rolled onto her side. "This way," she instructed, tucking herself up against him. With his hand holding his engorged penis, he was searching for her vagina, pushing, entering. It was new. Exciting. She was not Louise. He was not Franklin. She pulled his hands to her breasts and pushed them up and down, forcing him to massage them.

She forced her hips back against him, urging greater penetration, more movement. He had never felt so wonderful inside of her.

She moved against him, setting the pace, the rhythm.

His breathing was rapid as his body grew ever more frenzied in its thrusts, his hands still grasping at her breasts.

Something was going to happen. She could feel it, perched on the other side of a dark barrier, waiting to blanket her with mysterious, elusive sexual fulfillment.

A nugget of warmth radiated from deep inside of her and sent out ever widening circles of wonderful, warm, intensely pleasurable sensation.

It was beautiful. Glorious. She was exploding with pleasure as she allowed the sensation to take her where it would. To rapture.

Afterwards, her satiated body feeling wonderfully heavy and languid, she felt puzzled. After all this time of waiting for Franklin to make it happen for her, she'd made it happen for herself.

She wanted words of love. She wanted him to tell her it had never been more wonderful, but he just held her for a time, then returned to his own bed without his customary "Thank you."

She wondered if next time he would lift her gown as always. How costly had her experiment been? She had soiled his pure image of her. She had seduced him.

And yet she was glad to be his wife. She loved Franklin. It seemed she always had. He was more important to her than her parents and sister, and she cared more about him than any other human being. Being a good wife to her husband was more important than sexual fulfillment. They would march through this life together and share its sorrows and joys. Their baby grew inside of her. They were as bound to each other as trees to the earth.

Book Two

★ ★ ★

1940–1945

CHAPTER

THIRTEEN

"Well, it's not the tropical adventure I had envisioned," Babs Gentry said, drying herself with an Army-issue towel.

"It could be worse," offered Elaine Carter, as she picked her way across the rocky beach to the tin-roofed shelter. The two had finished doing their morning laps across the "pond"—an area of ocean protected by a shark net. "When Robby said we were going to the Philippines, I thought we'd be living in a beautiful, open-air palace of bamboo and mahogany, enjoying a fabulous social life in exotic Manila, and just look what I got. Corregidor! But at least we have breezes out here, and the mosquitoes aren't as bad as they are in Manila."

"I think it's pretty," Louise said. "The tropical flowers are fantastic." But when she'd arrived a month ago, her initial reaction had been disappointment. It wasn't the romantic tropical paradise she had envisioned, and seemed stark after beautiful Fort Sill.

Standing sentry to the entrance of Manila Bay, the tiny island's military outpost was aptly nicknamed "the Rock." The base did have amenities to make life pleasurable for its American inhabitants—an officers' club, a golf course, tennis courts, a motion picture theater, a chapel and a small library—but these scarcely compensated for heat, boredom and the pounding monotony of artillery fire.

At Fort Sill, Louise had quickly become oblivious to the sound of distant artillery firing. The big guns were used day and night to train future artillerymen. But on an island only a mile wide and two miles long at its greatest dimensions, the guns of Corregidor were hard to ignore. The island was spotted with twenty-three huge open gun pits armed with sea defense batteries. Outdated, some of the pieces required as many as thirty men to fire. In recognition of the air age, a few worn-out antiaircraft guns had been mounted. And Franklin had been assigned to the island in anticipation of field artillery pieces being brought in to defend the island from a landward attack. Thus far, however, his battery was practically gunless and was training alongside the coastal artillerymen. Training for all the batteries, however, was difficult. Ammunition was often in short supply. Gasoline for the ack-ack generators was rationed. The American officers grew more and more testy. Did Congress want the Philippines defended or not?

Babs and Elaine explained that the highlight of life for the wives on Corregidor had been excursions with their husbands into Manila for shopping, concerts, theater or for dining at the luxurious Manila Hotel or the Manila Officers' Club. But since news of the Japanese-German alliance, stepped-up training schedules were making the trips into Manila less frequent. The entertainment of bored wives was not important enough to utilize boats, husbands or precious gasoline.

Like Franklin, Bab's husband commanded a battery of Philippine Scouts from the 91st Regiment. Elaine's husband was a military engineer working on expanding and ventilating the already extensive tunnel system that crisscrossed the island.

Louise could sense the lethargy among the island's contingency of wives. The small quarters with their sweating concrete walls and identical rattan furnishings did not inspire great housekeeping efforts. And for only a few pesos a week, native servants would clean, garden and take care of children.

The wives scheduled their lives around midmorning coffee and afternoon bridge. They drank Bloody Marys before dinner and brandy after. They played golf and tennis and took swims in the ocean. Louise had arrived in time to experience the hottest months of the year, and most daytime activity—even military exercises—came to a stop during the heat of the day. Louise took long sticky naps that left her more tired than before. Sometimes, she played bridge and watched the other women drink too much.

"Aren't you afraid of becoming alcoholic?" Louise asked from her canvas beach chair. She averted her eyes from the late afternoon glare on the water and concentrated instead on the two women sharing the square of shade with her. Both Babs and Elaine were already on their second Bloody Marys. Louise abstained as usual, using her pregnancy as an excuse.

Babs, a tiny redhead from Missouri, nodded. "Yes, I do worry, as a matter of fact. I'm glad someone has the courage to say that word out loud. If we don't watch it, we're going to become alcoholics and ruin our husbands' careers."

"Frankly, I wish Tom would get another career," said the long-legged Elaine, lifting her glass in a solitary toast to the idea. "Coming straight from a West Point romance to Corregidor was a shock. I'm ready to call the Army a bad idea."

"Don't pay any attention to her," Babs told Louise in a mock whisper. "She's a spoiled Vassar girl. Doing without a gala social life and horseback riding at the same time has been hard on her, but her dad's a colonel, and she's regular Army to the core. She's just pouting because she can't have that gorgeous man of hers in bed every night."

"Well, my God, he goes off on maneuvers, practicing war with a bunch of little brown men, preparing to defend this godforsaken sweatbox of a country from little yellow men, while I, his sexy bride of seven months, after waiting three agonizing years to indulge in the carnal pleasures of his fantastic male body, am not only forced to sleep alone on occasion, but when he is around, he's an exhausted zombie. And it's too damned hot and humid for sex anyway. Damn right, I'm pouting. I hate this country. I hate the Army. I hate men. But do I love my Tommy."

"Your words are slurring, sweetie," Babs said, reaching for the thermos of Bloody Marys and dumping the remaining contents on the sand. "I think Louise will be good for us, Elaine. She wears a hat to protect her skin from this godawful sun. She isn't tipsy by dinnertime. She reads books and collects recipes. I'll bet her dresser drawers are neat as a pin. And I've never heard her say one ugly word about the

Army or her husband. Mangoes, anyone?" she said reaching into her basket. "Or how about a banana?"

Elaine made a gagging sound. "Oh, for an apple," she said, hands held heavenward.

"Am I that boring?" Louise asked.

"Boring, honey?" Babs asked, her mouth full of banana.

"Boring. Predictable. You make me sound that way."

"I didn't mean anything insulting," Babs said, worried creases forming across her freckled forehead.

"Hell, no," Elaine interjected with a toss of her blond ponytail. "I think we're both a little jealous. You seem to have mastered the fine art of acceptance better than we have."

"You're right," Louise said, slumping lower in her chair. "I'm boring."

Good old, predictable, boring Louise, she thought ruefully. Maybe she should at least get a tan.

Louise realized her stay on Corregidor would have been a lonely disaster without her two new friends. At Fort Sill, she'd had Cecilia Beckman. Here she had Babs and Elaine. Already she sensed a long road ahead with friends made and friends left behind. Her mother quit making them and had turned instead to books. But Louise needed the companionship of women to balance Franklin's dominant male presence in her life, and from the first day on Corregidor, her immediate neighbors in the row of junior-grade officers' quarters had been there to make her welcome and fill her hours. In spite of the mildew and humidity, Louise felt comfortable here.

But while she spent the lazy hours of her third trimester with Babs and Elaine, the world was seething. Hitler had made a joke of appeasement and gobbled up Poland. Britain and France had declared war on Germany. Women and children were being evacuated from London. In this part of the world, however, the threat from Japan was far more real than the emerging war in Europe. Everyone seemed to believe that the Japanese would eventually attempt a Philippine invasion. Louise constantly touched her pregnant belly, wondering what sort of world this child would be born into. Should she even be here? What if Franklin was wrong about the safety of military dependents? She would never forgive him if anything happened to her baby.

Two weeks before her July first delivery date, Franklin took Louise across the bay to stay in the Fort Stotsenberg quarters of Brigadier General and Mrs. Samuel Gardner, friends of his parents. And the following day, Maxine arrived.

"My goodness, just look at you!" Maxine said, regarding Louise's incredible girth. "I think you're carrying twins."

"The doctor says no," Louise said, feeling enormously glad to have her mother-in-law here with her. She wasn't her mother or her sister, but she was the closest to female family Louise could get.

Two nights later, her labor began. Maxine had gone out to dinner with friends and wasn't back yet. Louise tapped shyly on the Gardners' bedroom door. "I think it's time," she told the general when he opened the door wearing only shorty pajama bottoms. The hair on his chest was as white as that on his head.

"Already?" his wife called from the bed. "How exciting! Sam, you see if you can track down Franklin. And call Maxine. She left the number there on the pad by the phone. Tell her to meet us at the hospital."

After Louise had been installed in a labor room at the Army's general hospital in Manila, Maxine came to sit with her. In spite of the late hour, her short gray hair was carefully combed, her makeup fresh. Louise could imagine her no other way.

"Franklin's gone over to Caraboa for a night firing exercise," Maxine explained. "They're trying to contact him by radio."

"Can you stay here with me?" Louise asked.

"Of course I can. They have some sort of rule about only husbands in the labor rooms, but no one would have the courage to ask me to leave. I'm sorry I'm not your mother, my dear, or your sister, but Army wives are sisters in a way. I guess all women are at a time like this, so don't be embarrassed by anything. I screamed when Franklin was born. It can't be helped."

Louise doubted that Maxine had screamed or had ever done anything undignified in her entire life. She clung to her mother-in-law's hand and vowed that she would not scream. She realized it wasn't her own mother she wanted as much as her sister. And her daddy to tell her everything would be all right in his kindly daddy-doctor voice.

The screams came unbidden. The pain was endless, waves and waves of it, with only the briefest of respites. Her body sweated itself into dehydration. Her tongue was swollen in her mouth, her body exploding with the horrible, degrading, exhausting pain.

Louise wondered if she was dying and didn't really care. She hated Franklin for not being here. He could never understand what she had gone through.

No more children. Never. She wouldn't let him near her again. She wondered if the doctor could just sew her closed.

Soon it didn't matter that Maxine was Franklin's mother and the wife of a general. She simply filled the age-old role of woman-in-attendance, her hand an anchor in the sea of pain, her soothing fingers and voice reassuring. She kept promising it would end. And no, Louise wasn't going to die.

Louise soon ceased to be embarrassed by the nurses and doctors who came to poke fingers up her rectum to check her dilation.

I had no idea, Louise thought through the grinding pain. *No idea. Shouldn't someone have told me?*

Finally the smell of ether brought blessed oblivion, and when Louise awoke, she was the groggy mother of twins.

Maxine was there, beaming. "A boy and a girl. Franklin should be here soon."

Louise would doze, then awaken to make Maxine say it again. Twins. *Two* babies.

At last it was Franklin there. Crying. Thanking her. Kissing her. Kissing his mother.

The next time she woke, Babs and Elaine were standing by her bed, laughing and drinking a toast from their thermos.

And still she sank back into sleep until a nurse came, a tiny red creature on each arm. "Wake up, Mother," she said. "It's time to meet Baby Boy Cravens and Baby Girl Cravens."

Louise's uterus contracted painfully. *What have I done?* she thought as she held the two bundled babies. *What have I done?*

And she began to cry. She was happy and proud and scared to death.

"I feel like a cow," Louise said as Inez traded Peter for Pauline. Inez's flat brown face creased in a frown.

"Cow. Mooooo," Louise said as she wiped clean her full left breast with the wet cloth the Filipino girl had provided and offered its nipple to her two-month-old daughter. The tiny sucking mouth taking hold shot a shiver of pain through Louise's body all the way down to her toes, actually making them curl in her sandals. She cringed and caught her breath, then leaned back to enjoy the more pleasurable sensations that followed.

"Ah, yes," Inez said with a grin. "Missy make milk for babies like a cow." The girl actually knew a great deal of English, but her grammar and vocabulary could stand improvement. At first Louise insisted that they would teach each other. Inez would share her Tagalog, the local Filipino dialect, while Louise helped the girl improve her English, but she gave up on her little social experiment very quickly. All she seemed capable of doing was getting first through the day, and then the night, endless cycles of feeding, changing, bathing, rocking.

Inez had ten brothers and sisters—all younger. She carried Peter down the hall with a jiggling movement that seemed innate. Even Maxine had jiggled her twin grandchildren until she'd flown home to Hawaii. Louise was quickly learning to imitate them.

Maxine had amazed Louise. Her mother-in-law had rolled up her sleeves to do housework and laundry alongside Inez, freeing Louise to rest and care for her babies. When Maxine left, Louise had thanked her profusely, then cried. Tears came far too easily to her these days, but in this instance they were from genuine emotion rather than the feelings of inadequacy and lethargy that had plagued her since the birth of her babies. She would miss Maxine. Really miss her. "You'll never know how much your being here has meant to me," Louise had said, using a clean diaper to wipe her nose.

"Oh, my dear girl," Maxine had said, touching a handkerchief to the corners of her eyes. "I would not have missed it for the world. It's the best perk that rank has ever earned me, but I must get back to Harold. I think you and Inez can manage now that we've established a routine."

"I wish you lived next door," Louise said.

Maxine shook her head and straightened her shoulders. "None of that, Louise. We make choices. You chose a special man and a special way of life."

"But it would be nice," Louise said, clinging to her mother-in-law's hand.

"Yes, it would be nice," Maxine said, relenting. "I wouldn't mind being a grandmother with grandchildren underfoot. I might even bake a cookie or two. Or maybe I'd just teach them how to swim."

Choices. Had she really made them? Louise wondered. It seemed that she was just being swept along.

In the weeks that followed, Louise often wondered how she would have survived without the smiling, competent Inez. And with Franklin gone so much, it was comforting to have her and her young American husband living in the house. As good-natured as Inez, Mike Randall was from Kansas, a pudgy young private with stringy blond hair, who was assigned to the Fort Stotsenberg motor pool as a mechanic. He and Inez planned to open a garage in Wichita when his "hitch" was up. He didn't believe there was going to be a war. President Roosevelt would keep them out of it, he insisted.

Except for her two babies, Louise saw more of Inez than any other human being. She missed the easy camaraderie of Babs and Elaine back on Corregidor. But the deputy chief of staff from the U.S. Army Philippine Department had met Franklin on an inspection tour of the island's fortifications and taken an instant fancy to "Harold Cravens' boy." Franklin now served on the headquarters staff in Manila. An intelligence officer. His promotion to captain had followed shortly after his new assignment became official.

Louise hesitated to write to Marynell about Franklin's promotion. Franklin outranked Jeffrey, who was now a first lieutenant and still training national guardsmen at Fort McClellan.

After the birth of her babies, Louise had gone back to Corregidor only to supervise the packing of the few possessions they had brought with them to the Philippines. She and Franklin now lived in a lovely house next door to a major. Louise had gratefully accepted the upgrade in housing without question. Unlike the house on Corregidor, this one was more suited to the tropics, with more windows than walls and shaded by a deep, roofed veranda that opened onto a central courtyard planted with graceful palm trees and bougainvillea vines that twined their way to the roof. Inez and her husband had their own attached quarters across the courtyard from the family's bedrooms.

Pauline was getting drowsy, her nursing growing less frantic. At first, Louise had been too nervous to enjoy nursing her babies. Now she did. In fact, it bothered her that she enjoyed it so much. She found nursing just short of arousing when it could be accomplished peacefully without a second hungry infant fussing for his or her turn.

Her nipple popped out of Pauline's rosy little mouth, and the baby stared up at her mother with glassy eyes. Louise touched her smooth, moist cheek. "Pretty little baby girl," she crooned. And Pauline was pretty, but Louise worried that Peter seemed prettier.

Two babies. Louise felt blessed and cheated at the same time. One would have been sufficient for her initiation into motherhood, and she wished she could have had the same babies a year apart. She was too tired, too overwhelmed much of the time to enjoy her twins. Such greedy little creatures they were, sucking away her energy, her time, her looks and her husband's good humor when she had to tend to one of them rather than to him.

CHAPTER

FOURTEEN

*P*auline was sleeping. Louise leaned her head against the high back of the chair and allowed her eyes to close, but only for a minute. She needed to dress for the reception honoring the new commander of the U.S. forces, Major General George Grunert. Franklin insisted it was time she started going out again. The MacArthurs, President and Mrs. Quezon and all Franklin's new colleagues would be there.

With his new staff position and promotion, she knew their social life would be brisk. In fact, the social scene in Manila was legendary, complete with polo matches, golf tournaments, beach parties and frequent dances. Everyone had Filipino servants so child care wasn't a problem. Maybe she'd meet some other young officers' wives. She hadn't made any new friends since they'd left Corregidor.

She was curious to meet the legendary General MacArthur and his much younger second wife. The general was one of the rare officers who had built a military career without a wife at his side. His widowed mother had always acted as his hostess—and, according to gossip, driven off his first wife.

The general was no longer on active duty with the U.S. forces but was still the dominating military presence in the islands as military adviser to the Philippine army—such as it was. MacArthur's efforts to get military assistance from the U.S. Congress had been less than successful, and both Filipino and U.S. forces in the Pacific were ill-prepared for a confrontation with Japan. Franklin fretted constantly that Roosevelt and Congress did not take the Japanese seriously, that the U.S. president was overly influenced by Churchill. Hitler's Germany wasn't the only threat to world peace, Franklin would inform his nursing wife, pacing back and forth in front of her chair.

At first, the nursing had embarrassed them both, but since she spent so much of her time doing it, they had come to terms with it. Louise no longer felt like she had to keep herself covered in his presence.

Franklin would be home soon, and she needed to use the shower so it would be free for him. With great effort, Louise willed her eyes to open and rose to take Pauline to the nursery. Peter was still restless, sucking furiously on his fist. Louise leaned over his crib and patted him until he settled down.

She peeled off her clothes, making a face at the smell of her own body. Sweat and sour milk. Always.

After showering, she stood naked in front of the electric fan on the dresser, coaxing her clammy skin to dryness, then applying talcum powder to the rashes under her breasts, behind her knees, between her toes, in her crotch. The tropics were hard on skin.

When she heard her husband's footsteps coming down the hallway, she slipped into her robe. Franklin kissed her cheek, then pulled off his shoes and sat on the bed, leaning on pillows propped against the headboard, while they exchanged reports of their days. With her world consisting of dirty diapers and nursing infants, Louise never had anything important or exciting to say. Franklin, on the other hand, was concerned about the future of the world. She listened to tonight's tirade as she applied her makeup. The Philippines were being sacrificed. Roosevelt was getting terrible advice from George Marshall. The number of planes based at Clark and Nichols fields couldn't protect Manila much less the entire country. Louise knew her husband was suffering a bitter dose of disillusionment. The Army was only as good as the politicians in Washington.

Not even his promotion and a glowing efficiency report had soothed him. The Philippines didn't have a chance. The Filipino Army had no uniforms or guns for its new recruits. They were issuing papier-mâché helmets and training them with mock-up "guns" made out of bamboo. Long-awaited P-36s sat on the ground at Clark Field because the quartermaster corps in Washington couldn't be convinced that even planes based in the tropics needed Prestone to fly above twenty thousand feet. The Japanese weren't idiots. They knew a sitting duck when they saw one. Sometimes Louise offered comments, but usually she listened in silence. That was what Franklin needed.

He looked at his watch, then reluctantly stood and pulled off his shirt. "We need to be on time, Louise," he said, looking at her dubiously.

Louise touched her hair. She really should have washed it today but had forgotten or hadn't had the time or something. And she wondered if she should try to get the babies to nurse a bit more right before they left—for their sake and hers.

"I'll hurry," she promised.

She checked her face in the mirror. It was the first time in weeks she'd bothered with more than a dab of lipstick and powder. Her skin still had distressing brown pigment around her mouth—the mask of pregnancy, the doctor called it, promising it would fade in time. And no amount of brushing could give her hair back its former luster, but the doctor also promised that hair, too, eventually returned to normal. However, the stretch marks on her breasts and stomach, though they would fade, would always be with her.

While Franklin was in the shower, she coaxed underwear and stockings onto her still moist body and slipped extra padding in her bra to protect against leaks before putting on her white faille dress with the rhinestone buttons. She would be hot, but the dress concealed her still thick middle and full breasts. Her feet had grown two sizes like the rest of her, she decided, as she squeezed them into her white satin wedding pumps. She patted extra makeup on the brown skin around her mouth, and concluded she looked as good as she could manage under the circumstances.

"Maybe you need more jewelry," Franklin offered.

He was right, of course. She added pearls and changed her small gold earrings for larger pearl and rhinestone ones. They helped. And maybe a little more color on her eyelids would brighten her up a bit.

The reception was at the Manila Hotel, where the MacArthurs resided in the penthouse. Dressed in the flamboyant uniform of a field marshall in the Filipino army, MacArthur completely upstaged General Grunert and Admiral Hart of the Asiatic Fleet when he swept in with his entourage and swagger stick.

Mrs. MacArthur was stunning in a blue gown embroidered with silver. "So you're the young wife with twins," she said to Louise in the receiving line. "How busy you must be. Our little Arthur is a year and a half, and it takes a whole household of people to look after him. I'd love to see your babies. Why don't you drop by with them next week?"

Louise smiled and promised. She'd only taken the twins out a few times, always to the doctor. It took Inez and her half a day to accomplish that mission, but one didn't say no to MacArthur's wife. In the Philippines, MacArthur was more than just a retired Army general—he was a demigod.

After navigating the receiving line, Louise and Franklin went through the buffet line and stood awkwardly in the crowd of people attempting to balance drinks and plates. Shortly they were joined by two other couples, and the three men discussed Congress's unwillingness to appropriate additional money to fortify the entire country since the Philippines would be given their independence in 1946. "Talk about false economy," a major said sarcastically. "But I suppose if we don't stop the Japs here, there's always Hawaii or California."

The women stood to one side talking about domestic help and children. "Oh, you're the one with new twins," the major's wife said. At first the two women seemed fascinated, but soon stopped asking Louise questions about her babies and started talking about their own children. Louise sipped at her cocktail, the first she had had in months. And soon, a white-jacketed Filipino waiter exchanged her empty glass for a glass of champagne. But after only a few sips, she felt the champagne going straight to her head and realized the rich canapés were nauseatingly heavy in her stomach. There was no place to sit, and she shifted her weight uncomfortably from one foot to the other and tried to catch Franklin's eye. The conversation between the two women had progressed to childhood diseases when MacArthur's handsome Filipino aide-de-camp tapped Louise on the arm and informed her that Mrs. MacArthur wanted to see her on the veranda.

Louise felt the two women's eyes on her as she followed the officer across the room.

"Here, dear, sit down by me," the general's wife said. "I was watching you. You don't feel well, do you? Perez, get Mrs. Cravens a ginger ale and me a sherry. Take several deep breaths, dear. The air is cooler out here."

Louise did as she was told. "You're very kind," she said. She looked through the open French doors. Franklin was looking her way wearing a puzzled frown.

"There's no sense in you standing in there being miserable. You sit out here with me for a while, then we'll get that husband of yours to take you home if you don't perk up. You know, everyone, including the general, is certainly impressed with your young captain," Mrs. MacArthur said. "The general knows your father-in-law, apparently. Were they at the Point together?"

"No, ma'am. General Cravens served under him during the war. He said General MacArthur is one of America's greatest living heroes."

Mrs. MacArthur smiled. "You're a sweet-looking girl," she said. "Is your father regular Army?"

"Yes, ma'am. Medical corps."

"Do you play bridge, dear?"

Louise hesitated. "I like to play, but it's awfully hard for me to be away from two nursing infants for very long."

Captain Perez returned with the drinks and served Louise with a brush of his hand against hers. When Louise looked up at him, she was greeted by frankly admiring eyes. The man was slim and elegant, his smile revealing perfect teeth that contrasted beautifully with his smooth, brown skin. His uniform had surely been made by a tailor.

"What's the general up to, Perez?" Mrs. MacArthur asked.

"He's talking to President and Mrs. Quezon, ma'am."

Mrs. MacArthur sighed. "I suppose I'd better go be Mrs. General's

Wife. Why don't you stay here awhile, dear, and enjoy the breeze. If she starts feeling bad again, Perez, you tell Captain Cravens that Mrs. MacArthur said to take the poor girl home."

Captain Perez leaned against the balcony wall and crossed his arms across his chest. "You're very lovely," he said in his precise English.

Louise glanced after Mrs. MacArthur to make sure she had not heard. "Thank you," she said primly, wanting to add that she really wasn't, especially not tonight. Louise found herself wondering if her makeup still concealed the darkened skin around her mouth, if she'd eaten off her lipstick. She really should have washed her hair. It was difficult not to reach up and pat it a bit.

"Do you come into the city often?"

"No." She didn't explain that she had twin babies who kept her at home.

"I hope to see you again."

"I'm sure our paths will cross."

Franklin was coming across the room. Louise's heart began to pound furiously. He would be mad.

But what did he have to be angry about?

The two officers shook hands. "Your wife isn't well," Perez said smoothly. "Mrs. MacArthur thought the air would do her good."

Was Franklin looking at her strangely, or was it her imagination? Was she blushing or was it the heat?

Louise listened a minute to determine which baby was crying. Peter. That meant the crying would continue. Sometimes Pauline got her thumb in her mouth and drifted back to sleep, but Peter never did.

Her breasts responded, the milk pushing forward. She glanced at the clock. Less than an hour since she had nursed Pauline.

"Baby's crying," Franklin said, his voice groggy.

"I know," Louise said wearily. Why couldn't he have functioning nipples, too? She stayed tired all the time, dozing off in the middle of conversations, meals, baths. She could even sleep leaning against the utility porch wall, waiting for the washer tub to drain.

"There, there," Louise said, picking up her four-month-old son. The babies were smiling now, developing personalities. She adored them, worshiped them. They were the greatest miracle imaginable. Her babies. Peter and Pauline. But she wished she weren't tired and miserable all the time. She wished she didn't feel the essence of her self slipping away. What really mattered, though, was caring for her babies and nuzzling their wonderful little bodies, nibbling precious little toes, making them smile silly toothless grins. She loved them more than Franklin and resented it when he touched her. She used up all her passion, all her physical desire on her babies.

Jiggling as she went, Louise carried Peter out on the veranda in search of a breeze, but the air seemed as heavy and still out there as it did in the house. At least it wasn't raining.

It had rained almost forty inches in the last month. The walls became so moisture-laden that the electrical wiring often short-circuited, and when there was no electricity, Louise and Inez washed diapers and uniforms in the bathtub and wrung them out by hand. Louise's hands were red and cracked. Clotheslines crisscrossed the bathroom, the kitchen, the nursery and finally even the living room.

The incredible humidity aggravated the babies' diaper and heat rashes, turning them to impetigo. Both twins slept only in snatches. Nursing was often the only thing that soothed them, and Louise sometimes did her chores one-handed with a suckling infant at her breast. Her nipples became as raw and cracked as her hands.

When she looked in the mirror, which was infrequently, she thought of the elegant Captain Perez saying she was lovely. Would anyone ever say that again?

Peter was gumming her neck, furiously searching for a nipple. "Just a minute, honey. Let Mother get comfortable first," she whispered into his tiny ear. Louise walked around the veranda to the other side of the courtyard. The air was moving a bit here, carrying the heavy scent of jasmine.

She sat on a wicker chair and opened her gown. She didn't bother with sponging off her nipples anymore. She and the babies were all one, sharing bacteria, colds, rashes, life.

Peter always took hold more voraciously than Pauline, but Louise had learned to steel herself for it. Her toes no longer curled.

"Little pig," she whispered to him. "Mama's little piggy boy.

Tastes good, huh? You are going to be bigger than me pretty soon. I think a couple more weeks of this nursing stuff will be enough, don't you think so? It's time for Mother to stop being a cow and start being a woman again."

But she'd miss it when she weaned them, Louise realized. She wondered if she'd ever feel as connected to anyone again as she felt to her two helpless little babies. She really wouldn't want their father to nurse them if such a thing were possible. They were more her babies than his.

Louise leaned her head against the high back of the chair. Sometimes it was impossible to stay awake when she nursed, but she worried about the babies falling off her lap. And when out of desperation she took a baby to bed with her, she worried that she or Franklin would roll over on the child in the night and suffocate him or her. Did all mothers worry this much? Already, she was getting two lines between her eyes from frowning so much. She'd have to concentrate on not doing that. Pregnancy had already stolen away girlishness. Now motherhood threatened to steal away youthfulness altogether.

Her eyes were so heavy that she had to close them. Her head rolled forward, and she jerked it back. She concentrated on the night sounds, but what she was hearing wasn't insects or nocturnal birds. Voices—from the open window behind her. Inez and Mike.

"You know what I'm going to do now, don't you?" Mike was asking, his voice deeper, huskier than usual. "You like it, don't you? You want me to put my tongue inside you."

"Oh, yes, Mikie. Please."

Louise did not move, did not breathe. She listened to Inez's moans and gasps. She'd never heard sounds like that before.

She should leave. She shouldn't sit here and listen. It was unforgivable—the worst invasion of marital privacy imaginable. What if Peter cried, and they knew she was out here?

But with eyes staring into the steamy night, she listened to the foolish prattling and heavy moans of passion. Mike, the preacher's son. Inez, the housemaid. Unbelievable.

Peter seemed to sense a change in his mother and nursed with greater vigor, his strong jaw working hard. Louise could feel the rush of her milk.

"Together," Inez was gasping. "Let's do it together. Please, honey baby. I'm so close."

So close? With his mouth he was making her so close? Louise sucked in her breath. Could that be?

"See how big you've made me," Mike said, his voice even stranger.

"Oh, *si*. Is beautiful. I kiss it. I make love to it."

The sounds became distant, muffled. Louise felt dizzy, almost faint. She gasped, no longer able to hold her breath. Peter's nursing became ever more frenzied, tugging at her nipple with all the suction his tough little jaws could muster.

Mike was moaning now—loud, rasping moans, oblivious to the open window. "Did you like that, baby? I could feel you coming. God, I could actually feel you. Oh, sweet Jesus, you've got me there, baby. I love you. God, oh, God, I'm starting, Inez. Can you feel it, baby? I'm coming. Sweet Jesus, I'm coming."

Once again Louise became aware of the night sounds all around her, now mingling with the sound of heaving panting from the open window. She closed her eyes and saw two gaping mouths, two trembling naked bodies—one brown and one white—intertwined. Louise was panting, too. Trembling.

Her insides were open. Peter's sucking was so beautiful. Her nipple was connected to something deep inside of her that was tugging and opening and imagining. A tongue thrusting. A penis made hard and big with lust. A beautiful man with teeth white against brown skin telling her she was lovely, that he wanted her.

Her mouth opened. Sounds came in her throat. Whimpers. She couldn't stop them and prayed that Mike and Inez remained locked in oblivion. It was happening to her. That wild, erotic sensation was taking over her body, owning her, penetrating her. *Oh, my God. Sweet Jesus.*

Louise remained in the wicker chair as long as she dared, waiting for her body to calm itself. Peter had fallen asleep but not soundly. Carefully she rose from the chair on rubbery legs and crept back to the other side of the veranda.

In the nursery, she stood over Peter's crib, patting him until she was sure he was asleep, adjusted the fan so Peter got a breeze, then tiptoed back to bed. The moonlight was bright from the windows, making the white sheets look silver. The fan on the dresser needed oiling.

"Babies okay?" Franklin mumbled, reaching over to touch her hip.

"Yes, but I'm not."

She felt him becoming more alert. "What's the matter?"

"I heard Inez and Mike making love."

"You what?"

"I was nursing Peter by their window. They were making love—with their mouths. I could hear them talking about it."

"Oh, my poor darling," he said, rolling his body toward her. "I'm so sorry. That must have upset you."

"Yes, it did." She accepted his comforting arms, his kiss on her forehead. "Have you ever had a woman take you in her mouth?"

She felt his body stiffen. "Only whores do that."

"Inez isn't a whore."

"No, I suppose not, but she's a native girl. She's not like a white lady." He withdrew his arms.

"Mike's not a native," she persisted.

"He's a young boy. Young boys experiment."

"Have you ever had sex that way? Did you ever experiment?"

"My God, Louise, it's disgusting even to hear you talk about such things."

"I don't think it's disgusting when people do it out of love."

"Are you saying you'd like to do that?" His body was tense, his voice full of warning. She was walking on thin ice. But still she went on.

"No, not *that* necessarily. But you should have heard them, Franklin. It was so *passionate*, like they were dying or being born or something incredible. I just wonder what it would be like to *feel* like that."

"Have you thought about having a man in your mouth?" he asked. His hand strayed down to his crotch.

"No. Not until tonight. I didn't know people did that."

"And it excited you?"

Yes, Louise thought. And she was feeling it again. The excitement of sex with no boundaries. She and Franklin had always had such rigid boundaries. She wanted to experiment. She wanted to touch him with her hands and her mouth. She wanted his mouth on her. She wanted them to fondle and look at each other and excite each other with their words. She wanted to do whatever made passion come like it had in that bedroom across the courtyard.

"And it has excited you?" Franklin asked again.

"Yes, I got excited listening to them."

He moved so fast, she gasped.

He was hovering over her, his face very close to hers, his hands pinning her shoulders against the mattress. "You're not that kind of woman, Louise."

"Why do you keep saying that? Maybe you don't know what kind of woman I am." But now she was afraid. She wished she could take it all back. Franklin's hands were hurting her.

A baby began to fuss. Peter. Again.

"You are too fine a person for that, Louise. Think of those babies. They deserve a mother who's above such thoughts."

"You're hurting my shoulders," Louise said.

His fingers dug more deeply. His breathing was becoming ragged.

"Please, Franklin. Go see about Peter, and leave me alone. I'm sorry, okay? I should never have brought it up. You're right. We're not like that."

Both babies were crying now, and Franklin stumbled out of bed. Shortly he brought Pauline to Louise. While she cuddled her whimpering daughter, she could hear Franklin pacing with a crying son. Maybe there was going to be a storm. Everyone seemed so restless.

It was funny to hear Franklin cooing and talking to a baby. He called Peter "old man."

She dozed, but awakened when Franklin took the now sleeping Pauline from her breast. Louise didn't even remember offering it to her.

She knew from the purpose in Franklin's movements that he

planned to make love to her. She didn't want it now. She was groggy, the excitement gone.

He surprised her when he took the nipple vacated by Pauline in his mouth and nursed at it. Just for a moment, but she knew he tasted the milk.

In a rush of tenderness, she opened her legs and put her arms around his shoulders.

She had disturbed him terribly, and now he needed to reclaim her. She understood. She told him she loved him and caressed his back—a strong, male back with flexed muscles hard under her fingers. She didn't mind when he went on and on, holding back, making it last. Louise concentrated, willing herself into passion, to thoughts of what could be, to thoughts of a man who was not her husband.

Finally, in a violent frenzy, Franklin slammed into her harder and harder. He even cried out. Like Mike had done. His voice was loud in the quiet room. Louise held her breath, waiting to see if the babies woke up. Then she felt a rush of feeling in her belly, her thighs, not as intense as she had felt earlier, but she relished the feel of it, and with concentration, she held on to it.

Then as Franklin held her, kissing her damp hair, her neck, her shoulders, touching her milk-filled breasts, whispering words of love, he said it again—she wasn't that kind of woman. Louise understood. They were locked together in the prison of his needs, and he needed for her to be a certain kind of woman. She would continue to be that woman for him, but sometimes she would let her thoughts stray where they would.

And she understood that there was another side to her husband's sexuality, one he had acted out with other women. She wondered if he still did.

CHAPTER

FIFTEEN

At the sound of Matt's crying, Marynell automatically swung her feet to the floor and hurried across the hall, clucking soothing words even before she reached his bed.

"It's okay, honey. Mommie's here."

Mommie. It came more naturally now.

"Wet," he said.

"No kidding," Marynell said sarcastically, leaning over to kiss his forehead before she pulled off his pajama bottoms.

His diaper was soaked. He wet every night, even if she got up in the night and took him to the bathroom. The doctor at the post hospital assured her that little boys often wet in the night well past their third birthday. Or fourth.

He sucked his fingers while she changed him, then held out his arms to be picked up.

She knew she compounded the problem by taking him to bed with her. He liked it too much curled against her body and slept more soundly with her than in his own bed. And most of the time she liked it, too—the sweet feel and smell of him, the way he wanted to be near her.

"One more night, Tiger, then we've got to stop our little clandestine affair. Your daddy will be coming home at the end of the week, and I want to get some cuddling of my own."

Safe in the big bed, Matt slid his arms around her neck and buried his face against her shoulder. She patted his sturdy little back and felt him fall quickly back to sleep.

It had been hard for both of them with Jeffrey gone for almost three months, his unit and others from Fort Sam Houston sent on training maneuvers at Camp Shelby, Mississippi. He was fighting a make-believe war in preparation for a real one. Matt asked for his daddy constantly, watched for him at the window. Marynell was lonely and restless. Her world had shrunk to this apartment and caring for one small boy. Without Jeffrey's evening homecoming to look forward to, her days seemed devoid of structure.

Back at Fort McClellan, she and Matt had started the habit of waiting for Jeffrey on the front step, dinner cooking on the stove. Marynell would be wearing a fresh blouse, fresh makeup. She liked Jeffrey's appreciative smile when he drove up, but he didn't seem to have the same need as she did to talk throughout the evening. She didn't have anything important to say, and his gaze would sometimes stray back to his newspaper, but she would babble on, needful of his adult presence, hanging on his every word of praise for dinner, for a new furniture arrangement. She was becoming her sister, Marynell thought ruefully. But Jeffrey was a nicer man than Franklin. She wasn't afraid of him or his displeasure, but she was afraid of other things.

Once he had been very late—a flat on the way home. She walked to the corner and back a dozen times, praying to see the familiar green Ford. When he finally came, she erupted into a tirade. Why hadn't he called? He had scared her half to death. He wasn't ever to do that again. Then she had cried.

She'd put her life in his hands. Everything depended on Jeffrey, on his continued love, his success, his staying alive.

Jeffrey had made love to her dutifully and well during the first months of their marriage, even slipping over into passion on occasion, but always with a part of himself held back. After the intensity of their honeymoon, they both found it difficult to be uninhibited with a little boy in the next room. But on the nights when they had wine as a prelude and Jeffrey made it last, Marynell usually had an orgasm. She cherished those times when, satiated with lovemaking, she would curl against her husband, secure in her marriage. Sometimes Jeffrey would be ready to come before she was close, and then she faked her own passion. It was easier than allowing herself to get close and come away with nothing. But satiated or not, she liked to sleep touching him, to wake in the night and hear his breathing.

He never spoke of Elise. Marynell worried that it was his dead wife he thought of when they made love. If his grief had passed, he would talk about her: "Elise and I used to do that." "Elise had a dress like that." "Elise never could make a pie." Anything.

Marynell did not fully understand how she had gone from never wanting to love again to needing very much for this man to love her. The specter of her past was still with her, and at times she was repulsed by her husband's erect penis, by his very maleness, but the continual worry over whether he really loved her made her vulnerable. Just being married to him had given her new definition; his love could make her whole. If a man like Jeffrey could love her, she could feel worthy and normal and good.

This boy sleeping beside her needed her, but he would always love his father more.

She wanted to be loved as completely as Jeffrey loved his son, as completely as he had once loved Elise, as completely as a man could love a woman. She wanted to become so necessary to his life that she wouldn't have to feel afraid.

Or did men ever truly love completely? Their lives seemed so full, so important; marriage was just a part of life for them.

The past three months without Jeffrey, alone in a strange city with her new stepson, had seemed an eternity. Jeffrey hadn't written, but he called periodically. With Matt usually there pulling at her skirt and Jeffrey speaking from a public phone, the calls were awkward, never as intimate as she would have liked. Still, they exhilarated her. She hated to be gone from the house for very long, fearful of missing one. But traffic was terrible in the booming city, and errands took forever, especially the trip out to the Fort Sam commissary, where groceries were considerably cheaper.

With the ever-increasing number of officers assigned to the vast military installation near San Antonio, junior-grade officers were being evicted to make room for newly arriving field-grade officers.

Newly arriving junior grades weren't even put on a waiting list for housing. Jeffrey's quarters allowance wasn't sufficient to cover the rent of their furnished duplex apartment in east San Antonio, but with careful management of his salary, Marynell got by. The apartment was tiny but attractive with Mexican tile floors and a grillwork railing separating the living room from the dining room. The furniture was worn and drab, and there was no yard for Matt. But Marynell made chintz curtains and bought a little fence to make a play area out of the front porch. Before his father left, Marynell took Matt to the park every day before his nap, but now she sat on the porch with him, reading, the door ajar so she could listen for the phone.

She wondered how often during the day Jeffrey thought about her.

Friday, he was coming home. She wouldn't let Matt take a nap Friday afternoon so he would go to sleep early. She'd serve a fantastic dinner complete with candlelight and wine, and she'd tell Jeffrey she was pregnant.

Three months pregnant. Would he be upset that she hadn't told him sooner? She could have written to him or told him during one of his calls, but she needed to see his face when she said the words. She practiced saying them all the time. "We're going to have a baby." One of their own to cement their marriage.

But having a baby was also part of her fear. The dynamics of her marriage were so fragile. How would a baby change them? Whom would everyone love the most? Marynell kept wondering if she was asked to choose between motherhood and Jeffrey's total devotion what her choice would be.

She thought of her sister's letters glorifying motherhood. Louise's love for Franklin was dutiful, with all her passion invested in her babies. Marynell sensed that marriage was safer that way.

Would Jeffrey feel the same about sex after he knew she was pregnant? Marynell wondered. She wasn't ready to be sanctified yet. She wanted to make Jeffrey crazy with desire, but not so crazy he couldn't hang on long enough to make it happen for her. After years of masturbating herself to orgasm, she had been shocked at how much stronger they were when Jeffrey made her come. No comparison, she thought, as she turned her back from Matt and cupped her hands between her legs to ward off the desire that was building there. Friday, she promised her body. With the light on.

Please, dear Jeffrey, be thinking about me, too. Come home more in love with me than before.

And wouldn't it be nice if he came home with two silver bars on his shoulders instead of one?

Franklin was already a captain. Marynell tried not to let that fact matter, but it did.

The military band was playing "Stars and Stripes Forever." With Peter in her arms, Louise made her way through the crush of women and children to the railing. It seemed unreal, like a scene from a Hollywood movie—a troop ship, streamers, flags, patriotic music, weeping women, men in uniform waving frantically—only somehow the scene was ridiculously reversed with the men in uniform on the dock and the wives and children on board the troop ship.

Shortly before Christmas, the Navy had announced that all its military dependents in the Philippines were to be evacuated to the United States. Louise had been shocked. Nothing in the press had indicated that tensions between the Philippines and Japan had escalated to that point. Not yet. But at the end of January, Franklin gently informed her that the Army would be following the Navy's lead. An evacuation of Army dependents was being organized. Soon, she and the twins would be sent home. Indeed, the Philippine High Commissioners Office had requested that all Americans other than military personnel and diplomats prepare to leave the islands.

She had clung to Franklin and cried.

War seemed much closer now, and war meant death and destruction and fear. Everything would change. She would be alone with two babies. Life without Franklin would seem purposeless. It was for him she cleaned and cooked and fixed her hair.

Yet it would be good for them to be apart for a while. Sex was less careful now, but Franklin still clung to his rituals. And Louise was always listening for a baby. After almost nine months, Peter still woke crying in the night. Franklin said she was spoiling him by always racing to pick him up. Once, he had insisted she let Peter cry. "He'll go back to sleep when he knows you're not coming." Finally, Louise could stand it no longer and bolted. Peter had cried so hard he'd thrown up. His body was flushed, his heart pounding in his little chest. Franklin said nothing when she finally returned to the bed, but she knew he was awake. She could not go back to sleep until she heard his breathing deepen.

And for a time at least she wouldn't have to listen to Franklin's lectures on money and protocol, on the idiocy of President Roosevelt.

Melva, the young sergeant's wife she was paying to help her with the twins during the voyage, joined her at the railing with Pauline, looking out over the vast mob of khaki-clad men for her own husband.

Louise had already located Franklin. He had maneuvered his way to a place on the pier directly below them. He was waving, yelling something. Circles of sweat darkened the underarms of his uniform. Louise yelled back. "I love you, my darling. I love you." But her words were lost in the pandemonium.

Tears streamed down her cheeks. The ship was moving, opening a band of black greasy water between them. Oh, God, how would she endure without her Franklin? She didn't want to face responsibility alone. She didn't want to buy a car or have a checking account. She wanted her husband to take care of her.

Franklin was waving wildly with both arms, calling to her. Her husband. She was sad and proud. He was a good officer and a good man, and he would serve America well.

Please, God, keep him safe for us.

The band was playing a song from her father's war. "Over There." *We won't come back 'til it's over, over there.*

As the train slowly rolled to a stop, Louise saw them out the train window. Marynell's hair was longer and shone in the sunlight. Jeffrey was in uniform. Matt, wearing a red plaid jacket and matching cap, was holding his daddy's hand. They saw her and waved. Marynell bounced up and down, one hand protectively on her belly, the other blowing kisses.

Louise was overcome with relief. Finally, her journey was over.

The twins had had diarrhea. Louise had not only used and discarded all their diapers but had used up much of the babies' other clothing as substitute diapering. A sympathetic porter had even smuggled her dish towels from the kitchen. Louise realized the whole episode would make a great story when she got to San Antonio, but living it seemed pretty grim.

She had brought along a satchel of food for the three of them since visiting the dining car seemed imprudent for a mother traveling alone with nine-month-old twins. For two days she had been a prisoner in the tiny roomette with her sickly babies. And Louise didn't feel too well herself. She suspected she was pregnant but couldn't face that thought just yet.

The kindly porter supplied hot tea for her and fresh milk for the babies. The second night, he pirated a roast beef dinner. His name was George, he told her, and he'd been a porter for thirty-seven years. His fourth grandbaby was just about the age of the twins.

And now the porter had come to carry Pauline off the train to the arms of her waiting aunt. He wouldn't take the money Louise tried to press in his hand.

"No, ma'am. You left a husband over there to protect me and mine from the Japs. I wouldn't think of taking no money from you." Louise felt like hugging him, but white women didn't hug colored men, even kindly ones with white hair. She shook his hand instead.

"God, you look awful," Marynell said as they hugged around two babies. "You poor darling, you even smell bad. It's been a nightmare, I take it."

Louise nodded dumbly, willing away tears of self-pity, relishing the feel of her sister's touch, her sister's voice. She had made the right decision. When the fighting began, Jeffrey would be shipped out. She and her sister would wait out the war together in San Antonio. It was as good a place as any. They'd have commissary privileges and free medical care at Fort Sam, where Jeffrey was helping train great waves of new inductees coming through the post.

Louise hugged Jeffrey, then leaned over to kiss Matt, who had the same two fingers in his mouth as always and was warily eyeing the two strange babies.

"I can't believe how he's grown," Louise said. "Such a handsome boy—like his daddy."

Jeffrey grinned. He didn't seem as much like Franklin as Louise remembered. He kissed her cheek and gave her arm a squeeze. "We're glad you're here," he said. "Marynell has been counting the days."

Louise basked in her brother-in-law's smile and thought of Franklin's cool reaction to her family. Jeffrey made her feel welcome, and she was grateful.

"Just look at these two precious darlings," Marynell said, caressing first Pauline's cheek, then Peter's. "Finally, I get to spoil my niece and nephew."

Louise patted Marynell's round tummy. Six months along. She kissed her sister again. She was going to cry after all. She just couldn't help it. "My God, Marynell. How did we get from Mary Baldwin to here?"

"Come on, honey. Jeffrey will fix us one of his very best martinis. And I've got a casserole ready to put in the oven. You're home."

Jeffrey thought of the night Matt was born as he sat with Marynell during the endless hours of her labor. Elise hadn't labored as long, her athlete's body doing a more proficient job at birthing.

Louise hovered on the other side of Marynell's bed. A sister-in-law had sat with him that night, too—Elise's sister, Karen.

He remembered so well the worry, the relief when it was over, how overjoyed he had been when he first held Matt in his arms. A son. They were a family. It was the most meaningful night of his life. Elise had been ecstatic with pride.

Marynell screamed and grabbed at his hand as another pain took her body. Her hair was wet and matted against her pale forehead. Her lips were parched and cracked. How much more of this could she stand, he wondered, wishing there was some way he could suffer it for her.

"You're doing great, honey," Louise told Marynell. Jeffrey watched as Louise put a piece of ice in a cloth and held it to her sister's lips.

Louise was pregnant, her waist starting to lose definition, her breasts grown fuller. A lovely woman, his new sister-in-law. Louise reminded him of Karen. Both women had married too young and were overwhelmed by strong-willed husbands. But away from their husbands, a quiet radiance showed through.

Jeffrey had enjoyed the past three months, feeling husband to both Marynell and Louise, father to three children. The sisters had blossomed in each other's company, and he played with the children in the evenings to give Louise and Marynell time alone at the kitchen table, lingering over their coffee after the dishes were done. After the three parents had tucked the children in bed with proper ceremony and kisses, they would play cards and listen to the radio. He would pour sherry for Marynell, but Louise preferred one of his beers. He liked to listen to their chatter and found he could talk more easily with both of them than he could when it was Marynell and him. Sometimes one woman would plop herself down on the floor in front of the other's chair for an impromptu shoulder rub. Jeffrey marveled at how much they touched—hugs, pats, locking arms when they took walks. He had seldom touched his sister or brother. Janet had been ten years older and died of tuberculosis at twenty-two, but even before she got sick, they had studiously ignored each other. He and his younger brother, George, had fistfights until they started hurting each other. From then on, they only shook hands. Jeffrey had never been connected to either of them like his wife and her sister were to each other. And to their children. And he touched more, too—Marynell, Matt, the twins, even Louise on occasion. Pecks on her cheek, pats on her arm.

Louise had been looking for a house to rent, one large enough for both sisters and their children, and their mother, if need be. Marynell would move in with her when the time came—when he went to war.

When? Jeffrey wondered. Germany had overrun Greece and Yugoslavia, invaded Russia. The British were being routed by Rommel in North Africa. The United States couldn't stay out of it much longer.

War. After all, it was what he'd studied at West Point. A part of him welcomed the reality of war—to see what sort of a man he was. Not that war had been romanticized at West Point. The glamour was in manhood itself. The military provided an opportunity to take manhood to the limits, to test oneself physically, mentally and morally. And the reward for surviving was a man's knowing that he had met the test and won. Jeffrey remembered how in awe cadets were of officers who had been cited for valor in the last war. The stories behind the ribbons on their chests were told and retold. At the academy, no other men—not scholars, diplomats, humanitarians, clergymen, artists—were as revered as valiant warriors. But there was also the risk. Death. Pain. Amputation. A man finding out he wasn't valiant after all.

Death before dishonor. Could he do that? Jeffrey wasn't sure.

The first thing he'd thought when he was promoted was that reconnaissance officers were first lieutenants. Forward observers. The most vulnerable of all artillerymen. Casualties waiting to happen.

He prayed that he'd be a captain before he faced combat, really prayed, even knowing it was selfish of him, when no one ever wanted to die.

He closed his eyes as Marynell grabbed at him again, fighting her own war. Any semblance of bravery had long ago left her. As Jeffrey listened to his wife's screams, he had a sense of how it would be in the war. Screams in the night. Death sought as a relief.

Marynell's fingernails dug into the back of his hand. "Not much longer, baby," he promised. "Not much longer." He prayed his words were true. Or if they weren't, he longed for them to take her off to delivery so he could wait with Louise in the quiet of the waiting room away from Marynell's agony. He had felt a man's guilt through all of this. He was to blame. *God, let it end soon.*

The waiting room, however, held its own brand of agony. It seemed encased in a time warp with the hands of the clock all but paralyzed. The air was heavy and stale. Two waiting sergeants sat with their hands hanging between their knees, their backs hunched over. But Jeffrey couldn't sit. He walked up and down the room, went to the bathroom, walked more. Then he had to return to the bathroom. His nerves must be affecting his bladder.

Louise sat in a corner staring out a window into the night as they waited. From time to time, he'd sit down by her. "It shouldn't be much longer," she would tell him.

It was dawn when the nurse finally came with her cheery smile and good tidings. "It's a boy, Lieutenant. Congratulations."

Jeffrey grabbed Louise and hugged her. He wasn't even embarrassed at the tears of relief that came pouring out of his eyes. "God, I'm glad that's over," he repeated again and again. Louise hugged him back.

A boy, he thought, letting the knowledge sink in. He had sort of hoped for a girl. He loved Matt so much he was afraid he didn't have any love left over for another son and reasoned that love for a daughter would come from a different compartment. But it would be nice for Matt to have a brother. His name was going to be Eric. Erin if it had been a girl.

Eric and Matt. *Two* sons. How about that?

Five and a half months later, Louise had her baby at the Fort Sam hospital with Marynell and Jeffrey in attendance.

The doctor had promised that having a second baby was easier. For a time, she believed him, but the pain intensified, becoming as white and hot and dehumanizing as before. It angered her that once again Franklin was not with her. She hated the Army for doing this to her. And she hated Franklin, too. He was where he wanted to be—with MacArthur's staff in Manila, waiting for war with bated breath.

She had had a feeling all along that the baby would be a girl. She would name her Margaret Anne, using her mother's and Maxine's middle names. But when Marynell touched the tiny fingers of her niece for the first time, she called her "Maggie" and the nickname stuck.

Jeffrey wired the news to Franklin. His response came the next day. "Dearest Louise, we are blessed. Please kiss Margaret Anne for me. I am so proud of my wife and three children. Love always, Franklin."

Louise was nursing her two-week-old daughter by the upstairs window of her bedroom when she saw Jeffrey's car pull into the driveway. He was in uniform. On a Sunday afternoon. The twins were napping.

Maggie fussed to have her meal interrupted. Louise heard Jeffrey greeting the Mexican woman who was living in during her convalescence.

Jeffrey was sitting in the living room when Louise came down, carrying her whimpering baby. She knew as soon as she saw his face.

He and Marynell had just heard the news on the radio. The nation was at war.

The Japanese had bombed Pearl Harbor. He was on his way to report in. The base was on alert. The entire country.

"Marynell tried to call you, but the lines must be jammed. She says for you to pack up the kids and come over."

Louise's first thought was for her in-laws at Fort Shafter on Oahu. And then Franklin. The Philippines would probably be next. Or the mainland.

It had begun. Louise closed her eyes and prayed. For her husband. For them all.

"Do you think there'll be an invasion?" Louise asked, clutching more tightly at her baby.

"No one knows." Jeffrey touched Maggie's cheek, then awkwardly hugged both mother and infant.

Louise nodded. "I love you and Marynell so much. I'm afraid for us all."

Jeffrey's lips brushed hers, and he was gone.

In June of 1942, Jeffrey was sent to Fort McPherson, Georgia, a training hub for activated guard and reserve units. Marynell and the two children joined him there in July, after Matt recovered from a bout with measles.

In October, Eddie arrived in San Antonio with Elizabeth and their household goods. He was to report to Camp Dix to be processed for overseas duty. Africa, he speculated. Elizabeth and their furniture would wait out the war with Louise in her big two-story house on Page Street. When Jeffrey was shipped out, Marynell and her boys would join them. Eddie liked the idea of his family being together—unless the bombs came.

The tremor in Elizabeth's right hand had been joined by a slight but constant bobbing of her head.

"Doesn't she realize she's doing that?" Louise asked her father.

"It's an involuntary palsy," he explained, "common in the elderly."

"But she's not old."

"I know. Take good care of her, honey."

Louise and Elizabeth were impatient for Marynell to join them. They decided how they would arrange everyone. The three women would each have a room of their own—Elizabeth insisted on taking the tiniest bedroom, which was little more than a storage room. Matt, Peter and Eric would share a room, as would Pauline and Maggie. Louise searched the secondhand stores until she found a round kitchen table big enough to seat eight. She thought of all the hours she and her sister and mother would spend together at that table, sipping their coffee, sharing their lives.

War would bring the three of them together again.

CHAPTER

SIXTEEN

*L*ouise put away the last of the pans and hung the damp tea towels on a line strung across the back porch. Marynell finished wiping off the counters and poured three glasses of iced tea.

"I'll get Mother," Louise said and went down the long hallway to the front porch.

Elizabeth spent much of her time on the broad porch, swinging back and forth in the porch swing with one of the older children or rocking in the wicker rocker with a toddler.

Strange how seldom Elizabeth read anymore unless it was a picturebook for the children. Sometimes she held an open novel in her lap, but mostly she just sat, her head with its slight bob, like a cork floating in an almost calm pond, as she watched the occasional car drive down the tree-lined street or returned the greeting of neighbors strolling by. When a grandchild came to be held, the book was pushed aside. If asked, Elizabeth would come around back and pull weeds in the garden or hang clothes on the line, or she would help her daughters in the kitchen, peeling potatoes, making a salad. Almost daily she said how much she liked to watch her girls being together. But sometimes in the middle of hanging clothes or chopping vegetables, she would simply stop, say she was tired and wander off—usually back to the front porch in the odd shuffling gait she had developed.

Elizabeth was only forty-six. Her skin was still firm and youthful, the old beauty still there if one looked for it. Yet she seemed worn out, a person at the end of life rather than the middle. Her eyes stayed half-closed as though she hadn't the energy even to keep her lids open. The tremor now affected both her hands. When she held the saucer with her cup, the teaspoon rattled against the china.

"Marynell's poured the tea, Mother," Louise said.

Elizabeth's head tilted back. She regarded her daughter through squinted lids for a minute, her expression not registering. "Oh, yes," she said finally. "Is it time?"

Louise had planted a garden last summer, but with Marynell's help, this summer's was a much grander affair, and the inspection of the victory garden had become an evening ritual. Even if they had spent part of the day working in it, the three women, carrying their tea glasses, followed by five youngsters and the tan mongrel dog who had decided to live with them, would walk about the yard after dinner to inspect the rows of tomatoes, green beans, black-eyed peas, squash, okra, peppers, onions, corn, melons, turnips. The garden was a glorious success made sweeter when compared to Louise's mediocre crops of last summer. Marynell had spent the winter months reading books on gardening and taking careful notes. The sisters now understood about rototilling, thinning, fertilizer, watering, but most of all, they had discovered the magic of mulch. In the hot Texas sun, gardens didn't have a chance without a thick layer of cottonseed hulls or grass clippings to keep in the moisture.

"I'm sorry we forgot to plant English peas," Louise said. "Everything is growing so well, and we could have canned them for the winter."

"Well, we can still put up the green beans, tomatoes and okra," Marynell said. "Next year, I think we should plant strawberries so we can make jam."

"Maybe there won't be a next year," Louise said. "The Allies have beaten Rommel in Africa and the Japanese at the Bismarck Sea."

"Yeah. At least the tide seems to be turning. But I think it's safe to plan for next year's garden."

Louise knew her sister was probably right. The war would go on for another year at least. Maybe more. The Japanese and Germans were zealots who would fight to the bitter end.

Her marriage had been in limbo for more than two years, but the rest of her life had gone on. Strange how nothing was never all one way or the other. While she missed Franklin's masculine presence in her life and hoped and prayed constantly for the war to end, in many ways life here in the big house with three women and five children was quite satisfying. Already Louise was looking forward to their first foray into home canning. Louise loved the big kitchen and their noisy meals around the round table.

Of course, with all of them living under one roof, there was an unending stream of irritations and problems. Childhood illnesses got multiplied by five. The laundry was unending, the children's squabbling annoying. Louise thought Marynell was too strict with Matt and the twins. And she often found herself resenting her sister's know-it-all attitude, having always to be the authority on everything. But at least when she and Marynell disagreed, they argued. Louise had never argued with Franklin. And the frustrations of motherhood seemed less unsettling in this small world occupied with only women and children.

They had made acquaintances here in the neighborhood but had no real friends in town or on the base. Louise had been pleased when her in-laws had stopped for a visit on their way cross-country to Harold's new assignment in the War Department. Maxine and Harold insisted on eating family style in the kitchen with the high chairs and spilled milk. "Don't worry," Maxine promised. "Franklin will never know you didn't serve our meals in the dining room with china and sterling."

Around their grandchildren, Harold and Maxine seemed like any other doting grandparents. But Louise was intent on keeping all the children on their best behavior, and after four days of shushing and threatening, she had been relieved to wave good-bye as Harold and Maxine's train pulled out of the station.

Louise bent to pull a caterpillar from a tomato vine. Nasty thing. Matt jumped forward to grind it in the dirt with his toe. "Find one for me to kill," Peter demanded.

"Find your own," she told him.

"Amazing how pleasing it is," Marynell said as she surveyed the rows of green beans.

"Yes," Elizabeth agreed. "My mother always had a kitchen garden back in Seymour. She used to grow rhubarb for pies. Next year, *I* will plant some rhubarb."

"Strange how our lives are so tranquil while . . . " Louise's voice trailed off. There was no need to finish the sentence.

A victory garden seemed like such a tiny bit to do for the war effort, along with eating meatless meals, saving wastepaper and tin cans—even toothpaste tubes—for recycling, buying war bonds, donating used clothing and shoes for CARE packages. Of course, there were shortages to endure. The latest items to disappear from store shelves were hairpins and Kleenex, but it seemed petty to complain when she thought of the hardships in Europe.

She thought of the two maps on the wall of the kitchen—one of Europe, one of the Pacific. Jeffrey's and Eddie's pins were both in Great Britain. After serving in an evacuation hospital in Libya, Eddie had been promoted to lieutenant colonel and placed in command of a U.S. military hospital near Gloucester. His pin on the map was green. Louise worried about the buzz bombs, but otherwise her father should be safe.

Jeffrey's pin was blue and in Scotland. He was training troops once again. American forces were being amassed in England and Scotland. Eventually, there would be an invasion. Jeffrey had been to Gloucester twice to see Eddie. They liked each other, which pleased Marynell enormously.

Franklin's red pin was on the other map, still in Australia with MacArthur, frustrated in his staff job, eager for front-line duty. Guadalcanal had been taken without him.

She hadn't gotten any letters from Franklin in almost three weeks, and the last one made no mention of an upcoming campaign. But then, any slip of vital information brought a censor's black mark.

In spite of her husband's eagerness to prove himself in battle, Louise was grateful he was safely tucked away Down Under, and she didn't have to worry about him just yet. So many were dying. Franklin's cousin David, who'd been best man at their wedding, had been an early casualty, dying last summer at Tobruk where he'd been sent to observe British Eighth Army operations. And classmates of

Jeffrey's and Franklin's. The son of a neighbor. Local boys whose obituaries appeared daily in the newspaper. Gold stars on front windows.

And for two young mothers, just as frightening as war casualties and more immediate was the danger from infantile paralysis—or polio, as the newspapers were starting to call it. The disease was on its way to becoming a national epidemic. Every fever, every childish voice complaining of an ache struck fear in the sisters' hearts. Matt's summer kindergarten program was canceled, the city and post swimming pools closed. Louise and Marynell kept the children away from public places, which meant they mostly stayed at home. It was trying but safer. They knew most of their children's storybooks by heart and had been bored to numbness playing "Old Maid" and "Go Fish" countless times with Matt and the twins.

Matt was old enough to like some of the radio programs— "Captain Midnight," "Jack Armstrong, All-American Boy," "The Lone Ranger." Peter and Pauline liked "Buster Brown's Gang" on Saturday mornings. All three would howl with delight whenever Froggy the Gremlin plunked his magic twanger.

Women and children all waited eagerly for the postman's daily visit. Matt, Peter and Pauline loved to send off box tops for awards, and the women all made a great fuss over the arrival of V-mail, the photographed copies of mail written by the daddies and granddaddy. The children liked their grandfather's letters the best. Eddie always included a story about a dragon he had talked to on a London bridge or the giant teddy bear whose broken arm he had set.

Jeffrey's wrote of fear and homesickness. "I hope I measure up when the time comes. I'm not a born soldier, that's for sure. I know it's my duty to fight, but I pray to God that my sons will never have to go to war." He sometimes wrote of getting out of the Army after the war, perhaps opening a car dealership with his brother or teaching school. Marynell dismissed such notions as nonsense, but Louise knew her sister was worried. "If I'd wanted to be a schoolteacher's wife, I would have stayed in Amber," she said.

Louise embellished a bit when she read the parts of Franklin's letters intended for the children, trying to make their mythical father seem more real to them. He missed them all *very, very much*. He *loved* the pictures they colored for him. He could tell by the last snapshots how much they'd grown. Be sure to color pictures for their grand-parents. When she finished reading their part of a letter, Louise made a little ceremony of hugging the children for their daddy.

Louise only scanned the parts of letters in which Franklin adopted his authoritarian mode, still being the husband in charge from half a world away. Make sure the oil in the car was checked regularly. Be sure that her mother and Marynell paid their fair share of household expenses. Don't forget to write to his parents. Had she read the book he recommended? *The Army Wife* had been reviewed in the new publication, *Army Times*, and was reported to be an excellent presentation of the Army wife's role.

In the intimate parts of his letters, Franklin wrote of her beauty and their love. He took great comfort in having a fine, loyal wife waiting for him back home. He realized he'd never kissed her enough before. He dreamed constantly of making love to her. He wrote several times of a "new beginning." Louise liked that. It was what she wanted, too.

At times, the sweetness of his words brought tears to her eyes. "I can't imagine myself married to any other woman. You are so dear to me, so deep in my heart that my very life depends on your love. I live for you, and if I don't return from this terrible war, please know, my darling girl, that when I breathe my last, it will be with your name on my lips."

She wrote back to him the words he wanted to hear. She occasionally asked his advice about money or the car to make him still feel the head of the household. She described vignettes from the life of the good wife, the good family. She wrote words of pride in him and what he was doing. And words of love, missing, longing, but never of lust. Lust she must keep on a high shelf of a hidden closet.

But in her letters, she also let him see how well she was managing. On her own, she had purchased a house and a car. She paid the bills, balanced the checkbook, hammered nails, changed washers and cleaned out clogged drains. She found a mechanic and a banker who treated her like a responsible adult.

Their separation had been difficult, but in the long run Louise thought it would be good for their marriage. She would not go back to the childlike status she had occupied before. She and her husband would be partners facing life together.

Her new resolve did not go unnoticed. "I sense in your letters a growing maturity and strength," Franklin wrote. "And of course, that must be. You've been left alone with three young children and must make many decisions that a husband normally would make. But please remember, I need to find the sweet girl I married waiting for me when I come home. It's her image I carry with me."

After the children and Elizabeth were in bed, Marynell and Louise carried their evening libations to the front porch.

"Matt must be asleep," Marynell said when Mister Dog scratched at the screen door to join them. She got up to let the dog out, his evening job of enduring Matt's hug until the boy fell asleep apparently accomplished.

Mister Dog curled at their feet. Louise kicked off a sandal and scratched his back with her toes.

Marynell sighed. "Jeffrey's been gone nine months."

Louise started to point out that at least Jeffrey had been with Marynell for Eric's birth and enjoyed his first birthday. Franklin had never seen his twenty-month-old daughter—darling Maggie with her freckled nose, strawberry-blond curls and silly laugh.

"God, how I miss him. In bed and out." Marynell moaned. "What about you? Do you think about sex much?"

"Sometimes," Louise said, closing her eyes and enjoying the soothing motion of the porch swing. She was tired. The days were full. "With these children constantly crawling all over me, I'm not sure my body could stand any more demands made on it if Franklin were here. But I think a lot about just being with him, touching him in the night, knowing we can raise our children and grow old together."

"Sometimes I think I'd like you and me and Mother and the kids to stay here like this forever, yet I want Jeffrey so much it makes me ill at times. I dream about him coming home constantly, yet worry when it actually happens—it will be a disappointment. Things that you want a lot are often less than you'd hoped for when you get them."

"That's not so," Louise said. "The children aren't disappointing, and we wanted them a lot."

"Yes and no. I wanted a baby of my own more than anything and love Eric more than I ever thought possible. But he's naughty to Maggie and refuses to stop pooping in his pants. And Matt's a tyrant to the twins and is ruining his teeth sucking on those damned fingers. He'll probably graduate from college with his fingers in his mouth. And if they all don't stop picking their noses and playing with their bottoms, I'm going to leave them for foundlings."

Louise laughed. "They dug up that squirrel they buried last week."

"Ugh. The little barbarians."

"Matt told Peter and Pauline he'd give them each a nickel if they touched it. Pauline is now five cents richer. I told her she should have bargained, made him pay a quarter. Then she'd have enough for another stamp toward her next war bond."

Louise finished her wine and put the glass on the window sill.

"You want to go in and listen to the radio?" Marynell asked.

"After a while. Let's have another round and just sit. Remember when we thought Mother and Daddy lived such a boring life?"

"Yeah. Maybe they were just recuperating from raising us."

At ten, they went inside to listen to the late news. Mussolini had been overthrown by the Fascist Grand Council and was in prison, newscaster Kaltenborn reported. The pompous dictator in prison. Strange. Louise thought of the newsreels with him giving speeches from a balcony overlooking a Roman square full of people cheering him fervently. To her, he seemed a silly caricature with his clenched fist, jutting jaw and theatrical poses. A joke of a man, yet he had caused so many deaths in his quest for power. And now his country was to be a battleground for Allied and German forces. Already Palermo in Sicily had been declared secure by General George Patton.

Men were dying even as she and Marynell sat here safe in their living room. Lives unfinished. Broken-hearted parents. Children left fatherless. Widows facing life alone. Sometimes Louise wished for a different sort of marriage, but Franklin was a fine, worthy man, and she didn't want to be a widow. She wanted Franklin to come home to her and the children. And Jeffrey to Marynell. More than anything.

Marynell went to bathe first while Louise locked up and picked up a bit, putting storybooks on the shelf, toys in the wooden chest in the hall.

Finding a comfortable house to rent in San Antonio had proven impossible with the tremendous influx of military personnel, so Louise had bought the big old frame house near Fort Sam using the down payment Franklin's parents had loaned to her. A strange feeling, owning a house after a lifetime of military quarters. She painted and wallpapered at will. For once, hers didn't look exactly like all the other houses on the block.

When she turned out the light in the kitchen, a shaft of moonlight illuminated the maps on the kitchen wall. Three pins cast three tiny shadows. She thought of the men they represented. Gentle Jeffrey, who had become her brother before he went off to war. Her daddy, who was the dearest. And Franklin, who was the most important.

She touched the pin in the South Pacific. "What are you doing at this moment, dear Franklin? Are you thinking of me?"

There wasn't any hot water left. Louise had to settle for a sponge bath.

The last thing before bed, she looked in on the children. Pauline and Maggie were wrapped up together like two kittens. Maggie's bottom was still dry. Louise would stop the night diapers soon. Her youngest was an easier child than the twins had been, or maybe she was an easier mother.

The boys' room was across the hall. Now six, Matt seemed so big, not a baby anymore at all. He and three-year-old Peter were like brothers, with a mutual passion for bugs, toy airplanes and guns. But Matt was teaching him to bully the girls.

Eric's bed was empty. Most nights he slept with his mother.

Louise still enjoyed a sleepy child crawling in bed with her in the early morning, but at night she was tired of children.

Light came from under Marynell's door. Louise tapped and opened the door a crack. " 'Night, Marynell," she whispered.

Marynell held up the book she was reading on home canning. "Guaranteed to put one to sleep fast. 'Night, Sis."

Louise finished a letter to her in-laws and started one to her dad before giving in to weariness.

In the warm darkness, she curled into her pillow. She hadn't been truthful with Marynell. She thought of sex more than she was willing to admit.

She still conjured up thoughts of General MacArthur's handsome young aide-de-camp, who had flirted with her in Manila.

And like her sister, Louise also fantasized about her husband's homecoming. Scenario after scenario. A new beginning.

At this moment, she wanted his warm, sleeping body beside her. After all this time, it still seemed unnatural to sleep alone.

Elizabeth had Parkinson's. After the disease was diagnosed, the tremor and muscular weakness became markedly worse, almost as though it had been waiting for a name to fully demonstrate itself. By Christmas, she needed help going to the bathroom, getting in and out of the tub. They turned the dining room into a bedroom for her so she wouldn't have to go up and down stairs.

The doctor insisted the disease was not immediately life-threatening, only crippling. She could live on for years. "I don't think she wants to live for years like that," Marynell whispered over a late-night cup of tea with a glance over her shoulder to the closed dining room door.

"I'm never quite sure what Mother's thinking," Louise admitted. "She just seems to accept everything without question."

"There's some of that in you," Marynell said.

"I know," Louise admitted, "but I'm changing."

By the fall, it became apparent the disease was impairing Elizabeth's lungs. Fluid accumulated. She recovered slowly from a bout with pneumonia, only to be stricken again within weeks.

On Christmas Day, 1943, the sisters sent a cable to their father: "Come home at once. Mother is dying."

Elizabeth's doctor notified the Red Cross, requesting an emergency leave for Lieutenant Colonel Edward Rodgers, U.S. Armed Forces Field Hospital, Gloucester, England.

Louise and Marynell had been taking turns at the post hospital, but they hired a Mexican woman to look after the children and began their death watch. Elizabeth kept telling them to go on home. The children were more important, and it wasn't right to postpone their Christmas.

An exhausted Eddie arrived December twenty-ninth. He had flown in one military transport to Newfoundland and caught rides on three more to make his way finally to Fort Sam.

"Then it's true," Elizabeth whispered when she saw her unshaven, travel-worn husband walk into her hospital room. For the first time, she cried, tears rolling down her still unlined cheeks.

Her breathing was labored, each breath an effort. Her feverish body was skeletal beneath the blanket. Carefully, mindful of the tube coming from her nose and the other from a vein in her arm, Eddie gathered his wife in his arms. "Oh, my dear precious wife," he said. "My darling Elizabeth."

Marynell and Louise tiptoed out into the corridor, closing the door behind them.

"I can't stand it," Marynell said, her shoulders shaking with sobs.

"Me either," Louise said as she reached blindly for her sister. Just when she thought she was too weary to cry anymore, the tears came again.

They walked the halls for a while, then went down to the canteen for lunch. The act of eating seemed almost a sacrilege. Their mother was dying upstairs, and Louise had no appetite, but she had discovered that she must eat something or her head ached so terribly she became nauseated. And her mother's dying would be easier to get through without a sick headache.

Eddie sat with his wife during the afternoon and evening. Every sentence seemed to begin with "remember when."

Elizabeth died just past midnight. They thought she was unconscious, her respirations coming only a few times a minute. But she lifted her hand to signal them, and they leaned close to hear her gasp, "Don't cry. It doesn't matter."

Eddie grieved through the next days, weeping a lot, telling them repeatedly how much he had loved their mother, how much he would miss her. But he also kept reminding them that life went on. Louise would have preferred for him to say that life would never be the same without her. But then, that went without saying, she supposed.

They buried Elizabeth among the white markers at Fort Sam Houston National Cemetery. A bugler played "Taps." The cemetery was beautiful but impersonal, with no family or friends buried close by. Louise wondered if her mother would have preferred her family's plot back in Indiana, but she had never said, and it was wartime. Travel was difficult at best. And a place would be left beside her for Eddie. Maybe that was appropriate for Army spouses, to be homeless together for eternity.

Eddie stayed only three days after the funeral, using the time to get to know his grandchildren. He taught the three older children simple card tricks, and he patiently read *The Little Engine That Could* over and over to Eric and Maggie. He took the whole brood with him to visit old medical corps friends out at Fort Sam.

He cried when he left. "My family. My girls. Everything changes. I love you all so much." The sisters and their children waved as the train pulled out of the station.

"I feel like an orphan," Marynell said.

Louise did, too. She wasn't sure why. They'd lost their mother, but surely their father would come back to them. He was vigorous and healthy, and he loved them.

After Eddie had gone, Louise and Marynell attempted a belated Christmas for the children, but neither sister's heart was in the task.

After the children were tucked into bed, each with a new toy in their arms, the sisters sat late at the kitchen table, drinking too much brandy and becoming maudlin, recalling every mothering thing Elizabeth had ever done.

"She was so beautiful, like an angel," Marynell said, tears streaming down her face.

"Like an angel," Louise agreed.

In the night, Marynell left her sleeping child and came to her sister's bed. They hugged in the darkness and remembered when they were girls and their mother was young and life was simple.

"I loved her so much," Marynell sobbed. "Do you think she knew that?"

"Oh, yes," Louise said. "I'm sure she did."

CHAPTER

SEVENTEEN

"**A**nd I've got something for you men a whole lot better than mules," MacArthur said, gesturing with his famous corncob pipe toward Franklin, who turned to wave at a private waiting a quarter of a mile down the road.

The khaki-clad general, his hat pushed back at a jaunty angle, was standing on the hood of a jeep, addressing the members of the 99th Field Artillery, a newly arrived battalion from Fort Bliss, Texas, along with other components of the First Cavalry Division.

The battalion and their 75mm weapons had seen lots of geography but no fighting in the two years since Pearl Harbor. Originally sent to Colorado to be trained on skis in anticipation of a possible invasion of Europe from the north, the 99th was then sent to barren Fort Bliss, Texas, to join the First Cavalry Division and train for fighting in the jungles of the South Pacific. They had embarked for Australia from Camp Stoneman, near Pittsburgh.

The First Cavalry had been converted from mounted to bantam truck operation shortly after the outbreak of the war, but the 99th was still classified as a pack battalion, and Franklin knew its men were expecting replacements for the mules and horses they had left in the States. Instead, a convoy of thirty new jeeps was now winding its way over freshly graded roads into the First's raw, new encampment area north of Brisbane. A number of wooden-floored tents had been erected in the grove of tall pines. A primitive wooden structure served as headquarters. The headquarters compound had already taken on a shipshape look, with white-painted rocks lining walkways and a carefully lettered sign built across the drive announcing "Division Headquarters."

Most of the several hundred men cheered as the jeeps rolled into view. Only a few older officers and seasoned noncoms remained stony-faced. They had packed artillery pieces in the last war. For them, horses and mules were as much a part of the artillery as howitzers.

MacArthur acknowledged the cheers with a pontifical smile and wave. Then he continued his speech, explaining additional jeeps and trucks for the battalion were being unloaded at Brisbane. He urged the men to spend the next months preparing themselves for the days ahead, for "their rendezvous with history." MacArthur liked that phrase. Franklin had used it in a speech he'd written for the general several months ago, and it now made its way into every extemporaneous delivery.

Becoming a speechwriter had not been of Franklin's choosing. The careful notes he had kept during his investigation of the existing political and military climate in Australia had pleased MacArthur when he arrived from Corregidor. In those first weeks, he kept Franklin at his side to brief him for meetings and interviews, and very quickly Franklin found himself preparing "remarks"—and making phone calls, dictating letters, operating as a sounding board, becoming indispensable.

Franklin tuned out the general as he scanned the faces of the artillerymen. They ranged from the middle-aged officers and noncoms to smooth-faced youths. But the adolescent eagerness of the first U.S. units to arrive in Australia was gone. In spite of the devastation of Pearl Harbor, the first wave of men had arrived thinking the Imperial Army with its little yellow soldiers was a bit of a joke. The Japanese couldn't possibly be a match for mighty America. After all, the real war was being fought in Europe and Africa.

America and its soldiers now understood the war in the Pacific was quite real and was going to be a long, hard one.

The taut look of fear crept onto many of the young faces as they listened to MacArthur drone on about the war ahead, about a bloodthirsty enemy, about sacrifice. Franklin felt it himself. Fear. It pulled the skin tight across his forehead and formed a rock in the pit of his stomach. He'd spent a month under siege on Corregidor, yet in a way he was as uninitiated as these men. On Corregidor, he'd seen men die, but he had yet to meet the enemy face-to-face.

If he had stayed on Corregidor, he would either be dead now or rotting in a Japanese POW camp. Of course, at the time of his departure, there was still hope that supplies and reinforcements would be on the way for the besieged forces on Corregidor and Bataan, but even in February of 1942, Franklin had already suspected that the American and Filipino troops were sacrificial lambs left to keep the enemy away from Australia as long as possible. Still, he never voiced his suspicions and prayed his fellow officers were correct. Sixty thousand men would not be abandoned.

But when the chance came to leave, Franklin jumped at it. He had no desire to be a martyr, and POWs didn't get promotions. Franklin remembered once snapping at Louise when she asked if he couldn't trade on his father's rank and get them a better place to live when they arrived as newlyweds at Fort Sill. Of course, he would never use his father's influence to get ahead in this man's army. Yet he knew things came to him because of who he was. The reason he'd gotten off Corregidor was because he was General Cravens' son. And he suspected MacArthur had once had a crush on his mother. The old general asked about her too much, remembered things Maxine had said and worn thirty years ago.

Franklin could almost imagine the discussion that had taken place when it was decided to send an official escort from the garrison along with President Quezon and High Commissioner Sayre when they left the island to form a Philippine government in exile in Australia. General Cravens' articulate son would do a good job of handling the press on the Australian end. He could tell them how grim the situation was on the Rock and on Bataan.

When Franklin said good-bye to MacArthur, he'd asked the general if he'd be seeing him in Australia.

"I don't know, son. But just in case, look things over, will you? I understand the Allied forces in Australia are pretty piecemeal, and not much coordinated training has taken place so far. Whoever is ultimately put in command will have his work cut out for him. I've arranged for you to remain with Quezon for a while, and that should give you license to snoop around a bit. And here are letters of introduction to the military attaché at the American embassy in Melbourne and to a few of the shrewder Aussie journalists. You might prepare a complete roster of what Allied units are stationed in Australia and where—along with a complete itemization of vehicles, arsenal, the works. A report on the strength of the Aussie divisions in North Africa would be helpful, too. Regardless of what Churchill thinks, they'll have to be recalled if Australia is to be defended. You might start thinking about reorganization. And I'm still counting on you to give a favorable accounting of the brave men fighting in the Philippines."

"Most assuredly, sir."

"If this is to be my last hurrah, I'd like to be remembered well."

"But sir, Roosevelt has promised . . . "

MacArthur held up his hand to stop Franklin's next words. "Mrs. MacArthur says to send her regards to your wife. And please remember me to your parents, especially that pretty mother of yours. My mother always thought highly of Maxine. Said if I'd had any sense, I'd have married a woman like her. I did, finally."

Franklin watched as MacArthur bid farewell to Manuel Quezon. Both men had tears in their eyes. The frail old president took a signet ring from his finger and gave it to MacArthur. Quezon's health was failing rapidly. Franklin doubted if the two old friends would ever see each other again.

Sayre helped the old president down the gangplank onto the deck of the *Swordfish*. Franklin offered his smartest salute to Philippine General Romulo and to MacArthur before escorting Mrs. Quezon aboard. It crossed his mind that he might be safer staying on Corregidor than running the Japanese blockade in a submarine, but the die had been cast. Franklin turned for one last wave, one last salute. MacArthur, standing with his hands behind his back, pipe jutting from his mouth, responded with a nod. "God be with you, son," he called across the strip of water.

In Australia, Franklin learned the bitter truth. The men on Corregidor and Bataan had indeed been written off. Their only function at this point was to keep Japanese invading forces occupied as long as possible. There had even been talk that, by choice, MacArthur, his wife and son would share the fate of the garrison.

Now, however, as Franklin watched MacArthur perform for the men of the 99th, he wondered if the general had really planned to "go down with the ship," or if it was just another case of the old man's grandstanding. There had been a footlocker stashed on the *Swordfish* that was reputed to hold MacArthur's medals, his and his wife's will and family mementos. It was addressed to a bank in Washington and was to be held in safekeeping until claimed by their heirs. Yet the indomitable man who said farewell to Franklin on the north dock at Corregidor hadn't seemed like he was ready to leave the struggle to others. But whatever the general had decided for himself, Franklin didn't approve of his exposing his wife and son to such danger. Mrs. MacArthur and the boy should have been sent home with the other military dependents back in the spring of '41. Franklin had been shocked to discover they weren't to be among the passengers on the *Swordfish*. He also didn't approve of other things MacArthur had done, like the dispatches sent out from Corregidor indicating the general had been present at battles on Bataan when Franklin knew he had not left the island since arriving there Christmas Eve from besieged Manila. And why in the hell hadn't MacArthur stored more food and medical supplies on the island and on Bataan if he'd planned for U.S. and Philippine forces to make their last stands there?

But Franklin conceded that MacArthur was the only living American hero, the one who knew the Japanese like no other Allied general did. The Australian government and press had demanded he be rescued in order to lead Allied Forces in the Pacific. In the end, Roosevelt had been put in the position of ordering MacArthur to leave Corregidor, and history would never know if he had planned to leave anyway.

In the year since, Franklin had served MacArthur well, and now he wanted his reward. He had personally petitioned the general for an assignment with the 99th Field Artillery but as yet had no answer. Franklin feared he would spend the entire war being introduced as Harold Cravens' boy, writing inspiring speeches for the general, composing careful dispatches and press releases. Franklin knew military history. He could always find a parallel or precedent. MacArthur liked that. Franklin had ingratiated himself right into a dilemma. The crusty old general had created a special staff position for Franklin and sometimes even gave him a chance to offer an opinion on battle plans, but Franklin needed a chance to prove himself at the front lines. He wanted to return to his wife a hero. He wanted to make his father proud. And he wanted a war record that would earn him promotions and assure his future career.

Almost weekly, Franklin heard of some member of the West Point Class of '38 who had passed him in grade. Franklin feared a stalemated career more than he feared battle itself. Surely MacArthur understood how important it was to let a young officer have his own "rendezvous with history."

MacArthur was droning on, telling the artillerymen about the heroes of Guadalcanal and Bougainville and New Guinea. The march toward Japan had begun, and they were to join it.

The assembled men were getting restless. They already knew they were to be part of invasion forces making landings on Pacific real estate they had never heard of before. The only thing they hadn't realized was that instead of leading mules onto beachheads they would be packing and pulling their equipment with this impressive row of new jeeps.

Two staff sergeants in front of Franklin were whispering. "Why in the hell didn't they tell us to leave them harnesses back in Texas?" the older man was saying. He punctuated his words by spitting tobacco juice.

"What about the veterinarian? Think Doc can cure a jeep of colic?" the other man whispered back.

"Sure am glad I learned how to ski. That's going to come in real handy in the jungle."

Franklin winced.

. . .

"Babe Rude is dead," the voice called out in the darkness. Franklin assumed the caller meant Babe Ruth.

"Roosevelt fucks Betty Grable," another voice said.

Franklin stretched his legs out in front of him and leaned against the sandbag wall of the fire direction center. He wondered if learning such phrases was part of all Japanese soldiers' training, or if some smartass Jap here in the Admiralties had dreamed up this particular form of distraction for the American invaders.

"The stars at night shine big and bright, deep in the heart of Texas," sang out another Jap voice from the darkness.

Franklin hated the night callers, but at least they helped keep him awake. Sleeping at night could be a fatal mistake since Jap soldiers infiltrated the perimeter after dark, creeping up on foxholes to bayonet their occupants, bellying their way up to gun emplacements and tossing in grenades. They did more damage at night than in the daytime.

In Brisbane, Franklin had spent most of his nights thinking about his wife. On only three occasions, had he sought out the company of a woman—two times with Aussie drivers, the other time with an American nurse. He would never see the same woman twice. Other men were stupid that way—even some officers—and would get involved.

Here on Los Negros, his thoughts were only of his wife. He thought incessantly of the moment when he could hold her again and inhale her scent, touch her hair, hear her voice.

In his fantasies, Louise was lovelier than ever. Dressed in white, she radiated an aura of love. Always, she fell into his arms crying. She was slimmer than before, like a girl, her hair long and silky.

He tried to place his children in these scenes, but they always disappeared after the opening shot. The twins, who'd still been babes in arms when Louise left Manila three years ago, were regular little people who sang songs and got into mischief, according to Louise's letters. And Maggie, whom he had never seen, was a funny, cute two-year-old with red-gold hair. He had little sense of his three children and thought of them mostly when he read Louise's letters, visualizing his family living the days she described. He thought of his parents more than his children. Mostly he thought of Louise. At times, he even imagined her a widow receiving his posthumous Congressional Medal of Honor or weeping in front of a tombstone bearing his name. A woman like Louise would never remarry. He'd had an aunt like that, widowed from the first war. Her duty to her husband went on after his death as she raised her children to revere their dead father's name.

The most fearful scenarios were those fleeting ones in which he was maimed. Missing a limb. Hideously ugly. Emasculated. But he purged those thoughts as soon as he caught them creeping in through the crevices of his consciousness. In dreams, however, they were beyond control. He would jerk awake in his foxhole, sweating, heart pounding, the vise of fear constricting his chest.

One night a young corporal had been there beside him. Corporal Hooks, the one they called Preacher. The boy's hand was on Franklin's shoulder. He realized he'd been shaken awake.

"You okay, sir?"

"Yes. I'm fine." But his voice was trembling.

"Those dreams can be pretty bad, huh?" Hooks drawled. He was hunkered down beside Franklin, his hand still resting on Franklin's shoulder.

"Yeah, pretty bad." Franklin sat up. The soldier withdrew his hand. It had felt nice. Human.

"I remember when I was a little kid back home, and my mom would come. Now, I pray to God. It helps."

"Where you from, Hooks?" Franklin asked, not wanting the boy to leave.

"Burkburnett, Texas, sir. Used to be an oil boomtown. Now it isn't much. But my people are there."

"You got a girl back in Burkburnett?"

"Yes, sir. A mighty fine girl. Her name's Sally. You married, sir?"

"Yes, a wonderful woman named Louise. I miss her a lot. And I've got three kids, one I've never seen."

"I know that Mrs. Cravens is proud of you, sir. I wrote my folks about how proud I was to serve under a West Pointer."

"Even one who has nightmares?"

"I imagine even MacArthur himself has nightmares."

"Why do they call you Preacher?" Franklin asked.

"I've got the call, sir. I'm going to seminary when I get home."

"Well, pray for us, okay?"

"Yes, sir. And you pray, too, hear."

Franklin saluted the boy in the half-light. He'd have to tell Louise about Preacher Hooks in his next letter.

On the way to Los Negros, Franklin had tried to record every detail in his mind, imagining that he would someday want to tell Louise about his combat experience. But to deal honestly with what had happened to him since arriving on this godforsaken place would mean sharing the horror and the terrible, numbing fear.

He could never tell his wife that he'd wet himself. Twice. The first time was in the landing craft when a volley from their own naval bombardment sailed over their heads—but at first he didn't know what it was. It sounded like screaming from hell. He'd thought he was a dead man, closed his eyes and waited for it. He didn't even realize he'd wet until he felt the warm trickling down the inside of his left leg. The scent of urine was all around him in the crowded craft of hunkered-down men. "Keep your heads down!" he called out needlessly since the word had gone around that a coxwain in the previous wave of landing craft had had his head blown off, but as the only officer in the craft, Franklin had needed to sound in charge. When the front end of the boat dropped, he'd leaped into the ocean gratefully. The chest-high water camouflaged his disgrace.

At first the fighting hadn't been so bad. A devastating naval bombardment had scattered defenders on this side of the island, catching the Japanese by surprise. Most of their larger gun emplacements faced the large harbor on the northwest corner of the island. The tiny harbor on the east was protected only by antiaircraft guns. While the Japanese scrambled to adjust their defenses, the landing party established a perimeter along the west side of the island's airstrip.

MacArthur came ashore only six hours into the landing. Photographers took his picture while he inspected gun emplacements, stared down at some of the enemy dead, encouraged the men. "You have performed marvelously," he told a group on the beach. "Hold what you have taken, no matter against whatever odds. You have your teeth in now. Don't let go."

He stopped by Franklin's battery. "Glad to see you made it ashore all right, Cravens."

"Thank you, sir."

"I sent a message to your father at the War Department. He knows you're here."

Franklin nodded. "I appreciate that, sir."

"Well, good luck, son, and to your men," MacArthur said with a salute to two awestruck lieutenants.

The men looked at Franklin with curiosity. They'd heard his father was a general. But Jesus, MacArthur himself had singled him out.

Franklin wet himself again when Corporal Hooks got his face blown away. Franklin was looking directly at him when it happened. In an instant, he didn't have a face. It looked like someone had slapped handfuls of bloody hamburger meat between his ears. He could still scream, even though he didn't have lips or teeth. He screamed and screamed. Franklin screamed, too, for the medics. Hooks was silent by the time the medics came and carried him away. Franklin prayed he was dead. Surely they wouldn't try to save him. Franklin's hands were shaking so hard, he put them between his legs. He was wet.

At least he hadn't lost his shit, Franklin consoled himself, remembering. If he was going to do that, he'd have done it that second night ashore when, just at dusk, he'd left his foxhole to drag a wounded GI to safety. As he bent over the groaning private, out of the corner of an eye he saw movement in the deep shadows by the trees.

A Jap, with an arm raised. About twenty feet away.

Franklin sensed rather than saw a grenade being tossed. His action had been instinctive. The grenade hit the ground rolling. Franklin picked it up and threw it back. It hit the Jap in the stomach.

Franklin dragged the wounded man the remaining twenty feet. Already voices were calling for a medic. Somebody kept saying "Jesus Christ," over and over.

The wounded man had lost consciousness, but he was still alive.

When the medics arrived, a corporal told them excitedly about their captain picking up a live hand grenade and tossing it back.

"No fuck?" one of the medics said, casting a sidelong look at Franklin.

"No fuck."

Franklin turned away so he could smile. He wondered if he'd have some sort of delayed reaction to the incident. Jesus, he could be dead. But right now all he felt was proud. He could imagine the letters his men would write home. *The battery commander played catch with a hand grenade. A general's son who knows MacArthur. Volunteered for combat when he could have stayed behind a desk back in Aussieland.*

The next day, after the area was secure, Franklin went to look at the Jap's fly-covered remains. The body had already started to smell. It didn't take long in the jungle heat. The Jap's right arm and both legs were all but severed from what was left of his trunk. Hunks of flesh were hanging from the body. It seemed more like garbage than something human.

The man's face was surprisingly intact. Eyes bulging. The flesh was pulling away from the mouth. Franklin wondered about his soul. But then a Jap wouldn't have accepted Christ as his Savior. Franklin wasn't sure if that meant the Jap would go to hell, but surely there was no place in heaven for him. Many Americans considered the Japanese subhuman, not worthy of compassion. He wondered what the Japs thought of Americans.

When he was a kid, Franklin had examined with great care dead animal carcasses he'd come across in the woods. Once there had been a dead horse in a field, a maze of intestines erupting from its rectum. Franklin's reaction to the dead animals had been the same feeling he was experiencing now. Morbid fascination.

I could look like that now, if I hadn't tossed back that grenade. The thought was in his head, but he didn't really feel it. Maybe no one ever did.

He touched the severed arm with the toe of his boot, his stomach contracting. Gruesome.

There were no rings. No watch. Like a hunter picking a tooth from the carcass of a dead wolf, Franklin wanted a keepsake.

Then he saw the pin in the sand where the man had dropped it. The pin from the grenade. Franklin picked it up and put it in his pocket.

He wondered when someone would come along and bury the mess. Soon, he hoped.

It had taken several days. A bulldozer was brought ashore to deal with mass graves—there were over seven hundred enemy dead by that time—and to flatten Jap emplacements with their occupants still inside.

That had been a week ago. It seemed like an eternity. The 99th had moved their guns inland to support the taking of other island positions—a native village, an abandoned mission. Most of the remaining Japanese were dug in, but some still came out at night to scream strange messages in the darkness and take the offensive on suicidal missions inside the American perimeter. Thirty of them had gotten cut off from a raiding party and blown out their own guts with grenades rather than face capture.

The American casualties on Los Negros now numbered over two hundred with at least five hundred evacuated casualties. In military terms, a very small price tag to pay for this miserable little island made worthy by its airstrip and geographical position. As soon as the troops of the First Calvary cleared the area, planes would start landing, a stepping-stone on the road to Japan.

"Babe Rude is dead," came a voice from the jungle blackness. "Betty Grable is dead."

Jesus, Franklin thought, don't they ever give up? There couldn't be a couple hundred Japs left alive on the whole island.

Just before dawn, he awoke abruptly. Damn, he didn't like to nod off like that. Napping in the daytime was much safer.

He started to stretch, but the hair on the back of his neck stiffened. Pulling out his side arm, he peered over the side of the bunker.

A crouching Jap was preparing to come over the side with a fixed bayonet. Franklin raised his weapon, his finger on the trigger.

The man straightened, instantly appraising the situation. "And a good day to you, sir," he said in a clipped British accent before Franklin fired.

Damn, who in the hell was teaching these guys English? Franklin didn't want the people he shot to wish him a good day. Damned slimy bastards. Sneaking up like that. Not caring if they got killed. Expecting to get killed. Damn. And that one was an officer. Jesus. An officer.

He didn't like them to sound like people. He had to get that body dragged away from the bunker before it started to stink. Jesus Christ, didn't the guy have anything better to do than to commit suicide?

War wasn't what Franklin had expected it to be. It was so disorderly, not at all like training exercises at the academy and Fort Sill. Not precise like in the textbooks.

And he had never been so hot, so filthy, so uncomfortable, in his entire life. He had bugs in his crotch and rashes in every crevice.

"Babe Rude sends his love," he screamed out at the jungle.

With the morning light, news of the night's casualties began drifting in. Two signal corps guys had been found facedown in the creek. Corporal Clark over in A Battery had gotten a bayonet in the balls last night.

Several men crossed themselves.

One of the lieutenants put a protective hand over his own crotch. "Christ," he whispered.

Franklin prayed. If he got to go home, he wanted to be whole.

The Japanese had dug themselves into impenetrable bunkers made of huge palm logs. The cleaning up of the island would take weeks. The smell of death was everywhere. Sweet, sticky, sickening. But at least the perimeters were fairly secure. Soon he would be able to sleep through the night, bathe in the creek and wash some clothes.

And with the Japanese holed up in their pillboxes, Franklin would be able to practice the science of artillery as he been taught it.

He knew now that it was going to be a long war. And the taking of Los Negros had been easy compared to what lay ahead. He consoled himself with the fact that he had been tested. He had met the enemy and survived. And he wasn't a coward. He was especially grateful for that. But he didn't like face-to-face killing. Not at all.

Still, he liked being here with these brave men. He who loved sit-down dinners with china and crystal also loved eating slop out of a mess kit with his fellows. He was part of a family of fighting men. There was complaining, petty jealousy, lying, but there was also love, which Franklin felt as intensely as he'd ever felt anything before. His comrades in arms.

Hook's death bothered them all. A nice, decent young man whose simple faith had elevated them. Hooks was always telling them of God's love. In his memory, they had started saying "God loves you" as a greeting among the one hundred and seventy members of the battery. Franklin had dreaded writing a letter to Hook's parents, but once he started, it was easier than he thought. "He brought God to a godless place. And love. He was a good, brave man, and none of us will ever forget him." Franklin imagined them opening the letter, reading it, crying. He hoped they found some small comfort from his words.

And a good day to you, sir. The Jap officer hadn't been reciting a rote phrase. With that accent, he probably had a degree from Oxford. The man had gone out with style; Franklin would hand him that. He wished he'd thought to take a souvenir. The guy's brass, maybe.

CHAPTER

EIGHTEEN

"**I**s the mail here already?" Louise asked as she carried a sack of groceries in the back door.

Marynell, still in her housecoat, her hair uncombed, was sitting at the kitchen table, her hands folded across a letter.

"The mailman's a little early, isn't he?" Louise asked as she put the groceries and her purse among the unwashed breakfast dishes. "My, it was crowded at the store. They had syrup—real maple syrup! Only one per customer, but I thought maybe you could go buy a bottle, too. Imagine, pancakes with real syrup!"

Marynell pushed the letter across the table. "Read this," she said, her tone flat.

Louise picked up the letter, recognizing their father's handwriting.

No, Louise thought, as she scanned the letter. Her hand flew protectively to her heart. No. Don't let it be true.

He was married—to a British nurse.

"Martha is a fine woman," Eddie wrote, "so vital and full of life. We are very happy. I know your mother has been dead for only six months, but I'm no longer a young man, and I want to take advantage of the good years I have remaining. I hope you girls will understand and wish your old daddy well."

There was a photograph: Eddie and the woman, both in uniforms. She was short, a little thick in the waist, younger, neither pretty nor ugly. They were both smiling.

"I'm shocked," Louise said, sinking into a chair, staring at the photograph, at the smile on her father's face.

"I'm furious," Marynell exploded. "Absolutely furious! How dare he do that with Mother barely cold in her grave. Six months indeed! She died exactly five and a half months before the postmark on that letter, and no telling how long he'd been married when he wrote it. And no telling how long he'd been carrying on with the woman before that. No wonder he was in such an all-fired hurry to get back to England. He had a little English doxy warming his bed."

"You don't know that," Louise said, wondering. Had their mother's death been a gift, allowing him to marry this other woman? The pain of disillusionment pressed against her chest. He should have grieved for years. He should have whispered Elizabeth's name when he breathed his last, and his final resting place should be beside her at the national cemetery. Louise needed to believe her parents' love had been that strong. It was the foundation on which her own marriage was based.

"I'm going to write and tell him exactly what I think," Marynell said, her lip quivering. "How dare he ask us to wish him well."

They were interrupted by a herd of feet charging down the stairs. Pauline was calling "Mommie, Mommie!" She came racing into the kitchen, pigtails flying, Matt and Peter in hot pursuit.

"She took my pencils," Matt was yelling.

"They're *my* pencils," Pauline said, clutching a box of colored pencils against her chest. "This box has red. You lost the red out of your box."

"Did not."

"Did, too."

"Peter, whose pencils are they?" Louise demanded of her son.

Peter shrugged, unwilling to take sides. Louise knew they were his sister's. If they were Matt's, Peter would have said so.

"Marynell and I are having a very serious discussion. I want you boys to go outside and Pauline to go color in the living room. We will settle this argument later. And you boys leave Maggie and Eric alone. They got the sandbox first."

The three children looked at one another warily.

"Now!" Louise snapped.

The screen door slammed behind the boys.

Matt's voice rang out. "Last one to the swing is a rotten egg."

"That's not fair. You got a head start," Peter yelled indignantly.

"I want a cookie," Pauline demanded, her chin jutting and feet planted.

Louise pointed wordlessly toward the living room. Pauline took a reading of her mother's face, then turned and dragged her feet toward the hallway, reluctantly accepting banishment.

"I'm going to tell him she'll never be welcome in my house," Marynell continued. "In fact, I never want to see him again. Ever. He can't see the kids either."

"No."

"No, what?"

"You can't write a letter like that. You'd be sorry afterwards. He's our father and the children's grandfather, and he has a right to do what he wants with his life," Louise said with more conviction than she felt.

"But he shouldn't be allowed to be happy because our mother is dead." The end of Marynell's nose was red, her chin quivering.

Louise stared at the maps on the wall, at her father's pin in England. "We can't expect him to be lonely for the rest of his life just so we can continue to believe our parents had a perfect love," she said slowly, seeking reason as she formed her words. "Life isn't that simple. After all, you wouldn't be married to Jeffrey if Elise were still alive."

Marynell sat up straighter in her chair, her eyes narrowing. "Damn you for saying that! This isn't the same. Jeffrey wasn't sleeping with me while his wife was still alive. And when she was alive, he wasn't waiting around for her to die."

"Neither was Daddy," Louise barked back. "Mother's death was a tremendous shock to him. You know that."

Louise got up and walked to the stove. Her hands were shaking. Her voice had been too loud. "I'm sorry," she said, feeling the coffee pot. It was still warm. "I shouldn't have said that about Jeffrey."

She poured two cups of coffee and carried them back to table.

It was Marynell's turn to stare at the maps. Finally she sighed and took a sip of coffee. "Poor Mother, she was never happy, not really."

"I don't think that's true, and even if it was, I'm not sure we should blame Daddy. Sometimes people just get a second chance. He didn't plan it that way. Leave him alone, Marynell."

The coffee was terrible. Marynell had been experimenting with extenders again. Louise would rather have had one cup of real coffee than two of Marynell's concoctions. But her sister read every article about how to get around wartime shortages.

Maggie's voice was calling from the backyard. "Mommie, make them stop."

Louise rose and looked out the window over the sink. Matt and Peter were bombarding Eric and Maggie with green walnuts that had fallen from the neighbor's tree.

"You boys stop that right this minute, or you can't listen to your programs for a whole week."

The kids were getting impossible. Matt would be in first grade in the fall—and that should help some—but the twins would probably just squabble more when Matt wasn't around for Peter to play with. Where had she ever gotten the notion that twins were always devoted to each other?

Of course, part of the problem was their missing grandmother. It had taken Louise a while to realize that even after Elizabeth was all but chair-bound, she'd had a calming effect on the children, making them feel important by running errands for her, bragging about their artwork, taking an upset child into her lap, offering a haven from an angry mother or aunt, an abusive sibling or cousin. She would brush the children's hair in the morning and inspect their hands before meals—little things that had given structure to their lives.

Their mother's death had also changed the relationship between herself and her sister, Louise realized. They were often short with each other, still floundering to fill the void left by Elizabeth's passing.

And now their father's marriage would push them further apart. Louise was sad for them all.

The time had come for her and her sister's families to go their separate ways. With Mother's death and their father's marriage, they were really two families rather than one extended one.

Come home to us soon, Franklin, Louise thought, a wave of longing washing over her. She was ready to be a wife again, to have her husband at her table instead of her sister.

She and Franklin had been apart for more than three years. And Franklin's father, now an assistant chief of staff in the sprawling new Pentagon building in Washington, said the war in the Pacific would take another year, at least, maybe two. After the German defeat at the Battle of the Bulge, the war in Europe had turned for the Allies, but the other war seemed doomed to proceed island by island with a hideous cost in lives. The Japanese fought to the death.

Franklin had taken part in a landing on the Admiralty Islands in February and was still there, as far as Louise knew, although there had been another Allied landing at someplace called Hollandia. She hadn't had a letter in almost three weeks. The last one she received had been six weeks en route.

Fear was now part of her daily life. Whenever the doorbell rang, she jumped. Bad news came by telegrams delivered to front doors by old men or young boys.

Jeffrey was in Scotland, training. Still no combat. But his time would come when the Allies invaded Europe. According to the newspapers, the invasion was imminent. Great Britain was bulging at the seams with American and Canadian troops, ships and planes. Journalists were already calling it the greatest invasion of all time, predicting an incredible loss of life. Hitler would not surrender. He would lead his people over the edge of the precipice, taking as many Allied lives as possible with him.

Jeffrey had visited Eddie again in London. Louise wondered if he had known about the nurse.

Yes, she decided. Jeffrey had known. When Marynell had shared parts of her last letter, it hadn't sounded right. "Your father is well," but nothing of how much time they had spent together, what they had talked about, where they had eaten. Nothing about Eddie coping with a widower's grief.

Louise went back to the car for the rest of the groceries. When she came back to the kitchen, Marynell was gone, her half-full cup of coffee still on the table. Louise had to put the groceries away by herself.

She slammed cupboard doors. Damn it. She was angry, too. At her sister for going off to pout when the kitchen was a mess. At disgusting images of her father loving another woman. Chances were that Eddie had indeed been loving Nurse Martha for longer than five and a half months. Had he planned to leave Elizabeth when the war was over, or would he dutifully have come back to his wife, the British nurse a fond memory?

Louise picked up the photograph again. *So vibrant and full of life.* In other words, not like Elizabeth. She hated him for that. And understood.

She and Marynell avoided each other for the rest of the day. Louise fixed sandwiches for lunch, which Marynell skipped. The children were awful at dinner. Matt said the sausage looked like poo-poo, and the children refused to eat it. Pauline kicked Peter under the table, and when he retaliated, his milk got spilled. Eric whined because Marynell wouldn't let him have bread and butter until he'd taken a bite of green beans. Even Maggie's normally sunny disposition disappeared. "Make Matt stop looking at me," she demanded of her mother.

"He can look wherever he wants," Louise said.

With a smirk, Matt continued to stare bug-eyed at his younger female cousin.

"Matt, stop that," Louise said. "You're acting like a brat."

Marynell cast a hostile look in Louise's direction. Only *she* had the right to call her son a brat.

"Since I cleaned up after breakfast and did lunch alone, I think you should do the dishes," Louise said, heading for the front door. She already knew she'd put her children to bed early and read in bed. "Come on, kids. Let's go for a walk."

It was hard to sleep. Her father making love to another woman. Incomprehensible. She'd have to write to him. What a careful letter it would have to be. She couldn't possibly give her blessing—not yet. But she didn't want to lose her father, too.

That night, propped up in bed, she tried a few tentative lines:

"I won't pretend that I wasn't shocked at your news. And disheartened. I guess I needed for you to grieve endlessly for Mother to prove how much you loved her. But that is not what you needed.

"It will take a while for Marynell and me to grow accustomed to the idea that our father is married to a woman who is not our mother, a stranger. You must be patient with us."

Early the next morning, she heard Marynell in the bathroom. Louise stubbornly stayed in bed. Marynell could have her coffee alone.

But she had already put on her robe when the bedroom door flew open. "On the radio," Marynell said wide-eyed. "The invasion."

The sisters rushed downstairs to the living room and held hands tightly as they listened. An invasion of the Normandy coast. An estimated landing force of one hundred seventy-five thousand. Nine thousand ships and smaller crafts. Eleven thousand airplanes. Choppy seas. Swamped boats. Fifty-mile front. The First Army landed on both sides of the Vire River.

"All those men," Marynell whispered. "Does God even know he's there?"

Louise understood. Jeffrey seemed expendable, only a speck in a giant wave. It seemed wrong to pray for one life over all the rest.

"I wonder if he's thinking about me," Marynell said.

"I know that he is," Louise said. "You and the boys."

Jeffrey had taken communion the night before. He had his doubts about organized religion but kneeling there in front of the chaplain, taking the wafer on his tongue, sipping the wine had seemed an appropriate thing to do on the night before battle.

Since Elise's accident, he had avoided thinking about what happened after death. He didn't know if his first wife was in heaven. He didn't know if there was anything after death but decay, but now, alone with his thoughts in the bobbing landing craft, he found himself wondering if there was anything to it. What sort of afterlife did faith offer? Clouds and choirs of angels? Did things ever get dirty or broken? It all seemed like a fairy tale made up for the comfort of children.

He was less afraid of death—even the absolute death he half-expected—than he thought he would be. All around him, men were vomiting over the side from seasickness and fear, but Jeffrey's stomach was steady. And his head. He knew he wouldn't run and hide. He hoped the howitzers would make it ashore, that he and his men could do their part as Americans, as protectors of freedom. He might have lost his belief in war, but he believed in stopping Hitler. He would do his damnedest; then he wanted to put it behind him. No more uniforms, military discipline, scrambling for rank, training for war. If he made it through the war, he wanted a peaceful life. On a farm maybe. His boys could learn to ride horses and cut hay. Or they could live in New York and go to museums on Sunday afternoons. Or in a normal little town with old men sitting in the square. A river would be nice for fishing. He could teach school. Marynell, too. They'd get by just fine.

He closed his eyes and recreated the communion in his mind, tasting the wine through the salt of the sea air, feeling the texture of the wafer on his tongue. He swore on the body and the blood of Christ that he would end his military career. *Roosters at sunrise instead of bugles, so help me God.*

CHAPTER

NINETEEN

"Collect call from Major Washburn." The operator's voice was flat. Routine.

"Yes. Oh, my, yes!" Louise said. "Matt, run out back and get your mother. Your daddy's on the phone."

With a war whoop, Matt went tearing through the kitchen, the screen door slamming as he raced into the yard. "Mom, Mom, it's Dad! On the phone!"

"Marynell?" Jeffrey's voice across the static of miles. Louise felt goose flesh prickling on her arms, tears in her eyes.

"No, this is Louise. Marynell will be right here. Oh, my God, Jeffrey! Where are you? Are you okay?"

"I'm in New York. Just got off the ship a few minutes ago and fought my way to a telephone. Everyone else has the same idea."

The screen door slammed again. "She's coming now. I'm so happy, Jeffrey. So happy."

Marynell was wide-eyed, a clothespin still in her hand. She grabbed the phone. "Jeffrey. Is it really you?"

All the children were in the hallway now. Matt was pulling on his mother's arm. "Let me talk. Let me talk."

Louise sat on the stairs, and Maggie instantly crawled in her lap. "Matt and Eric's daddy is coming home," Louise explained. A daddy. Her children's only concept of a daddy came from their storybooks.

"Daddy? When are you coming?" Matt said, his voice trembling with excitement. "I'm big now. I can ride a bike. How many Germans did you kill?"

Marynell wrestled the phone away from her son. "I love you, honey. This is the happiest day of my life. Wait until you see Eric. He's wonderful. And Matt's half-grown. Yes. Call me as soon as you know when, and I'll be there. Oh, God yes, I'll be there. I love you so much."

Marynell grabbed Louise's hands and pulled her to her feet and spun with her round and round in the entry hall. "He'll be here in a week or less. He's coming home. Oh, dear God, my Jeffrey's coming home!"

Marynell stopped long enough to grab Matt's hand. The three of them spun around. Finally all seven of them were skipping around the hallway chanting "Jeffrey's coming home!" to the tune of "Farmer in the Dell."

"Hi, ho the dario, Jeffrey's coming home!"

Marynell stopped abruptly. "Oh, my God. Do you realize I've got to lose five pounds, do something about my hair, figure out what to wear, cook a banquet—all in less than a week?"

"I'll take care of the banquet," Louise said. "Then I think you and your husband should check in to a hotel for a few days. I'll hold down the home front."

Marynell nodded gratefully. "And I'll do the same for you when Franklin comes home."

She scooped down and grabbed three-year-old Eric in her arms. "Finally, my precious lamb, you're going to get a daddy. What in the world will I wear, Sis? Let's splurge on a roast if we can find one. And make him an apple pie. Except there's no sugar. Can we use honey to make a pie?"

Jeffrey should see Marynell now, Louise thought. If ever a human being looked radiantly in love, it was her sister. Louise felt a strange mixture of joy and jealousy. She and her sister had belonged to each other since Jeffrey left two and a half years ago, and now he was coming back to reclaim his wife.

Soon Franklin would return.

Louise looked forward to his homecoming with excitement and not a little trepidation. She had changed. She wondered about Franklin.

But she was anxious for her family to begin their new life. And she needed to be held and loved, to be a wife as well as a mother.

She closed her eyes, stealing a moment of anticipation. *Soon.*

And there in the middle of their celebration, she felt a stab of sexual desire.

The following Sunday, Marynell was weak with nervousness as she and her two sons left for the railroad station.

"You look beautiful," Louise assured her. "You'll be the best-looking woman there."

Marynell checked her image in the hall mirror. Her hat looked perky and her suit smart, but her face was pale and tight. As she pulled on her gloves, she forced a practice smile. "I wasn't this nervous when I got married," she admitted.

"Come on, boys," she said, straightening Matt's tie. "It's time for the next chapter."

Marynell almost didn't recognize Jeffrey. He was skinny, his hair thinning, his face different. They were surrounded by a sea of excited, crying, embracing people. The boys will always remember this, Marynell thought, the day their daddy came home from war. Happiness swelled up inside of her and made it hard to breathe, hard to talk.

Marynell navigated seven-year-old Matt into his father's arms for the first hug. Then she handed him Eric. Jeffrey's composure broke. His sons. His wife. His family. He had lived to come home to them. "Oh, God, Marynell, you're all so beautiful."

Eric was all eyes as his mythical father kissed him and cried real tears. Matt was sobbing, not even trying to be a big boy.

Then with Eric on one arm and Matt clinging, Jeffrey managed to slip his other arm around his wife. The eyes that looked down at her were overflowing with love. Marynell lifted her face to be kissed. His lips were tender beyond belief. It was the sweetest kiss of a lifetime.

"Welcome home, my beloved husband. Welcome home."

• • •

It was October before the homecoming call came from Franklin, two months after the first atom bomb had been dropped on Hiroshima with the second three days later at Nagasaki.

First there had been the pictures of the pitiful, wasted bodies of liberated American prisoners of war in the Philippines. Then the unfathomable horror of pictures taken at the liberated Nazi death camps. And now pictures of the hideously burned in Japan. Rotting flesh falling from living bodies. Over a hundred thousand killed with one bomb. Incomprehensible. One felt guilty to be alive, not to have suffered horrors beyond belief, embarrassed to be human.

Louise consoled herself that surely this was the end of war. Surely. If mankind had not learned the futility of war by now, the race was doomed.

After the atomic bombs, Japan had capitulated at once. All that death and suffering meant her husband was coming home.

Jeffrey had already reported for duty at Fort Bliss in the southwestern corner of the state. Marynell, her sons and Mister Dog were gone. And the letter had arrived from her father telling her he would not be coming back to the States but would stay in England with his new wife. They would live in the south on the channel—in a village near Hastings, and after he had tended to certification, he would open a small practice. Martha would be his nurse.

For weeks before Franklin's call came, Louise heart had jumped every time the phone rang. Finally, when there was a man's voice saying her name, she couldn't believe it was really him. His voice was familiar, yet different. Older. And not as excited as Jeffrey had sounded.

"Louise, are you there? It's Franklin."

"My darling, is it really you? Where are you? Are you all right? When can you come home?"

Franklin was laughing. That was better. "Hey, one question at a time." Louise laughed, too. Her Franklin was safe and would be coming home to her.

He would fly into Dallas in three days. He wanted her to meet him there for a second honeymoon.

Marynell was gone, and she'd have to find a sitter, but Louise didn't hesitate. "Oh, yes. That would be wonderful. I can hardly wait to hold you, to kiss you. I've missed you so."

The next day she went shopping, marching through downtown department stores with her three children, searching for replacements for her worn-out underwear. She felt foolish in a dressing room with three children as she tried on bras and slips, but they were making a day of it, including lunch at the Woolworth's soda fountain with a half dollar apiece to spend afterwards. And the children were getting new underwear, too, and pajamas. Suddenly it mattered how they all looked.

Reluctantly, Louise passed up satin and lace lingerie for more practical cotton. A mother of three just didn't seem a proper candidate for anything else, but she got the prettiest of the cotton bras and did succumb to one really lovely pink satin slip with ecru lace to wear under the beautiful pale pink suit she had bought months ago in anticipation of this reunion. And there was a smart little pink hat in the box on her closet shelf along with a pair of patent pumps still in their box. She would be all brand new for the first time since her marriage.

That night after the children were in bed, she took the white nightgown that Franklin had given her for her twentieth birthday from the bottom drawer of her dresser and tried it on. The woman who stared from her dresser mirror wasn't suited to a Victorian nightgown. She had no time for long hair and kept hers conveniently short. She'd given up protecting her skin from the Texas sun, and during long hours of gardening her face and arms had freckled and turned brown. Her hands were work-worn, their nails clipped short.

Louise took off the nightgown and examined her nude body. The stretch marks on her belly and breasts had narrowed and faded to pale silver. After nursing three babies, her breasts were no longer high and girlish. Her nipples were longer, browner than before. Her waist was less slim, but her arms and legs were firm and muscled. A girl's body no longer but a fine woman's body, and she was proud of it.

She folded the nightgown and put it back in the drawer. She didn't want to play the snow-white virgin anymore.

She had been married seven years—four of those years spent without her husband. She was not the same young, innocent girl he had married, but he would have to learn that for himself.

"I want another baby," Louise said in the darkness when his breathing had calmed. Her head was on his shoulder, her body cradled in an encircling arm. Even at this late hour, sounds of big-city traffic drifted up through the open fifth-floor hotel window, strange after years of the sleepy neighborhood in San Antonio.

"Why?"

"You never had a chance to enjoy babyhood with the other three, and you weren't with me for their birth. I think it would be good for us all—a family project for a family that needs to remake itself. And I want one more. I can't explain why."

"It's okay. You don't have to. I'd be proud to make you pregnant again."

They lay quietly for a time, then she felt his penis already stirring against her leg. Yes, Louise thought, he wanted to make her pregnant, to reclaim her. The idea aroused him.

She sat up and pulled the gown from her body, then lay back on the pillow and opened her arms. "Make love to me again, my husband. I've missed you so very much."

She loved the male feel of him, the smell of him, the taste of his kisses, the sound of his voice.

He talked to her while he made love, telling how thoughts of her had kept him going, kept him alive, given him a reason to live. How she was his center, his life, how he would die without her.

Louise could not believe such words. Never had she loved him more. He needed her.

He lost his erection as he explained to her in the darkness that he had fought bravely and well, that he had faced his own fear and won. Once his men had cursed him for refusing to retreat, and another time for leaving behind two dying men. Every time he had killed a man, he had done it for her and the children.

Louise thought of how her mother's cats used to bring tributes of death—mice, birds, lizards, even baby rabbits. Elizabeth never knew how to react. The cat was honoring her, but its methods were disturbing.

At the railroad station when Franklin had stepped from the train—a handsome officer with rows of ribbons on his broad chest—she had been overcome with pride. Her brave warrior was returning to her, thinner, weathered, older, a hero. Her knees had turned weak.

At the hotel restaurant, the mâitre d' and waiters kowtowed. Major this and major that. Again, she had felt elevated with the pride of being married to him.

"Yes, I want to put another baby in you," he was saying fiercely. "God, yes."

And he was hard again, pushing, almost savagely, not the Franklin of old. Louise arched herself toward him, willing her body to open, begging for the feeling she wanted desperately to come. He had killed for her. He needed her. He loved her. Her body was hungry.

She had almost reached that special place when he began calling out her name over and over, distracting her, and then became a gasping, dead weight on her body.

The feelings of open, raw desire mingled with the profound relief of having pleased her beloved husband produced not an orgasm, exactly, but rather a release from desire.

Other nights, when she was less nervous, there would be more. She knew that. But she wondered if a part of her would always be empty.

During the years they were apart, she had often made Franklin the lover in her fantasies, but now that he was back at her side, now that they had once again made love, she let go of the dream. She and Franklin were husband and wife, not lovers. And passion seemed the stuff of dreams.

She was grateful to the depths of her soul that he had returned to them. She loved him almost as much as she loved her children. Maybe that was how she loved him, as she would a child, a love beyond questioning.

How long would it take her to get pregnant? Louise wondered, touching her belly. She hoped she was already. A new baby. She felt a smile pulling on her lips. This baby was going to make her happier than the others. She already knew that. She was older, more accomplished at motherhood, calmer.

Louise buried her face against her husband's warm neck. "I love you," she whispered to his sleeping form. In the night, she woke often to touch him and listen to him breathe.

Book Three

★ ★ ★

1946–1954

CHAPTER

TWENTY

He wanted to discuss it again. Ever since they'd visited his family in Racine, Jeffrey had been exploring the idea, talking long-distance to his brother, making long lists of figures in a ledger, trying to prepare Marynell.

He had begun his new assignment as an instructor in the Air Defense Artillery School at sprawling Fort Bliss, Texas, near El Paso. Even though he said he liked teaching, Jeffrey was restless. He kept bringing up "the future."

Marynell wanted to put her fingers in her ears and block out his words. He couldn't be serious, she said. When he put a little distance between himself and the war, he'd realize how foolish he was being, how much he would be throwing away. My God, he was a West Pointer. He had served well in France and Germany. The Army owed him.

She stacked the plates and carried them to the kitchen. Resign his commission? Become a civilian? The idea struck her with dread. He wanted to buy a car dealership in Wisconsin with his brother, to risk their savings and future and become a car salesman!

"I'm just not cut out for an Army career," he said, following her into the kitchen carrying the meat platter.

"Why not? It's what you were educated for. It's what I thought I was getting when I married you." She put soap in the dishpan and turned on the hot water.

"Is it that important to you?"

"Yes, God damn it!" she said, turning to face him. "I don't want to be the wife of a car salesman. I want to be the wife of an Army officer. And think of your sons. God, Jeffrey, they're so proud to be the sons of a major. Yes, it makes a big difference. As an officer you're special. Selling cars, you're ordinary—just an ordinary guy in a sport coat, boot-licking to get ahead."

"And you think I don't boot-lick in the Army?" He was still holding the meat platter. Marynell took it from him.

"That's different. It's not to get someone to buy something. It's discipline, orders, tradition."

Jeffrey sighed. "Maybe you should join the Women's Army Corps. You're more suited to the military than I am."

"I'm suited to being the wife of an officer," she said, wrapping the leftover meat in waxed paper. "It's all I ever wanted to be. It's the only life I've ever known. I can't bear the thought of someday being at Franklin's promotion ceremony when he gets his first star, with you standing there in a civilian suit. Think how you'd feel."

"I'd feel happy for Franklin." Jeffrey thrust his hands in the pockets of his fatigue trousers and leaned against the counter. He was still wearing his boots, but he had removed his fatigue jacket, leaving his T-shirt and dog tags. He was still too thin. "Hell, Marynell, if I'm in some sort of competition with Franklin, I've already lost the race. I was two years ahead of him at the Point, and already he's ahead of me on the promotion ladder. I'm not brilliant. I wasn't the protégé of a national hero. And I've spent the last two and a half years discovering I don't like war."

"The war is over."

"For now. But we train for it every day. I teach men how to conduct one. War is the Army's business. Couldn't you love me at all if I was just a regular businessman? Or a schoolteacher? I still think about that sometimes—maybe I could go to graduate school and teach at a college."

"Silly boy. Of course, I'd love you no matter what you did," Marynell said and gave him a reassuring hug and peck. But deep down she wasn't so sure. This was going to be a bitter pill to swallow if he followed through with this car idea. She wanted the dignity of military life. And order—to know what was expected of you and what the rewards would be.

She wanted to strive and work hard, to do her part to propel Jeffrey along as a successful officer, to share with him the ultimate reward, when she stood by his side at the ceremony promoting him to brigadier general. The general and his lady. Their handsome sons, grown by then and perhaps themselves in uniform, to complete the family picture. She would be wearing a fur stole. A smart suit. Lizard pumps with matching bag. Impeccable, regal, like the Duchess of Windsor. Or Franklin's mother. Marynell lived her life for that moment.

Louise would have it someday. Marynell couldn't bear for her sister to have it and not herself. She knew she was being petty, but she couldn't help it.

So she and Jeffrey arrived at a compromise of sorts. He would stay in for a few more years in order to give the postwar Army a chance, but for his next assignment he would volunteer for an ROTC assignment at a college or university. In the meantime, they would enjoy their nice quarters at Fort Bliss, buy the boys a horse, go fishing in New Mexico.

Marynell congratulated herself on handling the crisis and threw herself back into the life of an Army wife. She was elected vice president in charge of fund-raising for the wives' club. She did sit-down dinners with style in spite of her budget. She extended her limited wardrobe with carefully chosen accessories, decorated economically by making curtains and bedspreads and found an elderly Mexican man who refinished some marvelous secondhand furniture for next to nothing. She thought it unfair that Matt got new clothes and Eric got hand-me-downs, but both boys always went off to school clean, pressed and shined. She charmed ranking officers and their wives with equal flair and took pride in the fact that Major Washburn's wife was much admired. Once or twice a month, she and Jeffrey went dancing at Fort Bliss's handsome officers' club. Jeffrey still danced beautifully, and in spite of his thinning hair was always as handsome as any man on the floor. Marynell made certain he asked the appropriate officers' wives to dance but not so much that she didn't have time with him. When the music was romantic and the lights dim, he still got an erection against her tummy. She liked that and whispered in his ear what they would do when they got home.

The secret to living well was orderliness. Marynell liked to look at her carefully kept calendar and know just what lay ahead. She liked to open a drawer and know precisely what was inside. She liked to reach for her husband in the night and know exactly what his response would be.

When they were growing up, Louise had been meticulously neat, Marynell haphazard. But now Marynell liked the hangers in the closet all turned the same way, pans with polished copper bottoms, freshly waxed floors. Jeffrey teased her that she worked harder than the Mexican woman who came in once a week. It was true. Marynell could clean a whole lot better than Benita.

Only her relationship with her children was sometimes a bit untidy. She hated losing her temper and raising her voice, but their bickering drove her crazy. And Matt was starting to resist her hugs and kisses. She'd always tried to be as affectionate with him as she was with Eric.

But even things with the boys had improved since Jeffrey had returned. Matt and Eric were nicer children with a father in the house. Marynell watched for signs of favoritism on Jeffrey's part. Did he love *their* son as much as he loved Matt? Did he think of Elise every time he looked at Matt? But he seemed equally devoted to both boys. The Washburns did family well.

Before sex, Marynell sometimes had an attack of anxiety and had to concentrate at calming herself, but she'd actually learned to make her heart slow down, her breathing even out. It was like giving a speech: a period of stage fright had to be endured, but once you got into the flow of things, it could be fun, even euphoric during moments of brilliance. When she drove past the gatehouse at the entrance to the post, she averted her eyes from the MPs standing guard there, but that was mostly out of habit.

Feeling a bit sorry for herself, Louise waved good-bye as the car backed out of the driveway. She had cooked the food and packed the picnic basket, and she would have to bake the pies from the blackberries they picked, but she would miss the excursion itself.

The baby was sick again.

Louise went into her quiet house and tiptoed into the dining room to check on Andy. She had set up his playpen in a patch of morning sunshine, and he'd been napping earlier. But he was sitting up now, holding his one-eared teddy bear, waiting for her.

Andy seldom cried. Such a patient little boy, more like his sister Maggie than the twins. His diaper was wet, his nose stopped up, his body hot with fever, but he just sat there waiting, trusting that his mother would come and make him comfortable.

Louise carried him to the cot in the downstairs bedroom. Designed for the live-in maids of a bygone era, the room served as Louise's sewing and ironing room and as a daytime changing room for Andy.

"Poor little lamb," Louise cooed as she cleaned out his nose. He whimpered and pulled away. If only he could blow, she thought. His breathing was still raspy, but at least he wasn't coughing as much. It was his fever that concerned her the most. He'd had two febrile convulsions—one at six months, the other only a week ago. Louise couldn't think of them without a stab of apprehension.

Andy lay quietly while she changed his diaper. He was so scrawny she could count his ribs.

"It's just you and me this afternoon, sweetheart. We get to do laundry, and maybe we can sew your bear's ear back on. I found it under your crib. Then I bet you'd like a little rocking while Mommie reads her new mystery."

She didn't really like mysteries, but they were quick, and she didn't have to feel happy or sad, just entertained. She never even bothered guessing whodunit and was content to let the author do all the thinking.

Louise stretched out on the narrow cot beside her baby. Andy scrambled to a sitting position and began patting her cheeks. "You love your old mom, don't you, honey?"

Andy answered in a series of nonsense syllables, complete with inflection. He showed no signs of walking or even crawling, but Louise decided he would probably talk early.

This fourth baby had in no way fulfilled the fantasies in which she had indulged herself before he was born. Andy had arrived early and weighed only five-and-a-half pounds. Louise's labor had lasted less than three hours, and she and Franklin had barely made it to the post hospital in time. Louise had been grateful and disappointed at the same time. She didn't suffer, but Franklin would never understand how much she had endured with the birth of the twins and with Maggie. She could never tell him except in the vaguest of terms, just like he never talked about the war in any meaningful way. And when Louise thought about all the other suffering in the world, much of which her husband had witnessed firsthand, birthing babies seemed inconsequential.

At least he'd been there with her this time, having returned only the night before from six weeks of paratrooper training at Fort Benning, Georgia. But he didn't weep with happiness. Neither did she.

The baby had not made their family closer. Rather, he had divided them, with Franklin and the older children on one side of an invisible line and herself and Andy on the other. Franklin did not know how to relate to a sickly infant and invested his fathering in his three robust youngsters, who had very quickly adapted to the presence of a father in their lives. When the five o'clock cannon sounded at retreat each afternoon, they raced to sit on the top step of the front porch and await his homecoming.

Franklin listened to the twins read from their first-grade readers, and he would patiently read stories to the three of them, but he refused to oversee the children's mindless card games. Louise still had to Go Fish and be the Old Maid.

Franklin took the twins and Maggie horseback riding and to parades. They watched as his battalion had its monthly parachute jump, trying to decide which of the hundreds of paratroopers strewn across the sky was their daddy. When Franklin got out his shoeshining gear, they ran to get their own shoes and shined with him. For him, they cleaned their room every Saturday morning and "stood inspection," even Maggie who was almost six. They adored Franklin and followed him around like little puppies. For a word of praise from their father, they cleaned their plates at mealtime. To

Franklin, they said "Yes, sir" and "No, sir." To her they said, "Hey, Mom."

Louise seldom had any time alone with her husband until after the children were tucked into bed. Then she and Franklin usually listened to the radio, read for a while and turned out the lights. Often, they had pleasant if dutiful sex. She felt as though they were replaying a script written for her parents.

Before Andy's birth, "the new baby" had been a topic of great discussion. The children liked putting their hands on Louise's belly to feel the movement there and asked if the baby could hear what they said, if the baby cried inside her, what the baby ate. But after Andy was born, nobody showed much interest in the tiny, sickly infant who took all of Louise's time. Franklin often seemed to resent the baby. He had wanted her to hire a sitter for the afternoon and go with them on the picnic. Maybe she should have. Franklin had been so pleased with himself when he came home to report the blackberries he'd found growing on the Fort Bragg reservation. All week, they'd planned to go blackberry picking.

More and more, she and Andy were left alone while the rest of the family went off together. Louise wanted to go with them, but what if Andy had another convulsion? What if the sitter forgot his medicine? What if he cried for Mommie?

Franklin was planning a trip to Williamsburg before school started. Already, Louise worried that Andy would be too sick to go. Franklin would be annoyed. She wondered if he and the other children would go on without her and Andy.

No, Andy had not changed their family for the better. She worried about him constantly. One of the doctors had used the ominous phrase "failure to thrive," when talking about him during one of his visits to the outpatient clinic.

Yet Andy was special. He was delicately beautiful, his hair fair and fine. His eyes were hazel like the other children's but seemed oversized for his narrow little face. His skin was so thin that blue veins showed through on his forehead.

Louise loved him fiercely. So much that it scared her. She almost resented her other children at times because they were so healthy, so robust, as if they had stolen away those things from her womb before it could produce Andy.

But then, she loved them all, and her family loved her. The children took her for granted, but they still came to her when they were sick or hurt, and they still wanted her hugs and kisses at night after their prayers. "You forgot to say you loved me," Peter had called after her last night.

Louise went back and cradled him and said, "Of course, I love you. You are the best seven-year-old boy in the entire world."

"What if I was a terrible boy like dumb Ralph in my room at school?"

"I would still love you. Mothers love their children no matter what. I'm just lucky that you happen to be the best."

"Am I the best seven-year-old girl?" Pauline called from the girls' room across the hall.

Louise kissed Peter again and went to assure Pauline that she was the best seven-year-old girl, then to tell Maggie that she was the best almost six-year-old girl.

"And Andy is the best baby," she added.

"But he's sick all the time," Maggie said.

"He can't help that," Louise said. "Pretty soon he'll be better, and he'll need his big brother and sisters to take him for walks and push him in the swing."

Louise began her preparations for their Williamsburg trip a week early, getting clothes laundered and ironed, making arrangements for a neighbor's child to gather the newspapers and mail, getting Peter's hair cut, getting the car serviced and the suitcases packed.

Franklin wanted to get an early start, and Louise was dressed, had packed a basket of snacks and had breakfast ready by six. While she cleaned up the kitchen, Franklin supervised making the beds and the children getting dressed. Then suddenly the house was quiet.

She knew they were waiting in the station wagon. Quickly, she did her checking—stove, fans, cellar door, back door, the upstairs toilet that sometimes ran.

She paused, going over her mental list. The horn sounded from the alley. Just lightly. A reminder. They were all waiting.

Louise grabbed her purse, then raced back upstairs for some pillows. The children slept better in the car with pillows.

The motor was already running. Franklin didn't look at her as she slid into the front seat. "You've known for days I planned to leave at zero-seven-hundred hours."

Louise felt a flash of anger. *Damn him!*

She read the children a couple of stories. Peter and Pauline played cards. Maggie said it wasn't fair for them to get to sit in the back and insisted Louise make them let her play.

Andy had fallen asleep with his head in Louise's lap and the other children were dozing in the back before Louise spoke to Franklin. "I want you to stop doing that."

"What?" he asked.

"Putting the children in the car and waiting for me with the motor running. And don't ever honk the horn at me again." She said each word carefully, not disguising her anger.

Franklin shrugged his shoulders in an exasperated gesture.

The silence grew heavy, but she would make him endure it for a while. Not long, though. Family vacations were stressful enough. By lunchtime, she'd have to say something cheerful to neutralize the tension. That was their pattern. Anything would do. *Look at that beautiful house! Did he think the children should take piano lessons?* And she would need to find an excuse to pat him or touch his hand. Whether he stopped waiting for her in the car with the motor running—only time would tell.

With no small amount of trepidation, Eddie came to visit that fall, first to Fort Bliss to see Marynell and her family, then to Fort Bragg for a week with Louise and her brood, who would be leaving for Japan before the end of the year.

Marynell had been polite to Martha but did not return her hug of greeting nor the one offered in departure. And Martha's offers to help out in the kitchen were politely declined.

Jeffrey took them on an excursion to Juarez and one into the national park. Eddie sensed the tension between him and Marynell. He could see it when Jeffrey disciplined Eric for his smart mouth—when he told Marynell that, no, he was not going to volunteer for the post athletic council even if it was one of the general's pet projects.

In private, Marynell referred several times to the fact that Franklin had been promoted to major a full year before Jeffrey. "He'll probably be a lieutenant colonel before the year is out. Of course, it does help to have a three-star general for a father. They take care of their own."

"Honey, Franklin's a dedicated officer, and I think any laurels he earns are deserved. At this point in his career, I suspect he has to be twice as good as the competition just because his father *is* General Cravens, and no one wants to be accused of favoritism. Jeffrey's just not as comfortable in a military career as Franklin, and it shows."

Marynell's mouth looked pinched. She turned back to the sink. "The boys are waiting for you. You promised to play a game with them," she said in dismissal.

Matt insisted on Monopoly. Eric wanted checkers.

"He cheats at Monopoly," Eric insisted, " 'cause I'm littler and can't add as good as him."

"I don't either cheat," Matt said indignantly. "You're just stupid, that's all."

"I'll tell you what, let's play Chinese checkers instead," Eddie suggested brightly. "I haven't played in years."

Matt scowled a bit, then grinned at his grandfather. "That's what they call a compromise, isn't it? We learned about that in school."

Eddie mussed his hair. "That's right, son, like if you boys want to stay up until ten and your mom says eight and you all three agree on nine." Eddie began putting the marbles on the board. "You know, I used to play this with your mother and your aunt Louise when they were little girls."

"Did my real grandmother play with you?" Eric asked. "Grandmother Elizabeth?"

"Sometimes, but she preferred reading to the girls. I did most of the game playing."

"Matt's got another grandmother, but he's only seen her once."

"Twice," Matt corrected.

"Yeah, but you were a baby the first time and don't remember. Mom said so. She said that Grandmother Elizabeth was the nicest lady in the whole world and that I would have loved her a lot if she hadn't died."

Matt looked at his grandfather. "I think Grandma Martha is a nice lady. Think she'd like to play with us?"

Eddie found himself drawn more to his stepgrandson than to Eric. Of course, Matt did pay more attention to his granddad, following him around, asking questions about England, wanting to know if he'd ever seen the king, if he ever cut people open.

Martha accepted Matt's invitation to join their game. Then Marynell and Jeffrey played a round. Marynell would warn Eric with her eyes when he was about to make a bad move.

Later, Eddie went upstairs with Marynell to tuck the boys in for the night. She hugged and kissed both boys, heard their prayers.

"They're good kids, honey," he told her. "You're doing a fine job with them."

"I wish Mother could see how they've grown. Eric doesn't even remember her. He has her eyes, you know."

"Yes, I noticed. Beautiful eyes."

"Do you think about her at all?" Her tone was challenging.

Eddie heard himself sigh. "Of course, I think about her, Marynell, just like you do."

With four children, Louise's household was incredibly busy. So many groceries, so much cooking, laundry, activity, noise. Things were always getting spilled, broken, torn. Children were forever getting comforted, reprimanded or praised. Amazing. Louise would have household help in Japan, she told him. A laundress *and* a maid!

Eddie felt like hugging Louise that first night when she accepted Martha's offer to make the salad. The twins started imitating her British accent, much to everyone's amusement. Maggie and Andy sat in her lap. Even Franklin was nice.

Franklin was more relaxed, less jealous about having his wife's relatives visit than he had been that time at Fort Sill. But he still needed to make all the decisions, and Louise still apologized too much—when she hadn't cooked enough potatoes, when the sugar bowl was empty, when she had forgotten to take his shoes to be repaired. Only now there was a tightness about her mouth, and sometimes she challenged Franklin. His sunglasses were wherever he had left them. She would fold the laundry as soon as she had time.

Eddie's older granddaughter, Pauline, was plain as a mud hen but affectionate and bright. "Tell us about the dinosaur on London Bridge," she insisted.

Eddie was pleased the twins remembered the stories from his wartime letters. Martha had a hard time keeping a straight face as he made up elaborate stories about bears who were nursemaids and kitty cats held captive in the Tower of London. Pauline was forever interrupting, though, telling him how *she* thought the story should go.

Peter, as beautiful as Pauline was plain, was beginning to figure out that his twin was cleverer than he was, but he seemed willing to let her take the lead—most of the time. She decided what game was to be played, who got what picture in the coloring book.

Maggie, with her reddish hair and freckles, was a charming child, who understood her own feminine powers even at six. At every opportunity, she held her granddaddy's hand and insisted on sitting by him at dinner. "I like you better than our other granddaddy," she whispered. "He's real nice, but he doesn't tell stories."

Then there was Andy, his mother's heart, all but ignored by his siblings. So delicate. Eddie wanted to cry whenever he held him. Eddie made him the hero of one of his stories. When Andy grew up, he helped Superman save the Americans from a Martian invasion. The other children weren't impressed. "There aren't any people on Mars," Pauline insisted.

"Well, there isn't any Superman either. It's just a story," Eddie said defensively.

Franklin was natural and loving with his three older children. With Andy, he was forced, and would relinquish him to his mother at first excuse. Eddie could sense Franklin's puzzlement at his youngest child. Everything else in his life had gone as planned—until Andy. Franklin was like Marynell. He needed for life to follow a plan.

Eddie cried when he left. So did Louise. And the children. "When are you coming back, Granddaddy?" they kept asking him. He said "Soon," but he knew it would probably be years before he saw them all again.

"Martha's nice," Louise whispered in his ear. He hugged her one last time and thought his heart would break.

"Is life with me worth the price you have paid?" Martha asked as they winged their way back across the Atlantic.

Eddie took his second wife's plump hand to hold. "Yes, dear girl, it is. I miss my daughters, and I would have been a terrific grandfather, but you're the comfort of my waning years."

It was true. Martha was warm and witty and wise. She knew how to laugh and enjoy life. She would go on a trip at the drop of a hat and loved to tease, to play jokes on him. And she mothered him. That was the best part, being mothered. He had never encouraged that in Elizabeth. Although he had been more genial, less stern than Franklin, he had been too much like his son-in-law—always the daddy, even to his wife. That had been a mistake. Eddie knew that now.

CHAPTER

TWENTY-ONE

The distant sound of sleigh bells drifted across the crisp air, and the American children who were gathered in front of the school started shushing one another. The Japanese children stood quietly in two careful rows on the other side of the flag pole.

Yes, it was definitely sleigh bells.

"There," an excited voice called. "It's him." And sure enough, coming from behind the general's quarters at the head of the parkway was a primitive wooden sleigh pulled by a pair of skinny white mules, and inside were a red-clad Santa Claus and two helpers dressed in green. The children shaded their eyes against the sun's glare on the brilliantly white snow. Santa Claus had found them, even in this northernmost American outpost of Occupied Japan.

Major Mike Williams, standing next to Louise, leaned close and whispered, "It was the closest I could come to a 'miniature sleigh and eight tiny reindeer.'"

"I think you've done a splendid job," Louise said. "I thought he'd probably have to arrive in a jeep. Where'd you find the sleigh?"

"My houseboy's uncle uses it to haul wood down from the lower slopes. I love Santa's suit," the sandy-haired major added. "I'm sure it's the first time he's come attired in red silk."

"The flannel I ordered from the Sears and Roebuck catalog never came," Louise explained, "and silk was the only red fabric I could find. The Japanese seamstress couldn't believe it either—or the dimensions I gave her."

Louise nodded to the leader of the hastily assembled band standing on the schoolhouse steps, and a jazzy rendition of "Santa Claus Is Coming to Town" rang out across the snow-covered school ground. The band, composed of volunteers from Franklin's battalion, boasting two harmonicas, a saxophone, an accordion and a fiddle, had been recruited by Major Williams, who was Franklin's executive officer. The post commandant had appointed the major president of the school board. It struck Louise as a rather peculiar choice since he was the only unmarried field-grade officer on their tiny military outpost. Louise had been "invited" to be the board secretary.

Standing with them on the front steps were the kindergarten teacher who also served as principal of Camp Younghans Children's School, the director of the Japanese orphanage whose children were their guests today and a Japanese interpreter. Both the director and interpreter were formally dressed in cutaway coats that had seen better days.

As the sleigh drew near, the American children sang along in high, excited voices. The Japanese orphans watched the procedures with solemn faces and runny noses, which they periodically wiped on the sleeves of their quilted jackets. Runny noses seemed as inevitable for Japanese children as black hair and brown eyes. Inadequate diet and cold houses, Louise supposed. Louise looked over to where her four children were standing. Peter and Pauline were unsuccessfully attempting to look blasé as they sang. Now eight and a half and in the third grade, the twins had discovered the truth about Santa and were facing their first Christmas as nonbelievers. Louise had made them promise not to tell the younger children—at school and at home. Maggie was clapping her hands and jumping up and down as she gleefully sang out the words. Just seven, Maggie was two years behind the twins in school and still very much a believer. Andy didn't know the verses, but he joined in on the chorus, his little face full of wonder. At two and a half, Andy was the perfect age for Christmas magic, and Santa had really come today, just like Mommie had promised.

Pauline came up the steps and pulled on Louise's sleeve. Louise bent over. "It's really Sergeant Bynum, isn't' it?" Pauline whispered in her mother's ear.

Sergeant Bynum ran a mess in Franklin's battalion and was by far the most portly member of their small military community.

"You think so?" Louise whispered back. "I thought it was Santa Claus."

"If Sergeant Bynum isn't dressed up in that suit, why isn't he playing his horn in the band?" Pauline asked, still whispering.

"Maybe he's busy making goodies for the party."

Pauline looked skeptical and went back to stand with her brothers and sister. With an impatient gesture, she pulled Andy's cap down over his ears, then reached for his mittened hand. Maggie noticed and grabbed his other one. Pauline had become quite the little mother of late, albeit an impatient one who referred to Andy as her "stupid little brother." But at least she didn't ignore him anymore. Peter and Maggie took Pauline's lead. Andy was the low man on the totem pole, but now he was at least allowed to be one of them.

All four of the children had on stocking caps in different colors with matching mittens, which Louise had ordered from the Sears and Roebuck catalog along with the clothes and the toys they would be receiving Christmas morning. Shopping at the post exchange was limited.

My children, Louise thought, allowing herself a moment of maternal pride. The lack in her life was not from want of satisfying children. Or from a fine husband who was also a caring father. The sometimes emptiness inside of her was a shortcoming in her own makeup. She had expected children and family to fill her up completely, and most of the time, they did—but not always.

Yet what was it she had expected out of life? When she was growing up, she never thought of more than this—a good man to marry, children to love.

Louise was glad this was the family's second and last winter on northern Honshu. Andy had been sick much of last winter, and this winter was beginning to look like more of the same.

In preparation for today's event, the wives of both the commissioned and noncommissioned officers had cooperated in bake sales and campwide bingo parties to raise money for the gifts to be distributed at the party. Louise had hoped the two sets of wives could cooperate on future projects but knew that some of the officers' wives might object. Military hierarchy was as carefully observed even at this tiny, isolated outpost of the U.S. Occupation Forces as it was in the more permanent posts in the States. Located in a small mountain valley north of Sendai, Camp Younghans had only two battalions and a few hundred dependents. The school had only fifty-five students in grades kindergarten through eight. The general and his wife had the only high-school-age children—two daughters, who studied at home by correspondence, helped out at the school and were occasionally allowed to date the younger lieutenants. They were riding with Santa in the sleigh dressed in makeshift elf suits.

With a jovial "Ho, ho, ho," Santa jumped from the sleigh, picked up a tiny Japanese girl and led the procession into the auditorium with the wary-looking child on his arm.

Like the rest of the school, the auditorium was surprisingly large. Whoever had planned Camp Younghans had not taken into consideration that the handful of dependents' quarters could not possibly supply enough children to fill so grand a school.

Louise, Major Williams and the wives of the committee helped the Japanese and American teachers remove the children's coats. All the Japanese boys had shaved heads. The girls' hair was all clipped identically in bowl cuts. Many of the children had splotchy skin on their faces, a reminder of recent impetigo sores.

Santa Claus served as master of ceremonies for the program. The American children sang several Christmas songs, and Pauline flawlessly recited the entirety of " 'Twas the Night Before Christmas." Louise cringed a bit at her daughter's dramatics.

Then the orphans sang several songs and a pair of older boys gave an origami demonstration, folding paper into flowers, birds, animals.

"And last on our program," Santa said, "eight-year-old Hameja Takaeta will sing a song in English."

The audience fell absolutely silent as the undersized boy began singing, a cappella, the familiar if strangely accented words in the purest, sweetest voice Louise had ever heard.

Tell me the tales that to me were so dear, long, long ago, long, long ago. Sing me the songs I delighted to hear, long, long ago, long, long ago.

That was all. For a minute no one applauded. Then the major started clapping loudly. Andy smiled back at his mother, clapping his hands excitedly.

Louise rushed to the front of the room and asked the interpreter if Hameja would sing another song.

"But he know only one song of English," the formally clad man explained.

"We'd love to hear him sing in Japanese," Louise said, but apparently she was misunderstood for after she had returned to her seat and Andy had abandoned his own seat to crawl onto her lap, the hairless Japanese boy—not much bigger than Andy—climbed the three steps up the stage and sang the same short verse once again. But no matter. It seemed as though the entire gathering was holding its breath while they listened, knowing this time the brief, haunting refrain would be all there was.

Louise's eyes misted. Next to her, the major took out his handkerchief and blew his nose. The two adults looked at each other over Andy's head and smiled. Mike Williams wasn't embarrassed. Louise liked that.

The American children applauded so long and loudly that little Hameja sang his song one last time. Louise hugged Andy against her chest, aware that the man beside her was sharing the pleasure of the moment. This time when they applauded, his shoulder brushed against hers.

The program ended with Santa and his elves distributing gifts ordered from catalogs by the ladies of the committee. Each orphan received a toy, mittens and a wool muffler. It seemed strange to see little Japanese girls holding decidedly Caucasian baby dolls. The Japanese boys got toy dumptrucks.

Santa said good-bye, and soon Sergeant Bynum appeared to supervise the refreshments. Pauline gave her mother a knowing look.

"The orphans were a brilliant idea," Louise told Major Williams. "I think the children will always remember this day. I know I will."

He shook her hand. Pauline was pulling at one arm, whining to leave. Andy was hanging on her opposite leg. Peter and Maggie were leaping about the stage.

"Well, have a nice Christmas," he said, still holding her hand.

"You too. Where will you have Christmas dinner?"

"At the mess, with the men. Sergeant Bynum will serve a feast, I'm sure."

"Would you like to . . . "

Major Williams shook his head before she finished the question. "I tried that last year with the Petersons. It's better to just go it alone."

That evening as Louise and the houseboy prepared dinner, her thoughts turned to the major. Mike. A widower with a child—like Jeffrey had been. His wife had died of polio. Their daughter was with her parents. He wasn't handsome but had a plain, honest face. He reminded her of Van Johnson. Franklin said he was a good officer but not brilliant, not a West Pointer. No stars were in his future.

She smiled as she thought of him blowing his nose when the orphan boy sang, like her father would have done.

And he had held onto her hand longer than necessary when he shook it. How susceptible she was to a bit of male attention. So silly really, but she still remembered a boy in high school who'd winked at her, and the Filipino captain who'd flirted with her after the twins were born. When she was old, she'd probably rock back and forth in her chair mentally reviewing her little list of every man who'd ever given her a special look.

At dinner, the children tried to explain to their father about the little orphan boy who sang. *They felt it, too,* Louise thought, pleased.

The following Saturday night at the officers' club Christmas party, Mike Williams asked her to dance.

"You look lovely," he said.

The song was "How Are Things in Glocca Morra?" Louise felt very aware of the major's hand at the small of her back. She wanted to put her head against his shoulder and close her eyes.

He pulled her a bit closer and put his chin lightly against her cheek. It was easier that way. No eye contact. Wordlessly, they danced.

He smiled at her when the music ended. "We dance very well together."

Louise smiled back, feeling foolishly pleased.

Franklin was standing by the table when Major Williams escorted her back to him. He was holding Louise's coat and scowling. Louise's heart jumped.

"We've got to go home," he said. "Semiko called. She's worried about Andy."

Louise felt a strange mingling of relief and fear. "His breathing again?" she asked.

Franklin nodded and helped her into her coat.

Andy's wheezing was the first thing they heard when they opened the door. It was worse than the last time. Andy's eyes were wide with panic, his lips blue.

Franklin sat with Louise and Andy most of the night, much of it spent in a steam-filled bathroom. They decided she would take Andy by train to the American hospital in Sendai in the morning. His illness was beyond the capabilities of the lone medical corpsman stationed at Younghans.

The doctor at the Army hospital in Sendai diagnosed asthma. He prescribed medications and keeping the boy calm. The weather was part of the problem; asthmatics did better in hot, dry climates. With luck, Andy would outgrow it.

"I don't understand it, " Franklin said when he picked her up at the train station in the nearby village of Jinmachi. "The other children are healthy. You and I are healthy. Asthma can go on for years. A lifetime. My God, Louise, you already stay away from half the social functions because he's sick. People are going to think you're a loner."

"I'm Andy's mother," Louise said, putting her arms more firmly around her son. "And he does have *e-a-r-s*."

As the winter grew colder and the snow piled high, Andy's attacks became more frequent. Louise watched him grow even thinner, more frail. The worst attacks came at night, but he also had them when he was upset or excited. She worked at keeping him warm and calm. While the three older children rode taxi jeeps to the airfield to watch the monthly paratrooper jumps or went off with Franklin to master cross-country skiing, to swim in the hot spring-fed pool in nearby Tendo, to explore the countryside or be honored guests at judo matches held in nearby villages, Louise stayed home, not daring to leave Andy. But how she hated staying behind. She, too, wanted to explore the mysteries of mountain communities and isolated Shinto shrines. And she hated saying no to the wives' club expeditions to the silk mills at Yonezawa, to Tsuruoka for a demonstration of silk screening.

She guiltily wondered if she and the children should leave Japan to seek a more agreeable climate for Andy. But where would she go? And she would only have to turn around and move again when Franklin was reassigned. She rode the train back to Sendai to ask the doctor if Andy could die during one of the attacks. "It's not likely," he replied. Louise didn't know whether to be relieved or not.

The other wives stopped asking her for bridge. Franklin went alone to a reception in Tokyo honoring the MacArthurs. She continued to volunteer at the school when she could and to help Mike Williams with school board business. He dropped by the school Monday mornings, and they had coffee in the teachers' lounge, papers spread out on the table in front of them, Andy on Louise's lap. Monday was her favorite day.

She thought all weekend about what she would wear. Sunday evening she washed her hair. And at the Saturday-night club dances, Mike would always ask her to dance—sometimes twice.

Louise helped with the Valentine party for the combined third- and fourth-grade classroom. Suddenly Mike was there, passing out Valentine treats he'd bought for the children. The surprise of his presence flustered her. Pauline had to remind her to cut the cake.

At the St. Patrick's dance, Mike sat in the corner drinking with two bachelor lieutenants. When he came to claim his dance from Louise, his speech was a bit slurred. "Too much Irish whiskey," he admitted. "It loosens the tongue, you know. It's making me say that I wish I could dance you right out of here."

"Oh? And where would you dance me to?" Louise asked.

"To a high mountain top where there was only you and me."

He exerted a gentle pressure on her lower back, drawing her closer. There was no mistaking the hard lump of an erection through his uniform.

"Do you mind?" he asked.

"I think the whiskey's had an effect on more than your tongue. You know, don't you, that we can never be more than friends?"

He didn't answer.

Louise couldn't sleep for thinking about the hard reality of Mike's erection. Her fantasies were filled with scenarios in which that erection slid into her body. She could feel herself getting wet, open. It was one thing to think about men who would never materialize, but Mike was a part of her life.

Monday morning at the school, he asked, "Are you happily married?"

"Reasonably so," she said, putting her cheek against Andy's smooth, fine hair.

Mike said nothing for a minute, his eyes on her face. "I'm glad," he said finally. "Colonel Cravens is a fine officer. The Six Seven Five is the best-run battalion in the division."

"Yes," she agreed. She had heard this before. Already a lieutenant colonel, Franklin was outstanding.

"Well, not exactly glad," he qualified. "I guess you know that I admire you. Hell, Louise, I think about you all the time."

Louise shook her head, warning him to stop.

"No, I want my say. I've enjoyed these Monday mornings. I go to sleep on Sunday evening with a sense of anticipation, and the only reason I go to those dances is to have you in my arms for a little while. But one dance just makes me want more. I've got my orders, Louise, and I'm leaving next month. I know I can't ask a married woman with four children to run off with me . . . "

Louise had to laugh. "No, you can't ask that," she said. "I'm about as married as a woman can be, but having you notice me has meant more than I can ever say."

His plain face was so earnest. Louise wished she could touch his cheek. "And I don't suppose you want me to ask if before I go we couldn't at least . . . " He looked uncomfortably at the boy in her lap. Andy looked up at his mother's face to make sure everything was all right. She gave his leg a pat, and he went back to his puzzle.

"No, I don't want you to ask that," Louise said, glad for the comfort of her son in her lap. It made her remember who she was.

"And believe me, I've thought about it. If there was a way . . . But thank you for wanting it. I'll never forget you."

They stared at each other. Louise wondered if the look on her face was as full of longing as his was.

"Andy, old man, could you do me a favor?" Mike asked.

Andy nodded.

"Would you go see if my jeep and driver are still waiting out front?"

Andy slid from his mother's lap and hurried off on his mission. Mike pushed the door closed and drew Louise to her feet.

She slipped her arms around his neck and met his lips as easily as if she'd been kissing him all her life. His tongue was in her mouth at once. It was a fine kiss full of passion and promises of what could have been.

Sadness pushed against her chest as she trudged home through the mushy snow, pulling Andy behind her on the sled. The sun was shining; the day warm. Spring was coming. Finally. Andy already seemed better.

Oh, dear God, what was she going to do without her Monday mornings, without the anticipation of Saturday-night dances with Mike?

She hadn't lied to him about her marriage, but since Christmas she had found herself thinking about Mike all the time. When Franklin made love to her, she thought of Mike.

She wasn't in love with the man, not really, but to Mike Williams she was someone other than Colonel Cravens's wife and the mother of his children. She felt special when she was with Mike.

She'd miss that feeling as much as the man himself.

The first of May, while a howling blizzard raged outside, Andy had his worst attack yet. As he gasped for air, Louise fought against panic. The trains wouldn't be running in weather like this, and she wouldn't be able to get him to the hospital at Sendai if she needed to.

All she could do was give him his medicine and rock him. Andy's wheezing seemed to fill the house. Franklin brought her brandy and sat with her through the night. When he took turns soothing Andy, Louise dozed on the sofa. "I want you to take him to Sendai as soon as the tracks are cleared," Franklin instructed. "You may have to take him back to the States to a specialist. We can't go on like this."

Poor Franklin. So used to giving orders. But he couldn't order a little boy to get well.

About four o'clock, Andy's breathing began to improve. Franklin carried him into their bed, and they slept the remainder of the night with their sickly child between them. When Louise woke, Franklin was dressed, leaning over her to kiss Andy's forehead.

"You okay?" he asked Louise.

She nodded and slipped her arms around his neck as he planted a kiss on her forehead. "You do love him, don't you?"

"Of course I do. I just wish he wasn't sick. It's been so hard on all of us."

As the doctor had promised, when the weather warmed Andy got better. And then Franklin got his orders.

Franklin would accompany his battalion to Camp Campbell, Kentucky. In the fall he would report to Fort Leavenworth, Kansas, where he would attend the Command and General Staff College. The college was a career plum, a landmark on the road to generalhood. Franklin was delighted. He called his father all the way from Japan.

Louise wondered how cold the winters were in Kansas.

CHAPTER

TWENTY-TWO

The children leaned against the railing, throwing coins into the water. Dozens of the brown-skinned youngsters swam below them, diving for coins tossed by the passengers aboard the U.S.S. *General Hodges*. The docks of Honolulu were ahead, the silhouette of Diamond Head to their right.

"What happens to the coins the children miss?" Maggie asked.

"They sink to the bottom," Louise answered, clinging to the strap of Andy's harness. She'd had a harness for Maggie going over, but now Maggie, like her older brother and sister, had to be trusted not to fall overboard. At least the calm waters and balmy weather of the South Seas made Louise worry a lot less about children being lost at sea. The January crossing from Seattle to Tokyo a year and a half ago had been a nightmare of storms and seasickness. Franklin had reported to his new command three months before, and Louise had had to travel alone with her brood. Every time a child was out of her sight, she had panicked.

On this crossing, Franklin was with them. He had decided the three older children could have the run of the dependents' area. Of course, they sneaked down to the lower decks to visit the soldiers, but their daddy didn't know that. She supposed she should worry more about them, but the tropical sun and gentle movement of the ship were like a drug. And Andy seemed like a different child from the sick, pitiful little boy of last winter.

One week of the month-long voyage was already over. Louise

wished they were going 'round the world. Even the simple shipboard fare tasted delicious, or maybe the sea air was playing tricks on her palate. But she was luxuriously happy.

Their family of six was assigned two staterooms, a large roomy one, befitting Franklin's rank, and around the corner a small one for overflow members of the family. Louise refused to allow the four children to sleep in a room by themselves, so she, Andy and the two girls slept in the more spacious stateroom with its two portholes while Peter and his dad occupied the tiny one without portholes. With a tinge of guilt, Louise enjoyed this respite from the marital bed and loved crawling into her upper berth and reading herself to sleep. She didn't have to cook, clean or do laundry. Andy didn't wake up sick. She felt like a grande dame on vacation.

And now they were to have two days of sightseeing on Oahu. Already, sounds of a welcoming island band drifted across the water. Franklin had come up beside her, his arm slipping around her waist. He touched her much more during the day now that he couldn't at night. She turned her face for a kiss. When they were at sea again, maybe she should send the children to one of the nightly movies alone—only then he'd expect her to do that every night, and she wasn't ready to give up her vacation just yet.

Franklin was sporting clean khakis and a fresh haircut. He was even more handsome now than when she married him, his features were more mature, his skin more lived in. If she were casting a battalion commander for a movie, she would choose this dark-haired man with his determined jaw and a mouth that could look ferociously stern or appealingly tender.

"Beautiful, isn't it?" she said.

Franklin nodded, his thumb easing upward to make contact with the slope of her breast.

"Dad, will we get to see Pearl Harbor where the Japs bombed?" Peter asked.

But Franklin didn't get a chance to answer. "What the hell!" he said as a body dove past them from an upper deck, followed by a second and third.

Three soldiers had shed their boots and shirts and joined the children in the water. Their fellow soldiers on the ship were hooting and whistling encouragement. A rain of coins began to hit the water. One of the soldiers dove and surfaced with a quarter held high. His buddies on board responded by throwing more. The Hawaiian children were almost frantic in their efforts to retrieve the coins.

Franklin swore under his breath.

"They're just boys themselves, Franklin, cooped up too long in an isolated Japanese valley," Louise cautioned. "Don't be too hard on them."

She could feel his anger, see it in his face.

"They are not *boys*," Franklin said between clenched teeth. "They are soldiers in the United States Army who just went AWOL."

"They'll come back to the ship when it docks. They'll have to dress for shore leave. Franklin, come on, don't ruin the trip for everyone. Show them you don't have a rule book for a heart."

But even as she spoke, Louise knew she was sentencing the three frolicking soldiers to the brig. Any chance they'd had of escaping the wrath of their commanding officer she had spoiled. Wives didn't tell officer husbands how to run their commands.

Louise watched the three soldiers swim with the native children toward a nearby beach as the tugs towed the ship into the docking area. Franklin was going to court-martial them. They'd be put in the brig for the rest of the trip, maybe face more imprisonment when they reached the States.

She watched Franklin rush away. He'd have to arrange for the Honolulu shore patrol to pick up the men.

The last night of the voyage, after the movie, an impromptu family talent show was held. Pauline recited the entire poem "The Highwayman" by heart in her most theatrical voice, then led a chorus of children in the "Paratroopers' Hymn" sung to the tune of the "Battle Hymn of the Republic."

Blood was on his risers. Blood was on his shoot. Intestines were a danglin' from his paratroopers boots. He ain't goin' to jump no more. Gory, gory what a hell of way to die . . .

"One of her own compositions, I take it," Franklin said with a droll laugh. He was sitting very close, holding Louise's hand, the first time he'd touched her since he'd had the three soldiers arrested.

"Could be. She's not wanting for ideas, but some are kind of tasteless."

Andy came to sit beside her. "Did you think the song was funny?" she asked.

He shook his head no.

"Well, maybe it's a funny way of saying paratroopers aren't afraid," she explained. "They are very brave, don't you think?"

Andy nodded, his expression thoughtful. He was so serious for a little boy who had just turned three. So sensitive and sweet—even his older siblings appreciated that now. They'd get mad at each other but seldom at Andy.

He stood up and whispered in her ear. "Are you still mad at Daddy?"

"No, I guess not," Louise whispered back.

Andy smiled.

"Why don't you go sit in your daddy's lap? I think he'd like that."

Franklin accepted the boy in his lap without a word. Louise wondered if Franklin noticed that Andy had gained a bit of weight.

They watched three wives lip-sync an Andrews Sisters song, "The Boogie-Woogie Bugle Boy from Company B."

Four young officers offered a bit of barbershop harmony that was surprisingly good. The only Negro officer in the battalion played a wonderful blues piece on his trombone. And finally, chairs were pushed to one side and recorded dance music filled the air. Everyone insisted the battalion commander and his wife have the first dance. Louise could hear her four children cheering the loudest as Franklin swept her into his arms. The music abruptly switched to Guy Lombardo's orchestra playing the "Anniversary Waltz."

"You remembered," Louise said.

"Eleven years ago today," Franklin said with a tentative smile. "I love you more than ever."

Franklin danced like the West Pointer that he was. Louise remembered those other dances, all those years ago, of being afraid their bodies would touch, of wanting so desperately to please him.

"How long are you going to punish me for doing my duty?" he asked.

Louise thought of the three young men in the brig. For an instant, she wanted to argue with him all over again. The "crime" had been one of youth and high spirits by three boys who surely did not consider the military their life, who had not been marching into battle but were excited to be arriving in legendary Honolulu. But what would be the point?

As other couples joined them on the makeshift dance floor, she allowed Franklin to hold her close. The moon was full, the stars never more plentiful, the salty breeze balmy. And he did love her.

"But we just got off one boat," Louise protested as she stood staring at the jaunty cabin cruiser. "And you don't know anything about boats."

"It's just a simple motor craft," Franklin said. "Peter and I will manage just fine. Right, big guy?"

Peter nodded vigorously, his father's buddy.

"You're a soldier, not a sailor," Louise continued, knowing she was disappointing everyone. Franklin had arranged the trip as a surprise for the children, an anniversary present for her, a way to combine romance with a family vacation. They were to sail along the southern coast from New Orleans to Apalachicola, Florida, where Jeffrey, Marynell and their boys would meet them for a combined family vacation. Jeffrey had an ROTC assignment at Florida State University in Tallahassee. Louise had thought they would buy a station wagon in New Orleans to replace the Plymouth they had sold in Tokyo and drive to Tallahassee.

But Jeffrey had already purchased a station wagon for them. It would be waiting in Apalachicola, where they would leave the rented boat. Franklin had planned everything. As he proudly showed her through the compact craft, he pointed out a galley stocked with food, a private roomette for the captain and his "wench" and sleeping accommodations for the children that did double duty in the daytime as benches. There was even a cubicle with a toilet and miniature basin.

"What's bothering you, Louise?" Franklin said as they stood alone in the tiny bedroom.

"I'm afraid. Boats sink. We're not sailors. It would be different if we knew what we were doing." Her switch to "we" was calculated. It softened her protest.

"Look, Louise, I spent the war in the South Pacific. We went everywhere in boats."

"But you didn't drive them."

"It 'drives' just like a car, Louise," he said, not trying to conceal his exasperation. "I've been planning this excursion for months. What in the hell are you afraid of?"

"Of all of us drowning. Such things do happen, you know."

"Jesus Christ! I can't believe I'm hearing this. I wanted to surprise my family, and now you accuse me of wanting to risk their lives. We'll never get out of sight of land. We'll spend every night in port. At the first storm cloud, we head in. That's in the contract I signed with the owner. I'm not going to take chances with my own family."

"We'll never get out of sight of land?"

"Never."

When would she learn, Louise wondered. In the end, he would have his way, but now she had spoiled things. She'd have to work at making up with him.

She looked at the peculiar bed built into the bow or stern or whatever. Finally, they would have a little privacy. She began by putting her arms around his neck. "I guess I'm just a big baby. It will be a wonderful trip. The children are so excited."

He did not return her embrace, but he did allow her to plant a kiss on his mouth.

The family slept on the boat that night and "set sail" the next morning. The first stop would be Bay St. Louis in Mississippi. Then Biloxi.

They fished and swam during the day and ate their evening meals on shore. They sang songs and played cards. Louise and Franklin took turns telling ghost stories and family history. Pauline wanted to hear the story of how they met. Franklin told an abridged version, leaving out the part about Cadet Gerald Worth and describing how he was smitten by the most beautiful girl at the dance, how he had known in an instant he wanted her for his wife.

"She was wearing a purple dress," he recalled, "that had sparkling things all over it. And she was so shy, I was afraid she'd turn into a dove and fly away."

Pauline actually sighed, then corrected her father. "The dress was lavender."

Louise relaxed. She had been wrong about the trip. It was a wonderful boat, not new, but well-kept, comfortable. She felt like a movie star as she sunned on the deck. Franklin had even thought to buy her a couple of new books. A Dorothy Sayers mystery. The newly published *Diary of Anne Frank* that she'd heard so much about.

The lavender dress. She still had it tucked away in tissue paper. Marynell had the wedding dress.

It was the third day out when Louise spotted the dark clouds on the horizon. They had weighed anchor and were fishing off Pensacola. Tomorrow she'd be with her sister again. She closed her eyes. Dear Marynell. They had been apart too long for two sisters who loved each other as much as they did. They'd sit at the kitchen table with their coffee just like before. Maybe Franklin would take a cue from Jeffrey and give them time to be alone. Yes, Jeffrey would see to it. He understood.

When Louise opened her eyes, the clouds were darker, closer.

"Franklin, I think we'd better go in."

He looked where she was pointing and nodded.

Peter drew in the anchor and Franklin started the engine.

But it sputtered and died.

He tried again with the same results. The auxiliary motor wouldn't turn over at all.

Louise looked apprehensively at the clouds. They were closer. Darker. She bit her lip to keep from telling him to hurry.

Franklin pulled back the door in the wooden deck. "Dad, look!" Peter said. Louise looked, too. The boat's wooden seams had been insidiously taking on water while they fished and sunned. The twin motors were standing in it.

She realized the boat was indeed lower in the water than before.

"Can you pump it out?" she asked anxiously.

Franklin nodded. "Peter, get that manual from the cabin."

Louise put a hand over her mouth to keep the words from coming out. He'd said he knew about boats. Why did he need a manual to start the pumps?

The waves washing against the sides of the boat were getting stronger by the minute. Louise herded the girls and Andy toward the cabin door.

"Mommie, look!" Pauline called, pointing toward the rapidly disappearing shoreline.

Louise put lifejackets on the girls and Andy, then one on herself, and carried two out to Franklin and Peter.

Waves were washing across the deck. "It's too dangerous for you to be out here," Louise yelled. "I think you'd better send an SOS."

When she got back to the cabin, there were several inches of water swirling about the floor. Pauline was hugging her little brother and sister as close to her as their lifejackets would allow.

Louise went to the door and called to Franklin, but the wind carried her words away. Holding onto the railing, she fought her way back to him. "We're sinking," she called. "Send the SOS now!"

The water in the cabin was rising fast. She gathered her children about her on the deck. They could hear snatches of Franklin's voice calling into the receiver. "SOS . . . carried out to sea . . . Pensacola . . . family of six . . . sinking."

Suddenly the boat lurched to one side. The deck was sinking under their feet.

"Jump clear," Franklin screamed.

For a horrible minute, it was only Louise and Andy being tossed about in a ferocious ocean. Then she saw Maggie and Peter clinging to each other, and holding Andy with one arm, she battled her way through the waves toward them. Franklin and Pauline were suddenly beside her. At least they were all together. Whatever happened, they would face it together.

The waves were impossible, constantly tossing them up and down, away from one another. Franklin made them join hands, but sometimes the force of the waves pulled them apart. They bobbed up and down like tiny helpless corks.

"Our Father who art in heaven," Louise prayed, screaming above the wind and rain, "hallowed be Thy name." Her family's voices joined her. Franklin's boomed. "Thy kingdom come, Thy will be done . . . "

What was His will, Louise wondered. They were adrift, alone, helpless in a godless ocean. Surely, they would die. But she begged Him anyway. *Please God. Not my children.*

Gradually, the sea began to calm itself. But the water was still choppy and darkness and chill were setting in. Andy couldn't survive a night in the water, Louise thought frantically as she rubbed on his legs and arms.

Throughout the inky blackness of the night, Franklin constantly kept pushing them together, reminding them to hold onto each other. They took turns rubbing Andy. Louise sang to them until her voice gave way. Then Pauline sang. Nursery rhymes. School songs. "Don't Sit Under the Apple Tree with Anyone Else but Me." "Doin' What Comes Naturally." Every song whose words she knew.

Louise's teeth chattered, and her body convulsed with shivers. Eventually she grew numb. She wondered if she was dying. She couldn't feel her feet. Franklin insisted his radio message had been heard, but he had no way of knowing. Surely, when they didn't arrive tomorrow evening, Marynell and Jeffrey would send out searchers. The Coast Guard. Could they find six little specks in such a big ocean?

Tomorrow evening. Could they survive that long? No food. No water. So cold.

Oddly enough, she slept, trusting Franklin to be vigilant, to keep them together. Off and on, waking with a start, grabbing onto Andy more firmly, rubbing him, making one of the others help her. He didn't have enough flesh to sustain him. Already, he was only half-conscious.

She heard Peter asking his father if there were sharks, heard Franklin shushing him.

Sharks. Vile monsters with hideous teeth that would tear them apart. No. Louise did not allow herself to think such thoughts. No sharks. Nothing below but water and harmless fish.

"Andy, talk to me, baby. When we get to shore, what's the first thing you want to eat?"

Andy mumbled.

Louise made him repeat his answer.

"Hot chocolate?" Andy nodded yes. That's what he had said. Yes, Louise thought, a big cup of hot chocolate with marshmallows. Andy would have a chocolate mustache, a dollop of marshmallow on his nose.

Finally it was dawn. No boats, no land. Nothing.

"Andy, kick your feet, honey. Please, for Mommie."

She got no response from him. He was blue.

Franklin helped her rub him. Frantically. Pauline took an arm, Peter another. They stretched him out in the water and rubbed and rubbed. Maggie was crying. "I'm sorry I called him stupid. I won't anymore."

Finally Andy began to whimper. "It's okay, baby," Louise said, kissing his face, his ears, his hair, the pain of fear and loving pushing against her chest wall.

"Aunt Marynell will send help soon," she promised. "And you know what I'm going to do. I'm going to buy you a puppy dog. A fat little puppy who will lick your face and make you laugh. A puppy you can sleep with every night. Your cousin Matt has an old dog who still sleeps with him every night. His name is Mister Dog. Pretty soon we'll be at their house, and you can pet Mister Dog."

The sunshine warmed the water and made it a dazzling silver that hurt her eyes. Louise closed them and dozed. They all dozed but Franklin. He kept herding them together. Strange how they were all the same size in the water, all equal, all powerless.

The sun had passed over their heads and was halfway to the horizon when Franklin started yelling for them to wave. "A helicopter. I can hear it. Wave everyone. Wave!"

Franklin took off his lifejacket and waved it in the air. "Wave, Louise!"

Louise opened her mouth joyously. They were to be saved. Thank you, God. Thank you. Thank you.

But something bumped into her. Something hard and large. She put both arms more firmly around Andy.

"Franklin, something's down there!"

They didn't hear her. They were waving, yelling for salvation.

Then the thing slid past her legs, and with one hard jerk, Andy was taken from her arms. Gone. Lifejacket and all.

The surprise took a half-second. "Andy!" she screamed. "Andy! Andy!"

Franklin and the others had paddled away from her toward the approaching aircraft. Peter had his lifejacket off, too, waving it.

"Franklin!" she screamed, as she ripped off her lifejacket. "Franklin, Andy's gone!"

Maggie, trailing behind the rest, turned.

Louise dove, forcing her body down, down, silently screaming her child's name. The water was colder, heavier. The green murkiness revealed no small boy, nothing.

With exploding lungs, she surfaced. Coughing, gasping. Franklin was swimming toward her. "Find him!" she screamed. "Oh, dear God. Please, find him!"

Again, she plunged beneath the surface and swam down as far as her body would take her. Where was he? God in Heaven. Please. Andy. Oh, God. Andy.

Nothing. Her lungs were bursting. She hung suspended in the gloom, turning, straining to see. Her baby. Her precious baby.

When she surfaced, the helicopter was hovering overhead, its propeller making choppy waves. Her other three children were screaming at her hysterically. "Mommie, Mommie."

She was aware of Franklin surfacing behind her as she dove again. Andy was down there. She had to find him. *Had to*. But her body rebelled, telling her she was too weak, too helpless. If she were strong, Andy would still be in her arms.

This time, when she surfaced, Franklin was waiting to grab her. The children were still screaming. They didn't want her to go down again.

A boat was approaching now. She tried to pull away from Franklin. He would want her to give up, to get in the boat and leave Andy. "Let me go!" She was screaming, but her voice was hoarse, alien-sounding. "I have to find him. Damn it, let me go." She hit at him, struggled against his arms.

"He's gone, Louise. He's gone."

"I won't leave him. I can't. I can't. Don't you understand?" She hated Franklin for being strong, for being a man.

She was aware of men reaching for her other children, pulling them out of the water.

"No, Franklin," she sobbed, but she knew the battle was over. "No. Don't make me leave him."

"He's gone, honey. Gone."

A man was in the water with Franklin. The two of them were dragging her toward the boat.

Louise fell to the deck and allowed the hysteria to take her. For once, she could not be strong for her family.

She crawled to her knees and beat her head against the metal deck until Franklin grabbed her. Then she beat at his chest with her fists. Why had he taken them out in that boat? Why? She couldn't stop screaming at him. At God. She would never stop screaming. The horror. The absolute horror. It couldn't be. It just couldn't be.

Maggie was there beside them, sobbing, trying to hug her mother's neck. "Please don't cry, Mommie! Please, don't cry!"

CHAPTER

TWENTY-THREE

"*I* wish you'd eat something," Marynell said, sitting on the side of the bed.

"I can't swallow."

"If you'll just drink some orange juice, I won't bug you anymore."

Louise allowed Marynell to help her sit up and took the required sip of juice.

"Do you want me to turn on the lights?" Marynell asked.

"No. What are the kids doing?"

"Jeffrey drove them to a matinee. Matt's in charge."

"And Franklin?"

"He went downtown to sign the papers on the station wagon. Then he and Jeffrey are going to drive to Pensacola for the coroner's inquest. He's worried about you, Sis. I am, too."

"I know. But I can't think about anything else. I'd rather die than go on thinking about it."

It had been a week. Louise knew she would have to relive the horror over and over again for a lifetime. The image of her child's death. A little body devoured. Louise felt her sister's arms surround her as the sobbing began again.

Her body ached with sobbing. Her head.

"Oh, Marynell, when I close my eyes, I can see it happening to him."

"I know. I know." Marynell was crying, too.

"It won't ever go away." Louise was wailing now, clinging to her sister. "Not ever."

"I know, honey. But somehow we'll learn to tiptoe around the nightmare. Oh, Sis, I hurt so for you, and I don't know what to do."

"You do the right things. You don't say anything about God and how the other children need me. You don't preach. I wish you could have known him better. You would have loved him, too."

Marynell took her sister's face in her hands. "Oh, Louise, I loved him. He was yours. I do love him. I do."

"He was so sweet. So precious. Is God punishing me because I loved him more than the others?"

"No. And it just seemed that you loved him more because he needed you the most."

Louise shook her head, then reached for a tissue to blow her nose. "No, I loved him the most. Franklin has decided that Andy didn't feel anything, that he was unconscious. He wasn't with him. He doesn't know. I hate him."

"It's Franklin's way of coming to terms," Marynell said, her voice full of warning. *Wives did not hate husbands.*

"God, Marynell, I hope he was unconscious, but I don't think he was. Franklin claims he would have died anyway—from the exposure. Why does he say things like that?"

Marynell was the only one she could cling to, Louise thought. Marynell was the only one who let her say the words out loud, who didn't tell her not to cry.

The Camp Campbell chapel was identical to all those other chapels on all those other Army bases. The Catholics came at nine on Sunday morning, the Protestants at eleven. But today was Tuesday. Louise sat in the front pew with her children on one side of her, Franklin and Marynell on the other.

A chaplain Louise had never seen before parroted a funeral service—an anonymous service in which Andy's name was never mentioned, only references made to a dear, departed child—but then everyone avoided saying his name. They looked away, embarrassed, whenever she did. Even the children.

They had cried at first. Hysterically. And still awakened in the night, sobbing with their fear and sorrow, sometimes crying for Andy, their bodies flushed and damp, hearts pounding. But during the day they carefully avoided mentioning their little brother.

They sat stiffly now in their Sunday clothes, Peter between the two girls, their eyes straight ahead, unsure how they were supposed to act.

Louise had insisted on the service, but now she was sorry. But without the service, they would have arrived at Camp Campbell as a family of five without acknowledging that they had once been six. That's how it would be at Fort Leavenworth. People might whisper rumors of their tragedy, but it would never be spoken of in their presence. The children would not discuss it with their new friends. It would be too embarrassing to have had a brother killed in such a hideous way.

Only Marynell would say his name. And her father when he had called her. Over and over he said, "Little Andy. Your poor little Andy." Louise broke down and couldn't speak. Franklin had taken the phone from her.

"Yes, it was horrible. The poor little guy was so frail, I doubt if he would have survived the ordeal if this hadn't happened. We'd been in the water twenty-four hours. Our only comfort was that he was unconscious and didn't feel anything. Yes, Louise is having a hard time coping. Write to her. Maybe she and the kids can come to see you next summer. It would give her something to look forward to."

Louise looked down the pew at her children in their Sunday school clothes. Taking them to visit her daddy in England. She would be freer to do things with the other children now without a sickly child to look after. She imagined a trip to England canceled because Andy was in the hospital and shook away the thought. Army families didn't take such trips anyway, unless they were being sent along with the daddy on government orders.

Her mother's two sisters from Seymour had driven down from Indiana for the service. They had never known Andy, but family went to funerals. Their black funeral dresses looked well worn. Maxine, impeccable in gray silk and pearls, and General Cravens, with six rows of ribbons on his chest, flew in from Washington and sat in the same pew with the aunts. Several of Franklin's officers and their wives sat a respectful few rows behind the family. A dozen or so baskets of flowers lined the communion rail. Mostly gladiolas and lilies. Funeral flowers. And the organ music was suitably funereal. The organist should be playing Andy's favorites—"Jesus Loves Me" and "I'm a Little Teapot," she thought. After all, it was a very little boy they were honoring here today even if there was no small casket, nothing to bury, no small body to hold for one last time before the lid came down for an eternity.

Louise clutched her gloved hands together. Bony hands resting on bony thighs. Amazing how much weight she had lost in just three weeks. Franklin got angry with her, ordered her to eat. The other wives had been kind, doing the commissary shopping, bringing in casseroles and cakes. They were living in temporary quarters with quartermaster furniture—actually a hospital converted into apartments. The bathroom in their apartment had four lavatories, two urinals and three toilet stalls. They'd live there until summer's end when it would be time for Franklin to transfer his battalion to another officer eager to have a troop command on his record. Then Franklin would report for his year of schooling at Fort Leavenworth.

Louise supposed she should be grateful that she didn't have to deal with settling into a new home just yet. Someone had put the dishes in the cupboard, clothes in the closet, arranged the sparse furnishings, installed the Maytag, which had accompanied them to Japan and back. Franklin had been washing loads of clothes for the twins to hang out. The hamper was full again, but she knew he was waiting for her to start functioning. An invisible line was drawn across this day on the calendar. Marynell and the senior Cravenses would leave in the morning, and Franklin was planning to put in a full day at battalion headquarters tomorrow. Once again, Louise would be in charge of the household. Shopping, cooking, washing, ironing, cleaning.

And Franklin's birthday was next week. Louise would be expected to bake his favorite cake—chocolate cake with caramel icing. And soon it would be time to organize the move to Leavenworth, start a new household, shop for school clothes. But part of her wished she could go on punishing her family forever for never saying Andy's name.

Andy's favorite cake was also chocolate cake with caramel icing, but she wouldn't remind her family of that. She had baked one for his birthday in May. They'd ordered him a Red Rider cowboy suit out of the catalog. His brother and sisters helped him put it on, grinning at each other behind his back. It was too big, but he looked pretty cute. Semiko had taken him next door to show the Brownfields' maid.

She wished the chaplain would finish explaining that death didn't matter. Maybe she'd stop coming to church. Franklin wouldn't like that.

What would the others do if she stood and asked the chaplain why his God had allowed her innocent, three-year-old son to be torn apart by a shark? But, of course, she wouldn't do that to her children, to Franklin.

Back at the quarters, more casseroles and desserts had arrived. The women tied aprons or tea towels over their dresses and busied themselves putting out a meal and making it seem like a normal funeral day. Louise had told Marynell not to come, but she was glad her sister was here. Marynell spoke for her, buffered her from the people who said hadn't it been a lovely service and weren't the flowers beautiful.

After the meal, robotlike, Louise went to the kitchen and automatically began to clean counters. One of the officer's wives hurried up to take the dishcloth from her hand, but Marynell shook her head. Leave her be.

Maxine had been trying to navigate Louise into a private conversation ever since she'd arrived. Finally, after the last guests had finished paying their respects, Louise allowed herself to be led to the bedroom. Her mother-in-law pulled a chair close and ordered Louise to stretch out on the bed and rest.

Louise sat on the edge of the bed instead. "If you're going to tell me to be a good soldier, that my other three children need me, that Franklin is worried about me, I've already heard it all. I've also heard about God and His wisdom and putting my faith in the Lord."

"So what is it you'd like to hear from me?" Maxine asked, reaching for Louise's limp hands. "Give up? Renege on your responsibility to your family and indulge yourself in private grief? What do you want me to tell you, Louise?"

"I don't want you to tell me anything. But if you must, I'd prefer to hear that Andy mattered, that he was precious and dear and life will never be the same without him. That being a good mother and wife doesn't mean I have to erase him and pretend he never was. I don't want to be stoic. I want to beat my breast and cut off my hair or my fingers. It was hideous. The nightmares kill me. Over and over. My little boy. Don't you understand, I can't just *go on*?"

"But you must," Maxine said softly.

"Don't say any more, Maxine. I know you mean well, but I don't want to be talked to anymore. I'll work this thing out in my own way in my own time. Right now I just want to be left alone."

Franklin was grateful for the call from his adjutant. A knifing in the C Battery barracks. He really didn't have to go. The victim had already been taken to the hospital, and the military police had arrested the assailant. But Franklin went first to the hospital. The private—his shoulder bandaged and face pale—was startled to see his battalion commander. The incident had been over a poker game. Yes, sir, he knew they weren't supposed to gamble in the barracks. Yes, he understood that disciplinary action would be taken. No, sir, he didn't want his parents notified. "Will I get a dishonorable discharge?" he asked.

Franklin looked at the very young face with a sprinkling of freckles across a sunburned nose. "Do you like the Army, son?"

"Yes, sir. It's the only place where I've felt like maybe I had a chance to amount to something. Back home in Mississippi, my family's just poor white trash. I want to wear my uniform when I go home on leave. I want my mama to see me in it. My record's been clean up to now. Honest."

"I'm sure it has. I'll see what we can work out."

Franklin went to the military police headquarters. The knife-wielding private was frightened. He hadn't meant to hurt anyone. He wanted his parents. Franklin placed a call to Henderson, Ohio, and explained to the boy's father what had happened. Both parents would come tomorrow. When Franklin reported back to the boy, he cried.

Franklin had an overwhelming urge to gather the frightened young soldier in his arms. But of course, he couldn't do that.

"You'll be assigned a defender from the judge advocate's office," he explained, "unless your folks want to hire civilian counsel. Your father said to tell you that he and your mother would stand by you, that they loved you."

"I was jus' playing around. I didn't mean to hurt him."

"Maybe the court will take that into consideration," Franklin said reassuringly.

Louise had accused him of having a rule book for a heart when he'd ordered a court-martial of the soldiers who jumped ship in Honolulu. Only last month. God, it seemed like another lifetime ago.

But he did care about the men he commanded. Deeply. And because he cared about them, discipline had to be maintained. Without discipline, an army wasn't an army.

It was sad, though. The boy wasn't bad. Only hot-headed. And stupid.

To put off going home a bit longer, he went to the officers' club and ordered a double scotch, which he carried to an isolated corner of the bar. The voice of Patti Page singing "Old Cape Cod" drifted from speakers in the ceiling.

God, what a day. But maybe now that they'd gone through the ritual of a funeral, Louise would begin to come out of it. They just couldn't continue as they had with her semi-hysterical crying jags or spells of staring off into space like a zombie.

He had tried to reason with her. "Even if you continue to blame me until the day you die," he told her, "you still have three children who need a functioning mother."

"Andy needed me more than the rest of you put together."

"He's gone, Louise. We have to pick up the pieces of our lives."

He wanted to tell her to be a good soldier, that good soldiers cut their losses and go on, but she would call him heartless, say she was a mother not a soldier.

It was hard not to replay her accusations over and over in his mind. That he had arrogantly thumbed his nose at the fates. That he really hadn't known enough about boats to undertake such a journey. That if just once he could have admitted to being wrong, Andy would still be alive. That he made pronouncements rather than face the truth. She was both right and wrong. He had to be strong because his family depended on him. Commanding officers made decisions, but no one could promise always to be right, only to do what seemed best at the time. In the war, he'd learned that nothing was accomplished by guilty hindsight. At first he had wanted to replay each man's death a dozen times, but it didn't bring them back. He'd learned to determine if there was a lesson to be learned from the dying, then to pray sincerely for the man's soul and deal with keeping the rest of his men alive.

So what lesson had he learned from his family's tragedy? Franklin asked himself. He already knew he was fallible. Surely he would now have greater respect for the caprice of nature. And fate. He would be forever sorry about Andy, but he wasn't going to sacrifice his family to remorse.

If only he could make Louise understand that he was not being callous, only pragmatic. And the weaker she became, the stronger he must be.

He nursed his scotch, wanting to make it last, for he would not allow himself a second. Already this one was eroding the dam that kept tears at bay. Poor little Andy. What he wouldn't give to turn back the clock.

Such a skinny little guy. Peter, Maggie and Pauline had sturdy bodies with flesh under their tanned skin. There had been nothing sturdy about Andy. When Franklin held the boy on his lap, he was always aware of the Andy's bony little bottom, his fragile shoulders and arms. Yet he was the sweetest, Franklin admitted. So eager to please. So delighted with any attention from his brother and sisters, from his father. But Franklin had resented that intense bonding between his wife and her youngest. He had been jealous of his own small child.

He should have done a better job with Andy. Louise didn't think he'd loved the boy, but he had. He just never quite understood how he and Louise had become the parents of a sick child. The other children were healthy. There were so many things now that he didn't understand.

Life was more like war than he'd thought. He had less control than he thought.

An image of that boy he liked so much in the 99th came to him. Corporal Hooks, who was going to be a minister, getting it in the face. That had been the worst—until Andy.

Dry, suffocating pain swelled upward into his throat. He mourned for his lost son, but he mourned more for the family they had been before the boy died, for the wife who once came sweetly into his arms.

A foursome came into the bar and cast a look his way. Franklin nodded at one of the officers. The post engineer. Bing Crosby was singing now, "Old Buttermilk Sky."

If only Louise would allow him to hold her. God how he needed that. But she wouldn't let him touch her.

He really had to leave before he put his head down and wept.

CHAPTER

TWENTY-FOUR

*L*ouise was just finishing the dinner dishes when the knock came at the front door.

"Someone get the door," she called. It would be one of the other children in the building asking if anyone wanted to play kick the can, an almost nightly ritual, weather permitting.

She glanced at the clock. Already eight. Everything took her so long these days. Sometimes she felt as if she was moving in slow motion. Sometimes she forgot what she was doing.

If only she could escape into sleep. But even after five months, the nightmares were still too vivid and the questions in the night too disturbing. Could she have held on to him? Did he feel himself being torn apart?

When she did sleep, she would wake bathed in sweat, her stomach heaving. She crept into the bathroom to change her nightgown, stare at her face in the mirror, wonder what was going to happen to her.

The knocking continued. Then she remembered the children had already gone downstairs—right after dinner. She'd made them come kiss her first and wait until she buttoned up their coats. They got tired of her constant kissing, hugging, touching, of her adjusting their hair and collars. She got tired of their arguing—with her, with each other.

They had promised to be back in time to do their homework. Peter hadn't been doing his. His teacher had called about it. Last week she had called about a playground fight.

Maybe the door was locked, although they seldom bothered in this

288

huge four-story building aptly called the Beehive, full of other officers-turned-students and their families.

Louise dried her hands and took off her apron. "I'm coming," she called.

It was two military policemen and Peter.

"Is Colonel Cravens in?" one of the men asked. Peter looked scared.

Louise invited them to step inside, then went down the long hallway to Franklin's study. She tapped on the door. "Franklin, two MPs are here with Peter." She sounded like her mother—Elizabeth's worried voice wanting Eddie to take care of things.

She hovered in the background while a T-shirt-clad Franklin listened to an expressionless military policeman explain that Peter and two other boys from the building were caught soaping the post commandant's car windows. The general had not been amused.

Franklin in his T-shirt seemed no match for the uniformed MPs with billy clubs and pistols at their belts. But his voice was firm and his shoulders square as he thanked the MPs for bringing Peter home. He would call the general. It would not happen again.

After the MPs left, Franklin turned to Peter. "Do you realize a report of this incident will be put in my permanent file?"

"I didn't mean no harm," Peter said, looking down at his feet. He was sweating, his wonderful dark hair wet against his forehead. He was getting so tall, on the verge of adolescence. She hardly knew him any more, this boy who made trouble and deliberately used bad grammar.

"Any harm," Louise corrected automatically. Franklin glared at her. Louise realized her turn was next.

Franklin was taking off his belt as he marched Peter down the hall. He'd never used physical force against the children until Leavenworth. Peter had received three beatings, the girls several spankings. Their family was falling apart.

She listened to the sound of leather against bare thighs. Five times she cringed. She shouldn't be letting this happen.

Franklin came out of Peter's room and called her to their bedroom. She sat on the bed. He closed the door behind him. "Do you realize that my entire military career depends on my success at the Command and General Staff College?"

Louise nodded and stared at the dust on the dresser. She wished there was some way to avoid this.

"Everyone keeps saying I'm brilliant," he continued, "but I'm not. At West Point, I worked damned hard to excel. It's the same here. I don't have time, Louise, for misbehaving children and despondent wives. It's bad enough that you don't go to any of the wives' functions, but you have not been fulfilling your responsibilities to this family. You let the children run wild. Their rooms look like pig pens. Their report cards were unacceptable in both academics and deportment. When was the last time you helped with homework? The girls wear dresses that haven't been ironed. Can't you at least hire a woman to come iron? And change the bed sheets? Hugging those children all the time doesn't make you a good mother. And when we have sex, you never move a muscle, never say a word. What is happening to us, Louise? How long will this go on?"

"I'm tired," Louise said with a flutter of her hands. Her mother's gesture. "I still can't sleep. In the night, I hate you because you sleep, and I relive the nightmare."

"And do you hate the children because they are alive? Would you rather one of them have died instead?"

She shouldn't have sat down. She didn't like him looming over her. What he said was unfair, unthinkable.

"You're glad it was Andy, aren't you?" she lashed back. "You always resented having a sick child."

He slapped her.

Louise put her hand to her stinging face. No one had ever hit her before. Ever.

The sound of the slap hung in the room. The reflection of their frozen bodies were captured in the mirror over the dusty dresser—a framed picture entitled "Marriage in Trouble."

"Oh, God, Louise. I'm sorry. I'm so sorry." Franklin knelt beside her and put his arms around her wooden body. "I'm afraid. I feel you slipping away from us. What is it you want from me? You know how sorry I am about Andy and that I would give anything to change things. But I can't."

Anguish was in his voice. He was probably afraid she was going crazy. Was she? It would ruin their family. Did the military forgive crazy wives? She wondered if a record of her insanity would go into Franklin's permanent file and if the omnipotent powers who decided on promotions regretfully shook their heads and passed over men with crazy wives and children who soaped the post commandant's car windows.

How long had she hated her husband, Louise wondered. Was it when he decreed that Andy had been unconscious when he died? Or before that? She could forgive his taking them out in that boat if only he'd acknowledged he was wrong, that he shouldn't have when he didn't know a damned thing about boats and ocean currents. But all he ever said was that he was sorry. Well, everyone was sorry. That wasn't enough. She needed for him to suffer, to beg forgiveness.

"Do you miss him at all?" she asked.

Franklin turned his back to her, but she could still see his face, contorted in pain, in the mirror. "I'm not a monster, Louise. Of course, I miss him."

What now, she thought. Where did they go from here? She actually felt sorry for Franklin. Was she weak or just human? Or perhaps it was because, in a way, she was just as responsible as he was. It was she who had misgivings about taking a boat trip: if she had refused to go, maybe Andy would be alive. But no, that wasn't fair either. She hadn't known that misgivings would end in tragedy, and if they hadn't gone, her family would have resented her. Dumb old Mom. Her thoughts made her tired. Maybe it was time to put an end to blame.

They would never be the same. But that acknowledged, maybe it was time to go on.

They were visiting Franklin's parents at the Presidio near San Francisco when North Korean forces invaded South Korea.

Franklin had been granted a month's leave following his graduation at Leavenworth. He'd finished twenty-second in a class of four hundred and forty—commendable, but he'd wanted more. Louise knew that he blamed her, at least in part.

The evening following the invasion, President Truman ordered the Air Force and Navy to give support to South Korean forces. Suddenly America was embroiled in another war.

"MacArthur will be running the show," General Cravens said as he carved the roast at Sunday dinner.

Franklin nodded.

MacArthur. Franklin's old mentor. Louise knew at that moment that Franklin would be going. She could see the excitement in his face, hear it in his voice.

She wasn't sorry. In fact, she'd welcome the time without him to finish healing herself.

And she even knew where she and the children would wait out the war. The house in San Antonio was empty. They'd planned to stop on their way to Fort Bragg to check on it. The realtor who managed it for them said the floors needed to be redone and the roof repaired before it was rented again.

Franklin's orders to Fort Bragg were canceled. He was put on stand by until his orders to the Far East could be processed. Louise knew his father had helped engineer the quick change.

On July seventh, Congress enacted the draft. The next day MacArthur was named commander of the United Nations forces. A week later, Franklin was on his way.

Louise drove the station wagon from San Francisco to San Antonio. The children didn't listen to her as well as they did their father. Maggie got sick. The fuel pump went out in Amarillo. But after three endless days, she arrived feeling quite proud for having accomplished the trip herself.

The house and neighborhood were shabbier, but Louise felt like she'd come home. She walked through the empty rooms, remembering. In the little bedroom that had been her mother's, she wept.

The realtor told her not to worry about a thing. He'd take care of getting the house shipshape. Louise thanked him kindly but said she could manage on her own.

She put a map of Korea up in the kitchen and wondered if this war would last as long as the last one. She couldn't believe there was another one already. If she had the power, she'd end it today. The thought of more death and suffering made her feel old and tired. She'd worry constantly about her husband. And when he came home to them, she'd be grateful for his safe return and welcome him gladly. But she couldn't help looking upon this time without him as a gift.

CHAPTER

TWENTY-FIVE

Almost in passing, Louise mentioned Franklin's promotion in her letter. "Franklin's a full colonel now. The children are proud."

The silver oak leaves on Franklin's shoulders had been replaced with eagles. Franklin was now only one grade away from a general's star.

Jeffrey had finally been promoted to lieutenant colonel while they were at Tallahassee. His students had held a beer bust in celebration. He came home drunk and happy, and he and Marynell made love and giggled long into the night. She told him over and over how proud she was of him. "Yes, but do you love me?" he asked.

"Of course, I love you," she had told him. "More than anything, Lieutenant Colonel Jeffrey Washburn. More than anything."

For a few months, her husband had held the same rank as her sister's. But not really. Jeffrey had been passed over twice as a major. Franklin had never been passed over.

Marynell wondered if she could tell Jeffrey about her brother-in-law's promotion without it sounding like an accusation.

The familiar strains of the "Washington Post March" drifted across the street from the New Post parade ground where the division band was practicing for tomorrow's parade and review. Medals were being presented posthumously to the families of the state's first Korean War dead. Mrs. Younger, the post commandant's wife, had asked Marynell to hostess the luncheon for the families at the officers' club. It was the second time the general's wife had called on her for special duty. That was nice. After only three months at Fort Sill, she was already an insider. She'd been nominated for vice president of the wives' club, and nomination was tantamount to election since Mrs. Younger had approved the slate.

Marynell looked around the living room of her gracious home, by far the nicest set of quarters they'd ever had. The charming house had been built shortly after the turn of the century and had spacious rooms, high ceilings, an impressive entry hall with a wide staircase. She had reveled in arranging the furniture, making everything just right for receiving their first callers, having their first party, hostessing her first luncheon. Only this morning, the wives of the thrift shop committee had met here, and the younger women had looked around with envy. But as much as Marynell loved the house, Fort Sill was a disappointment. Jeffrey was back teaching at the artillery school again. All he ever did was teach, when what he needed was a troop command. To make matters worse, he had requested the assignment.

And now Franklin was a full colonel.

Marynell returned her attention to the careful script of her sister's letter. Now that Marynell had had time to get settled, Louise wanted them to come for a visit. Louise was temporarily husbandless again—and only a day's drive away—while her husband was in Korea earning more accolades.

Marynell had tried to get Jeffrey to volunteer for duty in Korea, but he insisted he'd had enough of war for one lifetime and greatly preferred the science of war to the real thing. He planned to stay right where he was.

"I'm a good teacher," Jeffrey said. "I'm not good at other things."

It was that teaching award he'd won at Florida State, Marynell thought bitterly. He'd gone beer drinking with his students again to celebrate. Articles about the award had appeared in both the town and school papers along with a handsome picture of him reviewing the ROTC cadets astride a horse. There was even a story in *Army Times*. It was the first time an ROTC professor at any school had ever won a campuswide teaching award, and it had filled Jeffrey's head with notions of resigning his commission and teaching school. But it was just another phase she would have to manage. Husbands had phases just like children.

Marynell thought of the years she and Louise had spent together with their children in San Antonio during the war. She had missed Jeffrey, but until their mother got sick, those had been good, simple years without the complications of men and their careers. But they had always known it was only an interlude.

Marynell would have loved to take the boys to Texas for a visit, but now with this news about Franklin, she wasn't so sure. Her younger sister outranked her again, and Louise had become the sort of woman people referred to as "lovely." Marynell stood and looked at herself in the gilt-framed mirror over the handsome mantel. She still had her looks, but she'd put on weight, and unattractive little lines—like a pair of parentheses—punctuated the sides of her mouth.

Would people still consider her the pretty sister? Marynell wondered. Maybe it wouldn't matter who was prettier if her husband could just get his career on track. How many years, she wondered, before Jeffrey could reasonably expect a pair of eagles?

Louise didn't seem to care about rank, while Marynell cared a great deal. It wasn't fair.

Marynell refolded her sister's letter and replaced it in its envelope. What *did* Louise care about? What else was there but family and ambition?

They had seen each other only once since Andy's funeral. Maybe it was time she found out how Louise really was. They could visit the national cemetery together, put flowers on their mother's grave. Marynell closed her eyes, seeing them there together in that sea of graves.

And Jeffrey would enjoy a trip to Texas. San Antonio had been their first home. She'd talk to him and the boys about it at dinner.

Matt came in first. Already taller than Marynell, at thirteen he was a gangling boy with braces on his teeth, his father's dark eyes and hair, and skin tanned so dark people often asked if he was part Indian.

He allowed Marynell to kiss his cheek, then helped himself to a glass of milk. "Don't spoil your dinner," she warned automatically as she resumed peeling carrots. "We're having baked chicken and biscuits."

"You got honey?"

Marynell nodded, and Matt grunted appreciatively.

"Your clothes are muddy. Why don't you take them off down in the basement before you get mud everywhere?"

Matt returned from the basement in his briefs and undershirt, the evidence of his maturing body barely concealed. Marynell had to look away.

She resumed her paring. He probably had erections in the night. Already, her stepson was difficult enough for her to manage. She wondered how much raging hormones would compound the problem.

Matt liked living on an Army post again after the family's bout with civilian life at Tallahassee. He spent most of his time away from home—roaming around the Fort Sill reservation mostly—either on his bicycle or on Cannonball, the aging gelding they'd had since Fort Bliss. Matt explored unused bunkers, abandoned farms left when the reservation was enlarged in the twenties, forgotten Indian cemeteries. He looked for arrowheads along the creek beds, bird-watched with his binoculars. Matt seemed to prefer his own company to that of others—except his father. The boy adored his father. He and Jeffrey would go fishing in the Wichita Mountains, and last winter they had gone deer hunting in Colorado. Recently, they had taken up woodworking, with a jigsaw installed in the basement. They had made lamp bases, gun racks, picture frames.

Eric wasn't interested in making things, and he didn't like to fish and hunt. His passion was sports, and although Jeffrey tried, he was a terrible Little League coach and couldn't score one out of five shots with a basketball. It bothered Marynell that Jeffrey was closer to her stepson than her own son. It bothered her a great deal.

The boys themselves had worked out an indifferent truce over the years. With increasing frequency, however, the truce would be broken, and frightening, physical fights erupted. The last was over

Cannonball. Matt accused Eric of riding him too hard and not cooling him down properly. The boys were big enough to hurt each other. Matt was older, but Eric was strong. Eric had come out of the last brawl with a jammed finger, Matt with a black eye. Jeffrey had lectured them with tears in his eyes.

She heard Matt coming down the stairs and called him into the kitchen. He had on clean jeans and a knit pullover. His hair was even combed.

"How would you like to go to San Antonio and visit your cousins and Aunt Louise?"

He shrugged. "That'd be okay, I guess."

"I thought you'd be more excited. You and Peter were always such buddies."

"He collects baseball cards," Matt said, as though that explained things, and headed for the stairs. "And Pauline's bossy," he added over his shoulder. "Maggie's okay, though."

Soon Marynell could hear the radio from his room. He was too sophisticated for baseball cards, but he still listened to "Terry and the Pirates."

Eric came bursting in from baseball practice, cap on backwards, bat over his shoulder, shirt dirt-streaked. He looked like one of Norman Rockwell's *Saturday Evening Post* covers. The all-American boy. All he needed was a dog, but these days Mister Dog roused himself from his blanket in the corner only long enough to eat and relieve himself in the same spot just outside the back door.

Marynell dried her hands to touch his face, smooth his hair. "How'd it go?" The season had been hard for him, she knew, arriving at Sill after the teams had already been formed and having to work his way into the lineup.

"I got a couple of hits. Coach may move me to outfield for the tournament though."

"You let a few grounders slip through again?"

"Yeah. But Todd said his dad'll help me some after dinner."

Eric thought the trip to San Antonio sounded great. "Pete and I can shoot baskets and go bowling."

At dinner, she asked Jeffrey. "Gee, honey, I can't get away during a term," he explained, "but you and the boys should go. Why don't you go after Eric's tournament? Stay until school starts. You deserve it. I can come down for the weekend."

He looked forward to having them gone, Marynell realized with a sting of hurt. He could tinker in the basement or read his books every evening in peace and quiet.

"I'd have to miss the Ogles' party," Marynell said, unsure. She had had her green silk shortened. No one at Sill had seen it.

"Don't you ever get tired of parties?" Jeffrey asked.

"It makes me think of Mother," Marynell said as they took their iced tea out in the yard for a tour of the garden. It was less ambitious than their victory gardens had been but pretty impressive for a solo operation.

"I know. I've even planted rhubarb. Remember, she said she wanted to plant some. I made us a fresh rhubarb pie. Oh, Marynell, I'm so glad you're here," Louise said, linking arms. "I've missed you."

"Yeah. I've missed you, too," Marynell said, realizing how true her words were. "It makes me feel happy and sad to be here. I'm glad you kept the house."

"Franklin decided it was a good investment so near the base. We've never had trouble keeping it rented. For me, it's strange to come back to the time before Andy."

"You still have the nightmares?"

"Yes, but not as often. Things will flash across my mind that make me die a little. And sometimes I'll realize hours or even a whole day has gone by without me thinking about him, and then I have to sit down and cry. It's like I'm killing him all over again by not thinking of him more."

"Andy's a part of you, Sis, like your arm. You don't have to think about your arm."

Louise stopped to hug her sister. "Thanks," she said, her voice catching. She looked around the big backyard with its fruit trees and the elm with the tire swing. The sandbox was gone, the trees bigger, but otherwise it looked much the same. "Andy would have liked it here."

"Maybe he could have helped you mulch," Marynell said. "You're not using enough, you know."

The children came tearing around the house. "Can we go to the matinee, Mom?" Peter called excitedly.

"We thought it would be nice to do something special for company," Pauline said in her most grown-up voice. "Maybe we could stop for an ice-cream cone on the way home."

"No ice cream," Louise said. "I'm making spaghetti and meatballs for dinner, and I expect everyone to come to the table famished."

Louise went into the house for a five-dollar bill, which she gave to Pauline along with instructions that everyone could have one Coke. She expected change.

"Maggie, run get some Kleenex," Pauline instructed, "in case the dog dies."

Matt snorted. Maggie swung around and shook her finger at him. "Just 'cause you're thirteen doesn't mean you're too big for crying at sad movies. You be nice, or I won't love you anymore."

When Maggie returned with the Kleenex, Pauline marched everyone down the driveway, Matt and Maggie bringing up the rear. Maggie had grabbed Matt's hand and was chattering away.

"God, that Pauline is eleven going on forty," Marynell said.

Louise nodded. "She keeps us all organized. Matt and Eric seem to be getting along. I thought you said they fought a lot."

"Matt's distracted."

"Maggie?"

"Yeah, she's a little charmer."

The sisters walked around the house to the shade of the front porch. Louise sat on the wooden rocker, Marynell the porch swing. Just like before, Marynell thought. "What do you hear from Franklin?" she asked, pushing the swing slowly back and forth.

"He's back in Seoul since the city was recaptured. But I haven't heard from him since Truman fired MacArthur. I know he must have been shocked."

"It's good his promotion came through before all that happened."

"Why?" Louise asked.

"Well, Franklin was always MacArthur's boy—you know, his protégé. Jeffrey says it's a good thing Truman replaced MacArthur, because the old generals don't understand about limited warfare. All they know is going for broke, and the atom bomb ruined that possibility."

"It would be nice to think all that death and horror accomplished something. Franklin visited Nagasaki after the armistice, but he didn't say much about it except it was horrible beyond belief. He never talked much about the war—any of it."

"Jeffrey told me everything. He even talked about the smells. It was the kids suffering that he couldn't stand. And he said he was faithful to me. What about Franklin?"

"I never asked."

"Don't you care?"

"I'm not sure. Sometimes people are lonely, afraid, in need of comfort. And maybe a husband and wife don't need to know everything about each other."

"God, Louise. Do you think it was all right that Daddy was unfaithful to Mother?"

"Oh, Marynell, let's not go into that again."

Marynell pushed the swing harder. "I'll never forgive him. He's my father and I have to love him, but I'll never forgive him. I couldn't forgive Jeffrey, either, if he was unfaithful to me."

"You guys doing okay?" Louise asked, tiny creases appearing between her eyes. "You know, getting along?"

"Yes and no. Jeffrey's like Mother. He reads a lot, and I'm never quite sure what he's thinking. But I love him so much it makes me afraid sometimes. Without Jeffrey, I'd be nothing."

"Yes, you would. You'd be my sister."

Marynell said nothing. That wasn't enough and Louise knew it.

"You know we went to General Cravens' retirement ceremony?" Louise asked.

"Yes. Right before Franklin left for Korea."

"It was lovely. I'm just like the kids when it comes to parades. We all stood by Harold on the reviewing stand." Louise paused. Obviously there was more.

"Why do I have the feeling you brought this up for a reason?" Marynell asked.

"Army's not all there is," Louise said. "The general and Maxine are having to find that out. Oddly enough, he's accepted it with more aplomb than she has. He said he's earned the right to do not much of anything 'cept golf and maybe try writing a book. And he's starting an Army retirees club in Fort Lauderdale—for officers *and* noncoms. They moved to Florida for the climate but really have no roots there or anyplace else after all those years of moving from one Army post to another. And there're no more teas for Maxine to preside over. She admits it's hard for her to be just another old lady."

"I know what you're trying to say—that in the end it really doesn't matter, but I want those years of glory. And I can't help but think Maxine would be even more lost if she didn't have those glory years to look back on and remember when she was someone."

"Maybe," Louise said, leaning her head against the high back of the chair. Her profile was clean and perfect. Marynell struggled with a pang of jealousy.

"But what if Jeffrey doesn't get promoted?" Louise asked. "What if he's retired? Don't you need to be prepared in case that happens?"

"You sound just like him," Marynell snapped. "I know that's a possibility, and I can accept it if we've given it our best shot. That's all I ask. What's the matter with wishing for your husband to succeed? What in the world do *you* wish for if not that?"

"Oh, I want Franklin to get a star or two. He needs that, and the children want it very much. He has them convinced that if they don't behave themselves and do well in school, he'll never make it. Maybe it's true. Maybe they only promote men who have law-abiding children and dignified wives. But as for myself, I have no great expectations of joy and happiness when that happens. I think I'd be happier if Franklin would retire at twenty years, and we could go have a little farm someplace. But he's not 'specially interested in growing things."

Louise closed her eyes and rocked gently back and forth, enjoying the peace of this old neighborhood, her sister's presence.

Dreams. Yes, she did still have them. With this war as with the last one, she dreamed of Franklin coming back a changed man, but not so much in the romantic sense. She still longed for passion, but after so many years with a man she loved automatically, it was hard to believe her marriage would ever be otherwise. Other things could change, however. She was tired of forgiving Franklin for his authoritarian ways. She understood he was more comfortable being in charge, that indeed, he *needed* to be in charge. But she had needs, too, and she didn't want to return to that wifely limbo hovering someplace between childhood and adulthood that she'd had when he'd come back before. She would like to be a full partner in their marriage and help make decisions about money, about life insurance, about his career plans. She didn't want him to take up his old habit of going over the bank statement and asking what various checks were for.

Franklin had made out a hurried will before he left for Korea, setting up a trust fund for his wife and children and appointing his father trustee. If anything happened to Franklin, she would be on the dole to her father-in-law. She'd protested, but not too much, finding it difficult to discuss estate planning when her husband was going off to war. But when he came back, she wanted his will changed. She wanted one that acknowledged she had the ability to make decisions about her and her children's future.

There were other dreams. Fantasies really. Of her owning a charming little restaurant and greeting people at the door who knew her only as the proprietor, who gave no thought to who her husband was.

Of romantic escapades with occasional men she'd met. The man who fixed her roof. The principal at the grade school. Her behavior toward them, however, was always proper.

Of Mike Williams—with whom she had not always been proper—of how it would be if she ever saw him again.

And there were thoughts of what it would be like when the children were grown, when it was just Franklin and her. She tried to imagine a more carefree relationship, with hand-holding and laughter, but she suspected they would spend carefully managed years of meals on time and social obligations fulfilled until they faced the starkness of retirement and old age. Sometimes, she caught herself speculating on what her life would be like if he died first, but that was foolishness. More than likely, she'd die young like her mother, and Franklin would be the one to love again.

Louise surveyed her handsome family gathered around the dining room table—together once again. Franklin was an older, more handsome version of the West Point cadet she had married almost fourteen years ago. Peter, at twelve, was still the most beautiful human being she had ever seen, with dark hair, a strong jaw, thick lashes rimming large hazel eyes, a full mouth that managed to be sweet and determined at the same time. Pauline's eyes were not so large, her hair less dark and rich than Peter's. His square jaw did not translate well on her face. How difficult it must be for her to be less beautiful than her twin brother. Maggie, at ten and a half, was an imp with reddish gold hair, laughing eyes and a mouth that was already sensuous.

Louise had met Franklin in San Francisco for three breathless days of making love, talking nonstop, eating, drinking, sightseeing—a time of *déjà vu*, reminding them both of his homecoming from war in the South Pacific.

Last night, she had brought him home to his children. A spotlight illuminated a banner hung across the front porch. "Welcome home to the world's best dad." As soon as the car stopped, the front door flew open and three barefoot, pajama-clad children came bounding out amidst cries of "Daddy, Daddy!" and bear hugs and tears.

And tonight they were having the formal celebration of his homecoming, belatedly celebrating his promotion, and just today the news had come that he was to be awarded the Legion of Merit for his work with the Armistice Commission Support Group in Panmunjom.

After Truman fired MacArthur, Franklin had been relieved of his United Nations Command staff assignment and sent to Panmunjom, where he was entrusted with the housing, feeding, health, safety and comfort of the members of the Armistice Commission and their staffs. He claimed the job was like being a mayor of a town. But Louise knew he'd turned a lesser assignment to his advantage, playing host to high-ranking diplomats, politicians and military men from a variety of United Nations member countries, making many important friends and earning a prestigious medal.

She'd splurged on a standing rib roast and set the table with white lace and the good china. For dessert, there was chocolate cheesecake. The children had made another banner for the wall. "We love our dad."

After dinner, Franklin poured champagne all around and lifted his glass. "To my beloved family. I'm so happy to be with you again."

Peter surprised them all by standing and offering a toast of his own. "To our father, who makes us very proud. I'd rather be the son of Colonel Franklin Cravens than any other kid in the world."

They were looking at her now.

Louise stood. After several glasses of wine and now champagne, she felt light-headed and melancholy. She thought of Andy, who would also have been proud of his daddy. She would like to acknowledge his memory but knew her family would look away, embarrassed, not understanding her need to do so.

She lifted her glass. "To our reunited family and a lovely future." And to Franklin, she said, "And I'd rather be the wife of Colonel Franklin Cravens than any other woman in the world."

She emptied the glass, then walked around the table and pulled Franklin to his feet. Slipping her arms around his neck, she gave him a lingering kiss while the children applauded.

In bed, she recalled the words of her toast. She never thought of being another man's wife, but she did sometimes think of another man loving her.

Book Four

★　★　★

1956–1967

CHAPTER

TWENTY-SIX

Maggie hadn't expected to like Daniel Norton. She and her classmates at the American high school in Frankfurt had known he was coming for weeks. The new general's son, the youngest of three sons. A ninth-grader. One of his brothers was at West Point, the other on active duty. Daniel had been attending a private school in Virginia but was now joining his parents for the remainder of their European assignment.

The General Nortons had come to Frankfurt from NATO headquarters in France. He replaced the division commander, the legendary General Andrew Jackson "Stonewall" Sheen, who had died of a heart attack while skiing in northern Italy. During World War II, Sheen had escaped from a German POW camp and while on his way out of Germany was said to have single-handedly derailed a German troop train.

If Steen's replacement had a less colorful history, his wife had a ferocious reputation for whipping wives' clubs into shape. She was big on projects for the ladies.

Rumor had it that the new general's youngest son was a creep with buck teeth and pimples. Another said he was a stuck-up snob. After all, he'd gone to a *private* school. From the minute Maggie saw him in the principal's office, she knew neither rumor was true. He didn't have pimples; his teeth were beautiful—like the rest of him. And the shy smile he offered her didn't seem one bit stuck up.

He had blond, wavy hair, dark blue eyes, a man's body and a

beautiful mouth—full and strong and sexy like Tab Hunter's mouth. Tab Hunter, with his boyish good looks, was Maggie's current heartthrob. Pauline liked the almost brutal looks of Jeff Chandler, but that was because he played Cochise in several movies that Pauline had seen over and over. Maggie suspected her sister fantasized about an Indian brave carrying her off to the tepee for a thorough ravishment ending in pledges of eternal love. She'd had a few such fantasies herself even though she suspected eternal love in a tepee would have its drawbacks.

Maggie preferred fantasies starring Tab Hunter-like boys who were beautiful in their tuxedos—or dress whites—when they danced with her on moonlit terraces and wanted to make love to her on beautiful beaches or in mountain lodges. And, of course, they would beg to marry her and devote the rest of their days to making her happy.

Poor Tab might be on the verge of losing his starring role in her fantasies, Maggie thought as she escorted Daniel Norton up and down the halls of the high school, showing him where his classes met, introducing him to his teachers, arranging to sit with him in the lunchroom.

"I'll kill any girl who looks at him," she told Pauline as they rode the bus home after school.

"What was that?" Peter said over his shoulder from the seat in front of them. "You're going to kill the competition? Who's the guy? Do I need to do a big-brother act and tell him if he so much as lays a finger on my little sister, I'll break every bone in his body?"

"It's the new general's kid," Pauline announced.

"Shut up," Maggie said, horrified. "Someone might hear you."

"I hear he's going out for football," Peter said. "A back. Means he can run fast. Sounds like he's going to need to."

Maggie punched her brother's back. "You don't run fast when Cindy Sue Miller comes around batting those false eyelashes."

"That's not all that's false about Cindy Sue," Pauline chirped.

Peter turned around. His neck was red above his Frankfurt Eagles letter jacket. "They're not false," he said indignantly.

"Which?" Pauline demanded. "Her lashes or her 32D bosom?"

Peter moved to the back of the bus, a pained expression on his face. Sisters were a cross to bear.

When they got off the bus on their tree-lined street in a part-German-civilian, part-American-military neighborhood, Peter broke into a trot. "'Bye, Ladies. I'm starving to death. And if there's any of that blueberry pie left, I plan to get to it first."

"That's not fair. You had two pieces last night," Maggie called after him.

"Don't worry," Pauline said. "There's none left. Let's make fudge when we get home. I'm having a chocolate attack."

"We have to fix dinner, you know," Maggie said, thinking her sister's waistline looked like she'd been having a few too many chocolate attacks. "It's Mom's day as a Gray Lady at the hospital."

"We can make fudge and meat loaf at the same time," Pauline said.

"How can I get him to like me?" Maggie asked her sister as she jumped out of the way of two tricycle-riding youngsters.

"Considering my less-than-vast experience with the opposite sex, I'm hardly the person to ask," Pauline said irritably.

"But you've been on dates," Maggie insisted.

"Yes, *both* arranged by the ladies of the dance class committee."

"You went to the honor society banquet with Bill Neely."

"His father drove us. Daddy came to take us home. Big deal. Besides, he scratches his crotch all the time. It's embarrassing."

"Well, if you wanted a boy to like you, what would you do?"

"Ask him to a Sadie Hawkins Day party."

"I can't wait that long."

After dinner, Maggie waited until she and her mother were alone in the kitchen. "Mom, how can a girl make a boy like her?"

"Well, I don't think a girl can *make* a boy like her, anymore than he can make her like him," Louise said as she cleaned out the sink. "It just happens."

Maggie hung the clean pans on the rack over the stove. "But if it was going to happen eventually, isn't there something she can do to hurry it along?"

"I suppose she can ask her mother if she can invite him to dinner, but if she's only fourteen, her mother might think she's too young to have a boyfriend."

"Yeah, but she can talk her mother into it—you know, promise only to see him at school and in the family living room—that kind of stuff. And she's a very mature fourteen-year-old. And her mother is *very* sensitive and progressive."

Maggie recognized the look her mom was giving her. It said *I know I'm being manipulated, but you're kind of cute.*

"Does her mother know the boy in question?" Louise picked up a tea towel and a handful of wet silverware.

"No."

"Does he have a name?"

"Daniel Norton."

"The new general's son?"

"Yeah, he's a doll. Now don't you dare laugh, but Mom, I think I'm in love—really, truly in love, and I don't know what to do about it."

"You might ask your brother for advice."

"No. He'd tease."

"Well, nobody ever promised the road to true love was an easy one," Louise said as she untied her apron.

Peter teased, but Maggie insisted.

"Well, why don't you just tell him you like him and see what happens?"

"I couldn't do that."

But she did—in a note, passed in German class. "I like you. Do you possibly think you could see your way clear to sit by me on the bus this afternoon?"

A European tour with his two daughters—Eddie had spent months reading brochures and making arrangements. In the spring, so the children would still be in school. Marynell came from Oklahoma, Louise from Frankfurt, meeting their father and Martha for two days in London, then on to Folkestone to see their house. From England, Eddie and his daughters would fly to Athens to begin their tour. Martha, concerned about a sick sister, stayed behind. "Besides, I've already been to all those places," she explained. But Louise suspected her father's wife wanted him to have some time alone with his daughters, especially since Marynell was still cool to her.

At Heathrow, they met their tour guide and traveling companions, three families with children, a couple on their honeymoon, four pairs of widows who eyed Eddie with great interest and six middle-aged couples, all discouragingly nondescript.

Already, Eddie had reverted to form and took charge, carrying all three sets of tickets himself, asking several times if his daughters had their passports, even suggesting they go to the bathroom before they boarded the plane.

Louise and Marynell exchanged looks. In the bathroom, Marynell said, "Can you believe him? You'd think we were ten. Do you suppose he treats his wife that way?"

"Her name is Martha," Louise reminded her. "I think they're both that way, fussing over each other."

Marynell said nothing.

On the plane, Eddie ordered champagne. "To my beautiful daughters and our wonderful adventure," he offered as a toast.

"To us," Louise said, lifting her glass, "I still can't believe I'm away from my children for two more weeks. Incredible."

The timing was perfect. Her children would be on a school-sponsored tour of Scandinavia for most of the days she was away, so she didn't have to feel guilty about being gone, although Franklin had certainly tried hard enough to make her feel that way. He was frequently away on maneuvers, four times in the past year, but he liked her at home when he was there. She could sense his struggle to find some worthy reason why she shouldn't take the tour with her father and sister. He wasn't sure it was safe. She would miss a reception for a visiting assistant secretary of defense. He didn't like to eat out by himself. "You can cook something at home," Louise offered. "Or I'm sure Frau Ogle would cook something for you on the days she comes in to clean. I'll leave plenty of groceries."

"I wanted us to go to those places together," Franklin protested. But they'd been in Germany a year, and most of the European travel he'd promised had yet to materialize, and Franklin would probably have his orders by fall. They'd taken a couple of weekend trips in West Germany and a skiing trip to Austria during the children's Christmas vacation, but Louise had longed especially for Italy and Greece.

"Franklin," she said, stroking his face to make her words more palatable, "I hope we can do some traveling together before we go back to the States, but this trip with my father and sister is a rare opportunity that I plan to enjoy."

The weeks before her journey were strained. Why was it so difficult for him to allow her any life outside the context of their marriage? Louise wondered. When the last of their mother's sisters died, she and Marynell had shared her estate. Louise felt oddly proud suddenly to have money of her own and joined a women's investment group that met every other Wednesday evening at the NCO club. Each member contributed a modest amount to a fund that was invested and tracked. In the process, they learned about stocks and bonds, about CDs and treasury notes. Louise liked the idea of an activity for women other than bridge or teas, and she wanted to learn how to invest her money wisely and turn it into more money. But Franklin would get home late on meeting nights and dawdle over dinner. And of course, the dishes were always waiting when she got home. If they were going someplace together, he would have insisted one of the children wash them. She found herself wondering if the club was worth the trouble with all the rushing, all the nervousness it caused her.

The night before she left on her trip, Louise reached for Franklin, rousing him to make love. It was her way of making peace. "I don't like you going someplace without me," he confessed in his ardor. "I want you here in this bed every night."

Yes, she thought, whether he was in it or not.

The hotel in Athens was disappointingly new and American, and Louise's sandals rubbed a blister the first day as they trudged behind their guide visiting the Acropolis, the Temple of Olympian Zeus and other antiquities—all wonderful but packed with other international visitors. The tourist business had seemingly recovered fully from the war. The next day, she wore more sensible oxfords on their daylong cruise to three islands, which were also overrun with tourists. From Athens, they bused their way across Greece, and Louise began to relax. She had no responsibility but to sit back, look at the fantastic scenery and enjoy the company of her father and sister.

In Delphi, after dinner, the tour guide marched them up a steep hill to a "typical *taverna*" for a bit of Greek nightlife. Almost immediately, small dark men with sensual smiles and admiring eyes started asking both Louise and Marynell to dance. Marynell refused, but Louise smiled back and found herself being taught the steps and propositioned at every turn.

"You ought to see yourself," Marynell said disapprovingly when Louise returned to the table to catch her breath and have something to drink.

"Oh, come on, Marynell. It's fun. Stop sitting there clutching your purse against your chest like the widow ladies and come take a spin."

"Go on," Eddie encouraged. "I'm not any good at that skipping around. I'm better at the waltz."

"Those men are after sex," Marynell said. "They collect tourist ladies like trophies."

"I know," Louise said with a laugh. "It's exciting. God, tonight at least five of them have suggested in varying degrees of English proficiency that I go off with them. Others do it with their eyes."

"Louise!" Marynell said, with a glance at Eddie. But he was busy explaining to one of the widows that he was danced out.

"I don't want to go off with them," Louise said. "I just want to dance. For once in my life, I want to be frivolous. It feels so good not to have to be Mrs. Colonel's Wife or good old mom."

She pulled Marynell to her feet and did an impromptu mazurka with her sister to the clapping and repeated cries of "Oppa!" from both Greeks and Americans. Marynell smiled, then laughed. "You look eighteen," Louise called out.

Finally they stopped, breathless, and were surrounded by eager men. Marynell scooted back to the table. How strange, Louise thought. Marynell used to be the one who chased the boys. Now she was a bastion of propriety.

At the end of the evening, Louise bought a round of drinks for her dance partners. Five very young men circled her and raised their glasses. "*Yasas!*" they toasted.

"Cheers," Louise offered.

"Race you home," she challenged her sister as they left the tavern.

"Act your age, Louise," Marynell said. "You wouldn't behave this way if Franklin were along."

My age, mused Louise. *I'm thirty-seven. And I haven't had much fun. Tonight I did.* Surely it's all right for thirty-seven-year-olds to have fun once in a while. And no, she wouldn't act this way if Franklin were along. She would have sat in there with her purse clutched against her bosom like Marynell lest some randy young male mistakenly ask her to dance.

I love Greece, she thought as she skipped down the steep hill. *I hope God doesn't decide to punish me for having so much fun.*

The next day they went to Hydra and caught the overnight ferry to Brindisi on the Italian coast and were met by another bus and driver. His smile for her seemed special. *My goodness*, Louise thought and looked in her compact mirror to see if she had changed. She decided she had. She didn't look proper.

From the bus window, Louise tried to translate some of the words on signs, using a small tourist dictionary. And she did managed a cheerful "*Buon giorno*" and "*Grazia*" when the bus stopped at a bank in the city of Bari so everyone could change money. She received another beautiful Italian smile for her effort. And again when they stopped for coffee.

In their absence, the bus had been blocked in by half a dozen illegally parked cars. Volunteers came from the bakery shop and shoemaker's to lift the tiny vehicles out of the way so the driver could manipulate the bus into the intersection. A monumental traffic jam resulted with dozens of honking cars demanding passage from four directions. Three policemen, each sporting enough gold braid to do an admiral proud, arrived on the scene. A crowd collected. Women with baby carriages. Men from the barber shop with soap still on their faces. Butchers with blood on their aprons. Diminutive nuns in habits. More policemen. Everyone talking at once.

Italy. Already, she liked the country, Louise thought with a smile when they finally got under way.

And after three days of watching the country pass by her bus window, Louise decided she must have been Italian in a former life. She hadn't known such beauty existed.

Always gregarious, Eddie seemed less interested in scenery than in the company of his peers. He participated in bridge games and visited up and down the aisle of the bus in between stops at picturesque towns for a meal, a visit to the local church, a quick tour of shops. When Marynell tired of discussing children and husbands, she retreated into a novel, looking up occasionally when Louise pointed out a mountaintop town in the distance, a view of the ocean. Louise didn't doze, didn't read, didn't visit except when her sister or father wanted to. She sat contentedly hour after hour looking out the window, speculating about the lives of people who lived in the towns and villages, what prayers they said at their great and small churches, what sorrows they carried to their strange aboveground cemeteries.

Before they reached Venice, the driver announced that the bus needed a new carburetor. Their one-night stay at the seacoast town of Amola would be extended to two while a new one was brought from Bologna. Unfortunately, they would have to cut their planned two-night stay in Venice to one, but the tour guide assured them there would be time to see everything. Louise smiled to herself. They only scratched the surface as they rushed through towns and cities. She'd lived in Frankfurt for a year and was still discovering new things at every turning in a city becoming modern but still rich with a traditional German past. But they could manage the glories of Venice in an afternoon and evening. *No problemma.*

Amola had been billed on the tour itinerary as a typical Adriatic fishing village. The tour guide bragged that it was not on the tourist circuit—this was their chance to see "*Italia pura.*"

The town was charming, built on a hill that sloped gently down to a boat basin peppered with dozens of fishing boats. And instead of a tacky new tourist hotel, the Albergo dei due Galli—the Inn of the Two Roosters—was old and charming and built on a timeless piazza near a medieval clock tower that chimed the hours. The widows complained about shared bathrooms, but Louise, Marynell and Eddie agreed the Rooster Inn was perfect.

Dinner was served in a front courtyard bordering the central square, which soon filled with children playing, young people courting, families taking an evening stroll. Tommaso, the English-speaking proprietor, hovered about Louise. When she rewarded him with a smile, Marynell whispered, "Don't start *that* again."

"What?"

"Flirting."

"Innocent flirting, Marynell. It's nice to be noticed. And Tommaso's kind of cute, don't you think?"

"In a coarse, peasant sort of way, I suppose."

"He runs a nice establishment. This is the best food we've had on the trip," Eddie offered, pouring another glass of wine from the pitcher and helping himself to another piece of bread. "Martha would like it here. Maybe I'll bring her someday."

"It's nice that Martha likes to travel. You two are happy, aren't you?" Louise asked.

"We are. I know that bothers you girls some, but I was happy with your mother, too. The years you girls were growing up were some of the happiest of my life. These are good years, too, though. Just different. I hope you'll understand someday."

"We do," Louise said, patting her father's arm and knowing she spoke only for herself, and only for part of herself. The other part of her would have had her father burn candles at the altar of her mother's memory forever.

They walked after dinner, up and down narrow streets paved with white stones polished to an incredible sheen by hundreds of years of footsteps. When they got back to the inn, Eddie announced he was ready to call it a day. The sisters went into the bar.

A smiling Tommaso was polishing the glassware. Behind him, a framed picture of the Madonna overlooked the rows of liquor bottles. "Ah, the beautiful American ladies, *buona sera*," he said, and without asking poured each of them a brandy.

"You have a lovely inn," Louise said.

"Yes, it is nice, but not mine. This is the hotel of the brother of my wife."

Louise liked his smile. And his weathered face. He looked like a peasant from a Fellini movie, not tall but with thick arms and chest, with blue-black hair and work-worn hands. His eyes, however, were an un-Italian blue, and he had a bit of a paunch. She thought of Franklin's hard, flat belly, the product of nightly sit-ups.

"Where did you learn English?" she asked.

"I cook for American officers after the war—at Milano. You like my brandy?"

"It's excellent, isn't it, Marynell?"

Marynell nodded politely.

"I make the brandy myself. And the wine."

He leaned on the bar with his elbows, his folded hands very close to Louise's. His nails were clipped short. There were dark hairs growing across the back on his hands.

When he smiled at Louise and asked if she wanted some fruit and cheese, she smiled back and nodded. "Yes, that would be lovely."

"He's no different from those boys in Greece," Marynell warned while Tommaso made espresso for three young men. "European men are like that. Sex means nothing to them but a conquest. Let's finish our brandy and go to bed. I'm tired."

"You go on to bed. I'll sit here for a while."

"Louise, you are the wife of an officer in the United States Army—a full colonel. You have three children and responsibilities. I will not permit you to flirt with that man like someone common."

"I just want to talk to him, Marynell, and I am very well aware of who and what I am. But I'm in Italy for the first time in my life, and I think this very nice Italian man will tell me stories about his town and let me practice a few words of Italian. I'm having a good time, honey. Is that so terrible? I feel—grown-up."

"You promise you won't let him seduce you?"

"I promise. On my honor as the wife of an officer and gentleman. Go to bed."

CHAPTER

TWENTY-SEVEN

*L*ouise and Tommaso stayed up until dawn talking. She could not believe their mutual outpouring of words, like they'd been waiting all their lives for someone to talk to. It was more intoxicating than wine.

Sometimes he had to search for the right word in English, and sometimes Louise had to use another word to make herself understood, but those were minor inconveniences. She was envious that he knew two languages. She'd studied French back at Mary Baldwin but remembered next to nothing.

He told her how he respected his wife and loved his two daughters, but his wife now preferred prayer to dancing and sex, and the daughters were all but grown. He seldom went to his home in the inland town of Lugato, preferring to live at the hotel and fish from Amola's jetties and beaches. Tommaso explained that his brother-in-law had a second, grander hotel in Lugato and left the running of the modest Two Roosters Inn to him. The daughters used to come to him on weekends—they liked his cooking—but now they were being courted and seldom came. He had failed his wife. If only he could understand what she was afraid of, maybe he could have helped her to enjoy life. Never once in all her years had she traveled the thirty kilometers to the sea. He feared she would die never having seen the sea. "A tragedy, no?"

Louise had to agree.

She was lucky, Louise told him. Her husband was a fine man who loved her and their children very much. She had managed on her own for more than four years during the Second World War and another year and a half when he went to Korea, but when he came home he expected her to step back into her old role. Her daughter Pauline was a bit like her father. Peter was gentle, Maggie trusting. She'd had another son, but he was dead. Andy.

How strange to be so honest with a man. She and Franklin had never talked like this, Louise thought, realizing how short her and Franklin's conversations usually were. Children. Finances. Schedules. Feelings were seldom discussed. After the last guests had left the bar, Tommaso found her a jacket and they walked down to the beach. The moonlight on the water was breathtaking, and the town behind them looked untouched by the twentieth century. Louise felt as though she had floated away from reality on a long, unwinding tether. Reality would eventually reel her back in, but it was pleasant leaving it for a while.

Taking his arm seemed the most natural thing in the world. Tommaso helped her walk out on a rocky jetty of the boat basin and showed her his favorite fishing rock. "I always catch the best fish here. Tomorrow I cook *un pesce specialmente per l'Americana bellissima.*"

Louise repeated the Italian phrase. Tommaso had her try a few others. She carefully repeated the words after him.

"*Brava!* In three month you speak as a native."

A lovely idea, she mused, sitting beside him on the rock, to be here for three months and learn Italian. But that could never be. She'd been in Germany for a year without learning much of the language. Of course, she spent most of her time with her family and members of the American military community, and it no longer seemed important to learn German—or anything new. She knew enough right now to carry her for the rest of her life. She knew protocol and etiquette. She knew how to check over her children's school assignments for spelling and grammar and how to keep house. She knew how to say the right thing and when to keep her mouth shut and how to conduct a dinner party. And she knew how to accommodate her husband in bed. When she was young, she thought it would be important to learn about art and languages. She'd studied art history and French during her two precious semesters at Mary Baldwin. Why? she wondered. What had her younger self thought she would do with such knowledge that was now mostly forgotten? Her mother had told her not to marry young—to finish school and travel first. Would she herself say the same thing to her own daughters?

"And what do you think about with such a serious face?" Tommaso asked.

"That you are right. I could learn to speak Italian in three months."

"But your voice tells me that when you go from Italy, you will not return."

"That's hard to know. My life is not my own."

"Yes, it seems that way sometimes. But perhaps we make our own prisons. Do you like fishing?"

"I've never tried."

"If you ever return, I will teach you."

They walked some more, miles up the beach, past sleeping villages, tiny farms. "I like this way better," he explained. "In the other direction is a new hotel. First class. With tennis and golf. Why would someone come in Italy for tennis and golf?"

"I don't know. They must be the same people who insist on hamburgers and Coca-Cola wherever they go."

"During the war, the beaches were forbidden because of the mines. Some children from Amola were killed from them. Still, when I walk here, I think of the years that I could not."

And he talked of the war—of starvation and fear and death. "You know the smell of war?" he asked. "It smells of excrement."

He explained that the soldiers would either be in the trenches or marching, and they would never have the opportunity to relieve themselves. Then the bullets would start flying and the bombs falling. Fear was an incredible purgative, he explained. There were no showers, no way to stay clean.

Tommaso was wounded and went home to recuperate. Then Mussolini was deposed, and he never went back. The family's land was often in the cross fire between Germans and Americans, and his father lost his leg to it.

While Tommaso and his father were recuperating, the Germans

occupied his family's farmhouse. The officers were demanding and often cruel, but the soldiers were young, homesick and called his mother "Mama." Tommaso's wife hid in the attic with her two babies. Finally he had sent her home to her mother. She felt safer there. His family was relieved to have her gone.

Often there was no food for days. One night, their last cow was killed in the strafing, and they dug a pit for roasting. The whole village came to sing and dance and fill their bellies. It was the most wonderful party he'd ever known.

Louise found herself wondering about Franklin's war experiences. Had there been wonderful parties when no one knew what the morning would bring? Had he ever soiled himself out of fear? She'd seen his medals, read the commendations, knew he was brave, but since their first night together after the war, he'd spoken of that time only with other men, and more recently to Peter. When she asked him about it, he would grow distant. Finally she stopped trying. She suspected that the war he related to Peter was not the war he actually lived, but perhaps he needed to forget the smells and dying and misery and fear. How separate the worlds of men and women were, how rare to meet a man on common ground.

Tommaso took her back to his seaside rock to watch the sunrise. "This has been one of the most beautiful nights of my life," she told him.

"And for me. I will never forget. But we have tomorrow and another night, and you must sleep. I think your sister will be not pleased with you."

"I know. It can't be helped."

Hand in hand, they climbed back up the hill to the town. At the door to her room, he put his hands on her shoulders, his lips brushed her forehead, her cheeks, her lips. "*Ciao, Louisa. Dormi bene.* Sleep well."

Marynell was white-faced with fury. "Here I've been worried sick, and just look at you."

Louise regarded herself reflected in the half-light. She was still wearing Tommaso's jacket and looked tousled but serene. "I look fine," she said.

"You went to bed with him."

"No, dear, I did not."

Louise kicked off her shoes, dropped her skirt on the floor and fell across her bed.

"I think you owe me an explanation," Marynell said, her voice quivering.

"We watched the sun come up. Please, go to sleep, Marynell. Everything is fine. Really."

She would sleep four hours, Louise vowed to herself. No more. Then she would see him again.

"You'll spend the day with Daddy and me, won't you?" Marynell asked, suspicious.

"No. I'm going fishing."

"What will Daddy think?"

"He will think I am going fishing unless you make it out to be something more. I'm exhausted. Come on, honey, go to sleep."

Marynell was still asleep when Louise woke up. She dressed quietly, took extra pains with her makeup, then wiped half of it off.

Her heart was pounding as she walked into the empty dining room. The rest of the group would be off on a walking tour of the village. They were to visit the church, the market, a bakery, a candle factory and a goat farm. Then they would have a buffet lunch at the fabulous new hotel north of town. There would be time for shopping, of course. Busy, busy, busy. The tour guide was good at his job. He had taken a minor emergency and turned it into an adventure.

The matronly waitress brought her coffee with hot milk and a hard roll. Louise wanted to ask about Tommaso, but she didn't.

She stared out the windows at the sea. So beautiful. Could one ever grow accustomed to such beauty?

She heard footsteps. She waited without turning, imagining him. He stopped behind her, put his hand on her shoulder.

Louise closed her eyes.

"You are well?"

She nodded.

"Shall we go fishing?"

"Yes."

She was doing something she had never done before—living for the minute.

He took her in his ancient truck to a deserted beach. They forgot to fish, but Louise tied up her skirt and waded out in the surf. She felt like a child. Last night they were serious, but today was for fun.

They hiked up to a tiny mountaintop hamlet and shopped for their lunch. Sitting on a wall that formed one side of the piazza, they enjoyed a fabulous view of the seacoast below as they ate bread, cheese and fresh apricots accompanied by hearty red wine. They had a contest to see who could spit apricot pits farther. He won.

They found a spot of grassy shade on the hillside for a nap. When they awoke, it was time for Tommaso to get back to the inn to supervise the preparation of the evening meal.

Louise wanted to help. She put on a big white apron and chopped vegetables, sliced bread and helped serve. Eddie decided to join her and got a white apron of his own. Their traveling companions— except for Marynell—thought it was wonderful fun. Eddie convinced the Italian waitress to join him in singing "Arrivederci Roma" as they carried dishes in and out of the kitchen. So corny. A wonderful evening, Louise thought. She wouldn't have missed Amola for the world. After dinner, one of the widows accompanied a sing-along on a hopelessly out-of-tune piano that sat in the corner of the lobby. Then the tour guide organized them into teams for a game of charades.

Marynell left the others and shyly came into the kitchen to sit by her father at the long wooden table. Tommaso jumped up to get her a glass of brandy. "I don't like charades," she explained.

Tommaso asked Marynell about her children, what Oklahoma was like. She answered reluctantly, not wanting to be charmed. "I understand we are leaving very early in the morning," she said finally. "I think we'd better get to bed. The dinner was lovely, Tommaso." Marynell and Eddie rose together. Louise stayed put. "I'll be up later," she said.

Marynell looked to her father for support. "Are you sure, dear?" he said. "Tomorrow afternoon, we'll be in Venice, and you'll want to be rested."

"I'm going to learn how to make Italian coffee in one of those little pots," she said, as though that was explanation enough.

"Well, then, I'll see you in the morning."

"Sis, I think you'd better come with me," Marynell said evenly.

"Good night, Marynell. Leave the door unlocked."

When they were alone, Tommaso said softly, "I make trouble with your family."

"It's nothing I can't handle."

"Handle?"

"Manage. Take care of."

After coffee, they walked in the square, then up and down the narrow streets of the village. At the end of one street, they climbed a hill to the church and sat for a while in its cool, quiet sanctuary on pews worn by the centuries.

"Do you believe in God?" she asked.

"I think so. I don't like the priests, but I like this place. It's holy to me. And you? Do you believe?"

"Sometimes. Not often. But if God had anything to do with bringing me to Amola, I thank Him sincerely."

Tommaso touched her hand and looked questioningly at her face. She turned her hand over, twined her fingers with his, accepting what would come, watching as he slid to his knees and buried his face in her lap.

Louise caressed his hair, the Madonna looking peacefully down from her ornate frame, and Christ in eternal agony from his cross. Banks of fluttering candles illuminated their holy faces.

Louise knew she would be sorry for the rest of her life if she didn't make love with this man. Perhaps she would also be sorry if she did. Perhaps guilt would ruin her marriage, her life. But could one isolated night of love possibly be that important? She wanted this Italian man very much, and the wanting filled her up. She, who had never been a risk-taker, was prepared to take this one.

But then, hadn't she known this day would come if for no other reason than curiosity? Ever since Mike Williams, she had known. She needed to know what sort of woman she really was—the white-gowned Madonna of Franklin's fantasies or another sort altogether.

She leaned forward and kissed Tommaso's hair, stroked his shoulders and neck. "My darling," she whispered. "My beautiful Tommaso."

Then, still on his knees, he lifted his face and kissed her with incredible tenderness. She closed her eyes and relished the feel of his lips. She was young again, and his was a kiss of young and innocent longing.

As they walked down the hill arm in arm, the mistiness in her eyes made halos around the street lights, around the moon hanging over the water.

The lobby was deserted. His apartment was on the first floor, behind the front desk. Moonlight streamed through the open window. Louise smiled to herself, thinking that the fates had managed to write a wonderful setting for her indiscretion.

He took off his shirt before undressing her, telling her over and over that she was beautiful, and in the moonlight, her body flushed with longing, she was. Reverently, he touched her breasts and thighs. When they embraced, the feel of flesh against flesh took her breath away. And under her fingers, she felt the roping scars on his back, the wounds of war. But he wasn't a soldier, she reminded herself. Not really, not like Franklin. Just a boy who'd been drafted.

She sat on the bed while he removed his trousers. Then they were both naked in the moonlight, free to kiss endlessly, to touch with excited fingers, to whisper words of love, over and over. His passionate whisperings were in Italian. It didn't matter that she couldn't understand him. The sound of his voice, his language excited her.

Then his mouth was at her breast, silenced, while he nursed her to more desire than she had ever felt before.

"Now, please," she begged, and she thought when he lifted his head from her breasts that he would enter her. But no, he wanted to love her first with his mouth. Louise couldn't believe what was happening to her. This was how it could be, how it was supposed to be. And she knew that later, in the night, she would put her mouth on him. Now, she could be glad that Franklin had never permitted such a thing. It made this night all the more special.

And finally, when their bodies could no longer stand to be apart, he entered her. Louise cried out. Again and again. She clutched at his shoulders and her body arched toward his, melting with him. She was beyond wonder, beyond understanding. Beyond anything but sensation and total surrender.

Tommaso fell against her and wept. She couldn't tell him enough times that she loved him. Over and over, like a broken record, like an idiot, the words kept pouring out of her mouth. She couldn't stop to think of other words.

But even as she said the words, she wondered. Did she love the lovemaking or the man himself?

He pulled her head to his shoulder and stroked her hair, her back, but still her heart pounded in her chest. She couldn't be calm. Not yet. Her hands wanted him. Her mouth. She kissed his neck. His chest. She couldn't kiss him enough. Everywhere. Gratefully. Greedily. She wanted to take a bite of him. To crawl inside of him. She adored him. Adored his body. Adored feeling this way, being this way.

When they came together again, it was wild and free. Unchartered.

Marynell stared at her sister in disbelief. Her open suitcase lay across the unmade bed. She held her folded nightgown in one hand, her slippers in the other.

"I just want a few days," Louise explained. "Out of an entire lifetime, is that so much to ask?"

"But you're a married woman. An officer's wife," Marynell said. "What you've done already is terrible enough." She looked down at the items in her hands and dropped them onto the folded clothing in the suitcase. "You can't. I won't let you."

"I hoped you'd understand," Louise said, rubbing her hand over the polished wood of the night table. "I need to do something just for me."

"But what about your husband and your children?" Marynell looked wild-eyed. Afraid.

"This has nothing to do with them," Louise said tentatively, as though testing the words.

"Of course it does. You're betraying Franklin's trust. Without our families, our marriages, we're nothing," Marynell said, her voice tremulous. She was going to cry. "If you stay here with that man, I'll tell Franklin."

Louise sank onto the bed beside her sister's suitcase. The suitcase had been Marynell's college graduation present from their parents. She had taken it on her honeymoon. "What would that accomplish?" Louise asked.

"My God, Louise, the man is a peasant. He probably doesn't even speak grammatically correct Italian. And you're committing adultery." Marynell was crying now, tears breaking loose and rolling down her freshly powdered cheeks.

"Give the man credit, Marynell. He speaks two languages, which is more than either of us can say. And would you be less disturbed if I was 'committing adultery' with a man who had a title?"

Marynell marched across the room, stopped in front of the window and turned, wiping her cheeks hard with the back of her hand like Pauline used to do. Behind her, out the window, were the sky, the beach, the ocean. "What will Daddy say?" she demanded. "What will the other people say? They're already whispering."

"I don't think Daddy'll pass judgment on me. He gave up that right when he was unfaithful to Mother. As for the others, tell them I'm sick. Tell them I was called home. Tell them whatever you want."

Louise rose to stand beside her sister. She wanted to slip her arm around Marynell's waist but didn't dare. "I'm truly sorry if I embarrass you, honey, but I have to stay. I still love Franklin, and I don't want to change my life. I just want a little bit of something else. I have the chance to steal a few days out of my life with a man who is sweet and passionate. That chance may never come again."

Never come again. Was that what this was all about? Louise wondered. A lovely man had come along at a time when age and need permitted her to break out of the careful emotional boundaries in which she had lived her life. But she didn't want to analyze motives. All she could deal with was feelings. For a time, she would be free.

"This trip was supposed to be a time for you and Daddy and me to make up and be family again," Marynell taunted.

"And we've done that. You go on to Venice and Switzerland. I'll meet you and Daddy in Paris at the end of the tour. We'll do Paris together just like we planned. I promise."

"Don't you realize that that man is probably telling his friends in the village about you right now. 'The American lady is really a hot one.' I just can't believe my own sister is being so common."

"I doubt if he's saying anything of the sort. Tommaso's a gentleman."

"A gentleman!" Marynell stared at her sister. "Now I've heard everything. You're crazy, you know. He's an uneducated cook, and you are risking your marriage for a few days of *sex* with him."

"I'm not so educated myself," Louise said, her voice deliberately soft in an attempt to counter the edge of hysteria in her sister's voice. "And I also cook. I'm not risking anything unless you decide to tell my husband, and I don't think you'll really do that."

Marynell looked away first, and Louise regarded her sister in profile. At thirty-eight, Marynell was still attractive, her skin no longer girlishly fresh but smooth and unlined. Her waist was thicker, but not much. Her hair, however, was faded, and she didn't dazzle any more. People didn't turn for a second look. Louise longed for the Marynell of old. That Marynell might have understood.

"I'm going downstairs for coffee," Marynell announced, slamming her suitcase closed and dragging it toward the door. "It's time to put the suitcases out. Come on, Sis, it's not too late. If you hurry, you can get ready." Her voice was pleading. *Please, don't do this thing that threatens everything we have lived our lives for.*

Louise felt herself wavering. Perhaps too much pure joy would shatter her like a pure, high note shattered crystal. And she could not even imagine the heartache if Franklin were to find out.

There were children down on the beach. Three little boys with a dog. Running, laughing. The dog ran out in the waves to fetch a stick. And far out on the rocky arm of the boat basin, an old couple was fishing. They had been there the day before. Tommaso had talked to them, asking them about their catch, about their health, if they thought his American friend was pretty. They had grinned and nodded. The old man had winked at her. Tommaso talked to everyone. A trip down the block to the tobacco store for cigarettes took him an hour. On the way back he gave half of them away to old men sitting on park benches. People came to the hotel bar at night expecting conversation along with their coffee or whiskey.

She was still standing by the window when Marynell returned. Marynell looked at her sister's clothes still scattered about the room. "You're really staying."

"Yes."

"They're loading the bus."

"Did you tell Daddy?"

"Yes. He's on his way up to tell you good-bye. I won't tell anyone else."

"I know."

Marynell came to stand beside her at the window. "It is beautiful here." She sighed. "Maybe I'm a little jealous. You look so radiant."

Louise slipped her arm around her sister's waist. "Do you understand, just a little, why I want to stay?"

"I understand why you want to, but I still don't think it's right. Aren't you afraid God will punish you for being wicked?"

Wicked. No one had ever called her that before. Was she? A wicked adulteress. "I think I'm more afraid of paying a price for daring to be happy even for just a few days," Louise answered. "Everything does seem to have a price."

Eddie came, tapping softly on the open door. "You're sure you want to do this?" he asked.

"Yes."

"Be careful, sweetheart," he said with a good-bye hug. "Don't throw away a good marriage. Don't get your heart broken. And don't expect too much."

"You sound like Mother," Louise said.

On the bus, Marynell stared out the window, seeing the beauty but not caring, feeling empty and betrayed.

She thought of the price she had paid for the sweet, young lust she had shared with a soldier from New York. She had almost ruined her life. She still carried the scars.

She wondered what price Louise would pay for her days in Amola.

. . .

That night after making love, holding each other in the silvery darkness, Louise told Tommaso about Andy. His arms comforted her as he allowed her to relive the horror once again, understanding that her need to tell him was part of the loving. He cried with her.

Here was a man who wept from the power of orgasm and for a small dead boy he had never known. A sweet man. Andy had been sweet. That's what she loved best about him. Louise began to tremble, grief and love all mixed up together.

And when he asked to see a picture, Louise turned on the light on the dresser, and naked they sat side by side on the bed while she fished about in her purse for her wallet then sorted through pictures and cards until she found her smiling four-year-old son. Tommaso took the picture and kissed it.

Maybe she was really in love. Louise didn't know if she should be happy or sad. Would her time with this man make the rest of her life easier or more difficult?

CHAPTER

TWENTY-EIGHT

*L*ouise shared the train compartment with three German businessmen, who talked and smoked their way across France, and two French nuns, who fingered their beads and occasionally murmured softly to each other. Louise sat in her corner, mentally preparing herself for homecoming. She didn't even try to soak up the French countryside, unable to absorb anything further. For her, the trip was over.

She'd been grateful for Paris, however. She would have hated to go straight home to Franklin. She needed the time to put Tommaso behind her before stepping into her husband's arms. The three days of sightseeing in Paris with her sister and father were subdued, but it was hard not to be affected by the city, especially at night with its lights and street life. Louise liked that about Europe—the way people enjoyed the night. Eddie and Marynell asked her no questions about Amola; Louise volunteered nothing.

The worst moment had come over dinner last night. They had been talking about their visit to the Louvre. Quite abruptly, Marynell demanded of their father, "Would you have come back to Mother if she had lived?"

Eddie took a sip of wine before answering. "I think so, but then I never had to decide. The fates intervened. Elizabeth was a beloved duty, Martha a love. It would have been a hard choice."

"It wouldn't have been if you'd never taken up with Martha in the first place," Marynell accused, with a pointed look at Louise.

Louise and Eddie glanced at each other uncomfortably. He motioned to the waiter. "We'd like to order after-dinner drinks," he told the man.

"No, none for me," Marynell said, pushing back her chair.

But today, caught up in the emotion of farewell, Marynell invited Eddie to bring Martha for a visit.

"Yes, I'd like that," Eddie told her.

Marynell had thrown her arms around his neck. Then suddenly the three of them were embracing. Crying. Saying how much they all loved each other.

Now Louise was alone again with her thoughts.

Tommaso. Leaving him had brought physical pain—in her stomach, her chest. "Will you return to me ever?" he asked. They stood at the train station in Ravenna, people rushing all about them, crates of fruit stacked nearby, a small band playing a farewell for a dignitary in a striped suit.

"I can't," Louise said. "But you'll always be in my heart."

"Not ever?"

She looked away.

She would not write to him or call him. Franklin would get his orders any time now. He'd requested Fort Sill. She would never see Tommaso again. It had to be that way. He was once in a lifetime. Franklin and family were real life. And the price of having a great love was the pain of leaving. With his characteristic excessiveness, Tommaso had promised that when he breathed his last, her name would be on his lips. Or was it excessive? Whose name would she be saying?

But that was too melodramatic. His memory would soften and fade. When she was old, she would probably ask herself if it had really happened.

In Franklin's letters from the South Pacific, he had written that if he died, he would be thinking of his beloved wife at the end.

But that was then. Would he still?

Louise decided he would. The thought made her squirm, made her adultery seem all the worse. Even though her husband found her

less perfect now than before, he still carried the image of the innocent young woman he had married. That wife was the one he made
love to.

Tommaso had asked to keep Andy's picture. Just thinking about
that now in the stuffy smoke-filled compartment made Louise cry. She
dabbed at her eyes and tried not to sniffle. The men didn't notice. The
nuns did.

Franklin was waiting for her at the station. She thought of when
he'd arrived in Dallas, returning to her from the war. This time, she
was the one who'd been far away.

As he drove them home, Franklin kept patting her leg, but
complained about Frau Ogle's cooking, about having to come home
to an empty house, about her missing an important reception. There
was a bottle of wine chilling in the refrigerator, he announced. Louise
understood. That was his signal he wanted her back in their bed,
needed sex to make things right again.

Numbly, she gave.

For four days she and Tommaso had been like two children,
discovering each other's bodies, their own sexuality. They'd raced
down the moonlit beach and plunged naked into the surf. With him,
she was uninhibited, sensual, wanton. She had crawled inside of her
fantasies and made them come true.

Surely, no man was ever as passionate as Tommaso. And she had
loved the sex as much as the man.

She dreamed of Amola, Tommaso's voice so real inside her head
it woke her.

She fought for control. There was the rest of her life to be lived, and
she couldn't always be thinking of what could never be.

Like a deep-sea diver decompressing to reenter the world, Louise
lay beside her sleeping husband and forced her mind to go over her
schedule for the upcoming week. She had to get control, to remember
who she was.

She would go to the commissary in the morning to replenish her
empty larder before the kids came in tomorrow evening. She'd fix
chicken fried steak, mashed potatoes and gravy, Waldorf salad,

chocolate cake for dessert—her family's favorite meal. The children would be excited and full of Scandinavian adventures. The best of family life was evenings around the dining room table.

Tuesday would be a full day. In the morning, she had the library cart at the hospital. Tuesday afternoon was bridge. Tuesday evening PTA. Franklin was president.

She was taking Elaine Carter to lunch on Wednesday—for her birthday. Dear Elaine, with whom she'd shared those months on Corregidor before the twins were born, was with her once again. The Army was like that, tearing apart friends only to reunite them again years later. Elaine was Louise's best friend in Frankfurt, the person with whom she could rage when the general's wife was being impossible. At each posting, there had always been at least one wife with whom to exchange secret looks at receptions and wives' club meetings, who understood it was all a game but that not playing it made waves. A sister for a time.

So many farewells.

Don't get melancholy, Louise warned herself.

Thursday evening was couples' bridge. Friday there was a dance at the officers' club.

Saturday evening, they'd probably go the movie at the base theater. Sunday, there was a new chaplain to hear. A black man, Louise was proud of the army for that.

A good life.

She considered tucking her body against Franklin's back. But she might wake him, and she didn't want to make love again. Not tonight.

She had to do something, however, or she was going to cry. Quietly, she slid from the bed and went downstairs. Maybe a bit of brandy would help her get back to sleep.

There wasn't any brandy. She had sherry instead, like her mother would have done.

Jeffrey was waiting when Marynell got off the airplane at Washington's National Airport. His civilian clothes disappointed her. She had wanted the romance of being met by her handsome, uniformed husband. People would have turned to stare when he took her in his arms and kissed her like a scene out of a movie. Jimmy Stewart and June Allyson.

But the kiss was lovely nevertheless.

"I'm glad to be back," she said, clinging to her husband. "I've really missed you. *Really* missed you."

"We've missed you, too, honey. I'm afraid we three guys aren't very good at batching it."

"I'd be disappointed if you were." She was happy to be walking beside her husband, holding his hand. He looked pretty damned good even in a sport shirt, even without a hat covering his receding hairline.

"Where are the boys? I was hoping they'd come with you."

"Matt is camping in West Virginia with a couple of friends. He'll be back Sunday. Eric has a ball game in Richmond."

Her family had adjusted to life in the Washington area better than she had. Jeffrey was stationed at the Pentagon, and they had rented a house in nearby Alexandria, Virginia, one that had a roomy basement for Jeffrey's woodworking tools. They seemed so civilian now—Jeffrey even wore civilian clothes to work much of the time, someone in authority having decided that so many uniforms in the nation's capital made the country seem militaristic. Jeffrey was a member of an interservice team making a yearlong feasibility study on the possible elimination of selected American military bases and the possible consolidation of others. Such studies had been done before, but bases were seldom eliminated. Members of Congress got very upset if a base in their district was threatened.

Marynell felt cast adrift not living on a post. But she had made friends with two other Army wives who lived on her block and had been invited to join a bridge club of off-post wives. She took pride in making the best of things. At least it wasn't as bad as Florida State, where Army was a college course.

She chattered on the drive home. About her daddy's funny little English cottage on the channel. Anecdotes about their assorted traveling companions. "And Paris. Oh, Jeffrey, I see what you mean. It was so beautiful. I want us to go there together. In France, I kept remembering names of places you had been during the war. I hope you get a European assignment next. You deserve to see peacetime Europe."

The house was dark, the lawn overgrown. But Marynell felt a surge of relief as the car rolled to a stop. Home.

The living room had been picked up, but the dining room table was covered with several weeks' worth of newspapers. She was afraid to look at the kitchen. Tomorrow.

She stood in the entry hallway, taking a minute to adjust.

The house was nice enough—a pseudo colonial with a big backyard for a garden. Marynell did like having a garden again. And it had been fun to paint and wallpaper. Walls in government quarters were all cream-colored, wallpaper against regulations.

"You must be exhausted," Jeffrey said as he started up the stairs with her suitcase.

"Not too exhausted for a bath and a welcome-home drink with my husband."

She added scented oil to her bath water and took the time to shave her legs. Feeling a little self-conscious, she put on her one sexy nightgown. She hadn't worn it since their last anniversary. Number seventeen. Louise had been married nineteen years. She and her sister would soon be middle-aged.

Her nipples and pubic hair were clearly visible through the sheer black fabric, and she found the sight of herself in the bathroom mirror arousing. She didn't look middle-aged.

She slid a finger into her vagina. Wet. Nice.

She put her finger to her tongue, tasting what Jeffrey would taste. He hadn't done that in a long time. She worried that he didn't want to anymore.

Jeffrey had a bourbon-and-water waiting for her. Marynell turned the radio on to mood music, propped a pillow against the headboard and leaned against it. The drink tasted good. She'd have two. Sex was always better after two drinks, and she needed good sex tonight. Time and again on the flight from London, she'd closed her eyes for a moment of anticipation.

Over the years, their sex life had been glorious at times, but more often than not, it was simply affectionate. But that was the nature of marital sex. Everyone knew that, and she and Jeffrey were no different. Still, in the last three or four years, sex had become increasingly infrequent. That was her fault as much as Jeffrey's. Maybe more. She needed to work at it more. More touching. Candlelight dinners when the boys weren't home. More bedtime drinks. More sex talk. And passion even if she had to pretend. She didn't mind when she came to sex dutifully, but she couldn't stand it when Jeffrey seemed that way.

"Well, tell me some more about your trip," he said politely, like one would speak to an aunt. *Tell me all about your tour of all those rose gardens in Georgia.*

Marynell heard herself talking too fast, using too many superlatives. She didn't mention the stop in Amola. She had wondered if she would break her promise to her sister and tell him. Louise's secret would be safe with Jeffrey, and Marynell liked the idea of sharing such an intimacy with him, of telling him about her dismay and pain over the entire episode, of her great disappointment in her sister. But what if he only shrugged? What if he *didn't* say he was shocked and that he was so grateful theirs was a marriage built on trust and fidelity?

Her sister's behavior had shaken her. Louise, always so good, had made love with a man she hardly knew. Marynell still had trouble believing it. It was one of the most shocking things of her entire life. Yes, she thought, making a mental list. Rape. The Japanese bombing Pearl Harbor. Her mother's death. Newsreel pictures of the liberated death camps. Her daddy marrying that nurse. Andy's death. Her sister being unfaithful to her husband.

The rape had affected her the most deeply, she realized, more even than her mother's death. It had changed her more than she allowed herself to acknowledge. The fear would always be there inside of her. Bad things over which she had no control could happen. But the even currents of her daily life kept such thoughts safely buried. As long as she had a full social calendar, attractive clothes, a weekly hair appointment, a clean house, a faithful husband and sons who loved her, she was fine.

Her sister's betrayal of the careful life eroded Marynell's confidence. But Louise promised it was just a fling. She wasn't going to leave Franklin. She would be good from now on.

So why do I feel so frightened? Marynell wondered. Louise had been a perfect wife and mother. Her husband's future was secure. Her son would have no trouble getting a West Point appointment. Her daughters dreamed of military weddings. Louise already had everything that was important, yet she had wanted something more, something outside her ordered existence. It made Marynell's head hurt to think about it.

She held her glass out to Jeffrey for a refill.

As soon as he was gone, Marynell hurried to the bathroom for aspirin. Her face was pale in the mirror, and she brushed on some color.

She sat on the bed and rubbed her temples. Jeffrey was taking a long time. On the radio, the Four Aces sang "True love's a many splendored thing." True love. A man and a woman being faithful forever. A beautiful song. She wished she could make it play again when Jeffrey came back. Marynell went to lean over the banister to call down and ask if he needed help, but the kitchen light went out and she dashed back to bed.

"Well, what's been going on around here?" she asked as she accepted her drink. "How's your life been?"

"Fine. Same old stuff. Eric lives and breathes baseball. Matt's either under the hood of that old truck or driving it God knows where. Says he wants to be a forest ranger."

"He'll get over that. What about you? How's work?"

"I write memos. And I write memos in response to memos. My job title should be memographer."

"Did General Thompson like the speech you wrote for him?"

"Oh yes. Now, I'm actually writing one for our illustrious chief of staff. 'When Is It Time to Close the Old Fort Down?'"

"Fantastic. You must really be good at it. That's how Franklin got in so good with MacArthur—writing his speeches."

Jeffrey sipped his drink.

"Did you go to the Thompsons' party?"

"No."

"Oh, Jeffrey, you promised. Now you make me feel bad that I left. You really should have gone. The guest list must have read like a Pentagon who's who."

"Yeah. Probably so."

His tone said not to pursue it. She didn't. He was in another one of those moods—just inches away from saying he wanted to resign his commission, but he'd gotten over it before, and he would this time. Writing policy speeches for the Pentagon brass was getting him noticed. Of course, it was the Pentagon that had brought on this new restlessness. He was past due for an overseas assignment. That's what they both needed, but in the meantime, the Pentagon exposure couldn't hurt.

The drink was making her light-headed. She touched her neck and trailed her fingers along her shoulder. Her skin felt good.

She wanted him to say something nice to her, that she looked sexy in her black gown, that he'd missed her terribly, that it was going to feel wonderful making love to her, that he loved her.

"You okay, honey?" she asked.

He looked at her, his expression softening. "Yeah. I'm fine. You know, you really are one fine-looking woman."

"You know how much I love you, don't you?" she asked, touching his face.

He nodded. "You're more woman than I ever deserved."

Marynell turned out the lamp, but there was enough light from the window for her to see him down the rest of his drink in one swallow.

"Honey?" he said, feeling the wetness on her face.

"I missed you," she said. "Make love to me, darling. I love you so much that I get scared sometimes."

"Ah, Marynell. You don't know how I need to hear you say that."

Afterwards he told her. He turned on the lamp and faced her, his head cradled on his arm. Surely she realized by now that there would be no promotion to full colonel, to brigadier. "I want to get out now before they retire me. With my cadet years, I have twenty-five years of service. I can retire at half pay and still have enough time left to do something else."

Marynell was rigid for a moment. She could feel the hysteria taking hold, grabbing at her throat. Jeffrey tried to pull her to him, but she scrambled from the bed, grabbed her old cotton robe from the back of her closet door, and began to pace up and down the space between the bed and the dresser, weeping bitter, frightened tears. He should try harder. If he really worked at it hard enough, he could make it happen. Maybe Franklin could help him. Franklin had influence. What was going to happen to them?

Jeffrey waited until she had run down and sunk bewildered and exhausted into the corner chair.

"I've wanted to resign my commission for years, Marynell," he said softly. He was sitting up now, his back to the headboard, his nakedness covered with a sheet. "You know that, but you've always talked me out of it. My career never really was on track—not like you wanted it to be. The next generation of generals was ear-marked years ago—the guys like Franklin, if they kept their noses clean. They're given the troop commands, sent to the career colleges, given the opportunities to shine—but that sounds like bitter grapes when the truth of the matter is, I never had it in me to shine. I was never a heavy hitter. Guys like Franklin, Peter, Danny Norton were born to a military life. You were, too. I knew it was a mistake for me back in my West Point days, but I didn't want to disappoint my parents and Elise. And I didn't have a grand desire to be anything else, so I stayed and graduated in the bottom half of the class. My classmates started passing me in rank almost before my diploma was dry. Poor Marynell. I wish I'd known how impor-tant all this was to you back at Fort McClellan. I could have told you then."

"Are you sorry you married me?"

"No, but you're sorry you married me, and in the end, it's the same thing."

"You don't know that you won't get promoted. It could still happen," she said woodenly.

"I don't think I want to wait to find out."

"So what about me?" Marynell demanded. "What about what I want? Doesn't that matter? Is it all what *you* want?"

"You're still a beautiful woman. Maybe we should get a divorce, and you can find a man who will make you proud."

"A divorce!" Her voice was shrill.

Then suddenly, she had a hideous thought. "There's someone else. You've been seeing someone else. This is just a ruse to get me to leave you."

He took too long to answer.

"My God, Jeffrey. Not you, too. My father was unfaithful to my mother. My sister screwed some dumb Italian on this trip."

She enjoyed the look of shock that registered on his face. And he thought Louise was so damned perfect.

"No, I haven't been unfaithful to you, Marynell, but I have been writing to Karen. We call sometimes."

Karen. It took her a minute to realize who he meant. Elise's sister. Matt's aunt. Matt had visited her in Wisconsin.

"What are you telling me?" she demanded.

"That it's time for us either to start over or go our separate ways. I can't give you your fondest dream, Marynell. I'm sorry about that. I always wished that we could share a dream, and I never understood why you cared so much about what other people thought, why you worked so hard to impress people who didn't really matter. At least twenty families live on this street, and the only ones you've bothered with are Army. I met the Sanchezes next door while you were gone. They're great—a lovely old couple. You never even told me they'd invited us to dinner."

"I didn't think you'd be interested in two elderly Cubans." Marynell longed for another drink. For the evening to start over. She was Alice falling down the damned well. No control. Things happening to her over which she had no control.

"No. *You* weren't interested in two elderly Cubans. All you care about is Army. You love the damned Army more than you love me."

"That's not so," Marynell said, pulling her robe tight over her nakedness. An old, ugly robe. She should have thrown it away long ago. Wives should look pretty for their husbands. "I just needed something to work for. What else was there? I wanted you to be successful. I wanted to be married to a successful man. Is that so terrible? I wanted to work hard and have something to show for it, like when I plant a garden and take care of it and have fresh vegetables to cook for my family."

"God, Marynell, you never hedged your bets. I'd give anything to make you happy, but—"

"Happy!" Marynell shrieked, starting her pacing again, using both hands to keep the front of her robe closed. "Happy is something you wish for your children. All I wanted was secure and safe." She spun around to face him over the foot of the bed. "Calling another woman! Writing to her! You were calling her tonight, weren't you, while I was up here waiting for you to make love to me?"

She waited for him to deny it, but he closed his eyes and leaned against the headboard.

"Damn you, Jeffrey. I never did that. Not once have I even thought about being unfaithful. I hate men. Men don't care what women think or want. You just rape us and leave us to crawl home alone."

She threw herself at him, meaning to hit him, to hurt him, but he grabbed her and held her tightly against his bare chest.

She struggled halfheartedly against him, then began to sob.

"Is that what happened to you, Marynell? Did some man rape you and leave you frightened for the rest of your life?"

"Don't leave me," she begged. "I could stand anything but that. Please don't leave me."

He rocked her back and forth like he used to do with the boys when they were little, and kissed her forehead, stroked her back. "No, baby. I won't leave you, not if you love me."

CHAPTER

TWENTY-NINE

*A*n MP checked her father's ID, then stepped back from the car to offer a smart salute. "The Artillery Center" read the well-lighted, red and gold sign at the main entrance to Fort Sill. And indeed it was forever pulling its own back for schooling and training or to conduct the schooling and training for others.

Maggie was certain fate had intervened on her behalf. Major General Fenworth T. Norton was currently post commandant of Fort Sill. She and her Danny boy would be together again.

The whole family was sitting upright, peering through the night at their new posting. Maggie remembered Fort Sill from when Aunt Marynell and Uncle Jeffrey lived here. A pretty place. Old. Dignified. Even at night, it looked Army—a white-curbed, well-trimmed, litter-free oasis in a disorderly world.

Finally, Maggie thought with tears in her eyes. Poor Danny. He must be standing on his ear by now. When she had called him from her grandparents' home in Florida, she promised to be there by early evening on Sunday, but it was now after eleven.

The trip back to Danny had been an endless one. After they'd docked in New York, claimed their beagle and station wagon, both of which had been sent on an earlier ship, the family drove first to Virginia for a week with Aunt Marynell, Uncle Jeffrey and the cousins. A long week. Eric was a spoiled brat with Aunt Marynell waiting on him hand and foot like he was some sort of prince. And Matt was sullen. He didn't want to hear about Danny. Christ. Just because Danny was a general's son, Matt accused her of being as stuck up as his mom. Maggie cried. She didn't want Matt to hate her. They'd always been best buddies. After that he was nicer, but they didn't talk about Danny anymore.

Maggie suspected that Matt liked her more than he should, and after all, they weren't blood cousins, but he made her feel uncomfortable. Unrequited love was okay for books but too sad for real life. She wished Matt had a girlfriend. She wished he was as happy as she was.

Her mom had sure been happy to see Aunt Marynell. Maggie wondered if she and Pauline would be that glad to see each other when they were grown. Dad actually got testy when Mom and Marynell stayed gone too long on their shopping expeditions or disappeared too long for back rubs. Daddy always wanted Mom to pay more attention to him than anyone else. Both women cried when they said good-bye. Maggie didn't like to see her mother cry.

From Virginia they had driven to Florida to see Grandmother and Grandfather Cravens. Grandfather kept wanting to give her money and getting her confused with Pauline. Half the time, his fly was unzipped. That really upset Daddy. He kept taking his poor old father aside and making him zip up. Grandmother didn't seem as formidable as she used to. She wanted to touch them a lot, but Pauline and Peter kept their distance; so Maggie would sit by her grandmother and hold her hand. Such old hands, skin dry as parchment, blue with veins. It was hard to imagine being that old.

The family had left Florida early yesterday morning for the two-day drive to Oklahoma. Hans, the beagle they had acquired in Germany, had been restless and refused to ride in the back of the station wagon. He was continually hopping over the backseat to walk across her and Pauline, leaving their shorts-clad legs crisscrossed with red marks from his toenails.

Daddy wouldn't let her and Pauline listen to Elvis Presley on the radio but insisted on singing along in an exaggerated baritone whenever "The Yellow Rose of Texas" played, which was frequently. It made them giggle. They'd never heard their daddy sing except at church.

Peter either sat up front with Mom and Daddy or crawled in the back among the suitcases to nap. Her father did all the driving although her mother kept offering to take a turn. Pauline and Peter were sixteen but didn't have driver's licenses yet since the legal driving age in Germany was eighteen. They both planned to take their driving test tomorrow morning first thing.

They stopped first at post headquarters so Dad could report in with the OD and pick up the keys to their quarters. Not much longer now.

Her parents started reminiscing about living on the post as newlyweds. Her father put an arm around his wife's shoulders. "Wonderful memories," Franklin said. Louise turned to kiss his cheek.

"Come on, Mrs. Cravens, you can do better than that," he chided as they pulled up in front of a set of two-story red-brick quarters. And they really kissed. Maggie approved. Her mother had been so quiet since Virginia. Daddy needed to cheer her up.

"I'm glad to be back here," Franklin said. "Fort Sill is the home office for artillerymen, and so many people I've served with are stationed here."

Yes, Maggie thought. Like the post commandant.

She had called Danny from Frankfurt after her father had made the announcement about his next assignment. She hadn't even asked permission but walked straight to the phone and placed a call to him right in front of everyone. The call had gone straight through, and almost at once, the Nortons' striker was answering.

When Danny came to the phone, she told him she loved him, right there in the front hallway with her listening family sitting around the dining room table. Then she crept with the phone into the tiny storeroom under the stairs for a few private words. Danny was in a closet on his end.

"We don't have to wait anymore," Maggie told him. "I was sorry we didn't do it on your last night here. If you'll buy some rubbers, I'm ready. I think about it all the time. I love you so much, and I want you in me, Danny. I want us to make love."

"I wish we were older, Maggie. I want to marry you."

"I know. But maybe this will make the wait easier."

She hung up and went back to her family. Peter didn't even tease. Pauline looked a little flushed. Mom and Daddy were talking in more-normal-than-normal voices about the crisis in the Middle East. Eisenhower had refused to sell arms to Israel. Nasser was being courted by the Soviets. They didn't say Maggie should have asked first before making a transatlantic phone call. Maggie hadn't been able to eat her dessert.

Their handsome quarters were located in the area of Fort Sill known as New Post, right next door to where Aunt Marynell and Uncle Jeffrey used to live. Maggie would have preferred Old Post, where the post commandant's quarters were.

They unloaded the car. The quartermaster had delivered cots and basic furniture for them to use until their whole baggage arrived from Germany and their furniture from storage. The phone was not connected.

"I have to go see Danny," Maggie announced.

"Oh, honey," Louise said. "It's midnight."

"He's waiting for me. Peter can drive me."

"He can't without a license."

"I'll walk then. I remember the way. Matt and I used to ride over there on bikes. Danny can bring me home."

Her mother and father exchanged looks. "I'll drive her over so she can say hello, then bring her right back," Louise said.

"No." Franklin was in civilian clothes, but he was giving an order.

Maggie started for the door. Peter and Pauline stared in wide-eyed disbelief at this younger sister who dared defy their colonel father.

Without looking at Franklin, Louise grabbed the car keys from the newel post and raced after her.

"I don't want to come right back," Maggie said as her mother unlocked the station wagon.

"Be thankful for fifteen minutes, young lady. It's late, I'm tired and your father's angry."

In the car, Maggie asked, "How come you remember what it was like to be young and Daddy doesn't?"

"Your father and I were never young," Louise said flatly.

Maggie didn't bother to ask for an explanation. Just a few more minutes and she could touch Danny. Her heart was pounding, her palms and underarms were sweating, her crotch moist.

"I love him, you know."

"I know," Louise said.

"Why are you driving so slowly?"

"I am driving twenty-five miles an hour just like the signs say."

"Please, Mom, just a little faster."

Louise obliged. They passed the headquarters building with its empty flagpole. The hospital.

"We're almost there, aren't we?" Maggie asked, straining to recall post geography. She didn't really remember the way.

"Yes, we're almost there."

Danny was waiting on the screened front porch of the impressive post commandant's house with its two ornamental brass cannons on either side of the doorway. He made the short front walk in two galloping steps as the station wagon pulled to the curb. Maggie was out of the car in a flash.

They crashed into each other's arms. Six months it had been. An eternity. Danny lifted her off her feet and spun her around. "Maggie, Maggie, Maggie," he said as his mouth found hers.

Greedily she kissed him. His arms were strong around her, his body firm, his eager penis hard in his blue jeans as it pressed against her belly. Soon, she thought. Soon. More than anything in the world, she wanted to give herself to him completely. They had done everything else. There wasn't an inch of each other's bodies they hadn't touched and kissed. They had satisfied each other with their mouths and hands, time and again, but she had made him stop short of the ultimate act. But no more. She was his and he was hers. His penis would be the first and only ever to enter her, and his coming would fill her. Totally. In a few years they would make babies. She loved him as much as it was possible to love another human being. More. "Danny, Danny, I'm home, baby. I'm home."

With Maggie's arms clinging to his neck, her legs wrapped around his middle, Danny clumsily walked around the side of the house for a few minutes of privacy, of hands inside of clothes.

Trembling, Louise watched from the station wagon as they

disappeared into the shadows. "Oh, my God," she said aloud, fists of her own longing grabbing at her insides.

She wanted to beat her breast and keen like a primitive, grieving squaw. In her mind, high wailing pierced this fine old Army neighborhood with its sleeping families who surely knew better than to permit raw feeling to invade their careful existence.

But she wept quietly. She wept for her own lost passions and for those two children and their vulnerability. Life was not kind to those who dared to soar into the rare, pure air beyond mountain peaks, and they would have to discover that for themselves.

Where are you, my darling Tommaso? Are you well? Do you think of me still?

She hit her head against the steering wheel to fight against images of white beaches and a playful surf, of a laughing, blue-eyed Italian with an unmilitary belly that hung just a bit over his belt.

Better never to have known.

CHAPTER

THIRTY

*T*here were certain places outside Bologna where a man could turn down a country road, drive slowly, and a whore would appear from behind a tree.

Twice, in the summer of 1936, Tommaso and two friends had made Sunday journeys to Bologna. Three youths on two motorcycles looking for sex. All the way from Lugato.

Tommaso wondered how the whores got there, who took them back to their homes. They disturbed him, these women who sold their bodies. Did their mothers know? Did they like sex? What happened to them when they got old?

Some of the women only did men in cars, but not all of them. Matteo talked to them. He was older—almost twenty. Tommaso watched the negotiations, feeling strange and nervous and not sure he really wanted to do this but what would his friends think if he didn't? Most boys used whores for their first time. A man needed to be experienced.

The boys parked their motorcycles well off the road. Both times, the women had a blanket stashed in the underbrush. The price was two lire per boy—in advance. Matteo went first. The first time, Tommaso had had to masturbate himself to an erection. He avoided looking at the women's faces while he had his turn.

The second Sunday afternoon on the way back to Lugato, they drove through the small town of Signano, their cycles leaving a trail of dust as they rounded the square a second time for the benefit of the old men sitting there. The motorcycle—an old Morini he had rebuilt—was Tommaso's most prized possession. He'd saved to buy it since he was thirteen. When he rode his motorcycle, he felt important. It didn't matter so much that he was just a laborer who loaded trucks at the cannery.

On the edge of town, Tommaso waved to a girl standing in the doorway of a fine, two-story house with green shutters and roses climbing on an iron fence. Shyly, as though her upper arm was bound to her body, she returned Tommaso's wave.

The following weekend, he went back to Signano on his own. The girl was still standing in the doorway just as though she had never left.

Tommaso asked for a drink of water. She was pretty but short with heavy breasts, the type of girl who would thicken with her first baby. And already, there were two frown lines between her eyes.

But even though she said very little, her eyes were interested. And she seemed like an angel after the heavily painted whores with their hard eyes and tight, gaudy dresses.

Her name was Julianna.

Tommaso went back the following week. Julianna's widowed mother fixed him coffee. They sat in the parlor, the signora rocking while he and Julianna looked at a family album. All his life, Tommaso had been able to talk to anyone. He struck up conversations with nuns and Gypsies and the aging *principessa* who lived on an estate outside Lugato and rode into town in a shiny black car with a driver. But to Julianna and her mother, Tommaso could think of nothing to say. His shirt grew moist. Sweat trickled down his forehead.

He didn't go back for almost a month. He didn't go to Bologna either. When he visited a second time, the signora actually smiled when she saw him at her door. Julianna looked down at her hands. This time, after serving coffee, the signora left them alone in the parlor, her steps heavy as she climbed the wooden steps to the second floor, the floor creaking as she walked down the hallway, and a door closed firmly overhead. Tommaso sat silently with Julianna on the high-backed love seat while a clock ticked loudly on the shelf above them. Julianna didn't stop him when he touched her hand, when he turned her face to kiss her. He hadn't wanted to kiss the whores. Julianna's lips were soft and yielding, her breath warm and sweet. She smelled fresh and clean, like clothes dried in sunshine. She didn't protest when he slid his tongue between her lips. When he put a tentative hand on her breast, she looked away but didn't stop him.

She never stopped him from doing anything.

They had little to say to each other. During the week, he would think of a few polite questions to ask after the signora had climbed the stairs, but once he asked them and she'd supplied answers—yes, she was feeling better; yes, the peaches were especially sweet this year—they'd lie on the rug in front of the love seat. He'd lift her skirts and push aside her underclothing.

Afterwards, Tommaso would desperately want to leave but would force himself to sit for a while longer. She'd excuse herself for a few minutes, come back with her clothes straight and her hair combed. She had nice hair, long and thick and shiny brown. He would ask a few more polite questions and sip the sweet liqueur she served him.

In the beginning, he would invite her to take a ride on his motorcycle or walk to the square for ice cream, but she always said no. It was too cold or too hot. She had a cough or a headache. The only place he ever saw her was in the parlor. He never even stayed for dinner.

Tommaso did not love the silent girl with the heavy breasts, but the prospect of sex was overwhelmingly seductive—though he'd always felt the press of disappointment on the drive back to Lugato. He wouldn't go back anymore, he'd promise himself. He'd look around for another girl, one he could talk to. By nighttime, however, he would be thinking of Julianna again, wanting her, needing to push himself in her soft, warm flesh and feel that feeling like no other. Even so, he'd often skip a week, knowing that mother and daughter were waiting for him, wondering why he didn't come. He never missed two Sundays in a row. The drive to Signano was erotic with anticipation. For years afterwards, whenever Tommaso went down that same road, lined on each side with tall cedars, he would remember those glorious motorcycle rides with the wind on his face, the power of the machine under him, his penis hard, knowing Julianna would be there to receive his youthful lust.

He worried that he was obligating himself by going back. Did it mean he and Julianna were engaged even though no mention was ever made of marriage and the future? Matteo said if you had sex with a nice girl, it was assumed you intended to marry her.

But was Julianna a nice girl? She hadn't been a virgin, and surely that let him off the hook. Or at least Tommaso didn't think she had been. There had been no blood. She had not cried out in pain. But he kept this information to himself. In case he had to marry her, he certainly didn't want anyone to know he hadn't been the first.

Of course, he would eventually marry someone. Only priests didn't marry. He just wanted to make sure he didn't repeat his parents' bleak marriage. And there was no hurry. He wanted to do things first. His dreams varied. An aviator. A merchant marine. An engineer on a train. A truck driver. A soldier, with medals on his chest and a beautiful woman on his arm. Always he dreamed of something that would take him away from Lugato to a place where life was less predictable and people stayed young longer and marriage did not mean an end to laughter. In Lugato, men a scant half dozen years older than he was already seemed tired and old. They worked in fields or in the cannery from sunup until sundown then shuffled home to an indifferent wife and another child every year until finally his wife would go sleep with her daughters, leaving her husband to an empty bed. Then the men would spend their evenings at the bar, playing cards with other men whose wives were finished with babies. It always seemed to Tommaso that his father loved his cronies more than he loved his wife and children, that the only time he hurried was in the evening when he was heading for his favorite bar. But then Tommaso had been the last child of seven, and maybe it hadn't always been that way. After the war when his mother died, Tommaso's father wept and tore at his hair. Once a week for the rest of his life, he hobbled to the cemetery on his wooden leg to put fresh gladiolas in the urn on her grave. "Your mother was a saint," he would tell his children, wiping his eyes with a soiled handkerchief, "a blessed saint." Tommaso supposed she was if not ever doing anything wrong meant one was a saint. He could hardly remember his mother doing anything but cooking and going to church Sunday morning in her black dress—like Julianna. And by that time, Tommaso was playing cards every evening at his favorite bar. He had become his father.

But before Julianna whispered with downcast eyes that she was going to have a baby, Tommaso still thought he had a choice in this life, that there had to be another way. Surely it was possible to have love and laughter, but never once had he thought he would have them with Julianna. He was using her like he had used the whores. What he did not understand was why she permitted it. Maybe she liked it more than he thought, but she was so quiet, so still.

Tommaso knew about safe days. But he trusted her to tell him if it wasn't all right. After all, there was no way for him to know.

Unless he asked.

Always, after he arrived, the signora would serve coffee, then climb the stairs, leaving the two young people alone to their devices, until Tommaso obligingly got her daughter pregnant.

By then, he'd been coming to the house in Signano for over a year. And he knew that Julianna was twenty-six and that her fiancé had run out on her five years ago. He supposed humiliation kept her from walking in the square. He felt sorry for her.

Tommaso wanted to blame the mother. Before he'd come along, Julianna's mother thought she had a spinster daughter on her hands. The signora's younger daughter was safely married to a dentist. Her son had married a stupid woman but had used his inheritance from his father to buy a small hotel and was prospering. Two other children had died. Only Julianna remained. An embarrassment. The signora had made it very easy for Tommaso to trap himself.

For he knew he had only himself to blame. Had he thought he could just keep going back forever without ever having to pay the price?

His father was raking leaves when Tommaso went to him with his dilemma. "Are you certain the baby is yours?" his father asked.

Tommaso nodded. No other man could be so stupid.

"Then you have to marry her."

"I don't love her."

"It doesn't matter. Marriage is for housekeeping and children and respectability. You can love your children."

Julianna and her mother cried during the ceremony. Tommaso didn't understand why. Wasn't this what they wanted?

He and Julianna embarked on a wedding trip to Rimini in the small truck he had gotten in trade for his motorcycle. Julianna cried and vomited until finally he turned the truck around and took her home to her mother. She spent her pregnancy in bed, nauseated, with her mother hovering. They lived in her mother's house, and Tommaso worked in his brother-in-law's hotel. He liked working there better than at the cannery. Sometimes he waited tables or tended bar, other times he worked behind the desk. His brother-in-law was as humorless as his mother and sister, but a decent man who treated his employees with respect.

After the baby was born, Julianna bled for almost six months, one of them spent in the hospital. When sex finally resumed, she became pregnant almost at once. Again nausea took her. And when their second daughter was born, Julianna almost died from blood loss. After that, they only made love in the days immediately following her period—if at all.

Tommaso loved the babies, but Julianna hovered protectively whenever he played with them, the two lines between her brows now deep furrows. She screamed in panic if he tossed a baby in the air.

The war offered escape. Conscription into Il Duce's army seemed a reprieve from life. But not for long. His brother Paulo was killed in Ethiopia, his friend Matteo in Greece. Tommaso himself was wounded in Sicily. During those weeks in a field hospital near Messina, he discovered how much he wanted to live, even though it meant returning to a bleak marriage. He wanted to see his daughters grow up and enjoy the company of family and friends. The happiest day of his life was when two aging uncles came to take him home.

He insisted Julianna and the girls come live with him in his parents' house. By then, his father had lost his leg and suffered from a terrible infection, and his mother needed help. There were two injured men to nurse, and first one nationality of occupying soldiers, then another—Germans, Americans, British and even Canadians—taking up residency in the house and barn. But soon Tommaso sent Julianna back to her mother's house. She was useless crying in the attic, hiding from the soldiers. Besides their ill-fated wedding trip, her time at the farm in Lugato was the only time his wife ever left Signano.

The time after the war was good for Tommaso. He liked working for the Americans and living in Milano, going to visit his wife and daughters only once or twice a month. The money was good. He learned English and cooking. Life was varied and exciting. But the Americans went home in 1947, taking their jobs and their money.

In 1950, when his brother-in-law bought the hotel in Amola, only thirty kilometers from Signano, Julianna refused to move there. The sea air would be bad for her lungs, for her daughters' lungs. The smell of fish upset her stomach.

Tommaso went without her. He missed his friends at the bar more than he missed his wife and children. But he found that he loved the sea. It brought him peace and acceptance. And he liked living at the hotel. There were always people around to talk to, and he took pride in his cooking, in a well-run establishment. Everyone knew it was his brother-in-law's hotel, that his wife was a strange woman who stayed in her mother's house. Tommaso didn't have to explain himself. For several years, his daughters came to him on weekends. He let them run barefoot on the beach and sleep with the windows open.

Eventually, however, they stopped taking their shoes off. They might cut their foot or get a disease, they told him. And their windows were kept closed at night. Sleeping in a draft caused joints to stiffen.

Their mother's words.

Tommaso found pleasure in the sun and the seasons and the tug of a fish on his line. He looked forward to the first cigarette in the morning and the last one at night, making a ritual of their smoking. He relished the smell of cooking food and liked to watch people enjoy what he had prepared. And he loved the men who came nightly to the hotel bar, gossiping, arguing politics and, like him, refusing to be sad.

Marcella, a widow almost twenty years his senior, came often to his bed. Her thighs were bigger than his, but she was kind and comfortable, and Tommaso felt much affection for her. But eventually, her children decided she was too old to live alone and sold her house, arranging for her to live a part of the year with each of them. Marcella became like a child again, her activities supervised. Tommaso visited her Sunday afternoons in whichever kitchen she was currently cooking. She didn't live very long, though, without her own house. Sometimes Tommaso trudged up the hill to the cemetery and put flowers in the urn on her grave. It made him think of his father.

On Marcella's tombstone, her children had had an epitaph inscribed. "Sainted Mother who lived for her children." Tommaso smiled at that. He hoped all those other sainted mothers interred here had a few secrets from their children, that their lives had been more than black dresses and pots of pasta. But he suspected that was not the case and wished he had made Marcella feel more special.

Tommaso didn't dream anymore about flying airplanes and going to distant places. He was satisfied to live out his years in his beloved Amola by the sea. But sometimes he ached with loneliness for the love he had never known. Just once, he'd like for a woman to look at him with love in her eyes.

He'd think of that as he stood on his rock, casting his line.

For years after the beautiful Louisa had passed through his life, when he fished, when he walked alone on the beach, he would pretend she was with him or plan how it would be if he ever saw her again. Then he simply remembered. She had been his star, his shining moment.

Sometimes he felt blessed that he had known love; other times it made him feel unfathomably sad.

He rejoiced in his grandchildren, who all but lived with him in the summertime. After years of saving, he bought an interest in the hotel from his brother-in-law and took pride in becoming a man of property, in having something to leave to his daughters when he died. He got foolishly attached to a yellow mongrel dog who took up residence at the hotel.

When Julianna died, he wept, but he seldom visited the Signano cemetery. He told his daughters that he didn't want to be buried there, that Amola was his home. But they looked at him with narrowed eyes, and he knew he would spend eternity next to the woman he had married.

It was amazing how little he thought of her.

CHAPTER

THIRTY-ONE

"I want to lose weight," Pauline announced to her mother as they drove back to the high school from her orthodontist appointment.

"Fine," Louise said. "Your clothes would look better if you were a few pounds thinner," she said, glancing at her watch. She was supposed to pour at Mrs. Norton's semiannual tea, honoring the latest group of new officers' wives, and as the ranking newcomer, Louise was to do the honors at the tea table. Teas. Not her favorite activity, but one should not be late when one was the pourer.

"A *few* pounds?" Pauline challenged, slapping an ample thigh for emphasis. "More like twenty. I'd like to try out for the senior play next month. How many pounds can I lose in a month?"

"Not twenty. Five maybe. But you'd be surprised how much difference five pounds can make. Do you want to figure out a new diet this evening after dinner? I think we need to be a little more stringent than last time."

Pauline nodded. "I cheated a lot last time. But I want it more now. Really I do."

Louise looked in her daughter's direction, trying to visualize a slimmer Pauline. Actually, she would be attractive enough if she lost weight, but she would probably always be overshadowed by her more beautiful brother and sister. "Then for starters, when you get home after school," Louise suggested, "leave those last two pieces of pie for your brother and sister. You can have an apple."

"It's not fair," Pauline said with a melodramatic sigh. "No one else in the family has to watch what they eat."

"Never count on things being fair," Louise advised, hating her own prim voice, but she continued with the same old line. Her children groaned but expected it. "Fair is for livestock shows and homemade pickles." Pauline parroted the words with her.

"Now if we undertake this project, you've got to do your part," Louise said. "I'm not going to make you special low-calorie meals only to have you smuggle candy bars to your room like last time, and I'm not going to be a policeman. I'll see that the right food is there, but you've got to eat it and leave the rest alone."

Pauline nodded. "I will, Mom. You'll see."

Louise dropped her daughter off at the high school, then drove too fast back to the post, checking her makeup in the rearview mirror at stoplights. They'd had to wait forever to see the orthodontist, but he'd been pleased. By Christmas, Pauline would be out of braces. Poor baby. Her brother and sister not only had undeservedly slim bodies, they had naturally straight teeth.

Maggie, with her strawberry-blond curls and ready smile, had found instant popularity at Lawton High School. When one of the sophomore cheerleaders got mononucleosis, Maggie was voted her replacement. And her home room had elected her student council representative.

Peter had won a starting spot on the high school football team as linebacker, and Danny Norton was a second-string quarterback. The Nortons and Cravenses—with both Franklin and the general in civilian clothes—had been going together to the Lawton games in the town's WPA-built stadium. Afterwards, they would meet the children at Luciano's Via Roma for the latest food rage—pizza pie. Colonel Cravens' son was a more important player than the general's, so rank somehow got neutralized, and an easy camaraderie prevailed. Even when the males got hot under the collar about the officiating or the coaching, the females teased them to good humor. "I suppose you and Franklin could do better," Louise would challenge the general.

The only thing out of kilter with those evenings was Pauline. At the big table in the back of Luciano's would be the two old married couples along with Danny and Maggie, and Peter and his new girlfriend—the vivacious Belinda, also a cheerleader, her father the post engineer. And then there was dear Pauline, alone, with no boyfriend, no cheerleader outfit, braces on her teeth, chunky thighs, not adorable. Pauline had been listed first in the high school honor roll for the first nine weeks, but that did not compensate. Life was indeed unfair, Louise decided as she passed the old stone guardhouse and turned onto the narrower streets of Old Post.

Louise wondered what the senior play was going to be, what part Pauline wanted. She hoped it wasn't the ingenue. More likely they'd let her spray silver streaks in her hair and play the ingenue's mother.

The Old Post parade ground was encircled with cars, and Louise had to park on the far side. Like a little girl late to school, she hurried down the deserted sidewalk to the general's quarters. It was too hot for a suit, but the calendar said November. She paused at the front door to dab the perspiration from her brow, to catch her breath, to put on her colonel's-wife demeanor.

"Louise, how are you, my dear?" Mrs. Norton said with her hand graciously extended. Mrs. Norton had bluish-white hair, regal bearing, impeccable taste. She looked every inch the general's wife. "What a charming hat. Is it new?"

"Thank you, but no, it's far from new," Louise said. "I'm sorry if I'm late. Pauline's orthodontist was running behind."

"Those things happen," Mrs. Norton said smoothly. Her rose-colored suit was perfect with a creamy silk blouse and cameo brooch. "Come along now, and I'll introduce you to our new wives before we serve."

The first floor was full of wives, all in hats, most in suits, some with flair, some matronly, some—like Louise in her navy suit, navy pumps and pearls—meticulously neutral. Three or four of the wives were obvious misfits—bleached hair, too much makeup. All had half smiles firmly in place. Sometimes Louise's face actually ached after a tea or reception from all that careful smiling.

The Nortons' home was like a museum, reflecting their thirty-plus years of world travel. The finest of Oriental rugs covered polished hardwood floors. Heavy German furniture mingled with delicate Japanese and French antiques. There were Czech crystal and Middle Eastern mosaics. Along the walls of the study that adjoined the large living room were dozens of photographs of General Norton with military and diplomatic dignitaries and of the smiling Norton family in various stages of maturity in front of world landmarks.

It made Louise think of her in-laws' home—even down to the pictures of the general with MacArthur, Eisenhower, Omar Bradley, Mark Clark, George Marshall. The Army made certain there were cameras whenever its brass gathered. Maxine Cravens didn't have teas any more, but the old general's health problems gave her purpose and were helping her cope with his retirement. His stroke had badly frightened them both, and while his recovery was gratifying, leaving him with only a limp, Maxine looked after Harold with sincere love and a fierce determination to keep him functioning and active as long as she could. In a way, the senior Cravenses seemed oddly content among their possessions and cats. An invitation to Eisenhower's second inaugural and Mamie's follow-up phone call had pleased them, but they didn't seem to mind the prospect of watching Harold's old colleague sworn in on television. Leaving the tending of cats, house plants and rose bushes to others for a few days and traveling to Washington for the event were not considered seriously. Louise had talked to her mother-in-law only yesterday. Maxine was more excited over Harold's upcoming cataract surgery than she was about the inauguration. She talked of nothing else, quoting the doctor, reading from the list of pre-op instructions. When Franklin got on the line, Louise realized he was hearing the same information.

Mrs. Norton whisked Louise around the room to introduce her to wives she had not previously met, then navigated her to the tea table. Wives had schedules to keep. Teas, bridge parties, rounds of golf, meetings ended at four or shortly thereafter, with mothers of grade-school children being excused a bit earlier. Husbands came home shortly after five. The evening news was at five-thirty. Dinner was served at six.

Louise put on her own gracious-lady airs, smiling, asking in a genteel voice if the ladies wanted tea or coffee, one lump or two. The ornate silver tea service was a treasure, the Royal Worcester china elegantly rimmed in gold. The ladies all played their roles well as they filled their plate with finger sandwiches, tiny cakes, a spoonful of nuts, then accepted their cup, offering an appropriate bit of small talk to Louise.

She felt herself getting depressed. Funny how she could go for weeks, even months, then suddenly, she found herself asking what in the hell she was doing.

But these were nice people—good women who loved their families, who needed some sort of structure to get through their days on this earth. Their lives were not so different from those lived by proper ladies everywhere. Perhaps the hierarchy was more firmly ingrained in the military than elsewhere, the ceremonies more ritualized, but those were only trappings.

A number of the officers' wives got teaching jobs these days and lived at the fringe of military life. The verdict was still out as to how much damage their second paycheck would bring to their husbands' careers. Louise thought it would be nice to teach school, to do something, but she had no degree, no training, and Franklin, she knew, would not approve. Louise wondered if her sister had ever considered going back to teaching. Jeffrey, she knew, would support anything that made Marynell happy.

Belinda's mother was waiting for her cup of coffee. Cream. No sugar. "Belinda tells me Peter's been accepted at the Air Force Academy. I know you must be proud."

"Yes. Peter's excited about being a part of a new tradition. His class will be only the fourth to graduate from the academy. Of course, his father would have preferred West Point, but Peter wants to fly. Is Belinda still planning on Boston University?"

"Well, she's wavering a bit on her parents' alma mater. So many of her friends are going to the University of Oklahoma, and Boston's awfully far from Colorado. I think she's more excited about the prospect of going to hops with Peter at Colorado Springs than she is about going to college."

"I remember the hops at West Point," Louise said. "It's a very special time."

And it had been. Franklin had a been a special young man then and was now a special forty-three-year-old. Sometimes she felt smug pride at being the wife of such a man. He would no doubt become a general, and she could even look forward to that, to beautiful quarters and servants doing the things she no longer wanted to do, to being a general's wife in her own particular style—maybe a book review or a speaker at the teas to give them substance. A Great Books group added to the officers' wives' club activities, an occasional Saturday morning coffee for the working wives. Collecting no-longer-needed baby paraphernalia and household goods for struggling soldiers' families. Providing scholarships for noncoms' children. Joint projects with civilian charities and women's groups.

Other times, she wondered what would happen if she just retreated into vagueness like her mother had done, no more meetings, no more tea poured from silver pots.

Mrs. Norton came to survey the table from time to time, sending the Negro striker scurrying back to the kitchen for refills. Two of the new officers' wives were Negro. Louise wondered if they could have white strikers should their husbands ever become generals.

"Louise, dear," Mrs. Norton said at one point, "I wonder if you could stay for a few minutes after the others leave."

Louise knew what she wanted. Franklin was irritated that Louise had told Mrs. Norton she needed to think about accepting the chairmanship of the post's Girl Scout Council. What was there to think about? The asking had only been a formality. He was right, of course. She should have just accepted graciously, said she would be delighted to serve.

"I would like to announce your appointment at the Juliet Low Tea," Mrs. Norton said over a glass of sherry. The striker was quietly clearing away the scattering of cups and plates from the vacated room.

"Of course, I'd be glad to serve on the council," Louise said, taking only the smallest sip from her glass. When she was a general's wife, she'd serve scotch or wine, anything but sherry. "But I don't think I'm qualified to be the chair. I was never a Girl Scout myself, and my girls were never very active. I'm not very familiar with the program and thought perhaps a mother of one of the more active girls might be more appropriate."

"There's a senior high troop, you know. Maggie might enjoy participating next year."

Maggie—a Girl Scout in a green uniform with a merit-badge sash. Maybe she could wear the uniform when she sneaked out at night to have sex with Mrs. Norton's son.

Maggie would be furious if she had to be a Girl Scout. How far did this woman's power go?

"I chaired the Fort Sill Girl Scouts when we were stationed here in the thirties," Mrs. Norton was saying. "I think it's an appropriate responsibility for one of the younger colonel's wives."

Apparently, it was settled. Louise would oversee dozens of leaders and hundreds of girls, fund-raising, camp arrangements, awards banquets, the works. "I'll try to do a good job," Louise said, vowing that when and if Franklin became a general, she'd never force such things on unwilling wives. There were enough gung ho ones like Marynell.

Of course, Louise reminded herself, she had just been thinking how she wanted to do "something." Why wouldn't Girl Scouts suffice?

But she needed something outside of her assigned role as a colonel's wife, something just for herself. She'd taken up needlepoint. That was nice. She liked going to bed at night with something done that wouldn't be undone even if it was only a row of stitches. But she'd already completed covers for the dining room chairs and a wall hanging. One household needed only so much needlepoint.

"And I do think Maggie will enjoy scouting," Mrs. Norton was saying. "The children are growing up too fast, you know, and they're too young to be seeing so much of each other. Danny really must concentrate more on his studies. Quite frankly, he spends more time on the phone with Maggie than he does studying. The general and I have discussed sending him away to a prep school in Washington if the situation doesn't improve."

How much did the woman know about Maggie and Danny's relationship? Louise wondered. Did Mrs. Norton think that putting Maggie in a Scout uniform and sending her off to camp was going to stem the tide of sexuality? Yes, Maggie and Danny were too young. Yes, they could ruin their lives. But while Louise didn't approve herself, she understood and saw no humane way to end it. Even if the Nortons sent Danny away, he would still come home vacations and in the summer. Maggie was not yet sixteen, Danny a few months past, but Louise did not doubt for one minute that they loved each other, that they would marry the minute Danny graduated from whichever military academy he decided to attend.

To ensure anonymity, Louise had driven Maggie across the Texas line to Wichita Falls to have her fitted with a diaphragm. The doctor was disapproving but complied. Franklin would be furious if he found out, Mrs. Norton appalled.

"Maggie is very busy with her school activities," Louise said firmly, placing her still-full sherry glass on the coffee table. "I really think she's outgrown scouting."

You can have me, but you can't have my daughter, she thought. Maggie's time would come soon enough.

CHAPTER

THIRTY-TWO

I will not sleep with him, Pauline vowed as she finished putting on her makeup. *I absolutely will not sleep with him.*

She debated about whether to wear a sweater or a blouse. Sweaters were sexier, but blouses were easier to get out of.

Stop thinking like that. She wasn't going to be getting out of anything, she reminded herself. Good grief, she'd only seen the boy once. Darrin was his name. A Phi Delt from Altus. His butt was fatter than hers.

In high school, she didn't have dates. Not ever. She'd been the girl they called to find out if Amy or Cindy or Susie liked them. Good old Pauline.

She chaired the decorations committee for the prom, but no boy asked her to go. She went with two other girls—Nickie Bellman and Susie Clark. Nickie had bad skin, and Susie was pear-shaped. And like Pauline, they made good grades.

No one danced with any of them. The three girls left early in Nickie's car and drove to Lake Elmer Thomas in the wildlife preserve, where they sat at a table in the deserted picnic area and drank the bottle of bourbon Susie had stolen from her parents' liquor cabinet. It was a pretty night with the moonlight reflecting on the water and illuminating nearby Mount Scott, which was small as mountains go but looked rather majestic rising up out of the flat Oklahoma prairie. Halfway through the bottle, they got maudlin. They'd be best friends forever. They liked each other a whole lot more than those other stuck-up kids, 'specially those dumb boys who fell in love with cheerleaders.

But what if no boy ever liked them? What if they never had a date, never married, ended up like Miss Weatherspoon, the algebra teacher, who was old, ugly, unmarried and disliked by all?

"We could be medical missionaries in the Amazon Basin," Susie offered. Pauline thought they might have a ranch in Wyoming. Nickie suggested anthropology in Africa.

They held hands and kissed some, taking turns being the boy. Nickie touched Pauline's breasts. But it was all halfhearted. There was no substitute for a boy. More than anything, they wanted a boyfriend to go on dates like other girls.

By the time they arrived at the breakfast at the post gymnasium hosted by the officers' wives' club for the entire senior class—town and post—Pauline was feeling sick. Her mother diagnosed her problem without asking, made excuses and drove her daughter home, stopping along the way for Pauline to throw up.

Louise fixed an icepack for Pauline's head and lay on the bed beside her. "Poor baby," she cooed while Pauline cried miserably against her mother's shoulder.

"My head hurts so bad. *So bad.* And I wish I were pretty and popular and had a boyfriend," Pauline sobbed.

"Shhhh," Louise said, stroking her daughter's hair. "Your time will come. Someday, my darling, you will have far more than the girls you now envy. Now, just lie still and try to sleep."

"How do you know that?" Pauline asked, wanting to believe.

"Because I'm your mother. Because you are bright and special and I love you."

"Not very logical," Pauline complained, but she had never appreciated her mother more. "Will you tell Daddy I got drunk?"

"No. But don't make a habit of it, okay?"

"I won't. Believe me, I won't. Have you ever been drunk?"

"No, but I suspect that's a shortcoming," Louise had said. "Go to sleep, baby. Everything will be fine."

At the University of Oklahoma, Pauline missed her mother more than her sister, but she wished her sister were here now to help her decide which skirt made her look less overweight, whether to wear perfume or cologne, whether the pearl earrings looked better than the hoops. Except maybe it didn't matter. She'd probably lose one or both of the earrings in the boy's car, and they were more interested in her big tits than the way she smelled.

During the first week of classes, Pauline and one of her new pledge sisters had been having a Coke at the student union, their pledge ribbons proudly displayed on their blouses. In the next booth was a boy Pauline had known at Lawton High. A town boy. They'd taken speech together when she was a sophomore and he was a senior. Robbie Todd. He remembered that she was Peter Cravens' sister but had to be reminded of her first name. He called the following afternoon to invite her to meet him for a Coke at the Copper Kettle. Pauline was stunned. A boy had actually asked her out. She dared hope college would be different.

The Copper Kettle was full of students, including several Tri Delts, and Pauline felt enormously proud to be seen there with a boy. He wasn't a frat man, but he was kind of nice looking and didn't abandon her for the pinball machines. They ordered a second Coke, and he told her she'd gotten prettier. Pauline flushed with the pleasure of it all, her thighs and underarms growing moist.

It was dark when they left the Kettle, and Pauline hoped he would invite her for a hamburger or a pizza. They could make an evening of it—she'd even pay her own way. "Have you seen *Vertigo*?" she asked. "Some of my pledge sisters saw it at the Boomer last night and said it's real scary."

But Robbie headed his Chevy toward the river and the maze of lovers' lanes that wound among sand dunes. Parked on a secluded path, he begged to see her breasts. That's all. Just let him see them. He wouldn't touch, just look. Promise. He even sat on his hands.

He told her that her tits were good enough for a centerfold. They were the greatest tits he'd ever seen. Big nipples. He was nuts about big nipples. Just one little touch. Please. They were so pretty.

Robbie just kept begging and telling her how pretty she was, and she kept letting him touch and bare just a little more flesh. She started thinking about true love and marriage. He was two years older. Maybe she wouldn't even finish school. Her mother had never graduated. Of course, Pauline had always wanted to marry Army, but she hadn't counted on Robbie sweeping her off her feet. He really liked her. He thought she was pretty.

She kept pushing his hand away as he attempted to roll her panties down her hips. But somehow they got pushed down anyway, far enough for him to get his hand between her legs and start probing. "No, you can't do that," she said. But he did. First his finger went in, then her panties disappeared from her thighs and shortly, with her head crammed against a door handle and her right knee jammed against the steering wheel, he pushed his penis in her. She told him she loved him. He said "Oh, baby" about fifteen times and collapsed on top of her.

She thought about all those fantasies she used to have about Indian braves. She would cling to the brave's strong, brown body as his pony carried them across the prairie to his tepee where, their flesh glowing in the firelight, she was entered slightly against her will. There had never been a car in her fantasies, yet here she was in a front seat with a steering wheel poking painfully in her side, her head at a right angle to her neck, the circulation in her left leg cut off.

Awkwardly, she and Robbie uncoupled themselves. As she sat up, she could feel a gush emptying itself all over the mohair upholstery of his Chevy. Her virginity. It would stain, she supposed.

Robbie didn't call her the next day or ever. She had spotted him only last weekend at the Lawton High School homecoming game. But she pretended that she didn't.

"Love your hair, honey," Betsy Fitzpatrick said as she whizzed by the open door of Pauline's room. Breezy, confident Betsy lived across the hall. A Kappa pledge. She was already pinned to a Beta.

Her new haircut and permanent wave did look nice, Pauline had to admit, glancing back at the mirror. It was short and wavy with fluffy bangs. She'd worn a pageboy or ponytail for years, but Maggie had been up last weekend and insisted Pauline get her hair cut like Liz Taylor's in *Cat on a Hot Tin Roof.*

Pauline stepped into her old standby straight black skirt. Everyone else was wearing pleated plaid this fall, but Pauline knew that pleats and plaid were a deadly combination for her.

Worrying about her weight and counting calories had become a way of life. She'd lost ten pounds her junior year in high school and during her senior year had struggled to get her weight below one hundred and fifty. On one wonderful morning in August, she had actually weighed 149. Her mother had bought her a new dress to celebrate. Now, she fought a constant battle to stay below one sixty. Just one evening of beer and pizza could put on three pounds.

She decided on a pink turtleneck sweater and added matching pink lipstick, pink bobby socks with her loafers, a black scarf, gold hoop earrings and her gold charm bracelet. Not bad, she decided, smiling at herself. She was still in love with her straight teeth. Her looks were improving, but she was still on the wrong side of that invisible line separating good looking from not so good looking. She had been rushed by several sororities because she'd been valedictorian at one of the state's largest high schools, and she often wondered if she'd made the right choice in pledging Delta Delta Delta. Tri Delts were perky and cute. Three of this year's cheerleaders were Tri Delts, an unheard-of achievement. And the sorority boasted more campus beauty queens than any of the other houses. Pauline was supposed to help raise their grade-point average and had been elected scholarship chairman for her pledge class.

Pauline was certain her sorority sisters didn't screw indiscriminately—if at all. Even the girls who were engaged professed to be saving themselves for marriage. Pauline felt ill at ease whenever conversation turned to sex. It felt as though a neon sign must be blinking on and off across her forehead. *I fuck*. Last night after pledge meeting, Mary Beth Sanger had almost cried because Prissy Timberlake said Grace Kelly had had an affair with Bing Crosby when they made *High Society* and had not been a virgin when she married Prince Rainier. Mary Beth adored Princess Grace and had a picture of her and the prince on her bulletin board. She insisted that Grace had saved herself for marriage, that she wasn't the sort of woman who had sex before marriage. "On what do you base that opinion?" Prissy challenged.

"You can tell by looking," Mary Beth said. "She looks pure and good, and she was raised Catholic. Besides, a prince wouldn't marry a woman with a sordid past."

Pauline didn't care if Grace had or had not been a virgin on her wedding night, but it did bother her that her pledge sisters unanimously seemed to equate virginity with goodness. She'd overheard a Sigma Chi in her freshman composition class insisting he could tell at a glance if a girl was a virgin. Two other boys nodded their agreement. She wanted to ask them to glance at her but was afraid of their assessment. She'd gone back to the dorm from class and spent a lot of time in front of the mirror. What would give her away? She longed for smaller breasts. When she weighed 149, they weren't as big. Grace Kelly had a lean, almost boyish figure. And sleek hair. Pauline wondered if perming her hair had been such a good idea after all.

Pauline understood her own behavior very well, and her freshman psychology class only reinforced that understanding. She slept with boys to feel better about herself, to feel loved. It was so simplistic, it was laughable. Of course, in the long run, sex only made her feel worse, but while a boy was hot and lusting, she felt slim, pretty, desirable.

What she was, however, was cheap, disgusting and pitiful. She hated herself. She was a girl who couldn't say no, and not saying no filled her with self-loathing. She wanted to be good. Short of that, she wanted to be loved like Maggie. Maggie and Danny had been sleeping together for a year and a half, but they fucked only each other.

It was only December first, and Pauline had already gone all the way a total of eleven times with five different boys. She carried shoplifted condoms hidden away in the secret compartment of her billfold. She had bought the billfold because it had secret compartment.

And she didn't even like the sex itself. She liked the boys to want it, to say pretty—or dirty—things to her. She preferred pretty but anything that indicated the boy had been thinking about her, had been wanting her made her weak and easy. When they were humping away on top of her, however, with her neck scrunched up against the door handle, she wanted to cry. And she was disgusted when she had to stuff Kleenexes or toilet paper in the crotch of her panties to keep the boy's cum from leaving telltale wet spots on the back of her skirt when she hurried into the dorm right before curfew.

She worried constantly about holes in condoms and pregnancy. She panicked when the boys started rubbing their naked thing around on her during foreplay lest one of those little tadpole sperms pop out ahead of its buddies and find its way into her vagina. Every month, she was weak with relief when her period began. Every month, in a toilet stall of the dorm bathroom, she promised God she'd stop.

And as fearful as the prospect of pregnancy was, the fear of being found out was even worse—the fear that people would turn and look at her on campus and whisper to their companions. Trash. Slut. Nympho. How much did boys talk? She worried that maybe they talked a lot. *Tell her she's pretty and she'll fuck.* Darrin was the third boy from the Phi Delt house to ask her out. What if the man she married learned of her disgusting past? What if her sorority sisters found out? She simply had to stop. She read about an operation in France where they stitched the hymen back together. She'd like to do that, to be a virgin again and start over.

Since plebes couldn't come home, the family was going to see Peter at Colorado Springs for Christmas. He'd promised to get her a date to the plebes' Christmas hop. Her date wouldn't know she went all the way, and the dances were carefully chaperoned so there'd be no opportunity for sex. Her secret would be safe.

Pauline could hardly wait for Christmas. She fantasized constantly about meeting a fine young man like her twin brother, a boy who would respect and love her, who would want to marry her. The Air Force Academy would be the closest thing to starting over she'd probably ever get. She was going to diet extra hard. And do sit-ups every night.

The phone rang. "Your date's here." The voice belonged to Penny Curtis, one of her Tri Delt pledge sisters. Penny had been on the front desk last Saturday night when Pauline went out with the second Phi Delt. Maybe Darrin wouldn't be wearing his Phi Delt pin. Penny would wonder about a girl going out with fraternity brothers.

"Man, you look great," Darrin said with a low whistle. He had on a navy sweater over a white shirt with his frat pin over his heart. "All you Tri Delts are great looking. I'm sure glad you were free tonight."

Pauline's heart sank.

CHAPTER

THIRTY-THREE

"But I don't want to go to the University of Texas," Maggie said. "All this time, I've planned to join you and all our Lawton High friends at OU."

Louise dished up the rice pudding, observing the exchange between her daughters. She was surprised at Pauline's suggestion that she and Maggie go to Austin in the fall. She had assumed her older daughter would be anxious to get back to OU for her junior year and to her friends. She'd even won a scholarship as an outstanding journalism student.

Pauline and Maggie were spending a lonely summer as new residents of Fort Hood, Texas, where Franklin was newly assigned as commander of Division Artillery for the Second Armored Division after attending the one-year course at the Army War College in Carlisle, Pennsylvania, a required rung on his climb to a star. Louise and Maggie had spent the year with him in Pennsylvania, their household strangely quiet with Peter and Pauline in college, Franklin once again spending most of his time studying, Maggie missing her Lawton High friends, in a holding pattern until she could return to Oklahoma and attend the university.

The Beckmans, their friends from their newlywed days at Fort Sill, were stationed at Carlisle. Louise and Cecilia went antiquing in the Pennsylvania countryside and played duplicate bridge. They both wondered at times why they weren't happier when they had successful husbands and satisfying children. "Sometimes I feel like a little windup doll," Cecilia said, "with no mind of my own. If Johnny would get an ROTC assignment, I'd go to graduate school. I was happiest when I was in college."

Yes, Louise had agreed. She'd always regretted having only that one year at Mary Baldwin. But then if she'd stayed in school, she probably wouldn't have married Franklin, and she wouldn't be the mother of the same children. There was no point in thinking about it now.

Franklin had finished third in his class, much better than his standing at Leavenworth when Louise was trying to put herself back together after Andy's death.

He was pleased with his assignment on an armored post. Tanks instead of field artillery. Diversification, he pointed out. He thought that was important.

But Maggie and Pauline hated not knowing anyone, and they hated Fort Hood. While most Army posts were old and charming, stark, uninviting Hood had been a World War II–era camp and only made a permanent post in 1950. The nearby town of Killeen had lost any semblance of rural charm with the advent of pawnshops, bars and cheap housing built to serve the continual stream of military personnel that trained there during World War II and Korea.

For Louise, life here at Hood was pretty much like that at any other posting, except their quarters were nicer. Brand new. All their accumulated possessions had never looked better than in that spacious, decidedly contemporary house, and Louise had personally tackled the landscaping of the yard. Everyone told her the hot Texas sun baked the gray clay soil to cement and was fit only for growing weeds, sage and scrub oak. But Louise made friends with the owner of the Killeen Seed and Feed, who shared his secrets of coaxing selected grasses and plants out of the clay. All her spare time was spent weeding and dragging hoses about the yard with Hans the beagle following her around if it wasn't too hot. Her yard was prettier even than the general's. Even her roses thrived, and she had a small vegetable garden out back. Franklin would walk about the yard with her after dinner, full of praise. He was pleased that the Cravenses' yard had become a topic of cocktail party chatter. "This winter, you'll have to start a garden club for all the wives, and maybe we can have lots of pretty yards next summer," Mrs. General Harmon suggested during a reception for a visiting British general.

Louise cringed, hoping Mrs. Harmon would forget by the time winter rolled around. Maybe the general would be transferred.

She did join a book club at the town library, however.

The civilian members, mostly senior citizens, really didn't care that her husband was a colonel. Louise had stopped being embarrassed about reading so much. Maybe she was getting to be more like her mother all the time, but so be it. She liked female authors better than male ones. Taylor Caldwell, Daphne du Maurier and Pearl Buck were her current favorites, but with a few exceptions she read whatever book was assigned for the next club discussion. She read while Franklin watched television. She read while he wrote professional articles for the *Army Magazine*. She propped a novel by the stove when she cooked and by the bathtub when she bathed. Franklin complained about too many grilled hamburgers and bacon and tomato sandwiches, but Louise ignored him with only a twinge of guilt. There were still the rounds of parties and committee meetings, but at least Mrs. Harmon was in favor of informal dressing in the summertime, and bare legs and sundresses were allowed at most functions.

Summer was almost over, however. Peter had already come and gone, his one month leave from the Air Force Academy split between his parents and Belinda. Danny had visited from Washington, where his dad was now stationed. In the fall, the garden would die, stockings would again be required, and she would have no children in the house to mother. There would be only herself and Franklin in the biggest house they'd ever lived in.

The idea of the girls going to school in nearby Austin was an appealing one.

"But why do you want to transfer to the University of Texas?" Franklin quizzed Pauline. "You've done well at OU, the past two years, even won a scholarship. You're going to be treasurer of your sorority, and your senior year you'll probably be Tri Delt president and named an outstanding senior woman. At Austin, you'd have to start all over, and it's twice as big as OU."

Pauline stirred at her small serving of pudding, her shoulders sagging a bit. "I just thought it would be nice to be closer to home. You and Mom could come to the football games and fine arts stuff in Austin like you did at Norman before you moved to Pennsylvania. I missed you guys."

"It would be nice to have the girls close to home," Louise offered, taking Pauline's side. "We wouldn't be able to see them as often if they went to Oklahoma."

Pauline looked at her mother gratefully.

"It's only a five- or six-hour train ride from Norman," Franklin said.

Louise's gaze met Pauline's. What was Pauline afraid of at Norman? "Sometimes a fresh start is for the best. Would you like that, honey?"

Pauline nodded.

"I would, too," Maggie said indignantly. "In Norman, at the University of Oklahoma, I'm signed up for rush. All my friends from Lawton are expecting me, and I think I deserve the college of my choice after having to spend my senior year as a nobody at a new high school in Pennsylvania when I would have been head cheerleader if we'd stayed at Lawton. Geez, Pauline, I thought you loved it at OU with all the sorority stuff and the football team winning all the time. I thought you wanted to be my big sis, show me the ropes."

"The football isn't as great as it used to be. Texas has beat OU two years in a row," Pauline offered with a shrug.

"Is there some reason you don't want to go back to OU, young lady? Something you're not telling us?" Franklin demanded.

Pauline shook her head. "No. Not really." She took a bite of her pudding.

"Then it's settled," Franklin announced. "And Maggie, if you do half as well at OU as your sister's done, you'll make your mother and me very proud."

Pauline's chin went up. That helped, Louise thought. She did love to make her father proud.

The next day, on their way back from the post exchange, Louise asked Pauline why she wanted to change schools. "Is it a boy, honey?"

"I wish there was 'a boy.'" Pauline said. "Boys don't like me. In two years, not one boy has ever wanted to go with me. Every girl from my pledge class has been pinned or dropped at least once. Four of them are engaged."

"But I thought you had lots of dates."

Pauline shrugged her shoulders. "Sometimes. Never for the big dances. Never for anything nice."

A surge of hatred shuddered through Louise's body. Damn all those boys who didn't like her daughter. She wanted to take Pauline in her arms. She wanted to cry.

They stopped while a company of men doubled-timed smartly across the road. Louise found their uniforms, their deep voices sounding out the cadence, their very maleness, offensive.

"Do you want to try again with Austin?" Louise asked. "We could plan a different strategy."

"You mean try to make Daddy think it's his idea?"

Louise kept her eyes on the road, unable to meet her daughter's challenging gaze. "Well, not exactly," Louise hedged, "but maybe there's a good reason we haven't thought of."

"It wouldn't do any good. You know how Daddy is. Once he's said no, he never takes it back no matter how good the reasons are."

Yes, that was true, Louise thought. Franklin was inflexible. And judgmental. He was probably little different from the young men who had hurt her daughter time and again, yet Pauline loved her father without reservation. And she knew the first one of those boys who gave her a chance would also have her love.

Franklin had entered the United States Military Academy at West Point in 1934, and now in August of 1960 he was being promoted to a brigadier general. Somehow, for an event twenty-seven years in the making, the celebration did not seem grand enough. Maybe after the parade on Saturday morning, Louise would feel her husband sufficiently honored.

General Harmon had conducted the actual ceremony in the commander's office this afternoon, with dozens of officers and some of their wives crowding into the room. Louise wished Peter could have been there, but at least the girls hadn't left for school yet and were there to smile proud tears as a pair of stars was pinned on their father's shoulders. Louise's eyes filled, too. She was so proud. Of course, the promotion would mean another move to a more important job. Louise thought of their beautiful quarters, her yard, her garden. She should have known better.

Mrs. Harmon had corsages for the three Cravens women. A photographer snapped a picture of Louise giving her husband a congratulatory kiss. The picture appeared that evening on the front page of the *Killeen Daily Herald*. The girls loved it. Louise studied the picture carefully. She and Franklin were both still slim and youthful, and the kiss had been a sincere one. They looked more like lovers than husband and wife.

All during the evening friends dropped by, most with a teasing remark about the newspaper photograph. The phone rang constantly as the news followed the Army grapevine across the country and colleagues called their congratulations. Most of the callers were West Point classmates.

Jeffrey called. In his soft-spoken way, his words sounded more heartfelt than the rest. Louise listened on the extension while he told Franklin, "I've never known a man who deserved it more. The Army needs more like you. Marynell and I are delighted."

Louise had already talked to Marynell. She'd called her this morning right after Franklin had come home to tell her the news. The girls had just left for their morning job teaching post youngsters to swim. Louise knew the minute she saw her husband's face.

He was so proud of himself. Even though she sat in his lap, laughing and crying with her happiness, she felt like his mother. Her boy had done well. It was the most important day of his life.

They talked about the promotion ceremony that afternoon, how excited the children were going to be. Louise would have to get ready for lots of company this evening. He'd be honored at a parade on Saturday.

Franklin needed to hurry back to the office, but he kissed her with passion and asked with a boyish grin, "Tonight, after the party?"

"You bet, *General* Cravens. Tonight." And she saluted.

Then she called Marynell. "You're the first person I've told," Louise said.

"I'm glad one of us made it," Marynell said. "Congratulations, Sis."

"Do you still love me?" Louise asked. Jeffrey was retired now. A civilian.

"Does that worry you?"

"Yeah, a little. No, not really. You're my sister. You have to love me."

Marynell laughed. "That's true, but I won't pretend it doesn't hurt. I would have been a terrific general's wife."

"Yes," Louise agreed. "Much better than I'll be."

"You're very lucky," Marynell said.

"I know. I have a good husband, and my three living children are fine, healthy human beings. I have everything I want and need."

"So why do you have to keep reminding yourself?" Marynell had asked.

Franklin called his parents twice during the evening. He wasn't quite sure his father understood, but his mother said her bridge buddies had come over to celebrate with her, and they had all toasted him with champagne. She and Harold would be there for the parade on Saturday. She'd already made plane reservations and taken Harold's uniform to the cleaners.

It was after ten before Peter could get free and return his parents' call. Louise, on the extension, listened but said little.

"I think you know, Dad, how proud I've always been to be your son. You are the epitome of a military officer, and I've always known I wanted to follow in your footsteps."

Franklin's voice actually broke. "Having a son like you means more to me than any star."

Franklin offered to help her straighten up after the last guests had left, but Louise slid into his arms. It was time for him to claim the final prize of the evening.

First, however, she made him wait while she went to the bedroom to light a pair of candles and put on her peignoir set. Franklin brought two glasses of champagne for one last toast.

In bed, she teased him about how strange it was making love to a general, but gradually the lovemaking became passionate. They both needed the night to be special, and Franklin wanted to satisfy her—he touched her, making her wet, talking to her, telling her how lucky he was to have such a wonderful family, how he'd gotten through two wars with thoughts of her, how the promotion was as much her honor as his.

The candlelight made his eyes glow, illuminated the sheen on his moist shoulders.

She told him again how proud he made her. She told him how much his children loved and respected him. All this while he made love to her, the same movements and patterns of the last twenty-two years, lovemaking carefully choreographed long ago. But tonight was special. He needed her pleasure more than his own. He was almost like a lover.

After looking forward to it for years, Maggie didn't have as much fun rush week as she'd thought she would. Each day, rushees were cut from the next round of parties and went home heartbroken. Their pain suddenly made the Greek system seem less exciting and worthy, but Maggie dutifully followed in her sister's footsteps and pledged Delta Delta Delta. At least the Tri Delts weren't as intimidating as the Kappas and Pi Phis, who wanted to pledge her only because she was a general's daughter. And the Tri Delts didn't wink all the time like the Thetas or talk in little-girl voices like the Chi Omegas. If it hadn't been for Pauline, however, Maggie would have preferred the athletic Gamma Phi Betas or somewhat unpretentious Delta Gammas. It was the fall of 1960. In June of 1964 she could marry Danny. Sorority life would help make the years pass more quickly.

"As much as I like Danny, I predict you guys will break up," Pauline said as she unpacked Danny's picture and put it on the desk of her sister's freshman dorm room. "In my two years here, I've never known of one high school romance that survived. There're just too many goodies in the cookie jar."

Maggie just smiled and continued trying to figure out how to fit her wardrobe in the tiny closet.

"It's a long time until Christmas," Pauline continued. "And in Colorado Springs, you won't have much time alone with him."

"Nothing worthwhile ever comes easily," Maggie said.

"Thank you, *mother* dear," Pauline said with exaggerated sarcasm. "Why don't we needlepoint that bit of wisdom and hang it on the wall? So if you don't date, what will you do?"

"Study. Make friends. Be your sister."

Pauline's expression softened, and she offered a sisterly hug. "Thanks. I'm glad you're here. College life hasn't been all it's cracked up to be. I'd rather spend time with you than some of the jerks I've dated."

"Maybe this year will be different," Maggie said.

Pauline wondered. No matter how hard she tried, she ended up having sex with every boy who asked her out. Sometimes she held out for two or three dates, but it always came to that. And then they'd drop her after a while—for a nice girl, she supposed, or a cute one.

Pauline had seen three movies this semester in which a young girl had died of a botched abortion, but even so, she got up at daybreak and drove a borrowed car to southside Oklahoma City. A chiropractic office. Dr. Melvin M. Goodpasture, D.C. At least it wouldn't be performed on a kitchen table.

She'd told two different boys the baby was theirs. Between the two of them, she had collected enough money for an abortion. One of the boys supplied her with Dr. Goodpasture's name and offered to drive her but was openly relieved when she declined. Pauline wasn't sure which boy's sperm had impregnated her. It really didn't matter.

Pauline wanted to tell her sister and had started to several times, but she hadn't and wasn't sure why. Maggie would not have judged her. But Maggie would be uncomfortable with an abortion, and Pauline didn't want to debate the issue. She had already debated it enough times in her head.

Her initial reaction had been to run home to her mother, but that route would have gotten her to a Salvation Army Home for Unwed Mothers to have a baby for adoption. In some ways, Pauline would have preferred that, but it would mean her father would have to be told. She could have survived her sister, brother and mother knowing, even some of her Tri Delt sisters, but Pauline simply could not bear for her father to know. She loved her mother, but she worshiped her father. He thought she was a good girl. He told her how proud he was of her excellent grades, her responsible behavior. Pauline knew he doted on Maggie, but then, who wouldn't? What she had was her father's admiration and respect. Before he left Fort Sill, whenever her name had appeared in the *Lawton Constitution*, announcing her election to honor societies or her participation in campus activities, she loved the way her name was followed by "daughter of Col. and Mrs. Franklin Cravens of Fort Sill." And now the hometown news would be sent to Killeen. "Pauline Cravens, daughter of Brig. Gen. and Mrs. Cravens of Fort Hood." On more than one occasion, she had heard her parents' friends comment on how outstanding their daughter Pauline was. Last year, she had been chairman of the university's Dads' Day celebration, and her father had taken the weekend off from his all-important studies at the War College to fly all the way back to Oklahoma for the festivities. Their picture had appeared on the front page of the Sunday edition of the Oklahoma City newspaper. They were standing under a banner that said "Welcome OU Dads." Franklin had been in uniform, his arm around his daughter's not-too-thick waist, and he looked proud. That was the framed picture Pauline kept on her desk—her father and her.

No, she didn't want her father to know. And she wanted to change her ways. Those two thoughts were the result of hours of middle-of-the-night agonizing. More than waking up beautiful or finding a prince to marry like Grace Kelly had done, Pauline wanted to get through this nightmare with no one finding out, and she wanted to stop screwing boys.

She had grown up wanting to marry a military man like her father and to be a gracious and admired officer's wife like her mother. And although she loved history and literature and wondered about graduate school, she knew it was only an alternate plan to keep panic at bay. No Air Force cadet had fallen in love with her during her visits to the academy. She still screwed boys, who asked her out only because she was that kind of girl. No boy was ever going to give her his fraternity pin, and one of these days the Tri Delts were probably going to lift her sorority pin if she didn't straighten up. There was a morals clause in the sorority charter; she'd looked it up. One of the pledges last year had been asked to depledge because she went out with a married man. The sorority had its standards.

Pauline had thought going to the University of Texas might have helped; it would have been nice to be someplace where no one knew what a horrible person she was. Maybe she wouldn't have gotten pregnant in Austin.

A heavy black woman in a white nylon jacket and brown nylon slacks was waiting in the empty reception room with its dusty rubber plant and cracked vinyl furniture. "You bring Kotex?" she asked.

Pauline held up a grocery sack.

"And the money?"

Pauline reached in her purse and pulled out a roll of assorted fives, tens and twenties.

The woman counted it.

"Follow me," she said and led Pauline down a long hallway, past the rooms where regular patients were treated, to a windowless room in the back of the building. Two galvanized steel sinks and an old Maytag wringer washer lined one wall. A laundry room. She might as well have opted for a kitchen. Pauline removed the lower half of her clothing as instructed and crawled onto a padded treatment table.

The black woman talked about her aching feet while she scrubbed Pauline's pubic area. "It's hard being on your feet all day. Don't get no standing-on-your-feet job if you can help it, hear. I sure wish I could get me a sit-down job, but you got to have some training for that. My sister works in a tailor shop. Sits down all day."

Dr. Goodpasture was old. His white jacket was clean, but he hadn't shaved in days. He called Pauline "sugar." The black woman's name was Loretta.

Loretta put a folded cloth over Pauline's face and told her to breathe deeply. When she woke up, it was all over. She hurt, but the pain was not unbearable.

"Could you tell if it was a boy or girl?" Pauline asked.

"I didn't look, sugar," the doctor said. "You don't need to know that anyhow. It was just a thing. No boy. No girl. Just a thing."

They elevated her feet and left her. She could feel the bleeding. It seemed like a lot. If she bled to death, what would they do with her? No one knew she was here. Loretta hadn't asked for a number to call in case of emergency, and Pauline hadn't volunteered one. Maybe they'd dump her alongside a country road. She'd be a headline in the student paper. Her father would know after all.

Pauline was aware of voices as the clinic opened for business, as patients came and went.

Loretta came back from time to time to change her pad and give her sips of water.

Pauline felt heavy in the body and light in the head. She even dozed a bit between the painful cramping that grabbed at her insides and wrung out big globs of blood that soaked the inadequate Kotex pads. The leather table felt slimy.

"You need to go now. It's night," the woman said, flipping on the overhead light.

Pauline covered her eyes. "I need another pad."

"They're all gone. You go now. I need to lock up."

The woman gave her two folded hand towels to stuff inside her panties and, with a meaty arm around Pauline's waist, supported her while they walked out to the car. Pauline had to stop every few steps. She felt so dizzy.

"You stay off your feet for a few days, hear," the woman said, " 'specially tonight. And drink lots of liquid. If that bleeding don't stop, you go to an emergency room at a hospital, hear. Tell 'em you did it yourself with a coat hanger. Don't you go giving them the doctor's name. He's a good old soul and helps lots of girls in trouble—white and colored. Sometimes he does the poor ones for free."

Loretta opened the car door and eased Pauline inside. "You really should have made the no-count that did this to you at least drive you home. Hope you don't have far to go."

Pauline started to tell her she was driving twenty miles to Norman but didn't bother. It wasn't Loretta's problem.

"Don't you let no boy put his tool in you 'less he's wearing a rubber, you hear," Loretta said before she closed the door. She reached in and patted Pauline's shoulder. "I don't want to see you back here no more. It's too hard on a woman, having 'bortions and babies and men always after her for what they can get."

Pauline touched the woman's hand and nodded.

She managed to get herself in and out of a drugstore, where she bought a large box of super Kotex.

In the car, she replaced the soaked towels with two pads. There was a lot of blood. With her forehead against the steering wheel, she sobbed. *Dear God, help me. I'm sorry. I'm so sorry. I don't want to die.* Longingly, she eyed a pay phone at the corner of the building. She could call Maggie. *Come get me. I'm bleeding and scared to death.*

But she reached for the ignition. She'd gotten herself in this mess, and she'd get herself out.

The drive to Norman was endless. So much traffic. The oncoming headlights kept blurring. Pauline couldn't control her sobbing.

On the outskirts of Norman, she pulled into a closed Texaco station to replace the pads again. She threw the soiled ones and the bloody towels into a trash barrel.

The parking lot in back of the Tri Delt house was full. She drove around it one more time to make sure. Nothing. Pauline heard herself wailing. "No. No." She had gone as far as she could go. She parked behind the housemother's Pontiac, leaving the key in the ignition.

It took the last of her energy to crawl up the back stairs. It was Monday night. Chapter meeting. The halls were deserted. No one saw her.

She changed her pads and prayed into her pillow. "I'm sorry, God. Really sorry. I shouldn't have done it. I won't fuck anymore. I promise."

She wondered if she was falling asleep or dying.

Vaguely she was aware of her roommate coming in. "We missed you at chapter meeting. Not feeling well?" Teresa asked.

"Stomach virus," Pauline explained.

"We nominated Claudia for yearbook beauty," Teresa said, changing into her chenille bathrobe. "It really killed me to vote for her, but she'll win for sure. Looks like five pledges won't make their grades. You go back to sleep. I'll study upstairs. You sure you're all right? You look awful white."

Pauline changed her pads twice more in the night and drank a lot of water, as Loretta had instructed. The bleeding wasn't any worse.

Toward morning, the flow had definitely lessened, but Pauline fainted in the bathroom. She opened her eyes, and there she was on the floor by the showers, her cheek resting on the cool tile floor. She changed her pad and drank more water, then pulled a hidden candy bar from her desk drawer and lay in the darkness eating. For once, she didn't have to feel guilty about candy.

In the morning, over Pauline's protests, Teresa called Maggie at the dorm. She came by before class. "Jesus, Pauline. Teresa's right. You look awful. I'm going to call a doctor."

"No," Pauline said, trying not to show her panic. "I've just got a virus. And maybe a bit of a hangover. A bad combination. I was sick all night, but I'll be all right if you just bring me some toast and coffee."

Apparently she was going to live. She'd still have to study for finals and Christmas shop as though nothing had happened. Pauline wondered if she would feel guilty for the rest of her life, but it was too late for doubts.

She felt so weak, it was an effort to lift the cup of coffee to her lips. But beyond the weakness, deep down inside of her, she felt a new strength growing. She could ruin her life or change it.

CHAPTER

THIRTY-FOUR

"Do you ever hear from the Italian?"

Louise looked up, startled. In four years, Marynell had never mentioned Tommaso. They never spoke of that trip. Louise wasn't sure she wanted to now.

"No. I never gave him an address. We both knew it was . . . " She paused. Was what? Two ships that passed in the night? A fling? A fairy tale? She could think of no appropriate term. "We never intended for it to be anything more than a lovely memory. Does it still upset you?"

They were sitting at the kitchen table of Marynell's Alexandria home, the dinner dishes done, the men in the living room watching a basketball game on television.

Louise hoped this was the first of many such nights. Finally she and her sister were living near each other and would be able to call daily, have lunch, be together. That helped compensate for having to move again so soon. She'd had only one summer with her wonderful yard and garden at Fort Hood. She wouldn't be there when the bulbs came up this spring, when the roses bloomed. She'd leave the yard at Fort Myer to strikers. Except she wanted roses. And wisteria. And fresh tomatoes.

Jeffrey had retired three years before, but he and Marynell had stayed on in Alexandria, waiting until Eric departed for college, still undecided about where they would eventually live. For now, Jeffrey was teaching American and military history at a private school that prepared young men for the academic rigors of military academies, and he refinished furniture for people who answered his classified ads in the newspaper.

"Sure, it still bothers me," Marynell said, cradling her coffee mug with both hands. "You broke the rules, yet your husband is a general and mine's refinishing old chairs in the basement. Your children are doing well. You look good. It's hard to understand."

"One of my children is dead," Louise reminded her.

Marynell looked down, embarrassed. Obviously, she hadn't thought of Andy.

"Your children are also doing well," Louise said.

It was true. After a disastrous freshman year at the University of Richmond, then dropping out a year to "find himself," Matt had enrolled at the University of West Virginia and was finishing a degree in forestry. And Eric, after a year at the same expensive prep school where his father now taught, was attending the University of Arizona on a baseball scholarship. But Louise knew that Marynell was disappointed—especially with Eric, who had decided to forgo West Point. He was supposed to have had the brilliant military career that eluded his father.

"Yes, my boys are fine," Marynell said. "Jeffrey is fine. Everyone is fine. I'm sorry I sounded so bitchy."

Was the secret of success not to care too much? Louise had wanted Franklin's star but not with the passion Marynell had wanted one for Jeffrey. And she was proud of Peter, but a nonmilitary career for her son would have suited her just fine. In fact, she would have preferred it. The idea of her son flying fighter planes in the next war was not a pleasant one—and there would be another war. Southeast Asia was seething. The high hopes brought by a bright new administration had already been tarnished by the Bay of Pigs fiasco and an ugly wall across Berlin.

Her children were smitten with Kennedy and his fine rhetoric. "... pay any price, bear any burden, meet any hardship, support any friend, oppose any foe to assure the survival and success of liberty." Even Franklin, who had voted for Nixon, approved of Kennedy's buildup of NATO and his appreciation of the military. Louise wasn't sure. The president seemed too much like an actor playing a role. And she wasn't sure she believed in paying any price.

Peter was finishing his third year at the Air Force Academy, an officer in the cadet corps and currently ranked third in his class—the Class of '62 would be only the fourth class to graduate from a school that had quickly become a tourist attraction, with its isolated mountain setting and futuristic architecture. Eddie looked forward to seeing the school firsthand. He'd written that he planned to come to Peter's graduation. "It's not every old officer who gets a chance to see a grandson get such a fine start on his military career."

But Louise wrote back and suggested Eddie come this June for Matt's graduation instead. "Marynell would take it personally if you chose Peter's graduation over Matt's. We'll have a reunion. The children. The husbands. Everyone. Bring Martha, too."

After Matt graduated, he would work for the U.S. Forestry Service. He wanted an assignment in the Southwest so he'd be near his brother and could support the Arizona State baseball team. Marynell had gotten misty-eyed when she told Louise. After years of antagonism, her sons were becoming brothers.

"Have you thought anymore about renewing your teaching license?" Louise reached for a cookie. Homemade chocolate chip. She used to make cookies, too. Now she often felt an outsider in her own kitchen. Sometimes she wished she could cook and serve, and their current striker could preside at the sit-down dinners.

"The teaching license bit was your idea, not mine," Marynell said. "I have mixed feelings about working. After all, I only taught that one semester, and I'm not sure I still have it in me. And I'm still old-fashioned enough to think a wife shouldn't work."

"Times are changing. I'd certainly consider it if I had finished college."

"Oh, sure. The first working general's wife in the history of the world. You could consider it all you want," Marynell said, breaking off a bite of cookie, "but Franklin would never stand for it."

"I didn't really mean now," Louise admitted. "But before, it would have been nice to do something—teach, do landscaping, work in a library, own a restaurant. I'm not qualified for much, though. At least you've got a degree. I wish you'd get interested in something, start planning a new life."

"I liked the old one." Marynell's mouth was tight. Little creases radiated outward from her upper lip.

"Come on, Marynell. You're a better person than that. Lots of people have to start over for lots of different reasons. You're beautiful, educated, charming. Your husband loves you. Your boys are friends."

Marynell held up her hands in protest. "I know. I know. Shall we open our hymnals to number one hundred and fifty-two. 'Count your many blessings, name them one by one. Count your many blessings, see what God hath done.' "

Louise didn't say anything.

Marynell got up and busied herself pouring coffee. "I feel old and passed over," she said as she resumed her seat. "Nothing turned out like I thought it would."

"Then make some changes. Go to work. Have another baby. Take up a sport. Find a cause. And for God's sake, get rid of that gray hair. It doesn't become you."

And it didn't. Louise had been appalled to see the change in her sister. More than Marynell's hair had grayed. What happened to her beautiful sister with the sparkling eyes and the rich brown hair? Louise had rushed to a mirror and examined her own reflection. Did she look as drab as her sister?

Marynell put a hand to her hair. "You don't have any yet, do you?" She said it like an accusation.

"Not many. I still pull them out. But my time is coming. And you need to pay more attention to your makeup. My goodness, Marynell, you used to take such pride in your looks."

"And you used to be a mouse." Again, Marynell sounded accusing. How dare Louise become unmouselike and show up her older sister.

Louise changed the subject. "When Daddy and Martha come, do you want them to stay here or with us out at Fort Myer? Do you realize it will be the first time we've all been together in years? In fact, I guess we've never all been together—not with all the children, Daddy, the husbands, Martha."

"They can stay with you. You'll be settled by then. It still seems like Daddy should be with Mother."

"And Andy *should* still be alive, but that's not the way it turned out," Louise said sharply.

"Do you still think about him a lot?" Marynell asked.

"Andy? Yes."

"And the Italian, too?"

"Yes, about both of them. At odd times. I dream of Andy. I daydream of Tommaso. Sometimes the dreams are nightmares, and Andy's screaming for me to help him, to pull him back. We're underwater, but I can hear him. I wake up in the night crying because in my dreams I can still hear him and see him, even touch him. I used to touch Andy all the time. It was like that with Tommaso. I couldn't touch either one of them enough, and I felt so connected to them. I miss that."

Louise held up her hands and looked at them. No-longer-young hands.

"But it's been so long." Marynell reached for Louise's hand. The men were cheering in the living room. "Did you see that?" Jeffrey was saying.

"Yes. So long." Louise lifted her sister's hand and caressed it with her cheek. "Isn't it strange that we're getting old?"

"I'm too old for another baby."

"You've thought of it?" Louise asked.

"Tried it. Nothing happened. I don't think about it much any more. Forty-two is too old for babies, and I don't think I have the energy. I'll just wait for grandbabies."

"Franklin sold the house in San Antonio. I cried. I wanted to think that somehow you and I would get back there with the next generation of babies. It was *our* house. But the neighborhood was getting run down. Army people didn't want to rent it anymore."

Louise was surprised to see tears spring in her sister's eyes. "Those were good years, weren't they?" Marynell asked.

"Yes. It's funny how sometimes when I remember us back then, I put Andy there with us. He would have loved his grandmother Elizabeth."

"Yes, they would have sat on the porch swing by the hour," Marynell agreed. "He would have been her favorite."

"I need a hug now," Louise said.

"Me, too. I'm sorry I'm so crabby. I love you, Sis."

"I love you, too, honey."

"I'm glad you're here. I've been counting the days. Really. I need my sister to help me sort all this out."

They took coffee and cookies in to the men, then Marynell led Louise to the basement. The clean odors of linseed oil, varnish and raw wood greeted them as soon as Marynell opened the door. There was a set of stripped ladder-back chairs lining the far wall, waiting for the next step. But what caught Louise's eye was a pair of chairs in the middle of the room. Beautiful chairs, modern but reminiscent of Shaker designs, made by a master craftsman who had loved the wood into form. "Did he refinish those?" Louise asked. "My God, I've never seen such beautiful wood. Rosewood, isn't it? And the chairs. They're works of art."

"Jeffrey made them," Marynell said shyly, proudly.

Franklin arrived from the airport with Peter just at dinnertime. Peter was the last of the family to arrive, fresh from his third-year finals, resplendent in his cadet uniform, going first to his grandfather for a hearty handshake and hug, full of congratulations for his cousin Matt, enduring his sisters' and mother's hugs and kisses, the beagle's excited yelping.

The whole family. Marynell, Jeffrey and their boys. Louise, Franklin and their three youngsters. Eddie and Martha. All reunited at Louise and Franklin's Fort Myer quarters. Tomorrow they would go to Morgantown for Matt's graduation.

The sight of Peter made Eddie teary. He wondered why. He hadn't cried three days ago when Matt picked Martha and him up at the airport. Or when Maggie and Pauline arrived from Oklahoma, Eric from Arizona. But in a way, Eddie himself had started the process that brought Peter to a military career. He had stayed in the Army after the First World War and raised two little girls destined to become military wives. Peter's uniform filled Eddie with pride and fear. Young, beautiful men died in them. He knew that better than most.

Louise had already lost one son. Surely God would not be so cruel as to rob her of another. For Eddie had no doubt another war would come along. One always would. He didn't believe that after World War I, the war to end all wars. And after World War II, he had still wanted to believe the world had learned something. But Korea came so soon afterward, taking away his final vestiges of hope that men could exist without war.

Eddie hadn't prayed for years, but he would pray for Peter. He didn't know what else to do.

And darling Maggie would marry a pilot. She positively glowed when she talked of her Danny. The phone rang during dinner, and when Maggie realized it was Danny calling from Colorado, she changed into the most beautiful young woman in the world, eyes misting, smile full of rapture. Eddie had to turn away. Matt turned away, too, to hide his pain.

Eddie couldn't help but think how Elizabeth would have enjoyed this family gathering—as long as she didn't have to cook. But then the girls always managed the kitchen better than their mother. When their daughters left home, he cooked more than Elizabeth. And in England, he cooked more than Martha just to have something to do. He was retired now from active practice and only treated the minor ailments of neighbors and friends. Of course, his and Martha's meals were simple. They didn't digest fancy food too well anymore. But except for Martha's occasional bouts with arthritis, they had their health. They still found joy walking along the shore when the days were warm and enjoyed touring about England and Scotland by bus in the summer and fall, their tour mates as fascinating as the castles and cathedrals. They didn't travel much out of the country anymore, except for an occasional ferryboat ride to Calais or Flanders. The flight to America had been tiring for Martha. Him, too. They probably wouldn't be coming for other graduations.

"I hope the rest of you grandchildren understand," he told them over coffee. "I came to Matt's graduation to honor you all. You're good children and have made your parents proud. And I will buy each one of you a plane ticket when you are ready to visit Martha and me. That will be your graduation gift."

They had all cheered—Matt, Eric, Pauline, Maggie and Peter. He wondered which ones would come.

They left the dining room table and dirty dishes to the black striker, Private Washington, and went to sprawl around the living room, where Franklin brought out the brandy. The young people helped themselves to rounds of beer from the refrigerator.

As Eddie sipped his brandy, he felt a fog of melancholy enveloping him. These few days were the first and probably the last for this particular mingling of family. Martha caught his eye from across the room and shook her head. She knew his moods. If they were alone, she would remind him they only walked this way once, that they were luckier than most, that she loved him. Eddie shook himself a bit. He hadn't come all this way to feel sad.

With little prompting, Eric brought his grandfather up to date on his baseball career. Eddie was impressed. All-state. *Sports Illustrated* High School All-America. No wonder he'd gotten a scholarship. And he'd been named the most outstanding freshman in the Pac Ten.

Eric was a cocky young man with the body of an Adonis. Marynell's eyes followed him wherever he went. Flesh of her flesh. Marynell still hoped Eric would change his mind about forgoing a military career. "Talk to him, Daddy," she'd said yesterday after lunch. She'd invited Eddie and Martha to see her home, to look at the incredible furniture that Jeffrey made. "It's not too late," Marynell insisted. "His uncle Franklin could help arrange an appointment to West Point for a year from this fall. Eric's grades are adequate. Baseball is so worthless."

"He's getting an education in Arizona, and baseball is what the boy has always wanted, Marynell. And I'll tell you, if he ever goes pro and makes it to the World Series, I'll bring my old bones back here to see it."

"You sound like Jeffrey," Marynell had said.

Pauline pulled a footstool over to sit by her grandfather's chair. He reached out and patted her. She was almost pretty when she offered a small smile over her shoulder. For years, she'd been the overweight adolescent in snapshots. Now she was thin, and while she wasn't pretty like her sister, Pauline would be attractive if she didn't laugh so much. A brittle, artificial laugh. And when she wasn't smoking, she nervously chewed her thumbnail. When Peter told her she looked terrific, she asked if he needed glasses.

"Are you still thinking of graduate school?" Eddie asked her.

Pauline shrugged. "Maybe. I'll see how things go my senior year."

In other words, she'd wait and see if she met Mister Right during her senior year. Marynell had kept up her Army contacts, and now that Pauline was here for summer vacation, Eddie gathered that Marynell planned to start fixing her niece up with eligible young lieutenants. The one next Saturday night was a *West Pointer*, she'd announced triumphantly to Pauline. Eddie noticed that Louise tuned out when aunt and niece started conferring about the list of eligibles.

"Don't you want Pauline to marry Army?" Eddie asked Louise when he helped her carry the cups and glasses to the kitchen.

Louise leaned against the sink, her arms folded. "I want her to marry a good man. I don't care if he's a custodian as long as she loves him, but I shouldn't judge. She's just following in her mother's and her aunt's footsteps. We set our caps for Army."

"Has it been such a bad life?"

"No. Of course not. Franklin and I have been as happy as most."

At forty-one, Louise was more beautiful than she had ever been in her life. Her face was unlined but mature and wise. An artist should paint her, Eddie thought, with sunlight on that thick dark hair, with her chin lifted to show her smooth ivory throat. Did Franklin see it? Did he see this lovely woman who reflected a full knowledge of the world in her sometimes green, sometimes hazel eyes, or did he still see the chaste young girl he had married? Eddie wondered if she ever thought of the man in Italy. Tommaso.

They went back to the living room to make the final plans for tomorrow, the caravaning of three cars to Morgantown for the graduation ceremony. Marynell and her family said good night.

Tomorrow would be a busy day. Eddie followed his wife's broad bottom up the stairs to the guest room.

Martha knew without asking that he needed to make love to her. The middle-aged passion of their beginnings had waned, but they still enjoyed each other. Usually he could enter her although he seldom ejaculated. But there was sweet comfort in connecting with her and feeling the golden warmth of potency returning to his loins. Even her plumpness was pleasing to him—Freudian, he supposed. His big mama. Crawling inside where it was safe. Sometimes, however, thoughts of Elizabeth's ascetic slimness were hard to shake. Yes, he still missed Elizabeth at times. He went weeks, even months, he supposed, with only passing thoughts of his first wife. Then a memory would click on, like the way her girlish arms came around his neck in the night, awakening him with her desire. That part had been poignantly sweet, except sometimes he had wondered in which fictional hero's role she was casting him.

Being with his daughters made him think too much of the past. He hid from it in Martha's flesh, in her scent, in her sighs. She lifted a heavy breast to his mouth. "Mother loves her boy," she whispered. "Mother loves him so much."

The University of West Virginia's graduation was impersonally large, but earlier in the day, the School of Forestry had held its own small convocation for thirty young men and three young women. Matt had received an award for his senior paper.

Matt was a quiet, handsome boy with brooding dark eyes—even as a baby, he'd been that way. Eddie wished he knew his stepgrandson better. But then he didn't know any of his grandchildren, not really, he thought as he tuned out the ponderous musical offering from the university symphony. That's what he had given up, the price he had paid for Martha. He knew her grandchildren better than his own. He was not without regret.

But he couldn't imagine having spent the last fifteen years any place but the quaint little stone cottage by the channel. They had a good, simple life, and Martha was a part of him the way Elizabeth had never been. Martha wanted to be with him for himself; with Elizabeth, Eddie suspected any kindly caretaker would have sufficed. She had been a butterfly on an outstretched finger, beautiful to behold but belonging someplace else. He hoped she'd found that someplace. A heavenly library full of books, perhaps, with no one expecting anything of her except to rock a baby now and then or read a story to a child.

When the last of eight hundred graduates had finally received their diplomas, Matt's family found him in the milling crowd. Jeffrey was so proud. He kept patting the boy, finding excuses to touch him. In Europe, it was easier for fathers. They were allowed to kiss and hug their sons for a lifetime. Eddie wondered if Jeffrey had thought of Matt's real mother, that she should have been here.

After the graduation ceremony, they returned to Louise's for the celebratory dinner. Eddie had forgotten the excess of American dining. So much food. Standing rib roast and baked chicken. Mashed and sweet potatoes. Green and jelled salads. Hot rolls and sweet muffins. Corn on the cob and fresh green beans. Apple pie and chocolate cake. Marynell had made the pie and salads. Private Washington's hot rolls were the best Eddie had ever tasted. He knew without asking that Louise had made the cake. He remembered the meal Elizabeth had served when Louise brought her new fiancé home for the first time. An engagement dinner with cold cuts and store-bought cookies.

Elizabeth again. She had come with him this trip. He supposed it was only fair. She was their grandmother, not Martha.

There were toasts all around. Eddie had waited until last. He stood, lifting his glass. "To Matthew Washburn, son, brother, grandson, cousin, nephew. Our congratulations on your accomplishment, our wish for a satisfying life preserving nature and beauty in this great land. You've chosen a worthy profession, and I salute you. And I salute my other grandchildren who will soon tuck their sheepskins under their arms and go forth to meet the world. And I think we should remember tonight other loved ones who would also have been proud—Matt's first mother, your grandmother Elizabeth and dear little Andy. Life is a gift, children. Make the most of it. Don't take anything for granted, and don't regret in your old age opportunities you didn't embrace in your youth."

He hadn't intended to remember the dead when he raised his glass. Maybe he shouldn't have, Eddie thought as he sat down. Age was dulling his judgment. But Martha patted his hand approvingly. Louise smiled gratefully as she dabbed at her eyes with her napkin, and the young people looked down at the table, embarrassed. Franklin and Marynell looked stunned.

CHAPTER

THIRTY-FIVE

Pauline wished she could hold hands with Peter as they watched their veiled sister come down the aisle on their father's arm, but they had to watch from their respective sides of the altar. Pauline leaned forward, needing at least to meet Peter's eyes. He nodded and winked. Their baby sister's wedding day.

Maggie looked glorious. In this setting, on this day, in that dress, she seemed like a princess, her prince waiting for her at the altar. But Pauline was certain that no prince and princess—real or fairy-tale—had ever been more beautiful, more in love than Danny and Maggie.

The wedding wasn't exactly like the ones the two sisters had planned throughout the years of their girlhood, but it was pretty close. The chapel wasn't West Point's, but it was at a military academy. It was June Week, and the groom was uniformed and gorgeous. Maggie was wearing their mother's wedding dress, the same dress Aunt Marynell had worn when she married Uncle Jeffrey. The veil was new and different, and the net overskirt had been replaced with a fuller, whiter one appliquéd with lace flowers and white sequins, but it was still recognizable as the dress from the white-and-gold leather album that Pauline and Maggie had pored over on winter afternoons.

Pauline had attended a West Point wedding last June. Nickie Bellman's younger sister had married a cadet, and Pauline had driven up for the wedding and a reunion with her old high school buddy.

Nickie wasn't married yet either. She was terribly bothered that her younger sister had beaten her to the altar. "More than age, having your younger sister getting married first makes everyone start treating you like a spinster," she told Pauline. "My aunts keep telling me that there are worse things than never getting married. They don't itemize their worse-things list, but I'm sure they'd include things like the end of life on this planet as we know it, terminal disease, the loss of more than one limb."

And now Pauline was cast in the same role—the older sister serving as *maid* of honor at her younger sister's wedding—at her *beautiful* younger sister's wedding to an adorable man. Pauline had worked hard not to love Danny herself. The day was bittersweet, full of joy and jealousy, good wishes and fear. Only Aunt Marynell understood how it felt.

Marynell and Jeffrey both looked quite civilian. He was almost bald and wore a regular blue suit like a businessman would have worn. Marynell was less glamorous, more subdued. "I kept thinking at your mother's wedding how it wouldn't be so bad if I had had a fiancé or at least a steady boyfriend," she sympathized with her older niece. "By the time I got married, Louise was pregnant with you and Peter, and I had to share the limelight. It was all right though. I was so relieved to get that ring on my finger. Your mother can't possibly understand what you are going through. She had a West Point miniature almost before she knew what one was. Just a freshman. Imagine. Franklin just swooped in and decided the little waif was for him when I was the one out looking."

After Pauline moved to Washington following her graduation from the University of Oklahoma, she and Marynell had developed a real friendship. Marynell had stayed in touch with selected Army friends around D.C. after Jeffrey's retirement and continued to seek out information about eligible young officers stationed there. And she would ask her friends to arrange blind dates for Pauline. Marynell was incredible.

Pauline had lived first with her parents at Fort Myer, then in a Washington apartment shared with another girl who also worked for a senator. Pauline worked for Senator Kerr of Oklahoma, a public relations position Danny's father had arranged. General Norton now had his third star and had no trouble calling for a favor from political friends made during his stint in Oklahoma.

Her roommate envied Pauline's dates with lieutenants, but none of them had stayed in her life long enough to become a real boyfriend. They backed away when Pauline made it clear her object was matrimony—not sex. "The right one will come along," Marynell insisted. "Just wait and see."

And last night at the rehearsal dinner at Colorado Springs' elegant old Broadmoor Hotel, Marynell had asked in that special conspiratorial tone she used when talking about prospects, "Remember Jerry Wilhite?"

"No. Should I?"

"His younger brother was a friend of yours at Fort Sill," Marynell explained. "He said he met you at a picnic at Lake Elmer Thomas."

"He must be George Wilhite's brother. George was Peter's friend, not mine. I didn't have any boyfriends, and I don't remember meeting a Jerry Wilhite."

"Well, he certainly remembers you. He's stationed at the Pentagon," Marynell said with a wink, keeping her voice low. Louise didn't approve of husband-hunting.

In many ways, Pauline felt closer to Marynell than to her own mother. Louise kept telling her to find a man to love and worry about his profession later. And not to be in such a hurry. "You can be married for the rest of your life. Enjoy being free and unattached. Go to Europe for a couple of years. The world won't end if you aren't married by the time you're twenty-five, and it won't end if you marry other than a military man. If you have to choose between love and the prestige of being an officer's wife, take love."

"You wouldn't say stuff like that in front of Daddy," Pauline accused. They had been shopping for Louise's mother-of-the-bride dress and their satin wedding shoes. Maggie had floated on ahead. The closer her wedding, the more diminished her ability to concentrate became. Displays of pots and pans drew her like magnets. As did china, linen, infants' wear. She'd get lost from her mother and sister like a preschooler.

"I'm talking in general terms, Pauline," Louise snapped. They were both tired. It had been a long day, and she still hadn't found a suitable dress. Louise looked too young for beige lace and too old for blue taffeta. "Your father and I have managed very well. But maybe we would have done better if I had been a little more grown up, if we'd known each other a little better. I married too young. I wish I'd finished college. I wish I'd learned a little independence. It would have been good preparation for marriage."

"You haven't told Maggie to go Europe."

"Maggie and Danny are different. They have their own world, their own civilization, and they've known each other for years. I don't think they're capable of waiting. But you're talking about an abstraction, a man you don't even know, much less love."

"Hurry up, you two," Maggie said. "I want you to see these adorable tea towels."

Louise and Pauline made a face at each other. "I'd rather sit down and drink a tall one," Pauline said.

"We don't have time. Your father will be wanting his dinner," Louise announced.

"But we haven't found your dress yet," Pauline protested.

"It will wait," Louise had said firmly. "Your father is expecting us."

Maggie and Pauline had always agreed that their parents had a good marriage, but each sister had different reasons for thinking so. Maggie insisted their parents' affectionate kisses and pats signified marital passion behind their closed bedroom door, but Pauline was sure that any sex her parents shared was dignified. What her parents shared was deep respect and abiding affection. Pauline wanted respect more than passion. She wanted to be like her mother and have a man like her father treat her well. It seemed to Pauline that most Army officers honored their women, especially West Pointers with their courtly manners and uniformed gallantry.

Pauline had not had sex since her abortion. She had given up sweets and sex cold turkey and found a job in a city full of young Army officers.

Pauline suspected her mother looked at Maggie and Danny and longed for the passion she'd never had, but then her mother had also never had an abortion. She had never faced rejection and never been cheapened into a nameless slut. Franklin Cravens was the only man her mother had ever dated, kissed, loved, and he honored her. Pauline felt oddly superior. She knew better than her own mother what was important in a marriage.

Except that she herself looked at her radiant sister and felt a tiny gnawing of doubt. Pauline would like for a man to adore her the way Danny Norton did Maggie. Adoration might be worth waiting for if she could only be sure it would come along.

Jerry Wilhite. She didn't remember him, but his brother had been tall and gangling, not at all cute. Their father owned a furniture store, but he was retired military. Wilhite's Fine Furniture on Sheridan Road. She hadn't realized George had a brother at West Point. George had been painfully shy, and she was sure he'd never screwed girls at the drive-in. She wondered about his brother.

The organ sounded as celestial as the one at West Point, with the sound soaring through all that vaulted space. The colonel chaplain's voice soared, too.

"For as much as Daniel and Margaret have consented together in holy wedlock, have witnessed the same before God and this company . . . "

An illustrious company, to be sure. She'd never top this wedding, Pauline thought, but now with only a twinge of jealousy. Her mother was right. Danny and Maggie belonged together. Their names had been inscribed together on a book someplace since before the world began. Even lust between them was probably beautiful—a sacrament. Maggie said she would die for Danny, and Pauline believed her. But as it was, she would live for him, have babies for him, stay beautiful for him, stand radiantly at his side someday when he became a general like his father.

Heads were bowed for the Lord's Prayer, then the chaplain gave forth his final blessing. Pauline folded back her sister's veil for Danny to kiss his bride. Then Maggie turned to kiss her sister, and tears filled Pauline's eyes. She loved them both.

. . .

As they gathered for the photographer, Louise embraced her new son-in-law. "Thank you for making my daughter happy. I guess you know I already love you like a son."

Danny nodded. "Maggie got it all from you. I couldn't help but love you, too."

At the reception, Marynell took charge of organizing the receiving line. Louise was grateful. She felt oddly out of touch as she shook hands with two hundred or more people, somehow remembering their names, pulling her gracious-lady mode out and letting it take over.

Everyone needed to comment on how attractive, beautiful, handsome, perfectly matched the newlyweds were. "I just can't take my eyes off them," Mrs. Norton admitted, dabbing. People stared with amazed smiles. Was it Maggie and Danny's physical beauty or the love in their eyes—or both? Whatever, *it* was a potent force that dominated the room in spite of all the brass and politicians. Only Franklin's father seemed unaffected by the newlyweds. "Not nearly as pretty as my Maxine was as a bride," Harold Cravens commented, forgetting he was speaking to the bride's mother and that he was the bride's grandfather. Maxine kissed him on the cheek. "Sweet, old fool," she said affectionately.

At first, Maxine had said they wouldn't come to the wedding, that the old general wasn't up to the trip, that she was still upset about their terrier's death. But Franklin had insisted that his mother, at least, come to Maggie's wedding, and rather than leave Harold, Maxine increased his dosage of Ritalin and brought him along. Once again in uniform, his shoes spit-polished, Harold looked a bit like the general of old as he visited with Danny's father, trying in vain to find comrades in common. But General Norton was of a different military generation, and Harold was out of touch. He remembered names and dates from the past with uncanny accuracy, but he had a hard time sorting out who all these people were here today. He used to command a division; now he fretted about his new glasses. Three different times, he showed Louise the red marks they were making on the bridge of his nose.

Louise parked Maxine and Harold on chairs by the string quartet and went to stand with Pauline and Marynell while the bride and groom cut the wedding cake. Pauline reached for her mother's hand.

"Are you cold?" she asked.

Louise shook her head no, but she was.

Gorgeous Danny in his dress uniform was smiling down at Maggie. His profile as pure as Peter's, his smile as sweet as her Andy's had once been. He was a good man. Yet he shared his soul with a warrior who would willingly march off to war hand in hand with death. And her own son would, too.

War. The business of her husband, her son and now her daughter's husband. How Louise hated it. It made her love them less because they loved it so.

She put an arm around Pauline's shoulders to steady herself. She'd had too much champagne, too much tension, too much emotion, not only from her daughter's wedding, but from preparing to move. After two years in Washington, she was once again being uprooted, the furniture already in storage, the dog transported to his new home at Marynell's, the time again at hand to bid farewell to her children, her sister. She had gone with Franklin to Manila on the brink of World War II, and now she would go with him to Saigon on the brink of a new war there.

God, she was tired. She should have known better than to drink all that champagne.

Pauline was gesturing toward her father. Franklin hurried over to take his wife's hand, concern on his face. "Are you all right?" he asked.

"Yes, a little exhausted, I guess. But fine." And her gracious-lady self offered a reassuring smile, to receive her general husband's kiss on her cheek.

"You sure, honey? You look a little pale."

"Quite sure." She pointed across the room. "Come on, you two, it's time for Pauline to catch the bouquet."

Franklin looked puzzled. "How do you know she's going to be the one to catch it?"

"Silly boy," Louise said, linking arms with him and Pauline. "Her sister will throw it to her. Just like I threw mine to Marynell. Sisters stick together."

She offered Franklin a knowing grin when the bouquet landed in Pauline's outstretched hands. She still had her arm linked with his. An anchor. Her children were grown. Franklin was the constant in her life.

She lifted her face for a kiss.

CHAPTER

THIRTY-SIX

*T*heir footsteps echoed in the empty rooms as Louise and Pauline walked through the apartment. There were only six rooms and an entry hall, but the rooms were large with lots of windows.

"It's not as grand as anything you're accustomed to," Pauline said apologetically. "But it was the best I could find in the price range you suggested without going all the way to Fairfax or Wellington. And you said spaciousness was more important than amenities."

"I've no need of anything grand," Louise said, standing in the middle of the living room. The painted walls were too dark, the wooden floors in need of refinishing, but there was a wonderful flagstone fireplace and the windows in the living room were high and arched. Actually, if she was of a mind to, the apartment could be made quite attractive, but Louise didn't know if she was of a mind to. Six months in Saigon had been draining, and this was the fifth time in six years she'd had to make a home out of empty rooms. After Fort Sill, there had been Carlisle, Fort Hood, Fort Myer, Saigon and now back to Virginia. God, how many times had she moved over the past twenty-seven years? And her mother before her. Lately, many American wives were opting for the term "homemaker" over "housekeeper." Military wives surely deserved the designation more than most.

With Franklin staying in Saigon to finish his assignment as special liaison between ARVN, the South Vietnamese army, and the various components of the American military, this apartment was to be just

410

for her—and Maggie, if she decided to come to Washington when Danny was sent to Southeast Asia, as he surely would be. The apartment wouldn't have to please a husband, impress VIPs or stand the scrutiny of other officers' wives.

Louise had opted to come back to Washington to be near Pauline, who was still unmarried and unhappy, and Marynell, who now lived only an hour away in Fredericksburg, Virginia. Jeffrey had bought part interest in a small furniture factory there, and Marynell had reluctantly put her name on the substitute teacher roll and begun taking night courses to get her teaching certificate renewed.

Louise had also invited Pauline to live with her, but she didn't want to be an unmarried daughter living with her mother. She said it seemed too "spinsterish," and she had her own apartment and a roommate.

Marynell had been overjoyed at her sister's return to the Washington area. "With Franklin gone, I can see you whenever I want," she said gleefully. "You won't always be looking at your watch and wondering if you dare have one more cup of coffee and risk the wrath of your demigod husband. You won't have to hang up the telephone the minute the lord and master walks in the door."

"What terrible things to say!" Louise said, pulling away from her sister's embrace.

"Then deny it," Marynell challenged. "When I'm around you, I realize how lucky I am to have Jeffrey."

Louise had turned away, her eyes suddenly full of tears. "I'm sorry you think so poorly of my husband. You've never really liked him, have you?"

"Let's say we've tolerated each other. Don't cry, Louise. I'm sorry. Sometimes I wish you'd stand up to him more, but I understand. When you do, he makes you pay. It isn't worth it."

Louise had been angry. Marynell had no business talking about Franklin like that. She was still jealous about Franklin's career, Franklin's star. It wasn't that Franklin demanded his wife's presence—he *needed* her. She stopped talking on the phone because she wanted to welcome him home, to ask of his day. They needed each other. That's what marriage was all about.

But Jeffrey was an easier husband. No question of that. Louise sometimes wondered if she wasn't as jealous of Marynell's life as Marynell was of hers.

And as she looked around the apartment that was to be her home, already aware of how she would arrange her furniture, she realized how much she looked forward to living near her sister and her now-grown daughters with no restrictions on the time she could spend with them. She and her girls could shop, drink beer, sit up into the night talking. She could go to Fredericksburg for weekends. Marynell could come into town for the plays or concerts and stay the night. Jeffrey wouldn't mind.

And Cecilia Beckman was living in the D.C. area. Johnny was also in Nam. Louise could luxuriate in friendship and family.

But then war had always provided her respite from marriage.

"The apartment is fine," Louise said. "I know how tight housing is in the Washington area and how hard you must have looked to find a place for me."

"All your things won't fit," Pauline said, still unsure.

"I know. I'll leave some of the furniture in storage." Louise sat down on a window seat overlooking an alley and the back of another apartment building. She'd have to put some sheer curtains over the window, but it would still be a nice place to seek the winter sun with a book.

"What will you do?" Pauline sat down beside her.

"Do?"

"Without Daddy, without kids, without a social life?"

"Spend time with my sister and my girls. And Cecilia Beckman's living here. I can volunteer someplace. Read. I've thought about going back to college, but that seems silly for a woman my age. I'm not going to launch a career, I'm years away from a degree, and when your father returns next year, I'll move again and return to committees and functions, I suppose."

"You never really liked all that stuff, did you? Teas. Committees. And you hated Girl Scouts. Right?"

Louise laughed. "Yes. That was a low point, all right. Running the

Protestant Sunday school in Frankfurt was no picnic either, but we had to keep all you little Army brats from turning into Huns, or so Mrs. Norton thought. I really must love Maggie a lot to accept her marrying the son of my chief nemesis. Mrs. Norton was in Saigon, you know—organizing as usual. The general commanded VCOR. Since Franklin's technically his own boss, I didn't have to get involved, but he thought it best not to offend the wife of a higher-ranking officer. I helped with the Christmas party for American military kids, but I used my work at a Vietnamese orphanage and trips with Franklin as excuses not to be involved in other things."

Louise paused, remembering the insanity of American officers' wives planning functions, playing bridge at the club, consuming too much alcohol, pretending everything was normal when nothing was. "Funny how nothing is ever all good or all bad," Louise continued. "I hated to leave your father, especially since he shared this job with me more. It was as much diplomatic as military, and we talked a lot, traveled together, met so many people, but I sure was glad to get away from Mrs. Norton's constant phone calls and 'suggestions.' And the city has been seething since the assassination of President Diem and his brother. The whole country. After we got word of Kennedy's assassination, I felt like the world was falling apart. I wanted to come home."

"Was Saigon scary?" Pauline asked.

"Oh, yes. Cong terrorists were infiltrating everywhere. The military dependents should have been sent home months ago, but Johnson thought that would be too much of a political statement. A major's child was killed in a car bombing. And bodies of American military advisers were being shipped home daily. Mrs. Norton set up a roster of ladies to go out to the air base and see the caskets off. I admit I approved of that bit of organizing—sad as it was. I hate to think of what will happen when the all-out war starts."

"Maybe that won't happen."

Pauline's shoulder was touching hers. Louise liked that. She reached for her daughter's hand, needing more. "North Vietnamese regulars have crossed the Seventeenth Parallel. Your father says the U.S. will have to send combat troops now," Louise said.

"I wish Daddy weren't still over there."

Louise kissed her daughter's hand. "I know, dear, but your father's a soldier."

"Are you sorry you married a soldier?"

"Of course not. I'm very proud of your father. We always worry about the ones we love no matter who they are or what they are."

The two women grew silent for a time, the quiet heavy in the empty apartment.

"Your father and I had dinner with Jerry Wilhite before I left," Louise said.

"Oh?"

"Yes. He called and introduced himself. He said his younger brother was a friend of yours and Peter's at Lawton High School, but I remembered that you'd gone out with him a few times while he was still stationed at Fort Myer."

Pauline nodded. "One of my many nonconquests."

"He's stationed up in the mountains as an adviser to Montagnard tribesmen. He's quite a linguist, apparently. He studied Japanese at West Point and has already mastered Vietnamese. He's coming back next month to teach at the academy. He wants to see you, Pauline."

"I wrote him, but he never answered."

"I know. He told me. He said he tried but couldn't think of anything to write back. He wasn't sure if you were just being nice to a serviceman overseas or were interested in him. He's very unsure of himself when it comes to women."

"You sound like you're matchmaking. How come? I thought you didn't approve."

"I also don't approve of your unhappiness. If getting married is what you want, then that's what I want for you. I had hoped that it would 'just happen' for you like it did for your sister. I hated the cold-blooded, calculated way you and Marynell have gone about searching for *a* husband."

And she was tired of standing on the sidelines for years watching her daughter be rejected by an endless stream of men. Even after she had slimmed down and acquired some style, her intensity scared men away. If she hadn't been so desperate, they might have pursued her, but Pauline had never learned coyness. Maggie hadn't either, but Maggie didn't need it.

Louise compared her daughter's young hand to her own aging ones. How smooth and soft the skin was. Her long, manicured nails glamorous.

Jerry was a quiet, shy, homely boy who needed a woman like Pauline to organize his life. Louise doubted if he'd ever had a real involvement with a woman. If true love eluded Pauline—and it seemed that it might—then being safe and secure was the next best thing. Jerry seemed safe. He wouldn't hurt her, and Pauline had been hurt quite enough.

It was a beautiful, bright February day. They drove into Georgetown, buttoned up their coats and walked a bit, arm in arm, up and down the quaint streets before stopping for lunch. She and Pauline took a table in front of the fireplace, and the waiter brought mugs of hot cider. Louise ordered the colonial meat pie, and Pauline a salad, as always.

Over lunch, Louise launched the next phase of her campaign.

"When Jerry calls you, don't scare him away with your terms," Louise said.

Pauline frowned. "What do you mean?"

"Maggie says you tell every man you go out with that you will not go to bed with him, and unless he's interested in pursuing a serious relationship, not to call you again. Is that true?"

"Well," Pauline said, picking at her salad with her fork, "not exactly, but something like that. I decided a long time ago that I was going to be completely honest. I'm scared as hell of never getting married, but I guess I'm even more scared of getting involved in a meaningless sexual relationship and getting dumped. I'd rather get dumped *before* I go to bed with a guy."

"I respect your feelings, but you don't have to make pronouncements," Louise said. "That scares men away. Perhaps you should consider giving yourself and the man in question time to find out if a serious relationship is something you both want."

"But what if he expects sex?" Pauline couldn't quite look at her mother.

"Say no."

Pauline broke off a piece of bread and buttered it, then put it down on her plate. "I'm more comfortable with saying no up front."

"I don't think that will be necessary with Jerry. He's very shy about women, but if he does start getting physical and that isn't what you want, then just tell him you're not ready yet. You can be kind about it." Louise reached across the table and patted Pauline's hand. "Let him court you, honey. Let him bring you flowers and take you romantic places. Don't tell him to go away unless he's looking for a serious relationship. Let him think he's pursuing you. Men need to feel they're in charge, even shy ones like Jerry."

"It all seems so dishonest. Why can't you just put your cards on the table?"

"Because that's not the way the game is played."

"You didn't play games with Daddy."

"No. When we got married, I was too inexperienced for games, but even so, I discovered very quickly to go easy on honesty. You measure it out in small, palatable doses at precisely the right moment." Louise wished she had ordered a real drink. She shouldn't be saying such revealing things to her own daughter. Or maybe she should have said them years ago.

"Danny and Maggie aren't like that," Pauline challenged. "She tells him exactly what she thinks. Then they have a terrible fight and make up."

"I've told you before, Danny and Maggie are a special case."

Pauline lit a cigarette and blew the smoke away from her mother. "You and Daddy never fight," Pauline said thoughtfully.

"No. Almost never." Louise took a sip of water to avoid meeting her daughter's gaze.

"But do you always agree with him?"

"No. But there's usually no point in telling him."

"Then what's the point of having an opinion if you can't voice it?"

Why indeed, Louise thought. Pauline was right, of course. But she was also unmarried. Choosing her words very carefully, Louise picked her way through an answer.

"Your father and I have evolved a marriage in which we can both be comfortable. Yes, I would sometimes prefer a more egalitarian relationship, and he wishes I'd be more dedicated to my role as an officer's wife. In any relationship, you have to pick your conflicts. There's no point in arguing about overcooked eggs, but you might want to challenge . . . "

Challenge what? Louise tried to think when she had last challenged Franklin. She dug in sometimes, but mostly it was easier to avoid conflicts. She kept things from him like Peter's traffic tickets and Maggie's diaphragm. She had lied to him about how much groceries cost so she could afford to buy more expensive clothes for the girls, that Maggie was spending the night with a girlfriend when she was out with Danny all night, that one or the other child had a virus when they were hung over. She went to teas and receptions, served on committees to avoid confrontation. She didn't visit her sister as much as she would have liked because Franklin didn't like her to be gone from him. She didn't go to movies he didn't approve of and read in private books he would question. She was far more liberal politically than he, but Franklin didn't know it. Her friends needed to be selected from the ranks of officers' wives. She still wrote to a friend who'd divorced her major husband and moved to Colorado to be a potter, but Franklin didn't know about the letters. She never had more than two drinks in his presence, and there had been times in Saigon when she wanted more. When she bought clothes, it was always with Franklin's approval in mind. She didn't tell him that she had started coloring her hair for fear he would not approve.

A log fell in the fireplace, sending a spray of sparks. Louise jumped. "Mom, are you okay?"

"Sure. But I just realized I'm not exactly the right person to be giving you advice. I need to go to the ladies' room. Would you order me a brandy?"

In the basement restroom, Louise leaned against the wall and held a dampened paper towel across her forehead. The meat pie was heavy on her stomach. On the other side of the wall, a cook was upset. "Sour cream, you idiot! Not whipping cream."

Someone tried the door. They'd have to wait.

She never fought with her husband. Until this moment, Louise never realized what a damning commentary that was on her marriage. She lied, placated, coddled, deceived, manipulated, accommodated, but she never fought.

How could she go back and face Pauline? Pauline had always idolized her father. She, Maggie and Peter thought their parents had the perfect marriage.

She stared at her face in the mirror. Soon she wouldn't be pretty. Soon she would be old. She'd been married her entire adult life.

In all those years, she and Franklin had never even tried to have a real marriage, and it was more her fault than his. She had allowed him to live his life unchallenged, unexamined—always the authority figure, always in charge, or thinking he was in charge, and that amounted to the same thing. He was same man she married because she had allowed him to remain that way. She had made inroads but never had the courage to renegotiate the terms of their marriage, always using the excuse that he could not change the way he was, but in doing so she had denied him the opportunity to try. Poor Franklin. Poor her. And her poor children who held them up as the ideal.

She found herself thinking of Tommaso, of Italy, of the one time in her life when she felt completely herself.

The doorknob jiggled again.

She closed her eyes and felt the sea breezes, tasted the wine. Her fingers ached for the touch of his hand.

"It took almost six months of kid-glove handling, but he proposed," Pauline said triumphantly, holding up a ringed finger.

Maggie jumped up from the sofa with a squeal and flew across her sister's living room for a hug. "Oh, Pauline, that's terrific! God, I'm so happy for you. Let me see that ring. Look, Mom, a West Point miniature just like yours."

Louise hugged her older daughter. "That's wonderful news, dear," she said. "I know it's what you wanted."

"Yes. This is a celebration dinner. I even bought champagne."

"Aren't you just thrilled to death?" Maggie bubbled.

"Well, after all the hemming and hawing around, when the boy finally got the words out, it was a bit anticlimactic. 'Pleased' would be more the word for it. We're getting married next month at West Point—in the chapel." She grinned at her sister. "I thought at least one of us should fulfill the girlhood fantasy."

"We'll have to unpack the wedding dress and get it ready," Maggie said. "I think I'm going to cry."

They all hugged again. *I want to remember this night*, Louise thought, *with both my daughters so happy.*

And Peter. After eight years of an on-again, off-again relationship, Peter and Belinda had called two months ago to say they'd gotten married. Belinda was three months pregnant, but Peter sounded sure and happy. He had always loved her and was thrilled about a baby. Louise believed him. Peter was at Edwards Air Force Base in California, waiting.

Danny was stationed on the *Enterprise* in the Tonkin Gulf, also waiting.

Pauline popped the cork on a bottle of champagne, and Maggie lifted her glass. "Here's wishing happiness to the world's best sister."

"To my darling daughter Pauline," Louise said, raising her glass. "May all your dreams come true. I can't tell you how smug and satisfied it makes me feel to know my three children will all be married to nice people. And now, let's see if we can get a phone call through to your father. He'll be so pleased. A West Pointer. Then we need to call Peter and Belinda—and Marynell."

Louise sipped her champagne while she placed the call to Franklin's office. It was early in the morning in Saigon. She tried the apartment first. After a half-hour wait, the call went through, but just barely. She and Franklin yelled at each other until she was sure he understood the call was not an emergency, that Pauline was engaged to Jerry Wilhite. Pauline took the phone and listened intently, then began nodding her head. "He says he's proud of me." She was crying again.

Maggie had her turn on the phone. Yes, she was fine. And Danny, too. He was flying daily training missions. "I love you, Daddy. Stay safe."

Louise took the receiver back. "I love you," she yelled. "Take care of yourself." Suddenly her husband's voice was very clear, very close. "And I love you, too, Louise. Don't ever forget it. You are my life."

His life? She knew she was very important to him, that he needed her very much, but the Army was his life. If she died, he would grieve sincerely for a time, then find another well-behaved woman to be gracious, to be there for him when he needed her. For he did indeed need a wife to love in his way. And no, she wouldn't forget it. He was *her* life, and she'd be glad to get him home. She wanted her husband out of Saigon before the bombs started falling.

Peter and Belinda weren't home, but Marynell was thrilled that one of the blind dates arranged by her had resulted in a husband for Pauline.

"How's teaching?" Louise asked her sister.

"I'm surviving," Marynell said with a sigh, "but just barely. The kids love to give substitutes a bad time. They talk back and lie about what the regular teacher has them do. I just hope it will be better when I have a classroom of my own. Maybe I can learn to like kids again. But Jeffrey's happy. He goes to work looking like a common laborer, but I'm beginning to realize how unhappy he was all those years."

"I just wish you could both be happy at the same time," Louise said.

"Me, too. I know I whine a lot, but I'm working on it, Sis. Really I am. Having you close by helps a lot."

"Can you come up next weekend?" Louise asked. "We'll talk wedding nonstop."

"You couldn't keep me away. Jerry Wilhite was my idea, remember, and I intend to take *full* credit."

Louise laughed. "You deserve it. Pauline and I are both grateful."

The champagne was making her light-headed, Louise realized. It felt nice, but she wished for Peter and Franklin. She hoped Peter and Belinda could come to the wedding. How fine it would be to hug her beautiful son once again, feast her eyes on him. She'd like to pat Belinda's pregnant tummy. A grandchild. The next generation. Her eyes got misty again.

Pauline bustled about her tiny kitchen, putting the final touches on dinner, talking through the open pass-through. She still lived in the same apartment, but she was alone now. Her roommate had gotten married. Maggie had already moved in with her mother in the Alexandria apartment by the time Pauline's roommate moved out; otherwise Louise suspected her younger daughter might have moved in with her sister instead. Louise was selfishly glad to have Maggie living with her.

She and Maggie lived very simply. For the first time in years, Louise had no household help, but it seemed foolish to have someone in to clean when she had nothing but time.

A household with two women made Louise think of the war years in San Antonio with Marynell. Of course, this time there were no children. In Saigon, she had done much of the cooking, leaving cleaning up to a Vietnamese maid. Franklin even came home to lunch if she was going to be there. He was cranky if she wasn't there when he came home in the evenings, but sometimes she deliberately made other plans just to exercise her right to do so. Their evening ritual included a beer or cocktail before dinner. And a bit of brandy afterwards. Franklin always had a stack of paperwork and newspapers to read, but he still wanted her in the room with him. Often he read to her. "Say, did you see this article about Westmoreland in the *Times?*" Even if she said yes, he'd read it out loud anyway. For years, he'd been doing that but never once had she told him it annoyed her. Years ago, she wouldn't have had the courage. Now it seemed too late. *Franklin, dear, you've been annoying me for the past twenty-six years.*

Here in Alexandria she seldom bought a paper, relying on television for her news. She changed her bed sheets infrequently. With no male body in the bed, no sex, she didn't need to.

She volunteered two afternoons a week at Walter Reed—once again manning a library cart—and at Cecilia's insistence had enrolled in a European history class at Georgetown University. She felt old and out of place in the lower-division class but loved the lectures, the readings, learning. She envied her girls their jobs. Senator Kerr had died, and Pauline now worked for his successor, Fred Harris. Maggie was teaching history at a private school in Alexandria. Louise suspected her daughter was a very good teacher. They talked history sometimes. Even argued. It felt good.

Pauline's ratatouille was superb. "You'll have to drive us home if I have any more wine," Louise told Maggie as Pauline refilled her glass.

"Don't go home," Pauline said eagerly. "We can have a slumber party—put on pajamas, get tipsy, gossip. We can sleep late in the morning. Jerry's driving down tomorrow, and we'll make him take us all to lunch."

The next day, Louise watched Pauline and Jerry together. The three women talked about the wedding, with Pauline working hard to draw Jerry into the conversation. He didn't say much, but he smiled fondly at Pauline. His parents would drive up from Oklahoma. A few of his and Pauline's friends from D.C. would come. And of course some of his new colleagues at West Point. But it would be small and quiet. He was sorry General Cravens wouldn't be there.

Jerry and Pauline liked each other, Louise decided, but they weren't in love. She thought of Danny and Maggie, of they way they couldn't sit next to each other without holding hands, sharing looks, smiles, squeezes.

Yet at one point Jerry swallowed hard and said, "Mrs. Cravens, I want you to know that I will always love and respect your daughter. She's the best thing that's ever happened to me, and I'm grateful that she's agreed to become my wife." He even blushed.

Pauline had never liked herself very much. Maybe Jerry was exactly what she needed, Louise thought. She doubted if Jerry would inspire passion, but sincerity was important, too.

Passion was such a funny commodity anyway. Danny and Maggie thrived on it. Marynell was afraid of it. Franklin had little need of it, and Pauline seemed much like her father.

As for herself, she had learned to invest her passion in her children, a good book, a sunny day.

Jerry would have to stop calling her "Mrs. Cravens." She wondered if he could be comfortable with "Louise." Danny called her "Mama Dear," a pet name he had invented for her in Frankfurt when he and Maggie were still in high school. He'd come swooping in the back door, never knocking, hug her and ask, "What've you got to eat, Mama Dear?" She admired Danny's courage. He wasn't intimidated by anyone—not his own parents, nor those of his girlfriend. When he and Maggie were caught skinny-dipping in the middle of the night in the Fort Sill officers' club pool, the MPs brought them to Franklin, unsure of what of what their role should be when the commanding officer's son erred. Bathrobe-clad, Louise had hovered in the background. "What in the hell were you two thinking about?" Franklin raged. Danny had shrugged. "We're just kids, sir. Sometimes kids screw up." Louise felt as though Danny belonged more to her than to the always proper, forever bossy Mrs. General Norton with her blue hair and cool gaze. Louise hoped she could love Jerry, too. If he made Pauline happy and content, she would love him out of gratitude.

After lunch, Louise and Maggie drove home through heavy traffic. A civil rights rally was scheduled at the Lincoln Memorial, and the countless vans and buses bore slogans. "Let My People Go." "We Shall Overcome." "Washington or Bust." "God Bless All Americans."

A dented brown van was parked in front of their apartment building. Eric, Matt and a pregnant black woman with her hair ornately done in braids and beads were sitting on the front steps.

Maggie was out of the car in an instant, running to her cousins' embrace. First Matt, brown as an Indian, dark eyes full of pleasure, picked her up and swung her around, then engulfed her in a hug. Eric, his sandy hair sun-bleached, kissed her broadly on the mouth. Maggie jumped up and down like a five-year-old, clapping her hands. "I don't believe it. I just don't believe it. God, Eric. Long hair. Headband. I bet Aunt Marynell could just croak."

"She hasn't seen it yet," he admitted.

"You look positively square next to these two," Maggie told Matt. "Where's *your* long hair?"

"The U.S. Forestry Service frowns on it." He hugged her again. "You look great, kid. God, it's good to see you."

The young woman was Leah, a graduate student from Berkeley who'd decided to drop out for the year and travel to the freedom marches. She patted her belly. "I wasn't planning on my friend here, but we'll make the best of things." Leah had met Eric and Matt at a civil rights rally in Denver during her trek eastward, and they had joined forces.

"What does your mother think of your coming here?" Louise asked her nephews.

The brothers looked at each other. "We thought we'd surprise the folks after the rally," Eric said.

"She doesn't know you're activists?"

"She knows but has decided to pretend it's just a phase," Matt explained.

"Our phone calls are about health and weather and when are we coming to see them," Eric said. "She preaches to me a lot about me going back to school, finding a nice girl and getting married, that kind of stuff. If she chooses to believe we're about to join the Young Republicans, we let it ride. You know how Mom is. But now that Dad's retired, it's not as bad as when she'd get hysterical if we did anything she thought would damage his precious career."

"Well, try not to get arrested," Louise said.

"Do *you* approve?" Eric asked.

"Yes. But don't get hurt, and stay out of trouble. Do you want to stay here?"

"No. We've got sleeping bags," Matt said. "But we'd love a free meal. Then why don't you and Maggie come into the city with us and look around?"

Louise said no and Maggie yes at the same instant. They laughed. "Why not?" Maggie asked. "I won't tell Daddy."

"And we won't tell our mom," Eric said with a wink.

"I'll tell you what. I'll go only if you boys tell your mother, and Maggie tells her father. Maybe I need to make a statement, too."

Matt grinned. "All right!"

Maggie and Louise fed the three lunch. The cousins insisted that Louise change into a pair of Maggie's blue jeans for the afternoon. She felt incredibly gay, sitting on a mattress in back of a van on her way to a demonstration—and wearing blue jeans! Mrs. General Cravens. How delicious.

Traffic came to a standstill, and they parked the van near the national cemetery and hiked across the bridge.

Although nothing compared with the famous rally last summer when Martin Luther King had made his famous "I Have a Dream" speech, an impressive gathering of people—whites and blacks of all ages—congregated on the mall in front of the Lincoln Memorial. Could there really be a world like this, she wondered, where people are—if not equal—at least more equal than they were now?

Louise was glad she had come.

They sat on the grass, listened to the speeches, sang the anthems of the movement. The speeches were emotional, naïve, moving.

"I'll bet out of all these people, we're the only officers' wives," Maggie observed.

"Would Danny approve?" Louise asked.

"Approve is too strong a word. I don't think he'll care that I came as long as I don't get into trouble. Military types are supposed to be apolitical, but I suspect he and Peter aren't as different from Matt and Eric as they appear. They just have careers they care about. And the flying. In the Air Force, they can soar."

"How do you guys feel about Nam?" Maggie asked her cousins.

"We won't go," Eric said.

Matt nodded his agreement.

"What if you're drafted?" Louise asked.

"We've thought about Canada," Matt said. "Even prison. We're not sure if we want to go that far, but the civil rights movement has taught us to stand up for what we believe in, and we don't believe in killing any more than we believe in racism."

Pacifists—the sons of a military family were pacifists. Louise thought of that irony often in the days to come. Her nephews. Marynell would probably be humiliated when she realized the truth about her sons. Louise wasn't sure what Jeffrey's reaction would be. Franklin would be horrified. Maggie apparently omitted that when she wrote Franklin, though she did write about the rally.

Franklin's letter to Louise was chastising. "I was surprised to learn from Maggie that my wife and daughter had taken part in a so-called civil rights rally that interrupted traffic and commerce in our nation's capital. I am disappointed, to say the least, not so much at Maggie, who is young and idealistic, but at you, Louise, who are old enough to see how destructive such demonstrations are to our country and to our country's image abroad—and at a time when the energies and emotions of our citizens should be focused on the very real threat of Communist domination. Civil disobedience has no place in an orderly society. People must solve their civil grievances through the courts. I shudder to think of the next generation of draftees who will fight the war that is escalating all around us here in Vietnam. Military effort and strong nations are built on discipline. I trust that you will use better judgment in the future."

Louise tore up the letter. God, that man could be pompous at times. She was afraid the stars on his shoulders made him even worse.

But in a way, she understood. He was like Marynell and needed the safety of absolutes. Marynell was learning that she couldn't order up a world on her terms. She wondered if Franklin ever would.

She wrote him back. "There are two sides to most issues. In a perfect world, civil rights grievances would be solved in the courts, and I can understand your preference for this more orderly way of dealing with such problems. But after years of frustration, I can also understand why black Americans feel they have the right to challenge inequality through civil disobedience. I believe that in our imperfect world, without such measures, they would wait forever for justice. This is my opinion, and I would appreciate your respecting my right to have one."

Then, to soften her words, she wrote how much she missed him, how lonely a house was without a man.

In response, he offered only one sentence in an otherwise rambling letter. "As to your comments on civil disobedience, sometimes I feel like I don't know you at all."

CHAPTER

THIRTY-SEVEN

*I*t was Franklin's voice on the phone. "Is Maggie there?"

"Yes. She's up in her room. Why?"

"Don't let her go anyplace. I'm coming home."

"Franklin, is something wrong?"

But already he had hung up.

Louise replaced the receiver but remained seated on the bench in the hall. The maid was humming tunelessly in the kitchen. Sounds of the lawn mower slowing and stopping came from the open windows. The smell of freshly cut grass mingled with that of furniture polish and dinner cooking.

For no reason, Louise stared at her hand on the receiver, at the West Point miniature protecting her wedding band. It was almost five o'clock. He would be coming home soon anyway, yet he'd called to say he was coming to see Maggie.

Louise realized her hand was trembling. Hurriedly, she withdrew it from the phone and tucked it in her lap. No. It wasn't what she thought. Not that. It was something else.

Slanted shafts of light from the front windows cut across the living room rug. Such a handsome room. High ceilings framed with fluted moldings. Marble fireplace. Polished wooden floors and Oriental area rugs. The sixteenth home of her married life. She'd counted them up as they moved into this fine old house in a lovely Alexandria neighborhood. A civilian neighborhood for a change, with Maggie living with them now that Danny was doing his second tour in

427

Vietnam. Franklin was stationed at the Pentagon as chief congressional liaison for the Joint Chiefs of Staff. A major general now. Incredible. They'd had a lovely reception in honor of his promotion at the Army and Navy Club. His parents hadn't come this time. Harold was bedridden in a nursing home. Maxine hovered. No one could bathe him, feed him, care for him to her satisfaction so she did almost everything herself. She would probably come live with them when Harold died. At eighty-two, Maxine was still remarkable.

Louise looked at her watch. Franklin would be awhile. He'd hit the worst of the rush-hour traffic.

The door to Maggie's room opened. *No, don't let her come downstairs. Don't let her see my face.*

But her daughter's footsteps were on the stairs.

"Have a good nap?" Louise called out.

Maggie yawned as she sank down on the bottom step. "Yeah. Those fourth-graders wear me out. Who was on the phone?"

"Your dad. He's on the way home. Why don't you go see how dinner's coming? Make sure Phyllis doesn't forget my pie? It should be done by now."

So silly for her to bake a pie. Phyllis could probably make one that was just as good. But with a maid, there wasn't much for Louise to do around the house so she intruded on Phyllis's kitchen and worked alongside the gardener in the yard. And she'd taken up needlepoint again, which she brought with her to meetings and coffees.

"How about a little wine?" Maggie asked. "You look like you could use a little pick-me-up."

Louise nodded. Maggie headed down the hall for the kitchen, and Louise followed her as far as the study. She turned on the television and perched on the edge of the sofa.

Her heart was pounding too hard, as though she'd just run upstairs. She willed her daughter to stay in the kitchen. Maybe she'd cut up the salad greens for Phyllis. She heard the two women laughing. Phyllis liked Maggie. They went to NAACP meetings together. Far more liberal than her sister, Maggie agreed with her cousins on most issues, except about the war. She defended the war. The war had to be right. Danny was fighting in it.

Danny.

Louise felt ill. She went upstairs and looked for something in the medicine cabinet to calm her stomach. Then she tidied up her desk, stalling.

"Mother, I've got your wine," Maggie called up the stairs.

They sat in front of the television. A major escalation of the air war in Vietnam. In New York and Berkeley, demonstrations against the war. Quintuplets born in Australia.

Louise heard a car stopping out front.

Maggie followed her into the hall. Franklin took off his hat and put it on the table by the front door. He looked tired, defeated, with his shoulders sagging. He met his wife's gaze, nodded, then turned to their daughter.

Already, Maggie's hands were at her mouth.

"Danny's missing, honey," Franklin said with a helpless shrug. "He was shot down yesterday. Our intelligence people just got the word."

"Missing?" Louise repeated. Maggie was absolutely motionless.

"He and his navigator have been officially listed as missing in action," Franklin explained. "He reported he was going down in the mountains northeast of Nam Dinh, near the coast."

"Did they eject?" Louise asked.

"We don't know," Franklin said. "There's no visual report on the crash. His wing man had taken a hit earlier and limped back to the carrier."

Maggie uncovered her mouth. "What happens now?"

"Not much, I'm afraid. The intelligence people said that if the crew lived through the crash, we can assume they were captured. All we can do is hope our sources are able to get some information, or that the Hanoi government lists him as a prisoner of war."

"Do his parents know?" Maggie asked, too calmly.

"I understand that General and Mrs. Norton have been informed. I haven't talked to them yet."

"Would you ask for a written report of everything the intelligence people know so far?"

Louise stepped into Franklin's arms. They watched as Maggie, her back straight, went to the phone and placed a call to her in-laws in Hawaii.

"I know he's alive," she told them repeatedly. "I know he's alive." Then she told about his last letter, how he won the carrier Ping-Pong tournament, how the Protestant chaplain was a former Olympic sprinter.

When she hung up, she turned and started up the stairs.

"Maggie?" Louise called as she hurried after her. Louise followed Maggie to her room and closed the door behind them. Maggie sat in her wicker rocker and began to rock.

"He's not dead, you know. He's a part of me, and I'd feel it if he was dead, and he promised he'd come home to me. He promised."

She asked her mother to make phone calls . Pauline and Jerry at West Point. Peter and Belinda in California. Jeffrey and Marynell drove in from Fredericksburg.

Phyllis, her eyes red from crying, served a late dinner. Maggie was calm, even ate some roast beef, assuring all of them that Danny was not dead, her father agreeing with her. "Danny's a fine officer," Franklin said. "If there's a way to come out of this, he will."

Maggie nodded at her father's words, then asked Phyllis to bring in Louise's freshly made cherry pie. She had a note pad by her plate, making lists of friends and relatives who needed to be notified.

"Have you told Matt and Eric?" she asked Marynell.

Marynell and Jeffrey exchanged glances. Marynell buried her face in her hands and began to cry.

"The boys are in Canada," Jeffrey explained. "They called day before yesterday from Toronto. Eric received his draft notice, and they'd made this pact. . . . "

"Jesus Christ!" Franklin roared. "I can't believe we've got draft dodgers and heroes in the same family."

"Matt and Eric are following their consciences," Louise snapped.

"You mean they're traitors!" Franklin said. "They have no right!"

"Of course they have a right. They may pay the consequences, but we can't tell them what to believe," Louise answered.

Franklin, his neck a bright red, slammed his fist down on the table, making the dishes jump and Marynell gasp. "My God, Louise, how can you sit there and say such a thing when your own daughter's husband has just been reported missing in action?"

"I can say it because I believe it, Franklin. Danny, Peter, Matt and Eric are all doing what they believe is right."

Jeffrey gave Louise a grateful look. Marynell looked down at her plate. "I've never been so ashamed," she whispered. "Never."

Silence settled over the table as the grandfather clock in the hall began to strike midnight. Stricken, the family seemed to hold its collective breath as they silently counted twelve deep bongs.

As the clock fell silent, Maggie began to scream.

Louise stayed with her throughout the night. "When will I see him again?" Maggie kept asking. "When? Oh, Mom, there's no way to know. It may be years. How can I live years without Danny? I can't. I just can't. Nothing matters without him."

Louise could offer no promises that everything would be all right. All she could do was hold her daughter and cry her own anguished tears.

"Nobody ever loved anyone as much as I love Danny," Maggie said.

"I know, honey. I know. And he loved you back. Remember that."

"Do you think that he's thinking about me now?"

"Oh, yes. If he's alive, you can rest assured that he is thinking about his darlin' Maggie."

"He's alive!" Maggie said trembling, and began screaming again. Franklin, Pauline and Marynell came rushing in. Jeffrey hovered in the doorway.

Franklin sat beside Maggie on the bed and gathered her in his arms. "Come on, honey. You're Mrs. Daniel Norton. Danny needs you to be strong and to pray for him and to believe in him."

Maggie listened and nodded.

"I'm going to call Walter Reed and have them send someone out here with a shot to make you sleep," Franklin said. "Maybe when you wake up in the morning, there'll be some more information for you."

"Will you stay with me, Daddy?"

"Yes, honey. Your mother and I will always be here."

• • •

In the weeks and months that followed, Maggie continued to teach, continued to look young and pretty, her wonderful golden-red hair a curly halo over vivacious green eyes. She even laughed out loud at times. But no matter what the topic of conversation, she turned it around to Vietnam, to Danny. She talked of Danny obsessively. And was quick to justify the war, to chastise those who condemned it. While Maggie was much admired for her bravery, her obsession frightened people away. Louise warned her that people would start avoiding her if she didn't stop being so evangelical.

And indeed, friends stopped calling. Maggie cried when she realized her colleagues at school were doing TGIF these days without her.

It was Franklin who found her an MIA sister, the daughter-in-law of a Pentagon associate. Maggie moved in with the woman—Janet, a bank teller. Maggie found other sisters. Often weeks would go by with Louise and Franklin seeing her only at dinner on Sunday.

Louise enrolled in another class. The Sociology of Women. She found sisters, too. This time she wasn't the only middle-aged person enrolled. The professor believed in small-group discussions. Maybe it was because of the anonymity offered by a college classroom or perhaps the candor of the professor herself as she moved about the room, but the women talked. Women who didn't love their husbands as much as they thought they should. Women who hated their husbands. Women who puzzled over the sexual politics of marriage. Women who sacrificed for their families and wondered in middle life if the price had been worth it. Others certain it was.

And after class, still stimulated, they'd go for coffee to continue the discussions. Even the professor. But even these sessions never lasted long enough. There were jobs to return to. Children and husbands to see to. Even the professor had to rush to pick up children, shop for groceries, feed a husband.

Louise never told anyone—not even the professor—that her husband was a general.

And she never so much as hinted to Franklin about the true content of the class. "It's just a beginning sociology class. The roles of people in society." He didn't approve of her taking college courses. There were so many young radicals on campuses these days. It was unseemly for a woman of her age and position to attend college classes. What did she hope to accomplish anyway? Poor Franklin. He didn't know how to deal with a wife who deliberately contradicted his wishes.

In the night, so often, they talked about Maggie.

"What will happen to her if he doesn't come back?" Franklin would ask in the darkness.

"I suppose she'll continue teaching, marry again. She's young."

"But she'll never get over it."

"No. I don't imagine she will. I'd feel sorry for any man who tried to follow Danny."

"I really admire her, the way she loves him."

"Yes, she's loved Danny for a long time. But it's always been a young love."

"What's that supposed to mean? I'd say Maggie's love has more than been put to the test."

"No, they'll never know how much they love each other unless they're married a long time, raise children together, face sadness together."

"Like we've done?" Franklin asked.

"Yes. We've lasted."

"You've changed, Louise."

"And you liked me better before?"

"Yes. Now I'm never quite sure what you're thinking."

And he had been sure before. Not correct, perhaps, but sure. Louise felt a pang of guilt. Wives should not puzzle their husbands.

She turned into his arms. "I think that I'd like for you to make love to me."

Book Five

★ ★ ★

1968–1971

CHAPTER

THIRTY-EIGHT

The weather was perfect, the Italian countryside as beautiful as she remembered. The Adriatic Sea on the left was a perfect sheet of azure, the hills on the right lush and green, patterned with vineyards and orchards.

"It's Tuesday," Louise mused as she rounded a curve. "I'm missing a reception at the Danish embassy."

A distant hilltop village came into view. Maybe they'd stop there for lunch if they didn't have to walk too far after parking the car. Eddie could only take so much hiking up steep stone streets.

Eddie grinned, turning the lines radiating from his eyes into deep creases. "A reception? I know you're broken-hearted."

Her father looked every one of his seventy-eight years. His hair was white and wispy. His flesh hung loosely from his body, reminded Louise of an old basset hound some relative had back in Indiana.

And for the first time, Eddie no longer had to be the daddy in charge. He was willing to be chauffeured, to allow Louise to make all the decisions.

He had presented himself to Franklin as a lonely old man needing one last trip with his daughter before he retired to the rocking chair for good. But actually, he was managing the trip rather nicely. His knees gave out if he asked too much of them, but he had a surprising amount of stamina for a man of his years. He and Martha didn't travel much anymore—more because of Martha, who now relied on a cane to get around. Louise suspected her father had masterminded this trip because he was worried about her. Sometimes she hadn't bothered to hide the discontent in her voice during their weekly phone calls. It was no cheaper to call England from Paris than it had been from Washington, D.C., but the fact that her father was just across the channel made Louise reach for the phone more often.

She and Franklin had stopped at Folkestone last fall on their way to Paris to visit in the wonderful cottage by the sea. But after two days, Franklin had grown restless, eager to get on to his new assignment on the staff of the supreme commander, Allied Powers, Europe, and had cut his stay short, leaving Louise to loll awhile with Martha and Eddie, to walk along the cliff and shop in the village, to work in the garden and play cribbage or gin rummy with her father and Martha in the evening in front of the television set.

Louise had called her father that first Monday morning after arriving in Paris and every Monday morning thereafter, preferring a time when Franklin wasn't around. She edited herself too much when her husband was listening.

Her phone calls now originated in Brussels after SHAPE headquarters had moved there following France's abrupt departure from NATO. And she had just been getting to know her way around Paris. Another move.

Throughout the winter and spring, her conversations with her father got progressively longer. They exchanged family news. Made plans for Louise's next visit to England. And they shared their day-to-day lives. He'd planted two rows of radishes and one of onions, set a cocker spaniel's broken leg. She'd bought Flemish lace tablecloths for the girls, gone to the fourth social function in a week, the one last night at the Danish embassy. Her social skills seemed to be slipping, and sometimes she said something inappropriate. Occasionally, she drank too much. And if she didn't find someone interesting to talk to, she'd find a corner to sit in. Franklin would critique her behavior on the way home. She had learned to tune him out, and this irritated him more than the original offense. "Louise, are you listening to me?" She'd pat his cheek—or kiss it. "No dear, I'm not. So why don't we just drop it."

Louise realized she was too candid with her father, didn't bother to disguise her restlessness. And after all, she loved being back in Europe, was thrilled by the scenery and sightseeing, enjoyed her twice-weekly French lessons. So why did this malaise cling to her like talcum powder to damp skin? Age was part of it—only one more birthday before fifty. She kept asking herself if the rest of her life would consist of aimless days, protocol evenings, passionless nights.

She and Franklin lived in a palatial home near the American embassy. A soldier polished the floors and served the meals cooked by a French-speaking chef. Another soldier served as her driver. The opulence was numbing.

She would have even welcomed a committee meeting or two—anything to give her life structure. She called her children too much. Peter and Belinda were in Iran. He was a major now, and their son Benjamin was almost three. Pauline and Jerry were stationed in Alaska. He was a lieutenant colonel, and their daughter Jessica had just had her second birthday. And Maggie. Franklin had wanted Maggie to come with them to Europe, but she had her teaching job and was involved in the formation of a national organization of MIA-POW families. She'd moved into a larger apartment and lived with two other MIA wives—Anita and Holly. Most of her friends were also MIA wives, sisters in their plight, in their shared limbo.

While her father always had time for her calls, Louise sometimes felt like her calls to her children were an intrusion. An international call was a mandate to take time and talk. They couldn't blithely announce they were about to eat or on their way out the door and offer to return the call in the morning, with papers to grade and meetings to attend. But Maggie usually sounded rushed. Pauline would yell to her waiting husband, "Just a minute, honey. Mom's on the phone." Peter would talk a few minutes, run out of things to say and hand the phone to Belinda. Often a receiver was put to a child's ear. "Say hello to grandmother." Benny and Jessica—her snapshot grandchildren.

After a while, Louise resorted more to writing her children though she was aware that a letter could also be an intrusion of sorts, requiring either an answer or a guilty conscience. Belinda and Pauline both periodically dashed off short notes that said little and were sent along with the padding of children's artwork and family snapshots. Maggie's letters were longer but more infrequent and full of apology for not having written sooner. Like her last letter.

I'm sorry I haven't written in so long, but I've been very busy. Really. Last weekend, Janet, Holly and I went on a retreat in Shenandoah National Park with a group of MIA-POW families living in the area. Some of the women and parents are starting to side with the antiwar activists. We've had some real heated discussions, and a couple of the women left in a huff. We all desperately want the fighting to stop so the POWs can come home, but we hate to see the government giving in to the antiwar movement. If America just gives up, what has been accomplished by the loss of all those American lives? I try not to think about Matt and Eric. I don't want to hate my own cousins.

On the evening news last night, there was some footage of POWs being held in Hanoi that had just been released by the North Vietnamese. It made my heart stop. The film was of poor quality and the men haggard, but one of them could have been Danny. He was in the background and visible for just a second. I went down to the TV station and had them show it to me again and again. I wish I could be more sure. But he's alive. I know he is. He's with me every minute of each day. I never stop thinking about him, and I know he's thinking about me.

Work is work. I come home every night with a stack of papers to grade and lesson plans to make. I have an accelerated class that I really enjoy, but I have to do twice as much preparation. Some of those kids know more than I do. The students think they're the only ones counting the days until vacation. Ha! Yet when I'm not teaching I have too much time on my hands. I'm considering your offer of a ticket to Belgium, but I'm so paranoid about leaving town for fear a letter will come from Danny or the Air Force will have some news for me—finally. One of the MIA wives in Baltimore got a letter! Just like that—out of the blue. One of those dictated things saying he was being treated well, followed by a bunch of Commie propaganda. But it was his writing, his signature! His wife knows he's alive! All last weekend while we were on the retreat, I kept imagining the phone ringing in our empty apartment. But I miss you guys, and probably I can pick a time when Anita and Holly will be here, just in case . . . I could use a little spoiling from my mom and dad. I'll write soon. Really.

Love to you both,
Maggie

Marynell always answered letters promptly. She liked her new principal. She had a terrible student teacher this semester. Next summer, she and Jeffrey were going to Canada to see Matt and Eric. Eric was married and had a little boy, Seth. Marynell was willing to make a truce with her sons so she could hold Seth in her arms.

Jeffrey and I talk about baby Seth all the time. Yet I'm so nervous. I said so many things to Matt and Eric that should have gone unsaid. They knew how I felt without all those ugly words. I keep remembering what you said that night Danny was reported missing—that everyone has the right to pursue their own conscience. Having my sons run away from their patriotic duty is the worst humiliation I've ever borne, but they're alive when others are dead. Or missing like poor Danny. And I'm glad for Seth. Such a funny name for a baby, but it's growing on me. He'll have to be a rugged individualist with a name like that—don't you think?

I hope Eric's wife likes me. I hope she'll let Seth come visit when he's older. Jeffrey can teach him to make things. I've missed having a family around the table. Jeffrey and I go to a cafeteria most evenings. I hate it, but who feels like cooking after a day in the classroom? We both cook on weekends. I feel like Mother and Daddy with both of us puttering around in the kitchen, getting into each other's way. Jeffrey made curry when I had the faculty over for dinner. It was delicious, but he didn't want me to use the good china and crystal. I did anyway. And the sterling hollowware. What's the point of having it if I can't use it? The table looked magnificent, just like before. I need for people to know what we came from. Jeffrey said I distance myself from people by acting that way, but I feel distant. They've led such narrow lives. Some of the teachers were *born* in Fredericksburg.

One of my sixth graders won the state essay contest for the American Legion. When they interviewed him for the newspaper, he said I was the best teacher he'd ever had. Imagine. I cried. Of course, for every kid who thinks I'm a good teacher, there are six others who think I'm a mean old biddy. Which I am. But not all the time.

Love,
Marynell

The phone calls and letters gave Louise something to talk to Franklin about in the evening.

Sometimes, she almost welcomed the arrival of yet another engraved invitation, usually bearing an embassy crest of some NATO country. The invitations gave her something to write in the squares on her calendar, and she had come to dread the empty squares more than the events themselves. Louise had started taking a greater interest in her wardrobe now that she had more money to spend on clothes, discovering that there was pleasure from looking well turned out, and she liked her husband's compliments, even flirted with him when she felt pretty. The only time they made love was when they'd been to a party. The combination of wine in his veins and a flirtatious wife in evening clothes made him amorous. As they were being driven home, he'd whisper to her that he wanted to make love to her, that she had been the most beautiful lady at the party. Usually, she had consumed more wine than he had. The wine made sex almost exciting.

More often, however, Franklin just talked, even after he got into bed. His voice droned on and on, lecturing in great detail about SAC, long-range ballistic missiles, the Soviet buildup in Eastern Europe, his irritation with the French for pulling out of NATO, the Vietnam peace talks in Paris. The war went on. Growing numbers of Americans wanted to throw up their hands and belly up to Communism. The fools. They didn't deserve to call themselves

Americans. Did they want their children to grow up Communists? Sometimes, she listened and cared a great deal; other times, she wanted to put her hands over her ears. Those nights, Franklin simply talked himself to sleep, dropping off in midsentence. Louise would curl away from him, enjoying the quiet as she drifted off to sleep.

Franklin was happy. For that she was grateful. It meant she had to deal with him and her marriage on only a superficial level, retreating into her own thoughts, her books. She longed for a woman friend. But her husband's rank distanced her. And she found the other generals' wives tedious. She understood now why her mother had gotten vague.

Franklin didn't seem to notice her withdrawal. But then the household was run efficiently by servants, and Louise always put her book down when they talked. Biographies were her current passion. Of Madame Curie. Mary Pickford. Mary Magdalene. Elizabeth I. Eleanor Roosevelt. She preferred women's lives. But she had read about Freud recently, and Michelangelo. She still read mysteries some, but avoided fiction that was thought-provoking, that asked questions but offered no answers.

When Franklin was ordered to Milan for a month to represent the American military at a conference on upgrading NATO's defense mission, he wanted her to go along.

Italy. She wasn't sure she really wanted to be reminded of that other time, but there was no real reason not to accompany her husband. And once there, she enjoyed the food, the sound of the language. She took great interest in Milan's museums and churches, its magnificent Duomo, but it was a bustling industrial city with little of the rural Italian charm she remembered. "Remember our trip?" she asked Eddie on the phone, the second call that week. "Italy was so lovely then."

"That Italy is still out there, honey. Go find it."

"With my driver?" she asked sarcastically. "Or perhaps Franklin's aide-de-camp?"

"What about one of the other wives?"

"I don't have friends anymore, Daddy. I'm too tired to make them, only to say good-bye and have to find replacements. Besides, Franklin's rank puts distance between me and other women. And other generals' wives have this annoying habit of starting most of their sentences with 'the general says.' Of course, I'd probably do the same thing if I wanted anyone to pay attention to me, but I don't have much to say anymore. Maybe I can convince Franklin to take some leave before we go back to the States, and we can travel a bit."

Two days later, Eddie had shown up in Milan unannounced. Louise was thrilled, Franklin polite.

"The country's unstable, and there are too many terrorists, too many kidnappings," Franklin insisted when he realized what Eddie wanted. "I don't think it's safe for the wife of a high-ranking American military officer to travel about Italy unescorted."

"I'll be with her," Eddie said firmly. "And we won't be in a staff car with two-star flags fluttering from the fenders. We'll rent a nice inconspicuous little European car. No one will know who Louise is."

Before Franklin could offer further protest, Louise told him she was going. Just like that. She wasn't quite sure what she would have done if he'd challenged her. Probably kissed her father good-bye and sent him back to Martha. Then again, maybe not.

She'd packed her suitcase quickly, before Franklin could put some impenetrable obstacle in her path. They left next morning.

Her father was an easy traveling companion. In Venice, he had sensed her fascination with San Marco and dozed on a bench while she explored the cathedral's Byzantine excesses to her heart's content. And he wandered aimlessly along the canals with her until his knees began to bother him, and he took a water taxi back to their hotel so she could enjoy walking unhampered. She thought of her first trip in Europe when men flirted with her. She still got an occasional bold look, but not like before. She was older. And the excitement in her eyes had been replaced with mild curiosity.

With no advance reservations, they had taken lodgings in a modest tourist-class hotel.

"Shall I tell them who you are?" Eddie teased. He seemed to think it a great joke that the major general's wife was staying in a tiny hotel with the bathroom down the hall.

From Venice, they had gone to Ravenna but stayed only a day and a night to see its famous mosaics. Like Venice, it was full of tourists. And now they were driving aimlessly south, toward the distant hilltop village where they'd have lunch. Tonight they would sleep in some yet-to-be-determined place.

Eddie served as navigator, with his map and guidebook usually open on his lap. Louise followed his directions mindlessly as they poked along. They drank homemade wine and ate too much pasta wherever they stopped. They pulled off the road to take in the breathtaking views. Louise had a camera, but she seldom used it. She wanted to live the moment and not worry about recording it.

The road wound its way through orchards and vineyards. Eddie waved at men working in the field.

Louise put the car in second gear for the steep grade up the hill, climbing toward the tiny town at its rest. "Montebenso," the sign said. She parked as close as she could to the gate in the ancient city wall, then leaned over and kissed her father's cheek. "Thank you."

"What for?"

"Rescuing me."

Eddie hugged her for a minute. "My pleasure, dear girl," he said.

They made their way slowly up the steep street into the center of town and had lunch on the balcony of a tiny restaurant. They could see all the way to the sea over a patchwork countryside of greens and browns, dotted here and there with villages and farmhouses. No one spoke English, but with the help of her dictionary Louise managed to order a wonderful lunch. Pasta, of course. And fish. Fruit and cheese.

"Do you miss Martha when you experience something beautiful?" Louise asked over the last glass of wine.

"Not when I have you to share it with. And Martha couldn't have climbed that hill. Won't be long until I can't either." He lifted his glass to Louise. "I'm glad, dearest Louise, to be out in the world again, to be here with you, to share places and food and thoughts with you I've never shared with anyone else."

That afternoon Eddie made a great show of examining his map.

"How about that! Unless I'm mistaken, we're close to that little town where we stayed that time the tour bus broke down."

Soon the name appeared on a sign. Louise's heart fluttered in her chest.

"See! Amola," Eddie said, pointing triumphantly. "Wasn't that the name of that town? What say we stop for coffee and a sweet?"

Louise wondered suddenly if this was why her elderly father had brought her on this one last trip.

But surely not. That had been another time in her life. And fathers don't arrange opportunities for their aging, married daughters to stray from the path of respectability.

He looked at her eagerly. "Just a drive through if you don't want to stop."

"Just a drive through," she repeated and turned off the autostrada and headed toward the sea.

In her fantasies she had returned to the quaint little town many times.

But not for years.

She still thought of the long-ago Italian man and that time with him, but memories had dimmed, and she no longer conjured up fantasies of return. When she closed her eyes, she couldn't see his face. Only in an occasional dream did Tommaso become real again, and then with such clarity that she woke in a daze of sadness and longing.

She could smell the sea before cresting the hill. And suddenly, there was the town, nestled in the distance around its small bay, the arms of the boat basin encircling a scattering of fishing craft. The water was dazzlingly bright and clear, and between the ancient buildings the dazzling white stone streets were visible. She'd forgotten about the white streets. Like a pearl, Amola glistened below them.

Louise pulled the car off the road. "This is far enough."

"Fine," Eddie said agreeably. "The view is pretty, isn't it? Maybe you should get your camera out."

Louise just sat. "I can't go down there."

"Why?"

"It's been twelve years, Daddy. I'm old. Maybe he's dead. Maybe he's forgotten me. Maybe he doesn't work at the hotel anymore. He'd laugh at me, coming back like this."

"He's down there, honey. He remembers you."

Louise turned and stared at her father's face. "How do you know?"

"Martha and I came two years after you girls and I had been here. Tommaso asked me to call him once a year just to tell him that you were okay."

"You've called him?" Louise shook her head in disbelief.

"Yes. Just to tell him you were fine," Eddie hurried on. "I told him when the kids got married. Stuff like that. He told me when his wife died and his grandkids were born." Eddie's words poured out in a rush. "I'm sorry if I overstepped, honey, luring you back here. You seemed so unhappy."

Louise didn't want to know that Tommaso's wife had died. Why did he have to go and tell her something like that?

As she digested her father's words, her breathing became more difficult. She felt like she was being suffocated. All those long-buried emotions puffing themselves up like dried-out sponges filling with water.

"What is going down there supposed to accomplish?" she demanded angrily.

"I'm not sure. It just seemed like you needed something."

"Like when you first reached out to Martha?"

"I suppose." Eddie slumped against his seat. Louise knew she was disappointing him, but what had he expected of her? That she'd go rushing down there and live happily ever after like a princess in a fairy tale?

"And Jeffrey," Louise added. "I think he came very close to leaving Marynell for someone else. But he didn't. He was honorable and stayed."

"So now there are two unhappy people where there might have been only one," Eddie snapped.

"But his leaving would have devastated Marynell. And they're doing better. How can someone be happy at another human being's expense?"

Eddie sighed. "When Jeffrey and Marynell came to see me last year, she asked again about your mother. Would I have left her if she lived? Marynell is obsessed with that. Jeffrey kept apologizing. I think she came all that way to bring it up again, although they were supposedly on their way to France for Jeffrey's pilgrimage to the battlefields and cemeteries."

"Yes," Louise said. "Apparently Marynell was as moved as Jeffrey by seeing those places. I think she finally understood why he needed to put the military behind him."

"But her foolish bitterness will never go away. Jeffrey did not give her what she wanted out of marriage, and she will live out the rest of her life as an ordinary woman in an ordinary town with an ordinary husband."

"We all come to that in the end. Look at Franklin's parents."

"Yes," Eddie agreed. "And Martha and me. But Marynell doesn't think of that. She only thinks of what might have been. You should have married Jeffrey and given Franklin to her."

Louise realized she was still clutching the steering wheel. She let go, opening and closing her cramped hands. "So, what do we do now?" she asked, more to herself than her father. Amola beckoned below them. Franklin and years of shared family history stood behind her.

"You would have gotten yourself here before you and Franklin went back to the States," Eddie said. "I just got you here sooner."

"Perhaps," Louise said. "I might have walked through the streets of Amola and stood outside the hotel. But I would never have gone inside."

"Maybe you won't now either. Maybe it will look shabby. Maybe you and Tommaso will shake hands, then we'll have a drink and be on our way. But don't you think the rest of your life will be easier if you know that the possibility isn't still here waiting for you?"

"But what if it is?"

"Then you can turn your back on it and apply for beatification, or live the last years of your life for yourself."

"Maybe there's more of Marynell in me than you realize. Part of me still wishes there wasn't a Martha. Part of me hasn't forgiven you either. I could never leave Franklin. Never."

"No. I suppose you couldn't. But where did Amola fit in?" Eddie asked, his gaze on the distant town. "Was it just a fling?"

"Yes, but it backfired."

"Yes. Passion is hard to turn your back on."

"So is responsibility."

Eddie nodded, then took out his handkerchief and blew his nose.

"God, Daddy, you're a hopeless old romantic. Passion has other names, you know, like adultery. Cheating. Playing with fire."

Louise started the car, waited for an old, dented truck to go by, then maneuvered the car around. "Look at that map of yours," she ordered, "and figure out where we can spend the night. Inland. I don't want to look at the sea."

Dutifully, Eddie unfolded his map.

But she went no farther. Another truck was coming from the west. She pulled over to let it go by, then sat there, sweating hands clutching the wheel, heart pounding. If she drove away, that was it. For the rest of her life. Nothing between her and death but proper, sedate wifehood, an occasional dutiful visit from busy children and bored grandchildren. Even Maggie, who had needed her so much when the news about Danny first came, now had her fierce sisterhood with other MIA wives.

Marynell needed her, Louise supposed, but she was weary of her sister's self-pity. It made her angry the way Marynell had changed, but sisters were for life, and Marynell was the only one she had. She wouldn't admit it to her father, but Louise had wondered for years why Jeffrey stayed. Maybe for the same reasons she herself did.

"Will you drive?" Louise asked. "I seem to be stuck in neutral."

"No. I won't drive," Eddie said, tracing a road on the map with his finger.

"You really called him once a year?"

"On New Year's Day. Three o'clock in the afternoon. He would answer the phone saying my name. '*Ciao, Signor Eddie. Buon Anno.*'"

Her father had brought her all this way, but ultimately the decision was hers. Her hands hurt. Her head hurt. And her chest.

With tires spitting gravel, Louise turned back around. It was a small car, but still the effort made her perspire. Maybe her father was right. Maybe she would not have been able to leave Europe without a return to Amola.

The Inn of the Two Roosters was smaller than she remembered it. More worn. But clean. That part hadn't changed. The windows sparkled, and the rows of glasses behind the bar. The floors were polished to perfection, the walls freshly whitewashed.

The same gaudy picture of the Madonna resided on a shelf over the bar, and there, beside a vase of plastic roses, in its own tiny frame, was Andy's picture. Louise was stunned. Andy. She remembered the night she had shown Tommaso that picture, how he had cried for her little lost son.

Funny little Andy with his big serious eyes and his tentative smile. Precious child. After losing him, she'd never been the same. Andy, who had filled her heart more than any other human being.

Until Tommaso.

She found him fishing from his favorite rock. When he saw her approaching, he stood and shaded his eyes against the setting sun.

Slowly, they approached each other. She could see the change in his face as he realized it was really her.

At first there was just a touching of hands, shy smiles, an examination of the years on each other's faces.

He was completely gray, heavier. Deep creases radiated outward from blue eyes that were less blue than before.

"You have never left my heart," he said.

"Nor you mine," Louise admitted. "Those days with you were the best of my life."

"I want to hold you, but I smell of fish."

"It doesn't matter," Louise said.

And so they embraced. The feel of him was solid, incredibly sweet. He did indeed smell of fish—and sweat, of the sea and life.

Throughout that first evening, Louise ate her meal and drank her wine in a fog of sweet anticipation. She didn't know what would happen afterward, but tonight she would make love to Tommaso. Her flesh knew it and tingled. She kept touching her own skin and marveling at the sensation there, and finally, she had to reach out and touch his arm. The rough hair, the weathered skin, the sinewy muscles of a man who had labored long years. Nothing had ever felt more erotic.

Tommaso smiled at her. Eddie kept blowing his damned nose.

They stayed for a week. Louise supposed it was strange to be with one's lover *and* one's father, but the two men liked each other. They fished while Louise watched, drugging herself with sunshine and beauty, taking pleasure in the camaraderie of the two men. At mealtime, Eddie shuffled about the kitchen, helping out. Again, Louise was content to sit and watch. She felt strangely passive after a lifetime of being the gracious hostess, the hovering wife and mother. She listened while the men exchanged stories of family and wartime. She wished there was some way she could make time stand still, for she knew this would end. Amola was not real.

She had forgotten how much she loved the sea. Tommaso taught her to ride the waves, to snorkel for calamari. One night, after the kitchen was cleaned, they built a fire on the beach, and when their bottle of wine was empty, Eddie put a message in it and set it adrift. He refused to tell what he had written, but they made up stories about who might find it.

In bed, it was as though she and Tommaso had never been apart. The passion and love had endured. Their bodies were young in the moonlight.

She wondered how long they would make love every night if they stayed together. Intellectually, she knew the hunger would lose its edge, the intensity diminish. But it felt as though they could be this way forever.

The whole town knew. Everywhere they went, people smiled indulgently. It was impossible for Louise to walk beside Tommaso without holding his hand, impossible to keep her eyes from following him when he was across the room.

"Do your friends know I'm married?" she asked.

"They asked if you are a widow. When I say no, they assume you are divorced. Everyone knows that Americans divorce. I see no reason to say otherwise. It would confuse them. In Italy, we have only two classifications for our women—good and bad."

"And I am neither?" Louise asked.

"I think everyone is some of both. What I think about you, *mia cara*, is that you have been trapped for many years in a loveless marriage."

"No. That's not true. My husband loves his good wife. He doesn't know her very well, but he loves her. And I love him because he needs for me to."

Tommaso knew now that Franklin was an Army officer, that she had no real home. But he didn't question her about her husband, and she did not volunteer Franklin's rank. It was too intimidating. She wondered if Tommaso would have had the courage once again to ask her to stay with him if he had known.

"I cannot offer you much," he explained as they sat under the arbor, watching the sunset. Eddie was down on the beach, wading with Tommaso's youngest grandson. "I will love you well and cook for you, teach you to fish. We can walk on the beach in the evening and listen to the music in the square. Your grandchildren can play with my grandchildren."

Louise shook her head. "I have a husband who needs me, children who would be disappointed. I'm too old to learn a new language, too old for such changes."

If not for Franklin, she knew she would stay. But she couldn't do that to him.

When the car was packed and ready to go, Tommaso embraced Eddie. Both men were crying. Eddie promised to call him on New Year's. They shook hands and embraced again.

Then Tommaso gathered Louise in his arms. She felt like her heart was being torn from her chest. She'd had so little time with him, not enough for a lifetime.

She wanted desperately to promise him that she'd come back, but she doubted if she ever would. She'd had her return trip. She wondered if asking for more would be tempting the fates.

When she and her father returned to Milan, she realized the fates had already extracted their price.

CHAPTER

THIRTY-NINE

*T*hey decided to stay the night in Florence and drive on to Milan the next day. "Sure you don't want to take a few days and explore Florence like we'd planned?" Eddie asked.

"I need to get back to Franklin, Daddy. We've already been gone longer than we said we'd be, and he sounded testy when I called Tuesday evening."

Louise had no doubt that Florence was the treasure trove her father had promised, that seeing Michelangelo's works was in itself worth a trip to Italy. But already, she was on her way back to her husband after having spent the most beautiful week of her life with a man she loved far more passionately.

She had moments of panic. What if Franklin sensed some difference in her? What if he guessed her secret? But she'd been touring with her seventy-eight-year-old father, she reminded herself, and surely that would make her above suspicion. The deceit ate at her, made her stomach raw and her head throb. She thought of other times she had deceived her husband—usually to avoid family conflicts. She felt no guilt over those wifely deceptions. She tried to convince herself that what happened at Amola had nothing to do with Franklin and their marriage, that it was just a little respite from real life, but that wasn't so. If it was, she wouldn't feel guilty.

Their hotel was north of the old center of Florence in an area of newer apartment houses and office buildings, but charm and a view of the river were ridiculously expensive. The Albergo Borgo was new and modest. While the bellman unloaded the car, Louise gravitated toward a newsstand in the square. The evening papers hung in rows. Something about a large picture under the bold headlines bothered her. A man in uniform. The skin on her forehead grew tight with apprehension. As she drew closer, her breathing slowed. Stopped.

It was Franklin.

A row of identical Franklins. The same picture stared at her from rows of stacked newspapers from other cities. Roma, Milano, Bologna. Newspapers in other languages. French. German.

"*Ha un giornale in inglese?*" Louise asked in her careful Italian.

"*Si,*" the man said, handing her the *Herald Tribune*. Nixon's picture was on the front page. He was in Moscow for the summit meeting. And halfway down the page was a story whose bold headline blared "American General Kidnapped in Italy."

Very conscious of each step she took, feeling as though she would shatter if she stepped too hard, Louise made her way back across the square past benches of old men smoking cigarettes and young mothers with children.

Eddie was checking in. Mutely, she handed him the newspaper and watched the expression of disbelief pass across his face. "Oh, my God," he whispered.

Sobbing, Louise fell into her father's arms, but they brought little comfort. Her husband was in mortal danger. Maybe he was already dead. She felt ill and frightened.

Eddie guided her to a far corner of the lobby, away from the eyes of the startled desk clerk and bellhop.

"I should have been with him," she wept as she sank onto a sofa. She really did feel nauseated. It was hard to deal with that and her tumbling thoughts.

"Why, so you could have been kidnapped along with him, or killed?" Eddie's voice was harsh.

"You know what I mean," Louise said, surprised. It had been years since her father had used that tone of voice with her.

"You mean you feel to blame? Yes, I suppose there's a big book in the sky where someone looked up your punishment. 'Unfaithful wife—husband gets kidnapped by terrorists.' "

"That's not funny," she said angrily, fishing in her purse for a handkerchief.

"It wasn't meant to be," Eddie said, handing her his. He sat down beside her. "Look, honey. This is going to be difficult enough without a lot of self-recrimination. Bad things happen. Now stop blaming yourself. Okay?"

Louise nodded. This time there was more comfort in his embrace. She put her head on his bony old shoulder and cried for a time. But soon she would have to stop. They needed to make plans. They needed to get themselves back to Milan, to whatever waited there.

They left immediately. Eddie offered to drive but seemed relieved when Louise said that she could manage. Even in the middle of the night, the traffic was heavy. Trucks, mostly, shook the car as they roared past.

Eddie tried not to doze, but his head would fall back against the seat, leaving Louise to her thoughts. He was right, of course. What had happened to Franklin had nothing to do with her. But she felt so wretchedly at fault.

My darling, Franklin. I love you and want you to be all right. Wherever you are, please know that.

She wanted to make a bargain with God, to promise never to leave Franklin's side if she got him back. But if there was a God, she doubted if he ever listened. And was she really sure she wanted to make that promise?

So without promises, without bargains, she hoped for the safe return of her husband. It was a physical act, this hoping. Her entire body focused on it. Her heart beat with it. Her fists closed around it. Her eyes closed with its intensity. *Please.*

In Milan, they went immediately to police headquarters. Peter had already flown in from Iran. "My God, Mom, where in the hell have you been?" he demanded in his father's voice.

Louise reached for her father's hand.

Peter insisted on taking all phone calls, giving details to family and friends, informing journalists that his mother was unavailable for interviews.

She insisted on calling her daughters herself, however. And Maxine.

"I want to come," Maggie sobbed.

Louise closed her eyes, wanting Maggie here with her. But then Pauline would feel she had to leave little Jessica and come all the way from Alaska. And there was nothing either one of them could do. "Peter says it could go on for weeks, honey, months even. You've got your job. Just hang tight. I'll call you every day."

Maxine kept asking in her quavery, old-woman's voice for Louise to say it all again. "But I don't understand. Why would someone kidnap Franklin?"

"We don't know, dear. Probably someone wanting a political figure released from prison—or something like that."

"In Italy? I thought you lived in Belgium now. I sent Franklin's birthday card to Belgium."

"He was in Milan for some meetings. Maggie says for you to come to Washington and stay with her for a while. You can wait for news together."

"No. Harold eats better when I'm there to feed him. I won't tell him about all this. He wouldn't understand. I'm not sure I do. You mean you have no idea where Franklin is?"

"No. Not yet."

"Will he be all right, Louise?"

"I hope so."

"It's hard to think of him as a prisoner. Franklin's always so . . . You know."

"Yes. Your friend next door—Mrs. Simpson—can she come over and stay with you?"

"You mean in case Franklin is killed."

"No. I mean just to have someone to worry with."

"Yes. She'll come if I need her. Or the minister's wife. Louise, my sister's dead, you know."

"Yes, dear. I know."

"If Franklin dies, you'll be the one to bury us. In Arlington. You'll do that, won't you?"

"Of course, I will. But let's pray he'll be okay."

"Yes, I'll pray. I prayed to have him. All those years ago. I thought I'd die if I didn't have a baby. But that prayer got answered. I'm frightened. Are you frightened, Louise?"

"Yes. I very frightened. I love you, dear. I'll have Maggie call you every day. At the nursing home if you're not at home. Okay?"

When the call to Alaska went through, Pauline cried so hard that Jerry took the phone. "Do you want us to come?" he asked.

"Not right now. I'll keep you posted. Take care of Pauline."

"Are you all right?" he asked.

It seemed a stupid question, but she knew he meant well. "I'm holding together," she told him. Yes, holding together. A million fragmented pieces of her self.

By afternoon, a Communist terrorist group called the Domenica Rosa had claimed responsibility. As proof they held Major General Franklin Cravens, they had sent newspapers in Milan, Zurich and Paris a photograph of Franklin holding yesterday's Milan newspaper with his picture on the front page. That picture in turn appeared in the evening paper. Not only in European newspapers, Louise supposed. Probably everywhere. Maggie would see it in Washington, Pauline in Alaska, Maxine in Florida. Louise made another round of phone calls. Everyone felt better. At least they knew he was still alive.

Louise was drawn again and again to that second picture of her husband. She kept picking up a newspaper and staring at it. The photograph was of Franklin, no doubt of that, but he had changed. He was a man no longer in control. His face had lost definition, his T-shirt-clad shoulders seemed less broad. She wondered if tomorrow another picture would arrive of Franklin holding a picture of himself holding a picture of himself. She thought of the little girl on the box of Morton's salt: a picture within a picture within a picture into infinity.

She found herself worrying about silly things. Would they let him take a shower? He got a headache without his morning coffee. Was he thinking about her? She took one of Eddie's sleeping pills. Maybe sleep would clear the fog from her brain. But she dreamed of Franklin being pushed off a boat, sinking beneath the sea.

She got up and crossed the living room of their suite. The door to

Peter's room was ajar. He was in bed, propped up against the headboard. "I'd like the hug now that you forgot to give me this morning," she told him.

He opened his arms, and she snuggled up against his chest. A man's chest. Only yesterday he'd been a little boy.

"I'm sorry, Mom. This is such a godawful mess. You know it could end badly?"

"I know," she whispered. She could hear the beating of his heart. Feel it.

He touched her hair—an automatic gesture, she supposed, for a woman in his arms.

"I worry about Dad, and I worry about you," he went on. "God, how would you ever manage without him?"

Louise relished the moment of closeness a bit longer, then sat and smoothed her son's thick hair, looked at his beautiful face in the half-light.

"I would be infinitely sad if your father did not return, Peter, but I would manage, just like I've managed without him through three wars. Why do you insist on thinking of me as helpless?"

The next day she stared at her own picture in the newspaper. She and Peter, with Eddie behind them, were coming out of the hotel elevator, looking puzzled at the crush of reporters, photographers, television cameramen waiting to accost them. How strange to be a news item. How strange to have the sort of thing that only happened to other people be happening to her. A story in *Time* magazine. She felt that any minute she'd wake up and find out it hadn't been real.

She wondered if Tommaso had seen the picture.

Probably. He would know by now that she was the wife of a high-ranking officer.

How would that make him feel? Would he rethink everything from this new perspective and be embarrassed that he asked her to give up her stately life for a simple one in Amola? Would he wonder if such a grand lady really loved him, or if she had just been on a holiday?

No, he wouldn't think that. He knew she loved him. He would

worry about her. Feel frustrated because he could do nothing for her. Think of her every minute.

She thought of calling him, or asking her father to call him, to say that her days with him had been the best of her life. But he knew that already. And her time with him was over.

Her allegiance must be totally to Franklin. All her thoughts, her emotions. She felt as though she were locked in a mortal battle with fate. If she diverted her attention even for a minute, she would lose.

After the invasion by the press, Peter requested that an additional security guard be stationed in the lobby of the Grand Hotel Milano, where he had arranged for them to stay. The apartment where Louise and Franklin had been living was being searched for clues. No one was allowed to enter it. Louise gave a police detective a list of things she needed.

A pair of Army intelligence officers arrived to interview Louise. Had Franklin received any disturbing phone calls, visitors or mail prior to the kidnapping? Had he been acting strangely in any way? When Louise explained she had been away, they questioned her about that. Why had she left at this particular time? Where had she gone? When had she last talked to her husband? Louise was acutely uncomfortable. She had things to hide.

They wanted to know Louise's assessment of Franklin's physical and mental health, how she thought he would react to confinement and torture. Peter kept trying to answer for her. Finally she'd had enough. "Peter! Will you stop that? You can give your own answers, if you like, but please allow me the same privilege."

An Army physician arrived to listen to Louise's and Eddie's hearts and prescribed tranquilizers for Louise, which she refused to take.

Then a chaplain arrived to pray with them.

Louise lost her temper. "I know you mean well, Peter, but if I'd wanted a chaplain or a doctor, I'd have asked for one. Now, will you stop treating me this way? You are acting like your father."

"What's wrong with the way my father treats you?" Peter was shocked. Indignant. "I've never known a man that has more respect for his wife than he has for you."

"He respects me because I don't break his rules. From now on, I'll take my own phone calls and find someplace less opulent for us to stay. Or see if I can get that apartment back. I'm not in the mood for gilded furniture and brocaded walls."

At the end of the week, she and Peter put Eddie on a plane, sending him back to Martha. He didn't protest too much. He was tired and, Louise suspected, not well.

She and Peter moved into the apartment where she and Franklin had been staying. Their days fell into a tiresome pattern of meeting with military and civilian officials, American and Italian, being told the same things over and over. They had no further clues.

Louise took the train to Rome to speak personally with the American ambassador. Was he satisfied that everything possible was being done? Couldn't the American military intelligence be put in charge of the investigation?

She sat on a velvet sofa in the ambassador's opulent office, declined a cup of coffee and listened while he told her the same thing that the American consulate in Milan had—and the American military authorities. The crime was committed in Italy. The Italians were in charge.

"They're very committed to finding your husband, Mrs. Cravens," he said in a decidedly Bostonian accent. "Believe me, they are. They are fearful of Italy becoming a haven for international terrorists, and they would like nothing better than finding those responsible for kidnapping General Cravens. They want to show the world that terrorism will not be tolerated in this country. And you may not be aware of it, but American military intelligence is very involved in the case."

She had the afternoon to kill before taking the evening train back to Milan. She had some minestrone and a salad at a street café while blue-jean-clad tourists and well-dressed Italians strolled past. It seemed so stupid to be in Rome when she was sad. She didn't want to go sightseeing. She couldn't make herself care about the expensive clothing displayed in boutique windows along the Via Veneto. She strolled into the huge park filled with statues, fountains and young lovers.

She felt so old and tired. What made her think anything was important except family? If she could just get Franklin back, she'd forget about being in love.

During the wars, she had felt the same way, had wanted only one thing—to have her husband home safely. And even after years of growing away from him, even after sometimes wishing they could both go their own ways and come together only for family celebrations, she wanted him back.

When she returned to Milan, she insisted that Franklin's photograph be displayed in public places. The police ignored her request. She hired someone to do it. A poster bearing Franklin's photographs started appearing on fences and walls, alongside graffiti and memorial photographs marking death anniversaries of beloved sisters and brothers, sainted mothers, respected fathers. She placed ads in major metropolitan newspapers throughout the country, offering a ten-million-lire reward for information that would lead to the recovery of American General Franklin Cravens. The following week she ran the ad again, making the reward twenty million.

"Mom, we don't even know he's in Italy," Peter said when she talked about running the ad for a third week.

Then Domenica Rosa announced in a statement sent to several European newspapers that Franklin had been tried by a "people's court" and found guilty of imperialism. The penalty would be death unless the American government paid a ten-million-dollar ransom.

The Italian police received a tip that the American general was being held in a warehouse in Bologna, and another that his body was buried in an orchard near Palermo in Sicily. Both rumors proved false.

A third tip that Domenica Rosa had an arsenal of weapons hidden in a boathouse in Castelamara di Stabia near Naples proved correct. After a three-day standoff between Italian police and the terrorists, an explosion destroyed the boathouse and the people inside. The police reports stated that the bodies of four men and one woman were found in the rubble. Two were identified as Libyan nationals. The other three were burned beyond identification. But Louise and Peter were assured that both bodies belonged to smaller men than General Cravens.

Then there was silence. The days dragged by after the boathouse incident. Two weeks. A month. Two months. The reporters stopped following them. Peter requested an extension of his emergency leave.

Louise prepared simple meals in the efficiency kitchen. There was no oven and only a tiny refrigerator. She marketed every morning with her shopping bag like an Italian housewife. She and Peter took long walks. Played cards. Watched television. She tried to read but couldn't concentrate.

Peter treated her formally, almost coldly. He was disappointed in a mother who did not idolize his missing father.

He saved all the newspaper and magazine clippings about Franklin's disappearance, saying it was important to keep a record. Louise understood. The very volume of attention that Franklin's kidnapping received in the world press proved what an important man he was, made him even more important, made Peter even more proud.

He kept reading things to her. Just like Franklin. Impatiently, she would grab the paper or magazine from his hand and read it for herself. Or pretend she was.

Peter speculated that the leaders of the terrorist group must have been killed in the boathouse explosion, that perhaps they were regrouping, trying to decide how best to use their captive.

General Kevin McIntosh, a classmate of Franklin's at West Point, arrived in Brussels to take over his NATO job. He made the journey to Milan to pay a call on Louise and Peter, to offer his condolences and support.

Peter hitchhiked flights to Teheran several times to see his family, leaving Louise to maintain the vigil alone.

Four months after his father's disappearance, Peter's military superiors ordered Peter to return to Iran and complete his assignment there.

Louise waited on by herself another futile month before returning to the house in Brussels. Maggie kept begging her to return to Washington. Marynell, too.

"Come home, Mom. We need each other." Maggie said.

Home. Such a wonderful word. Louise had never had a real one.

She and assorted furniture simply followed Franklin around, but Washington had been more of a home to her than the other places she had lived. There, she had been just another general's wife in a city with hundreds of generals.

In Washington, she could once again be anonymous. And she would have Maggie and Marynell nearby. It would be better than waiting by herself in this chilly palace, feeling that she had to dress carefully every time she walked out the door because she was the wife of the missing American general. And it would be easier to put Tommaso out of her mind in America.

Franklin deserved a better wife than she was. He deserved someone like Maggie whose every breath was a prayer for his survival. But Louise realized she could not continue living with guilty thoughts. Almost from that first moment, when she saw the newspapers in Florence, she had begun a conscious process of purifying her thoughts. It was obscene to think of her lover when her husband was in peril. And she knew she could not enjoy freedom if it came to her at the cost of Franklin's life.

She had even gone to church a few times, kneeling in Brussel's thirteenth-century Cathedral of St. Michael, trying to feel one with all the faithful who had knelt there before her, trying to find a faith that once had been automatic. If she found it, perhaps she could beg for forgiveness, promise to be a good wife for the rest of her days in exchange for her husband's life. But Andy's death had robbed her of faith; the potential of another tragedy did not renew it, and Christians weren't supposed to strike bargains with God. She couldn't shed the feeling, however, that her sins against her marriage had brought about Franklin's kidnapping. She had been with Tommaso while five hooded men clubbed Franklin's driver and aide-de-camp and dragged Franklin from his staff car. But, of course, she was being silly. The fact that it had happened while she was in Amola was just a coincidence. She knew that. And she didn't.

CHAPTER

FORTY

Jeffrey and Marynell wanted her to come to Fredericksburg with them for the weekend, but she had shooed them and Maggie away, saying it was time she spent her first night alone in her new apartment.

"You're sure?" Marynell had said. "Jeffrey and I can stay a few more days."

"That's just putting off the inevitable," Louise said. "You both need to get back to work, and I'll be fine. Maggie's just across town. You guys are a phone call away. Go."

Marynell picked up Louise's telephone one more time just to make sure it was working. They had already called the NATO offices in Brussels and the police in Milan to give them Louise's number. And Louise had called Pauline in Alaska. A depressing conversation. They usually were these days. *No, there wasn't any news. Yes, I'll call the minute I hear anything.*

"It's hard for us to know how to conduct ourselves," Pauline had complained. "We've stayed away from social events for over seven months now. And with the holidays coming up . . . "

"Now we know how your sister has felt all this time," Louise said with a bite in her tone.

"Don't be mad at me, Mom. I'm worried sick about Daddy. You know how much I love him, and I feel privileged to be the daughter of such a great man. Sometimes I think I love him more than you do. I don't see how you can be so calm about all this. I'd be frantic. I'd be in Italy looking for him myself."

"And where would you suggest I look?" Louise said dryly.

"I don't know. I guess that's unfair of me. I know that Marynell thought you could wait for news in Washington just as well as over there, but it just seems more appropriate for you to be in Europe. Peter and Jerry think so, too. Now it seems like you've given up. I just want him to come home so we can all get on with our lives. Danny, too. I feel guilty sometimes because I have a husband."

"Don't," Louise said. "No matter what happens with your father or Danny, enjoy your life."

"Jerry got a wonderful efficiency report," Pauline said. "He should be a full colonel soon. I'm very lucky."

"Yes, you are. Jerry's a fine man."

And they had a sound marriage, Louise thought as she hung up, a careful marriage based on mutual ambition and a shared appreciation of the military life. In the last snapshot they had sent of three-year-old Benny, he was wearing a T-shirt that said "West Point Class of '88."

"Pauline thinks I should have stayed in Italy and found Franklin myself," Louise said when she hung up the phone.

Jeffrey and Marynell soothed her. "Pauline's just upset by how things are dragging on," Marynell said diplomatically.

"She's more worried about appearances than how you feel," Maggie said. "She'll get over it."

"We'll come back next weekend," Jeffrey assured Louise as he put on his mackinaw and picked up his toolbox. "You make that list, now, as you come across things that need fixing. I'll build any shelves you need, and I'll fix the leg on the dining room table."

There were hugs all around. Darling Maggie, in a fatigue jacket, her mop of sandy hair pulled back with a rubber band, her long-legged frame too skinny. At twenty-seven she was lovely and ripe. Her youth was being wasted. She and Danny should be making love and babies. Louise hated the war that had done this to her daughter, that left her in a seemingly endless limbo. But she kept her opinion to herself. Maggie equated patriotism with blindly supporting the government and its war. And soon—one way or the other—the waiting should be over. The peace talks finally seemed to be getting someplace. Or was it the massive antiwar demonstrations? Whatever. Some U.S. troops had been withdrawn. With a truce, the POWs could be released. Danny was still listed as missing in action, but Maggie had already bought a new outfit to wear to his homecoming. Like a religious zealot, her blind faith that Danny was still alive had gotten her through these last two years.

The next hug was for Marynell, who had settled for a thickening waist and graying hair. If she was going to live an ordinary life, she had decided to look the part.

Jeffrey, his hands and nails permanently discolored from wood stains, was slim and youthful looking in spite of a bald pate with its fringe of gray hair. His handmade furniture was in great demand and had won several awards. He had done most of the work on their new home himself. It was a gem of a house with wonderful paneling, built-in bookcases and cabinets, and parquet floors, all of the most carefully selected woods, works of art.

Marynell was proud of the house. "We couldn't have had such a wonderful house in the Army." Jeffrey had beamed when she said that.

"You're my brother and dear friend, " Louise told Jeffrey as she hugged him.

As the door closed behind them, quiet settled over her new home. She would be alone now.

The apartment was nicer than the one she and Maggie had shared when Franklin was in Saigon. Marynell had found it for her, obviously thinking a major general's wife needed lodging suitable to her station in life. The Georgetown address was needlessly expensive, but maybe she wouldn't be here very long.

Louise added a log on the fire Jeffrey had built, poured herself a glass of wine and tried the solitude on for size.

"Franklin, where are you?" she said out loud from the corner of her sofa.

She thought of Pauline's accusation. Could she have made a difference if she stayed in Europe? She had felt so useless. No one knew what to do with her.

But even as she had made the arrangements to leave, she felt guilty. Franklin did not have the comfort of family. Why should she?

"See what it's like not knowing," Maggie had taunted her mother. "But Daddy's alive, and so is Danny. We have to believe."

Louise admired her daughter's faith. But Danny was Maggie's life, her reason for being. For Louise, Franklin was the husband of a dutiful marriage. She desperately wanted him to be alive, but she wouldn't feel that her life was over if he weren't.

In fact, she could imagine a lovely life without Franklin. But if she were ever to have her freedom, she didn't want it to come with his death—the ugliest of gifts. And if he were alive, she would stay with him whether out of loyalty—or lack of courage. She was his wife.

She missed Franklin. Not Tommaso. Tommaso wasn't a part of her daily life. He lived only in her fantasies. Franklin had been the presence at her table, in her bed. Franklin was the father of her children. She had been his wife for many more years than she had not.

There was still no clue as to Franklin's whereabouts. It was as though he had dropped off the face of the earth. How long did one wait? What if in a year, or five years, she still didn't know if she had a live husband or a dead one? Maggie would wait until she had an answer, however long that took. But Louise was not young.

She was aware that many in the American military and diplomatic communities thought Franklin was dead. But a silent death made no political statement, Peter insisted. If the kidnappers had killed him, surely they would let the world know. Louise hoped her son was right.

Peter's letters to her were formal, his mother's image a bit tarnished. He'd gotten his orders for Scott Air Force Base in Illinois. When he was once again Stateside, maybe they'd mend the bridge, Louise thought as she sipped at her wine and let the dancing flames work their hypnotic spell. Peter preferred for his mother to be an extension of his father rather than a person in her own right. But then the girls were like that, too. A strong, affectionate father and a gentle, selfless mother. Tommaso said everyone wanted mothers to be saints. He took her to the cemetery and showed her the epitaphs. Women who lived only for family.

During the months of waiting in Italy and in Brussels, she had found no escape in books and had too much time to think. Maybe here in this new place, she could at least read again. Go to movies with Maggie. Watch the talk shows on television. Johnny Carson. Dick Cavett. Or was it wrong to distract herself when Franklin might be in a dank cell with no books, no comforts at all? Or in a shallow grave?

Louise shuddered.

All around her in her new Georgetown living room were mementos of her years with Franklin. Porcelains and tapestries from Japan. Rattan chairs and a teak coffee table from the Philippines. American Indian pottery from Oklahoma. A collection of steins from Germany. She'd been married to Franklin for more than thirty years, yet the possessions most dear were the ones from before that time, ones that had decorated all those Army quarters where she'd spent her childhood with her parents and Marynell. The mantel clock. The hunt scene that always hung over the buffet in the dining room. The Boston rocker where her mother petted her cats. Would her girls someday feel that way, revering the mementos of childhood over those of marriage?

Maggie had suggested her mother get a cat or reclaim Hans, the beagle, who had been living with Marynell and Jeffrey. But Hans went to work with Jeffrey and was happy following him around all day. And she wasn't ready for a cat and a rocker. Not yet. Whether Franklin came back or not, she had to find something to care about other than a pet.

She put another log on the fire and poured a second glass of wine. Could she stand years of such solitude punctuated only by family visits? The thought of loneliness didn't bother her as much as being purposeless. Her mother-in-law had found meaning in caring for her sick and senile husband. Maggie found purpose in her role as the nobly waiting wife. Peter had his career. Pauline, like her Aunt Marynell before her, was totally engrossed in her role as officer's wife. With Jerry's every promotion, Pauline became more gracious, calmer, more regal.

And Marynell at least had a job to get up for in the morning. Louise suspected her sister enjoyed her work more than she admitted. When she and Marynell ran into her students in a Fredericksburg grocery store, the kids responded too brightly for Marynell to have been an indifferent teacher, but outside the classroom Marynell, too, often assumed her martyred role. Life had disappointed her, her children were an embarrassment. To find acceptance, Marynell would have had to forgive Jeffrey for not being like Franklin, and she hadn't done that yet. She'd been thrilled, however, when their house had been featured in the home section of the *Washington Post*. And there were moments between her and Jeffrey when genuine affection erupted, but Louise worried that Jeffrey would always have to court her, always have to find new ways to bring an unqualified smile to his wife's face.

The wine was making her drowsy. She wasn't supposed to think about Tommaso. She'd made that bargain with herself. No more guilt if she stopped thinking about him, but two glasses of wine took away her control. Would she ever see him again?

Sometimes Louise felt that she could manage just fine if she could only touch Tommaso at night as she fell asleep. She would be the good Mrs. General's Wife, a pleasing mother and grandmother, a charming hostess. But when she turned over to sleep, if she could just wrap her body around Tommaso, feel the sturdiness of him, inhale the smell of him, hear the sound of his breathing, then she could be happy.

The onslaught of approaching headlights was relentless, with people returning to the city after the weekend. For years now, she and Jeffrey had lived where other people weekended, longer than she'd ever lived anyplace in her life, yet it was still hard for Marynell to believe that she would live the rest of her life in Fredericksburg, Virginia. The Peaceable Kingdom, Jeffrey called it.

It would feel good to sleep in her own bed tonight, Marynell thought as she reached over and rubbed Jeffrey's neck. "Tired?" she asked.

"Yeah," he said, murmuring appreciatively.

She kneaded the knots in his neck as he drove. He'd put in quite a week, determined to do everything he could to leave Louise's new home shipshape. It was the least he could do, he kept saying. She'd fix him a toddy after their baths. They could curl up in bed and look at the mail.

"Do you think Louise will be all right alone?" he asked. "It still seems like she and Maggie should live together, or that she should come live with us for a while, at least until she knows what her situation's going to be."

"Women like a place of their own," Marynell said with a yawn. She stopped rubbing, letting her head fall back on the headrest. She was tired, too.

"Would you?"

"I do, silly. For a woman, a place of her own means not having some other woman in your kitchen, rearranging your cupboards, turning the water glasses down when you keep them up. Whether or not a man is in residence is a whole different issue."

"Will Louise be all right?" he asked again.

"She'll manage. Thinking of her alone like that makes me realize how lucky I am to have a lovely husband to look after, who looks after me."

Jeffrey reached for her hand. "Has it been so awful for you, having our life turn out like this?"

"No. It just took getting used to. I've wasted a lot of time being jealous of Louise, but look at her now. What a mess. And I don't think she's ever been all that happy. We have a better marriage than she and Franklin do."

"Does that mean we have a good marriage?" he asked with a squeeze.

"Yes," Marynell said, bringing his hand to her lips.

"I've always loved you," Jeffrey said.

"No, not always. It took you awhile to make up your mind, but then you loved me more than I deserved. I think I've always loved you though, deep down. I just got so disappointed for a while. I still feel it when Franklin gets those damned promotions, but maybe it doesn't mean as much as I thought it did."

Did it? Marynell wondered, cradling her husband's hand in her lap. When she got around ordinary people and they started assuming she was ordinary, too, she had moments when she wanted to scream at them that she had been destined for better than Tuesday-afternoon teachers' meetings with chalk dust under her nails. Her sons had not been exceptional, and she hated having to listen to people whose children were. Her husband had not brought her prestige, and she avoided wives of prominent men in the community. Even her good looks had faded, when she had assumed she would always be better looking that other women her age. And Jeffrey no longer turned heads either, when he used to be so handsome in his uniform. Now they were an ordinary-looking middle-aged couple.

She remembered how her mother always scraped the icing off cake before she ate it. Marynell never understood that. For her, the purpose of cake was to have something to put icing on, a pink rose from a birthday cake a prize.

Jeffrey was supposed to have provided the icing. She hadn't expected life to be plain cake. She hadn't expected the most remarkable facts about her to be that her sister was married to a two-star general and her sons were draft dodgers.

Women have to love their children. But they didn't have to love their husbands. And Marynell loved Jeffrey with a warm, comfortable love that was growing with the years. And that, she knew, was rare. Maybe Jeffrey was the icing on the cake after all.

The phone woke Louise. A different sound than the phones in Brussels. At first she thought it was the grandfather clock. She was still on the sofa, but the fire had burned down. The phone rang a second time. She glanced at the clock as she hurried to the hall. Midnight.

Had something happened to Jeffrey and Marynell on the way back to Fredericksburg?

Or was it something else?

With a pounding heart, she put her hand on the receiver and offered a silent prayer. Please. Nothing bad. If the call was about Franklin, let him be all right. Let him still be himself.

It was an international call. She recognized the hollow crackling, the seconds of delay. She put a hand on the table to steady herself.

A male voice said, "One moment, please." There were other voices in the background.

Then a voice speaking to her. At first, she didn't realize it was Franklin's. So weak, and raspy. But he was calling her Louise, telling her he was alive, telling her he loved her until he had to stop in a fit of coughing. Nasty, gagging coughing, full of thick phlegm.

She sank into a chair. "Oh, my darling. My darling Franklin." Her body began to shake, sobs filled her throat. "Where are you? I'll come now. Tonight."

But there was a different voice, with a southern accent. A Colonel Chambers, explaining. Franklin had escaped. He had pneumonia and dysentery. His arm had been broken during the abduction and never properly set. The general was being stabilized at an American military hospital in Frankfurt and would be flown to Walter Reed tomorrow or the next day.

"Let me talk to him again," Louise said.

"Franklin, can you hear me?"

He coughed again and said yes.

"I'm so grateful, my darling. We've all been sick with fear."

"I escaped," he said.

"I know. You are so brave."

"I had to come home to you, Louise. That's all I could think about—coming home to you."

CHAPTER

FORTY-ONE

A national hero. That's what the newspapers called him. Those three words helped give meaning to the pain and humiliation he had suffered during more than seven months of captivity.

So much had been written about him in the months since his return. Again and again the retelling of his escape, how the American general had been held, usually in cold and darkness, in a storage room in an abandoned mountain villa north of Bolzano near the Swiss border, how in spite of malnutrition and constant pain from his broken arm, he managed to kill a guard with a shard of glass he had found embedded between two floor boards, and then using the dead guard's forty-five to kill another guard.

With other captors in pursuit, wearing ill-fitting boots he had taken from one of the dead guards, he had walked miles through snow and cold before taking shelter from a blizzard in a makeshift lean-to. It had taken him two days to make his way down from the mountain and find the farmhouse where he collapsed. It was several days before Franklin regained consciousness and made the attendants at the hospital where he had been taken understand that he was the missing American general.

The newspapers stories reiterated Franklin's World War II triumphs. His father's before him in World War I. His son Peter's and his son-in-law Jerry's service in Vietnam. And, of course, the story of Maggie faithfully waiting for her MIA husband to return. A family of heroes.

They were all there, standing with Louise. Peter, Belinda and Benjamin. Next came Pauline, Jerry and Jessica. Both Belinda and Pauline were pregnant again. Maggie was standing by her mother. And in front of them, filling up the hospital auditorium, were military colleagues from the Army's Joint Chiefs of Staff to the sergeant who had been Franklin's driver during his last Washington assignment. In the front row were Jeffrey and Marynell, poor Jeffrey looking decidedly out of place in his tan suit. The media were out in force. Half a dozen television cameramen ringed the room. Cameras flashed.

Only his parents were missing, Franklin thought. His father was senile and bedridden, at the end of his days. His mother wouldn't leave him. She was so proud, Maxine told him. Her son, a hero. She said she thought Harold understood. He had recognized Franklin's face on television.

"You really think he understands?" Franklin asked.

"Well, maybe not everything," Maxine admitted. "But you are his pride."

His father's pride. Franklin had to close his eyes a minute to compose himself.

A congratulatory message was read from President Nixon before General Stallings read a statement of his own. A national hero.

Franklin understood the Army was trying to make the most of his exploits, which came at a time when antimilitary sentiments in this country were at an all-time high, when the Army was plagued with race riots and drug addiction, with draft dodgers and deserters, with a public who referred to soldiers as baby killers. In these waning days of a disastrous war, the Pentagon brass was thrilled to have an unqualified hero for a change.

Franklin wished he had a picture of his family's faces at this moment. *This is my finest hour*, he thought, but he wasn't sure how much longer his feet were going to bear his weight. The pain in his right foot where his two amputated toes used to be was bothering him. He reached for Louise's arm. Peter moved in from the other side, and the two of them helped support him. Better. If they made a movie of his life, who would play the starring role, he wondered to distract himself from the pain. Gregory Peck maybe. Julie Andrews could play Louise's role. Or Deborah Kerr.

He had insisted on wearing his uniform, insisted on standing. He reminded himself how lucky he was to have a foot at all. At first there was talk of amputating more than the toes. He could not have escaped a medical discharge with only one foot.

Two missing toes were no problem. And his right arm had been operated on, reset, and would be functional again. The pneumonia and the lingering effects of malnutrition still plagued him some. But he was almost recovered. In another month, he'd be ready for reassignment.

He thought of the family celebration planned in his hospital room after the ceremony. He would tell them then about the plum he was being offered. Louise kept talking about retirement. In fact, he was irritated with her going on and on about how he'd given enough, that it was time for them to make a life just for themselves, how they could hire Jeffrey to build them a perfect house. They could grow things, she said. Grow things? Where had she gotten such a notion? And then she had suggested they buy an inn in Vermont and had even brought in a realtor's pictures of some little hotel that was for sale.

During his months of captivity, he'd forgotten that Louise could be irritating. He supposed she meant well, but he was not ready to be turned out to pasture yet. His next assignment would be a dream come true, the reward for being brave and living up to the standards he had been taught so long ago as a cadet. *The superintendent of West Point.* What every man who had ever graduated from the academy had longed for would be his. He would move into the select crowd with Westmoreland, MacArthur, Robert E. Lee. And after that, another promotion. Someday, he could be the joint chief giving out the medals.

General Stallings was reading the commendation now. So much they couldn't say in the commendation. How those bastards had treated him like an animal. Made him live in his own filth. Left him to the pain in his arm that got worse each day. The man in charge had been killed in the boathouse incident. The ones remaining were stupid, unsure of what to do with him, waiting for word from someone in Libya. He had known he would kill them if given the chance. Thoughts of killing them and being reunited with Louise had kept him alive. She was his beacon, beckoning to him from the other side of pain and despair.

He felt Louise's gaze on his face and turned to give her a reassuring nod. He was all right.

God, how wonderful she looked. Her skin was still clear and unwrinkled, her chin firm. Her hair was mostly gray now. He hadn't thought he'd like that, but after the initial shock he saw how much it suited the woman she had become. Anyone who saw the handsome, gray-haired woman in the elegant red suit would know she was special.

How far she had come from the scared girl he had married. His mother had doubted his wisdom in choosing a girl like Louise, but he had been right. He had taken a pliable girl and molded her into the perfect wife.

Well, almost perfect. She had gotten a bit headstrong with age. Like his mother.

But usually, she was still his darling Louise. A woman to make a man proud. Soon he'd be getting out of this place and could make love to her again. Recently, he'd been waking in the night with wonderfully reassuring erections. It was time.

The Distinguished Service Medal was impressive. General Stallings pinned it on his uniform. Franklin offered a smart salute. With Peter's help, he stepped to the microphone.

"I want to thank you all for coming, but I want to assure you that I only did what any American military man would have done under the circumstances. I thank God that He has allowed me to return to my family and the service of my country."

As Louise watched, tears welled in her eyes. She was so grateful—and so proud of him, for him. A hero. How was it that she was the wife of such a man? She still felt like a bashful young woman from Mary Baldwin College, trying to measure up as a date for a West Point cadet.

The pride that swelled painfully in her chest was almost maternal. Franklin was so pleased with himself, pleased that he had brought honor to her and their children and their country.

Pauline's and Maggie's faces were both tear-streaked. Peter was fighting for control. They loved their father with a love that approached worship. It was Franklin's standards they always tried to live up to, his respect they sought. She had always been just good old Mom, and their love for her more automatic. They knew she would love them no matter what. There was no need to work for it.

With Franklin installed in a reclining chair back in his VIP hospital room, Peter and Jerry popped the corks on champagne bottles and greeted the endless stream of visitors who stood in line in the hallway to take a turn congratulating General Cravens, to shake hands with him and his family.

Franklin fairly glowed, any pain forgotten. He joked with visitors, accepted their congratulations with hearty handshakes.

Louise sipped the champagne, enjoying herself. How lovely to have her beautiful family reunited.

Then, after the guests had gone, his eyes on his wife, needing her approval most of all, Franklin told them about West Point. The superintendent. Peter cheered. Pauline and Maggie hugged their father's neck. Then Belinda. Jerry stepped forward to shake his hand.

Louise was stunned.

West Point. A life of smiling graciously while entertaining visiting dignitaries, reigning over the distaff side of academy life. A life of sherry, Ultrasuede, insincerity and isolation.

"I can't," she told Franklin when they were finally alone.

"My God, Louise, this is what we have lived our entire lives for—an assignment like that. Think of the recognition. Think of what comes after."

"I don't want to dress up and be charming. I can't do that anymore. Can't you just stay in Washington?"

"I don't understand. Everything I've ever done has been to make you proud and happy."

"Then make me happy by retiring. What about that hotel in Vermont? I saw an ad in the newspaper for a Christmas tree farm for sale in West Virginia. Or we could take college classes. Learn to fish. Take long walks and learn about each other. Learn to talk to each other."

She was babbling. Franklin had the strangest look on his face. Hurt. Puzzlement. But she couldn't stop. "Oh, Franklin, we don't have many good years left. If you take this West Point job, you'll be on track for another star, and then it will be years before you retire. You'll probably be chief of staff someday. There won't be years left over for anything but being old. We could do something for *both* of us."

"I don't understand you, Louise," Franklin repeated. "It's *all* been for both of us."

She knew that he really believed that. For both of them. Maybe it had been.

"But it's always been what you've chosen for us, and I've never asked for otherwise. Now I'm asking. If you insist on West Point, I'm warning you, Franklin, I will stay on in Washington, in my apartment. You can come see me on weekends and holidays. But I simply cannot play the role of superintendent's wife at West Point."

She didn't come to the hospital the next day, her way of showing she meant her words. But did she? Did she really think Franklin would retire and devote the last years of his life to marital bliss? He thought they had it already.

Peter came to talk to her. In uniform. Dark hair, dark eyes like his father. But a sweeter person than his father. Less arrogant. "For God's sake, Mom, Dad has an opportunity to be one of the most important military men of his generation, and you want him to grow Christmas trees?"

"How does Belinda feel about your career, Peter? Does she want you to wear that uniform for the next twenty or thirty years? Does she ever long for a real home? Does she still want to train horses?"

"Yeah. We talk about it sometimes. But Dad's different. Special. I can't imagine a wife who wouldn't be proud to serve a great man like that."

"And because he's great—special—I have less of a right than other wives to say how we should live?"

Peter nodded. "Yes, I guess so. A special responsibility."

"And if Belinda talks you into retiring, will your children always hold it against her because you never had the opportunity to be a great man like your father?"

"Why have you changed, Mom? You used to be so . . . "

"Perfect," Louise said, finishing the sentence for him.

"No, I was going to say 'happy.' But that's not the right word either. Maybe I just never thought about how you were before."

After he had gone, Louise sat in her lovely living room for a long time. The grandfather clock and her heavy, thudding heart ticked away the minutes of her life. Her grandchildren's toys and books looked out of place in such an adult room. Belinda had taken Benny and Jessica to a matinee. Pauline was at the hospital. Maggie at work. The quiet was oppressive, suffocating. Louise wanted to scream. To break something. To start running and never stop.

The next day, a hospital chaplain waylaid her on the way to Franklin's room and asked to speak with her.

He led her into a tiny two-pew hospital chapel, where he told her how worried General Cravens was about her. He tried to counsel her about a wife's duty.

"Go to hell," she told him most ungraciously and left him sitting there.

The following Saturday morning, they brought Franklin home from the hospital. Leaning a bit on his cane, he walked out the door with his arm in a sling but otherwise looking fit.

Pauline and little Jessica were staying another week or two. Peter, Belinda and Benny were leaving in the morning for their new assignment in Illinois.

Franklin looked around Louise's apartment without comment— this place she planned to keep as her home rather than do her duty and accompany him to West Point. They had not mentioned West Point since the day of the ceremony, but tension had hung in the air between them.

While Jessica and Benny watched cartoons on television in the living room, the adults sat at the dining room table, and Maggie served the coffee cake she'd baked. Pauline poured coffee.

Louise looked around the table at her family. Her children looked at one another uncomfortably. She knew they were planning to confront her, to talk some sense into her. A united front. She'd been expecting it.

"I'm leaving this afternoon," Louise told them before Peter had a chance to clear his throat and begin.

"For how long?" Pauline asked. "Will you be back for dinner?"

"No, I'm going to England to see my father."

"Have you taken leave of your senses altogether?" Franklin said, pushing his cup away. Coffee splashed into the saucer. "You don't just announce that you're going to England without . . . "

"Without what, Franklin? Without asking your permission?"

CHAPTER

FORTY-TWO

*E*ddie stood at the window and watched Louise coming up the path, her heavy sweater a darker gray than the sky. She'd spent much of her time walking—or hoeing the garden, getting it ready for spring planting. He hadn't planned on a garden this year, but Louise didn't know that. Maybe he'd try one more year if his tired, old body would permit it.

His heart ached for her, this unhappy daughter. Dearest Louise.

He loved her the most. For years, he had denied it. Fathers love children equally, and daughters were not to be loved more than wives. Of course, when the girls were little, he hadn't known how much he would love Louise. He worried more then about favoring the vivacious Marynell, whose smile and outrageously affectionate ways melted his heart with great regularity. He had to remind himself at times to pay attention to Louise, who always hung back and allowed Marynell to play center stage.

But something had happened to Marynell the summer before her senior year at Mary Baldwin. Eddie never quite understood that failure of spirit he had witnessed so helplessly. Marynell had been forced to reassemble herself in order to survive and had emerged as a tightly controlled woman who allowed herself to experience love and laughter only in carefully prescribed doses.

Was it because he lost that first Marynell that he had discovered Louise? Perhaps. But Eddie didn't waste much time anymore trying to figure out why things had happened; he simply accepted his plate and digested what he could. As Louise matured, his appreciation of her grew, and the love that had always been there blossomed. Far more than Marynell, Louise was a mingling of himself and her mother. He could see in his younger daughter so much of his beloved, ethereal Elizabeth, yet Louise also reflected his own brand of pragmatic romanticism. They both believed that life had to have love to succeed. It was as simple as that.

That Louise should have married a man like Franklin was a tragedy. In her husband's presence, she was guarded. Even her laughter was stilted. Both of them would have been better off with someone else. So many times he had thought if he could revise history, he would have switched his daughters' husbands and given Marynell the general and Louise the furniture maker.

And now, Louise had fallen in love with a man very much like Jeffrey. Tommaso, who cooked and fished, who enjoyed laughter and was not ashamed to cry. And he loved Louise in return. Adored her, and that made Eddie love Tommaso.

Just thinking about the two of them together brought tears to his eyes. Louise and Tommaso were like teenagers, unable to conceal their delight in being together, touching constantly, smiling, whispering endearments. The women who worked in the hotel would nod and exchange indulgent smiles with Eddie. They all basked in love's glow.

Eddie smiled as he remembered a rainy afternoon cleaning fish at the metal sink in the inn kitchen and listening patiently while Tommaso launched into a lengthy tribute to Louise, how intelligent she was, how beautiful, how graceful, how kind, until finally Eddie held up a malodorous hand to call a halt. "My God, man, we're not talking about the Madonna."

"No," Tommaso had said, his face quite serious. "For me, she is higher than the Madonna. But sexy."

Then he blushed that he had said such a thing to Louise's father. Eddie chuckled. Then burst out laughing. "A sexy Madonna! Now that's really something."

And Tommaso laughed, too. That's how Louise found them. She

didn't ask about the joke but stood in the doorway, a look of pure pleasure on her face.

Tommaso had made Louise young again.

For Eddie, Louise was the most cherished person on the face of the earth. Martha was the comfort of each day and would be with him when he breathed his last. He wanted her and no other to kiss his lips in death, but he suspected when he took his last breath it would be with Louise in his mind and heart. Louise was blood of his blood, his link with her mother, the person most like himself.

And now he felt an almost frantic need to see her life settled before he died. He wouldn't live much longer. Every morning now, he felt older than the day before. It seemed impossible that his younger daughter was almost fifty years old, and he was approaching death. He couldn't decide if life had been short or long. If it had been worthwhile or wasted. If it mattered.

Funny how much he thought about Elizabeth now after years without her. He had found a good life after she died, better in many ways than if she had lived. Yet she was still so much a part of him. He didn't believe in heaven, but he found himself speculating about what sort of marital arrangement he would have if there were one. His life divided neatly in two: the Elizabeth half and the Martha half. Which half deserved heaven more?

When Louise arrived at their house with less than a day's notice, he and Martha left her alone. Just being there with them seemed to soothe her. When Eddie asked if she wanted to talk, Louise said, "Not yet." He hadn't asked her again.

She seemed to want nothing more than to share their simple life. While they napped, she walked or dug in the garden, then she'd help prepare dinner and sit with them for their television shows. Television people were as much his friends as the folks in the village. And he was devoted to his cozy bed tucked under the eaves and no longer fretted because he spent as many hours in it as out of it.

Martha was still napping. Eddie had dozed a bit but had awakened when Louise went out. He lay there, seeing his daughter in his mind's eye as she walked the path along the cliff to land's end. He got up in time to stand by the window and watch her walk back.

Louise had almost reached the gate when she stumbled and fell to her knees. When she made no attempt to get up, Eddie's first instinct was to rush to her, but she didn't seem to be in pain. She knelt there, her hands folded as though in prayer, staring out at a muted sea that matched the sky.

Eddie reached for his worn jacket. Louise was standing when he reached her, her hair blown loose around her face, her cheeks pink with the wind and chill. Not a beauty like Marynell had been, but Louise had a quiet loveliness that made one want to look again. A full mouth like her mother's. Sensual really. He wondered if Louise knew that. He used to tell Elizabeth, and sometimes he would see her examining her mouth in the mirror, trying different looks with it. He buttoned Louise's sweater up to the top button like he had when she was a child and turned the collar up against the chill, then walked her around the side of the house to the bench he had built by his tool shed. The bench was sheltered, yet they could oversee the tilled black earth of the garden and the timeless gray waters of the channel beyond. The air smelled of salt and freshly turned earth, of approaching spring and a world that would go on without him. "And now, Louise," he said, "we must talk. Why have you come?"

Squinting, she stared out at the water. "I'm not sure," she said hesitantly. "Franklin's been assigned to West Point. I don't think I have it in me, Daddy, to be the wife of the superintendent of the United States Military Academy with all that pomp and tradition. I try to tell myself it's just another assignment. You know, I was a serious little girl and a serious young woman, and now I'm hovering on the brink of being a serious old one. I feel like I've never been a child. I'm too old to make changes, yet I think how few good years I have left and I'm afraid not to."

"You were a child in Italy," he offered.

Louise sighed. "But that wasn't real. I don't think there's any such thing as happily ever after."

Eddie took her hand. It seemed older than her face, with prominent veins and a scattering of brown freckles that hadn't been there in her youth.

"No," he said softly, "but maybe there's such a thing as more happy than not for the rest of one's life. Why don't you go back to Italy for a couple of months and see how it feels?"

Louise regarded him with widened eyes. "What am I supposed to do? Call up my general husband and tell him I'm going AWOL?"

"No. But you can call him and tell him you need a few months to decide about the rest of your life."

"I don't have the courage," Louise said flatly, withdrawing her hand and burying it among the folds in her skirt. "When it comes to Franklin, I've always been a coward, like Mother was with you. Did you know that she was afraid of you?"

It was Eddie's turn to sigh. "Yes, I did. Habits get set so early, and young husbands think they have to be that way."

"I feel responsible for him, Daddy. In his way, Franklin needs me very much—like the way I used to need you and Mother. What did it matter if I made an A or won an award if I didn't have someone meaningful to tell? When Franklin gets his promotions and medals, he needs a proud wife at his side."

"Yes," Eddie agreed. "Franklin needs you. You are a fine and noble wife, and perhaps nobility has its own reward."

Was that all she had wanted of him? Eddie wondered two days later as he watched her make preparations to depart. He had played the devil's advocate so she could argue her case, and now she was going back to her husband and a life designed for someone else.

They left before dawn for the drive to Heathrow, stopping at Tunbridge for coffee and a pastry. Louise's flight was delayed, and Eddie sat with her. They people-watched and passed the time gossiping about family—first about Pauline, who was striving in every way to be the perfect officer's wife, the way Marynell used to be. "Only it's working for Pauline," Louise said. "Her husband's probably going to make her a general's wife."

"Poor Jeffrey," Eddie mused. "I often wonder if he made the right decision by staying with Marynell."

"I think he did. He's not the sort who would make a new life at someone else's expense. Marynell would never have recovered if he'd left her. And I think she's come to appreciate him more as time goes by."

"Franklin's not like Marynell," Eddie interjected. "He'd survive just fine—as soon as he found another dutiful wife."

"We're not talking about Franklin," Louise snapped.

Chastised, Eddie watched a young mother on the bench across from them trying to manage three small, restless girls while her bearded husband in a black suit read his newspaper. They were French. The girls looked like their mother, petite, white skin against black hair. One of them clung to her mother's arm, her face flushed with fever, and the other two whined with restlessness. The woman held a wet handkerchief against the sick child's forehead and kept hushing the other two with nervous glances at her husband. Eddie didn't feel kindly toward the man or the wife.

He'd never been as bad as that man, or Franklin, but Louise was right; Elizabeth had been afraid of him. Never once in twenty-seven years of marriage had she argued with him. Never once. Never refused him sex. And he had never considered the implications of her behavior. The first time Martha said, "Not tonight, dear," Eddie had been shocked. But how reassuring it was on the nights when she reached out to him.

Ah, Elizabeth, how was it with you? he wondered, his mind drifting back over the years. *Did you love me? I wish we'd learned about each other. I wish I could change the way things were.*

Louise was talking again, about Marynell, saying that visiting the boys in Canada had mended their family. She had a grandchild to love, and Matt and Eric had promised they would accept clemency if it was offered.

"Matt came to see me twice, you know," Eddie mused. "From Canada." He's the only one of the grandchildren who ever came, and he's the one not of my own blood. I like him. He doesn't fret about unimportant things. He brought the black woman, Leah, with him the first time, and her little boy. They were good together, but Leah wanted to marry a black man, and I always thought Matt was in love with Maggie. The second time he came alone. He's alone too much."

"I wish he'd tell Maggie how he feels."

"He can't do that, not until she gives up on the dream of that husband of hers coming home. Danny. I never met him, but I remember the look on her face once when she was talking to him on the telephone. Matt saw it, too."

"Poor Matt."

Their conversation was interrupted by an announcement on the public address system of a gate change. A gate change for a flight to Milan.

Italy. Eddie watched as Louise lost herself for a minute, then struggled to regain her train of thought. She couldn't. Her shoulders slumped, and tears sprang to her eyes.

"Don't you think you're entitled to a few months, honey?"

"But Franklin needs me," Louise protested.

"Yes, but does he care enough to find out what *you* need?"

"That's different," she said sharply.

"Why?"

Her chin jutted out. "Because I'm wiser than he is. I understand how things really are. Besides they'd all hate me. I'd never get to see my grandchildren. I'm not tough enough for that."

"How often have you seen those grandchildren up to now? Army people don't 'see' their grandchildren, not like you mean."

"No, but the prospect is always there. That's important, too. When Marynell and I were growing up, we didn't see the folks back in Indiana more than every other year or so, but it was good to know our grandparents even if we didn't have Sunday dinner twice a month."

"But, tell me, Louise," Eddie said softly, taking his daughter's hands in his, "what will you think about when you preside at the tea table, pouring for the West Point ladies from a sterling pot?"

She said nothing as he opened her purse and extracted the ticket. He looked at her, his eyes questioning.

Louise sat very still for a long moment. Hardly breathing. Wanting something so much it felt like she would die of the wanting.

She reached for the ticket and put it back in her purse. "I must go home first," she said.

CHAPTER

FORTY-THREE

Maggie picked her up at the airport. "Everyone flipped with you taking off like that," she said as they drove to Louise's apartment. "Daddy was furious. And hurt. What gives?"

"I'm not sure," Louise said. "Pauline said your father is doing well."

"Hey, wait a minute. I'm not ready to change the subject yet. Dad says you don't want to go to West Point."

"Something like that."

"You're not thinking about doing something crazy, are you? I know you haven't exactly reveled in Army wifehood, but Daddy would be lost without you."

"Are his needs more important than mine?" Louise asked softly.

"I always thought you needed each other. We kids always thought you two had a terrific marriage."

"In some ways it was—constant, safe. We had wonderful children. But with you kids gone—"

"Well, obviously you don't throw away thirty-one years of marriage because of an empty nest. What would be the point?"

"Yes. Since I already have one foot in the grave," Louise said sarcastically.

"Come on, Mom. You know what I mean. You've passed the point where starting over makes any sense. What would you do? Where would you go? What would it accomplish?"

Louise leaned her head against the seat, wondering if Maggie was right. Because she had a limited number of good years left, did that diminish their importance? Or make them more precious? She honestly didn't know.

"I read that there've been more antiwar demonstrations," Louise said firmly, her voice signaling that this time the subject would stay changed. "I'm sure that upsets your father."

"Yeah. He was upset. Got into a real rage. 'Civil disobedience has no place in civilized society!' he said. He thinks the president should call out the Army and put a stop to them."

"And you?"

"I don't know. The peace talks don't seem to be getting anywhere. If we're going to abandon ship, I wish we'd go ahead and get it over with—and get everyone home again. I want to know if I have a husband or not."

Poor Maggie. Even her unquestioning patriotism was wavering. As was her unquestioning faith that Danny was still alive.

Franklin and Pauline stood up when they walked in the door. Jessica clung to her mother's skirt. Franklin's arm was in a sling, but he looked hale and fit. And stern. Pauline, too. Louise tried to embrace them, but both father and daughter were stiff. Her granddaughter, too.

Pauline made Louise feel like an intruder in her own apartment. In three weeks' time, Pauline had rearranged the furniture and the kitchen cabinets. Louise had to search for a water glass. Franklin's things were scattered about her bedroom.

Pauline, looking more pregnant in just three weeks, served the lasagna she had prepared. Maggie had brought a pie. Louise told them about her father and Martha. They listened politely.

She asked about Franklin's recovery and got perfunctory answers. He was walking—weather permitting. Three miles a day. Yes, the insert in his shoe helped his balance. No, he was not in pain.

She tried again with Jessica. What had she named her new teddy bear? There was a present for her in the suitcase. A tiny china tea set all the way from England. But Jessica had picked up on her mother's distance. She looked at her grandmother with wary eyes.

Louise felt panic rising in her breast. How was she going to get through the rest of this evening? How could she go into that bedroom with Franklin, sleep in the same bed with him as though nothing had changed? And with Pauline and Jessica sleeping in the guest room across the hall, how could they discuss anything?

And she wasn't sure yet just what she wanted to discuss.

"When do you report at West Point?" she asked when Franklin emerged from the bathroom. He limped without his special shoe. Louise was sitting on the side of the bed, already in her gown and robe.

"In a month," he answered. "We can go up next weekend and look around. I'll make arrangements for you to look at the superintendent's quarters."

"I plan to stay here in Washington for the time being," she said. "I don't want to go to West Point. I haven't changed my mind about that."

He sank onto the bed beside her. "Why, Louise? I've been crazy since you left, wondering what the hell's going on."

"I'm tired. I feel like I did after Andy died. Tired." And she thought of that other scene in a bedroom at Fort Leavenworth. A marital crossroads. She stared at their reflections in the same mirror over the same dresser. The same people, only older. The same marriage. No different.

"But you pulled yourself together then," Franklin insisted. "You can do it again."

"I don't want to." She felt so sorry for him. So very sorry for him. There was no way she could make him see, no way she could make him understand.

"You want to stay tired?" he asked. "I think you need to see a psychiatrist, honey. In fact, I've talked to a Doctor Dickenson at Walter Reed."

"God damn it, Franklin. Do you think just because I don't want what you want that I need a chaplain or a psychiatrist? I am a person, you know. I am entitled to my own thoughts, my own desires. I don't always have to agree with you."

"And what do you desire?"

"I told you before I left. I want a new life. I want something beautiful in the years I have left. I want love and sharing. I don't want to be a puppet wife for the rest of my years."

"I want you to see the psychiatrist, Louise," he said, his words measured. The last-warning voice. "There are medications, therapy."

"Shut up about a psychiatrist! I don't want some Army shrink telling me my duty. I'm not happy. Make me happy, Franklin. Ask my opinion sometimes and listen when I give it. We've had different politics for years, but you've assumed all this time that I vote like you vote, think like you think. Let's renegotiate the terms of this marriage. I've made my life fit yours all these years. It's my fault really. We should have had this conversation years ago, except years ago there were little children, a family to protect. Now, the children can survive on their own. I want a new life. I want us to start over again, to go on a honeymoon and never come back. I want us to learn how to talk to each other, to laugh together, to make love like lovers do."

She took a deep breath. "I just can't go to West Point with you. I can't pour teas, or sip sherry, give luncheons, stand in receiving lines, host VIPs, be honorary president of the officers' wives' club. I never was very good at all that. Apparently you are committed to going, and maybe you should if it means so much to you. I want you to go without me. It won't hurt your career—not now. You're too important. If we're not going to retire, I at least deserve a sabbatical."

"So you stay in Washington, and I go up there looking like a fool. Why should I agree to a scheme like that? What do I get out of it?"

"A wife."

"What in the hell is that supposed to mean?"

"Another solution would be a divorce."

The word hung heavy in the air between them. An ugly, shocking word. He looked at her, puzzled.

Then he exploded.

She tried to quiet him, acutely aware that Pauline was hearing every word. But he didn't care. Let her hear what an ungrateful, uncaring woman her mother was.

When he started repeating himself, Louise got a bottle of vodka from the pantry, orange juice from the refrigerator, and they drank and talked their way into the night. Angry words and poignant. Quieter now. Private.

"You never forgave me for Andy," he accused from the chair in the corner of the bedroom.

"Yes, I did. Years ago. But you never forgave me for not idolizing you like the children did. You wanted love on your terms. Why couldn't we have been like your parents? They were best friends. Lovers. He valued her judgment. They discussed things. We never discuss things. You just make pronouncements."

"I always thought my father was less of a man for allowing my mother to run the show like she did."

She stopped and stared at him. "Good grief, Franklin! Your father adored your mother. They were the happiest married couple I've ever known."

"I've given you everything, Louise. Everything."

"No, you haven't," she said, refilling her glass and sitting on the edge of the bed. "You haven't given me the right to change, not me or our marriage. You wanted me to stay forever young and innocent. Well, I'm not," she said defiantly.

"What are you saying?" He eyed her suspiciously. "Have you ever been unfaithful to me?"

"Yes," she said, knowing the liquor gave her too much courage. Could this really be her, speaking the truth to her husband after so many years of duplicity?

"You've been with another man?" His voice was rising again.

"Yes. I have." Already she was sorry. But now there was no going back to the way they were.

He wept. Openly. With sobs and tears. This man who hid his tears when their son died, who never let anyone ever see him cry.

Pauline knocked on the door.

"Go back to bed," Louise told her.

"But Daddy . . . "

"Go back to bed, Pauline. This is not your business."

"How could you betray my trust?" Franklin asked, blowing his nose with the Kleenex she handed him. "How could you defile our marriage?"

She knelt in front of him, wanting to touch him, to soothe. But she knew he'd pull away. "Have you ever been unfaithful to me?" she asked. "You have, haven't you? We've been apart too much."

He didn't answer for a long time. "It was during the war," he said finally. "But it's different for a man. It's just lust."

Louise wondered which war. She'd heard him talk about the liaisons some officers made at Panmunjom with Korean geishas. Did he do that? Or in Australia? In Saigon? "I did it for lust, too," she said softly. "Why couldn't you lust after me?"

"I'll never forgive you. Never. I trusted you. I thought you were perfect. All that time in that filthy, freezing cellar, I thought of my beautiful Louise, waiting for me. I thought that even if I died, you'd be true to me."

"Why would you think a thing like that? If I died, you'd marry again. Some nice lady to stand beside you and reflect your glory."

"Weren't you ever proud of me?"

"God, yes! But I got tired of being proud. I needed other emotions. I got tired of belonging to that life. You and the Army wanted too much. Blue hair. Mink stole. Smile. Smile. Smile."

"But I loved you," he protested.

Loved. Had he used the past tense on purpose, Louise wondered?

"I love you, my darling," she put her hands on his shoulders. "I always will. I'll always be here for you, if you'll let me."

Did she mean that? What if he surprised her and offered forgiveness?

If he did that, she decided, then maybe their marriage deserved another chance.

Oddly enough, after the words had run dry, they made love. Sweet love, that made her cry.

The next day, Franklin told her once again that it was unacceptable for his wife to live apart from him.

They were once again in the bedroom, Pauline in the kitchen feeding Jessica. A wife belonged with her husband, Franklin said in his sternest voice, standing in front of the window, his hands behind his back, and she had a duty to him and their marriage.

She hated that tone of voice. It made her stomach knot. Still. Could she really stand listening to it for several more decades?

"And how could I trust you?" he asked. "Every time I look at you, I'm going to see an unfaithful wife. Who was he, Louise?"

She turned away.

She wavered often in the days that followed. Pauline left, tight-lipped, teary-eyed. Louise wondered how much her daughter had heard but hadn't the courage to ask. Franklin moved into Maggie's apartment until time for him to report at West Point. Louise wandered about her suddenly empty apartment, trying to think which possessions she should keep to begin a new life, which things Franklin should take with him. How could he possibly set up a household by himself? Would that fall on poor Maggie's shoulders? Louise wondered if she should offer.

Several times a day, she would start to call Tommaso, then stop. She wasn't sure anymore what she wanted of him.

"Fence sitting can be hard on the ass," her father told her during one of their unsatisfactory phone calls.

Franklin invited himself to dinner. He brought flowers and wine. *Why, he's courting me*, Louise thought in surprise and felt a flush of pleasure. After dinner, when he started dictating the terms on which he would take her back, she found herself listening to him. He wanted to spend the night, and she almost let him. She felt guilty saying no.

It was Jeffrey and Marynell who convinced her to go.

"You guys think I should go to Italy?" Louise asked incredulously.

They both nodded. She was in their living room, a fire burning in the fireplace, good smells coming from the kitchen. Marynell had lost weight and was celebrating with a pair of size-ten jeans. She was wearing an orange sweater, her hair shorter, newly tinted a soft brown. The jeans were a little snug, but she looked good—younger, like someone who liked herself.

Jeffrey, as usual, was wearing a plaid shirt and a pair of jeans that were far from new. He was more kindly looking than handsome now, the sort of man whom a woman would feel comfortable asking for directions.

"But what about Franklin?" Louise demanded. "What about Peter and the girls? What about my grandchildren?"

"What about Louise?" Marynell asked softly.

"I can't believe that you of all people would encourage me to leave my general husband."

"I feel sorry for Franklin," Marynell admitted. "Terribly sorry. But I think you need to try something else. It might be a disaster, and if it is, you can come live in Fredericksburg with us."

Jeffrey handed Louise a beer and nodded his agreement. "We think you should at least give it a try."

"But why?" Louise asked.

"Because we're getting old." Marynell said. "Because I haven't forgotten how you looked in Amola. If that man over there can make my sister look like that again, I want him to do it. I got real sick of being the long-suffering Marynell. Now I'm getting pretty sick of my long-suffering sister. I didn't appreciate what I had. You don't know when to give up. Go on, Louise. If you fall flat on your face, we'll help you pick up the pieces."

"But if I go, that's the end of my family. There's no coming back to that."

"Kids want their mother and father to stay together in case they decide to come home for Christmas. Family's not like it used to be when everyone lived in the same town forever."

"Maybe so," Louise said, "but I still need them and care about them."

Marynell nodded. "I love my boys, and I loved the years they were growing up. I adore little Seth. But in Canada, I realized how separate we've all become. No matter how much you love your kids and care about what happens to them, they go their way, and we still have our own lives to live. I wish I'd figured that out a long time ago. Day in and day out, it's Jeffrey who counts. Jeffrey who puts up with me. Jeffrey who sees me as I really am and loves me anyway."

Marynell reached for her husband's hand. "Besides," she said with a grin, "we could come stay in that hotel for free. A second honeymoon. God, it was pretty there."

Louise closed her tear-filled eyes and reached blindly for her sister. "I'm not brave," she said.

Marynell knelt in front of her and hugged. Jeffrey sat on the arm of the chair and held her hand. "No," Marynell agreed. "You're not brave, and it will be hard. Don't go if you don't really want to. But we just thought that you should know that not everyone in the family thinks you're crazy."

Out of guilt, Louise gave almost all of their household goods to Franklin, keeping mostly things that had belonged to her parents and mementos of the children. How many times had she broken up a household and moved on? But this time was different. Gut-wrenching.

Louise stored her possessions in Marynell's attic and took only two suitcases with her. She felt too uncertain for more.

She didn't call Tommaso. She was too uncertain for that, too. In a rented car, she drove from Milan to Amola, thinking all the while she'd stop soon, call Franklin and beg forgiveness, then turn around and go home—to West Point where she belonged, where their marriage had begun. Full circle. She even had imaginary conversations with Franklin. Sometimes, the conversations went well, other times, he was indignant—of course, he didn't want her back.

The autostrada was full of crazy drivers who frequently drove three abreast in two lanes. Most of the exit signs were for places she'd never heard of. She couldn't remember how far a kilometer was. She didn't want to live in a foreign country, to be forever alien. She was a spoiled American, used to abundant hot water, phones that worked, mail that arrived on time. Franklin or no Franklin, she should go home where she belonged.

But eventually she parked near the piazza in Amola and stared across at the hotel with its two-roosters sign. It was the first of May, but the day was cold and drizzly. She was sweating, her heartbeat erratic.

Maybe she didn't love Tommaso except in a fairy-tale way. In fact, she didn't think she loved him at all. At this moment, she didn't love anyone, except her sister and her daddy. Had she lost the love of her children and her husband to come here to this foreign place and ask a vacation lover to take her in?

She cried again. That's all she did anymore, cry. She should have gone back to England instead of coming here. Never left Washington in the first place. She had had a safe life with Franklin. Her children's respect. Now she had nothing.

She didn't go to the hotel but walked on the beach instead—away from the town. For miles she walked, until the muscles in her legs ached with exertion and her teeth were chattering. She was cold, wet, hungry. And afraid.

By the time she walked back to the hotel, she was shaking with cold and exhaustion. And crying again. Damn.

He was behind the bar, a ledger open in front of him, reading glasses perched on the end of his nose. A dubbed episode of "I Love Lucy" was playing on the television set in the corner. Four old men were playing cards.

She waited in the archway until Tommaso saw her, then she stepped backwards into the deserted lobby.

Then, in an instant, there were his arms, his lips, his voice whispering her name. The sweet, passionate man of her dreams. Tommaso. It seemed that she did love him after all, for her heart was about to burst.

She made no promises. He asked for none. She would go carefully through each day, trying not to think about the next. She would agonize and cry and miss her family. At times, the pain would far outweigh the joy. But Tommaso was a patient man. He had waited years for her to come. He would wait years more for her tears to dry.

The following year, Louise returned once again to Folkestone. Eddie was ill and wanted her to visit him now rather than come for a funeral. In fact, he didn't want a funeral. He was to be cremated, his ashes scattered from the cliff near their cottage.

"What about Marynell?" she asked her father when she arrived. "Shouldn't you have called her, too?"

"Marynell would want to deal with remorse and regrets," Eddie said. "The time for that is past."

"I think she would have surprised you," Louise said.

"Maybe so, but there's not time now."

He had chosen to die at home with Martha as his nurse. Already the cottage smelled of disinfectant and stale urine, like a hospital. At times, Martha's eyes were red, but otherwise she was strong. Eddie needed her to be strong, she told Louise. She'd cry when he was gone.

Sometimes father and daughter reminisced, but the talking tired him. Mostly he wanted Louise to read to him. Anything. He didn't listen much. He just liked the sound of her voice.

Her father's sunken face and wasted body bore little resemblance to the man who had raised her. Even his voice was different—thin and raspy. But the words were her daddy's.

"Are you happy with Tommaso?" he asked.

"Yes, but I miss my children and grandchildren. Nothing is ever all one way or the other, is it?"

"No," he agreed.

"Mother once said that the best one can hope for is to be content—and I am, much of the time. I know now why you live by the sea. And I live with a kindly person who values me for what I am. But there was contentment before from being the good mother and the good wife." She stopped. What's done was done. Papers had been filed; Franklin was divorcing her. The good ladies of West Point had already found a perfect wife for Franklin. A former cadet hostess, whose husband had died in Korea. They were to be married in the fall. Louise was glad; it made her feel less guilty. She could relax now that there was no going back. She was just beginning to understand how much of a difference that made. Tommaso sensed it, too.

Eddie slipped in and out of wakefulness. Louise would be reading and realize he was asleep. He never slept very long.

"I dream all the time," he told her. "Just now the four of us were sitting on the seawall near Biloxi eating watermelon."

"The rinds floated out to sea like little boats," Louise remembered. She had shaded her eyes and watched them for the longest time.

"I'm surprised you remember. You and Marynell were little girls, Elizabeth so young. She'd made matching mother-daughter sundresses, pink, with ties on the shoulders. My three girls. Three heads of beautiful hair shining in the sunlight. Three sunburned noses. I remember wishing that time would stand still, that the four of us could go on being the same forever."

After only two days, Eddie was noticeably weaker. He told Louise she could go now. When she protested, he held up a hand. "It's my right," he said.

When it was time to go, she knelt at his bedside and buried her face against his frail chest. There was little left of him but bones. She felt his hand in her hair. She stayed like that, knowing when she lifted her head, it would be over. She would never see him again.

When she was seven or eight, she'd had pneumonia. Her daddy would carry her downstairs to sleep on the sofa in the daytime and carry her back up to her bed at night. How Louise had loved being carried up and down those stairs by her daddy. Like a princess. She couldn't imagine a world without her father's love.

"It's time," he said. "You'll miss your plane. Tell my friend Tommaso that I love him for loving you."

"Thank you, Daddy, for taking me back to Amola, for knowing me better than anyone else."

He nodded weakly.

"I don't want you to die," she sobbed. "I need my daddy."

"I know, honey. But I'm very old, and it's past time. Be as happy as you can possibly be."

"First, tell me that you know how much I love you."

"I know. And I love you, too, my darling child."

Book Six

★ ★ ★

1973–1984

CHAPTER

FORTY-FOUR

*P*auline was not waiting on the platform.

Louise waited a little, then picked up her suitcase and followed the crowd of people heading toward the depot. After four years of Italian, it was strange to hear German being spoken all around her.

How long ago had it been since she had ridden that other train into the Frankfurt station? Franklin had been waiting on the platform when she arrived from Paris, returning from the tour she had taken with her father and Marynell. 1956. Seventeen years ago.

She'd seen him out the window as the train rolled to a stop, felt her heart stop along with the train. Dear God, how difficult that had been, greeting Franklin, pretending everything was the same, that she was still the good and chaste wife she had always been.

Franklin, in his summer khakis, a colonel then, had carried her suitcase as she walked along beside him, asking how he had been, listening to him grumble about solitary evenings in an empty house. It wasn't until later that he'd asked her about the trip, feigned interest as she told him about the quaintness of her father's home, about thrilling to the antiquities of Greece, the beauty of Paris and Rome.

He was never comfortable with anything or anybody that divided her allegiance from him. If he hadn't held so tightly, would it have made a difference?

She remembered the days that followed. She would have erased Tommaso from her life if she could have. Put her life back as it was. She was so full of regret. Sadness. Guilt. In hindsight, Amola seemed sordid. And out of guilt, she became even more accommodating, even more the passive wife.

Louise surveyed the group of people waiting at the entrance to the station concourse. What if Pauline didn't come for her? Maybe one of the children was sick, or she had changed her mind about her mother's visit.

Louise shifted her suitcase to her other hand. If Pauline didn't come, she'd take a taxi. She had the address in her purse. It would be all right.

Then Louise saw her up ahead. A well-dressed American woman in a brown coat with a fur collar. Boots. White kid gloves. Careful hair. Careful expression.

Pauline endured her mother's embrace. *I will not cry*, Louise promised herself. *I knew it was going to be difficult. It's my grandchildren I came to see.*

Of course, that wasn't true. Mostly she had come to see her daughter, hoping against hope Pauline's icy heart would melt once they were together again.

"She reminds me of Andy," Pauline said.

"Yes," Louise agreed, pressing her lips against the silky hair on Sara Jean's head. A sweet, delicate child. Eyes too big for her face. And patient like Andy had been, sitting in her playpen, waiting quietly until her mother came for her.

Three-year-old Chad, having cookies and milk in his highchair, was as robust as Sara Jean was frail. And demanding. Spoiled. Jessica was a skinny seven-year-old with bright eyes and a sprinkling of freckles across her nose. She had rushed in after school, eaten her snack standing up, anxious to change clothes and go next door to her friend's house. But she had accepted Louise's embrace and questions graciously. "We're so glad you could come to visit us." "Yes, I like school. I can run faster than anyone in the room, boy or girl." "Yes, I like living in Germany." Then she looked to her mother for permission to be off.

"They're beautiful children, Pauline. Thank you for letting me come, dear. I know it's hard for you," Louise said.

Pauline shrugged. She was too thin. Too tense. This visit was hard on Pauline, too, Louise reminded herself, as she watched her daughter scratch at the back of her hands, stir her coffee a second time. "Well, it seemed ridiculous to live in Europe and not let you see your grandchildren," Pauline acknowledged. "At least that's what Maggie said. And Marynell."

Louise bit her lip. Concentrated. No tears. "Frankfurt is a wonderful city," she said. "I'm sure you're enjoying it here. Remember how we'd go down to Old Town on a Sunday afternoon and watch the street performers?"

"Yeah. And buy pastries. I started my fat period here. There's hardly any Army stationed here anymore. We don't socialize much. I wish we could transfer to Munich."

"Being here makes me think of Maggie and Danny," Louise said. "Remember how she was so certain that she loved him from the very first day? And she did."

Pauline nodded. "I wanted Maggie to be here when you came. That's why I kept putting you off. But she's so busy with her newfound cause, and I'm not sure she can afford the ticket."

"You wanted her as a buffer," Louise acknowledged.

"Yeah. Something like that. I thought it would be easier with her here."

"I'm glad you started writing me about the children." Louise inhaled the sweet baby scent of the child on her lap.

"Maggie said I had to. She talked me into inviting you. Promised she'd come, too, then backed out. I think I've been duped."

"Now that I'm here, how do you feel?"

"Well, I don't hate you. But I don't love you anymore either, at least not like I used to when I thought I was lucky to have such a perfect mom. And I feel sad. It should be you and Daddy here together. Do you have any idea how difficult it's been to have a notorious mother like you? How painful? And now Maggie's starting to go crazy, too. Making public statements that the government isn't doing enough to find out what happened to the MIAs. Getting Jerry all upset. Daddy's furious with her."

Louise wrapped her arms more closely around Sara Jean's frail body as though the baby could shield her from harm. *Notorious*. She hadn't wanted to cause pain. "Maggie wrote how hard it was for her when the POWs came home," Louise said. "She kept hoping for a miracle."

"I was, too. I'd watch those live broadcasts of the guys coming back, getting off the planes, kissing the ground, sobbing as they embraced wives and kids and parents. God, it really tore me up. I can imagine what it did to Maggie. And every time a face appeared in the door of a plane, I'd look to see if it was Danny, even though I knew Maggie would have been notified if he'd been among the liberated prisoners. And of course, every time the phone rang, I'd pray it was Maggie saying they'd found him, that he'd be on the next flight."

Pauline handed Chad a handful of raisins, which he slapped away. "No, you can't have another cookie," Pauline chastised, standing to lift him from the highchair. "Why don't you go get a book for Grandmother to read to you while I cook dinner. You want some more coffee?" she asked Louise.

"No. Later. Tell me, now that I'm here, are you very sorry that you invited me?"

"I don't know, Mom," Pauline said, sinking back into her chair. "I'll never get over what's happened, if that's what you mean."

"Would it matter if I told you I'd been unhappy for years? That I love Tommaso very much?"

Pauline's chin went up. "No, that doesn't help at all. I don't want to hear that you were unhappy all those years when I thought you had a perfect marriage. And you didn't have to fall in love with that man. Things like that don't *just happen*. When did you meet him, anyway? Maggie and I haven't been able to figure that out, and Aunt Marynell won't talk about it. Said we were still too young to understand. Too young! Can you imagine? That statement was followed by a lecture on what a good mother you'd been, how much you loved us, how Daddy never really appreciated you. Well, that's not the way Maggie and I saw it. Peter either. We thought he appreciated you a lot. And then one night, he was screaming at you for being unfaithful. I thought I'd die. Of all the things I never thought my mother would do. . . . "

Louise felt beaten. Old. Wretched. She had dreamed for months that once reunited, they could be mother and daughter again. How she wanted that, needed that. "In many ways your father did appreciate me," Louise said carefully. "And I appreciated him. But I needed something else."

"Yes," Pauline said wryly. "A Latin lover. Well, maybe part of every woman wants a Latin lover. But that doesn't mean you have a right to run off and find one."

Louise felt her insides shrivel. She had loved her children more than anything. "I think it's time to end this conversation," she said wearily.

"Maggie thinks he must have been living in Belgium while you and Daddy were there. Or was it in Paris? You couldn't possibly have known him very long. What did Daddy do to deserve that? What, Mom? Make me understand."

"Pauline, I hope with all my heart that your marriage is a beautiful thing, that it continues to bring you all the love and happiness you deserve. But if it didn't, would you feel obligated to devote the rest of your life to it?"

"Absolutely. Marriage is for more than love and happiness. It's who you are and who your children are. And besides, I wouldn't hurt my kids like that."

Louise fished in her pocket for a Kleenex. "I won't stay for three days," she said. "If you'll just let me spend tomorrow with the children, I'll go on home."

"Yes, maybe that's best. I didn't mean that about not loving you. I do. I guess that's why it hurts so much. Maggie says that since there's no going back, we should wish you happiness. Well, I can do that now. I hope you're happy, and that's a whole lot more than I could say before."

Blindly, Louise handed over Sara Jean and went to her room to cry. She cried again the following evening at the moment of farewell. Pauline cried, too. "I love you, Mom. Really I do. And I need you to love me." And the two women clung to each other. Louise kissed her daughter's hair, her face, her mouth.

She wanted to say that she hoped someday Pauline would understand. But to understand would mean she had faced the same pain. And Louise would not wish that on her daughter.

The ride home was endless. She'd called and left a message for Tommaso with the desk clerk saying that she was coming home early. Tommaso would know the trip had not gone well. He had been worried about that, fearful that Pauline wasn't ready yet. "Your Maggie, perhaps. And Peter. But not Pauline. Your leaving made her too afraid. Perhaps she sees too much of herself in you. Of her father in her husband. You must be patient with her."

He was waiting at the station. She knew he would be, but seeing him there was even better than she'd thought it would be. She was home. That man was her home. It hadn't been easy to come to that. She resented that she had made all the sacrifices, done all the leaving behind. And she would lash out at him. Hate him for having grandchildren who came to see him and hugged his neck. But he understood her resentment, didn't deny her right to feel it, the right to feel it deeply. He never told her to buck up, to be a good soldier.

Always, he reminded her she had the right to leave. Or to live with him only part of the time if that would help. "I do not want to be another prison for you," he'd tell her. "You are free. Always free."

"My marriage wasn't a prison!" she said indignantly.

"You called it so yourself."

"Well, I can say that. You can't. Just like you can say your wife was pitiful, but all I say is that I feel sorry for her sad life."

"Not pitiful. Afraid. Like your Franklin. Like Pauline."

Sometimes she had to get away from him. His goodness got on her nerves. She hated the isolation of being forever foreign. Usually she went no farther than Florence or Bologna to buy newspapers and books in English. She could read Italian but hungered for words in her native tongue. Novels especially. Novels had to be in English. She'd gone to visit Martha a couple of times, once to find solace after she'd gotten word of Maxine's death. Maxine had outlived Harold by only six months, her purpose for living dying along with him. Louise had loved Maxine but had given up the right to tell her good-bye, to go to her funeral. She'd had to do her grieving alone.

She had tried to write Maxine, needing to explain why she had left Franklin, but the words wouldn't come. *I've left your son for another man.* There was no good way to say it.

But Maxine had written her.

"I'm so sorry for you both—and disappointed. From the very first, I knew you weren't the right girl for Franklin, but I loved you, anyway. I guess I still do. Part of me says you should have stayed and done your duty no matter what, but another part hopes you have found the life you were looking for."

She had closed with good-bye.

"Did Daddy have to get away from you at times?" she asked Martha, who still lived in the same house on the channel, now with a younger, widowed sister.

"Oh, my goodness, yes. Usually, he'd go off to prowl in London, see a few American films. Or to golf a bit in Scotland. He missed you all terribly. Cried over photographs and letters. Got angry with me because of all he had left behind. But most of the time, he was glad to be here with me. We were best friends, you see. As we got old that became more important than other things, although some of the other things were quite nice in their time." And she had blushed.

Louise longed for her family. Not continually, for her children and her sister had long ago ceased to be a part of her everyday life. But when she thought of her children, it was with pain. No matter how she rationalized that she had a right to her own life, the pain of knowing she had disappointed them and hurt Franklin was still heavy. She wondered if it would always be so.

Winters were the worst, with great melancholy clouds of bone-chilling fog blanketing everything. It was the second winter that she decided to leave forever, to go home to Maggie and Marynell. Tommaso had wept over her decision but had not begged her to stay. But when the moment of farewell actually came, Louise couldn't bear to walk out the door. And now she felt strong enough to go to America for just a visit. Next summer. She knew she would return to Amola. Always would.

She stepped from the train, and Tommaso opened his arms to her, held her against his chest, didn't tell her not to cry. "You are the most loved woman in the world," he said. And she knew she was.

In his pocket, he had a kitten. A tiny little creature too young to be without a mother.

"I found it on the rocks at low tide. I'm sure its littermates were drowned. Perhaps we can find a home for it."

Louise cuddled the tiny animal against her neck and felt its purring. "Perhaps," she said. Baby animals had their own smell, just like baby people.

"Perhaps we can give it to one of the children in the square."

Louise had to smile. She was still crying, but she smiled. He knew she wouldn't give the kitten away. It was his way of distracting her from sadness. Like a rose on her pillow. A look across the room. His way of saying life was happy as well as sad. Of getting her to smile through her tears.

A kitten. So obvious, but it was working. A kitten was irresistible. So was the tentative look on Tommaso's face, a look that said *I love you* and *What can I do to help you feel better?*

They ate a late supper in the hotel kitchen, sitting at one end of the long work table. But he turned the lights low and put a candle in an empty bottle. And he opened a special bottle of wine. Louise ate with the kitten sleeping on her lap.

"Tomorrow night, I will take you dancing," he said.

"Yes, I'd like that."

Tommaso loved to dance. Wonderful mazurkas, twirling her round and round the floor. And dancing close to Neapolitan love songs with her arms around his neck.

By the time she crawled into bed, Louise was drowsy from the wine, the trip, emotion. She curled up against him, thinking how pleasant it would be tomorrow evening after the music and dancing, after making herself pretty for him, and flirting with him, and being a bit wanton on the dance floor when the lights were low, to come home to lovemaking. But tonight she wanted only his closeness. Strange how not having to make love was one of the most loving gifts of all.

CHAPTER

FORTY-FIVE

*P*eter's flight from California had arrived first, and he was waiting for her at the gate. How handsome her twin still was, she thought as she welcomed his hug. She'd always been jealous of Maggie's beauty but proud of Peter's. Even out of uniform, he was a remarkable looking man. Pauline felt such pleasure in his touch, his smile, and he seemed as glad to see her as she was him.

While they waited for his suitcase, they discussed Maggie and ticked off status reports on spouses and children. Belinda was taking night classes in accounting. Benny was a bookworm, Missy a tomboy.

Jerry had received a commendation medal for his work in revamping the training program at Fort Benning, Pauline reported. Jessica and Chad were fine, Sara Jean sick too much.

"God, it's good to see you," Pauline had said, slipping her arm around Peter's waist and leaning her head against his shoulder for a moment. "I can't remember the last time I had my twin to myself, even for just a few minutes. Maybe when we're old, we can have adjoining rocking chairs at the rest home. I miss you."

"And I you," Peter said, kissing her hair. "Are you happy, Sis? Everything okay?"

"Yeah. Except I miss Mom, and this business with Maggie causes problems with Jerry," she admitted. "I don't think I can forgive Maggie if Jerry doesn't get his promotion because of all this terrible publicity."

"Jerry's a terrific officer. I don't think they'll judge him because of his sister-in-law."

"*And* his mother-in-law," she reminded him. "God, it was bad enough when the whispers were just about Mom. Now they've got twice as much to whisper about."

"You've always worried too much about 'they.' "

" 'They' have a way of weeding people out," Pauline insisted. "At least Carter's pardoned our draft-evader cousins. We're supposed to go to Fredericksburg tomorrow to see everyone. How are we supposed to greet our turncoat cousins?"

"How about 'Welcome home?' It'll be good to see them, Sis."

Pauline shrugged. "The only reason I'm going is because I don't want to hurt Marynell and Jeffrey. They deserved better than those two."

After retrieving his luggage, they went outside to look for Maggie. Pauline had wondered if she would even show up, but after a fifteen-minute wait, she came driving up to the appointed spot outside the baggage claim area. Her greeting was cool. She knew, of course, that her brother and sister had come to Washington to gang up on her. She was wearing blue jeans, which annoyed Pauline. She could have dressed up a bit, put on some makeup. Her close-cropped hair was no more becoming in person than it had been on television. Maggie was, it seemed, bound and determined to be faithful to Danny even if it meant making herself unappealing.

Her car was dirty and had a badly dented front fender. MIA slogans covered her bumper. Pauline didn't understand how someone who had been raised military didn't maintain higher standards. Of course, with all her notoriety Maggie's teaching contract had not been renewed, and Pauline doubted if her sister's government pension was sufficient to cover expenses. But she had brought it all on herself, and it didn't cost anything to clear litter out of the backseat.

The three of them said little on the drive to Maggie's apartment, allowing her to navigate through the rush-hour traffic, waiting until they could face one another before the discussion began. Maggie looked annoyed when Pauline lit a cigarette. "I thought you promised Jerry you'd quit."

"I don't smoke around him," Pauline said defensively.

"Well, I don't like people to smoke in my car."

"Yes, you do keep it immaculate," Pauline countered. She pointedly took two more draws before putting it out.

The meeting of the three Cravens siblings had been Jerry's suggestion, and Peter and Pauline agreed to try one more time to reason with their younger sister. Their father had washed his hands of her. Their mother had abandoned them all. Jerry claimed it was up to Maggie's sister and brother to put a stop to her outrageous behavior. It was hard to measure how much damage all this publicity was doing to her husband's and to Peter's respective careers. And poor Daddy. First an embarrassing divorce and now an infamous daughter. And him a national hero.

Jerry had waited to leave for work yesterday morning in order to watch the "Today" show segment in which Maggie appeared. "That sister of yours," he had muttered. This time she had really gone too far, claiming on national television that the government had lied to her, bugged her telephone, had her followed and opened her mail, all to monitor her antigovernment activities. "They'd like to catch me selling drugs or taking money from the KGB," Maggie had insisted during her interview. "They'd like to make people think the militant MIA wives are publicity hounds or crazy or in cahoots with Hanoi, and that we couldn't possibly have legitimate complaints about the way our MIAs have been forgotten."

But at least she hadn't gone into the ridiculous story she'd told them last month when she claimed a CIA undercover agent had tried to have an affair with her and get her hooked on drugs in the process.

"They'll do anything to discredit me," she had wept into the telephone. "I'm scared, Pauline. I'm not sure how far they'll go."

"I don't for a minute think that the Air Force or the CIA or anyone else is interested in whether or not one of the MIA wives gets involved with a man," Pauline insisted, grateful that Jerry wasn't listening on the extension. "But if you insist on being so paranoid, why don't you stop calling attention to yourself with all this political activism? If you're so scared, then just stop, God damn it. Just stop! You're embarrassing your family, and just think of what Danny would think if he were alive. My God, Maggie, you're disgracing his memory."

"Go to hell, will you," Maggie had shrieked. "Just go to hell. You've got what you want in your nice tidy little life with your perfect children and your perfect husband, so you don't give a damn about me and Danny just so long as I don't make waves."

Pauline leaned her head against the wobbly headrest of Maggie's car and closed her eyes. Sometimes she felt as angry with her husband as she did with Maggie. How many times had he told her "You've got to do something about your sister" when there really wasn't anything she could do? After years of Jerry appreciating his wife's family connections, now they were a liability to his career. First her mother. The scandal of Mrs. General Cravens leaving her husband had rocked the military world. Since then, whenever Pauline and Jerry walked into a room, the wave of whispering would begin.

And now people were whispering about Maggie, too. It was so unfair. Jerry was an outstanding officer with a fine war record in Vietnam, his wife a general's daughter who entertained beautifully and dressed with impeccable taste. Pauline was playing her part perfectly, but offstage distractions were ruining the show.

Only occasionally did Pauline recall that time in her life when she hadn't been perfect, when she screwed every boy who asked her out. She still worried that Jerry would somehow find out.

She had almost told Jerry her sordid secrets during the first years of her marriage when she discovered she could actually love the shy, considerate man she had married. But Pauline had heeded the inner voice that begged for caution.

While no longer shy, Jerry was still considerate most of the time, except that he had become more exacting with rank and maturity. He was fond of saying he could forgive mistakes, that everyone made them. What he couldn't forgive was willful misconduct.

Pauline was pretty certain that he would consider promiscuity willful misconduct. And abortion? She had no idea how the knowledge that she had once been pregnant with another man's child would affect his love for her, but she had no intention of finding out.

And with the exception of a brief bout of postpartum depression following Jessica's birth, she had never permitted herself to speculate about the fetus aborted by the Oklahoma City chiropractor. Never.

She and Jerry had settled into the respectful, comfortable years of middle marriage. Their children were satisfying. Jessica, beautiful, bright and athletic, looked like her aunt Maggie. Chad made them all laugh—a seven-year-old comedian who was silly about everything. Sara Jean was an angel adored by them all.

At times Pauline wanted to tell Jerry that she couldn't do a damned thing about Maggie, that her sister was a grown-up woman and had a right to conduct her own life as she saw fit. But instead, Pauline would promise to write Maggie again, to call her, to get Peter to write letters and make calls, to ask her father if he wouldn't please break his silence. Pauline remembered criticizing her mother for never disagreeing with Daddy. She didn't understand then that wives placate husbands however best they can. That was why she had come to Washington—to placate Jerry.

For nothing she or Peter had said or done had any impact on Maggie. Their sister, once the superpatriot, was obsessed with her new cause. She preached her one-sided sermon to waiters in restaurants, clerks in grocery stores, cab drivers, anyone who'd listen. The government was sacrificing the MIAs.

Yesterday, the "Today" show's Tom Brokaw had been a willing listener. His first question asked if her illustrious family supported her MIA activities. That set her off. "No, my family doesn't support the war against the government that I and other MIA families are waging, a war to discover the truth about our loved ones," Maggie said in that evangelistic voice she used for her radio and television appearances. She was wearing a tailored suit. With her short hair, she looked like a butch attorney. If Danny ever came back, he would hardly recognize her.

Jerry cursed. "My wife's sister. Jesus! Do you realize a record of her activities is in *my* file?"

The television interview had taken place in Maggie's apartment. There in front of the fireplace was the catalyst for this particular interview—a tombstone that had been delivered to her apartment the week before. Congress had declared all MIAs to be presumed dead, and government regulations said all dead servicemen were entitled to a grave marker. *Sans* cemetery addresses for the phantom dead, some fool had decided to send the granite tombstones to residences of nearest kin. Two deliverymen with a tombstone on a dolly appeared unannounced at Maggie's front door. She, of course, pounced on the tombstone in her living room as another example of an insensitive government for whom the MIAs were simply embarrassing numbers. Maggie had babbled on about live sightings that had gone uninvestigated, about offers of ransom first from the Viet Cong, then from the Hanoi government, that had been ignored, about cover-ups and lies to the MIA families.

"Do you really believe that twenty-two hundred Americans have disappeared without a trace?" she demanded of Brokaw.

That was when she launched her favorite tale—how she'd seen the name of Danny's navigator on the list of returning POWs and contacted him. They had both ejected, he told her. The navigator had been captured immediately and never saw Danny on the ground, but he was certain Danny had gotten out of the plane alive. And yes, he'd told the Air Force this information upon his release. Why hadn't someone from the Air Force passed it on to her? Maggie asked. Why did she have to find it out on her own? Because they wanted her to continue thinking her husband had gone down with his plane. They didn't want troublemaking wives demanding to know the fate of men they'd already marked off their list.

That discovery—that the government never bothered to tell her that Danny had apparently survived the crash—had been the end of patriotism for Maggie. Almost overnight, she had shifted her allegiance within the MIA group to the antigovernment faction. At their gatherings, they exchanged stories of the lies that had been told, of live sightings that had been ignored by the government.

And now the whole issue had been swept under the rug with the declaration that all MIAs were dead.

It had been ten years since Danny was shot down. Pauline didn't know if Maggie's activities were still motivated by unfailing love or only by obsession. But since the POWs had been returned and the MIA issue put to bed by the government with a legislated death for all the missing, Maggie had gone crazy. She couldn't believe the government she had supported all that time wasn't going to produce a husband for her in exchange for her loyalty.

Two years ago, Congress had passed the Freedom of Information Act, which had given the MIA families additional fuel for their accusations. When previously closed files were examined, families claimed the information they had been given did not agree with written records.

If Maggie hadn't been the daughter, granddaughter and daughter-in-law of generals, few would have taken note of her at all, but as it was, she had become a national spokeswoman for all those people who wouldn't give up, who wanted a miracle.

In a way, Pauline understood. It was her sister's way of keeping Danny alive. Pauline had always envied Maggie her perfect love, but she didn't anymore. It had ruined her life. Other women grieved sincerely, then went about the business of rebuilding their lives. But not Maggie.

"You're losing your sanity over this," Pauline told Maggie when at last they were seated in her living room, the engraved tombstone like a fourth presence.

Daniel Edward Norton

Captain, USAF

Distinguished Flying Cross

MIA activist publications—*The Bamboo Connections* and *The Insider*—were scattered across the coffee table, Maggie's picture on the cover of one of them. On the wall was a framed poster showing forlorn American prisoners behind barbed wire. The caption read "Bring our loved ones home."

"What would you have done?" Maggie had demanded of her sister. "If there was a possibility that Jerry was being held captive, would you just let him rot because it would be 'embarrassing' to the government and your family if you dared demand that someone do something?"

"Maggie, it's been ten years," Pauline reminded her. "Do you honestly think if any of those men were still alive, the government would ignore them?"

"I am well aware how long it's been. And yes, I do think the government would and has ignored them. Twenty-two hundred human beings don't disappear without a trace. Our government has taken the convenient way out. It's made a pronouncement just like Daddy used to do."

Pauline looked questioningly at Peter. Couldn't he shut her up?

"Congress proclaimed they were all dead," Maggie continued with a snap of her fingers. "Just like that."

"Sometimes pronouncements are in order," Peter said. "What would you have the government do—pretend all those men were still alive?"

"They could have continued carrying them as MIAs until they knew the truth. They could do more to find out the truth. You guys know how much I loved the Air Force, but they didn't really care about me—or Danny. We'd become an inconvenience that Congress decided to legislate out of existence. No more MIAs. No more MIA wives. Only widows to pension off. An end to all that accruing salary."

"How long are you going to leave that thing sitting there?" Peter asked, tilting his head in the direction of the tombstone.

"Until I get Danny back."

Peter gave an exasperated shrug. "Danny's not coming back, Maggie." He sounded like Daddy when his patience was worn thin. "The sooner you acknowledge that," Peter continued, "the sooner this family can get back to normal."

"Normal. Now that's a joke!" Maggie said. "Our mother leaves our general father for an Italian cook. The general father won't talk to me unless I promise to be a good little widow lady. Our cousins are draft dodgers. My sister has become the biggest tight-ass of all time with my brother not too far behind. Just your nice, basic, All-American family."

"Don't you care about any of us?" Peter asked, holding a scotch-and-water with both hands.

Maggie's expression softened. "Of course I care about you. I just see you differently now. I see the world differently. I don't care about the same things you care about—politics, prestige, power. I'm beginning to understand about Mom turning her back on it all."

"And if Danny were alive, what would he care about?" Peter asked. "He was career military, Mag. He'd understand about cutting losses and getting on with the campaign."

"You sound just like Daddy," Maggie accused. "Why couldn't they just tell it to me straight? What the hell are they trying to hide, Peter?"

"Maybe there have been inadvertent errors made in reporting to you and some of the other MIA families. But if there was a prayer anyone was still alive in Southeast Asia, the military would pursue it. You're just obsessed with an unrealistic daydream. Danny is dead, Maggie. Find someone else. Make babies. Get on with your life."

Maggie starting crying. "Don't you think that's what I want to do, damn it!"

Pauline gathered her sister up in her arms. Peter hugged them both.

"We love you, honey," Pauline said. "We just get frightened for you."

Peter grilled steaks on her tiny balcony, and Maggie poured another round of scotch.

Maggie let her brother and sister shove the grave marker in a closet. But she wouldn't back down. "I'll agitate until I get my husband back, dead or alive."

"Then I hope the next set of remains Hanoi returns is Danny's," Peter said. "I hope to God."

And then what? Pauline wondered as she flew back to Georgia. What would Maggie do, if she could finally bury Danny? No career officer would be interested in a woman who had been a political activist. Maggie would end up like Aunt Marynell, married to a civilian and teaching school year after year. But how could she settle for something so lackluster after Danny?

A picture of Danny had flashed onto the television screen during the "Today" interview. Goose flesh broke out on the back of Pauline's arms as she stared at the unsmiling yet beautiful face of her brother-in-law in an official military photograph. Danny. Then abruptly the screen was filled with a wedding photograph of Danny and Maggie. A chill had cut through Pauline's body. What if he *were* still alive?

CHAPTER

FORTY-SIX

*A*fter fourteen years, what was left of Danny had come home. Remains. All that was left.

With Peter waiting at her side, Maggie watched the casket being lowered into the ground while her family and the Nortons waited at a discreet distance, the other mourners having paid their final respects and departed. Watching overall-clad cemetery workers fill in the grave was not part of the formal ceremony, but Maggie insisted on staying until the end.

The leaves were just beginning to turn, and Arlington was at its beautiful, melancholy best. She tried to find comfort in the beauty, but couldn't. She was sorry Danny had been buried on a hillside overlooking the Pentagon. No longer the faithful military wife, she wished he could have been buried someplace far away from Washington. In fact, she would have preferred a civilian service in a country churchyard, instead of an Arlington burial complete with horse-drawn caisson and rifles firing a final salute. But Peter kept saying that Danny would have wanted Arlington. His father was buried here. And Danny's mother would not have understood if her son was buried elsewhere. Mrs. Norton had rights, too. And his two uniformed brothers, who were here with their families. Danny had nieces and nephews he had never seen.

With a small tractor, the workers were filling the hole, covering what was left of her darling Danny for all eternity.

Maggie reached her brother's arm. *Oh, God, Danny, I loved you so much. I don't think anyone ever loved another person as much as I loved you. Have you been dead all those nights I lay in my bed aching for your love, longing for you to put a baby in me, crying out for you, begging God to send you back to me, touching myself and pretending it was you? How could I have been yearning for a husband who was already dead?*

Two men with shovels stepped forward to smooth the earth. Soon grass would grow. The tombstone she'd been sent four years ago would finally have a place to stand.

She really should have looked at the bones and touched them. Now she never could. She had wanted to do that, asked about it. "I want to view what's left of him." God, how shocked they had been at such a request. Only her mother seemed to understand. Her father, Peter and her Air Force case officer had told her that was unheard of.

"God, Maggie, that's the most morbid thing I've every heard of," Peter said.

"I've waited fourteen years for my husband to come home—it just seems like I should have something to touch one last time. In fact, I'd like to have a small bone to keep. Catholics keep relics of saints in their churches. Why can't I have a relic of my husband to put in a special place and burn a candle to every now and then?"

"Because people would think you're crazy, like they did when you wanted to keep that tombstone in your living room."

"Look, your precious Air Force sent it to me *sans* body, sensitive bunch of guys that they are."

So much had been done to her since then, Maggie thought, from threatening phone calls to the brakes on her car mysteriously giving out. Peter and Pauline said she was paranoid. Maybe she was. She didn't even bother to tell her father. He never answered her letters anyway, wouldn't accept her calls.

She wrote her mother instead. And called sometimes. But the long-distance phone calls were difficult with the meter ticking away. In the letters she could ramble on about Danny, about all that had been done to her.

Now it all was over. She was no longer an MIA wife but a widow. She had nothing left to agitate for. Her husband had, at last, come home.

She'd kept the tombstone in the coat closet until her current roommate, Celeste, also an MIA wife, had objected, saying it depressed her every time she hung up her coat. After that, Maggie kept it in her own closet, under a stack of blankets. Celeste had refused delivery on the tombstone sent to her, but she accepted the government declaration of her widowhood and found herself another husband. Maggie had fought bitterly with her, calling her a traitor to the cause. Celeste had come today, and they had embraced. She was pregnant. "Get on with your life, honey, before menopause sets in. This loyalty business gets to be a sick habit, like drugs. Find another man, and take the cure."

Maggie wondered if she'd be able to do that—get on with her life. Find a replacement for Danny. Have babies.

The arms she had longed for all those lonely nights had been reduced to bones in a casket. Almost a full skeleton, the Air Force had assured her. And a skull, of course, with teeth that matched Danny's dental record perfectly. Danny's remains had been returned in a batch of eight. Maggie knew the wives of three of the men. They had called one another to grieve, to admit they were relieved that the nightmare was finally over.

And her family was relieved.

She hadn't asked them to come, but they all had anyway. Her mother, all the way from Italy.

And after six years of not speaking to her, her father was here. In spite of herself, Maggie felt grateful.

This was the third time her mother had been back. Six years ago she had come for two months. And last year. Both times Maggie hadn't wanted her to leave, had felt angry all over again when she did.

And now Louise had come back to say good-bye to Danny. Danny and her mother had always loved each other. Danny hugged her more than Peter did, more than he hugged his own mother. Louise had cried when she stepped forward to touch Danny's casket.

Her father was more impressive than ever with three stars on his shoulders, a corps commander. Maggie wondered how her mother felt about that, but she had turned her back on the life as much as the man. Maggie sympathized with her mother's dissatisfaction with military life, but it was still difficult for her to accept her leaving her husband. Maggie got tears in her eyes every time she heard Tammy Wynette sing "Stand By Your Man." That was her credo. She would have stood by Danny if he'd been a bank robber, a murderer, anything.

She wondered how Danny would have felt about the Air Force now, if he would be like Peter and have second thoughts about staying in. Peter was considering early retirement, claiming he had discovered that piloting was more important to him than a military career. With his Air Force flying days drawing to a close, Peter and two of his fellow Air Force pilots were thinking about starting an air charter company out of Golden, Colorado. Belinda was pushing for it. She wanted a home. "And they can fight the next war without my husband," she said defiantly. Pauline couldn't understand how either of them would willingly give up the only life they'd ever known.

Eric and Matt hadn't come. Eric was a high school coach in Ashley, North Carolina. Matt managed a logging camp in Virginia. They could have been here with the rest of the family. It seemed sad for them not to be, but Maggie understood. A military funeral for her husband who had died in the war didn't seem an appropriate place for the cousins who had boycotted that war.

She should have called them, asked them to come. She remembered how they used to hug her, lifting her up off her feet and spinning her around. Today she would have had to settle for a sedate funeral hug, but she could have clung to them for a minute, let them know that she didn't want to lose them, too.

Uncle Jeffrey was famous for his furniture. And prosperous. A special section in *The New York Times* on American crafts had called Jeffrey one of the country's premier artisans, who created functional art of the highest caliber, and indeed, some of his pieces were being purchased by museum collections. Jeffrey looked less military with each passing year. He was still slender, but spit and polish had long since gone out of his life. Marynell looked wonderful in a blue suit and matching coat. In fact, Marynell and Louise both looked lovely—two aging sisters who wore their years well. Several people had whispered that word to Maggie. "Why, you're mother looks lovely." It surprised them. She wondered how they expected her to look.

Last night, when they had picked their mother up at the airport, Pauline had tried hard to be reserved, but failed. They all cried, even Peter. "I miss you so," Maggie sobbed, clinging to Louise like a child.

Louise was wearing slacks and a sweater. Her hair was gray but soft and full. She was tanned and had pierced ears. That fascinated Maggie. Her mother with pierced ears.

Maggie fixed dinner for everyone at her apartment. Louise was obviously tired from the flight and nervous about being with her children. She asked dozens of questions, wanted to see pictures of her grandchildren. She was staying a couple of months and looked forward to visiting everyone.

Over dessert Louise tried to tell them about her life in Amola, but Pauline cut her off. "Please, Mom, we don't want to hear about your life with him. It still hurts too much. We had dinner with Daddy and June last night. We can't even have dinner with our mother and father at the same table. I used to think you were the finest woman I'd ever known. You can't imagine how I admired you."

Belinda jumped up and started clearing the table. Jerry grabbed a couple of plates and followed her to the kitchen.

"Come on, Pauline," Peter chastised. "We can do without that."

"You feel the same way," Pauline accused. "Don't deny it."

"What specifically did you admire, Pauline?" Louise asked, care-fully folding her napkin and pushing away the remainder of her pie.

"Your loyalty," Pauline said. "We thought you would be loyal to Daddy until the day you died, like Maggie was loyal to Danny."

Louise looked from one to the other of her children. "Well, apparently I wasn't the woman you thought I was." She had excused herself then, saying how tired she was from her journey and gone to bed.

"Hey, you were pretty rough on her," Peter said, refilling his wineglass from the jug on the table. Maggie nodded for him to refill hers.

"Well, I can't stand to see you and Maggie acting like everything is all right, like she's still dear ole Mom."

"She is still our mother," Maggie said. "I know how you feel, honey, but there's no point in beating a dead horse. I'm glad she's here."

"Me, too," Peter agreed. "She looks good. Softer. Pauline once said that Mom and Dad had a marriage of respect. Maybe Mom missed the passion. Maybe this man . . . "

"God, Peter, that's disgusting," Pauline snapped.

"What is? Passion, or a mother being passionate?"

"I think it's time for you to forgive her, Pauline," Maggie said.

"I can't," Pauline said. "I want to. Really I do, but I just can't."

That was when Maggie decided she would go back to Italy with her mother. She hadn't told any of them yet, not even Louise herself, but the more she thought about it, the more she wanted it. Desperately. To be mothered.

The gravediggers were finished, the earth smoothed over the grave. There was nothing left to do but walk away, but Maggie's knees went weak. She wanted to give in to the weakness, to fall to her knees and burrow her way into the raw earth. Peter held her arm tightly.

It was really over.

"What do I do now?" she asked.

When Peter didn't answer, she looked at his face. He was crying.

She had marveled all day at her own composure, but at the sight of her brother's tears, it left her.

"He was the best," Peter sobbed. "He was like a brother. I'm so sorry, Maggie, that it ended like this. I'm sorry for the rotten time I gave you when all you were trying to do was figure out some way to keep him alive. I'm so sorry."

She buried her face against her brother's uniform. He sobbed with her. There would never be another Danny.

Maggie stayed in Italy three months. The woman living in the pretty little hotel in Amola was so different from the woman who'd raised her. She smiled and laughed more. She acted silly sometimes. She challenged her daughter to races along the beach and could almost win. She was openly affectionate with Tommaso, something that continued to shock Maggie. Her mother was gray-haired and past sixty, but in the morning she often had the whisker-burnished skin of lovemaking.

Tommaso was a weathered, kindly man who smiled with his whole face. He stayed in the background, allowing mother and daughter to spend time together. But Maggie's curiosity got the best of her, and she would wander into the kitchen to ask how he made the tomato sauce, did he have any more of those incredible pears. Where was he during the war? Would she get to meet his daughters? And he would ask things in return. She found herself telling him about growing up an Army brat and her involvement in the MIA wives' organization, explaining how she no longer had a role to play.

"Your mother tells me you are a teacher. A fine thing to be a teacher."

"Yes, I suppose. I'm ready to get back to it. Now that I'm a respectable widow lady, maybe I can find a job."

"Were the few years you had with your Danny worth all the pain?"

"I think so. Love is always worth the price." Then she thought about what she had just said and laughed. "I think I've just been tricked."

He grinned. "Tell me about Danny. Did you laugh with him?"

Maggie knew she was being charmed, but Tommaso was funny and a good listener. She still felt uncomfortable when he and her mother were together, however.

"It makes me angry to see you happier with another man than you ever were with Daddy," Maggie admitted to her mother. "It seems so unfair."

"And you blame me?"

"I don't know. Not as much as before. But would it have been so awful to stay with Daddy and keep us all a family?"

"No, it wouldn't have been awful, but I wanted something else. I used to spend a lot of time reliving the past and trying to think of ways

I could have changed things, but I don't bother with that much anymore. Perhaps I wasn't ready for happiness before. Now, tell me of your father. June seems very nice. I want so much for him to be happy."

Maggie returned home in time to spend Christmas at Carlisle Barracks with Pauline and Jerry. Her mother and Aunt Marynell used to talk about the maiden aunts in Indiana, and now Maggie was filling that same role for her nieces and nephews. Without children and family, Christmas would have no meaning. Last Christmas she'd been with Peter and Belinda. And next Christmas? Maggie didn't want to think about it.

As they cleaned up after Christmas dinner, she begged Pauline to go see their mother.

"I have a family to look after," Pauline said, carrying her sherry glass with her to the kitchen. "Sara Jean's asthma is worse than ever. I'll be glad when we get back to Washington, and I can rely on Marynell. She flew up here to help the last time Sara Jean was in the hospital. My aunt is more of a mother to me than my own mother."

"Take Sara Jean along. The sea air would do her good. Don't you miss Mom, Pauline? I miss her something fierce."

Pauline's shoulders sagged. "I can't go. Not yet anyway."

CHAPTER

FORTY-SEVEN

*P*eter had flown in from Colorado—in a company plane. Eagle Charter. Peter and two other former Air Force pilots had scraped together every cent they had to buy three planes and rent a hangar. He and Belinda had borrowed from assorted relatives to put a down payment on an antiquated farmhouse near Fort Collins that they were redoing themselves. Free of military restrictions, Peter's hair was longer, and he sported a bushy mustache. Last Christmas, when Maggie, Pauline and her family came to share their Rocky Mountain Christmas, Pauline took one look at her brother and burst into tears. "I just don't understand what's happening to this family. We used to be so respectable."

"You have enough respectability for all of us," Peter had said, grabbing his twin and tickling her neck with his mustache.

A wreath had arrived from Pauline yesterday for Maggie to place at the Vietnam War Memorial. And she had called last night. "I want you to know I love you very much. Regardless of our differences in the past, I wouldn't have traded you for any other sister in the world, and I hope the monument brings some peace to you and the whole country."

Aunt Marynell and Jeffrey had driven up from Fredericksburg to be with her and Peter for the afternoon. And Matt came, but he kept hanging back, not quite sure if Maggie would want him to be part of the dedication of a memorial to her husband and all the others who died in that war. Finally, she linked her arm with his. "I'm glad you came, but you don't always have to wait for a family gathering."

"I'm never sure how anyone feels. It seems best to just stay out of the way."

"I feel like you're my darlin' cousin Matt. And you don't need to stay out of my way."

Maggie longed for her mother, but it was nice to be surrounded by family. They understood the importance of the day. The whole country did. The healing had finally begun.

Earlier, after the speeches and military ceremony, the press of people in front of the monument made reverence difficult. But now, at dusk, Maggie and Peter had come back to have some private moments. After touching Danny's name again, Peter went his own way to touch the names of the men who had been his comrades in arms, his friends.

At last Maggie was alone with her thoughts.

Daniel Edward Norton. Maggie reached out and traced the name carved among so many others on the shiny black granite. Her own reflection looked back at her, names carved across her image, Danny's across her heart.

Her precious Danny. No one would ever love her more, but finally, she was letting go. He was a memory, not an organic part of each day and night. She no longer conjured up dreams of him coming home, of making love and babies with him.

Yet only last month she had discovered that the remains returned to her couldn't possibly have been identified as Danny's. Maybe the nagging suspicion had always been there. She and others among the most vocal of the MIA family members had been conveniently neutralized when remains were returned to them. A woman in Nebraska had become suspicious and exhumed the remains she had buried. She'd held a press conference to reveal a forensic anthropologist's claim that no positive identification could possibly have been made on the basis of a few bones and bone chips.

Maggie hadn't looked at Danny's file for several years, not since her activist days. There had been no reason, and there hadn't been any reason last month. Maybe it was only that the dedication of the Vietnam Memorial was drawing near, that she was going through her own last rites. She had taken Danny's pictures down from her wall in anticipation of a suitor she hoped would soon enter her life. Danny's clothes no longer hung in her closets, a drawer in her dresser was no longer filled with his personal possessions. She packed a foot locker with what she couldn't bear to give up and donated the rest to the DAV and AMVETS. And she went to look at Danny's file one last time, needing to read for herself how the identification on his remains had been positive, how the teeth matched Danny's dental records and the evidence of a childhood fracture in the femur matched an X-ray from Danny's medical records. At first, she thought she had the wrong file. There must be two Daniel Edward Nortons. But the Social Security number was the same. Her name was there. His parents.

The written report on Danny's remains bore no resemblance to what she had been told by Air Force officials. Seven bone fragments, two ribs, a tibia, seven metacarpals. That was all. No skull. No teeth. No femur that had once been fractured and healed.

She stared down at the document, struggling for comprehension. Then, as realization sank in, round black holes began floating in front of her eyes. Her chest grew too tight for breathing, the skin on her head tightened, squeezed at her brain. She wondered if she was going to faint.

She concentrated first on forcing the black holes in her vision to fill themselves. Then she worked on her breathing. Deep breaths. Slowly.

She sat there for a long time, looking again at the report, making sure she wasn't crazy. What now? Dear God in heaven, what now?

Her first impulse was to rush to a pay phone and call Peter and Pauline. She could tell them triumphantly that she now had proof that there had been a conspiracy against her just as she had always claimed. She wasn't crazy or paranoid. They'd be sorry when they realized she'd been right all along. The government had lied about Danny's remains and probably everything else.

Vindication. Maggie could feel the adrenaline pouring into her bloodstream.

She ticked through the names of journalists and television

broadcasters she knew, trying to decide who'd get to break the story. She'd call a press conference if she thought she could get enough media people to come.

And she'd need to see a lawyer, get a court order to have the remains at Arlington exhumed. Could she do that? She knew she should have used a civilian cemetery.

She'd go in the night if she had to, dig them up with a shovel. She'd prove to the world that she'd been duped.

It was all so obvious. She had been one of the most vocal in criticizing the government's handling of the MIA issue. She had claimed she would continue her protests until she knew once and for all what had happened to her husband, so they presented her with some bones to shut her up. And to how many others? Vocal MIA wives conveniently turned into pacified widows.

Could Danny still be alive?

Mentally, she composed a letter to her mother, explaining the situation. *So you see, the battle continues. I'd rather have a baby, but what can I do?*

But Maggie knew exactly what her mother would write back. *Let it go.*

And suddenly, Maggie had realized she wouldn't call her sister and brother, a lawyer, experts, anyone. She wouldn't even write the letter to her mother—someday maybe, but not now. The government had won. She didn't have the energy or the courage or the faith to take up the battle again. After all this time, in spite of the deceit and lies, she could no longer make herself believe that Danny was still alive. All she wanted now was a warm male body in the night and a baby to make them a family. She didn't even care if she found passion. Comfort would be enough.

She had noticed the bearded man with the crutch earlier, during the dedication ceremony. He was alone, forlorn-looking, wearing faded jeans and a torn fatigue jacket with airman's stripes on the shoulder—a staff sergeant.

And now he was leaning forward on his crutch to touch a name near Danny's and almost lost his balance.

Maggie reached out to steady him.

He was crying. She looked at him.

"My cousin," he said. "We grew up together. I came here today to see his name—and the others. You can't imagine how long I've waited for this day."

"Yes, I can," Maggie said, still not looking at him. "We've all waited for it. I hope it helps."

She touched Danny's name again. She wanted to kiss it, but she didn't with the stranger standing beside her.

"What year did your old man buy it?" the man asked.

"He was shot down in 'sixty-seven," Maggie said, "and listed as missing."

"Tough shit," the sergeant said emphatically. "Real tough shit. Sixty-seven. That's when I lost my leg."

Maggie forced herself to look at him again. He was leaning heavily on his crutch. He needed a haircut. He was wiping the tears from his face with the back of his free hand. His chest heaved as he fought for control.

She wasn't sure why, but Maggie opened her arms to him. He stumbled against her and put his head against her shoulder and cried. Awkwardly, she held him and stroked his back, feeling like she was a kindergarten teacher comforting the child of a giant. She held him for a long time.

Finally, he backed away from her. "I'm sorry."

"Don't be. You live in Washington? Can I take you someplace?"

"Naw. I'll hang around awhile. There's a bus that goes back to the VA Hospital at nine."

Maggie extended her hand. "Maggie Norton."

"Carl Tucker." He switched his crutch to his left armpit and extended his right hand.

"Would you like to have dinner with me and my brother?" she asked.

"Naw. You don't want to mess with me, pretty lady. My stump has never healed, and neither has the rest of me. I've have a hard time putting all this behind me."

"Me, too," Maggie said. "And it's been a long time since anyone called me pretty."

She took him to her apartment and cooked spaghetti for him and Peter. Peter was wary but polite. Conversation was careful during the meal, but when Maggie brought out a bottle of scotch, both men got talkative. They got maudlin about the monument. They talked about Nam and life after Nam. Carl described how he'd been wounded during strafing, his leg too mangled to save. "I used to wonder if I'd feel better about losing it if I'd lost it doing something wonderful like saving a buddy or a kid. I don't think about that now. I just wish I could get used to having it gone, but given a choice between getting my head straight or getting my leg back, I take a straight head. I hear screaming in the night. It wakes me up all the time."

Peter described how he'd taken a hit on his tail and been forced to eject. His life raft failed to open, and he tread water all night before the rescue helicopter spotted him and picked him up in the morning. "I kept thinking about us floating in the water after that boat sank," he told Maggie. "I could almost hear Mom's screams when Andy disappeared. I kept telling myself that one family couldn't have two sons eaten by sharks. Or could it? Jesus, remember how she beat her head against the deck? I couldn't think about Andy for years. I learned how to turn off thoughts about him as easily as I turned off a radio. It was much easier than remembering. But after a few hours in the water, I started talking to him. Toward morning, he started talking back. I'd forgotten so many things about him until he started talking about Joe, his dilapidated old teddy bear with almost all the stuffing gone, about hunting for Easter eggs in the snow, about us teaching him how to play Old Maid, how he was afraid that the monster under his bed was going to come out and eat him, so he'd come get in bed with me, and I'd tell him how I used to be afraid sometimes. He was such a good little kid. He sure was afraid of that monster. 'Beastie,' he called it. Oh, Jesus." He got up and looked out the window. The clock on the mantel became louder in the silence.

Maggie blew her nose and poured another glass of scotch, deciding tomorrow's headache would be worth the price. "Daddy wouldn't let us have nightlights," she remembered. Andy had gotten in bed with her some, too. She'd forgotten about Beastie. "I could have done without knowing I almost lost my surviving brother," she said. "I didn't know you'd had to ditch. Is there much else I don't know?"

"Yeah. As I look back, the miracle is that I survived. At first it had been exciting, living on the edge. I knew I could finesse myself out of whatever trouble they threw at me. After Danny went down though, I didn't feel like that anymore. I was just waiting for my turn. And after it was all over, I started wondering about the people I'd killed. I couldn't do that again. I couldn't kill."

"Me neither, man," Carl agreed. "I'd pull my own plug first."

Maggie thought of Danny. How would he have felt by now? And why did men keep going to war if the ones who came back felt like these two? But there were also men like her father and Jerry, who served without questioning, who took satisfaction in a task well done regardless of the cost. Maggie closed her eyes and prayed that any babies she had would be girls. She didn't want to send sons off to war.

It was almost midnight when she and Peter drove Carl back to the VA hospital. He was scheduled for a skin graft on his stump the next day. His fourth. Carl wasn't optimistic. He might have to give up on a prosthesis altogether.

Peter invited Carl to visit him in Colorado. "There's a lot of Nam vets in Colorado," he said. "They find towns in the mountains. Like me."

Maggie visited Carl every afternoon, first at his bedside, then pushing his wheelchair to the lounge at the end of the hall.

But one day he asked her not to come back. "I've been thinkin' about Colorado. There's a VA in Denver. Maybe I'll go. And you need to find someone who doesn't scream in the night. I'd wake up that baby you want to have. I wouldn't be any good for babies."

She wanted to protest but knew he was right. "But I can't just abandon you," she said.

"Just come once a week," he said. "And don't kiss my cheek anymore. It hurts too much for you to get close."

As Maggie followed the winding road through the officers' residential area, she wondered which of these houses had been her mother and Aunt Marynell's when they lived at Fort Belvoir all those years ago. Granddaddy Eddie had run the hospital here. Her father had come here from West Point to ask Eddie for his younger daughter's hand in marriage. The quarters were practically identical, but Maggie wanted to know exactly which one had been theirs. When she wrote her mother next, she'd ask.

A freshly painted sign announced the residence of Col. Gerald M. Wilhite. The packing boxes had been hauled away, every window had curtains and pots of flowers bloomed on the front porch. Pauline was incredible.

Maggie had been thrilled when Pauline called to tell her about Jerry's orders for Belvoir. She wanted to feel part of a family again. Usually, she drove down to Fredericksburg once a month or so to see Marynell and Jeffrey, but that wasn't the same as having her sister and her sister's children close by. Of course, Pauline could be a pain, and Jessica was a bit tiresome at times with her perfect manners and high marks, but Chad and Sara Jean were dear.

Pauline waited until after lunch to discuss the list of prospective "escorts" she had compiled. A widowed colonel who Pauline claimed was absolutely charming. A divorced major whose wife had had a drinking problem. A bachelor captain who was only six or seven years younger than Maggie. And a widowed chaplain who looked like Anthony Perkins. Maggie remembered when Aunt Marynell had played the same role for Pauline.

"I appreciate your efforts, honey," Maggie firmly announced, "but I don't want to go out with or marry anyone military."

"Why not?" Pauline demanded.

As always, Pauline was impeccably groomed, her hair too coiffured for Maggie's taste, her clothing too conservative. Maggie wondered if her sister ever put on a pair of jeans. But then their mother didn't wear jeans when she was an officer's wife. And she had cooked wearing starched aprons like a television mother.

"Lots of reasons," Maggie explained. "There might be another war. And after years of being my own person and setting my own rules, I can't imagine dressing up and going to teas. Can you imagine a military man wanting me—and my checkered past? I want a settled life with a house and garden, like Peter and Belinda have. If I hurry, maybe I can have a kid or two to take to Italy in the summertime when I visit Mother."

Pauline looked away at the mention of Italy. She'd never gone. Maggie doubted if she ever would.

They were sitting in Pauline's living room, which after only a week of settling in was already a perfect example of the tasteful eclectic decor often found in military homes. Pauline's version leaned toward elegance, with mahogany furniture, thick Oriental rugs, oil paintings in heavy gilded frames. A silver urn held cut flowers on the coffee table; another graced the dining room table. A glass-fronted cabinet gleamed with an impressive collection of sterling hollow ware. Last time Maggie had moved, it had taken her weeks to empty all the boxes and make order out of the chaos. Of course, Pauline was efficient, had excellent taste and never procrastinated, while Maggie had become a self-acknowledged slob.

Pauline was sipping her afternoon sherry. Maggie had drawn a frown from her sister when she asked for a beer.

"You aren't still seeing that one-legged vet, are you?" Pauline said it like an accusation.

"No, except for an occasional visit. But Matt's come to see me a couple of times."

"Matt! You're *involved* with Matt?"

"Not involved. We just hang out. I may go see him. He says he's got a really great cabin with a front porch that overlooks a lake."

"Well, I know Matt's not a blood cousin, but really, Maggie, it hardly seems appropriate. In fact, it seems . . . "

Maggie held up her hand. "Don't say it," she ordered.

Pauline sighed and refilled her glass from a crystal decanter. Then she held the glass to the light and stared at it. "For years, when I dreamed about Jerry getting a star, it was always with my family in attendance, my mother on my father's arm, my brother in uniform, you and Danny together. Now that it's about to happen, everything has changed. My family certainly has disappointed me." Pauline sighed again and took a sip of sherry.

"Oh, come off it, Pauline! What gives you the right to sit in judgment? I'm thrilled for you and Jerry, but dreams haven't come true for the rest of us. We've had to manufacture new ones."

"I'm not 'judging,' " she said defensively. "But what am I supposed to do? Applaud?"

"It wouldn't hurt."

With great dignity, Pauline rose from her chair and went to the hall closet. She returned with a framed photograph. "I came across this in the move," she said, thrusting the picture of their parents' West Point wedding into Maggie's hands. "It makes me cry every time I look at it. What the hell am I supposed to do with things like this? Daddy sent me all this stuff before he married June—all the family mementos, letters he'd written to Mom during two wars, our baby books, family albums, school papers, report cards. Happy Mother's Day cards to the most wonderful mother in the world."

Maggie studied the wedding picture. It was the one with the crossed sabers. She remembered it hanging by the dresser in her parents' bedroom in Japan. After that, after Andy died, her mother must have relegated it to a box. Was that when her parents' marriage became so polite?

How beautiful they both had been. So young. Franklin had an arm protectively around his bride's shoulders. She was smiling. Had they loved each other then, or was it only timing and circumstances that had brought them to that wedding long ago?

"It doesn't matter what you do with it," Maggie told her sister. "Burn it all if it bothers you. This picture is just an instant in time. I had a wonderful wedding, too, but what did that guarantee? Put this away and take off your proper-lady clothes and put on something less intimidating. I'd like to take you to my favorite dive for an evening of jazz, shrimp and beer."

"But I don't have a sitter for Sara Jean."

"Sara Jean has a father, doesn't she?"

Maggie went with Marynell and Jeffrey to Jerry's promotion ceremony. Jerry's commanding officer, a General Rice, who headed the Army Combat Development Command, did the honors, then Pauline stepped forward for her moment of recognition—a kiss from her husband, a handshake from General Rice. "Congratulations, Mrs. Wilhite. You must be very proud."

Pauline had never been a pretty girl, but she had become a handsome woman—almost regal with head held high and confident eyes. Her mink stole was elegant with her emerald-green shantung suit. She had what she wanted out of life and looked very proud. Maggie was happy for her—deeply, profoundly happy.

Maggie wondered what she herself would have been like if Danny had lived, if Danny had earned a star? She tried to think of herself as a handsome general's wife, but she had become haphazard, unconventional. Pauline accused her of looking like a windblown gypsy. Maggie couldn't decide if it was life that had shaped her or if she was just becoming more like herself the older she became. No, she didn't know what she would be like if Danny were still alive.

But such thoughts were too heavy to bear on this day of celebration. Her Danny would stay forever young, forever pure, forever in love with the girl she had once been.

After the reception, Maggie hurried home to meet Matt. On the way, she stopped by the VA to pick up Carl.

"Maybe your cousin doesn't want to meet me," Carl said reluctantly.

"He said the same thing about you. Relax."

Over the first six-pack, Carl announced, "For a long time, I hated you guys. I couldn't bear to have someone saying all those poor bastards had died in Nam for nothing. But now I don't know what any of that shit meant. I don't know if you were right or I was. At least you still got two legs."

"Seeing you makes me feel like I should apologize for them," Matt said. "And I feel less certain than I used to. I'm not sure if there are any right answers."

Maggie served spaghetti à la Tommaso. She wished she had some of his wine to go with it. The men drank more beer and finally the talk switched from Nam to sports.

While they watched the Redskins and Bears on the living room TV, Maggie sat at the kitchen table and wrote to her mother.

. . . Daddy and June were at the ceremony, of course. She's wearing a chignon now and looks very dignified, kind of like an aging Princess Grace. Daddy looks marvelous and, thus far, is managing retirement better than I thought he would. He's on the International Olympics board and is considering an offer to be commandant of a military college in Georgia, but I don't think he'll accept it. He wants to buy a house near D.C., but I understand June wants to buy a small inn in New England, and Daddy's actually considering it. Isn't that ironic? I remember him having a fit when you wanted to do that.

Jeffrey's lost a lot of weight. I don't think he's well. Marynell said he's been having some tests done. I can tell she's worried sick. He's a wonderful man.

Enclosed is an article about Jerry masterminding the rescue of two hostages in Iraq. He's sure to get a medal and is supposed to be part of the cover story in next week's *Newsweek*. I think they hurried through his promotion because of it. When Pauline called to tell me all about it last week, she cried and cried. She's so proud of him. I wish you could have seen her today. She looked marvelous. She was born to be a general's wife—like Danny's mother and Grandmother Cravens. Chad wants to go to West Point like his dad. Jessica is a cheerleader and quite popular at high school. Sara Jean is so frail, it breaks my heart. When Pauline and Jerry are away, she stays down at Fredericksburg with Jeffrey and Marynell. In fact, I gather that she goes down there a lot. Marynell tutors her when she has to miss school. Sara Jean still seems like an innocent child—like our Andy. Strange to think that Andy would be a man in his late thirties now.

Matt's staying the night. You can read into that whatever you want. He sends his love. He's been writing to Peter and is thinking about moving to Colorado to work for the state park department. He likes high mountains. Claims they make people humble. Like the ocean.

Maybe I'll go, too.

I understand now that sometimes you have to give up on one dream and find another. Part of me will always feel guilty because I'm not still carrying banners and making speeches for the MIAs, but I've passed the torch. Last year, I found out that the bones I buried probably aren't Danny's, but instead of sweet hope surging back through my veins, I wept at the thought of having to start it all again. I guess part of me will always hope and dream that Danny is alive, but I can't live my life for that. It was thoughts of you, Mom, that gave me courage to reclaim my life—to put down the banner and live at last in peace.

I guess I'll always miss Danny. Our love was the best part of my life. But he's gone, and I want to have a baby before I'm too old.

I think a lot about a baby. I think of a son or daughter of mine digging in the sand alongside Tommaso's grandkids at Amola, with you and me sitting under the arbor while he fusses about, making the children laugh, bringing us fruit and wine. I don't think I'd have to look away now when he stops to give you a kiss.

I love you, Mom, and think of you every day. I'm glad that you've found some happiness, and I'm grateful that I can finally accept your right to have done so.

Do you think I'm too old to have a baby?

Maggie

Maggie's baby, Louise thought as she stared toward the beach, seeing an image of this future grandchild digging in the sand.

Matt. Did she dare hope? Louise clasped her hands to her breast. Maggie and Matt. How right that would be.

She reread her daughter's letter and cried a bit. She cried for Maggie who wasn't happy yet but trying. For Pauline who thought she was. Especially for her sister who was facing the greatest sadness of her life.

Dear Jeffrey. He was dying. Marynell had called to tell her, to ask her sister to be there when the end came.

"I'm very lucky, you know," Marynell said. "It took us awhile, but Jeffrey and I kind of blossomed, don't you think?"

Marynell and Jeffrey had come last fall. Their second visit. The first time had been just for two weeks in the summer. But this time Louise insisted they come in the fall when her little world was at its most beautiful. Marynell was newly retired from teaching, and they stayed through November. Three wonderful months. The four of them made a family—Tommaso and Jeffrey like brothers, she and Marynell cherishing each day together. Sometimes the four of them would link arms when they took their evening walk on the beach. Louise had never been so happy.

She dried her eyes on her apron, tucked her letter in its pocket and went to help Tommaso in the kitchen. It was his youngest granddaughter's confirmation day, and he was preparing a family feast. She liked his family but being with them made her long so for her own.

The kitchen smelled of garlic, onion, fish, oregano. So much food. It looked like they were feeding an army.

Tommaso looked up from his chopping. "The letter is good news?"

"It surely is. But I need for you to stop that and hold me for a while."

CHAPTER

FORTY-EIGHT

"You came for Danny's funeral," Maggie's letter said. "I think you need to come for the beginning of my new life."

Louise carried the letter with her as she walked on the beach. She would walk awhile, then stop and pull the letter out of her pocket, stare at her daughter's handwriting on the envelope and smile. When she got far enough down the beach for privacy, she kicked off her shoes and ran in the surf. She laughed and called out her joy to the gulls. Maggie was marrying Matt. It was enough to make one believe in fairy tales or a god or good forces in the universe.

Louise opened her arms to the heavens. "If there's anyone up there I should be thanking," she yelled to the white clouds and blue sky, "then I do so. Thank you from the bottom of my heart."

Back at the inn, she had to explain the relationship to Tommaso. "They're not really cousins," she said. "Matt was Jeffrey's son by his first wife."

Pauline would disapprove, of course, but she'd get over it. Maggie and Matt were going to live in Colorado, in the mountains. She was going to look for a teaching job. Matt would work as a forester for the Colorado Park Department.

After dinner, Louise and Tommaso walked up the hill to the church, where they lit a candle for Maggie and Matt. Louise was hardly a believer, but she liked the small ritual performed in this cool, ancient place. And she liked the look of Tommaso's face in the candlelight as he prayed for the happiness of her darling Maggie.

Even in bed, she couldn't stop smiling. "I feel so good," she said, turning into Tommaso's arms. "So blessed. I want you to kiss me for a long time."

"Is that all?" he asked, nibbling on her ear.

"Well, what else is there for an old man and an old woman?"

"You're right," he said. "Kisses only."

"I don't believe you," she said.

"And why is that?"

"Your friend down there is giving you away."

Marynell offered to have the wedding at her house. Maggie accepted. "Right here in the backyard," Maggie said, taking her aunt's arm as they inspected the rose garden. "But do you think Jeffrey will be up to it?"

"I think it'd be good for him. He likes the idea of everyone gathering for a wedding instead of a funeral. But don't wait too long . . . " Marynell's voice broke.

"Are *you* up to it?" Maggie asked.

Marynell smiled and gave Maggie's hand a squeeze. "Absolutely. Do you kids have any idea at all how thrilled we are about this wedding?"

"Yes. We know. That was the first thing we thought of when we realized where we were heading—how pleased you and Mom and Jeffrey would be."

They sat on a bench under a maple tree. "I remember when this tree was just a sapling. Have you really lived here that long?"

"We built the house almost twenty years ago. We've lived our best years here. Does your mother know you're getting married?"

"I wrote to her. Does she know about Jeffrey?"

"I called her. We all talked for a long time. Lots of 'remember whens.' Jeffrey told her how much she's always meant to us. He's always loved Louise, and she loved him. I used to be jealous. She's promised she'll come when we need her."

"Oh, Marynell, how do you stand it? I know your heart breaks every time you look at him."

"Yes. But he keeps reminding me that we've had forty-four years."

"Forty-four *good* years," Maggie corrected.

"No. About half and half. That was more my fault than Jeffrey's. You know, Jeffrey and I have talked about building a gazebo on that little knoll for years. I think I'll have him design one for the wedding."

After Matt and Maggie had left, Marynell fixed a light supper. Jeffrey leaned on her arm while they walked about the yard—an evening ritual. They talked about the gazebo. Jeffrey wanted stained wood, of course. Nothing painted.

They sat in lawn chairs and listened to the sounds of evening. "If there's a heaven, I think it looks like our backyard," Jeffrey said.

Marynell started to cry.

"Hey, none of that."

"Oh, hush! I can cry if I want to."

"Do you think Maggie's too old for a baby?"

"No. I think she's already pregnant." Marynell reached in her pocket for a Kleenex.

"Did she say so?"

"No. But the bodice of that sundress was too tight, and it fit fine last month."

Jeffrey sighed contentedly.

His back hurt at night. Marynell gave him a painkiller and got the heating pad. Then she held him. It was worse for them both in the darkness. Fears got bigger and bolder. They took turns being strong. They told each other dozens of times a day how much they loved each other. Marynell wished she could invent another word. She felt that she had worn out the old one. But she said it now. "I love you," she whispered over and over, like a lullaby until she felt the Demerol and sleep take hold.

Jerry in uniform and Pauline in a silk dress sat with Peter and Belinda on lawn chairs arranged on the shady side of the yard. Eric and his wife, Sue, were behind them. The assorted cousins were sitting together on picnic benches. Benny had a girlfriend with him. Jessica was adjusting the bow in Sara Jean's hair. Jessica reminded Louise of Pauline at that age. Bossy. Sara Jean was so pale. Louise ached for Pauline to bring her to Amola, to the sun and the beach.

Marynell helped Jeffrey to his seat. He was ashen, wasted, but smiling. "I'm thankful that I lived to see this day," he'd told them all at dinner last night.

Eric, with tears streaming down his face, led the cheering. The rest joined in. Cheering, clapping, crying because dear Jeffrey was still with them.

"We've toasted the bride and groom," Eric said, standing and raising his glass to Marynell and Jeffrey. "Now I want to toast my mom and dad, who have taught us all an awful lot about living the past year. I guess you both know how much I love you, how much Matt and I love you. Admire you. Thanks. For everything."

Louise would stay on after the wedding. The doctor had warned that Jeffrey's next hospital admission could be his last.

Carl, in a wheelchair, played the wedding march on his guitar. Beautifully.

The back door opened, and Franklin and Maggie came down the back steps and across the yard. She was wearing a loose-fitting dress of ivory lace, flowers in her golden hair. Her grandmother Maxine's pearls were at her throat. Tucked away in her sleeve was her grandmother Elizabeth's handkerchief that she'd carried at her wedding to Danny.

Franklin still had a full head of hair, beautifully white. He wore a civilian suit for the occasion, but his military bearing still set him apart. He had come alone, his wife at a family funeral in Florida.

Very formally, he escorted Maggie to the new gazebo and the waiting minister and bridegroom.

Maggie and Matt had written the service themselves—personal words about growing up cousins, about why they loved each other, why they wanted to marry each other. And then the minister asked, "Who escorts this woman here today for her vows of holy matrimony?"

Louise was unprepared for Franklin's response. His voice was strong and clear as he answered. "Her mother and I are with her today and offer our blessing on this union."

His part played, he came to sit beside her. Louise tentatively touched his hand, and he opened it to her.

Hand in hand, they watched their pregnant, forty-three-year-old daughter marry her stepcousin. *Her mother and I.* A break with tradition, Franklin's way of acknowledging what once was. And oddly enough an image of those long-ago days on the boat before Andy died flashed across Louise's mind. Sunny days of fishing and laughing. It hadn't been all bad. In fact, there had been so much good. They had been a family. Day to day, surrounded by love and beauty, she had found peace and contentment. Her life was uncomplicated and good, and Tommaso had become all men to her—husband, father, son, friend. He was the other half of her body, the other half of her soul. But she missed her family, and that meant missing Franklin, too.

Under a canopy of nature, Maggie and Matt exchanged their vows in clear, certain voices. Wouldn't Eddie have loved this day. He'd be blowing his nose now.

Yes, a good day. The satisfaction of it filled Louise with pleasure as brilliant as the sunshine.

Her mother had once said contentment was the best one could hope for, but that wasn't enough. For Maggie and Matt, Louise wished happiness, and so much love.